THE FORTUNATE DEAD

THE FORTUNATE DEAD

DAVID PENNY

For Mum
Betty Penny 1928 - 2017
*Never without a book at her side or a joke on the tip of her tongue. And she called **me** cheeky?*

THE THOMAS BERRINGTON HISTORICAL MYSTERIES

The Red Hill

Moorish Spain, 1482. English surgeon Thomas Berrington is asked to investigate a series of brutal murders in the palace of al-Hamra in Granada.

Breaker of Bones

Summoned to Cordoba to heal a Spanish prince, Thomas Berrington and his companion, the eunuch Jorge, pursue a killer who re-makes his victims with his own crazed logic.

The Sin Eater

In Granada Helena, the concubine who once shared Thomas Berrington's bed, is carrying his child, while Thomas tracks a killer exacting revenge on evil men.

The Incubus

A mysterious killer stalks the alleys of Ronda. Thomas Berrington, Jorge and Lubna race to identify the culprit before more victims have their breath stolen.

The Inquisitor

In a Sevilla on the edge of chaos death stalks the streets. Thomas Berrington and his companions tread a dangerous path between the Inquisition, the royal palace, and a killer.

The Fortunate Dead

As a Spanish army gathers outside the walls of Malaga, Thomas Berrington hunts down a killer who threatens more than just strangers.

The Promise of Pain

When revenge is not enough. Thomas Berrington flees to the high mountains, only to be drawn back by those he left behind.

The Message of Blood

When Thomas Berrington is sent to Cordoba on the orders of a man he hates he welcomes the distraction of a murder, but is shocked when the evidence points to the killer being his companion.

A Tear for the Dead

As the reign of Moorish Granada draws to a close, dark forces gather to carve a new Spain. Can Thomas Berrington overcome the plot to destroy not just one civilisation, but two?

THE THOMAS BERRINGTON PREQUELS

A Death of Innocence

When 13 years old Thomas Berrington is accused of murder he must enlist the help of pretty Bel Brickenden to prove his innocence. And then another kind of death comes to Lemster.

THE THOMAS BERRINGTON BUNDLES

Purchase 3 full-length novels for less than the price of two.

Thomas Berrington Books 1-3

The Red Hill

Breaker of Bones

The Incubus

Thomas Berrington Books 4-6

The Incubus

The Inquisitor

The Fortunate Dead

Thomas Berrington Books 7-9

The Promise of Pain

The Message of Blood

A Tear for the Dead

PLACE NAMES

For many of the Spanish cities and towns which lay beyond the boundary of Andalusia the current Spanish name has been used, except where the town had a significant Moorish past, such as Cordoba and Seville.

I have conducted research on the naming of places within Andalusia but have taken a few liberties to make the names easier to pronounce for a modern day audience. Where I have been unable to find reference to the Moorish name of a place I have made one up.

al-Andalus … Andalusia
al-Mariyya … Almeria
Gharnatah … Granada
Ixbilya … Sevilla
Malaka … Malaga
Randonda … Ronda
Qurtuba … Cordoba
Sholayr … Sierra Nevada mountains

SPAIN 1487

MALAGA, ANDALUCIA

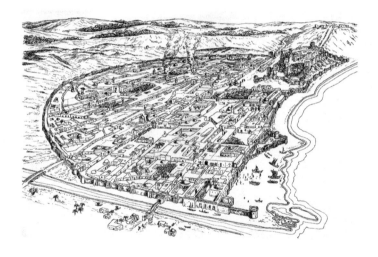

Map of Malaga, 1487, Copyright Thomas Shepherd 2018, based on an original on display in the Malaga museum. To view a larger image on my website click the map.

ONE

"Tell me, exactly, how did you manage to lose a body?"

Thomas Berrington stared at a wooden pallet, its surface stained by years of misuse. He wiped at his blood-stained hands with a damp cloth but it did little good. Only a long bath might make him clean again.

"I didn't lose it," said Lubna, her face set. "I delivered the woman to this pallet before noon and informed the mortuary officer of her location."

"Perhaps the family collected it. Did you check?" Thomas made little attempt to hide his impatience. Lubna had sent for him as he was attempting to set a broken leg where the bone had pierced flesh. He had fixed it as well as he could but suspected the man would lose the leg. That thought had put him in a foul mood.

"Of course I checked. Would I send for you if it was that simple? Nobody has come to claim her."

"Are you sure she was dead?"

Lubna gave him a glance that said more than words, perhaps not wanting to sour the atmosphere between them any more by speaking, and Thomas realised that

1

perhaps he was being too harsh on her. He had lost bodies in the past himself. The infirmary in Malaka was both large and busy, and sometimes he wondered how any body made its way to its family after it had stopped breathing. Thomas touched Lubna's shoulder, but she pulled away. Not forgiven yet, then.

He wondered if she was distracted by thoughts of the child she carried. Over six months now, beyond the time she had lost their first. They had been living in Ixbilya then for Thomas to attend the Spanish Queen. The loss had been on his mind of late, hers too, he was sure. He knew he may have been too attentive, too cosseting. Lubna was not a woman to be cosseted, even less so this last year. They had come to Malaka so she could attend the Infirmary, the place Thomas had learned his skills. That had been many years before, half a lifetime, and much had changed since. Except Malaka was still where people came to learn the skills of a physician, ever since Persia fell to the Mongol hordes.

It had not been easy for Lubna. As a woman, she was not made welcome, only accepted in the end because she was Thomas Berrington's wife, and everyone knew his reputation. A reputation that brought respect but little fondness. The lack of the latter didn't concern him. Ability and an open mind meant more, and Lubna possessed both.

"What did she die of?" he asked.

"Does it matter?"

"I'm curious."

"In that case, I don't know. She was admitted after a fall that damaged her skull, but she was recovering. She became conscious a day ago, and we talked briefly. She told me her husband had died recently and that her name was Dionora, but not her family name. The way she spoke it seemed as if she no longer wanted to live."

Thomas frowned. "Such a thing is possible."

"Which is why I wanted you to see her. Why I came for you. I have learned much this last year, but not enough to explain what happened to her. She was getting better, I am sure of it."

"We'll go to the clerk of records. The body might have been mistaken for someone else and handed over to the wrong family. It has happened before."

Lubna fell into step beside him. "How often?"

"Not often, I admit, but four or five times over the years. It's surprising how many people choose not to look at the face of a loved one after life has departed. Or perhaps not so surprising."

The administration offices lay close to the Infirmary, requiring the crossing of a busy street and ascent of marble steps beneath the onslaught of a fierce sun. It was as they climbed the steps that a commotion broke out behind them, and Thomas turned to see what the shouting was about.

A tall man walked up the street with a woman's body cradled in his arms. He was calling out at the top of his voice in bad Arabic, over and over, "Save her! Someone save her!"

It was all Thomas needed. He ran toward the man, knowing Lubna would not be far behind.

"What happened?" He reached out and touched the woman's face, his eyes tracking the greyness of her flesh.

"They threw her in the water like a piece of rubbish. I was too late." The man lifted his gaze to Thomas, his eyes tracking him. "Can you help her?"

Thomas reached to take the weight from the man, but he took a step back.

"I will carry her. Show me where."

Thomas led the way into the Infirmary, along corridors to an empty space he had spent most of the morning in. He was glad to see someone had cleaned up since he left.

He slapped the wooden table and waited until the man laid the woman down. Thomas put a hand on his arm and pushed him away, meeting resistance.

"I need space to work. Stand against the wall and don't come back until I say so." He waited, still pushing, unsure the man would give way, then all at once the tension left his body and he turned.

"Is she your wife?" It was Lubna asked the question, but Thomas caught the man's nod before he began to examine the woman's body. He took a blade and cut her robe away to reveal pale skin beneath, then turned and glared at the man when he began to come forward again. It appeared to be enough.

Thomas pushed the woman onto her side and pressed on her chest and back. He expected water to spill from her mouth but nothing came. Then he noticed the damage done to her body. Blood stained her thighs, and her back showed cuts and bruises.

"Who did this?"

"They threw her in the water when they were done. Like a soiled rag. I will kill them. Kill them all." The man spoke with a coldness Thomas was familiar with. He had experienced it often enough himself.

"Who did?" he asked again.

"Three men." The man raised his eyes and met

Thomas's. "But I know their faces. They will pay for this, but first you must mend her."

"Where were you?"

"A boat. I was in a boat. Too far." A shudder ran through him. "They knew I could see them, but they still did this. I was too far away. They knew I was too far away."

Thomas sighed. Malaka was normally a safe city, but these were not normal times, and there had been more strangers recently. This war, as all wars did, attracted violent men. They frequented the inns and markets. Stood on street corners looking for other men to fight or women to abuse. They took what they wanted when they wanted it. To some people, surrender seemed an easier choice, but this man's wife had fought back. Had she not she might have lived, unless her shame killed her.

"I'm sorry, but I can do nothing for her." Thomas laid his hand on the woman's swollen belly, waiting. "How far gone is she?"

The man glanced at where Thomas's hand lay on his wife and shook his head. "She is close. Weeks. I told her to stay at home in Sevilla, but she insisted on coming with me. And now this. They will pay. I saw their faces. They didn't even pretend to hide what they were doing."

Thomas felt a slight movement and looked toward Lubna. The man couldn't be here for what came next, but what came next would have to be done now, the sooner the better if there was to be any chance one life could be rescued.

He saw Lubna nod and leave the room, then began preparations. He would try to hold back from cutting until she returned with guards, but if it came to it he

5

had already decided to knock the man senseless before he began.

"What are you doing?" The man came to stand too close to Thomas, taller than he was, broad-shouldered, and Thomas wondered if he would be able knock him down if he needed to, and thought perhaps not. There was something familiar about him he couldn't quite place. Perhaps they had met somewhere in Malaka, or even when he had lived in Sevilla. Perhaps somewhere else, for the man was Spanish, and Thomas had spent much time in Spain, often against his will.

"I think I can save your child. Your wife I cannot. Surely one life is better than none."

"How?"

Thomas had trouble deciding if the man was too shocked by grief to understand.

"I'll have to cut, there isn't time for anything else."

Once more he detected movement, but it was faint, slow, and he feared he had left it too long. Lubna returned with two guards. They approached the man, who turned and faced them, his arms spread in a way Thomas was familiar with. He had seen it from those he had faced in the past. The guards had seen it before as well. They approached slowly, with care.

The man struck at one of them, a crashing blow that sent the guard reeling backward.

"Leave," Thomas said to Lubna, but she stayed where she was at his side.

He waited a moment, then cut the woman across the base of her belly and reached into the wound. He heard the man cry out, a great guttural roar. The guards had him between them now, but for how long couldn't be predicted. Thomas worked fast. It wasn't pretty, but it had no need to be. He found the child and eased it free, wiped the tiny body clean with a linen cloth, then cut the cord. He gripped the heels and held it up, slapped it on the back. He repeated the operation, then laid the infant beside its mother. He leaned close and blew into the open mouth, slid a finger in and cleared mucus. Laid his hand on its fragile chest and squeezed. Eventually he straightened and cursed. Too much time had passed. When he turned it was to discover the man stood alone, the guards having fled at the sight of what Thomas had done.

The man glared at Thomas, but there was no indication of any attack about to be launched.

"Now there are four men I must kill" He glanced to one side. "Or should I take your woman and kill her as you have killed mine? I see she carries a child too. It would be natural justice."

Thomas placed himself between the man and Lubna, stared up at his face. He had fought tall men before — big men, strong men — and trusted in himself. Lubna moved past him, began to press on the infant's chest, to manipulate its limbs.

"There was nothing anyone could do for her. Too much time has passed. If you can identify the men who did this you must report them so they can never do such a thing again."

"Oh, I will make sure they cannot do it again." The man's eyes continued to burn.

Thomas heard a noise behind and turned. The infant moved an arm, heaved air into its frail chest as Lubna lifted it in her arms. Lubna smiled as the child opened its eyes and stared at her as if in recognition.

Thomas stepped between her and the man. "Lubna

will prepare your wife. Come for her in an hour. She will check your–" He hesitated, glanced at the small figure Lubna clutched to her chest, "–your daughter too. Give me your name and I will make sure you can take them when you come." Another glance at the woman's mutilated body. "You will need to find a wet-nurse."

"I will stay."

"Then stay, but we still need your name," said Lubna. "There are rules."

The man didn't look at her, continuing to stare at Thomas, anger pulsing from him in waves.

"My name is Guerrero. Pedro Guerrero. Remember it well, both of you, remember it for when I come for you."

Lubna turned away as if he hadn't spoken. She made a makeshift cot for the child then fetched a bowl of water and cloths and began to wash the woman's body. Guerrero made no move. Neither did Thomas. He waited, watching as the anger finally began to loosen its hold on the man.

Guerrero turned away abruptly. "An hour, though I may be longer. It depends how long it takes me to find the men who did this."

Thomas watched him go, then took the newborn to a bench and started to wash the tiny body, amazed as always at the miracle of birth, even one as unfortunate and bloody as this one had been.

TWO

The clerk of records ran his finger down a list of names scribed in a thick ledger before coming to a halt. "Dionora Jinto Jiminez," he said, looking up. Thomas and Lubna had finally managed to return to their interrupted task. "She was admitted five days ago and assigned to Lubna as her primary carer. Death was recorded this morning. I have sent a message to her family. To her son." His finger moved to hover over a note written in the margin. He read it, frowned, and turned back several pages. "Her husband died here four weeks ago. Name of Miguel Jiminez." He read some more. "Broken skull caused by a fall downstairs, it says here. Found by his wife, brought in by their son." He glanced up again, said to Lubna, "Not one of yours that time." As if it was an accusation. "Strange, both dying within weeks of each other, but it happens more often than you might think."

"The family haven't taken her body, have they?" Thomas asked.

"It would be recorded if they had." The clerk shook

his head. "What do I tell them when they come, that they are too late?"

"Might another family have taken her in error?"

"It should not happen."

"But it does sometimes, doesn't it?"

"It is unusual," said the clerk of records.

"But possible."

"Possible, yes."

Thomas turned to survey the lesser clerks who worked at scribing records of births and deaths. He raised his voice. "Who of you knows this Dionora Jinto Jiminez?"

A hand rose. "I recorded her admittance, sir. I assigned her to Lubna, who gave her willow bark tincture and a little poppy when she grew distressed."

Thomas glanced at Lubna, who nodded. He tried to recall if she had spoken of the woman, but no memory came. Sometimes she would recount her day in detail, probing for information that might add to her education.

"You remember all of that?" he said to the man.

"I wrote Lubna's notes into the ledger, so of course I remember."

Thomas was impressed. Most clerks made a habit of not committing anything to memory for fear it might fill their heads with useless information and drive out what they needed to remember.

"And today?" he asked.

"We have not received the physicians' notes for today," said the clerk of records.

Lubna reached inside her robe, the movement drawing it tight to reveal the swell of her belly. "Mine are here," she said.

"No, no, you must follow procedure." The man shook his head as if he had been insulted. "You know to leave them with the ward clerk who gathers them together and brings them to me. Put them away."

Thomas let the idiocy pass for the moment. He looked away from the clerk and his men, thinking about what he knew. Had the body been misidentified and taken by someone else? Or even identified as a body lacking family, in which case it would be wrapped in linen and placed with the others that were unclaimed, to be burned at sunset. There was a place outside the city reserved for such, so the smoke and smell didn't disturb its citizens.

When Lubna tugged at his arm, Thomas glanced down. She made an impatient face, and he looked around to see the clerks had all returned to their duties.

"Let's go see what we can find out," he said, and Lubna nodded, following as he turned away. None of the men in the room looked up as they left.

Lubna stopped at the top of the marble steps outside the Administration building and Thomas turned back, concerned when he saw how tired she looked. She stared across the wide roadway, but he doubted she saw anything at all. When she became aware of his attention, she offered a smile.

"Why did you help that man? You could see as well as I his wife was already dead."

Thomas walked back up the steps and took her hand, feeling a tremble there. "We saved his child, didn't we? Besides, it is what we do. We help the sick and injured and despairing."

"I'm not sure saving the child was any favour. A man alone with an infant?"

"Should I have let both die, then?"

"No, of course not." Lubna looked at the crowded street, her eyes searching. "Do you think he's really going to kill those men?"

Thomas released her hand. "If anyone harmed you or Will, I would pursue them to the ends of the earth. So yes, he will try, I suspect, and might even succeed. He gave me the impression he was a man capable of offering retribution."

Lubna shivered despite the heat. "Sometimes the world doesn't feel safe. Not just Malaka — everywhere."

"Since when has it ever been different?"

"It used to be, in Gharnatah. I thought so, anyway. Is there any place that is safe? Where we could live our lives in peace and not have to worry about war, or men killing each other or other men's wives? This England you come from, is it safe there?"

Thomas started to laugh until he saw the want in Lubna's face. This was important to her, and he wondered how long she had carried the need without saying anything to him, and why she was raising it now. Was it the child she carried? His child and hers, the child she would bear this time.

"That man, Guerrero, should not have left his wife unprotected. She was alone beyond the city wall, on the rocks above the sea while he went off in some rowboat. No wonder she was attacked."

"A woman alone beyond the city wall is fair game now, is she?"

"That's not what I meant."

"It's what it sounded like to me."

Thomas went to put his arms around Lubna but she twisted away, sparking a flash of anger in him. They had both had difficult days, but it was Lubna who had lost a body. Or at least the Infirmary ... he was sure it was not Lubna's fault, though he was not sure she believed that.

"You know who he reminded me of?" said Lubna.

"Who?"

"That man. Guerrero. He could have been Mandana's double, separated by fifty years."

Of course, Thomas thought, the idea snapping into place in his mind like a lost answer that eludes capture.

"Except without the beard, the grey hair, and with two hands."

"Except those, yes." Lubna offered half a smile, and Thomas hoped it meant the start of forgiveness, but for what he wasn't yet sure. "It might have been just his height, I suppose."

"No, you're right, that's who he reminded me of as well, but I couldn't bring it to mind. Perhaps I didn't want to."

"I like to forget about him, too," said Lubna. "Isn't he due to visit again soon? You know my feelings on the matter, but I am only your wife."

"I don't remember. It's some time since he last came, so soon, I expect."

"You should turn him away and let him die."

The vehemence in her voice surprised him, but she was wrong. A physician couldn't decide who to treat based on whether they were good or evil.

Thomas began to descend the steps again just as a ragged figure ran through the crowd below toward a group of musicians who had begun to play, dancers swirling, their voices lifting in ululations. As he came closer, Thomas heard people laughing and jeering and saw it wasn't only the musicians who were being accosted but a well-dressed man he recognised as Ali Durdush, Grand Master of the Malaka Guilds, and almost certainly the richest man in the city, if not all of al-Andalus.

"What's going on?" he asked an onlooker.

"It's that idiot preacher, al-Antiqamun. Everyone is his enemy today. He has already torn Durdush's cloak and now it's the women he has it in for."

Thomas watched as the ragged-robed man, tangled hair falling almost to his waist, berated two female dancers. Four others tried to continue their dance, but the musicians were faltering. A few laid down their instruments and approached the altercation.

Attention diverted from him, the rotund figure of Ali Durdush bustled away. He glanced in Thomas's direction and offered a nod of recognition before moving on.

When Thomas looked back at the preacher, he had grasped the arm of one of the women and was trying to force her to her knees. The others had stopped dancing and gathered around. Voices were raised. And then a knife appeared. Sharp light flashed from its blade. Al-Antiqamun staggered back and fell to one knee.

Thomas pushed through the crowd. They had stopped laughing, but one or two now called threats. He reached the preacher and tried to find a wound, but before he could, one of the musicians pushed him aside.

"Let me finish him. This crazy man has been following us for a week and I will have it no more."

Thomas watched the blade dangle loose in the musician's hand, a drop of blood hanging from the tip. The man was short, slim, with corded muscle showing in his arms. His accent placed him from the north coast of Africa.

"Leave him be." Something in Thomas's eyes gave the musician pause. Thomas turned back to the preacher and lifted sections of filthy robe until he found the wound. A slash to the arm. Nothing serious, but it would need binding and a salve applied to prevent infection. He saw older scars and knew this was not the first attack on the man. Al-Antiqamun had no-one to blame but himself.

"I need to treat you." Thomas steadied the preacher as he rose. He was tall, with a wild beard that matched his hair. His face was surprisingly intelligent, but his eyes were bright with madness or rage.

"I need no heathen to mend me. Allah watches over his own." He looked beyond Thomas and scowled at the musicians who were packing their instruments away, about to move on.

"You should leave them in peace. They do no harm."

"Allah forbids it. Music. Dancing. Women wearing clothes designed to reveal their bodies. It is against what is written in the Quran." He looked around. "And where did that fat fool get to? I've not finished with him yet." His gaze returned to Thomas. "I know you, don't I?"

"Many do. And I know you, but not your true name."

"I am al-Antiqamun."

"That I know, but it is not your given name, is it."

"I am al-Antiqamun. I have no other name."

Thomas knew it was all the answer he would get, perhaps all the answer the man knew. The child he had once been was now lost amongst his visions of heaven and hell. Or vengeance. For that was what his adopted name meant in Arabic. Vengeance.

"You are the stranger." Al-Antiqamun's eyes were calm now the dancers had moved away. "They call you the butcher, do they not?" He smiled. "When Allah's fire cleanses this land of unbelievers, it will scorch the flesh from your bones, *qassab*." His head turned as he sought new victims. His gaze fell on Lubna, waiting on the steps for Thomas. "But your wife is devout, so she will live." Al-Antiqamun frowned as if considering whether such a gift was in his power to bestow. In his madness he no doubt believed it was.

Thomas turned away. The man could bleed to death for all he cared. Those who were already dead waited for him, and there were times he considered those the fortunate ones — all the trials and tribulations of life lay behind them. Not that he felt death had much to commend it either, and offered the choice he would always choose life, however hard it had sometimes proven to be.

He shook his head, annoyed at himself and his thoughts. He looked to where Lubna waited, patient, beautiful. Did she ever doubt, he wondered?

THREE

The mortuary was as still and silent as only a mortuary can be. A single living man sat in an alcove writing in a ledger. He glanced up when Thomas and Lubna entered. When he saw who it was he rose, shaking his head.

"She is still gone." He indicated the empty pallet. There were others, also empty, but none that were meant to be currently in use. The ebb and flow of death in the hospital meant that at times the room was often empty, at other times almost full. Now it was Spring and the weather was clement, there were none of the storms of Winter or the heat of Summer to accelerate a passing.

"When did you last see the woman?"

A shake of the head. "When Lubna brought her in. I do not make a habit of checking my charges. They have a habit of staying where they are left."

"Apart from this one," Thomas said. "Did anyone else come?"

"Physicians brought other bodies, but not so many.

You know how it is." The man was not young, into his fifties, and Thomas wondered if he had worked here when he first came to the Infirmary himself. If so he didn't recall his face.

"No strangers?"

"A strange boy is all. He wandered in, lost I think. Not like other people. Brainless." He tapped his skull, not in judgement, merely a statement of fact.

"Did he say anything?"

"Something, but I didn't understand him. He spoke Spanish and Arabic mixed together, and I only understand one of them."

"Was the woman here when he came?"

The man frowned, stared off into a corner of the room. "Yes, I think so."

"And when he left?"

"I think I would have noticed if he had carried a body out."

"You have been here the entire time since?"

"Apart from–" The man glanced at Lubna, making it clear he would prefer not to state the reason he might have briefly left his station.

"How many times–" Thomas started to ask anyway but was interrupted by a commotion from outside. Raised voices, male and female, and as he turned five individuals entered the mortuary. Two of them stopped as soon as they realised where they were and turned back. The clerk of records was one of those who remained, accompanied by two strangers, a man and a woman.

"Ah good, Lubna, you are still here." He turned to the couple. "This is the physician who attended your mother, she can explain the situation to you." With that he made a hasty retreat.

"Coward," Thomas said, but too quiet for anyone other than Lubna to hear.

"What have you done with our mother?" said the woman, hard-faced, her hair pulled tight in a severe bun. She was dressed so flamboyantly Thomas was sure Jorge would have approved, but dressing in such a way was not unusual in Malaka, where many different cultures rubbed against each other.

"My wife has done nothing with your mother." Thomas looked toward the mortuary clerk. "When you returned from your trips did you happen to notice her loss? Or the boy anywhere?"

"Boy? What boy?" The woman glanced at the man, presumably her husband, or perhaps brother, though they looked nothing alike. "Has a boy stolen our mother's body?"

"She is not lost, merely misplaced," said the clerk.

Oh, lost is what she is, Thomas thought, but said nothing, knowing it was important to present a united front to the couple.

"This boy," said the man. "Was he really a boy or only appeared to be a boy?"

"I thought him a boy," said the clerk. "But he was tall."

"Diego," said the woman, her face tight with a suppressed anger. "I told you he should have been taken away from them. Or drowned at birth."

"He is my brother," said the man, who turned away from the woman to address the clerk. "Was he dark-haired, friendly, always with a smile? But difficult to understand unless you know him well."

"Possibly." It was clear the clerk was unwilling to admit to anything until he knew what manner of trouble he might get into.

"Who is this Diego?" Thomas stepped closer to the couple. He glanced beyond them for a moment, but their companions were nowhere to be seen. "Is he family to you?"

"My brother," said the man. "My youngest brother. He is not … as other men."

"How much younger?" Thomas judged the man to have close to forty years, not so far from his own age.

"My mother had him when she was older than I am now. Too old. Everyone said she was too old, but they loved him all the same. Maybe loved him too much — more than the rest of us, anyway."

"They spoiled him," said the man's wife, for it was becoming clear that was who she was.

"Where do they live?"

"Has he truly stolen her body?" The man shook his head. "Diego might lack wits but he has a keen sense of right and wrong. He would never do such a thing. Though…" He ran a hand across his head, pushing back thinning hair. "It is true he has been distracted of late, as has my mother, ever since my father passed away. I am sure it was that which brought on her illness. Diego could not care for her, and she could no longer care for herself. We should have taken her in, but…" He trailed away with a brief glance at his wife.

"Who brought her to the Infirmary?" Thomas directed the words mostly to Lubna, who shook her head.

"The clerk of records might know," she said.

"I will not ask that man again. How long had she

been your patient?" He touched Lubna's arm and drew her away so their conversation would not be overheard by the son of the missing woman.

"Four days. No, five. Do you recall I asked you about her the night after she arrived? I asked how to force someone to eat when they had no wish to do so."

Thomas didn't, but there were times his own thoughts drove out everything else. He could converse, and even make a great deal of sense, but his responses were often automatic. No doubt he would have offered advice of some sort, though what it might have been he had no memory of.

"Was it hunger that caused her death?" He might have given too little attention to Lubna before, but now she had all of it.

"Not directly. She was sick in any case. I was going to ask for advice again tonight, but when I came this morning, she had died in the night." Lubna wiped the beginnings of a tear from the corner of her eye. Watching the movement, Thomas wondered if she was not too emotional for the profession he had hoped for her, and wondered if he had pushed her too hard to come to Malaka to study. Perhaps he should have been more sensitive to Lubna's needs. Or at least spoken with Jorge about them, who knew far more of such things. Lubna, no doubt, would have discussed her fears with Jorge even if she could not with him.

"It is possible this boy has taken his mother," Thomas said.

"Then the family will take care of it," said Lubna, with a touch of relief. "It is no longer our responsibility."

"I feel responsible," Thomas said. "Had I listened to

you, the woman might not have died. And now she has, I'm duty bound to see the matter to an end." He glanced at the man and woman. She was talking at him, her face inches from his. "Besides, I'm not sure it's for the best that woman is involved if the boy is vulnerable, and from what I've heard, he is. We should fetch Jorge; he is better at handling these situations than me."

"I can manage," said Lubna.

"I want you there too, but I want Jorge as well. Indulge me in this." Thomas didn't want to explain his reasoning. He was worried the boy might become agitated if they uncovered his theft. After the loss of one child, Thomas knew he was over-protective of Lubna, but knowing it didn't make it wrong. He would want her far away from any interrogation.

Lubna turned away, unconsciously crossing her arms in mirror of the woman on the far side of the room.

Thomas closed the distance to the couple. "Tell me where your mother lived."

"Near the Ataranzana. They have a house close to the other merchants. My father was clerk to the Master of Weapons until his death."

"Weapons?" Thomas said, but made an effort to stop his mind spinning off into creating some conspiracy theory. He waved a hand. "No matter. Can you show me where? I have someone I need to fetch first, but can you meet me here in an hour?"

"I am not staying," said the wife. "We have abandoned our children too long already." She cast a glance of pure spite at the man and turned away. Thomas watched her go, her movements stiff with barely restrained anger, and he wondered how people could live their lives in such a way.

When Thomas looked back at the man, he was shaking his head. "Two of our children have children of their own," he said. "We left them all together. We live side by side with her sisters. Not near my parents, but a nice enough neighbourhood. Well, I think so, anyway." He glanced at Lubna, as if wondering where he might find a wife as amenable, not to mention beautiful. Then he looked away, aware Thomas was watching. "Yes, an hour. I will find somewhere to pass an hour. Should we meet here?"

"At the main entrance on Salinas street," Thomas said. "An hour, no more."

FOUR

The man brought Thomas and Jorge to a good-sized house situated at the residential end of Iron Street and left before they went inside, pleading urgent business. *Cowardice, more like*, Thomas thought as he opened the unlocked front door and called out. There was no response, but he hadn't expected one. Although the house appeared deserted, he was relieved he had managed to persuade Lubna not to come.

A staircase rose to a narrow gallery, all the visible doors closed. Thomas tried the first door to his right on the ground floor. It revealed a place for cooking, but there was no residue of the smell of food and nothing on the table or shelves. It was the third door, into a large room flooded with sunlight from tall windows, where he discovered what had happened to the missing woman.

She sat almost upright in an ornate chair, cushions stuffed to either side to prevent her slipping. A blue tasselled rope was wrapped around her upper chest and tied behind the chair. A matching rope held back one of the curtains of a window, which offered a view along the street toward the tower of the Mosque and the heart of the city. Another corpse occupied a second chair, the two facing each other, as if their occupants had departed this life in mid-conversation. A notion soon disabused by the bindings holding each in place.

"You didn't tell me there would be bodies," said Jorge. "All you said was you needed my help." He started to turn away, a look of disgust on his face.

"I still do. There is a boy here somewhere."

"And two dead bodies." Jorge sniffed the air. "One of which, if my senses do not lie, has been dead for some time."

Thomas frowned, studying the male figure. Had the clerk of records not said the woman's husband died a month ago? Which meant this man could not be him. So who was he? " Dead at least four days, I would judge," he said.

"You would know about that better than anyone," said Jorge. "I still don't like it."

"I don't expect you to like it, I expect you to help me. Once you have talked to the boy you can go. If it makes any difference, I didn't expect the second body either."

"Just as long as this isn't another of your mysteries." Jorge looked from one chair to the other and pulled a face. "It looks like one of your mysteries. Didn't you say the father had died not so long ago? Could this be him?"

Thomas had barely glanced at the man's body. It too occupied a chair, this time tied with an orange cord. No doubt they would find its match on a curtain some-where in the house. The man's skin was beginning to darken as putrefaction took hold. The windows filled the room with both light and heat, and Thomas knew four days might have been an over-estimation.

"The father was claimed by the family and laid to rest beyond the city wall in the Christian burial ground, at least a month since. Who this man is I have no idea."

"Someone must be missing him," said Jorge. "We should try to find out who he is."

"See, you can investigate perfectly well without me."

"I didn't mean it that way, but it is common courtesy to try."

"Hm." Thomas looked around the room. Fine wall hangings. Expensive tables, and chairs of dark wood. A house in the Spanish style. It might be unusual elsewhere in al-Andalus but not in Malaka.

When he stood still and listened, he heard nothing. Or, not nothing, for noise entered from outside, at times rather a lot of noise. Raised voices, the cries of a trader. But within the house there were only the sounds that all houses make. A faint whistle as the constant wind from the sea caught at a corner. A creak as wood expanded or contracted. Nothing human. No boy, if boy he was. His brother had brought them here and made some excuse about being too busy to enter.

"We should at least inform the authorities," said Jorge. "Have the bodies taken away."

"The family will take the woman. As for the man ... you're probably right, we should ask questions. And much as it pains me to say it, you are also right, there will be someone who misses–" Thomas broke off. Held a finger to his lips.

Both of them stilled, listening. There had been a sound, faint, almost not there at all, but someone had moved in the room above. A creak of a floorboard. The scrape of a shoe against wood.

Thomas motioned Jorge to walk softly, turned, and made his way to the door, hesitated a moment then began to ascend the staircase, testing each riser before allowing his full weight to settle.

Another sound came. Two, perhaps three footsteps, louder now he was closer. And then a whimper, as of someone afraid.

Behind Thomas a stair creaked loudly as Jorge's extra weight pressed harder than his own. Whoever was hiding above heard it too and abandoned all pretence at stealth, as did Thomas. He caught the figure as it reached the upper corridor, moving away fast, but not as fast as Thomas. Whoever it was proved stronger than expected. Not a boy, not a boy at all, but a youth of near twenty years. As Thomas turned to him he discovered a figure that rose only two inches below his own height. He saw an expression of outright fear on the youth's face, masked by the softness of a mind troubled by little other than when his next meal might arrive.

"We are friends, Diego," Thomas said, assuming this had to be the woman's son, but the youth continued to writhe and try to pull away. There was a strength under Thomas's grip, and he was grateful when Jorge arrived to add his own, the youth clasped between them.

"Ah — ah — hurts!"

Thomas hesitated and loosened his grip, but only a little, waiting to see if the boy tried to flee. Instead his body softened and went slack.

"Diego?"

A fast nod. "Where are they?" His voice was slurred, the words hard to decipher, harder still because as the mortuary clerk had said some were in Spanish, others in Arabic, as if the two languages had become one. Perhaps, for this individual, they had.

"Your mother?"

Another nod. "And Pa. Ma and Pa. They do nothing. Sit there. All they do is sit." A look of helplessness crossed his face. "I have hunger. So much hunger." He glanced from Thomas to Jorge, back to Thomas, and then away, finding Jorge the less frightening. "Ma cooks," he explained. "But she … she just *sits.*"

"You took her from the hospital?"

A nod. "Saw here taken there, too."

Thomas wondered how to explain that the two individuals downstairs were dead, in a way Diego might understand, but suspected there was no need. He must know they would no longer wake.

"Who is the man?"

A look away. "Pa."

"Your father died a month since. I have spoken with your brother, they took him away and had him interred."

Another nod. "Diego bring back."

"That man isn't your father."

"He is a man. Pa gone, so Diego find another Pa. They are so quiet." A tear gathered and spilled. "I talk, ask what for dinner. But no words. So quiet."

"He is someone else's father. Don't they deserve to know where he is, Diego?"

"Nobody miss him. What happens to me?" More tears. "Ma and Pa, both gone."

"I will talk to your brother. Perhaps he will take you in."

A shake of the head. "No. Wife don't like Diego.

Afraid I hurt little ones. Diego never hurt little ones. Diego love them."

Thomas released his grip and took half a pace away, watching for any sign Diego might try to flee again. His running might make life easier for everyone else, but not for Diego him.

"This is Jorge," Thomas said. "He is a friend."

"Big."

"Yes, he is big, but so are you. Almost as big as Jorge."

Diego frowned. "No. Diego small." But he looked at Jorge and perhaps noted there was truth in what Thomas said. In turn Jorge looked back, and Thomas watched as his face composed itself and turned into that thing he found impossible to emulate. Jorge became someone it was impossible to dislike. And Diego responded. He reached out a hand. Jorge took it.

"I have a friend who makes good food," said Jorge. "Would you like to meet her?"

Despite the mixing up of languages when he spoke, Diego appeared to understand Arabic without any problem.

"Diego has much hunger."

"Then I will take you to meet Belia."

"Belia? A name?"

"She is my woman."

"Ma?"

"No. Like a wife."

"Your wife?"

"Like a wife."

Diego nodded. "Yes. Your wife. Diego know about wife. Is she pretty?" A sly smile crossed a face too guile-less to hide it.

"She is beautiful."

Another smile.

"And Thomas's wife is beautiful too."

"Thomas?"

Jorge nodded to where Thomas stood, forgotten. Diego didn't turn, not yet forgiving him for his capture.

"Good food?" he said.

"Very good food."

"And Ma and Pa?"

"Thomas will take care of them."

"Diego love Ma." More tears filled his eyes, emotions racing through his mind displayed unfiltered on his face.

"I know you do. Thomas will take care of her. He is a physician. The best physician in al-Andalus."

Diego sniggered and shook his head. "Nobody that good."

Not as stupid as his brother had made out, then, Thomas thought. He waited, silent, as Jorge led Diego toward the stairs. When he heard the front door close he descended to the room that carried the taint of death. He untied Diego's mother and lifted her to the ground. There would be sheets and blankets somewhere, and he would cover her before fetching the family. He checked the body briefly, because Lubna had come to ask his opinion, and he believed he owed her at least a cursory examination. The woman was not young, well into her fifth decade, and her arms and legs were stick thin. Lubna had said she was admitted with a head wound, and Thomas saw it clearly, the bruise now yellowing. It was a bad enough blow, but not enough to kill, and Lubna had said she was responding to treatment.

He rolled her onto her front but found nothing else

until he lifted her thin hair to discover a dark, fresh bruise on the back of her skull.

Thomas wondered if Diego might have attacked his mother. But as he peered closer he decided the bruise was more likely caused by an accident, a fall of some kind, and almost certainly what had led to her eventual death. He would ask Lubna if she had observed the mark, but there would be no blame if she had missed it. And no blame over the woman's death. She had no doubt bled into her skull, and no surgeon in the world could have saved her. It was strange the bruise was less advanced than the other, and he wondered if she had tried to get up and fallen while in the Infirmary.

And her first fall, if that had been what caused the initial wound, was it the same as her husband? Both of them? It seemed too great a coincidence, and Thomas wondered if he had been too quick to trust Diego. Had he pushed them both down the stairs? Thomas let the thought work itself to a conclusion and shook his head. He couldn't see it. Diego had loved both his mother and father, that was clear to see.

He rolled the woman over again and turned to the man, ignoring the stink that rose from him as he pulled the corpse to the floor, long used to such and worse. And then, because he couldn't help himself, he examined that body as well. Which is when he discovered what had killed him. No fall this time, but a knife, thrust into the man's chest from the side, no doubt piercing his heart. Thomas removed the man's clothing until he lay sad and naked beneath his gaze, but no other wound showed. A single blow. Either lucky, or administered by someone who knew what they were doing. Not an accident, but deliberate murder.

Thomas pushed a hand to clear the hair that had fallen across his face and sat on his heels. Why had the man been killed? And why had Diego brought the body back here? Had he witnessed the killing? Did that put him in danger too? Thomas knew he would have to report the man's death to the authorities but also knew nothing would be done about it.

He dressed the man again and rose to go in search of blankets. Lubna wouldn't be pleased, he knew, because now there was a mystery, and questions that already scratched at the back of his mind.

FIVE

Diego slept. Belia told him the man-boy had eaten at least three full meals then fallen asleep with his head on the table. By the time Thomas returned to the house, which for now they called home, perched beyond the city walls on a low rise overlooking Malaka, Jorge had put Diego to bed in Will's room, and now Thomas stood beside his friend on the wide veranda. West, a wide plain was dotted with trees and scattered fields growing rice, sugar cane, and an array of vegetables and crops. Sheep and cattle grazed small clearings, and reflected sunlight glittered from irrigation channels. This was a rich land, a good land, well cared for and well cultivated. Testament to those who lived there.

Thomas wondered if he lived here now. This fine house was meant to be temporary, but the longer he spent in it the less that seemed to be the truth. It was starting to feel like home, and that worried him, because his home was meant to be in Gharnatah. Except little remained for him in Gharnatah, and people there wanted him dead.

"I suppose you want me to talk to him?" said Jorge.

"I would only scare the boy."

"He's no boy, except up here." Jorge tapped his skull. He had stopped shaving his head when they left Gharnatah almost a year ago, and now his hair hung almost as long as Thomas's, but of course far better cared for. It had grown in a light brown, lightened even further by the sun. His chin and cheeks were smooth, not only from choice but because when Thomas had unmanned him at the age of thirteen he had interrupted his normal development as a man. Now, when Jorge tried to grow a beard it came in patchy, so the perfect skin of his face was, unlike Thomas's, unmarked by any stubble.

He looked magnificent.

Thomas couldn't recall a time when he had not.

"Which is why it is better you question him. We need to find out who the dead man is. There must be someone who misses him."

"Perhaps he has no family," said Jorge. "I have heard no rumour of a missing man, and someone missing almost a week would raise questions. You said he was stabbed — murdered?" He shook his head and let his breath loose in a long sigh, not needing to say anything to make his meaning clear. Murder. Again.

Thomas wondered if he could he turn his back on it, to ignore what had happened. He glanced inside to see Lubna had fallen asleep on a pile of cushions. The air in the house was scented from the herbs Belia used to create her salves and potions. Also scented by the presence of the two women. An itch of unease bothered Thomas. Their life here had grown settled, comfortable. Happy. He didn't want to destroy that contentment by taking up another investigation. He had seen too much death, and been the cause of too much as well. In a few months he would turn forty-seven years of age. A good span for any man. He had no intention of closing his eyes for good yet, but an easier life was a temptation. If only he could quell his curiosity. He felt it scratching at him as they stood there in the heat of early afternoon. Who was the dead man? And why was he been killed? It was clear to Thomas why Diego had taken the body to his house — as a replacement for his missing father, but where had he found him? No doubt it made sense to the boy, if no-one else. He would need talking to, questions posed. Thomas sighed.

"Let him sleep for now," said Jorge. "This evening will be soon enough."

"Can you read my mind now?"

"Of course, and have always been able to. You are an open book, Thomas Berrington. Your thoughts are like words written across your face."

Thomas smiled. "If that were true you could certainly not read them."

Jorge waved a hand, dismissing such trivial matters. "We should let him sleep. I doubt he's slept much since he took his mother to the Infirmary."

Which reminded Thomas of something. He glanced toward Lubna, pleased to see she had woken and was looking back at him. A smile softened a face already soft with sleep. Thomas left Jorge alone on the terrace and went to kneel beside the pile of cushions.

"Can I ask you something?"

Lubna nodded.

A shadow passed and Thomas glanced to one side to see Belia join Jorge on the terrace. They embraced, an easy familiarity between them. They had lived as man and wife for over a year now and, despite Thomas's expectation it might end at any moment, they still appeared to love each other deeply. He turned away to allow them a moment of privacy, though he knew neither cared if they had an audience or not.

"Tell me again, when was Diego's mother admitted to the Infirmary?"

"Four days, a little more by now. Wait here." Lubna rolled sideways, then rose in a single, lithe movement. She padded away on bare feet, small toes appearing from beneath her silk robe with each step. Thomas waited for her to re-appear, which she did before long, clutching a leather-bound book which she opened as she sat cross-legged. Thomas leaned close as she flipped through pages of paper made here in Malaka. Thomas knew their source because he had bought the journal for Lubna the day after they arrived, when they were still living in a small garret close to the fish market, before she had even been accepted into the Infirmary. He smiled to see how many pages were now filled with Lubna's neat script. A finger traced the notes, and she looked up at him, a frown creasing her brow at the intensity of his gaze, and Thomas knew he had been staring too hard, as he often did.

"Yes, four days," said Lubna. "A little after dawn, though I didn't see her until later in the day."

"Does it record who brought her in?"

"It does. A neighbour." Her fingertip traced through the notes. "He says he found her lying in the street near her house and brought her directly to the Infirmary. He must have told Diego where she was later on." Lubna's finger continued to move. "It wasn't a bad blow to the head, and as I told you she woke within two days. I was sure she would make a full recovery."

"I found the mark of another blow, beneath her hair," Thomas said. "I found it when I examined her."

"I checked everywhere. Her hair as well, as you taught me. I would have seen it if it was there."

"When did you last check?"

Lubna consulted her notes again. "*Al-Khamis*, so two days. Could the mark take that long to show?"

"It looked more recent. You said Diego came to the ward?"

"He wouldn't hit his mother. I refuse to believe it."

"Does he know you? Did you talk?"

"Briefly. He wanted to know when she was coming home. I felt sorry for him."

"I need to question him in the morning. I was going to ask Jorge to be there, but perhaps you would be better. I think Diego likes pretty women."

"I tell you again, he would not harm his mother. And I did not miss any mark on her head."

"I believe you."

"But you found it." Lubna appeared crestfallen, and Thomas reached for her hand, held its small heat within his own.

"You didn't miss it, because when you examined her it wasn't there."

Lubna frowned. "I don't understand."

"You will if you think on it for a moment." He waited, watching the play of thoughts cross her face, aware this must be how Jorge saw people, except with far more skill than Thomas could ever possess.

Lubna looked up to meet his eyes. "Who? Why?"

"I don't know. If I did we might be close to knowing

the answer to my other questions. Was there anyone else who visited the ward?"

"Several people. Relatives of other patients. A few scribes who were called to rewrite a will. You know the Infirmary better than I do, people come and go all the time, it is impossible to count or control them." Lubna's gaze explored Thomas's face, a frown forming on her own. "You're not going to let this go, are you."

"You know I wouldn't be the man you loved if I did."

"Sometimes I wonder about the love," said Lubna, but her smile negated the words. "I should have been more suspicious when she died, shouldn't I."

"She suffered a blow to the head. We both know there can be complications later. A damaged blood vessel within the skull can suddenly burst. Or it might simply have been her time to die. To be a physician means we must accept death in the same manner we accept a life saved."

"No." Lubna shook her head, her hair, loose now within the house, flew dark and shining around her face. "I will never accept that. We mend people. We do not watch them die."

"Then you will never make a good physician." Thomas knew his words might hurt, but they had to be said. "Do the best you can, use your skill, but you have to accept not everyone can be saved. And most important of all, put the death behind you. Don't dwell on it. Even if you think you have made a mistake, put it in the past. Learn from it, dismiss it, but never make the same mistake again." He lifted her hand to his mouth and kissed her palm, the silk of her skin bringing a sudden arousal he suppressed. "You will be a better physician for it."

"What, are you telling me not to care ... like you don't care?"

"I taught myself to move on. You'll have to do the same."

Lubna drew her hand away. "No wonder they call you the butcher." She closed the book and started to rise.

Thomas held his hand out. "Can I borrow that for a while?"

"Why? So you can mark my notes?" She held the journal against her breast.

"I want to follow the events associated with her admission and treatment."

"I did what I could to the best of my ability," said Lubna. "I realise I am not the great Thomas Berrington, but you said she might have died anyway."

"You are as good a physician as anyone I have ever known. And you will get better. Better than me, one day, I am sure of it, for as you say, I lack compassion."

"You always told me that was a benefit." But Thomas saw she was pleased at his remark.

"A man can change his mind, can't he? No doubt you have softened me." He held out a hand. "Am I allowed to read your notes?"

"Make of them what you will," said Lubna, passing them to him. "But don't you dare comment on them."

Thomas smiled and watched as she turned away, as enchanted by her as he had been the moment they first met those five years before.

Thomas flicked through the book, starting at the beginning, familiarising himself with the way Lubna made her notes. They were concise, a trait he approved of, sticking to the facts, the only embellishment being when she had changed a treatment and wanted to explain the reasoning. As he browsed, Thomas saw that the words he had spoken as flattery would turn out to be true. Lubna was both skilled and knowledgeable. She might well exceed him, if only she could harden her heart and make the difficult decisions required. But he knew if that happened she would no longer be the woman he loved.

Only after a time did he turn to the more recent pages. The notes relating to Diego's mother were scattered amongst others, but once again Lubna showed intelligence. Individual patients were clearly identified, a thin ruled line separating each examination, each learning she had made. Lubna recorded the name each time, Dionora Jinto Jiminez. A Spaniard living in a Moorish city. Thomas recalled Diego's father was also Spanish. Malaka was the one city in al-Andalus where such a thing could pass without comment. There was no city anywhere in the world that boasted such a varied mix of people.

When Thomas looked up, his neck ached from leaning over and shadows had moved across the floor. Little more than an hour of daylight remained, but it would be enough.

He went to look in on Diego where he slept in a hastily erected spare bed in Will's room. He lay on his back, arms straight at his sides, face in repose. Thomas saw in his features the man he might have become had he been more fortunate in his making. Handsome. Tall. Clever. But would that man have been as loving as Diego appeared to be? Thomas had met others like him, often surprised at their intelligence, the kind that others might do well to match.

40

Beside him, Will was curled against Diego's side, his own bed empty. Thomas stared at his son and experienced an ache in his chest. Jorge told him the ache was love. Thomas wasn't so sure. More likely something he had eaten that disagreed with him. Not that he didn't love Will, because he did, with every fibre of his being … even if he might not be his true father, a certainty still denied him.

He turned left through the wide door at the side of the house and walked toward the path that would take him to the northern Buenaventura gate, the closest to the Infirmary.

SIX

As Thomas made his way east toward the Muralla district where the Infirmary lay, a strong breeze tugged at his clothes and whipped his hair about his face. Far inland, beyond the peaks that loomed over the city, dark clouds promised heavy rain, and he wondered if it already fell on Gharnatah. He had given little thought to the city in some time and wondered if the ease of forgetting was a sign of some kind. He knew his life had changed over recent years. Was it an indication his certainties might be changing too? He had imagined dying in Gharnatah, hopefully at a good age. He felt fifty years approaching like a runaway horse, an age which had once seemed impossible to attain. Now he thought sixty years would be interesting, seventy a dream. If Thomas attained the age of sixty, Will would be a man of eighteen years, almost the same age as Thomas had been when he first came to Malaka with a letter of introduction from an old man he had met in the Pyrenees. What would Will become? A copy of Thomas, or something else? His own person, he hoped.

And then his footsteps slowed and he came to a halt. For a moment he had almost forgotten that Will might not be his true son. He was loved as a son, Will knew that, and Thomas felt it in his heart. But was he the true product of his loins? He had lain with Helena, that could not be denied, but still she refused him confirmation.

Sometimes Thomas saw Will act in a way that was so much a reflection of what he might have done himself certainty came. And then, at other times, especially as Will grew older and became more his own person, there seemed parts of him that had nothing at all to do with Thomas. Often he put that down to the boy's grandfather, Olaf Torvaldsson. Will shared the same wildness when fighting, the same sturdiness, the same stubborn streak. *But*, Thomas thought, *did it matter?* As far as he was concerned, Will was his and Lubna's, even if neither had been involved in his conception.

He started off again just as a rumble of thunder shook the air, but when he looked up, only blue sky lay above Malaka. Strange times bring strange weather, he thought, as he started off once more, heading toward Diego's house in Iron Street. Lubna had said a neighbour brought Dionora to the Infirmary. Most people would be home from work by now, and it was not such a long street he couldn't knock at every door. He had almost reached his destination when a familiar hoarse voice called his name. Thomas stopped, not needing to turn to know who it was.

"Have you forgotten it is forty days?" The skeletal figure of Abbot Mandana walked slowly toward him.

Beyond, a half dozen of his men stood watching without expression.

Thomas stared at the man. No, he hadn't forgotten, but had hoped this encounter wouldn't occur, and certainly he could do without it right now. But it was his own fault. He had allowed Mandana to soften his mind to what the man had done. Allowed himself to feel sorry for him. An old man. An old, sick man who might be dead already if not for Thomas's ministrations and Belia's salves.

"I'm busy," Thomas said.

"And you think me not? I am on a task for Fernando, but I made time to come to you." He held his left hand across his chest, cradling the stump that was all that remained of it.

"Then it will have to be later. Tomorrow even. You can find something to amuse you in Malaka tonight, I am sure, even a man of God such as you claim to be."

Mandana shook his head slowly, as if disappointed in one of his followers. "And I thought we had become friends."

"Then you thought wrong. Tomorrow, at my house. You know where it is." Thomas turned away. He had Diego's neighbour to seek and a mystery to solve.

"Was your journey worthwhile?" asked Lubna as Thomas slid the journal across the table to her. She sat between Jorge and Belia, all of them curious to find out what he might have discovered.

"I'm not sure. Possibly."

Lubna placed her elbows on the table, her chin on her fists, and stared at Thomas. "Explain."

He smiled. It was what he would have said.

"I found the neighbour almost at once. A smith who has a small business near the city wall. He claims he heard voices, an argument, and then the sound of running. When he looked out to see what was happening, he saw Dionora collapsed on the roadway and went to her aid. He says he could tell she was badly injured so took her directly to the Infirmary."

"Was it him who told Diego?" asked Lubna.

"It was. He knows the boy. I asked did he go into the house, but he said not. I asked did Diego appear to be acting suspiciously, but he said no to that, too. Then he asked me should he have been suspicious. So then I said no."

"That's a lot of no's. Did you find out anything useful?"

"Yes." Thomas smiled. "It might be a lot of negatives, but it tells me something all the same. Diego was upset, the smith said, which is even more reason to believe him innocent of attacking his mother." Thomas held a hand up as Lubna began to object. "It also tells me whoever that other man is who was in the house was not there at that time."

"Why would he be? Diego's mother would certainly not allow a dead body into her house."

"Of course not. So I went to the Infirmary and questioned those on the ward to find out if they saw anything suspicious. Most of them had seen Diego at one time or another, but he would come and go, away from her side most of the time. No doubt it was during one of these absences he found the man's body.

He must have been distraught. His father already dead, his mother sick. It's no excuse, but given the way he sees the world I can understand why he did what he did."

"I'm glad somebody does. What else?"

"As you say, a lot of people come and go. The clerks and other doctors didn't remember anyone in particular, apart from one of the nurses. She was on night-duty when a man came in. She said she might not have remembered him at all but he had no Arabic and his Spanish was truly awful. He was asking after Dionora, with a story that Diego's father had left funds the city had only recently become aware of. He wanted to know where they might be sent."

Jorge snorted but said nothing.

"Exactly what I thought," said Thomas.

"Did the nurse believe him?" asked Lubna. "I think I know the one you mean. She is sharp, observant."

"Her opinion of the man's story was the same as yours would have been. She sent him away, but it seems he must have returned."

"Is it he who killed her? Who struck that blow to her skull?"

"I believe so. It would help if I knew why she was killed."

"Sometimes there is no why," said Jorge. "You know that better than anyone."

"But I would like to know there is no reason, or if not what the reason is."

Jorge shook his head. "Sometimes you talk in riddles."

"Pa! Diego says he's awake."

Thomas turned to see Will standing in the doorway

46

and knew this conversation would have to wait until another time.

"Then go and tell him to come through."

"He is crying," said Will. "He said someone had died. I told him not to be sad but he won't stop."

"I'll go to him." Belia rose, stroking Will's soft hair as she passed. Hair that was as fine as silk, like that of his mother's.

Thomas held his arms out, and Will came to him, walking fast, trying not to run. He pulled himself onto Thomas's lap and lay against him, sleep not long departed. A long body for his age, beginning to lose the fat of childhood, though still far from a man. But Thomas could see he would be a fine man. As tall as his grandfather, and as handsome as his mother was beautiful.

"I like him," said Will. "Diego."

"We all do."

"He's a man but not a man. We talked."

"About what?" asked Thomas, afraid if he pushed too hard Will might lose the thread.

"His Ma and Pa. He misses them. He said he tried to keep them with him but you took them away. Even his new Pa, the one he brought home." Will looked up at Thomas's face. "Why you do that, Pa?"

"They were ... not alive." Thomas had no wish to hide the truth from Will. Lies never helped anyone, even when told in an attempt to soften the truth.

"Dead? Diego didn't say that." A frown formed on Will's face so slowly and deeply, Thomas almost laughed, and raised a hand to hide his expression. "How?"

"He was old, my sweet."

47

The frown remained.

"How old?"

"Diego's father had almost sixty years, his mother a little less." Thomas pictured the image of the corpse that Diego had sat in a chair. That man had been younger than sixty, but only by a few years. It had been close enough for Diego to accept him as his father. Or to persuade himself of such.

Will nodded. "You have forty-six years, Pa, don't you?"

It was Thomas's turn to nod.

"How much between forty-six and ..." He hesitated, thinking about it. "... and sixty?"

"Fourteen years."

"I have nearly five," said Will. "How much more is fourteen?"

"Almost three times," said Thomas. "You can work that out yourself. Use your wooden blocks and count them. I know you can count higher than fourteen."

"But not forty-six," said Will, and this time Thomas couldn't suppress a laugh. He pulled Will against him and kissed the top of his head, inhaling the wondrous scent of him. He saw Lubna's eyes on him, an expression on her face that filled him with warmth. And then Belia returned with Diego and the night turned into a strange kind of party as they all tried to cheer him up.

Thomas put thoughts of the deaths aside, but they returned as he undressed and slipped into the wide bed they had acquired after taking the house overlooking Malaka. He tucked his palms beneath his head and stared at the ceiling, thinking about what he knew and what he didn't know. The latter, as always, outweighed the former.

Lubna's voice came from the room along the hallway as she put the two boys to bed. No, Thomas corrected, one boy and one man. It was so easy to regard Diego as a boy, but he had the height and muscle of a full-grown man. It was only his mind that had refused to grow. Perhaps that was an advantage. Thomas had found little in adulthood to recommend it. But then, there had been little in his childhood to recommend it either.

He glanced up from his own thoughts as Lubna entered the room and closed the door behind her.

"Are they asleep?" Thomas asked.

"Not quite, but almost." She smiled as she unwound her *hijab*, dark blue silk that played through her fingers like water. "Will likes Diego, and Diego likes Will. But he is sad. Diego, that is."

"It will pass." Thomas watched Lubna loosen the ties on her robe, the skin beneath slowly revealed. The swell of a breast. The curve of her belly within which lay their child. This one, he hoped, would live, but the carrying of babies was dangerous work, the birthing of them even more so. But Lubna was married to the best physician in Spain, so he knew everything would be well this time.

"What is to become of him?" Naked now, Lubna walked to a marble bowl and poured water from a jug. She washed herself carefully, slowly.

Thomas shifted on the bed. "He has a family."

"Who do not want him. Or did I hear wrong when his brother was at the Infirmary?" Lubna towelled herself dry, turning, aware of what she was doing as she displayed herself to Thomas, signs of her own arousal showing.

"You didn't, but something will work itself out."

49

"He can stay with us for a while at least, can't he? For Will's sake?" She knelt beside the low bed and drew the sheet down so that Thomas was revealed, as naked as she was. Lubna smiled and reached for him.

Thomas caught her wrist, and Lubna frowned.

"Do you not want me tonight?"

"I do. But I spoke with someone else today and have not yet told you who."

Lubna laughed as she lay beside him, her skin against his, her fingers tracing the scars that marked his chest and arms, each of them familiar.

"Is it more important than what I want to do with you?"

"Likely not, but I need to tell you anyway, because Mandana is coming to the house tomorrow. Knowing him it will be at dawn."

"Is it forty days since he was last here? Does Belia know?"

"I told her earlier because she needs to prepare fresh salves." Thomas traced the underside of Lubna's breast, the swell of her belly where their child grew within. "I will treat him and send him away as soon as I can."

"Until another forty days have passed." Lubna sighed. "None of us know why you do it."

"I'm not even sure myself."

"We can talk of such matters in the morning. For now I want you to finish telling me what else you found out."

"Now?" Thomas reached for her, and she allowed it, melting into his touch, her skin silk and velvet, hot beneath his hands.

"It will make our loving all the better for the wait."

Lubna smiled. "And you can tease me a little while you talk if you wish."

"How can I recall anything when I touch you?"

"The great Thomas Berrington?" She lay across him, her mouth covering his, and whatever he knew or did not know was dashed from his thoughts as he submitted to her.

SEVEN

Mandana came to the house alone. He left his men a quarter mile away, where they lit a small fire to roast something over the flames. A rabbit or hare, something to break their fast with.

Thomas watched him come, slow strides, older now and with something broken inside. It was not just the loss of his hand but something else, too. The man had held a position, been admired and followed by hundreds. Now the dozen men on the ridge might be all he had left. He was back in Fernando's favour though, doing work others refused.

Thomas waited until Mandana stepped up to the terrace then nodded toward the side of the house and led the way to a small workshop. Lubna had made it clear she wanted nothing to do with the man. Belia the same. She had prepared the ointments Thomas had asked for but he would have to apply them himself. Thomas wondered if Lubna and Belia had not been so against his treating Mandana whether he might have stopped, but their resistance made his resolve only the firmer. Yes, Mandana had been an evil man and may still be so, but he deserved the same treatment as everyone else. Was that not what a physician did — treat all the same?

Inside the workshop he discovered they were not alone. Will sat on a bench, examining one of the pots Belia had left there.

"Madana!" He dropped down and came to the man, who knelt and took Will's shoulder in his one good hand.

"Ah, my little friend. Has your father been treating you well?"

Will nodded.

"And have you been good?"

Another nod.

"Then here, a small gift for you." Mandana reached inside his robe and drew something out, dropped it into Will's hand. The boy sped off and Thomas knew he would have to check later what he had been given. Mandana watched Will leave, staying on one knee after he had gone. "He grows fast." He turned to stare at Thomas. "I believe he will overtake you before he becomes an adult." Mandana held out his hand, making it clear he wanted Thomas to help him to his feet.

With a sharp exhalation of breath, Thomas obliged. "Do you have much pain?"

"More this last week, but I am used to pain, it is good for the soul. Do you have the treatments?"

"Show me your arm."

Mandana rolled his sleeve back to display the mottled stump where wolves had taken the hand years before. He had been lucky to live through the attack. Lucky to have been forgiven by Fernando after kidnapping his only son. Thomas still failed to understand what had happened to change the King's opinion of this man.

He leaned closer to examine the stump, palpated it inside his hand as he watched for any sign of pain on Mandana's face, but the man's expression was a mask.

"You wash it twice a day?"

"When I can."

"As long as the skin is unbroken any water will do if you cannot find clean."

"I will try."

"Try harder. There are signs of infection. If it takes hold there is little I can do for you. So wash, and wash often."

Thomas used warm water and a soap made by Belia, which filled the air with a sharp scent, before wiping Mandana's arm dry and applying the first of three salves.

Mandana closed his eyes and his face lost its usual scowl.

"You have a beautiful house here, Berrington." His voice was soft. "But I would advise you to move as far from Malaka as you can."

"Of course you do." Thomas finished with the first salve and left it to perform Belia's magic for a time. "Would you like me to return to England, perhaps?"

"Each of us has a home. Do you not miss it? But please, do not go until you have made me whole again."

Thomas laughed. "I'm sorry, but I can't conjure a new hand. And I miss my homeland not at all." As he spoke the words, Thomas came to realise his memories of the border country between England and Wales where he was raised had faded almost into myth for him. Green fields, rain, snow, ice on the windows, mud. It was not a memory he welcomed. He would rather turn his face up to the sun than have it constantly dashed with water.

Mandana opened his eyes and studied Thomas. "I may be giving away something I am not meant to, but even you must know the Spanish are coming. And coming soon." He held his arm out as Thomas wiped the first salve from it and began to apply the second, more astringent than the first, and he saw Mandana wince and say, "I liked the other better."

"Pain is part of the healing. And why should I fear the coming of Spain? I assume you mean the army?"

"Come this summer, Malaka will fall. You should not be here when that happens, not unless you plan to switch sides. I know you have been asked, and know too that you would be made more than welcome." He shook his head. "You are a fool, but all the world knows that."

"A fool with two hands," Thomas said.

"Yes, that is true. For now at least."

As Thomas spread the final salve, he watched Mandana's face, at ease for once, eyes closed, and a memory surfaced.

"I met someone recently who could have been your double. Without the beard, and with two hands. And much younger, of course."

Mandana smiled, his eyes still closed. "So nothing like me, then."

"Perhaps not."

"It was probably my son. He was in Malaka with his

wife, on Fernando's business. He told me what happened, and your part in it."

Thomas stopped his treatment, and Mandana opened his eyes.

"You have a son?"

Mandana smiled. "Is the world not a strange place? I did not even know it myself until two years ago."

"How?"

"Oh, the usual way, I expect. You are a knowledgeable man so I do not have to tell you how such is done."

"You are an Abbot, or were, at least."

"An Abbot with access to many places. Including ..." Mandana stared into space, his face changing, growing younger. "There was a religious order I helped. Women. And ... I admit to a weakness of the flesh. I am a man, like any other, after all. And if the Pope can have a wife and children why not an Abbot?" He shook his head. "Perhaps there are other children, I do not know, all I know of is this one. Pedro Guerrero, he calls himself, a name gifted him by the nuns. He came to me, came to find me after they told him who his father was."

"Why?"

"Did they tell him, or did he come to me?"

Thomas wiped the salve from Mandana's arm with a linen cloth. He leaned close to examine the wound. It looked better, but eventually the wound would kill him unless it was treated regularly. Something Thomas was reluctant to do.

"Either."

"The answer to both questions is curiosity. You would understand that, I am sure. He asked and they told him. They are women of God, after all, and must tell the truth. He came to me because he wanted to improve himself. I found him a position serving Fernando, and a wife. The rest he did himself." Mandana turned his head and stared at Thomas. "He told me what you did, and that if he gets the opportunity he will kill you."

"I saved a child. The woman was beyond the skill of any physician. Perhaps he should have taken more care of her. What happened was none of my doing. Tell him that, for if he comes for me it will be he who loses his life."

"I tried to tell him if anyone could have saved her it would be you, but his heart tells him otherwise. You live among heathens, Berrington, yet profess friendship to my King and Queen. Tell me, where do your loyalties lie?"

"Honestly? We are being honest now, are we not?"

Mandana nodded.

"Then honestly I do not know. Spain, al-Andalus, England. I have no loyalties anymore. No allegiance. All I care for are my family and friends."

Mandana gave a tiny smile. "As it should be. My son is here under instruction from Fernando. You and I know that Malaka will fall, and when it does we need to be prepared. My son is helping in that, but he had no idea the price of his service would be so high." Mandana rose to his feet, tall, skeletal, a broken man and nothing like the one Thomas had first met in Qurtuba over four years before.

"Now, are we finished?" Mandana pulled his robe around himself.

Thomas went to the workshop door and looked out, breathing untainted air as he watched him return to his men. Will and Diego were behind the house, crouching to study something in the dry grass. He hoped it was not a snake or scorpion but knew Will was careful enough, and he had taught him of the few dangers he might encounter. The animals, at least. People were another matter.

After Mandana had gone, Belia came into the workshop as Thomas cleaned up. She stood near him, saying nothing until he stopped his work and turned to her. He studied her face for a time as she continued to keep her silence, as always fascinated by her sense of otherness. She was a beautiful woman — only one of the reasons Jorge loved her — but there was more than beauty there. Sometimes Thomas found her staring at him and found the attention almost frightening, as if she could see through all the layers of his being to his very core — a place he would rather nobody saw, or even knew about.

"He's gone. My thanks for the ointments." Thomas touched her shoulder but she shrugged his hand off.

"He will return in forty days, will he not? I do not understand why you do this for him, Thomas. You owe that man nothing. Nothing at all."

"He has changed."

"Or you think him changed."

"And you don't?"

"I did not know him before, but I do not trust him now. Send him away the next time he comes."

"But you will prepare your salves for me in any case?"

"Not just for him. There are more deserving patients for them."

"Then I will tell him to come to the Infirmary next

time." He glanced at the door. "I might be able to catch up with him and tell him now."

"They have gone. I watched them mount horses and ride away."

Thomas looked beyond Belia as Lubna entered the workshop, the small space suddenly claustrophobic with the three of them in it, and he thought of the workshop he had left behind in Gharnatah and wished he could be there now.

"That man gave these to Will," said Lubna, holding her hand out.

"I saw him give him something. What is it?"

"Dice."

It didn't seem enough to explain Lubna's tone of voice until she tossed them onto the bench. They clattered against a wooden box, spun a moment and fell still. Thomas reached out and picked them up, then dropped them again so they skittered across the floor. He had taken them to be fashioned of pale wood or ivory. On closer examination he saw them for what they were, carved from the knuckle bones of a hand. Mandana's little joke. Or a threat.

When he looked up, Belia was smiling, as if she had won some kind of contest.

"One more time," Thomas said, "and then I will tell him to find someone else."

Thomas found what he was looking for far back in a drawer in the room he and Lubna shared. He carried the small objects inside his hand as he went in search of Will and Diego. Mandana had been a distraction, one he didn't welcome even while continuing to treat the man. He thought of his promise to send him away and wondered if he could do so. He had a sense it was better to keep the disgraced Abbot close where he could see what he was plotting. And then he wondered how much longer Mandana might have left on this earth. His stump had healed a little with Belia's ointments, but Thomas knew as soon as the treatment stopped the effects would soon reverse. Could he sentence the man to that kind of death? There would be pain, a great deal of pain.

He found Diego and Will together, once more near the patch of grass, and Thomas saw why. There was a cleared circle of dirt where they had been playing with the knuckle-bone dice. He knelt beside them, amused when Diego turned his face away like a loyal dog that knows it has done something wrong.

Thomas shook his hand, letting them both hear the rattle within. Then he cast the dice. Twin cubes of ivory larger than Mandana's gift, and hopefully with less fear associated with them.

"Pa!" Will reached out before the dice had stopped moving. He examined them, a smile forming. "Good dice, Pa. Thanks."

"They are for both of you."

Will nodded and held the dice out to Diego, who remained with gaze averted.

"I need to ask you some questions," Thomas said.

Diego's shoulders bunched a little tighter.

"How do you know what they are yet? They might be good questions."

"Diego knows things," said Will.

"Everyone knows things." Thomas tapped his son on the top of his head. "Even you know a few things."

Will cast the dice, eyes fixed on their dance until they became still, and Thomas watched his lips move as he totalled the count. A three and a five. No significance to the numbers, only the counting of them.

"I want you to do something for me, Diego. For me and Jorge. It means going into Malaka."

Diego continued to stare out to where mountains reared, jagged-peaked, hazy as the heat of the day built. Swirls of wind came and went.

"We can find somewhere to eat," Thomas said. "You would like that, wouldn't you?"

Diego liked to eat. It was as if the food presented by Belia was something he had never experienced before, which might be true, for she had acquired her skill at the stove from somewhere else even if she was born in Ixbilya.

Diego twitched his attention toward Thomas, but it would not stay there long and skittered away again.

"Will come too."

"Will has to stay here."

"Then Diego stay too."

Thomas sighed. "All right, Will too." He glanced at his son, who continued to roll the dice.

"Play," Will said, his attention half on Diego. "Show Pa what you can do."

Diego shook his head.

"Is it a trick?" Thomas asked. "What can you do, Diego?"

"No trick," said Will. He held out his hand, the dice resting on his palm. "Show Pa. Five and Five." He touched the face of one of the dice to show the number, its shape, to Diego.

Diego glanced at the dice, at Thomas, back to Will. Slowly he reached out and took the two ivory cubes. He turned them over, studying the numbers, and Thomas wondered how much he knew of them. He had not spent enough time with Diego, assuming he lacked any mind at all, and he knew he was wrong to have done so.

"Five and five?" Thomas said, confused.

Diego gave a sly smile and tossed the dice. They flew through the air, tumbled. One hit a stone and bounced to one side, rolled back. When they came to rest the upturned faces both showed a five.

Thomas examined Diego, whose attention had moved back to the mountains. He wanted to ask how he had done that, and how Will knew Diego could do such a thing. It was most likely a fluke, incapable of repetition.

"Ask him to do it again," Thomas said. "Different numbers this time. A three and a one."

Will laughed.

"What's so funny?" Thomas suppressed a moment of annoyance. He didn't understand what had just happened, and it sparked a small fear inside him. He was used to logic, to science and knowledge. This owed nothing to anything he understood.

"Diego doesn't know numbers, only ... only shapes. You want one and three?"

Thomas nodded.

Will picked up the dice, turned them in his small hands to show Diego the numbers. Diego stared, looked up at Will, and nodded. He glanced at Thomas and smiled. This was something he could do. He took the dice and cupped them inside his hands, shook them, and threw. As before the dice tumbled a moment before falling still. They showed a one and a three.

"How ..." Thomas said, but it was to himself, and he expected no answer — unsure if he even wanted an answer. He stood and offered his hand. "We should go into the city before it gets too hot."

EIGHT

Diego became agitated as soon as Thomas began to question him, even more so as the questions continued. He put his head in his hands, covered his ears, and cowered in the corner. Thomas had sent Will away because he didn't want to subject him to the topic that needed to be discussed. Now he knew he was wrong to expect Diego to accept it either. He had forgotten he was not a man in anything other than body.

"Send for Will," said Jorge. He gripped Diego inside his arms, but it was clear how difficult it was becoming to hold him. "They have formed a deep bond in a short time. Will can help."

"I won't have him involved."

"Will is stronger than you think."

"He is four years old!" Thomas said.

"Almost five. And he is your son. That must count for something."

Does it? Diego had grown restless when the others left. They had all descended into the city and eaten at an inn before coming to the house that until recently had been Diego's home. And then Thomas had sent Belia and Lubna away with Will.

The time spent inside Diego's house had been tense but manageable. It was only as Thomas teased from him the story of how he had come to bring a dead man home that Diego began to grow agitated. Thomas had expected such, which is why Jorge was with him. Diego liked Jorge. Or he had.

"Shh ..." Jorge stroked Diego's face, whispered soft words in his ear, too quiet for Thomas to hear, but he did not want to in any case. Instead he waited, because there was nothing else he could do.

Slowly Diego calmed. Not altogether — his eyes continued to dart from place to place, frequently rising to study the mountains that circled Malaka, as they had done earlier that day. The mountains that protected it from invasion except from the sea, and invasion by sea was difficult, even more so when the city had a tall, strong wall to protect it on that side.

"Is it far?" asked Jorge. They had left the house, following Diego's reluctant instructions.

Diego shook his head. Pointed.

Thomas looked in that direction. A wide street with well-appointed houses. At the end of it a narrow gate through the wall stood open to admit people in and out to the rocky ledge that lay beyond, and the sea.

"If you are good now, Belia will make you a special cake. What would you like?"

Diego looked at Jorge, clearly unsure of the bribe. Then he made his mind up. "Honey and sugar. But Ma say I can't have it all the time. As a treat."

"Then Belia will make you a honey cake," said Jorge.

Diego nodded.

"After you show Thomas where you found the man."

Diego pulled away, but strong as he was, Jorge was stronger.

"It will not take long," said Jorge, his voice hypnotic, calming. Somewhere a dog began to bark, out beyond the city wall, and Diego flinched as another joined in, then another until it seemed every dog in Malaka was howling.

"Think of the cake," said Jorge. "Belia will make it sticky so you will have to lick your fingers. Sweet with honey and sugar. Is it this house?"

Diego shook his head. "There." He pointed. "Yellow, next the wall."

The house rose three stories so the upper windows looked out across the wall. To one side, away from the road, it merged into the Ataranzana building. Jorge began to move, slowly at first, dragging Diego alongside him so he had no choice but to move his feet.

"How did you find him?"

"Noise," said Diego. "The scream."

Jorge stopped walking.

"What screams?" Thomas asked.

"One scream," said Diego.

"What man?"

"The *other* man, man with the knife. Hurting Pa not Pa."

"When was this?"

"Early. I come early because nobody at home and Diego hungry."

"Why did no-one else hear the scream?"

"Early!" said Diego. "I tell you, it was early. Light only just come but Diego hungry. All the city asleep."

Not true, Thomas thought, for in Malaka there were

always those who worked, or lay awake with worries, or came strolling home after a night spent in illicit pleasure. Someone else would have heard, but just as the city never slept it could also ignore sounds it did not want to hear.

"The small man cut Pa."

Thomas stared at Diego. "You saw this?"

A series of nods.

"And the man with the knife, you saw him too?"

Another nod.

"Show me where."

Diego pulled free from Jorge and strode toward the yellow house. Thomas ran to catch up, afraid he might escape, but Diego came to a halt in front of an arched entrance. This was no ordinary house but some place of commerce.

"You went in here?" Thomas asked, and again Diego nodded. Thomas held out a hand, and Diego took it, but it was Thomas had to lead him through the entrance. "Show me where it was."

He felt the tension in Diego's body, his reluctance, glad when Jorge followed close behind. Diego led the way to a flight of stone steps, hesitated again, and Thomas began to ascend them, pulling the boy along.

"How much honey cake can you eat?" Jorge asked. "Do I need to ask Belia to make a big one?"

"Yes." Diego nodded. "Big one. Diego like cake."

He slowed as they came to the third floor, and Thomas knew they were close to where the killing took place. Diego hesitated once more, then appeared to steel himself and stepped forward, walking fast as if he needed the momentum to get him where he knew he needed to be. Which was what appeared to be an office. Thomas looked along the corridor before entering, saw that the building they had entered extended into the much larger Ataranzana where the majority of Guild trade was conducted. This was no private house, but open to anyone who wanted to enter.

Thomas went into the office. "Is this where it happened?"

Diego shook his head and kept doing so, incapable of stopping.

"Where?"

The shaking turned to a slow nod toward a connecting door that stood partly open.

"In there?"

Nod. Nod. Nod.

Jorge went to Diego and put his arm around him.

Thomas went to the door and pushed it open, went into the next room. It was as near identical to the other as was possible. Each had a narrow window that looked west across the Wadi al-Medina, beyond it the dark-sand shoreline, behind it rich farmland that stretched as far as the eye could see.

"In here?" He looked back to where Diego remained unmoving. His head began to nod again.

"Where in here?"

Diego looked at Jorge, who smiled and drew him closer to the door. Diego came, resisted at the entrance, then came two feet inside. He pointed at a corner to the left of the window. Thomas went to it and knelt, his fingers steepled against the wooden floor.

There was a faint stain as if of spilled blood, but it looked as if someone had tried to clean it up, and he wondered if whoever did it had been suspicious or not.

He glanced at Diego. "Did you do this? Try to wash the stain away?"

Nod...

"Tell me what you saw. Where were you — not in here. In the next room?"

Another nod. Thomas wanted to question Diego harder but knew it would be a mistake.

"Can you show me? You and Jorge?"

Diego gave a half-smile. It had become a game. He dragged Jorge forward and stood him beside the desk. Then he went to the other door that gave into the corridor, turned and came back into the room. He began to gabble, nonsense words designed to hide the reality of what had happened here from himself. He pushed at Jorge, who yelled back and Diego grinned and pushed again until Jorge was caught in the corner of the room. Then Diego stepped back until several yards separated them.

Thomas frowned. "Then what?"

Diego crouched, came back toward Jorge. He struck out with his hand, punched Jorge on the side of his chest. Once only.

Thomas watched as Diego moved back again, drew himself to his full height, and approached Jorge once more. He made a strange gesture with his right hand, a sudden flicking motion that appeared to mean nothing. He looked at Jorge and frowned.

"Down," he said, and Jorge lay on the floor. Diego nodded, satisfied. He stood for a time, then turned and walked to the door and out into the corridor.

Thomas caught up with him before he could descend the steps and brought him back.

"And then you took him to your house?"

"Later. After the man came back and went again."

"What? The man who killed him returned? Why?"

"Diego not know." He wrapped both hands together.

"Had he left something behind?"

"Diego not know." The fingers curled around each other, squeezing so hard the flesh turned white.

"We will look after you," Thomas said. "The bad man can't hurt you now, not with me and Jorge to protect you."

"And Will," said Diego.

"Yes, and Will."

"Will is good fighter. He will save Diego."

Thomas suppressed a smile. "Yes. I want you to go with Jorge to the house. Tell Belia you want honey cake and she will make it for you. I need to stay here for a little while, but I'll be home soon."

"Danger, Thomas," said Diego. "Danger come soon."

"I'll be careful." Thomas walked to the top of the steps and watched them descend. Diego laughed at something Jorge said, but there was a tension in the sound, and for a moment he looked back at Thomas standing at the top of the steps.

Thomas turned to the office, wanting to examine it more closely, and almost lost his balance as it seemed the floor moved beneath his feet. There was a moment of disorientation, then he shook his head, dismissing it as a lack of sleep.

The room where Diego had witnessed the killing was one of several identical offices. Each contained a chair and desk, shelves that were empty. Thomas knelt and ran his fingertips over the floorboards where the faint stain marked them. He glanced at the connecting door and realised he should have had Diego show him exactly where he had been, how he could have witnessed the killing without being seen in turn. But the other room contained shadows and Thomas knew it might have been possible, particularly if whoever was here had been close to the window, their eyes adjusted to the brightness.

Outside a deep rumble of thunder sounded. Thomas glanced at the window, but the sky remained a cloudless blue. He knew he needed to find out who the victim was, which might offer a clue as to why he was killed. Then he shook his head. The man had been here, in this room. No doubt it was his office. All he had to do was find someone else in the building who would know his name.

He glanced around the room, unsure if it could tell him anything more. He thought about what Diego had shown him. Two men, it came to him then. That was why Diego had hunched over before he struck the blow. There had been two men, one taller than the other. One to kill, one to argue. That was what Diego had been doing when he babbled — arguing with the dead man.

Thomas walked to the window and leaned on the sill, staring out at the city wall and, beyond it, a sea that roiled as if a large shoal of fish swam beneath the surface.

"Thomas!" Diego's cry interrupted his thoughts. "Thomas, come away!"

Footsteps sounded loud on the floorboards and then Diego ran inside and careened into Thomas, arms snaking around his waist. But it was no embrace, rather an urging.

"Thomas, fast, come now. Now!"

Jorge appeared, breathing hard. "Sorry, he got away

from me. The dogs started barking again and he slipped away. Better do as he says or he'll get upset again."

Thomas scowled. They couldn't continually bow to Diego's disability. It would be like walking on eggshells and would do him no good either. He was about to say so when the sense of disorientation he had felt on the street returned. He put a hand to his head, afraid something was wrong with him until he saw Jorge do the same.

"Out!" shouted Diego, and this time he went, staggering down the steps and out onto the street as beneath his feet the ground shook. The sound of thunder came again, but now he was outside, Thomas recognised that it came from beneath his feet, not the sky.

He had experienced shaking of the earth before. Not often, but the land between Gharnatah and Malaka harboured hot springs that came from deep underground, and Thomas knew they were a sign of a weakness in the earth where the fires of hell rose close to the surface. Even as the explanation came to him, the earth gave a heave and he staggered to his knees. A keening noise filled the air, and only slowly did he realise it was Diego screaming. Thomas stayed where he was as the ground heaved again and another rumble came, accompanied by a loud crash as behind him a wall buckled. The building where the man had died tilted, a great crack running down one wall, and then in slow motion the walls folded inward in a great cloud of dust.

NINE

"Diego knew what was going to happen," said Jorge. He and Thomas sat on the wide terrace, the rest of the household asleep. Their own house was undamaged, but as they made their way through the streets of Malaka they saw others that had not been so fortunate. There would be dead and injured, but Thomas trusted someone else would be caring for them. He needed to think about the murder.

"As did the dogs," he said. "And the birds. Most people listen to their minds too much. Diego doesn't."

Wine had been acquired and drunk, and he was considering whether to open another flagon. Beyond them the shape of Malaka could be made out from the lights arrayed on the city wall. Small darker areas marked where houses had once stood. Beyond, the dark sea was over-arched with uncountable stars, a crescent moon just starting to emerge in the east.

"He insisted we turn around. And I don't mean just the earth moving. He knew you would be killed if we didn't come back. He knew, Thomas." Jorge was uncharacteristically insistent. He rose and disappeared into the house. When he returned it was with the other flagon of wine. He twisted the cork free and poured into both their cups before taking his seat. "That boy knows things."

Thomas thought of what Diego had done with the dice, then dismissed the idea forming in his mind as ridiculous, unscientific.

"We all know things. Even you."

Jorge offered a smile of blissful mockery. "Make little of it if you will, but the boy has an ability the rest of us lack."

"I won't argue the point, but I didn't witness it, only the result. For which I am profoundly grateful."

"So, where to in the morning?"

Thomas had told Jorge of the little he had gleaned from his interrupted examination of the office. The next matter was to find out who the victim had been. Word had been sent but nothing had come back as yet. The slowly decomposing body lay in the cool-room of the Infirmary awaiting collection. If no-one claimed it by the end of the next day it would be cremated, together with the other unclaimed bodies.

"Until we hear word who the dead man is, we can do little," Thomas said.

"So I can sleep late."

"You always sleep late."

"Then I can sleep late with an easy conscience. Why do you continue to pander to Mandana, Thomas? Belia told me she will refuse to make his lotions again." The expression on Jorge's face showed what he thought of treating the man who had once tried to kill them both. Except Thomas believed Abbot Mandana had changed.

74

He was still driven, still a weapon used by the Spanish King, Fernando, but something in the man was different. Since seeing that difference in Ixbilya almost two years ago, Thomas had treated Mandana's wounds once a month if the man found himself close to Malaka. The rest of the time he roamed the countryside with his small band of warrior monks, each of them half mad, on whatever mischief Fernando had set them.

"Have you considered the coincidence of Mandana being near Malaka when this man was killed?" said Jorge.

"Of course. But he is not the man he once was. Besides, what kind of business would bring him to kill a stranger here?"

"That is what we need to find out," said Jorge.

"We?"

"Are we not a team?"

Thomas smiled. "If I'm lucky, someone will kill him before another forty days pass and we will all be content."

"Oh, you are never that lucky. Only today, when Diego came back to save you."

Thomas sipped his wine, dark ruby red, rich in his mouth. Such treats were easily obtained in Malaka. Any weakness a man might indulge was easily obtained in Malaka.

"We should go to our beds," Thomas said.

"Yes, we should, once we have finished this flagon."

"I am drunk already."

"Good, because so am I." Jorge turned to stare at Thomas. "Will Lubna keep the child she carries this time?"

It was an impertinent question, far too personal, but from Jorge it was to be expected, and accepted.

"I believe so. She is healthy, the baby moves with vigour, and our life here is easy compared to Ixbilya. The journey you brought her on was hard, and there was plague."

"There is always plague. And the journey was so she could be with you."

"I know, I know. I meant no blame." And then, before Jorge could say anymore, as Thomas saw he wanted to, he said, "It was not your fault. None of what happened was your fault. I should have taken greater care of her."

"Like you did the Queen."

"Yes. Something like that."

"I sometimes wonder if Belia would like a child. Or more than one."

"Has she said so?"

"No ... but I still wonder. If she does I will ask you to lie with her. Lubna will allow it, I am sure."

Thomas laughed. "Oh, she is not as forgiving as you might think. And Belia might want a say over who lies with her. What if she wants a handful of babies?"

"Then you will be a very lucky man. She is..." But Jorge stopped, realising what he had been about to say was perhaps too much even for him. He drained his cup then filled both.

Thomas's eyes followed the line of the city wall, noting gaps in the torches where stone had tumbled as the earth shook. In the morning, masons would begin work. Malaka was a city of trade, a crossing point for all of the known world, and trade could never be interrupted.

Thomas eyed his half full cup and put it down.

"I'm going to bed. I will leave you to sleep late tomorrow."

Jorge nodded, quiet for once, staring out across the invisible sea.

Thomas looked in on Will, and because he and Diego now shared the room, checked on both of them. Will, tall as he was for his age, looked small beside his new friend, but they had become inseparable. He stared at Diego, the softness of his features, the thatch of dark hair on his head pointing every way but the right way, and wondered what mysteries he was privy to that others were not. He believed Jorge, believed that Diego had foreseen the shaking, had foreseen Thomas's death if he had not come to warn him. Thomas shivered, afraid of something he couldn't understand.

No-one had come to claim the body, but Thomas told the Infirmary not to dispose of it yet. He did what he had been about to do when the shaking of the earth interrupted him. He went to the Ataranzana and started at the other end of the puzzle.

Diego had gone to the location where the man had been killed for a reason. Early that morning Thomas had teased that reason from him, and with Jorge's help managed not to upset him too much. The office where the body had lain belonged to the man Diego's father worked for. From that it was a simple matter. The Ataranzana had records which revealed that the dead man was Zufar al-Zaki, Master of the Weapons' Guild. An important man, no doubt. A busy man. A wealthy man. A man with staff in his employ — one of whom had been Miguel Jiminez. It explained what Diego had been doing in the office next to the one al-Zaki was killed in. Unwilling, or unable, to believe his father dead he had gone in search of him.

As they were already in the headquarters of the Guild, Thomas thought it only wise to consult its leader. Ali Durdush was Master of the Malaka Guilds, the same man Thomas had seen berated by the mad preacher after Lubna had lost the body of Diego's mother. Thomas had dined with the man once soon after coming to the city, because Durdush considered an association might prove useful at some point. The Malaka Guilds were powerful, but so was the Infirmary. It was a consideration only on one side of the relationship, but it did allow Thomas access to the man, and his administrative staff, who would prove the more useful.

Durdush was young for such a position, but his family had been an integral part of the Guild for many generations; their wealth was spoken of in whispers. As a man blessed with controlling all of the Guilds in Malaka, Durdush sat at the centre of a complex web of trade and influence, a position a clever man could use to increase his wealth a hundred-fold. Or, as was rumoured in Durdush's case, a thousand-fold. Thomas didn't particularly like the man, but had to admit he was clearly not without intelligence and cunning, both traits the Guild valued.

He welcomed Thomas and Jorge into a large room situated at the top level of the customs buildings that overlooked the docks. A long corridor with smaller offices set off it stretched the length of the building to a second complex of offices at the far end. There was no sign of damage from the shaking here. This building had been built of only the best material, using only the best workmen.

"It is a pleasure to see you again, Thomas. And in better circumstances than the other day. Someone should take that preacher out in a boat and neglect to return him to shore. Who is your handsome friend?"

"Jorge. We work together."

"I see. Another miracle worker?"

"Something like that."

A brief frown crossed Durdush's face, discarded as quickly as it had come. "And to what do I owe the pleasure of your visit?" Durdush snapped his fingers, and a young man darted from where he had been hidden behind a pillar. "Fetch a box of the dates that arrived yesterday from Tunis." A smile at Thomas. "A small gesture of my esteem."

Thomas knew better than to attempt a refusal. Besides, Diego would enjoy their sweetness.

"Have you heard the news of Zufar al-Zaki?"

"News? What news? Please, sit." Durdush seemed genuinely puzzled.

"His body was discovered in one of the Guild offices next to the wall," Thomas said, watching Durdush closely.

"Today?"

"He was killed almost a week ago, but his identity only discovered today. I am sorry to be the bearer of such news. You must have known him well."

Durdush raised a shoulder. "Not as well as you might imagine. Al-Zaki was not an easy man to know, and had neglected his craft of late. He no longer practiced and showed little interest in commerce. Most of the Weapons' Guild duties were carried out by his clerk, I believe."

"Would that be a man by the name of Miguel Jiminez?"

Durdush shook his head. "I would not know that. You will have to ask my clerks for the information. Ah, here is the boy." Durdush looked relieved at the interruption. He nodded toward Thomas, who was handed a small box almost spilling over with sticky, dark fruit. "You can find a use for these, I trust?"

"My thanks. Was al-Zaki popular among the other Guild Masters?"

"Not popular, but not unpopular either. He was reserved. A private man, I would say. Not a good trait in one meant to foster trade, but many Weapons' Masters are the same. Men want swords, muskets, all manner of means to kill each other. It requires little in the way of conversational skill to sell them such. But he was not disliked either, though there were rumours his personal life was ... complicated."

Another man entered the room, and Durdush turned his head in obvious relief. The man leaned close, the words he spoke too soft to carry.

"You will have to excuse me, there is someone I have been waiting for. If you discover anything more, send a message. I am grateful you are looking into the matter, Thomas, I hear you have had success in the past." Durdush rose and left the room, his staff bustling after him.

"Do you think he has gold here?" asked Jorge. "He is trusting to leave us alone."

"Oh, I suspect someone is watching us." Thomas nodded toward narrow openings in two walls. It was not possible to see if anyone stood on the other side, but he would be surprised if at least one watcher was not in place. "Besides, what do you need gold for? You already possess the riches of a prince."

"Which you will not let me spend."

"One day."

"One day soon?"

"Sooner than either of us might like." Thomas rose. "Do you think Belia will like these, if Diego does not eat them all?"

"She will use them to help make a meal fit for a prince with no money."

Thomas moved to an arched window which looked over the dock. He caught sight of Ali Durdush as he crossed the flagstones toward a tall figure surrounded by a group of men, most of whom looked like soldiers apart from one, who was also tall, slim, and good-looking.

"Who has he gone to see? Someone you know?" Jorge narrowed his eyes. "I like that one."

Thomas shook his head. "A Spaniard, by the look." He offered a tight smile. "The Guilds see the way this war goes. They will negotiate to protect their position. Their trade."

"Then you are lucky you do not have to partake of it," said Jorge. "And the man Durdush is talking to is not Spanish. His dress is of the north, I would say." He smiled. "Perhaps even of your country, though my knowledge of English fashion is sadly out of date, and there is little point in asking you."

"None at all, and I am glad it is so." Thomas watched Durdush and the man talk, wondering what they were discussing. "But you are right, he does have the look of an Englishman."

"There is a look? Other than a pale face and bad teeth?"

"I do not have bad teeth," Thomas said. "Nor a pale face."

"I do not count you as English."

"My thanks. But you're right, he is pale, and I hear many of my countrymen have come to Spain. They believe there are riches to be gained in this war and want a share of them. That man already has riches though, I wager. Look at the cut of his clothes."

"They are not to my taste," said Jorge.

"No, I expect they are not." Thomas turned away, losing interest in whatever negotiation Ali Durdush might be involved in even if they did involve one of his countrymen. Or perhaps because they did. "We need to find out more about Zufar al-Zaki. The clerks will have an address for him. With luck his wife will be the jealous type who has had him murdered and our task will be complete."

"We can always live in hope," said Jorge. "Though that would not explain what happened to Diego's parents."

"His father died from a fall," Thomas said. "His mother ... well, that is more of a mystery, but no doubt one with an innocent explanation. I intend to talk to Diego. He may know something."

"Or nothing," said Jorge.

"Yes. Or nothing, which is the more likely."

TEN

"Save me from these women!" Thomas had come to al-Zaki's house with Jorge after a clerk reluctantly provided its location. It lay on the eastern edge of the city, at some distance from where most Guild members lived close to the Ataranzana. The house was in turmoil. A group of five young women milled about, each of their voices contributing to a meaningless cacophony.

The Weapons' Master's body had finally been claimed to be prepared for burial, but not by anyone in this household. Instead they had paid one of the numerous undertakers to perform the task. Thomas thought it likely none of the wives would even bother to attend the internment.

Jorge stood among the chaos with a smile on his face, used to such from the harem. For Thomas it was chaos. He stood beyond the doorway, listening until he understood exactly what was happening, despairing he ever might. The young women made up the man's harem, even if he was a supposed Christian. Religion ousted by lust — a familiar story.

"Would you like me to question them?" asked Jorge.

"Can you. And while you do I'm going to look around the house. Keep them occupied as long as you can."

Jorge smiled, and it was clear a reply was not necessary. Thomas turned away, glad to be freed from the chatter. Al-Zaki's house was not small, but neither was it overly large, and the furnishings and decorations were modest for a man of his position. It seemed the Weapons' Master had been no lover of frivolity, and Thomas thought of Jorge's brother, Daniel, who fashioned some of the finest swords in Spain. He too was a plain man, forever in Thomas's debt for the rescue of his daughter, not that either of them would ever mention the fact.

The sound of female voices grew faint as he entered a kitchen, a wide room, the stove cool. He wondered who did the cooking here, for none of the young women appeared either capable or willing. A housekeeper, a cook, someone paid to carry out the day-to-day tasks? Which meant there was someone else who would need to be interviewed. Thomas made a mental note to ask before they left.

He looked through the storage jars, not exactly sure what he was searching for, but unwilling to miss anything. He knew the house was not where al-Zaki had died, but it might be where he had been taken from. Another note to ask: when was he last seen? He turned with the intention of doing the asking now when, as he passed the foot of a staircase, he heard a sound from upstairs. He ascended the staircase.

There came a scraping of something dragged across the floor. Thomas tracked it to a large room at the end of the corridor where the air was perfumed with the scent of women. Four beds were set, one at each corner. In the centre of the room a young woman leaned over a chest, placing silk clothing into it. As Thomas entered, she spun around, a hand rising to cover her mouth. She was one of the younger members of al-Zaki's harem, her skin as shaded as Lubna's, hair as dark and lustrous.

"I am not stealing anything," she said, taking a step away from the chest, "only taking what is mine."

Thomas glanced at the chest but was uninterested in the contents. "What will become of you now, you and the others?"

"Why do you care?" A flash of spirit showed.

"I am investigating your master's death."

"Why?"

"He was an important man."

"Important men die all the time. Do you investigate all their deaths?"

"But your master did not die a natural death, did he?" Thomas took two paces closer, her scent enfolding him, and an unwelcome image of Helena, the concubine who used to share his life, came into his mind. The scent was almost the same, the spark of life in this woman's eyes reminding him of the woman whose sister was now his wife. Thomas thought the telling of it sounded more complicated than the living of it. "When did you last see him?"

The hand that had fallen to her side rose again, touched lips stained red from the application of beeswax and crushed flowers.

"Who killed him?"

"That is what I intend to find out. When did you see him?"

"A week ago ... ten days ... let me think ..." She stared into space, her eyes tracking a memory. "I shared his bed nine nights since. It would have been my turn again two days ago, but none of us has seen him since ..." More searching. "Eight days. Yes, I am sure of it, eight days. You can ask Alisha, for it was her turn to lie with him that night." A smile of raw cunning and mischief came and went so briefly Thomas half doubted it had ever been there. He certainly didn't know what it meant — he would need Jorge for that.

"Did anyone report him missing?"

"He would often be gone from home for long periods. His work, he claimed. Except the last time he brought me back with him."

"Brought you back? From where? You're not Spanish, are you."

"I met him when he crossed the sea to Tunis. I worked in a ... I worked there and he took a liking to me. He was a generous man." A frown. "Is that why he was killed? For money? But that is all still here, in the cellar. At least I think it is, I have not looked. We should do so. What if someone killed him so they could steal his gold?"

"I will make sure to look later," Thomas said. "So he might be gone for days at a time and none of you would wonder where, or why?"

"He did not speak to us of his work, or his plans."

"Did any of you see strangers in the days before he disappeared?"

"I did not, but you should ask the others."

"My companion is talking to them at the moment. What about his work? Did people not come here to discuss business?"

"Never. He was protective of his private life, of all of us. He worked in the afternoons only, and always returned before dark when he was at home."

"Worked where?"

"At the Ataranzana. You must know it."

"Of course." Thomas knew he would have to return to al-Zaki's offices. There would be staff there able to provide more information. He was beginning to believe these women would prove of little use. Their lives were too constrained, apart from which they lacked curiosity, which was a sin in Thomas's eyes.

"So you cannot think of anyone who might wish your master dead?"

A shake of the head. "No. Unless you consider his wife. His ex-wife, that is. She hates him."

"Ballix," said Jorge. "The wife lives in Ballix."

"Ex-wife," Thomas corrected. "That is what I was told."

They ascended the slope toward home, the city behind them but the scent of its fires and thousands of people reached them on the breeze.

"It's an arguable distinction. She applied to divorce him when the girls became too many and she grew tired of his infidelities. But a divorce requires the splitting of a man's assets, and so far al-Zaki has paid her nothing. Does that still make them married or not?"

"I'm no expert on divorce," Thomas said. "Nor do I wish to become one. She has a name? A given name?" He halted for a moment, the air burning his lungs. The beat of his heart sounded in his ears. He turned and surveyed the city, then looked east, but Ballix lay beyond the peak of Aranzo. Not so far in miles, but half a day on horseback. He knew they had to talk to the woman, but it would not be today. Inland, dark clouds hung over the peaks, and curtains of rain washed across them. The wind promised tomorrow would be wet, but tomorrow the journey would have to be.

"Gomez," said Jorge. "Gracia Bernel Gomez."

"She is al-Zaki's age?"

"No, of course not. He was a man who liked his women young, and willing. They told me she was no longer young, not as young as they are. She is almost as old as you."

Thomas smiled. "So old enough."

"Yes, old enough." Jorge punched Thomas's arm softly. "Have you rested up enough yet, old man?"

A rumble of thunder sounded as they approached the house, and Thomas knew they would get wet before they reached it. When they had moved to this house shortly after arriving in Malaka, he had wondered why its original owner had built it so far beyond the city walls. What did he have to hide, or who did he need to hide it from? But he liked the house. It was large, comfortable, and people could not find him easily, which suited him well. Thomas had grown tired of people who always wanted something from him. Now he intended to do only what pleased him.

He wondered if the pursuit of this mystery was something that pleased him or not. In the past he had been given no choice. The first time the Sultan of Gharnatah had brooked no refusal, and each time since there had been pressure brought. But now?

Thomas glanced to where Jorge strode ahead of him,

his youth starting to show in greater strength, and Thomas knew he was getting old. Perhaps it was time for a man to start thinking of taking life easier, to make the most of whatever years were left to him. Except he didn't feel old. Lubna was only twenty-five, and Will so full of life and curiosity it made Thomas younger than his years.

So why was he following the threads of this mystery? Zufar al-Zaki meant nothing to him. Was it only the confluence of circumstance? Lubna mislaying a body, Diego finding another? Thomas knew he had to question Diego more closely about his parents. He needed to know if their deaths were coincidence or something more.

Responsibility had gathered around Thomas until he could not turn aside from the search. Which is why early in the morning he and Jorge would saddle two horses and ride the twenty miles to Ballix to talk to al-Zaki's wife, and with luck that might be the end of the matter.

By the time they reached the wide terrace, heavy rain was falling, and both Thomas and Jorge were soaked. Lightning stuttered to die against the surrounding peaks, thunder coming almost immediately. Thomas was sure Diego would be afraid, cowering somewhere with his hands over his head, but instead he and Will stood on the terrace laughing, watching as the sky fought the earth. Water cascaded from the roof so close they could reach out and let it rush across their fingers.

Will ran to Thomas, hugged his legs then returned at once. Diego did not turn, mesmerised by the storm.

Thomas went to change, laughing as Lubna came to

assist in a way that was no help at all, until eventually he tumbled her onto the bed and she squealed as though that had not been her intention all along.

After, as they lay curled together, she said, "That boy is like a jay."

"Diego? Why, can he fly? It wouldn't surprise me at all."

Lubna laughed and ran a hand along Thomas's belly, her fingers tracing the scars that criss-crossed him, each of them familiar to her now. "He likes pretty things."

"So do I."

"Will brought me a box. There were a dozen trinkets in it. Your wedding band among them."

"Ah. I dare not wear it outside the house for fear I will lose it."

Lubna kissed his shoulder. "It's all right, Thomas, it's not the ring that binds us." She held her hand up, splayed the fingers. "See, I do not wear mine either."

"Would you if I did?"

"Perhaps."

Thomas ran his hand over the swell of her belly, held it there, waiting. It did not take long before he felt movement within, the baby turning, dreaming perhaps, and he wondered did babies dream inside the womb, and if so, of what? An image of the baby he had saved only a scant few days earlier came to him, and the damage inflicted to the mother. Had it been possible to save both he would have done so, but a decision had to be made. It was why they called him *qassab*, because he could always make such decisions.

He pushed the vision away, not wanting to think of it, not when Lubna lay beside him, their child nestled within her.

"I need to talk to him anyway, should I raise it?"

"He likes you," said Lubna.

"He likes you too, and Jorge and Belia and Will."

"He respects you, then."

"Was that intended to be 'Yes, you should talk to him'?"

"It makes sense, before it becomes an issue. He means nothing by it, he simply likes pretty objects. None of us mind, and it's not as if he's going to run into Malaka and sell them in the market, is it."

"He needs to learn," Thomas said. He stared at the open window, the sound of rain loud, the moisture of it touching his skin. It was nothing like the rain of England, which was tentative, shy, but never far away. When rain came to Spain it did so rarely, but always made itself known.

"Do you think his parents let him do as he wished?" he asked.

"We will never know."

"Children like Diego are killed at birth more often than not, once the parents see what they have brought into the world. Other times they are given more love than is seemly." He glanced at Lubna. "They were old, were they not?"

She nodded. "It might be one of the reasons Diego is as he is. There are records at the Infirmary telling of the condition, and an older mother is one of the factors."

"I'll talk to him," Thomas said. "When we get back from Ballix. In the meantime, you should keep an eye on him, all of you. Don't take anything from him, but try to ensure he knows it's wrong if you see him take anything again."

"Have you seen the rings he wears on his fingers?"

"Not especially."

"I'm sure he has one on every finger. Two on some."
She smiled. "Unlike someone I know."

"Do you think them stolen?"

"Not stolen. More likely they belonged to his
parents. They are none of them worth any great value,
apart from one which is gold and has a fine stone set in
it. Why are you going to Ballix?"

"Al-Zaki's wife lives there."

"I thought you said he had created a harem for
himself."

"Which is why she lives in Ballix. The harem seems
to believe she bore him ill will on account of them, and
the fact he had not paid any divorce settlement."

"She will not get anything now, will she?"

Thomas shook his head. "I imagine not."

"We will never divorce, you and I, will we." It was a
statement, not a question.

"No, we will not."

"I hope the rain stops before you have to go," said
Lubna, straddling him in a single lithe movement. "You
are not tired of me yet are you, Thomas?"

And again he shook his head.

ELEVEN

The rain continued, if anything falling harder, though how such was possible Thomas could not comprehend. It was like riding beneath a waterfall, one that was impossible to escape from. Water cascaded down mountainsides and gathered in stream beds that only the day before had lain dusty and dry. Now they foamed, carrying trees and rocks along with an unstoppable force.

Jorge said something, his words swamped by the incessant noise of falling water, and Thomas had to lean closer to hear.

"Could this not have waited until tomorrow, or better still the day after?" shouted Jorge.

"Never leave undone what must be done."

Jorge shook his head and scowled. "This woman had better know something."

"Even if she doesn't, the journey is worth doing. It is often the slow accumulation of facts that leads to an answer, even if those facts have no obvious bearing on the matter in hand."

"You do it on purpose, don't you," said Jorge.

"Do what?"

"Talk in words that make no sense at all. Not to ordinary folk, anyway."

They had originally planned to travel along the relatively level coastal route, but as they rode around the outer wall of Malaka it became clear the quantity of water foaming from the mountains would make that way impassable. Thomas had turned his mount north and east. They climbed the shoulder of the heights of Aranzo, following tracks disturbed by few other than goat herders. Here the water continued to be an issue, but the gullies were narrower and easier to cross.

They were late and would be later still arriving in Ballix. They would need to find accommodation for the night rather than risk the return journey in the dark. With luck the rain would have stopped by morning.

Ballix was second in size only to Malaka along the coastal strip of al-Andalus, with a fine fortress sitting atop a sharp hill within the town walls. The sea crashed and foamed at the base of the southern wall as they approached, the flat land surrounding the western edge of the town knee-deep in water. The crops here were flooded but would no doubt grow better as a result. The Wadi al-Cuevo flowed somewhere beneath the surface and they would need to take care to cross it at the ford or risk being swept away.

The gates were closed, as if someone wanted to keep the floodwater at bay, but they were admitted soon enough, and Thomas made enquiries of the guard, but he did not know the woman they sought.

"Before we begin I need something to eat," said Jorge, "and a cup or more of wine."

"And somewhere to spend the night."

"If we must." Jorge walked ahead of his horse, leading it with an occasional tug of the reins. The rain beat on his head, plastering his hair around his face. He refused to raise the hood of his robe, claiming it only delayed the inevitable soaking. Beneath his own hood, Thomas suspected he was probably right.

The streets were deserted, but their path brought them to a coffee house which, fortunately for Jorge, also served wine and spirits, despite both being against the laws of Islam. Al-Andalus had lost its rigour long since, and it seemed only the Imams and the lunatic al-Antiqamun cared anymore, and few listened to their preaching. It was a world in the process of falling apart, the seams tearing to let in strange, alien ideas of how life could be lived.

The coffee house also turned out to offer accommodation and stabling for the horses, which Thomas negotiated while Jorge found a seat on a stack of cushions. Business attended to, Thomas sank down beside him, still after all his years in al-Andalus uncomfortable at being so close to the ground. Around them men — and there were no women other than those who served them — drank dark, bitter coffee, drew smoke through hookahs, and poured wine from flagons. The air was sweet with the scent of hashish and opium, the room crowded. It appeared the population of the town had sought distraction from the storm raging outside.

Thomas leaned over to a dark-skinned Berber whose shoulder was little more than a foot from his own.

"Sir, perhaps you can help us. We seek a woman by

the name of Gracia Bernel Gomez. Do you know of her?"

The man turned clouded eyes toward Thomas. He stared at him for an uncomfortably long time before shaking his head and turning away. Thomas sighed. This was going to be harder than he had hoped. Then the man leaned across to his companion and spoke a few words. His companion spoke to someone else until the message had spread throughout the entire establishment.

Word came back slowly, person by person, until it reached the man Thomas had originally enquired of, who turned and leaned close, the scent of hashish strong on his robes.

"She is not well liked," he said, his voice as rough as his appearance.

"Then you will no doubt be willing to tell me where I can find her."

"For a consideration."

Thomas smiled. He watched the man's face change, his clouded eyes seeing well enough to catch the intent. And then he stopped smiling.

"Of course." Thomas reached into his purse, pulled out coins, and held them within his fist. "Where does she live?"

"With another woman at the foot of the Alkhazabah."

"That does not help me."

"This road we are on, follow it until it forks, then take the left-hand way. It steepens. Keep going until you come to a crossroads. Take the right-hand way. The house is on that alley. It is small and in need of repair. If you cannot find her, knock on any door and ask."

Thomas dropped one of the coins into the man's hand. "You say she is not well liked. Why?"

More words were exchanged, returning a little sooner than from the first enquiry.

"Perhaps because she lives with another woman." He showed teeth stained almost black, darker than the gums that held them.

Thomas shook his head and slipped two more coins into his palm.

The man grinned to show a single tooth. "I hope you have more coin for those two, they don't come free is what I heard." The old man turned away, leaving Thomas to stare at the back of his head.

"Does this mean we are going out into the rain again?" asked Jorge.

"I see no other way of talking to her."

"Perhaps I will change my clothes first, then."

"You're already soaked. Change when we return, then you won't soak both your outfits."

Jorge looked around at the interior of the inn. "Are we safe here?"

"I'll sleep with my sword in my hand if it makes you feel more secure."

Jorge laughed. "No, I don't think it will. All right, if we are going to go let's get it done. And I was just beginning to feel warm."

The man's directions proved accurate, and the house identifiable. It was one of the smallest in the narrow street and the most in need of attention. It stood two stories high, but neither looked tall enough for Thomas to stand upright in. He knocked on the door while Jorge tried to shelter beneath the overhanging eaves, but only managed to get wetter as water sluiced off the roof and splashed his legs.

Thomas waited, knocked harder when there was no reply. The sound of the rain masked any noise from within, so it came as a surprise when the door opened and a short woman of close to his own age stared out at him. She was pretty, with a narrow face and dark hair tucked beneath a red scarf.

"What do you want?"

"I am looking for Gracia Bernel Gomez."

"Then you have found her. What is your business?"

"You are Señora Gomez?"

"No, but she lives here. Again, what is your business?"

"I have news of her husband."

"Then she does not wish to hear it. Good-day, sir." She began to close the door.

Thomas used his foot to block it. She stared down, opened the door again then slammed it. Thomas winced but kept his foot in place.

"I will scream," she said.

Thomas looked both ways along the street. "Scream, for all the good it will do you." He shook his head, met the woman's eyes. "I mean neither of you any harm."

Jorge stepped into sight, and the woman's eyes shifted, clearly liking what she saw better.

"What news?" she said.

"I would tell that to Señora Gomez."

An expulsion of breath. "Very well. But remove your cloaks. We have enough water coming through the roof as it is without you bringing more in."

Thomas ducked inside, Jorge ducking more as he followed. There was a single room occupying the entire ground floor. A stove set into one wall burned badly and billowed smoke into the air. A second woman stood in front of it, stirring a pot that failed to entice the senses.

"These men want to talk to you, Gracia."

"What men?" She turned, no surprise on her face, and Thomas realised she must have heard the entire conversation. She was a handsome woman, her looks well maintained, hair still dark and skin unlined. She wore a long dress belted at the waist, the figure beneath voluptuous. Thomas thought she looked younger than her years, if al-Zaki's women had told him the truth.

"I want to hear nothing of that man unless you have come to bring the money he owes me."

"I'm afraid not. I bear sad news."

She snuffled a laugh. "What, is he dead? I would not call that sad news."

"Yes, your husband is dead."

"Good." There was no change in her expression.

"At the hand of another."

"That doesn't surprise me. Was it one of his girls?" Her expression was confident, almost challenging. "Well, you have delivered the news. I am sure you can find your way out, or does Olivia need to show you where the door is?"

Her companion came to Gracia and laid a hand on her shoulder. "Perhaps you should speak with them. The law states you are entitled to his wealth on his death."

"We divorced, you know we did."

"But he did not pay you what was due. That makes it void, does it not? In which case–"

"His harem will have spirited his wealth away by

now." Gracia finally stopped stirring the pot and turned to face them. She wiped her hands in a cloth and shook her head. "You do not know how Guild wealth works, do you?"

Thomas gave the question some consideration before shaking his head. When he had first lived in Malaka, learning all he could at the Infirmary, he had been no more than a young stranger, a subject of gossip, of speculation and, in some instances fascination. But he had taken no interest in the bustling commerce of the city.

"Guild Masters are wealthy individuals, certainly, but the riches of each Guild is held centrally and only distributed if requested or someone dies. They will make an arrangement for Zufar's family." She pulled a chair from beneath a table and sat, nodding that Thomas and Jorge could do the same if they wished. Her companion passed by, once more a touch on the shoulder.

"An arrangement for you, too?"

A tilt of the head. "Perhaps. Perhaps not." She pushed fingers through her hair. "I will have to go to Malaka to plead a case. It may help that he cheated me out of half his wealth as the law states I am entitled to when I divorced him. The Guild plays fair by its members." She offered a bitter smile. "Are his playthings still as silly as ever, or are they weeping and wailing?"

"Not weeping nor wailing," said Jorge.

Gracia turned her gaze on him, letting it explore what she saw, then gave a smile. "My, but you are a handsome thing, aren't you?"

Jorge returned the smile but said nothing.

"Do you know if your husband had enemies?"

Thomas asked before the two women started tearing Jorge's clothes from him.

"He was a man of influence, so of course he did. How was he killed?"

Thomas considered his response, then decided she deserved to know. Partly because he did not like the woman. There was something calculating in her he found grating.

"He was stabbed."

"Was it painful? I do hope so."

"Fatal, in any case."

"Was it you who examined him? Are you some kind of priest? You do not look like one, and your friend certainly does not. He has a look of sin about him."

"I am a physician at the Infirmary."

"Dressed like that? You surprise me."

"What knowledge would your husband possess that would bring about his death?"

"Nothing I can think of. And what makes you think he had knowledge? Could it not have been nothing more than an argument? And he is no longer my husband."

"Some Guild secret, perhaps."

Gracia stood abruptly. "It is five years since I left him. How am I supposed to know what he has done since or what he knows now? Ask those slips of girls he beds one after the other." She grimaced, and Thomas wondered who she hated the most, her husband or the women he had gathered around him.

"I take it you have not left Ballix in the last week?"

"Why would I?" She stared at Thomas. "Do you think I took a knife and cut my own husband?"

"I didn't say it was a knife."

"No — what else could it be? I am no expert on stab-bings, but if I were to stab someone I would use a knife, except in this case I would cut him slowly, little by little, until he gave me what I wanted." She tilted her head, examined Thomas. "How would you do it, sir?"

"I would not do it at all." Though a memory surfaced of when he was much younger, a memory of a different life, one he no longer recognised except when it returned in battle. He had often considered if it was that younger Thomas people saw which unsettled them, for he knew he could unsettle people without even trying. Except it appeared not to work with this woman.

"And your lover?" Thomas said, glancing at the woman at the stove, deliberately using the term to see a reaction, but Gracia simply smiled.

"Oh, she would start on his cock and balls I expect. We would do it together, with great care and pleasure." She held her hand up, and the woman came to her. Gracia turned her face up so they could exchange a kiss. "Except we did not. My husband and his harem are of no interest to me anymore. I have evicted him from my thoughts. Though I confess a little money would be welcome. We are not, as you can see, well catered for here. But at least we have a roof over our heads, even if it leaks."

As they walked back through the rain, Jorge said, "I see why people do not warm to her, but I don't believe she killed her husband. Which means our journey here was a waste of time."

"Knowing she didn't do it is worth the journey on its own," Thomas said. "And though she might not have done the deed herself, who is to say she didn't find someone else who did?"

"She has no money to pay an assassin," said Jorge. The streets were still almost deserted, water running through them as deep as their ankles, rushing down the cobbles to gather in deeper puddles in squares and courtyards.

"She claims poverty, but there were things in that house a truly poor woman would have sold when she needed food on the table. But you are right, I don't think she had anything to do with it, either in the act or in asking someone else. How would it benefit her?"

"She hated him."

"If people killed everyone they hated there would be few people left in the world."

"Only you and me, Thomas." Jorge slapped him on the back.

"No. Only you."

TWELVE

The rain had not yet stopped, but finally it was starting to look as if it might. A brighter line hovered over the sea, moving slowly toward land. It did not cheer Jorge, who continued to complain about how wet he was, but at least he was doing so less frequently.

"Tell me your opinion of her again," Thomas said, as much to stop Jorge's moaning as anything else. They had spoken of Gracia Bernel Gomez over a meagre supper and gone to their shared bed early. It had taken Thomas a long time to find sleep, his own thoughts and the rattle of rain on the tiles above his head keeping him awake. He had used the time to examine the facts he knew, but the sound of the rain grew so loud even that failed to distract him. Jorge had begun a soft snore almost as soon as the candle was extinguished.

"I believe she had no hand in his death. I told you as much, or have you forgotten already? It is a shame — had she been guilty we could have returned to our quiet life. Damn this rain, will it never stop?"

"Don't worry, you can't get any wetter." Thomas

drew his horse to a halt and lifted himself out of the saddle to ease the ache in his thighs. He wiped a hand across his face to clear the water before starting to move again. "The man who told us about them said we would need money. Did they look like whores to you?"

Jorge wiped his face and smiled. "They were good-looking enough, certainly, and experienced too I'd judge. Two women living together as they claim, without work, that would make it possible, too. But no, I don't think they're whores. Do you?" Another smile. "Did you hope they were?"

"No. I was thinking out loud and letting my thoughts run away with me. I'm looking for some reason why she might have her husband killed, but that wouldn't be it."

"She didn't. Why would she? Alive he might send her money, or change his mind and take her back. I would rather share a bed with her, with both of them, than all those girls of his together."

"You would?"

"She accused me of having sin in my eyes. She could tell because she knows sin too. She is a woman with appetites for men as well as women."

"Are you sure? You saw them with each other."

"And you continue to believe I bed only women. There is more wonder among the peoples of this world than you can envisage, my friend."

"Does Belia know of your philosophy?"

"Of course, and shares it. Did you think she would not? I am who I am, Thomas. I cannot change my nature, and she accepts me as I am."

"So you sleep with other people. Both of you?"

"Not since she has shared my life. But if I wanted to I could, and so could she."

Thomas shook his head. Jorge was right, he was too innocent for this world, but preferred to be that way. He could not even begin to imagine how Lubna would react if he tried to make the same argument to her.

They had reached a narrow pass between two high ridges. Behind them the sprawl of Ballix spread across the plain, backed by high peaks that rose to the wide bulk of Maroma. Water coursed from the flanks of the hills to cut deep channels through what little soil clung to their slopes.

Jorge rode on for a moment before turning back. "What, have you forgotten something? If so you go back on your own. We are a third of the way home."

"I thought I saw something." Thomas pointed to one of the closer hillsides, which rose near vertical from the track they followed.

"A goat, an eagle, a ghost?" Jorge pulled on his reins, his horse turning patiently. "Who cares?"

Thomas continued to stare at the spot but began to believe Jorge was right, for nothing showed and he kicked his heels into his horse's flanks to get it moving again. The path twisted upward, turning back on itself before resuming the direction they wanted. The rain lessened then stopped and a beam of sunlight cracked the clouds and fell to illuminate the broad valley they had ridden out of. This time it was Jorge who stopped to point.

"I assume what you saw wasn't that? A blind man could barely miss them."

From the north, along the far bank of the Wadi-al-Cuevo, which had re-emerged from the flood, a few men made their way from a roadway that emerged between low hills. Thomas leaned forward, narrowing his eyes, but the distance was too great to decide who they were. Then, as he watched, more men appeared. Carts came dragging small cannon. Others were loaded with tents and supplies. The numbers thickened to become an army. In their midst rode a man who could not be missed, his body encased in shining armour that glowed bright in a shaft of sunlight.

"Spanish," said Jorge.

Thomas nodded, a sense of dread lodging in his chest. The year was young, the campaigning season still a month off, yet here they were. Spanish soldiers led, if he wasn't mistaken, by a man he knew well. Fernando, King of Castile and Aragon. Which meant these men came with serious intent.

Others had noted their presence as well. Across the waterlogged plain tiny figures gathered only to splinter apart. Carts were hurriedly loaded, others made no effort to save their belongings as they streamed toward the still open gate of Ballix.

The town was ringed by high walls, well-defended, but there were not enough soldiers within to make a fight of it if the Spanish mounted a significant attack. Cut off Ballix and the supply route between Malaka and Gharnatah would be broken.

"He's a clever general," Thomas said, more to himself than his companion, but Jorge heard.

"It is Fernando, then, do you think?"

"It has to be. Only he would be allowed to wear such fine armour. He has come for war." As he glanced at Jorge, ice filled his veins. "This might be the end. The end of everything. Take Ballix, cut off Malaka. If it falls by early summer the Spanish will turn to Gharnatah, honed troops filled with the joy of victory. By the turn of the year al-Andalus will be no more."

"Al-Zagal isn't an easy man to defeat."

"You speak the truth. But look at them. There are ..." Thomas narrowed his eyes. "Five or six thousand, and still they come. They have cannon, siege platforms, and supplies enough for a month. Ballix will not last a week. And then there's nothing between there and Malaka."

"Malaka is a tougher prospect."

"Perhaps. But it has grown old and lazy the richer it has become. You met Ali Durdush so I know what you think of him. Malaka will fall inside a month. Spanish corsairs will line the docksides, bringing more troops from Cadiz." Thomas turned his horse. "We have to get back. We have to leave here."

Jorge spurred his horse to catch up with Thomas. "To where? Returning to Gharnatah is pointless. Where do you intend, Thomas?"

"I don't know, but we cannot stay here."

"And the dead man?"

"Damn the dead man. Lubna and Will are back there. Belia and now Diego too. They have to be taken to safety. I was a fool even to come here."

"No," said Jorge, "if you hadn't come we would still be living in ignorance. You always tell me it is better to know the truth than turn aside from it, however uncomfortable that might be."

"I say too many things, and not all of them are right."

"Well, that's a first. The infallible Thomas Berrington admitting he might be wrong."

"Sometimes I wonder why I love you as I do."

"My beauty, obviously. My–" Jorge stopped abruptly

as a group of men appeared ahead of them. They had been concealed behind a splinter of rock until the pair turned a corner.

Thomas came to a halt and glanced across his shoulder to discover a second group blocking the trail behind.

"Tell them you are a friend of Fernando's." Jorge eased his horse close to Thomas's until their sides touched.

"That would be a mistake."

"Not if you are persuasive."

"These men aren't Spanish."

"Brigands?" Jorge drew his sword and held it up, for all the good it was likely to do if it came to a fight.

"Moors." Then Thomas laughed and urged his horse forward. "Yusuf?"

The man at the head of the band of soldiers stood tall, broad-shouldered, no longer the youth who had worshiped Thomas but a leader, a general. Nephew to Gharnatah's ruler, al-Zagal, and brother to Muhammed who laid claim to the crown. Yusuf was now a man of twenty-one years and, though Thomas had not seen him in several years, he had heard of his reputation as a leader of men and a brave warrior. He dismounted and walked forward, only slowing when he did not receive the welcome he expected.

Yusuf looked beyond him. "Is it only the two of you?"

"Of course. Who were you expecting?"

A flicker of the eyes. Yusuf knew Jorge, of course.

"Are you with the Spanish? A scouting party?"

Thomas stopped, uncertain. "Do you forget where my loyalty lies?"

"Rumour has it your loyalty lies with Spain these days. Have you come on behalf of your lover Queen to spy on al-Andalus?"

Thomas took a step closer, ignoring the other men as they drew weapons. He hoped Jorge had sheathed his own sword, for these were all experienced soldiers.

"Since when did you start believing rumour? Have you forgotten all those lessons I taught when you sat on my knee? The lessons Jorge taught you when you grew and began to discover women could be something more than playmates?" Thomas slapped his chest. "Are we not friends?"

Yusuf stared at him for a long moment. The rain returned briefly then passed on.

"Where are you coming from?"

"Where do you think? Ballix, of course."

"The Spanish are there. Have you been with them?"

"It seems whatever I say you are not going to believe me. We are tired, and Lubna and Belia are expecting us at home. Let us pass and we can all forget this encounter ever happened."

"Lubna is with you? In Malaka?"

"Where else would she be?"

"I thought ..." Yusuf looked away, eyes tracking the steep inclines either side before returning. Something in them had changed. "Word is you had gone to your other woman in Ixbilya."

"There is no other woman for me than Lubna, you know that. We have been in Malaka a year and a half while she studies at the Infirmary."

"Is she good?"

Thomas laughed. "You know she is good."

"As good as you?" Yusuf rolled his shoulder, the one

that had been injured six years before, now almost completely healed.

"She could have fixed you as well as I did."

"Then she is good." Yusuf shook his head, rubbed a hand across his face, and released the breath from his lungs. "We are camped that way if you want to join us. You are welcome, both of you."

"We need to get home. I am–" Thomas cut off what he was about to say. Yusuf didn't need to know he was involved in the investigation of another murder, and the man had his own responsibilities. "Are you with your uncle's forces?" Thomas referred to al-Zagal, Sultan in Gharnatah and a feared warrior. "Did he know the Spanish were coming?"

"He sent me ahead to scout the area. He feared they might come early, but we are fortunate the rain is hampering them, and ..." Yusuf trailed off, studying Thomas. He offered a grim smile. "You know, for a moment I almost forgot I don't trust you."

Thomas held his arms out. "It is me, your friend. You can always trust me. Do you not know that here, in your heart?" He patted his chest.

"I want to. But my uncle says trust no man, for everyone betrays you in the end."

"He's thinking of Spaniards," said Jorge, his first words since they met.

"Take no notice of him," Thomas said. "All he understands is women."

"Yusuf knows that, for I taught him well."

Yusuf nodded. "Yes, you did. And my thanks." He shook his head and laughed. "I cannot continue to doubt you, either of you. How can I when we have lived so much of our lives together? But tell me, is it true you have bedded the Spanish Queen?"

"Who told you that?"

"It is common knowledge. Everyone knows it. Was she good? I expect she is a disappointment after Moorish women, no?"

"If I ever find out I will let you know. She and I are..." Thomas thought of some way to phrase it but knew he could tell only the truth. "We are friends, it is true, but nothing more. She loves her husband and country too much to betray either."

"But you *are* friends?"

Thomas nodded.

"And him?"

Thomas shrugged. "Not in the same way, but they know Jorge, certainly. And Lubna and Will."

"Gods, Thomas, are you sure you have not ploughed her? And if not, why not? I never took you for a fool."

"Believe what you will, I know the truth." He studied Yusuf. Handsome, strong, confident. He wondered how much of that would remain after an encounter with the Spanish. Tides of loyalty surged through him, dragging him relentlessly where they wished. He decided to risk his life, trusting to old loyalties. "Are you stupid like your brother, or incapable like your father?"

"You know I am not."

It seemed the gamble might work.

"And your uncle?"

"Is a great general."

"Do you believe the Moors can win this war?"

"We are great warriors, and this is our land." Yusuf looked around. "Even when it is as wet as this."

"That's no answer to my question."

"I cannot give an answer," said Yusuf. "It is not my place to give an answer. If you want to talk foolishness you should come and eat with us. We are camped close by."

"We cannot."

"Then at least walk with us, we go in the same direction for a while." Yusuf turned away, his men falling in behind, others ranging ahead to protect their leader. A few curious glances were cast at Thomas and Jorge, but if Yusuf accepted them so would they. For now.

Thomas reached out and gripped Yusuf's arm, holding him back while the others went past, until only the three of them remained.

"Do you think this war can be won?" he asked. "Not just this battle, but the war for the soul of al-Andalus?"

"It is not my place to ask such questions."

"But you think them, don't you? Just as I do."

"It is not my place," said Yusuf again. "But you are right, that does not mean I do not think on such things." He glanced ahead to where his men were now a hundred paces distant. Far enough for honesty, it seemed. Yusuf began to follow the narrow trail, room enough only for Thomas beside him. "You are right. This war cannot be won, not even with my uncle sitting as Sultan in Gharnatah." He stared down at his hands for a moment before looking up. "Tell me, Thomas, do you truly have the ear of the Spanish King and Queen?"

"I do. But not enough to obtain what you want. This war will not end at my wish or yours, else it would be ended already."

"My uncle is a great general, but he is forged from iron. He has no humanity, no flexibility."

"He keeps Gharnatah safe," Thomas said.

"My brother seeks to replace him."

"That will never happen."

"Do not be so sure. You have been away from Ghar-natah too long, even if I did believe you were in Ixbilya, not here. The Albayzin is in open rebellion against al-Zagal, and Muhammed and my mother encourage it. He would sit on the hill again if he can."

"Then the end will come even sooner." And because Thomas trusted Yusuf, trusted him more than anyone else in the ruling family, he said, "I believe Muhammed has been turned into an instrument of the Spanish."

Yusuf stopped, turned to Thomas. "I do not like him, but he is my brother, and he is a Moor."

"Who was held captive by the Spanish for near a year. There is a man, Martin de Alarcón, who was his captor that whole time. Except he is like no gaoler I have ever known. Martin is a clever man. He turned Muhammed to his will. Turned him to the purposes of Spain."

Yusuf shook his head, his gaze going to his men who continued to walk away. "It is true he has said some things to me that have made me wonder where his loyalties lie, but if what you claim is true then it is a hard truth to take."

"There is someone else who could sit on the hill," Thomas said.

"My brother has the stronger claim."

Thomas laughed. "Since when has claim ever mattered? Your father had the strongest claim, but Muhammed ousted him. He is not liked and you are."

"Being liked is no qualification to rule. If it was then Jorge would be Sultan."

114

"God help me, and God help Gharnatah," said Jorge, who waited patiently.

"It is a good place to start," Thomas said. "And you are a strong general. Olaf Torvaldsson tells me you are, and there is no better judge."

"And if I sat on the hill, would that stop the Spanish?"

"No, but it might make the ending easier for everyone. They grow tired of our resistance. You have seen it. When Ronda fell they allowed the people to leave with their belongings. Last year, at Wadi-Ashi, the town was stripped of everything and many enslaved. What will be demanded next year? All our heads on stakes?"

"You preach treason, Thomas."

"Not treason, but reason. I preach a chance to save at least something from this chaos. We are going to lose, but at least we can try to lose with honour intact."

Yusuf shook his head and set off along the track. Thomas glanced at Jorge, saw him watching without expression. Thomas wanted to say something but knew he could not. Rain came again, dashing across his face, and he started off and fell into step beside Yusuf. Ahead he saw the men had disappeared and wondered when that had happened, and where they had gone to.

"What you say is logical," said Yusuf. "As everything you say is. But I don't know if I can embrace such an idea." He held up a hand as Thomas opened his mouth to speak. "No, you have stated your case, and a strong case it is. I must think on it, tease through the implications and come to my own conclusions." The tension flowed from his body, and his steps sped up. "Are you sure you will not stay the night?"

"My thanks, but our families are waiting. You should

come with us, for tonight at least. Lubna would be pleased to see you."

"And I her. But I cannot."

They came to a fork in the trail, and Thomas saw where Yusuf's men had gone. They were waiting for their master on another track, even narrower as it cut through an almost vertical crevice in the hillside. Rain fell on them, water rose ankle high, but they ignored both.

"This is where we must part, for now." Yusuf pulled Thomas into an embrace, holding him for a long time. "I will let you know what I decide." He hugged Jorge, then joined his men and trudged away through the rain.

THIRTEEN

"You haven't talked to him yet, have you." Lubna spoke of Diego, who continued to take any object that sparkled or drew his attention.

"I will. Can I at least dry myself first and get something to eat?" Thomas let his wet robe drop to the floor where it lay like something dead, bleeding a puddle of water. "Or it might be better if Jorge tried."

"He already has, but he is too soft. It will be better coming from you."

"Am I not soft then?"

Diego would not meet Thomas's eyes as he sat him down, hands clasped together in his lap. He had wanted Will to be with him but Thomas said the conversation was for the two of them only. So far it had not gone well. Not gone well at all.

Diego claimed he had taken nothing. When Thomas showed him the wooden box filled almost to the brim with trinkets — knives for eating; a packet of salt; three of Belia's potion bottles, two of which contained enough contents to kill a man — he had started to cry and held his arms out to be embraced.

Thomas only stared at him, his face grim.

"It has to stop. If you want something, ask, and most times we will say you can have it. But you have to remember it is not yours. This, for example." Thomas reached in and pulled out a golden ring. "Do you know who this belongs to?"

"Yours," said Diego.

"That's right. It is the ring that marks me as husband to Lubna. It means a great deal to me."

"You never wear it," said Diego. "I watch. I see. Lubna wears hers but not you."

"It is too big and I fear losing it."

"So Diego keep it safe."

"It is my ring." Thomas reached out, took Diego's right hand in his and spread the fingers. "Do all of these belong to you?" Thomas tapped the rings on each of Diego's fingers.

"Mine," said Diego.

"Or your parents'?"

Diego pulled his hand away and wrapped it inside the other.

"What is theirs is mine."

"And your brother? Might he not want a memento of them?"

"He can ask."

Thomas reached for Diego's other hand but it was pulled away.

"Do not do that," Thomas said. "You are part of this family now and that has responsibilities as well as benefits." He held his hand flat. "Give me your hand, Diego."

The youth hesitated, and for a moment Thomas

thought he had gone too far and Diego would run from the room. He knew it was a critical moment, but was determined not to weaken now, however much he felt sorry for him.

He waited, staring at Diego, hoping his gaze didn't carry too much of the coldness he was often accused of possessing and which he did not understand. Eventually Diego unwrapped fingers that were twisted tight together and extended his hand.

Thomas took the wrist and held it firm when Diego sensed the tightness and tried to withdraw.

"This one," Thomas said, tapping a fine garnet set in a twisted silver band. "Where did you get this?"

"Ma buy it. Diego in market and like. Say I want and she buy."

"It is expensive."

"Ma tell me never worry about money."

"And this?"

The interrogation continued until Thomas tapped a gold ring set with topaz which had been jammed onto Diego's thumb, too large for any other finger. As soon as Thomas touched it Diego snatched his hand away.

"Present, from Pa."

Thomas reached out again, waiting, saying nothing.

Diego stared at his hand, up to Thomas's face, down to his hand.

A splash of sunlight fell across them as the clouds parted. It lasted only a moment before fading. From elsewhere in the house conversation reached them as Belia prepared the evening meal and Lubna helped. Now and again Will would call out, and Thomas heard Jorge's laughter. He did not begrudge Diego's presence in their extended family, but knew this moment was important. He had to learn what was acceptable and what was not.

More tears welled in Diego's eyes, but he was captured beneath Thomas's gaze. Slowly he unclasped his hands and extended the left one. Thomas gripped the fine ring and tried to pull it loose but it was fixed too firmly.

"This is not from your father, is it?"

"He was there. My new Pa. The one I find. He give me the ring."

"Is that true? He spoke those words to you?"

Diego shook his head.

"Because he couldn't speak, could he?" Thomas felt a welling of excitement and pushed it away. "He was already dead."

"Diego was there. Diego afraid man will come back. I take so he cannot."

Thomas stared at Diego. "What man?"

"One with knife. One who hurt Pa not Pa." He moved his right hand in small cutting motions.

"You saw it all?"

Diego nodded. "Close my eyes because I do not want to see. But I look sometimes. Cannot close my ears."

"Why were you there?"

"Looking for Pa. He go away and Ma sick. She miss him. So do I. So I went find him."

"But you knew he was dead. There was a funeral."

"They not let me go. I not believe them when they say. I go look. Know where he works. But there is another man."

It occurred to Thomas he hadn't given enough attention to Diego's real father.

"What did he do?"

"Pa?"

Thomas nodded. Telling the tale seemed to be relaxing Diego. There was still the matter of his stealing, but for the moment the story he told was more important.

"Scribe." Diego made a motion with his hand, as if writing.

"Who for? Did people come to him and he wrote for them, or did he work somewhere?"

Diego snuffled, shook his head. "I say already. Diego went to find Pa where he *work*."

"Your father worked in that building?"

A nod of the head. "Work for other Pa."

"Your father was clerk to the dead man?"

"What is clerk?" said Diego.

"Someone who scribes words for others. When goods arrive, when ships dock. A record must be kept of everything."

"Yes. Clerk. Pa clerk." A soft smile. "He bring me things from the ships. Small things. Ma too, he bring spice and pretty stones. Pa love us." Diego stared into space. "Pa loved me." He twisted his hands together, then as if coming to a decision, pulled hard at the ring circling his thumb. His face creased from the effort but slowly the ring worked loose, came off in a rush and flew from his grasp. It skittered across the floor and came to rest in a corner.

Thomas left it where it was.

"Not mine," said Diego. "Diego know not his. But so pretty."

"Was it on the man in that room?"

A shake of the head. "No, no. Other man. Other man lost it."

"The man with the knife?"

"No. Other man have knife. Man telling him to hurt Pa not Pa."

Thomas stared at Diego. "There were two men?" He held his fingers up, unsure if Diego understood the concept of numbers or not. Diego reached out and lifted a third finger.

"Three?"

"Pa not Pa too," said Diego. "Big man and small man." He raised a hand above his head, lowered it to his waist, no doubt both exaggerations. He began to nod, a movement that settled into a steady, odd rhythm, as if it offered comfort. Thomas allowed him the respite for a moment. How must it have been for him to watch the attack? No, not an attack, a murder. Thomas went to the corner and picked up the ring, slipped it into his pocket, not wanting to upset Diego further. With luck he might forget about it altogether. The mind was wondrous in the way it could sweep aside memories it did not want, and Thomas found those with different capabilities like Diego could at times do so more easily than others. They were the lucky ones, choosing to hold on only to the happy memories and expunge the bad. Thomas wished he could acquire the talent but knew it was not in his nature.

"If you saw the men again would you recognise them?"

But Diego only continued to nod. His mind had gone to some other place he would be difficult to extract from. Thomas knew he would have to come back to the subject another time so rose and left Diego to his thoughts. Outside he found Will playing with blocks and told him to go and comfort him. The others were in the big room, Lubna and Jorge sitting at a wide table. Belia stirred a pot whose aroma filled the air and brought saliva to Thomas's mouth. The food in Ballix had been barely edible, and he wanted to sit and eat and talk of other matters. War might be coming, but for tonight it could be locked outside. They had made a good life for themselves here. He wanted to retain it as long as he could.

He sat, pulled the ring out, and turned it in his fingers.

"What have you got there?" said Jorge. "Has Diego been teaching you how to pilfer, too?"

"It's a ring worn by the killer. He lost it, and Diego found it." He passed the ring to Jorge, who examined it, pulling a lamp close.

"It's valuable, but too gaudy. The property of a man who needs to shout his position to the world. I prefer more subtle adornment."

Thomas smiled, wondering why such a sentiment did not apply to Jorge's choice of clothing. He had changed into a long robe of fine silk after bathing, red and gold, that shimmered and clung to his body. The sleeves were widely cut so they draped onto the table-top like pooled water.

"There is something inscribed within," Jorge said, holding the ring out for Thomas to see.

He took it and peered at fine markings on the inner surface. He couldn't make out what they said, or even if they said anything at all. They might be no more than scratches acquired over many years. He left the ring on the table and walked through to the room he shared with Lubna, searched through the boxes he kept there until he found what he wanted — a fine lens fashioned in Naples and imported at great expense. With careful use it could magnify an object tenfold.

Returning to the table he set the eyeglass into the hollow of his right eye. Not scratches, but words. He moved the ring closer then away, farther away again. He reached across and drew the lamp close until it burned his hair and he jerked back.

Lubna came and leaned on his shoulders, the scent of her enfolding him.

"Can you read it?"

"Not quite. It would help if I knew what language it was written in, but without reading it I can't tell."

"Can I see?" She held her hand flat.

Thomas continued to peer at the fine marks but knew his sight was not keen enough. He laid the ring in Lubna's palm and handed her the glass. She had used such an instrument before, they were not uncommon among some physicians who wanted to examine a wound or mark more closely.

Lubna sat beside Thomas and used her hip to push him along the bench until she was closer to the lamp. Thomas gripped her long hair and pulled it back so she didn't burn it as he had done.

After a long while, Lubna placed the ring on the table.

"No, I cannot read it."

"Someone else, perhaps. Belia?" Thomas turned, but Belia shook her head.

"Lubna's eyes are better than mine."

"And I cannot read in any case," said Jorge.

"I cannot read it," said Lubna, "but I can draw it. I can see the marks, I just can't read them. They are not in Arabic or Spanish or Latin, or I would recognise the words. She bumped against Thomas again and smiled. "Go fetch me paper, slave."

Lubna's face screwed up as she held the glass against her left eye. Her right hand moved slowly across a sheet of paper as she transcribed what she saw. Thomas, Jorge and Belia leaned close, watching as a pattern emerged, but after a while Thomas knew it meant something only to him.

It took some time, but as the marks were joined together, he made out letters written in French, a language he had not read in many years and was not confident of reading accurately now. He leaned closer, his hand coming to rest on Lubna's shoulder.

She shook it off. "I'm not done yet. Wait, can't you?"

Thomas withdrew.

The letters formed and faded in his mind, washed aside as Lubna added fresh marks, and he knew he must find something to distract himself until she was finished. He straightened, easing an ache in his back — too long in the saddle, too long in the rain.

He found Diego with Will on the terrace, leaning out to watch the last of the setting sun, which painted vermillion glory across distant clouds. They were talking nonsense in a mix of Arabic and Spanish, both understanding each other even if no-one else could.

Thomas sat on a wide bench and patted his lap. Will ran across and leaped onto him. Diego came more slowly, no doubt still not forgiving him for their conversation, but he sat happily enough and leaned against Thomas. One child on his knee, a second at his side, that is how it felt to him, but not how it would look to anyone outside of the house.

"What have the pair of you done today?"

It was Will who replied. "We played with Diego's dice, then I showed him how to kill a man."

Thomas smiled. "Wooden swords, I hope."

"Pa! 'Course wood swords. Knives too. But Diego can never kill. He fights bad, and he pulls his blows." Will stroked Thomas's arm, drawing the sleeve of his robe up to look at a scar across his forearm. He touched it with a finger, a familiar game, even if he did already know the answer.

"France," Thomas said.

"When you was nearly killed?"

Thomas wondered if he had told his son too many stories of his past, but he wanted him to be both invulnerable and aware of the dangers of battle. The joys too, perhaps, for the fight held a cold, insidious joy he had indulged in at one time, when he was not so much older than the boy he held against him. Many of those memories brought a cold ecstasy he feared, knowing its siren call. He wondered if that was why he told stories to Will, to scare him, to make the wonder of men fighting men less fascinating.

"When I was nearly killed," Thomas said, smiling. "What about you, Diego? Do you like fighting?"

A shake of the head, a nuzzling at his side, and Thomas lifted an arm to draw Diego against him.

"That's good. I often think my son likes it too much."

"*Morfar* says good to fight," said Will.

"Yes, Olaf would. But remember it is his profession, and he has dedicated his life to war. When you grow up, I pray there will be no more war."

126

"*Morfar* says war good."

"*Morfar* is not always right in everything he says."

Will laughed, put a hand over his mouth. "You tell him that?"

Thomas returned the laugh. "No, I don't think that would be a good idea."

"It's done."

Thomas turned to see Belia in the doorway. He nodded, kissed the top of Will's head, gave one more hug to Diego, then extricated himself from their arms and legs and went inside.

When he leaned over Lubna this time he wasn't convinced the completed strokes were much better than when he had left. He rested on his knuckles on the table as he studied what Lubna had transcribed. He narrowed his eyes to blur the image a little, and as he did so he could read what was written there.

A mon frere bien amie E.

To my dear friend and brother. An ornate E ended the short phrase.

It meant nothing to Thomas, other than the original owner might have been brother to someone whose name began with an E. Was that person the killer, or someone the killer knew? It was just as likely he had stolen the ring. Except not the killer. Thomas tried to recall what Diego has said. Two men, one tall, the other shorter. One with a knife, the other in charge, issuing orders. And ... yes, he was sure, Diego had said the ring belonged to the taller man. How had he come to lose such a valuable object?

Thomas wanted to question Diego again but knew he could not, so instead he told the others what the words said. They looked disappointed, as though they had expected a sudden revelation placed before them.

Lubna's arms snaked around his waist, and she leaned her head against his side. "Did it belong to Diego's father?"

Thomas shook his head, reached out and picked up the ring, half surprised it didn't burn with associated guilt. "I believe it belonged to the man who ordered al-Zaki killed. This ring belongs to one of the men we seek. Find him and no doubt we find the other as well."

"He is French?" asked Lubna.

"Perhaps. But in England the nobility speak French more than they do English."

"Why? Did you?"

Thomas snorted a laugh and stroked Lubna's face. " I am sorry to disappoint you, my love, but I was never nobility."

"You told me your father was a ... what did you call him?"

"Oh, an important man in Lemster, sure enough, but no more than a Squire, not a Sire."

"Ah well," said Lubna, "I still love you even if you are not important."

"I am relieved to hear it." Thomas stared at the ring, flat on the palm of his hand. "Knowing what it says doesn't help us find the man though, does it?"

Will came running into the room, his feet skidding wildly on marble tiles.

"Someone coming!" He careened into the table, bounced off it, and slid against Lubna, who rubbed his arm where he had banged it.

"It's too late for visitors." Thomas stood and made

his way to the terrace where Diego still remained, staring out at the darkening track that led to the house.

A single man plodded up the slope, an unlit lantern swinging from his hand. Thomas watched him for a while then went to the door, opened it and stepped outside. He wondered if he should have brought a weapon then dismissed the idea. This was not the first unexpected visitor to come to the house. Every week or so someone would make the journey in search either of him or Lubna, sent from the Infirmary to seek advice or treatment.

The man was close before he noticed Thomas waiting for him in the growing shadows, and he stopped ten paces away.

"Are you lost, sir?"

"Are you Thomas Berrington?"

"I am. And you are?"

A shake of the head. "It does not matter who I am, only my message. I come from Ali Durdush, Master of the Malaka Guilds. He requests your presence at the Antequera gate at first light tomorrow."

"On what business?"

"I am only a messenger. My master will inform you of the purpose in the morning." The man started down the track before stopping and turning back. "Any message in return?"

Thomas shook his head. "No, no mess–" But the man had gone. Thomas watched, waiting until he saw a spark of light from the lantern as the day faded too far to allow a safe passage of the twisting path.

Lubna snaked her arms around him, pressing the swell of her belly against his back. "Who was that? Do they want one of us at the Infirmary?"

"It was a message from Ali Durdush. He wants me to meet him tomorrow."

"And Jorge?"

"He didn't say, but I expect he'll want to come. He always does."

FOURTEEN

"Why are we doing what Durdush wants without question?" said Jorge. "Remind me again, if you would. Oh, no, of course, because you can't, can you?"

"You were there at the gate," Thomas said. "We ride to talk with the Spanish. It's not as if we were offered much in the way of choice. Besides, do this for him and I might get some help from his clerks if not Durdush himself."

Ahead of them a line of twenty men wound their way along a stony track raised above a river bed. It would normally be dry at this time of year but now ran with foaming water.

"Will Fernando be there, do you think?"

"I doubt it. He won't want to talk directly. I hope he isn't."

Jorge laughed. "Durdush considers himself an important man, at least worthy enough to meet a king even if it is not his king. And Fernando likes you."

"I doubt he ever gives me a moment's thought." Thomas leaned forward, searching for Ali Durdush, picking him out by his girth and the richness of his robe. A knot of soldiers surrounded him.

"Ah, but his wife," said Jorge. "The delightful Isabel. I suspect she thinks of you often. You should bed her, you know. Everyone assumes you already have. Why deny yourself a pleasure you have already been judged guilty of?"

"She is Queen of Castile."

"Do queens also not enjoy a tumble with a handsome man?" Jorge glanced across. "Or even with you."

"I am married."

"I know." Jorge smiled. "We heard you last night. My thanks. The noises you made were most encouraging."

Thomas tried not to smile. "I didn't think you needed much encouragement."

"I thought you had grown more relaxed this last year, but you are still wound tighter than a crossbow."

Thomas watched one of Durdush's companions steer his horse to one side. He hoped the man was not waiting for them but suspected the hope was in vain.

The man fell in alongside them, almost the last members of the party. To right and left, taller peaks rose and the river channel narrowed. In places enormous rocks littered the ground, and from the pink freshness of the cracked sides, Thomas believed some must have been loosened by the shaking of the earth. The man rode in silence for a time, staring ahead. No doubt he had been picked for a task no-one else wanted.

Eventually Thomas grew tired of the wait. "Get it out, then. What does he want of us?"

The man glanced aside, as if surprised to see the pair of them.

"Master Durdush requests your presence in the front ranks when the meeting starts."

Thomas said nothing, staring at the man until he kicked at the sides of his horse and cantered back to his companions.

"You lack every social grace known to man, do you know that?"

"Why would I want social graces? Besides, he was an idiot. Durdush even more so if he thinks my presence is going to help. It is the only reason we are here, because he has heard I know the King."

"It would not kill you to act like a normal person once in a while."

Thomas ignored the comment, as he ignored much of what Jorge said. He loved the man like a brother, in fact far better than he ever had gotten along with his own brother. Jorge was as easy to live with as the silk he wore, but Thomas knew he could never be like him.

"I do hope Fernando isn't there," he said.

Thomas ignored Ali Durdush's request and stood as far back in the courtyard as he could. There were two score men from Malaka, not enough to form much of a barrier, and Fernando's eyes discovered him almost at once. The King tried not to show anything, but a faint smile lifted one corner of his mouth. That, or a scowl — it was often difficult to tell with the man.

Durdush had been introduced as Master of the Malaka Guilds but took no part in the negotiations which were conducted by al-Tagri's vizier, and proceeded at a slow pace. Fernando also said nothing, sitting in an ornate chair raised on a platform so he could look across the meagre gathering. This was how negotiations proceeded, Thomas knew, slowly and with no prospect of victory. The real work would be done outside this chamber, man facing man, deals struck on a whim and a handshake.

They had come to the supposed castle, which looked more like a fort down on its luck. The courtyard made up at least a third of the area, with the rest of the building rising to more than a single story only on one side. Auta Castle was the name given to the edifice, but castle it most certainly was not. However, it did boast a fine position on a hill above the Moorish town of Aprisco al-Majianza, though no doubt that name would change now it lay in the hands of the Spanish. A small settlement surrounded by rich farmland, no different to many of the other small towns that had fallen beneath the continual advance of Spain.

"Why are these proceedings always so dull?" asked Jorge.

"Because everyone knows nothing will be decided here. No-one is allowed to state such, but there must be seen to be great deal of talk."

"Do you think anyone would miss us if we slipped away?"

"Fernando would. He looks our way constantly."

"He's pleased to see an old friend."

"I'm not so sure. Surprised, perhaps, and old friend may be stating it too strongly. His wife, yes. Fernando likes me well enough, but I don't think he regards me as a friend."

"Then it must be me he looks at," said Jorge.

"Yes, that will be it." Thomas twisted, easing an ache

in the small of his back. Too long standing on hard cobbles while foolish men spoke foolish words.

"Durdush has noticed you are here at the back," said Jorge.

"He will also have noticed Fernando is aware of my presence, which is what he wanted. The man's a fool if he thinks that will sway anyone."

"So our job here is done and we can leave?"

Thomas was about to offer a retort when he realised Jorge was right, as he often was, though he would never tell him such. Instead he stepped aside and half turned away from the proceedings. Nobody appeared to notice other than Fernando, whose eyes had locked onto the movement. He offered a faint smile and the briefest of nods. Thomas took it as permission, whether that was the meaning or not, turned fully and walked through the gates that had been thrown wide in welcome.

Outside he surveyed the tethered horses and the two men who had been left to care for them. Mounting their own steeds would raise no question, but instead Thomas turned aside and followed a stone wall to a rough turret and moved past it.

"Ah," said Jorge.

"Ah what?"

"So you intend to do Ali Durdush's job for him after all."

Thomas laughed, a sound containing little humour. "There will be no agreement here. Or if there is it will not be one that survives the first skirmish. Malaka is doomed. Not tomorrow, not next week, but within a month, do not doubt it."

"I love your optimism," said Jorge.

"I know. There are times I almost believe the world to be a wonderful place, just as you do."

"But not often?"

"No ... not often." Thomas wandered away to the side, following a track that might have been made by human feet but more likely goats. Yellow-headed weeds grew dense here, nourished by the recent rainfall, making the most of their brief moment. He stopped and knelt, snapped off four stalks, and handed one to Jorge.

"What am I meant to do with this?"

"Asparagus," Thomas said. "It's good. Good for you, as well." He smiled. "It makes your piss smell, though."

"And you want me to eat it?"

Thomas stripped the hard nodules from the sides of one of his stalks and bit into it. "You know, a man could live off this land."

"Except everyone would know where he went by the smell of his piss."

"True. But look, the almonds are in blossom. In a few months there will be nuts." He stepped aside to stand beneath the gnarled branches of one of the trees, its trunk almost black, the branches thick with grey-pink flowers just beginning to fade. Thomas kicked his feet, unearthing several dark, stained husks. "See? These are probably still edible."

"For goats, maybe." Jorge looked around, but it was obvious he didn't see the bounty that lay all around. "How do you know all these things, Thomas? Are they in those books you're always reading?"

"Some, certainly. But if a man asks questions he will get answers."

"Just like you got answers from Durdush."

"He's hiding something, and I will get it out of him before we're done."

They reached a low rise. Beyond, the land undulated away to the base of peaks formed of grey rock. One ridge resembled a sleeping giant, his head resting on an arm, his belly fat from eating birds that nested on the slopes. To the west the land was softer. A group of a dozen men had made camp near a small stream, and a fire spiralled smoke into the air. Thomas wondered who they were — part of Fernando's army, or simply men passing through? The fact they were camped so close to Auta indicated they were likely not strangers.

Thomas sat on a rock and chewed on another twig of asparagus, used a stone to crack one of the almonds. The fruit within was dark brown, but the thin covering peeled away beneath his nail to reveal pale flesh. He held the kernel up to show Jorge.

"They are better fresh, but these will keep you alive if you get lost in the wilds."

"Then I'll have to remember never to do so. Look," Jorge pointed, "the meeting is over."

Thomas watched as men drifted from within the castle. Some mounted their horses and rode off, others stood around in discussion. Thomas narrowed his eyes but could see no Spaniards. He glanced toward the small group of men, but they showed no sign of moving. Not with Durdush, then.

"They've been sent away with their tail between their legs."

"How can you be so sure?"

"There's no-one to see them off, and see, that's Durdush in the first group heading back to the river. If the talks were successful he'd still be inside with the others, talking to Fernando. Al-Tagri might have sent his vizier, but everyone knows it's Durdush and the Guild that rules in Malaka."

"So it will be war?"

"It will be war."

Jorge thought about it for a moment. "Do we need to move elsewhere?"

"Nowhere will be safe until this war is done. Even then..." Thomas didn't finish, not sure what might happen after the defeat of al-Andalus. He dismissed the idea, judging he would no doubt be dead by then, caught up in the fighting. But he hoped Will would live, and Lubna and Jorge and Belia.

Jorge laughed, but not at anything Thomas had said.

"I take it that's who we're waiting for?"

Thomas looked up from his thoughts, glad of the distraction.

Fernando rode out from the rear of the castle. Thomas looked aside, saw that the last of the party from Malaka were well down the hill and would not have spotted the King of Aragon and Castile. Fernando saw the two of them on the ridge and steered his horse in their direction. The four soldiers accompanying him followed their master.

Fernando rode fast, pulling up in a scatter of stones. The man could always be trusted to show off; it was in his nature. So was killing. Fernando was known as a skilled general and soldier, equally at home killing Moors and issuing orders to kill even more.

He swung from the saddle and offered his hand to the sitting Thomas, who took it, allowing himself to be drawn to his feet and into an embrace that might have cracked a rib in a less strong man.

"I could not believe it was you at first," said Fernando, "but then I saw this one behind you and knew it had to be." He turned to Jorge and embraced him also. "It's good to see you're both still getting involved in matters that are none of your business."

"How do you know it is none of my business?"

Fernando laughed and slapped Thomas on the shoulder, a habit of his that was becoming increasingly tiresome. "Because I know you too well. That excuse for a governor thinks me a fool. It is the fat one who will do the deal, but it will have to be soon. I take it you know him?"

Thomas looked away, but the Moorish party had disappeared completely. He wondered if they would note the lack of him and Jorge. He knew he had a decision to make but wanted to put it off. There would be time later, and he would know more by then.

"Ali Durdush is no governor," he said, happy to admit that much, "but he is Master of the Malaka Guild, which might be regarded as a more important position. I assume you sent them all away disappointed."

"I didn't agree to what they wanted, if that's what you mean, but I left a chink of light they can believe offers something in the future. Why were you here with them, Thomas?"

"My presence was requested."

"But you are no diplomat."

Jorge laughed, making Fernando smile. "No, he is no diplomat, you are right in that."

"And yet he always succeeds in what he sets out to do." The smile left Fernando's face. "You know we are here for Malaka and will take it before summer comes." His eyes caught Thomas's. "Does Durdush really hold power? Should I be talking to him or this governor who sent a deputy instead of facing me? Al-Tigri, that is his name, isn't it?"

So he had known all along, Thomas thought, even if he had mispronounced the name.

"Hamad al-Tagri. A fearsome warrior by all accounts. I have not met him, but Olaf speaks of him with admiration."

Fernando knew the Sultan's general, Olaf Torvaldsson, from when he had visited Ixbilya over a year and a half before to attend Thomas and Lubna's wedding. The unlikely pair had struck up a mutual respect, coloured by the knowledge they might have to kill each other one day.

"Do I have to deal with both of them?" Fernando stepped closer to Thomas, too close, but he was used to such from the man. "What is the sentiment in Malaka? Will they surrender without a fight?"

Thomas shrugged. Fernando was placing him in a difficult position. They might be friends, but Thomas lived in Malaka, thought of himself as belonging to al-Andalus. There was a possibility he could lessen the impact on the city if he gave away information on who truly ruled there, but could he do that? Would it feel too much like a betrayal?

He decided to keep any information he had to himself, for now.

"The city doesn't even know you're at its gates. As for surrender, you have already pointed out I'm no diplomat."

"I'm not so sure about that anymore." Another slap on the shoulder, which made Thomas wince. "You will ride with me, and stay to eat? There is someone you will want to meet."

"You bring Isabel with you?" Thomas knew Fernando's soldiers remained far enough away not to overhear their conversation, otherwise he would have used her full title.

"Juan and Isabel, too."

Thomas knew he referred to their only son and heir to the crown, and eldest daughter. A serious girl of near seventeen years who had been betrothed to a prince of Portugal for over ten years without any marriage taking place. Thomas supposed such a condition was reason enough to dampen the spirit of a pretty girl on the cusp of womanhood.

"You bring your family to war?"

Another slap and this time Thomas almost retaliated. He and Fernando had fought in the past, supposedly in fun, but there had been something beneath the fun that made Thomas wary.

"We are safe enough here," said Fernando. "Is it not a fine place to set our camp?"

"Who did the fort belong to?"

"Someone who valued his life more than a roof. No doubt he will return once we leave."

"And the town?"

"The town wants to continue enjoying a quiet life. You will both come and eat with us, won't you? Isabel likes your friend."

"Which Isabel?" But Thomas knew the answer. Once more Jorge had woven his spell on any woman over the age of ten, and most below as well. He glanced at Jorge, who smiled, and Thomas nodded. "It would be our pleasure." And he knew he spoke the truth.

FIFTEEN

As they entered a wide room set on the upper floor of the castle, Thomas saw that Prince Juan wanted to come to him. But now, aged nine years, the ties of duty bound him to protocol. He remained where he was, trembling beside his mother.

Isabel, being Queen of Castile, apparently considered protocol did not apply to her. She smiled broadly and came in small, rapid steps to stand in front of Thomas, looking up at him.

"My husband neglected to tell me you were with the party from Malaka." She cast a glance at Fernando. "How should I punish him, Thomas?"

"He has brought me here now, your grace, so no punishment is necessary. How does Catherine fare? Well, I hope?"

A slight moue touched Isabel's lips. "If you had accepted my offer of a place in my court you would know the answer for yourself, but yes, she fares well. A sturdy little thing, thanks to you. And use my name, Thomas. Are we not friends? Are we not the best of friends?" Her hand came out, hovered without touching, then withdrew. "You will stay the night? We have much news to catch up on. I want to know all about your son and wife."

"Lubna carries another child." He saw a momentary cloud pass across Isabel's face. He could still not quite forgive her reaction when Lubna lost their first child and Isabel had banished her from her presence. "We will have a new addition to our family before the end of summer."

This time Isabel could not restrain herself and touched his wrist. She used the gesture to draw him forward. "Come, say hello to Juan and Isabel."

As they crossed the wooden floor, Juan gave up the effort at restraint and came to Thomas. He knelt to embrace the boy, who hugged him tight in return. He glanced at Juan's sister, who watched the encounter without expression. Thomas had never managed to spark any friendship with the girl, unlike Jorge. When he looked toward the children's mother, she was watching the encounter with a smile on her face.

"Thomas lives in Malaka now," said Fernando, perhaps considering the reunion had gone on long enough.

"Is that true?" said Isabel. "You always told me Granada was your home."

"Lubna is studying at the Infirmary. She will make a fine physician one day." He smiled. "No, she is already a fine physician."

"But not the best in Spain?"

"Not yet. One day though, more than likely. She needs to control her compassion before she becomes great."

A servant appeared from a doorway hidden behind a heavy drape. He announced their other guest had arrived and that dinner would be served shortly.

Thomas offered his arm. Isabel rested her hand on it, while Jorge did the same with the young Isabel, who could not manage to suppress a smile, no more than she could the flush that coloured her cheeks.

The dining room was more homely than the larger space they had met in, draped with Moorish hangings left by the previous owner, finely wrought lamps scattering points of light across the floor. The scent of rich food filled the air and half a dozen servants stood around, waiting for them to sit. A tall, slim man stood apart, his clothing marking him out as someone important, though his presence in this room with the King and Queen of Castile made that fact clear. Thomas saw the man stare at him in surprise. Perhaps he had expected to have the ear of Fernando to himself alone. Thomas studied him a moment, unsure if he was the same man Durdush had been speaking to outside the Ataranzana buildings after their meeting or not. He looked similar, his clothing too, but it had been at a distance and many men looked the same. For a moment Thomas wondered if Spain had not already opened unofficial negotiations with the Guild.

Fernando took a chair at one end of the table, Isabel the other. She patted the space beside her, making clear where she wanted Thomas to sit. The others found their own places. Thomas saw the newcomer take a chair next to Fernando and smiled. The man was ignorant of where real power lay in the room. He caught a curious glance cast his way and wondered what the stranger made of him. A rangy figure dressed as if he had only that morning ridden out of the North African desert, the dust of travel still on his clothes. He watched as the man examined Jorge, finding more to his liking there — once again making the wrong choice.

Juan sat on Thomas's other side, the young Isabel opposite Jorge, her eyes lifting often from an examination of the table to gaze at him. The servants fussed about, bringing knives for each, and plates. Large platters of food were set along the table. Fernando, as was his right, took the first morsels, choosing half a capon and slicing into it to release the juices.

Thomas waited for Isabel to make her choice, but she made no move. He leaned closer and kept his voice low. "Who is the stranger?"

She smiled and spoke loudly. "Sir, my friend here wants to know who you are."

Thomas scowled, but Isabel only smothered a laugh with her hand.

"You have the advantage of me, sir," said the stranger. His voice was cultured but cold, a voice used to issuing instructions with an expectation they would be instantly obeyed.

"As you do me." He did not want to make mention of having seen him with Durdush, if in fact he had, not in front of Fernando, in case it was not a meeting that should be broadcast far and wide. "I am Thomas Berrington, sir, a physician." He spoke in Spanish, though suspected the man was English, like himself, and would also know French, like himself.

"The finest physician in the whole of Spain," said Isabel. "He saved my son's leg, and saved my youngest daughter's life and mine both. He is a worker of miracles. We should petition the Pope to have him made a Saint."

The man inclined his head, but his expression showed scepticism.

"I am Richard Woodville, Earl Rivers," he said, his Spanish stilted and coloured by the accent of a rich man of the English shires. "My father knew a Berrington once."

"There are several of us still in England, I believe," Thomas said.

"John Berrington, squire to John Talbot, Earl of Shrewsbury. Is he a relation, sir?"

Thomas stared at the man, reluctant to reveal anything about himself, but Isabel reached across and touched the back of his hand. "Can it be, Thomas, two Englishmen who have acquaintances in common? Answer the man, is this John Berrington known to you?"

There was no way out unless he lied, and he would not do that to Isabel.

"He was my father."

"Died at the battle of Castillon, if I'm not mistaken," said Woodville. "Berrington ... Thomas Berrington." He mouthed the words as though tasting them and finding a lack of liking. "He had a son of that name, I heard. Can that be you?"

Thomas wanted to flee the room but knew it was impossible.

"I was beside him when he died, sir. But you are too young to know of those matters, they happened many years ago."

"You are right. I was barely ten years of age when Castillon was fought over. But tales of bravery are often spoken of around the firesides of the gentry." Woodville tapped the table with his knife, delving into a memory that was no doubt at best third- or fourth-hand. "I heard you served well. Is that true?" The note of disbelief was barely disguised.

Isabel leaned close. "Did you, Thomas? I would expect nothing less from you, but you have not spoken of this battle to me. How old were you?"

"I had but thirteen years," Thomas said, "and believed I would never see my fourteenth."

Another memory surfaced to Woodville, and his examination of Thomas showed a puzzled note of respect. "Of course ... Sir Thomas." A nod of the head in acknowledgment of the honour.

"Sir Thomas?" Isabel frowned. "What say you, sir?"

"It is a tale told among a few men of honour," said Woodville. "The boy who fought the French and killed many. The boy who treated the English, saving their lives. Although ..." He stared at Thomas, gave a slight shake of the head, and Thomas saw the man knew what else he had been rumoured to have done, but was going to keep that information to himself.

"This is true, Thomas?" This time Isabel laid her hand over his.

He saw Fernando note the familiarity and decide to ignore it. Instead he leaned toward Woodville. "Are you saying Thomas is an English Knight? Sir Thomas Berrington?"

"He is, your grace. Word has it that a degree of bravery was shown. Bravery for a grown man, let alone one so young." He turned again to Thomas. "But it is said you perished during the battle, or soon after, for nothing was ever heard of you again." He frowned. "I

147

can scarce believe you are that boy now full grown. And turned native, by God."

And much worse besides, Thomas thought. If only you knew all the truth of it. He tried to change the subject by talking to Juan, but Isabel was not finished with him yet. She leaned closer, her blue eyes capturing his.

"Tell me about this battle. Are you really Sir Thomas?" She smiled as if she could not believe such a thing. As Thomas could barely believe it himself.

"It was meant as a joke, I am sure," he said. "A poor joke at that. But yes, there was a prince there who bestowed a title on me. Whether he had the power to do so I neither knew nor cared. It is something I had forgotten about. All of it."

Isabel smiled. "But it makes you an important man."

"I don't want to be an important man."

"You already are." Her voice soft, her eyes on his. "Titles can be bought and sold, Thomas. Favours granted or taken away. Great men rise above all that. Do not dismiss an honour granted in good faith." She smiled. "I am sure I have offered you such before, only to be turned down."

"I do not seek honours. They mean nothing to me."

"But a great deal to other people." Her eyes finally left his and looked along the table. "That man, Woodville, he has changed toward you because you have a title. Sir Thomas. It has a sound to it, does it not? Sir Thomas Berrington of ... where did you say you are from?"

"Lemster."

"Perhaps not, then. It is a shame you are married or I would have found you a pretty lady of nobility."

"I am content with the wife I have."

"Yes, of course, and I understand why you are."

"What is he doing here?" Thomas asked.

"Woodville? He has been sent by the English King in search of a wife. His niece Elizabeth is the King's wife, his sister wife to the previous king, or so he tells us, so he has all the right connections to negotiate. And he bears a letter marked with the royal seal of King Henry."

"Is he looking for any wife, or a Spanish wife in particular? Not for the King, for you say he already has a wife. Who, then?"

"A connection between Spain and England would serve us both well, but I am sure he would be near as happy with a French or Flemish princess for his son."

"It has to be a princess, does it?"

"For a prince destined to be a king, of course."

"The English King is old," Thomas said. "And from what I hear not in good health."

"All the more reason to find a wife for his son. Henry has a boy almost the same age as Catherine."

Thomas examined Woodville, who was deep in conversation with Fernando. Yes, the man had the look of privilege if not necessarily money. He had no doubt worn his best garments to this meeting, but Thomas noted a tear in one sleeve where the stitching had pulled apart, and a stain on his vest. The clothing was of good quality, but not new. Thomas was no judge of fine clothing and would ask Jorge his opinion later.

As for Jorge, he leaned across the table toward the young Isabel, weaving his spell until the girl's cheeks flushed and her eyes sparked with a new-found merriment.

For a moment, contentment settled through him in this room, warmed by a deep fire, sitting beside a woman he carried high regard for, if not even love, and his closest companion nearby. Then he chastised himself for allowing such pleasure to overtake him. These two, King and Queen, were the enemy of everything he had ever wanted, determined to destroy his way of life and the lives of those around him. For a moment, he hovered on the crux of anger before pushing it aside. His life had changed a great deal and would no doubt change even more in the months and years ahead, and he determined to take whatever opportunity for pleasure he could as he turned back to Isabel to find her sharp eyes on him.

"What is it?" he asked.

She shook her head. "Nothing. Nothing at all." But a flush coloured her cheeks, just as it coloured her daughter's, and he wondered what fancies her thoughts had conjured in turn.

Later, after the table was cleared and they had all drunk more wine than they should, Richard Woodville approached Thomas as he stood next to the fire.

He proffered a nod, but even that carried an air of reluctance. "Sir Thomas."

Thomas scowled in return. "I am Thomas, only Thomas, my lord."

"You cannot take away an honour bestowed by the crown. It will prove useful to you when you return to England."

"I have no plan to do so."

"The King tells me you live amongst the heathen, and that soon their land will be destroyed. Would it not be sensible to return to your ancestral lands and take up a position in the west? That is where you hail from, is it not? Some small burgh along the border with Wales?"

Thomas nodded. "Yes, a small place. And you, Earl Rivers, where is your ancestral home?"

"I have a place in Bedfordshire. But call me Richard. We are both men of title, after all."

"Except yours is far above my own. You are related by marriage to King Henry."

"Still, we are exiles in a foreign land, so use my name. If you do return to England I could be of great help to you. It is true my niece is married to the King, and I am not without influence."

Thomas wondered at the boast, for his influence did not extend to his choice of tailor. There had been a war in England, Thomas knew. He wondered if Woodville had chosen the wrong side, saved only by his connection to the crown.

"Isabel told me about your sister and niece."

Thomas noted the slight widening of Woodville's eyes at his use of the Queen's name. He glanced across at where she was deep in conversation with Jorge and her daughter.

"Your friend is a charming man, is he not?"

"Too charming sometimes, but yes, he is. My closest friend in the world."

"He is a heathen?"

Thomas laughed. "He was born in Qurtuba, but was captured by the Moors. He is now a harem eunuch."

Woodville looked back to study Jorge. Isabel had joined Fernando, and both children had come to Jorge, leaning against him as he whispered tales their mother would no doubt disapprove of.

"A eunuch? You surprise me. He has ... there is something about him that attracts the eye, something very masculine."

"I can assure you he is not wholly a man, but he manages well under the circumstances."

"I understand you now reside in Malaka," The question was offered casually. Too casually perhaps, "and live among the Moors."

"I have made my home in their land, yes."

"Why do such a thing when you are obviously close to both the Spanish King and Queen?"

Thomas looked into Woodville's eyes. There was a coldness there, a sense of absolute entitlement. "I am sure you know as well as I do that being close to royalty is not without its dangers and responsibilities."

Woodville held his gaze for longer than would be comfortable to another man, but Thomas was not any other man.

"England has been a difficult land to prosper in these last years, as I am sure Spain is. War is a time of sacrifice, but a time of opportunity, too." Woodville's gaze took in Thomas from head to toe. "Those men who were here earlier, the Malaka Guild. What do you know of them?"

"Less than you, perhaps. I am sure I saw you in conversation with Ali Durdush the other day. Was it you or am I mistaken? Do you have one message for Spain and another for Malaka?"

Thomas watched Woodville stiffen and hoped he had sparked anger in him. He didn't like the man, but would try because he was the guest of Fernando. He reminded him of a dozen similar he had known in England. The man who his father had been Squire to, John Talbot, Earl of Shrewsbury, had been a different kind of man, his titles bothering him little, but there were enough others who lauded title over capability or loyalty.

He could see Woodville wondering whether to lie or not. He would be aware Thomas was close to Isabel and Fernando, and he obviously wanted something from them himself. Unless Isabel's tale of him coming as an emissary in search of a princess was true, but that seemed too convenient a ploy. And then the decision was made, as it had to be, to tell the truth. Or at least a version of the truth.

Woodville lowered his voice, turning away so neither Isabel nor Fernando could see his face. "King Henry has much sympathy for their majesties. We are both Catholic countries, after all, and I am indeed here in search of a wife for his son, Prince Arthur. But Malaka is a city of great wealth and influence, and it would be remiss of me not to open discussions with Durdush too. In case matters do not progress as we would all want."

"Not me," Thomas said. "I would see Malaka prosper. I would see Spain fail and al-Andalus grow greater still."

"Then it is fortunate we are here by the fire where their majesties cannot overhear you."

"They know my mind." But Thomas was unsure if he spoke the truth or not, and wondered if Woodville would betray his honesty to Fernando. Not that it worried him over much, for they knew his mind on the matter.

"And still they call you friend?" Woodville frowned, perhaps at the unfairness of such a situation. "England is a land of trade, as you know, and it would be remiss of my king not to foster such connections when he can.

I would be most grateful, Sir Thomas, if you would do me the favour of mentioning nothing about my meeting with Durdush to their majesties." He placed a hand on Thomas's shoulder. "It would be a kindness I can repay when you return to England." His fingers tightened, and he tried to show some kind of threat in his gaze, but it had no effect on Thomas who was used to far harder men, who were capable of delivering on such a promise.

SIXTEEN

Thomas was in a foul mood as he made his way through the corridors of the castle in search of the room assigned to him and Jorge. His contentment had been wrecked when Woodville asked him to keep his secrets and Thomas had not said no, as he should have. His anger was at himself more than the man, who he understood only too well. Even as a boy he had recognised the privilege and sense of entitlement of such individuals. The world was arranged to satisfy their whims, whatever the cost to others.

At last he reached what he believed was the room he was sharing with Jorge and knocked first, listening for any reply. When none came he entered, only to stop dead at the sight of Fernando examining the hangings on one of the walls.

"I am sorry, your grace, I thought this was our room."

"It is, Thomas, it is." Fernando approached, and Thomas turned aside as the man's fist came toward his shoulder, which he feared was already bruised.

"Do you want something of me?"

"Not me, my wife." He smiled. "She has questions for you that could not be raised at table."

"I…" Thomas hesitated. "It would not be seemly at this time of night. Servants talk, if only amongst themselves."

"Talk all they want, there is only one pair of ears such gossip might trouble. I trust you, Thomas, and I trust Isabel. She is in the dining hall. You will not be disturbed." This time Thomas was too slow and the punch landed with a solid thump.

Isabel stood in front of the fire, which had been re-stacked with logs. She turned at the sound of the door, a smile of welcome on a face that was pretty if not beautiful, a face Thomas found fascinating. Perhaps it was her power, or her humanity. This was a woman waging war with all the resources at her command, but still she cared for the small people. He had seen it at first-hand and admired her all the more for it. This was a woman of the highest privilege, but she respected others too. The distinction between her and Woodville only cemented Thomas's dislike of the man.

"Sir Thomas," said Isabel, offering a curtsey that was close to impertinence considering their positions.

"Don't call me that. It's not my due and means nothing to me."

She shook her head in frustration. "To you, perhaps, but to others it means a great deal. Do not denigrate the honour afforded you, even if it was long ago. I am sure you earned it." As Thomas stopped in front of her, she raised a hand to touch his face. "You are the bravest man I know."

"Perhaps you should make that the second bravest."

A moment's thought. "Yes, perhaps I should." She sighed. "Politics is so tiresome."

"I will not disagree with you, your grace." He smiled as she started to object, then Isabel laughed at the realisation Thomas had used the term deliberately to annoy her, and he said, "I will call you Isabel when you no longer call me *Sir* Thomas."

"Then it is done, cousin Thomas." She turned away, as if the moment had grown too intimate. "Come, I need to talk."

Thomas watched her walk to the table and sit. When she turned, it was to find his gaze on her and she frowned. "Have I changed so much?"

Thomas tried to smile, but it felt false. "No, not at all, but I have not seen you in two years. I was reminding myself of…" He ran out of words, unable to express the emotions that roiled through him when he looked at her. He saw her cheeks colour and wondered if she too might not share his disquiet, then shook his head. Ridiculous.

He took the seat at the head of the table, wondering if she had taken the one to the side on purpose, then dismissed the idea. He needed to stop over-thinking things. He sat back in the chair, stretching his long legs out.

"So, what are we to talk of? You know there are some questions I cannot answer."

A sigh. "One day I hope to persuade you to come to me, but until then you can keep your secrets." She placed her hands on the table and leaned close. "I want to ask about your countryman."

"Woodville? I know nothing of him. I only met the man tonight."

"But you know his kind, do you not, from when you lived in England. Was your father an influential man?"

"My father was–" Thomas cut himself short. Isabel did not need to know that Sir John Berrington was a bully who had time only for his eldest son, who in turn shared the same name and took after him almost exactly. "My father was not without influence."

He recalled a time when that influence was withheld, after Thomas had been accused of murder. His father could have stopped the trial at once had he chosen to do so, but he allowed it to run its course. At the time Thomas had wondered would he have intervened if the rope threatened, not so sure of the answer. But his father was dead, as was his older brother and mother. Only John Berrington, Thomas, and his sister had survived the sweating sickness that swept through Lemster in the late winter of 1453. He had himself succumbed but survived, at the time thanking a God he no longer believed in. Thomas and his sister, Angnes. He called the name to mind, half afraid he might have forgotten it. Only when Isabel touched his arm and spoke did he realise he must have spoken it aloud.

"Who is Angnes, Thomas? Another of your conquests?"

He smiled. "She was my sister. No, she *is* my sister. I pray she still lives, and if she does she will be almost your age by now, Isabel."

"What happened to her?"

"Life. And death. Nothing that hasn't happened a thousand times before. It was long ago, and you have questions for me tonight."

Isabel's eyes held his for a moment, her hand still on his arm, and he knew both of them sitting in this room, the Queen of Castile's hand resting against the arm of a man who might be considered her enemy, was beyond any form of protocol that could be imagined. But it was how they were, she and he, as close as sister and brother, because both knew to be closer could not be countenanced.

Finally, she gave a tiny shiver and sat up, her hand sliding away with the movement.

"This man Woodville, then. You know his kind, do you not?" All business now.

Thomas inclined his head. Yes, he knew the type, but so did Isabel. They were not so different, the nobility of England and Spain, the nobility of any country for that matter.

"He claims his niece is married to the King. Henry, is it not?"

"The last I heard, but you are more likely to know than I am. England has had several kings since I left, and there may well be a new one by now."

"It is Henry, I believe, of the House of Tudor. Woodville comes seeking a bride for his son, he claims, and my diplomats assure me his letter of intent is genuine."

"You have enough daughters to offer," Thomas said.

"But Henry has only the one son. A boy of two years. Arthur, I believe. How can we make a marriage with a boy so young?"

Thomas smiled. "You have a daughter the same age. They would make a match, would they not?"

She laughed. "I suggested as much but was rebuffed. He is, I believe, looking for someone older. Though why I cannot tell."

"You have older daughters, too."

"Isabel is pledged to Portugal. That cannot be broken or there will be another war before this one is finished. Joanna is difficult, and Maria is only three years older than Catherine."

"Are you saying you will rebuff his approach?"

"I do not wish to do that. A marriage between Spain and England would forge a powerful alliance, the two strongest powers in the world joined."

"So you are saying you would pledge Catherine to this young prince? Arthur, you called him? I had not heard of him until you spoke his name. I take little interest in my homeland anymore."

"You should, Sir Thomas." She smiled and leaned close again, once more her hand coming out, this time covering his, and Thomas turned his over so that their palms rested together and she allowed the intimacy as he closed his fingers through hers. "Tell me," she said, her eyes on their joining, "this Woodville, what is your opinion of him? The truth now, Thomas, for are we not the best of friends? You can tell me anything. Tell me whatever lies in your heart."

Thomas hesitated, but knew he had to speak. "I do not know him well enough to judge. He is like others of his kind, so you will know him better than I. But he..." Thomas hesitated before deciding he owed Woodville nothing. "I do not like him. He is not the kind of man I could ever like: privileged and arrogant without the skills to claim such."

Isabel laughed. "Well, I did ask for honesty." Her fingers tightened against his. She leaned closer, her voice dropping to a whisper. "And I agree with your judgement. Such men are a blight on both our lands, but nothing can be done about them. Politics again. If I

160

want an attachment between our countries, I must work with him."

"I believe he is here for more than the joining between two countries. He has another prize in mind as well. He may also be in discussion with the man Durdush who came here today."

Isabel closed her eyes a moment. "Men seek fortune in war, and Malaka is rich. That does not mean his offer to us is not genuine." She opened her eyes, her fingers tightening once more through his. "But I am not telling you anything you do not already know."

Thomas nodded.

"Then come join me. Your beloved al-Andalus is doomed. Do not condemn yourself to the same fate. Come be part of my court." A flicker of a smile. "Now that you are Sir Thomas Berrington a place can be easily found for you. Bring Lubna, bring Jorge and his woman. And bring your son, for Juan loves him as a brother. All of you should come to where you will be safe."

The temptation was strong. It was one Isabel had made before, and each time she did, Thomas rejected her. Would he be a fool to do so again? Or was the intimacy of the moment swaying his decision? He had seen this woman in agonies, had seen her in anger and sadness, had seen her with joy on her face, and he knew he loved her. But could he turn his back on everything else he loved, beyond this place?

Isabel must have seen the indecision in his face, or perhaps his fingers tightened against hers without knowing.

"You do not have to answer me tonight, but you know you can always come to me at any time and will be made welcome." Her fingers squeezed one more time before releasing their grip. She sat up, smoothing her hands across her clothes as if they had been disturbed in some way.

Thomas watched Isabel leave the room. He was tired, but knew sleep would prove elusive, and did not want to disturb Jorge who, by now, would be sprawled across the entire bed.

Twenty paces beyond the fort, the darkness was profound, and Thomas stopped and craned his head back to stare at the stars. He owned a copy of Nasir al-Din Tusi's work on astronomy, left in his house in Gharnatah, and knew he was looking at other suns made small by distance, and other planets circling his own sun, but that knowledge did not lessen the awe at how many suns there must be, and the distances involved.

A wind blew through the grass and there came the sound of a distant river rushing with floodwater. Then a human sound, a soft cough, and Thomas turned to see Richard Woodville walking toward him. Except as the figure came closer he grew less sure. This man walked differently, like a soldier, alert to the night. Thomas realised he had not been seen in the dark, so waited as the man came closer. His path would take him within ten paces. He wondered where he was going at this time of night, barely giving a thought to what had brought him here himself, because he did not have an answer. And then he discovered everything he had assumed about the encounter was false as the man stopped and turned to face him.

"You are Sir Thomas Berrington, I assume." The

words were English, their sound unfamiliar after so many years.

"You have the advantage of me, sir." Thomas replied in the same language, aware his accent would by now sound strange.

There came a flash of teeth in the dark as the man smiled. "I have heard that is a difficult task to accomplish. My name is Edward Danvers, and I am companion to Richard Woodville."

"He made no mention of a companion to me."

"He gives little thought to the work I do, little thought to me either. You are a man of nobility so I expect you are the same with your own companion. Though I admit he appears to be an easier proposition. Richard can be difficult at times."

"Did you follow me out here?" Thomas was curious to know what this man Danvers wanted, if anything. He was surprised at his candour. He couldn't make out the man's face, and it felt strange to be having a conversation with each of them half-cloaked by the night. It was easier to read a man when you could see his expression.

"Richard told me he met you in company with the Spanish King and Queen. That you appear to be friend to them both. The Queen in particular, he said. And that your companion is an interesting man. A eunuch, by God! A real eunuch. I have never met the such until this night."

"Do you want something of me, or is this meeting no more than two men who cannot sleep conversing to pass time."

"I welcome the chance to talk with another Englishman, that is all, and I have been told you are a clever one as well as fearsome in battle. There are few enough of us in Spain. You are from the Marches, I hear. Did you know Richard was commissioned to restore order in Hereford? That is near to where you lived, is it not?"

"Do you know the West?" Thomas asked.

"I was born and raised north of Salop, so I know it well. A lush country plagued by proximity to the Welsh. What made you want to live among unbelievers, Sir Thomas?"

"No Sir Thomas, please. I did nothing to deserve it. I live here because I choose to." Thomas was in no mood to explain why, equally sure Danvers was in no mood to listen to his explanation, long as it would be. "What does your master want with Ali Durdush? I saw them together only a few days ago."

"Is that right." Danvers softened his voice so that Thomas had to step closer to hear. "He tells me he is curious about al-Andalus. That is what you call it, is it not? Al-Andalus — land of the Vandals."

"As England is the land of the Angles. Does Richard know as much about this place as you? Does he care, or does he search only for a princess?"

Danvers gave a laugh. "Oh, Richard is always searching for a princess." He took three paces, closing the distance between them to a bare few feet. "You have met him, spoken with him, so you know how he is, and what he is. He relies a great deal on me. Allows me much freedom to work on his behalf, which I welcome. There is nothing worse than a master who is always looking over your shoulder, is there not? Or perhaps you would not know, as a man without a master."

Thomas could make out Danvers' face now and saw that how, close to, he would not confuse master and servant, if that was what they were. He turned aside. "I am tired and going to my bed."

"To lie beside your eunuch?"

Thomas almost stopped, then gave a shake of his head and walked on.

As expected, Jorge took up the entire bed. He mumbled when Thomas pushed him to make space, rolled to his back and opened his eyes.

"Oh, it's you."

"Were you expecting someone else?" Thomas sat on the edge of the bed, naked. He had nothing to hide from Jorge, and Jorge nothing to hide from him.

"A man came looking for you. I told him you were probably outside eating some disgusting plant or other. I said he would no doubt find you by the smell." Jorge rubbed at his head with both hands. "Did he find you? I mistook him for that Earl at first."

"He found me." Thomas pushed at Jorge again, who had once more spread out. "Are you going to be trouble?"

"I am never trouble."

"Ah, I must be thinking of someone else." He leaned over and blew out the candle, then pushed Jorge away for a third time.

Sleep eluded him.

He heard Jorge begin to snore but had not the heart to kick him when his foot slid across.

He was thinking about Richard Woodville and Edward Danvers, and what they might want with the Malaka Guild. And thinking of the Guild brought to mind the death of Zufar al-Zaki that was no doubt connected to his position in that Guild. The two items came together in his mind, circling each other like moths coming closer together.

Why did al-Zaki have to die? Because he knew something? Because he had threatened to expose someone? And could that someone be Richard Woodville, or was that only Thomas's dislike of the man made him think that? As sleep began to enclose him, the thought he had lost before came again, this time fully formed, and he sat up in bed.

Jorge groaned and rolled onto his front.

Thomas sat on the edge of the bed and stared into the darkness.

Elizabeth Woodville had been married to the old English King, Edward. Sister to Richard Woodville, Earl Rivers. And her initial as it might be scratched into a ring. An ornate E.

Thomas knew he was stretching coincidence to breaking point, but could not help wondering how he might find out if his faint suspicion had any reality in fact. Woodville was not a man capable of murder, but Diego had said it was the other man who struck the blow. A tall man and a shorter one. Thomas rose and went to his robe, finding it by touch, but the ring he sought was not there. He recalled setting it in a box in the bedroom at home. But it could be retrieved and shown to Woodville. It would be interesting to judge his reaction.

SEVENTEEN

Thomas and Jorge rode alongside an almost unbroken column of soldiers moving south through the narrow valleys of Axarquia, until that moment a region almost completely ignored by Spain. It was too rugged, too mountainous, and too rebellious. A string of white Moorish towns and villages straddled hilltops or nestled along riverbeds that dried out in summer and raged in winter. It was a land only the Moors wanted, a land only the Moors could make a living from. And now it was a land about to be turned into a battlefield as Spanish troops came to reinforce those already there.

The soldiers ignored them, either believing they were part of their army or local men foolish enough to ignore the soldiers in their midst. Now and then Thomas saw other Moors passing, also ignored for now. The unwashed stink of the soldiers hung in the air, together with the chatter of conversation uttered in half a dozen languages. Many of the men were mercenaries, others soldiers of fortune come to seek riches. Like Richard Woodville, perhaps. Thomas was sure his journey was on behalf of the English King, but was the man taking the opportunity to find a way to enrich himself at the same time? Or was he negotiating with Durdush on behalf of his King? Woodville didn't strike Thomas as a man likely to act beyond the orders given him. Earl he might be, but what Thomas saw was a coward, and a weak coward at that. Danvers was a different matter, but Danvers had no position.

Thomas put thoughts of both men aside. He wanted to think more on the murder, so instead of heading directly to Malaka, he followed the twisting roadway south toward Ballix. He wanted another conversation with Gracia Bernel Gomez, sure the woman knew more than she had admitted to on their first encounter. Whether what she had left unsaid made her guilty or not he was unsure of, only that secrets got people hurt. As the land flattened, they forged the Wadi al-Cuevo, now fully constrained within its banks, and passed through the western gate of Ballix without challenge. But when they arrived at the house it was to discover it empty. More than empty, there was an air of abandonment. A neighbour told them Gracia had closed up her house and moved to Malaka, together with her friend, the latter said with a smirk. The neighbour claimed not to know the reason for her going, but as they turned away she called them back to reveal it might have something to do with her claim to an inheritance from those girls. She said it with a smile of triumph, and Thomas could imagine the stories she had been told about al-Zaki's infidelities, sure that was how they would have been presented.

The town gates continued to remain thrown wide when they left, as they had been every time Thomas had visited, and he wondered how long it would remain the case. The Spanish horde continued to gather on the far side of the river. The lead cohort had erected tents and dug soil pits, settling in for a lengthy siege.

"Should we go and talk to his harem again?" asked Jorge as they re-crossed the river and took a road that ran alongside the coast, the ground marshy here. Thomas had chosen a simpler route to the one they had followed leaving Malaka. It was close to noon, the sun at its zenith, and the heat encouraged loud swarms of flies that settled anywhere bare skin showed.

"You would like that, wouldn't you?"

"Don't pretend they don't attract you."

"But I can control myself. Damn these flies!" Thomas cursed and adjusted his *tagelmust* so only his eyes showed. He reached into a saddle bag and withdrew another, this one dyed a deep red, and handed it to Jorge, who wound it awkwardly around his face.

"Perhaps we should have gone the other way."

"This will bring us back two hours sooner."

"There is a rush?"

"There is always a rush when a killer is sought. The more time passes the colder the trail grows. Have I not taught you that already?"

"Possibly. But you know I don't remember things as well as you and Lubna."

"In that case I will make sure not to tax your brain more than necessary." Thomas urged his horse toward the west, skirting an area of shimmering water where mosquitoes hovered thick as rain clouds, their constant whine carrying across the fetid surface.

"You can go to al-Zaki's house on your own, can't you?" Thomas said.

"I expect so. What are you going to be doing?"

"I want to pose more questions to Ali Durdush. Now I have done him this favour he might be willing to tell me the truth. And I need to visit the Infirmary. I have neglected my duties of late."

"I didn't think you had duties." Jorge waved at a cloud of dark, fat flies as they descended around him.

"I don't, but you know that has never stopped me in the past."

Jorge might have smiled, but the *tagelmust* hid most of his face, and even if it had not, the flies were too thick to see him clearly.

The sun was sinking toward the west when Ali Durdush admitted Thomas to his offices in the Ataranzana, his face dark with anger. "Where did you go? And why did you not do as I asked and make yourself known to the King?"

"Why do you think I didn't return with you?"

"You spoke with him, then?"

"And the Queen. I relayed the importance of your message to them both." Thomas wondered if mentioning Isabel was a mistake, but it was too late to take the words back.

"And his reply?"

Thomas walked to the wide window. Glass of the finest quality showed a barely distorted view across the harbour. Durdush's personal clerk stood to one side in an attempt not to be noticed, but his note-taking was loud, to Thomas at least, whose ear was tuned to the sound of pen on paper. Every word they spoke would be recorded, he was sure, but unlikely ever to be read by anyone other than Durdush and the clerk himself.

"The Spanish may be willing to talk," Thomas said,

his back still turned, "but you will have to involve the governor. You may be willing to surrender the city, but is he?"

"I reported to al-Tagri this morning. He continues to believe our forces can defeat the Spanish. He told me he has been tasked with protecting the city, not surrendering it." Durdush glanced at Thomas. "Soldiers."

"Soldiers protect us."

Durdush continued as if Thomas hadn't spoken, the kind of man who ignored what others said. "Do you think the Spanish will grant the Guild a charter to continue trading? To keep our houses and wealth and lands? I hear they have made such arrangements in the past."

"You would switch master so easily?" Thomas hoped Durdush didn't hear the judgement in his voice.

"Will they be so different to the ones we have now? It is said they are good rulers, fair to their people, fair to those they conquer." Durdush came to stand beside Thomas. He used his hand to indicate what lay beneath them. "All of this — the trade, the riches that flow through Malaka — all of it can be put at their disposal for the right terms. You will tell King Fernando that?"

"I have no plans to see him again."

"But you will, won't you, for Malaka?" There was little in Durdush's tone to indicate refusal was an option. "This city is too great, too important to be razed to the ground. Go to him and make it clear I will do anything I can to broker a peaceful transfer of power."

"And al-Tagri?"

"Leave the governor to me. He will see sense in the end."

Thomas turned to leave, then hesitated, as if his real

reason for coming was something trivial. "There is another matter, but I am reluctant to raise it."

"What matter? Will it take much time? I have a meeting soon and I have to arrange to see al-Tagri."

"There is an Englishman by the name of Richard Woodville. Is he known to you?"

Durdush gave the question little thought before shaking his head. "The name is not familiar."

"He also goes as Earl Rivers."

"Is that another name? You have strange names in England, do you not? Is one not enough for you?"

"It is a title," Thomas said. "An Earl is an important man, one who is close to the King. It is of similar rank to a Duque."

"There was an Englishman recently, but he did not tell me he was a Duque."

"What did he want?"

"He came to discuss trade, and much as I respect you, I will not discuss the secrets of trade with you." Durdush began to move away. It was clear he believed the discussion concluded.

"Do you recall the matter of the Weapons' Master, Zufar al-Zaki, that I brought to you? It was the same day I saw you with Woodville."

Ali Durdush shook his head. "Are you suggesting a connection? Zufar died. People die all the time, particularly old men. I do not see what connection that might have with this man." Durdush frowned. "He told me his name, of course, but I do not recall it at the moment, though I am sure it was not Woodville or Earl anything. I will have my clerk find it, he will have made a record of the conversation."

"I can ask him for you if you are busy," Thomas said.

"You would like that, wouldn't you? A chance to read the Guild's confidential records. If I consider it relevant I will let you know what name he used, but I am sure it is not the same man you speak of." Durdush started to turn away, stopped. "Who would want to kill Zufar? It makes no sense."

"He didn't kill himself."

"And you seek whoever did it?"

Thomas nodded. "I need to know more about the man. What he was like, who he worked with, who his friends were. People are killed for too many reasons. Once I discover the reason here, I will be closer to who struck the blow. I also worry that his death may not be the last. I would like to speak with the other masters. I know some, but not all. I would speak with each, if only to warn them, as I am warning you. Who is to say the matter will end with one death?"

Durdush stared at Thomas. "Am I in danger?"

Thomas said nothing, waiting.

"My clerks are busy men." Durdush waved a hand toward the window. "You can see the trade that flows through Malaka. You said there could be a multitude of reasons for someone to kill him; it may not be connected to the Guild at all. In fact I would be surprised if it was."

"If you allow me to question the clerks, I will of course pass your request for further negotiations on to Fernando before I pursue my investigations any further. It is not even so far to go now, as he currently sits outside the gates of Ballix."

Durdush stopped on his way to the door. "When might I expect his reply? It is no good waiting until the city is reduced to rubble."

"Within days," Thomas said. "I will see him within the week." He had no intention of doing so, but Durdush had no need to know that.

"And you will not take up too much of my clerks' time?"

"As little as I can."

Ali Durdush nodded. "Tell them I authorise it. Now I must go. You can see yourself out."

The clerk who had stood silent in the room the entire time, the only sound from him the scratch as he recorded their conversation, scribbled something more, tore the slip of paper in half, and handed it to Thomas before he followed his master out.

Thomas looked at what was written and smiled. The clerk was good. Very good. It was an authorisation for Thomas to speak with any clerk in the Ataranzana, but only on matters pertaining to the sad death of Zufar al-Zaki. It was worth nothing. Thomas almost screwed it up and dropped it on the floor but stopped at the last moment. He could try, at least, but would have preferred Jorge with him to decipher the language of the body he could not translate himself.

Below, a dark-sailed ship manoeuvred toward the dock until it was close enough for ropes to be thrown, caught, and drawn taut. Beyond the harbour wall other ships waited, some at anchor, others tacking to and fro while they waited their turn to unload their goods. The Ataranzana was a hive of industry, men working in a finely choreographed dance that brought ever more riches for Malaka, ever more riches for Ali Durdush and the Guild.

Thomas went in search of someone who could help. He had a scribbled note of introduction, nothing more.

He could as well have simply told whoever he sought that Durdush had approved his questions, but at least this way if anyone thought to check he had evidence.

On the dock the smell of the sea was strong, its sound constant, the cry of gulls even louder. Creaking timbers on the ships that had managed to dock and the thump of cargo being unloaded completed the cacophony, making a wall of sound that made it difficult to think, though nobody else appeared to notice. Perhaps because their labour did not require much in the way of thought.

Thomas saw a man writing in a ledger and started toward him, but a crash stopped him in his tracks, his nerves still on edge after the shaking of the earth. After a moment he saw it was no more than a wooden platform that had been dropped against the dark-sailed ship. Almost as soon as it touched the hull, even before it could be tied in place, men started down its slope. Dark of skin, dressed in leather jerkins beneath desert robes similar to those Thomas wore, these were soldiers from the shores of Africa. No doubt mercenaries, they were hard-bodied and transmitted a sense of danger. There were no smiles, no chatter as they spilled onto the cobbles before drawing into a loose cohort. A man dressed no differently but obviously of higher rank came to stand in front of them. His eyes tracked the group before he spoke a few words and turned to lead the men away.

Thomas saw the dock workers, like him, had stopped to watch their arrival. "Who are they?" he asked a nearby man.

"Gomeres. Best fighters in the world, but the worst neighbours. Steer clear of them, my friend, if you want to keep your guts inside you." The man grinned, spat an impressive stream of saliva, and moved off.

Thomas identified the man with the journal once more and moved toward him. He would find out what information he could about the other masters, then go to save Jorge from al-Zaki's women.

EIGHTEEN

Gracia Bernel Gomez's voice overrode a bird-like chatter as she tried to tell al-Zaki's harem that the house was not theirs and they had to leave at once. Jorge caught sight of Thomas and waved him inside, but he shook his head and stepped away. The street was busy with market stalls and traders, the smells of cooking food, spices, leather, cloth, and people thick in the air. The late sun cast a soft light over everything. Men and women moved among the stalls picking out items, some buying but most simply there for the entertainment. The last time Thomas had come to the house there had been none of this, but now he could see why a Guild Master might make his home in such a place. There were even three blacksmiths conducting some sort of business repairing broken catches, selling knives and swords, and taking orders for more. Their braziers added a layer of smoke that hung over the street. At one end Berber musicians played, the beat of their drums infectious, high ululations filling the air from silk-clad women who whirled and jumped high. Thomas was sure they were the same group that al-Antiqamun had attacked outside the Infirmary.

"You should come inside," said Jorge, joining Thomas on the street. "I haven't had this much fun in a long time." His eyes surveyed the scene. "Why can we not move somewhere like this? Do you think we could buy Diego's old house?"

"Don't you like it where we are?"

"Of course, I like it well enough, but it's ... quiet."

"Which is how I like it."

"Hm."

"I need to speak with Gracia alone. Is her companion with her?"

"I haven't seen her, but it's a big house and she may be avoiding Gracia, for the woman is in a foul mood. I wouldn't recommend talking to her at the moment."

"I have to." Thomas stepped to one side as a clutch of children, none older than eight, came running full tilt along the street with a trader in pursuit. "Can you distract al-Zaki's harem while I do so?"

Jorge took an apple from a stall and tossed the vendor a small coin, waving away the need for any change. He bit into it, any reply to the question deemed unnecessary.

Gracia was still berating the gaggle of women when Thomas returned to the house. He stood outside the room and watched her display of righteous anger, slowly coming to the conclusion it was false. He gave a shake of his head, unsure if he was reading the situation right, knowing he was not Jorge and not trusting his own senses. When Gracia glanced in his direction, he motioned with his hand and turned toward an empty room.

It was some time before he heard rapid footsteps and moved away from the window he had been looking through at the dancers.

"There you are," said Gracia, as if it was his fault. "I was beginning to think you had left."

Thomas shut the door before taking a chair. The room seemed to have no specific purpose, a sign al-Zaki had been a rich man. More than rich enough to pay Gracia her due after the divorce.

"Why did your husband refuse to pay your settlement?"

"Why should I answer your questions? You are a physician, nothing more." Gracia declined to sit and instead stood in front of the cold fireplace. "Yes, I asked about you when I came here. I was curious why you sought me out. What is our business to you?"

"Was it the women?" Thomas crossed his legs, picked at a loose thread on his robe. "Is that the reason you have returned to Malaka, to this house?"

"I have come to claim what is my due. From them, yes, and if not them then the Guild. I am owed."

"Owed enough to have your husband killed?"

Gracia took a step closer, her body tensing. She was a tall woman, strong in body and mind. Strong in her anger. *But is it justified*, Thomas wondered, *or no more than a cloak she hides behind?* Cloaks could be torn if enough force was applied.

"I—" Thomas watched as Gracia took a deep breath and tried to control herself. She glanced around as if seeing the room for the first time, but it must have been more than familiar to her. This house had once been her marital home. She would know every nook and cranny, every creaking floorboard and sticking door.

Thomas indicated the chair across from him.

Gracia studied it then pulled a different one across, the legs scraping along the floor. She sat, arms resting on her knees, leaning forward. "How would it benefit me to have him killed?"

Thomas raised a shoulder. "He is dead and you are here. You seek compensation and he is not here to deny you. Those women cannot exist without someone to watch over them. Man or woman. And they are very beautiful."

"He was always a fool for a pretty face. I was beautiful once."

"You are still a handsome woman."

"But it is not the same as beauty, is it."

"Did the first of them come while you lived under this roof?"

"Two. Zufar claimed it as his right under law. That a man — a man of influence, a man of wealth — was entitled to many wives. But they were never wives. They didn't love him."

"And you did?"

"Once."

"And now?"

"It is difficult to love a dead man."

"Where is your companion? Did she come here with you?"

"She is getting food for us. The two of us. What those ... those things do is up to them."

"What happens if you don't get what you want?"

"I will. This is my house. His money is mine. Those stupid girls haven't a brain between them."

Thomas smiled. "These all sound like reasons why

you would want your husband dead. A woman cast aside without a *diram* to her name."

"A dead husband can't pay me what he owes," said Gracia, her voice tight with controlled anger. "I didn't want him dead. I–" She stopped abruptly, pressing her lips tight together, and Thomas watched her attempt to regain some measure of control.

"Did you ever love him?" Thomas leaned forward in mirror of her. "Everything you say is what a guilty woman would proclaim."

"I did not have him killed. But nobody would blame me if I did."

"Oh, I think the Guild might have something to say on the matter, and they have their own guards who would be only too pleased to take you into custody. Do you know what happens to handsome women in prison?"

"You would betray me?"

"If you killed him it would not be a betrayal, it would be justice."

"Then it is fortunate I did not, even after all he did to me, the way he treated me."

"Can you prove you didn't have it done?"

Gracia laughed, gave a shake of her head. Only a trace of her anger remained. "I can prove I haven't left Ballix in a year — is that good enough for you?"

"You would have no need to leave Ballix. All it would require is knowing someone who could do the deed on your behalf. Such men are not in short supply."

"And how would I pay such men? You have seen where we live."

"And yet you are here, sitting in a fine house you

claim belongs to you. When do you go to talk with the Guild? Not with Durdush, I'm sure."

"They have those who administer the law, and a divorced woman is entitled to half her husband's wealth. I have an appointment first thing tomorrow."

"Surely a widow is entitled to her husband's entire wealth if she is still married to him," Thomas said. "I have little knowledge of the law, but if he did not pay you what you were entitled to does that not make the divorce void? Do you remain his wife, heir to all of this?"

Gracia's smile was tiny, sly. "And you claim to know nothing of the law?"

"It doesn't help me though, does it?"

"I did not kill him, I tell you. I did not have him killed. I don't see how I can prove it to you other than for you to find the man who did."

"Will you help me do so?"

"Me? I would be no help at all."

"In that you are wrong. Your husband was not chosen at random. What did he know that might have caused someone to kill him to keep it quiet? Who were his enemies? Men get killed in fights on the street, but this was planned, deliberate."

Gracia looked aside, and Thomas saw she didn't want to continue with the conversation but suspected she was aware if she left now it would only make him more suspicious. He was already convinced she had nothing to do with her husband's death, but she might have some idea who had struck the blow.

"If he had secrets, why would I know them? Is that not the nature of a secret?"

"I have secrets," Thomas said, "but I am sure my wife

can tell you every single one of them, even those I am ashamed of."

"And if you had lived apart for years would she know what your secrets were now? No, the same as I know nothing of Zufar's life anymore. I have my own to lead, with Olivia."

"And the girls."

"They will be going soon. I have made that clear."

"After you discover whether this house belongs to you or them."

"He never married any of them so if it's not mine it belongs to no-one. It will be claimed by the city, no doubt." She frowned. "Would the Guild do that to me? Take my house from me?"

"I don't believe the Guild is vindictive. If you have a case, make it and they will hear you out. If this house truly does belong to you then they will let you stay." Thomas stared into Gracia's eyes, trying to understand what it was she was hiding behind her show of confidence. "Tell me what secrets he had when you lived with him. Were there things he kept from the Guild?"

"I doubt it. He was a man driven by lust and honour both." Gracia turned as if to study something in the corner of the room, as if a memory sat there. "He was a boastful man, too. He would make extravagant claims, trying to impress us." Her gaze returned to Thomas. "He said so many things I made no effort to remember them, but I will try. Perhaps there is something I can recall which will offer a clue for you."

"You saw him recently? And you said us — do you mean you and Olivia?"

Gracia nodded. "Zufar was a man who craved to lie with as many women as he could, even at his age."

"So you have left Ballix in the last year. Why did you tell me you hadn't?"

"Because I haven't. He came to us on occasion, always on the pretext of business, claiming he was simply passing by and wanted to know how I fared. He would ... bring us a little money, out of guilt I suspect."

"And talk?"

"Yes. He liked to talk. Perhaps only with us, I don't know."

"But you will try to think of what he said, if there is anything that might be a cause for someone to kill him?"

Gracia nodded and stood, strode from the room as if glad to finally escape.

NINETEEN

"Men boast of their prowess all the time," said Jorge. "Apart from you and I, because we have no need to, I suspect. Do you think she will remember anything useful or not?"

They had come to a stall to eat, three low tables placed in what shade there was to be had. The food was good, but Thomas pushed his plate aside, no longer hungry. He waited until Jorge finished his own food.

"I think not. She didn't like me questioning her, and if she does know something she will no doubt keep it to herself or try to use it to her own advantage."

"Do you believe her involved in his death?"

"No. That makes no sense. Dead her life only becomes more difficult. She told me al-Zaki visited them now and again."

"Them?"

"I asked her that too and she said yes."

Jorge smiled. "So, apart from knowing he was a man with some stamina, we have no more information than we did. We should question the other masters. Probably it was a falling out over money or some such."

Thomas laughed. "Something. There, you have solved the mystery for me. People kill for many reasons, sometimes for little more than another man looks at them strangely, but–"

"In that case I'm amazed you're still alive."

"*But,*" Thomas said, "usually for reasons that make sense. Love. Greed. Fear. Envy. Revenge. Religion. Anger."

"And war."

"Yes. And war."

"And which of these do you think it is?"

"I don't know. Which is why I want to question the Guild Masters. I have an address in the street of Spice, and as it belongs to a woman, I will let you ask the questions."

Thomas stood to one side as Jorge spoke with Narjis al-Ishraq, Mistress of the Spice Guild. She had admitted them to her offices without question, offered coffee and small, sweet cakes as they sat on cushions around a low scrolled table inlaid with shards of ivory. From beyond the room came the soft buzz of female conversation where her staff worked on sifting and measuring spices from all over the known world. The scent of them filled the air like a rich perfume.

"I knew Zufar only a little." She smiled. "It is not likely our paths would cross with regard to trade, and he was not the sort of man who had much to interest me. But I cannot think of any reason why someone might want him dead. Perhaps you need to look into his past. He made weapons for anyone who would pay him at one time, though that was all some time ago."

Her gaze flickered toward Thomas, as if she knew he was the one behind the questions but was far too polite to ask. She was a handsome woman in her forties, slim, dressed in fine silks with her hands marked by henna. She kept her *hijab* across her face at the start, but loosened it as she grew more comfortable in their presence.

"And you have heard no talk, no rumour of anyone asking questions they shouldn't? Anyone seeking either al-Zaki or some other master or mistress?"

"If a stranger came they would go directly to the Guild. It is there that all negotiation takes place. As a mistress I am concerned only with my own business, the same as we all are. The Guild controls what wealth I hold, the wealth everyone holds in common."

Her reply sparked something in Thomas's mind. "So he had no wealth of his own?"

"Oh, some of course, we all do. Guild Masters are paid well for their service, and a portion of the entire profit of the Guild is distributed twice a year based on what proportion we contribute. But the bulk of what we make is passed over."

"What proportion would al-Zaki make to these funds?"

"Weapons are in demand, particularly now, so theirs would not be the lowest contribution, but it pales into insignificance against others."

"And spice?" Thomas asked.

"Is much in demand, even by the Spanish these days." A frown troubled her smooth brow for a moment. "In fact I think one of my girls said a Spaniard had been here only recently asking questions."

"What questions?"

"I didn't ask. Do you want me to fetch her?"

"Later. How many people do you employ?"

"A score, even, all girls — well, I call them girls, but some have sixty years. Each hand-picked for their sense of smell and taste." She called out, waited until a figure appeared at the open arch. "Fetch two of those sample pouches, and ask Ayesha if she can come here for a moment." She turned back to Thomas. "A small gift for each of you. You have women who cook for you?" A glance at Jorge. "Or perhaps you cook yourself?"

Jorge laughed. "Not me. Thomas has been known to, but I have never tasted his cooking and suspect I am fortunate not to have done so."

Narjis's laugh sounded like the sweet cry of an exotic bird. "No. He doesn't look like a man with time for the finer things of life, unlike yourself." She spoke to Jorge but fixed her eyes on Thomas. "He is not a Moor, is he, despite how he dresses."

Thomas didn't know whether to be pleased or insulted. He dressed for practicality and comfort, with little care how others viewed him. Unlike Jorge, who dressed to impress and even now wove his usual spell. And once again, however hard Thomas studied him, he could see nothing he did that he might not do himself. It was something innate in the man that others responded to. He closed his ears to the conversation as Jorge offered a compliment on the smoothness of Narjis's skin and the lustre of her hair, but then she said something that made Thomas lean forward.

"Now I think a little more on it, I did witness something, most likely the man who questioned Ayesha."

Jorge too leaned close, his eyes capturing hers and for a moment. Thomas caught the merest glimpse of the magic he could weave as he touched the back of Narjis's hand with a single finger.

"A man? A stranger?"

"A stranger, yes." Her eyes flickered from Jorge to Thomas, back to Jorge like a moth to a flame. "Like him. Not a Moor nor a Spaniard. But not like him. He dressed like the men of France or Naples. I see them come to conduct trade all the time, but this one was different."

"What did he say to you?"

"Not me, to Ayesha. He was asking about me, but when he discovered I wasn't a man he lost interest."

"How foolish of him. But if you didn't talk to him how can you describe him?"

"I was standing upstairs. I had only recently risen and was in no state to meet with anyone, but there are always girls to conduct trade."

"Can you describe him?"

"I was up here so did not see his face, but he was tall. Well dressed. Dark hair."

"How tall? Taller than Thomas, taller than me?"

"He was on the street, so it is difficult to say. But..." She thought a moment. "He was looking down on Ayesha, so he was tall, but how tall in comparison to either of you I could not say."

"Is there anything else? Did he have a beard? Wear a sword?"

"He was clean-shaven, I think."

"Clothing?"

"As I said, they were well made but looked old. He wore dark breeches and boots to his ankles, and had a sword on one side, a knife on the other." She gave a delicate shiver, as much for show as in memory, and Jorge stroked her hand, cupping it inside his, and she smiled. "Your friend reminds me of him a little. Do you think he had anything to do with what happened to Zufar?"

Thomas spoke before Jorge could. "I cannot tell, not for sure, but it is possible."

"Do I need to take care?"

"Everyone needs to take care."

"Then perhaps I should employ a man, someone tall and strong like you."

Thomas sat back, trying not to laugh.

Later, as they made their way toward the Infirmary, he said, "You did the same thing with both of them."

"What thing?"

"*Your* thing. They would have thrown themselves to the ground and let you ravish them."

Jorge smiled. "Only because they knew I wouldn't. Apart from which Ayesha wasn't interested in men, not really. She is like her employer."

"How can you tell? They looked more than interested in you."

"Which is why you couldn't tell. You should watch more and talk less."

This time Thomas couldn't suppress his laugh. "Me? Talk less than you? The entire world talks less than you."

Jorge walked on, saying nothing, as if to prove a point. They passed the end of the street where the market stalls still remained, the African dancers and musicians close by, and Jorge stopped to watch them.

"So tell me, what did this man say to Ayesha?" Thomas had stood aside while Jorge questioned her, knowing two of them might feel threatening, also knowing Jorge would be able to get far more from her than he ever could.

"He wanted to know if her mistress ever worked with the Weapons' Guild. In particular its master, Zufar al-Zaki."

"He said that name?"

"He did. Ayesha paid it no heed. She said it was little more than an excuse to approach. He kept looking past her, as if more interested in the building and who worked within."

"Did she say when this was?"

"A month ago, perhaps a little more than that. We should go and ask Narjis for confirmation."

"You would like that, wouldn't you."

"There are worse things in the world than talking with a beautiful woman." Jorge shook his head in wonder. "Ai, look at that dancer. Is she not wondrous?"

"What else?"

"She can dance like no-one I have ever seen."

"Ayesha," Thomas said. "What else did she tell you?"

"He could not speak Arabic and his Spanish was poor, so most likely he is of France, as Narjis said. A Sicilian would have Arabic and his Spanish would be better."

"And she is sure she can identify him?"

"You will have to capture him first, but yes." He glanced at Thomas. "He scared her, she said. He did nothing, made no threat, but she said there was something about him, that he would not hesitate to kill her in a heartbeat. Excuse me, I must, I simply must."

Jorge stepped away, his feet transforming from something plain into a vehicle for delight. The dancer he had been watching turned toward him, her arms stretched to either side, and Jorge spun around her, the silk of his robes flashing and swirling iridescent in the late sunlight. The woman laughed, nodded in admiration, and began to match him step for step. She was the more skilled, but Jorge possessed enthusiasm. As Thomas watched he realised he had never seen this side of his friend before and wondered where he had hidden such magic from him, for Jorge was a skilled dancer. Not as skilled as the woman, because this was her profession, but he matched her movement like for like. The pair of them had eyes only for each other. The musicians gathered close, amused, raising the tempo of their drumming, the fingers of the lyre player a blur. The deep sound of North Africa echoed from the walls of the buildings until it seemed to be the only sound in the world.

Thomas stood transfixed, all thought of the killer he pursued forgotten. And then, like all moments of wonder, it came to an end. The woman continued to dance, faster and faster, and Jorge stumbled, losing the rhythm.

She ululated a high cry that turned into a laugh and twirled around Jorge before embracing him and kissing him full on the mouth. Then she pushed him away with disdain, as if unworthy of her talents.

"You're a constant surprise to me," Thomas said.

"Is that a good or bad thing?" Jorge's breath came in

gasps. "Oh, but I tell you, for a moment there I was transported."

"Indeed."

"I must dance more often. I will teach Belia, and Lubna too if you wish, then you can dance with her."

"I don't dance."

"Then you're a fool."

"You should fight like you dance," Thomas said. "You will confuse your enemies so much they will be easier to kill."

"I would prefer to kill no-one."

"And if it is you or them?"

"Ah, then I will kill them. After I have danced, of course."

TWENTY

It was almost dark before they reached home, and Thomas wanted only to bathe, eat, and sleep. His head buzzed with information, and little of it made sense. They had spoken with a dozen Guild Masters but, apart from Narjis's Guild, nobody else had been approached. Provided they had been telling the truth. Thomas could not make sense of why she had been the only one, and could not. Zufar al-Zaki had been a weaponer, a profession that might be considered to offer some protection, had he been younger and still practicing, but even an old sword-smith would be considered dangerous. Experience counted for more than strength.

Why had this stranger been asking about al-Zaki at least three weeks before he died? And was the stranger not a stranger at all but someone Thomas knew? The description fitted Woodville. Ayesha and Narjis had described him as a man of France, but the description could just as easily fit an English nobleman. One down on his luck despite his connections. Thomas had already seen the good quality of Woodville's clothes and the state of their repair. He knew he had to confront the man. Take the ring and show it to him. End this. Yes, end it, for he was growing more convinced he knew who had killed al-Zaki. Not Woodville directly. Diego had said another man struck the blow, but that a taller man was in command.

Lamps filled the windows of the house with a welcome yellow light, and Thomas walked faster, leaving Jorge behind to catch up. He tried to dismiss his thoughts for the moment, knowing he could do nothing until morning.

Will must have heard him coming because he came running down the track and threw himself at Thomas, who had no alternative than to pluck him from the air before he fell. He hugged him, breathing in the scent of his hair, then lifted him onto his shoulders, the wriggling parcel of boy pushing the last vestige of the mystery from his thoughts.

"Belia told Diego off again," said Will as they reached the terrace, and Thomas saw Diego sitting on the far side, his face turned away.

"Has he been taking things again?" Thomas lifted Will to the ground and rested his hand on his head.

Will shrugged. "He cried. He's sad."

"Go inside and tell Ma I'm home and that I'm hungry and need hot water."

Once Will had gone, his hand in Jorge's, Thomas walked toward Diego, who watched him come, wary.

Thomas sat on the stone bench beside him. "I thought we talked about you taking things. You must ask first. Why did you do it?"

Diego shook his head, his gaze darting off to the side, anywhere but on Thomas.

"You cannot take things without asking first. What was it?"

"My ring," said Diego. "I wanted my ring. Belia has lots of shiny things but I not touch. I wanted my ring."

"It is not yours, Diego. It belongs to–" Thomas cut himself off, knowing he couldn't explain the ring had been the property of whoever killed al-Zaki. "It belongs to someone else." He was dissatisfied with himself and knew he was too tired to be having this conversation now.

"I know." Diego's eyes finally met Thomas's. "But it reminds me of Pa."

"He was not your Pa."

"But I have nothing of Pa's. Nothing of Ma's, and she had a lot of rings."

Thomas stared at Diego and then pulled him into a hug, the man-boy stiff at first, then his chest hitched as he began to cry, and Thomas kissed his cheek and held him until he stopped.

"Tomorrow we will go to fetch something from your house. Some of your mother's pretty jewels." He hoped he told the truth and that Diego's brother had not emptied the house. No matter if they had, they too could be visited, and Thomas was determined Diego should have his pick of whatever mementoes he wanted.

By the time they reached the wide room where the others were, Diego had forgotten he was meant to be sulking and ran off to play with Will, the pair of them whispering in a corner, and Thomas allowed the warm glow his extended family raised in him to wash away his concerns.

Four of them descended the track and passed through the Antequera gate into a city busy with making preparations for the coming of the Spanish army. Some shuttered their houses, others filled carts with their goods and headed out in search of somewhere safe, though whether such a place existed was becoming a question increasingly hard to answer.

As Jorge lifted Will from his shoulders where he had ridden the entire time they walked, Thomas said, "Can you remember where Diego's brother lives?"

"And the harridan of a wife. Why?"

"I want you to go and offer to buy Diego's house from them. I assume title has passed to the son."

"Why do you want to buy the house? We already have one."

"The Spanish are coming. Not yet, perhaps not for weeks, but we are vulnerable outside the city walls. Diego's house is big enough for all of us, and safer."

"What if he doesn't want to sell? I agree it is a fine house, but he might want it for himself."

"Offer him twice what it's worth, more if need be."

"We could always leave Malaka and go somewhere else." Jorge looked into Thomas's eyes. "But you won't do that, will you."

"Do you expect me to walk away?"

"The fighting will be hard when it comes. Inside or outside the walls, nowhere will be safe. I say leave. Go back to Gharnatah, or take Isabel up on her offer and go to her."

"The fighting won't last long. Durdush is already

petitioning al-Tagri to negotiate a surrender. Fighting is bad for trade, he says."

"Fighting is bad for everyone, particularly me."

"Will you go and ask?" Thomas said, and Jorge nodded and turned away. Will wanted to follow, but Thomas held his hand until he felt the small body stop resisting.

Thomas led his two charges away, one hand in each of his. When they reached Diego's house he was annoyed to discover someone carrying furniture out through the door, and wondered if his sending of Jorge wasn't too late.

"Stay here," he said to Will and Diego. "Will, look after him." He crossed the street. "Hey, what are you doing, this isn't your house."

"Says who?" One of the men dropped the end of a heavy table, not bothering to be gentle, and turned. He was as tall as Thomas, broader in the shoulder, with long hair and a beard that hid most of his face. The colour of his skin failed to mark him as Berber or Moor or Spaniard, only the green of his eyes giving any clue to his origins. Two knives were tucked into a wide leather belt.

"Says me," Thomas said. "Show me your paper if you have any."

"The house is empty," said the man. "That's all the paper I need. Now fuck off before I make you."

Thomas glanced back at Will and Diego. One of them had turned his head aside, not wanting to watch the confrontation. Will leaned forward, intent on what was about to happen, but at least he continued to hold Diego's hand.

"I don't want trouble," Thomas said. "All I want is for Diego to be able to enter his own house."

"Who the fuck is Diego?"

"The man who owns this house."

"It's empty. That makes it mine now."

"I already told you once. I won't do so again." Thomas didn't want to be the first to throw a punch, so waited.

He didn't have to wait long. The man took a step closer, within striking distance, but still Thomas didn't react. He tried to make himself small, make himself look weak, knowing the man was a bully.

"You've broken Diego's table," he said.

The man laughed and swung a punch. Thomas ducked beneath it without effort, still not responding. He took a pace backward, giving himself more space, and when the man swung again, harder this time, he sidestepped and punched him on the chest. It didn't look like a punch to hurt but he knew exactly where to place it, and the man staggered to one side. His companion dropped the other end of the table and came around it, reaching for one of the knives at his waist.

Thomas cursed under his breath, half wondering why such things always happened to him. Had Jorge been here he would no doubt have been able to talk the men into leaving.

Thomas kicked out to disarm the second man, let his leg swing around until it connected with the knee of the first. As the man sank down he raised his own knee and slammed it into his chin.

When he looked up the second man was backing away, palms up.

"He made me," he said. "I told him it must belong to someone, a fine house like this."

"Take him away," Thomas said. "And in case he thinks of coming back, tell him next time I'll kill him. Understand?"

The man nodded as he helped his companion to his feet.

A small body careened into Thomas, and Will clutched at him.

"Showed him, Pa!" he said.

"He was a fool."

"Big," said Will. "Showed him." He swung his fists in a frantic parody of the fight, such as it was, and Thomas knew his son had inherited something wild. Whether from him or his grandfather he couldn't decide. Perhaps from both. It would need training because he knew it would be impossible to suppress, and it would do Will no good if he tried.

TWENTY-ONE

While Diego picked through drawers and cupboards in search of pretty objects to take home, Thomas set Will to watch over him while he went to find someone who could fit decent locks on the doors and bars across the windows. It took him a while before he found a man willing to perform the task immediately, in exchange for a sum that might be regarded as robbery had Thomas not possessed enough wealth to buy all the houses in Malaka three times over. As the thought crossed his mind, he remembered that most of that wealth remained in his house in Gharnatah. All he had brought with him was a small box containing gold coins and some fine silver jewellery. He smiled, wondering if Diego might want to play with it. He had stopped feeling guilt at the way he had acquired such riches. When he returned, Will was on the doorstep trying to stop a man and woman from entering and about to fail.

"What's going on?" Thomas demanded.

"I was housekeeper here," said the woman. "I left some possessions. I only want to retrieve them."

Thomas looked her up and down, found nothing threatening. Her husband the same. He nodded.

"Come in." He accompanied them, following the woman as she ascended the wide staircase.

"I can find my own way well enough," she said.

"Like as not, but this house has already had items stolen from it."

"I am no thief!"

"Good. Then you won't object when I come with you." He glanced at the husband, who remained at the foot of the stairs. "Will, if he leaves that spot shout at the top of your voice."

"Shout," said Will, demonstrating the power of his young voice, determination on his face, and Thomas tried not to laugh.

After a significant waste of time it appeared the woman was mistaken and had not left anything behind after all. As she turned a circle one last time the scowl on her face told a story of failure. She and her husband had expected the house to be empty. As housekeeper, she no doubt knew exactly where Diego's father had kept his riches. Thomas shot the bolts across the door after seeing them out and shook his head, then returned to the room she had spent most time in. It was sparse, with a single window overlooking a side alley. A desk in the middle of the room faced away from what small view was available. Five swords hung from nails on one wall. Each showed more skill in its construction than the last, and Thomas wondered if they were gifts to Diego's father from his master.

He walked the floor, examining each board, but found nothing that might indicate a hiding place. Perhaps this was not the room. Perhaps there was no hidden wealth and his suspicions were unfounded. He was about to leave when Diego came in, his hand in Will's, who had to reach up to hold it, but even so it was clear who was in charge of the two.

"Pa's room," said Diego.

"He worked here?"

"No. Yes. Some."

"Where is his hiding place?"

Diego frowned, stared at Thomas.

"The place he keeps things safe."

"Ah …" Diego crossed at once to the oldest of the swords and took it down. He tapped on the wall, the sound hollow.

Thomas examined the wall, tapping his way along it. There was a space behind but he saw no means of accessing it, and then Diego turned and walked through the doorway. They found him in the room next door, a bedroom. He stood near to an alcove where clothes were stored. Thomas took them down and laid them on the bed. Close to the floor he found a loose board and prised it out. It came surprisingly easily, as well as the three next to it, and he set them against the wall. Sitting beneath was a small chest. Smaller than he had expected.

"Diego no touch," said Diego.

"You could take whatever you wanted, but not this?"

A nod. "Diego no touch."

As Thomas lifted the chest he saw an expression of fear cross Diego's face.

"It's all right — this is yours now."

A tear rolled down Diego's cheek, and Thomas wondered what was going to become of him. Could they take him into their rapidly growing family, or was that nothing more than a vain desire? He and Will had formed a deep attachment to each other, but that didn't mean his life would be any easier.

The chest was locked but the key for it simply lay on top, and Thomas opened it and raised the lid. Within lay coins and papers, some jewellery obviously meant to be kept out of Diego's reach. A small wealth, little more than any man who worked close to power might possess, and Thomas considered Diego's father must have been one of the most honest in Malaka. It was a sad testament to a life lived in service of rich masters.

He lifted out the papers then touched Diego's arm. "All this is yours now. Put your other jewels in the box and we'll carry them home." Thomas was aware if Jorge was successful at the task he had been sent on this house would become their home, but for now it was better to remove anything of value.

Diego turned without a word and left the room. After a moment Will followed, his constant companion.

Thomas left the chest open and went to the bed where he sat and leafed through the papers, curious what they might contain to warrant their place of hiding. Bills of sale for furniture, one for the fine bed on which he sat. The minutia of a life lived well if not richly. Then Thomas picked up a rolled length of paper which showed a broken wax seal on one end and held it flat. Thomas looked to the bottom of the letter to see who it was from. Zufar al-Zaki. It appeared to be a reply to something Diego's father had sent.

I am disturbed at the accusations you make against an esteemed colleague. I have spoken with the man you accuse, who assures me your suspicions are entirely unfounded. Take care who you accuse, for no man is irreplaceable.

Thomas read it twice, a third time. He sat tapping the letter against his palm, staring into the room but seeing nothing. Al-Zaki was dead. Diego's father, Miguel Jiminez, the man this reply was addressed to, was also dead, as was his wife. It was to Thomas's mind far too much of a coincidence for all the deaths to be unlinked. He thought of the report of a man at the Infirmary before Diego's mother died, and the bruise to her skull which had not been there when Lubna examined her. He wished he knew more about what happened to Miguel Jiminez, but perhaps he didn't need to. The note was from al-Zaki and said he had told a colleague about an accusation made against him. Thomas knew all he had to do was discover who that colleague was and the mystery would be solved. He almost laughed. All the suspicions he had wrapped around Richard Woodville would fade to nothing. This was an internal matter. A city matter and a Guild matter. Which meant he needed to go back to Durdush's offices to discover who al-Zaki was associated with. And then his good mood left him. He already had a list of Guild Masters. Whoever Diego's father had accused he would no doubt be on that list. He sighed and blinked, his awareness returning to the room as he heard footsteps.

Diego and Will returned carrying handfuls of rings, bracelets and necklaces. They tipped them into the chest and went for more. Thomas smiled, but it faded quickly as he turned back to the letter.

There was nothing to indicate when it had been

sent, but the ink was still dark and the paper in good condition.

He would like to see Miguel Jiminez's original letter to know who he had accused, and what of. An esteemed colleague. How esteemed? It had to be someone within the Malaka Guilds. Thomas realised of those he had already spoken to he had been asking the wrong questions. Now he would have to interview them again.

Diego and Will returned once more and it seemed they had completed their task because Diego closed the lid of the chest and dragged it back into its hiding place, but left the boards where Thomas had set them.

He rubbed his belly.

"Diego's hungry," said Will.

Thomas looked around the room. This was a fine house, far larger than a man, his wife and their one son would need, but a larger family had once lived here. Thomas knew it was a house that would suit them if they moved to Malaka, as he was sure they must do. It would also make his investigation easier.

"Has Diego chosen everything he wants?" Thomas asked Will.

"Lots."

"Where do you want to go now?"

"Out."

Definitely like his *morfar*, Thomas thought, reluctant to use two words when one would suffice.

Thomas took the papers from the bed and went through to the office, laid them on the desk, meaning to go through them again in the vain hope there might be something else that would prove of use. Diego stood at the window staring out, his shoulders bunched tight, and Thomas went to see what had disturbed him, the letter still in his hand.

A man stood on the far side of the alley and it was clear he was looking at the house. He was dressed in a leather jerkin and leggings, a short sword on one side, two knives on the other. He wore a hat of some kind with a wide brim which shaded his face. Not another one, Thomas thought, taking him for someone else who had heard the house of a rich man lay empty.

Diego curled his hands into fists and laid them against the mottled glass.

"What is it? Are you sick?"

"Unh," said Diego, and Thomas put a hand on his shoulder.

"What's wrong?"

"Unh," Diego repeated, nodding at the man standing below.

"Do you know him?"

"Him," said Diego.

"You do know him. Is he a friend of your father's?"

"Him," said Diego again.

As if he had heard, the man's gaze rose and saw them in the window. Thomas could make out most of his face, clean-shaven, dark-eyed, the distance too far to discern any specific colour. "He kill," said Diego.

"He's the man?"

"Man." Diego's head nodded like it might come off, and Thomas turned away to run down the stairs. When he flung the side door wide the alley was empty. He started down the steps and stopped.

He couldn't leave Will and Diego alone, but if Diego was right there was a chance he could catch the man who had killed Zufar al-Zaki. He decided to take them with him and trust nobody else tried to take possession of the house before the locksmith arrived. He returned inside, took the hand of each, and pulled them toward the door.

Diego resisted, feet sliding across the marble floor, head shaking.

"You are safe with me," Thomas said. "I need you to help me look for him. Will you help me, Diego?"

A harder shake of the head.

Thomas had an idea. "Why don't you hold Will's hand. He will protect you. Won't you, Will?"

"Yes. Will fights good, like Pa."

Diego looked between them and then made the sensible choice. Of course Will could look after him better than Thomas, and he took his hand and walked outside, leaving Thomas to catch up.

He stood on the street trying to work out which way the man might have gone, north or south. The fortified gate lay only a little way north, and from there a bridge led to the west. It would be busy now with those abandoning the city. Had the man come that way, would he flee that way too? If he was even fleeing. He had gone, but was that because he had been seen, or had he just decided there was nothing to keep him watching the house? And why was he there at all? Had Diego been seen when he witnessed the death of al-Zaki? It seemed unlikely, because if he had the man would have returned sooner to silence him. And then it came to Thomas. He was there because of his own investigation. His questions had stirred an ants' nest and brought the man after him, Diego, and his entire family.

"Here," said Diego, starting off to the south. Thomas followed, cursing his own stupidity. He should have been more circumspect, instead he had floundered around asking questions of everyone in the hope something might turn up. At least now they had a chance to catch the killer. End it now. Today.

A right turn followed by a left, another right and the Ataranzana arches lay ahead, together with the tall buildings holding offices, storerooms, and places of trade. No more than a hundred paces to the west lay the room where Diego had witnessed al-Zaki's death, but there was no man who looked like the one who had been outside the house.

TWENTY-TWO

The roadway was busy, a constant stream of people entering and leaving through the arched gates, and Thomas had to fight his way through the crowds. A smell of burning tainted the air, together with rotting fish. Here could be witnessed people from a score of lands. Here could be bought and sold anything the heart or body desired, and more besides. You wanted a mythic beast such as an elephant? One could be found and shipped across the narrow sea. You wanted a woman or man as slave — how tall would you like them to be, what colour their skin? As well as the exotic there was the mundane. Root vegetables, sides of goat and lamb and beef, crates of spices enough to last a lifetime, because in Malaka there was always spice. Thomas surveyed the men, looking for a specific face, pleased to see Diego's eyes flicking from man to man too, but if who they sought was here neither found him. He looked toward the towering building. Had the man they sought returned to the place of his crime? Thomas remembered the ring that had been lost, the engraving within it which might identify its owner.

Thomas entered the Ataranzana through one of the arches, then realised he had forgotten the way and had to ask Diego to show him. He had been here only the once, and the upper floors contained a myriad of rooms. Will trailed along behind. A memory surfaced, and Thomas went to the end of the corridor only to find it blocked off where the linked building had been damaged. The man he sought would know that too. He could not be looking for the ring because that would be lost now, or so he would think.

When he turned back he found Diego gone and Will with him. A flare of panic ran through his chest. He called their names but there was no reply. He turned and walked fast, glancing through each open doorway, then stopped abruptly as he glimpsed Diego standing at a window, looking out to where rowboats were pulled up on the shingle, unloading boxes and crates from ships anchored beyond the mouth of the river. It was slow, back-breaking work that might take an entire day to unload a single small caravel.

As Thomas put his hand on Diego's shoulder, the youth jerked away with a cry and moved backwards so he could no longer see outside. Thomas thought he had hurt him in some way. He turned and went to Diego, who stood with his palms flat against the stone wall, tears in his eyes.

"I'm sorry," Thomas said. "What's wrong?"

"Man," Diego said, head nodding. "The man. There!" He pointed, his hand shaking. Thomas went to the window. There were many men, over a hundred, and he couldn't make out one that matched the figure he had glimpsed outside Diego's house. He considered running outside but knew his current vantage point offered a better chance of finding his quarry. Except there was no-one there even half likely.

A group of men emerged from beneath one of the central arches and Thomas saw Ali Durdush at their head, an arm raised to point something out. Two of the figures standing beside him were familiar. Richard Woodville, the Englishman Thomas had met when he visited Fernando and Isabel, and his companion Edward Danvers, both of equal height and build. Woodville was clearly still pursuing his attempts to foster trade between Malaka and England.

Thomas took Diego's hand, Will grasping the other. He led them through the corridors and down stone steps, not sure if he was doing the right thing. He couldn't pursue a killer with these two alongside, but there was no-one else to look after them. He had been wrong to send Jorge off when he did, but it was too late to change that now.

As they crossed rough cobbles between the building and river he caught sight of Durdush and the group of men standing beside a stall selling coffee and sweet cakes. He sought out Woodville, curious what it was he thought he could negotiate with Durdush, what was worth the risk of entering Malaka for. Not that there was much risk. It was barely believable the Spanish were laying siege to Ballix little more than twenty miles away while here trade continued as it always had, as if this world was not about to be destroyed.

A man approached Woodville and Danvers, and Thomas narrowed his eyes. A man dressed in leather jerkin and breeches, a wide-brimmed hat in one hand, his head bare to reveal short hair. Thomas drew Diego and Will to the side, not wanting Diego to see the man again. He might become upset and draw attention. Thomas was sure it was the same man, he didn't need further identification. He led them to a row of tables set with goods for sale.

"Pick something for yourself." He held a coin out for each. "Don't move from here, I'll be back in a moment. Will, look after him, don't let him out of your sight." Thomas knew it was wrong to leave them but trusted his son, despite his youth.

Diego took his coin and turned toward the array of goods. He leaned over to examine a fine silk scarf. It was fashioned for a woman but pretty enough to attract him all the same.

When Thomas turned the corner the man stood close to Woodville and they appeared to be arguing. Danvers gripped the man's arm and pulled him away, his protests carrying across the square. They came toward Thomas, and he sunk beneath the cover of an arch, hoping they wouldn't see him. He lost sight of the pair and risked exposing himself, but when he scanned the area neither was in sight, and he cursed. Woodville was still with Durdush, but their discussion appeared to be coming to an end. Thomas knew enough of Durdush's ways to recognise the signs — the looks away, the dipping toward a clerk for information, the lack of interest. He had no doubt Woodville would find another meeting difficult to arrange. So intent was Thomas on watching the pair he didn't hear Danvers approach until it was too late to avoid him. The man came within feet, a smile on his good-looking face.

"We meet again. Is this where you live? Malaka you call it, do you not, you heathens."

"Your master would do well to cut short whatever plans he has with Durdush. The city will fall to the Spanish before the summer ends."

"Durdush claims that trade will continue, and I suspect he is right. This is indeed a fine port, with good links to the rest of Spain, to Africa and the East."

Thomas reached inside his robe and his fingers closed around the ring Diego had picked up. It had been nestling in his pocket awaiting a moment such as this, but he kept it hidden for now.

"Even as far as England for a sailor with enough skill," Thomas said.

"Indeed."

"I saw you arguing with a man. Is he known to you?"

"No. A stranger a long way from home, is all. Like you and I. A mercenary, I suspect, trying his luck with another countryman. He accosted Richard so I drew him aside. I was close to hitting him, the rogue."

"What did he want?"

"Money. He recognised a rich man and thought he could take advantage of him. I sent him packing."

"Another Englishman, you say? You showed courage. He looked as if he would be dangerous in a fight."

"I am not without resources. I have fought in the past and will in the future. It is why Richard employed me, before we became friends. If there is nothing else, I should return to him."

Thomas watched Danvers walk to Woodville. They leaned their heads together, a curiously intimate gesture, and words were exchanged. When Woodville raised his head he looked directly toward Thomas without expression, as if he didn't even recognise him.

Thomas released his grip on the ring. He didn't want to confront Woodville here. It would need to be done in private, out of view of Danvers, who did indeed look as if he could take care of himself in a fight. He was as tall as Thomas, and twenty years younger. Not a man you wanted close when accusing his master of murder.

Thomas turned away, aware he had left Diego and Will alone too long, then stopped when he saw someone run toward Durdush. A message was passed and Durdush bustled away, moving faster than a man of his stature had any right to do. Thomas walked over to the messenger and asked him what was happening.

"The Spanish have taken Ballix," the man said. "They march on Malaka itself within days."

When Thomas looked around, Woodville and Danvers had disappeared. He was unsure whether to believe Danvers that his encounter with the short man was accidental or not but could see no advantage either he or Woodville would gain from plotting against the Guild. If not for the ring he would hold no suspicion of Woodville at all.

It was late afternoon by the time Thomas returned to the Ataranzana. He had taken Diego and Will back to the house beyond the walls and told Jorge, who had managed to acquire the deed to the house, to prepare to move into the city in the morning. He was unsure why he had returned other than a sense that events were happening he didn't know enough about, and he needed to know more.

He found a clerk who agreed to show him where the papers of the Weapons' Guild were held. Thomas had conjured a story about Diego's father and needing to find a paper to confirm his ownership of the house that had been purchased. The clerk pointed out personal papers would not be held in his office, but Thomas told him he had looked everywhere else and this was his last hope. Eventually the clerk agreed. He stayed watching Thomas for a while, who worked through the papers as slowly as he could until the man left.

Thomas knew exactly what he was looking for, but almost missed it among the stacks of records relating to the import of iron and charcoal for the city's sword-smiths, and the export of finished weapons. Thomas noted some of the sums involved and re-evaluated his measure of the wealth flowing through the city. If what he saw related only to the Weapons' Guild he knew he could barely judge what value the city's wealth must be. He was scanning a record of the number of swords shipped to Gharnatah, barely reading the words, when the next sheet he took was what he had hoped to find. A man like Diego's father, a clerk, would never send a letter without making a copy for his own records. It had not been at the house, so it had to be here, hidden amongst the minutia of trade, as safe a place for a secret as any.

He scanned the note, then read it again several times before folding it, slipping it into a pocket, and standing. It told him what he hadn't known before — who Diego's father had accused.

He found Narjis al-Ishraq still in her offices, talking

with a slim woman whose long hair fell to touch her mistress's shoulder. Narjis looked up at the interruption, her frown turning instantly to a smile. She touched the girl on the waist and stood from where she sat cross-legged, her movement easy and lithe. She came to Thomas and laid her hand on his arm, looking up at him.

"What can I do for you? Did your woman like the spices?"

"We used the cumin and coriander with some lamb last night. It was delicious, but I'm here on a more serious matter. Do you know Izem Amreqan?"

"Of course, he is Master of Coin. An important man. Why?"

"Have you heard any rumour about him being involved in matters he should not be?" As he asked it Thomas was aware he might be trusting this beautiful woman more than he should.

Narjis removed her hand from his arm and turned away. She folded herself into a sitting position on the scatter of cushions before looking up and patting a space beside her. Thomas knelt and turned awkwardly, feeling her hand on his arm once more, and heard a laugh.

Narjis's gaze met his, sharp and probing. "Tell me why you ask. What matters do you refer to?"

"I'm not sure I know myself yet."

"But you are here, so you must know something."

Thomas studied Narjis while he decided how much to tell her, and whether to do so might not place her in danger. He wondered if her beauty didn't make him trust her too much, but then he had no reason to suspect her of any involvement and had to trust someone.

"Do you know a man by the name of Miguel Jiminez?"

Narjis frowned before giving a shake of the head. "Should I? Is he a Spaniard? Have I traded with him, or has Izem?"

"But you do know Zufar al-Zaki."

"Of course."

"Jiminez was his clerk."

"Was?"

"He is dead. Murdered, I believe, but it's too late to prove it."

"Murdered like Zufar?"

"Not in the same manner, but killed all the same." As he considered the facts, Thomas was aware the links he had forged sounded tentative in the telling. "He wrote a letter to his master which accused Amreqan in turn of theft, or planned theft, at least."

"Izem a thief? No — it is not possible."

"Which is what Jiminez was told, and now he is dead, and so is the master he sent the accusation to. If Amreqan is innocent of what he was accused of, why were they killed?" Thomas studied Narjis's face, which now showed fear.

"You think Izem killed them?" She shook her head. "If you knew him you would know how ridiculous the idea is. He is old, for one. Too old to go around killing people."

"He wouldn't need to do the act himself. In fact I'm sure he didn't. There would no doubt be another man who worked on his behalf."

Narjis frowned. "Are others in danger? Am I safe

here? Are my girls safe? That man who came — is he the one you seek?"

"You said he lost interest when he discovered you were a woman."

"Why would he do that? I am a Guild Master, the same as the others. Perhaps he already has a name and seeks a specific person but doesn't know Malaka or the Guilds." Narjis stood close to Thomas, breathing hard, the sweetness of her exhalations enfolding him. "I will take you to Izem so you can see the error of your suspicion. Ask your questions, find out if he is involved. If he is I will be your witness. I know I am safe at your side. If he is guilty of a crime, we will go to Ali Durdush."

Izem Amreqan's offices were on the top floor of the Ataranzana. A long corridor ran the entire length. Ali Durdush's office sat at one end, Amreqan's at the other. The two lynchpins of trade in Malaka, the Guild leader and Master of Coin. But when they arrived they were greeted by a clerk who knew Narjis but told them his master wasn't there.

"A man came for him," said the clerk, a pen held in ink-stained fingers.

"What man?"

"A stranger to me, but my master seemed to know him, which was good because his Spanish was awful. I barely understood a word he said."

A sense of dread started up in Thomas. "Where did they go?"

The man glanced toward Narjis, who offered a brief nod to let him know Thomas could be trusted.

"The storehouse, I think. I heard the man say something as they left about a consignment of goods which had questionable provenance. If that is true they would be held somewhere in the storehouse."

In the corridor Thomas gripped Narjis's shoulders. "Go to Durdush and tell him what I told you. Ask him to send guards. I'll go ahead. I fear they may be plotting another death."

As he turned away, Narjis caught his wrist. "Take care, Thomas."

He offered a smile. "Oh, don't worry about me."

TWENTY-THREE

The storehouse appeared empty as Thomas stopped at the base of the first flight of steps. Somewhere water dripped. A scurrying hinted at rats coming in from the river in search of easy food, but what he had hoped to hear was absent. Which might indicate Izem Amreqan had concluded his business, or Thomas had made the wrong choice and he was not here at all.

He pulled off his boots, set them at the foot of the stone steps, and began to climb. The air was clouded with dust from grain stored in large hessian sacks. It glowed in the beams of late afternoon light falling through openings in the western wall. Other scents touched the air, redolent with the scent of olives, coffee, and a myriad of spices. Somewhere here would lie a chamber maintained by Narjis al-Ishraq for the storage of her goods, and as Thomas passed the second floor he thought he caught a trace of their presence. Then he heard a sound from above. Faint, but definite. The sound a man makes when he is in pain but too weak to call out with any force.

Thomas climbed faster, his breath coming in gasps which he tried to stifle so as not to give himself away, but as he came closer he knew whoever was above would not hear him. The cries of pain increased in volume. Whoever was the cause of them had to be sure the warehouse was empty, or too confident to care. Thomas moved faster.

He reached to his belt and withdrew a knife. Two more floors, the cries above growing ever louder, not because the man who made them was growing stronger but because Thomas was closing the distance.

With one more floor to go Thomas stopped, leaning against a stone bannister as he caught his breath. Looking down he saw steps spiralling away in a dizzying twist. A cold exultation filled him at the thought he was about to capture the killer before more victims died, and he wondered who Amreqan was having killed now. He took a deep breath and readied to finish the climb just as a crash came from below. He leaned out into space to see four dock workers dragging a heavily laden cart through the wide doors. They began to unload barrels, each thumping hard to the ground. The men's voices rose loud in the echoing space. So loud Thomas didn't hear the footsteps of the running man until he was almost on him.

He spun around, slashing wildly with his knife, but failed to connect. There was a dark blur as the man came directly at him, sword raised to strike. Thomas cried out and raised an arm, knowing it was a foolish gesture even as he did so. What saved him was a shout from below as one of the workers heard Thomas's cry and came to the foot of the stairs. The attacker was distracted for a moment, and Thomas threw himself at his feet, hoping to trip him and send him tumbling down through the gap. He almost succeeded, grasping the man's ankle as he leaped over him. He tried to maintain his grip but the man was moving too fast. He stumbled, recovered, and ran on, descending at a breakneck pace. Thomas lifted himself to hands and knees, but all he saw was the top of a head and the back of a leather jerkin. It might be the man he had seen watching Diego's house, the same man who had accosted Woodville. Then again, nothing about him or his clothes marked him as different to a hundred other mercenaries in the city.

The workers around the cart made no effort to stop the man as he ran past and out through the open doors. Thomas cursed and got to his feet. He turned and began to finish the climb, hoping Amreqan would be present and his victim still alive. In that he was both correct and mistaken. The Master of Coin was indeed present, but tied to a stout chair, and showed no sign he noted Thomas's presence even when he reached out to examine a deep wound in his chest.

Thomas leaned close, drawing the edges of the wound apart. As he did so blood flowed more freely, and he pressed the wound shut again. As he did, the pain roused Amreqan.

"No more, please God, no more." His voice was little more than a flutter of breath. "I told you true, no-one else is involved. Have a pity."

"Involved in what?" Thomas said. Amreqan gave a start and opened his eyes. Only one of them still offered him any view of the world, and it darted in its socket as he took in Thomas's face, the room, the fact that only the two of them remained.

"I know you," he said. "You are part of it too, then."

"Not a part, no, but I seek the man who is. Tell me, who is he?"

Amreqan shook his head, his one good eye closing. A blood-stained tear rolled down his cheek. "I am not a brave man. I held out as long as I could. Too long." A corner of his mouth twitched as if he wanted to smile. "But they don't know everything." The eye opened again. "Has he truly gone?"

"He has."

"I remember now, you are a physician. Can you save me?"

Thomas knew the man was dying, surprised he could talk at all, but he nodded. "I will do what I can."

"Then I am in safe hands."

"Why did he do this? Were you not working together?"

A shake of the head, barely discernible, and Thomas opened the leather bag he was rarely without and removed gut and needle.

"The wound in your chest needs closing. Tell me what you can as I work. There will be more pain, I'm afraid."

He sensed a reluctance in Amreqan that was nothing to do with his wounds. Instead he saw the man was ashamed of his actions.

Thomas pretended to work on the wound, knowing he couldn't save Amreqan and unwilling to inflict more pain without need. It appeared that Amreqan knew he was dying too, and needed someone to know what he had done.

"Tell me why he did this to you." Thomas said.

"The others." The single eye searched for Thomas

again. "He wanted to know who else is involved. I told him no-one, but he didn't believe me."

"Involved in what?"

"Of course, how would you know? I have lived with the knowledge so long it feels as if the whole world must know it too. But it is only me. All the others are gone. Killed. Like I am killed."

"Which others? Al-Zaki? Jiminez? Who else? And what are you plotting?" Thomas pressed on the wound, hating himself for causing more pain to a dying man. "Tell me while you can."

Amreqan's breathing became more of a struggle, but it seemed his need to confess to what he had done over-rode the pain, for now at least. "Gold and silver. Riches. Wealth beyond dreams. Malaka is the richest city in all of Spain. Nobody is going to miss a single crate, but I needed help from outside. Not Spain, they would steal the gold for themselves, all of it. I was a fool to trust the man." A smile almost appeared. "But he is the fool."

"What did you tell him?" Thomas was afraid Amreqan would die without revealing what he knew, and all of this would be for nothing. He would be no further forward, no closer to catching the killer.

"The Alkhazabah," said Amreqan. "The Englishman knows what lies in the Alkhazabah, how I planned to free a single crate. One of three score. Small return for my duty to this city."

"What Englishman? And what is in the Alkhazabah?"

"I cannot…"

"Give me a name. If you want to be avenged tell me who did this to you."

"Avenged?"

"For the injury done to you."

Stay alive, Thomas thought, stay alive long enough to give me a chance. But it was a wish made in vain. Amreqan took a breath, as if steeling himself to reveal what he knew, but when he released it blood spilled from his mouth and ran across his chest, which did not rise again.

Thomas cursed and turned away, walked to the window. On the dockside, work continued as usual. Trade would never be halted in this place.

An Englishman, Amreqan had said. That could only be one man: Woodville. The man who had been here was one of Woodville's soldiers, perhaps the one Thomas had seen earlier. And what secret lay within the Alkhazabah? Someone must know. Amreqan would not be the only one trusted with such knowledge. There would be records, if Thomas could only access them.

He started down the steps, had descended halfway when he saw the corpulent figure of Ali Durdush waddle through the tall opening from the dock. Thomas went down faster, determined the man would answer him fully this time. If Amreqan, Master of Coin, was involved, it must cast suspicion on Durdush too.

TWENTY-FOUR

Ali Durdush refused to climb higher than the first floor. Thomas was grateful, because it took the man an inordinate length of time to get that far, which allowed him time to think. He left him to continue his wheezing ascent while he took four men to where Izem Amreqan lay and instructed them on disposal of the body.

"Dress him," he said. "Cover his wounds as best you can."

"What about his face?" One of the dock workers stared without curiosity at the damaged eye.

"If anyone asks, tell them he tripped and hit his head on a crate."

The man, satisfied he had a story, uninterested in what had actually happened, nodded and set to work with his companions to lift the body into a wooden crate. It would be lowered unceremoniously on one of the hoists that lifted bulky items in and out of the storehouse. Thomas trusted them to take enough care and descended to where Durdush waited.

"Is it the same as Zufar al-Zaki?" His earlier antagonism had faded with the news of another death. No doubt he was thinking he was as vulnerable as those already taken, and more knowledgeable. It was almost certainly the reason two strong, armed men were nearby.

Thomas glanced to where Durdush's guards stood waiting for instructions. "Can we talk in front of them?"

Durdush followed his gaze, lowered his voice. "They will repeat nothing they hear, but perhaps it is best if we move away a little." He waved a hand to tell the men to stay where they were as he turned. He led Thomas to the end of the open space. Sacks of olives stood to one side, leaking a residue of oil across the floor, the smell of it thick in the air. A wide, high opening revealed a view to the west. The stone bridge fortified at both ends was packed with citizens of Malaka streaming out, escaping before the Spanish arrived.

"Tell me, what do I need to do?" Durdush asked when they had put a hundred paces between themselves and the guards. "Is anyone safe from this killer?"

Thomas knew he meant members of the Guild, though it was obvious no-one in Malaka would be safe for long once the Spanish arrived.

"Amreqan was still alive when I reached him." Thomas stared at Durdush, looking for any reaction.

Durdush's mouth pursed in distress. "I have no wish to know the details."

"He spoke of the Alkhazabah, but didn't have time to tell me why that place in particular. Do you know what he meant?"

"What did he reveal to his attacker?"

"I don't know. He held some knowledge so close he took it with him to the next life. All he managed to tell me was it has something to do with the Alkhazabah. What would be there that he had to protect the secret to his death?" Thomas held the knowledge of an Englishman to himself for the moment, unsure whether to trust Durdush or not, wondering what Woodville was negotiating with the man.

Durdush stared through the opening at the fleeing crowds, his face expressionless, as if all emotion had drained from him. He glanced at Thomas. "There is only one secret held fast in the Alkhazabah, and it is good that Izem took it with him."

"Are you going to tell me what it is?"

"I do not know if I can trust you. Not with this. It is too big. Too important."

"Money." Thomas watched Durdush's eyes widen before he managed to regain control of his reactions. "Amreqan talked of gold, and I can think of nothing else that would be sought so ruthlessly. How much is held there? The Weapons' Guild gold? More than that? Amreqan would know, wouldn't he? He would know where everyone keeps their wealth."

"Yes, he would. And he would know this secret too."

"This, this, this!" Thomas slapped the wall. "Don't trust me with it, then. I no longer care. Let this man kill you all, torture you all. The Spanish are coming and we'll have more to worry about soon."

"That is the secret." Durdush's eyes met Thomas's. "That is the secret he died for, the others too." He washed a hand across his face, and with the motion came a decision. "If I tell you what Izem knew you cannot pass the information on to anyone else."

"My companion must know. I keep no secrets from Jorge."

"Only him, then, and he must be sworn to secrecy."

"If I ever find out what the secret is."

Durdush sighed, releasing the last ties on his reluctance. "The wealth of Malaka, the wealth of the Guilds, has been taken into the Alkhazabah. All of it." Durdush turned away, his voice low even though no-one was near. "A plan has been set in place to take it out of the city before it falls. If it falls. Arrangements have been made. Everyone has been sworn to secrecy."

"Arrangements to take it away? How many people know of the plan?"

"Only those who must, but that is still two score. Ships need to be brought close to shore. Men recruited to carry the boxes, though they have no need to know what they contain. There are many boxes. And the masters of each Guild know, of course, for the wealth belongs to each of them."

"And their clerks?" Thomas said. "Zufar al-Zaki wasn't the first to be killed. His clerk died first. Clerks know everything. How many are there in the Guild's employ?"

Durdush paled. "Hundreds. But all the masters are sworn to secrecy."

"Nothing is secret from a clerk."

"Only a handful of people know the details of how it will be done. The masters had to agree, of course, but the organisation was left to myself, to Izem, and a few others."

"Is one of that handful Woodville?" Thomas asked.

Durdush frowned. "Woodville? I don't understand what you mean. Why would that fool have anything to do with it?"

"Amreqan said he was conspiring with an Englishman. I can think of none other than Woodville."

"And yourself, of course."

Thomas scowled. "Of course — so it must be me. I have seen you several times with Woodville. What are you discussing?" Thomas came close to accusing Durdush, only holding back at the last moment, realising how ridiculous such an accusation would be. And how dangerous. This was Durdush's city more than it was the governor's.

Durdush continued to stare out at the exodus of Malaka's citizens, not looking at Thomas. "Richard Woodville and I are in negotiation regarding another matter entirely. One that is not related to Amreqan's death; one that is none of your concern."

"I want to see where this gold is stored." Thomas expected Durdush to refuse, or at the least to put him off. Instead he nodded.

"Come to my office, I will have a clerk prepare a note for you to take to the Coin Guild."

The Master of Coin's offices were easy enough to find. Thomas followed the same corridor he had walked only an hour earlier, but when he passed those used by Narjis al-Ishraq they stood empty, an air of abandonment to them, a few stray papers lay scattered across the floor. He had hoped she would still be there and might tell him something about Amreqan's offices before he went there. Word of the gathering Spanish had spread and people were saving themselves. Is that what explained

Narjis's absence, her empty office? Would she not have been privy to the same secret as the other Guild Masters? Why had she said nothing of it? *As was her right,* Thomas thought. Had she realised it was what the man sought when he came to her offices? If so she had hidden the knowledge well, and Thomas couldn't help but feel a sense of disappointment she hadn't trusted him more.

He wondered where the wealth of Malaka was to be taken. Would it be redistributed among whichever masters were left, or spirited away never to be seen again?

As Thomas approached the end of the corridor he saw movement in the large room at the end and slowed. A well-dressed man stood with his back to the door as he stared through the window. Thomas hesitated, then rapped on the side of the door.

The man turned. "Have you seen what is happening?"

Thomas entered the room. "Everyone is fleeing the city, yes."

"That, of course. But I mean this, the reason for it." The man lifted a hand, pointing toward something beyond the glass. Thomas approached and stood beside the man, who turned back to the window. The Ataranzana was the tallest building in Malaka, its upper offices presenting a view over the city wall, across to the rising bulk of the Rabita fort where al-Tagri plotted his secretive defence of the city, and further beyond to the steep slopes east of Malaka. Slopes that were now thick with soldiers. Spanish soldiers. Thomas scanned the ground and saw others coming along the narrow coastal strip.

"So," he said, "they arrive."

"Yes. They arrive." The man glanced at Thomas. "Do I know you? Your face is familiar."

"Thomas Berrington. Physician. You have the advantage of me."

"Oh, I suspect not." A smile. "My name is Cesare Padvana."

"You are not of al-Andalus then, nor Spain."

"I was born in Venizia, but that was many years ago. I am of Malaka now. As are you. Both of us strangers who have made this land our home. I have heard of you by reputation. If you are here to see Izem I'm afraid he's gone out on some business. I didn't know he was in need of a physician."

"He isn't. Not now, in any case. Your master is dead."

Thomas's words snapped the man from his lethargy.

"How? An accident? He wasn't young, but he was always in good health. Or was it his heart? He had complained about–"

"He was murdered. Like Zufar al-Zaki."

"Why would someone kill Izem? He and I are little more than clerks scribbling numbers into journals." He waved a hand at the shelves stacked against one wall. "Many numbers. Many journals."

"You record the wealth of the Guild," Thomas said. "Wealth that has now been moved to the Alkhazabah." Thomas was sure the man would have to know of it, as he suspected half the clerks in the Coin Guild would also know of the plan. He reached into his robe and drew out the letter Durdush's clerk had prepared and handed it across. "This note asks you to provide permission for me to inspect the storage of this cache of gold."

Padvana examined the paper for longer than necessary to glean its meaning. "How do you know of this? It

233

is the best kept secret in Malaka. If the population had even a hint of what we are doing there would be panic. They would believe we plan to abandon the city."

"And would they be wrong?"

"The wealth of Malaka must be protected. Do you have even the slightest idea as to the value of what is now stored there? No, I am sure you cannot. I am sure no man comprehends the wealth of the Guild." He stared at Thomas, a frown forming. "I don't understand your interest."

"At least four people have died to protect your secret. I would like there to be no more, and I would like to catch the killer. The killer of your master."

"As would I." The man didn't appear unduly upset at the death of Amreqan.

"Will you provide me a letter of permission or not?"

Padvana looked at the note again, then strode to the doorway and shouted a barked command to one of his clerks, the sharpness of it at odds with his behaviour so far.

"How long has this undertaking been planned?" Thomas asked when Padvana returned.

"It has been in place for many years, before I was even born. If it is inevitable Malaka will fall, then the wealth of the Guild is to be protected."

"Where is it to be taken?"

The man turned to face Thomas. "Do you take me for a fool?"

It was a good question, but one Thomas didn't have the time to give the attention it deserved.

"Aren't you concerned you might be in danger, too? Your master lies dead, and others before him. All connected through this mythical wealth–"

"Not mythical. The wealth of Malaka is as real as you and me. As real as this stone." He slapped his hand against the wall. "It is safe, and will remain safe." He moved to sit at a wide desk fashioned of expensive wood. "Am I truly in danger?"

"No, I suspect not. Unless you are also involved in the plot?"

"What plot?"

"You master revealed to me he planned to steal a portion of the gold. A small portion, he said, but even a small part would be a fortune."

Padvana stared at Thomas, his face expressionless. Slowly, he shook his head. "I don't believe you. How dare you accuse my master of such a crime."

"He told me the truth of it himself, not an hour since. Moments before he drew his final breath." Thomas watched Padvana for any sign of guilt, wishing Jorge was here. The man was not upset at his master's death, but that didn't mean he was involved.

"I should go to Ali Durdush at once and tell him of your slander on a good man's name."

"He already knows. I have just left him."

Rapid footsteps sounded and Thomas turned, half expecting guards come to remove him. Instead a slim clerk rushed into the room and handed a slip of paper to Padvana. He read the note before laying it face down. Thomas hoped it was his permission, but it seemed not.

"There is no answer," Padvana said, and the clerk departed as rapidly as he had come. "It is from Ali Durdush."

Thomas waited.

"It confirms my appointment as Master of Coin, and to instruct me should you come here to tell you

235

anything you want to know." Padvana released the air from his body in a long sigh. "It goes against my nature. Against the nature of the Guild. But I must assume the Master of the Malaka Guild knows what he is doing." A hand indicated one of the chairs. "Sit, Thomas Berrington. Unless you prefer something lower."

Thomas took a chair. Whatever Durdush's note said it had changed Padvana's attitude.

"What would you ask of me? There are some things I cannot tell you, but if I can, I will help."

So much for telling me anything I wanted to know, Thomas thought. He leaned forward. If Padvana knew something useful he might not even be aware of it himself.

"When did you start to move the gold?"

"Two months ago. Before the Spanish gathered at Ballix. Everything has been transferred now."

"You had planned this so long ago?"

Padvana lifted a shoulder. "Ballix and the surrounding towns were never going to offer much resistance. Unlike Malaka. Would you rather we allowed the Spanish to plunder everything?"

"It shows little faith in the forces arrayed here, doesn't it?"

"Boxes of gold can be returned as easily as they can be spirited away. It is a precaution, for I am sure al-Andalus will prevail." But his face told a different tale.

"Were you involved in the planning?"

"More so than my master, who had other responsibilities. I ... No, I am sorry, that is one of the things I cannot reveal."

Thomas believed the secret related to the transport of the boxes when the time came, but he also suspected it was unimportant. They would be taken away by sea, no doubt. To where didn't interest him. Malaka was finished — the Malaka of the Moors, at least. What the Spanish made of it didn't concern him because he would no longer be here.

More footsteps sounded, and this time it was what Thomas had been waiting for. Padvana took the sheet of paper, read it, and scowled. Then he folded the single sheet, melted a spot of wax, and applied a metal seal to close it. He stared at the letter for a moment then sighed and slid it across the desk. "Your permission. Use it wisely, for it allows you access to anywhere you ask."

Thomas took it without a word and rose to leave. It had already been a day so full of incident his head spun with too many thoughts. Any visit to the Alkhazabah could wait until morning, but in that he was wrong — it would have to wait far longer.

As he made his way past the Infirmary, heading toward the Alkhazabah, the tall figure of the master came out to stop him. "Thomas, thank the Gods. The city is sending a force to attack the Spanish, and they need you. You are the best battle surgeon we have."

TWENTY-FIVE

It was dark as a thousand soldiers picked their way across rocky slopes toward the forces of Spain that far outnumbered them. They were relying on the night, dawn still hours away, and the element of surprise. At the rear, Thomas led a horse laden with saddle bags which held potions, herbs, and instruments. He was thinking of the many times he had taken this same walk on different fields of battle. Of lives lost and lives saved. Of what he would witness and what he would do to save men or ease their passing. He knew there was nobody better suited to what the next hours would bring, for he was, was he not, *qassab*, the butcher: saviour of men of war.

The sky was clear, a million stars dusting the blackness. A faint glow from beyond the distant peak of Maroma showed the moon close to rising. Their band would need to be in the foothills to the east of Malaka before that occurred, ready to attack, but something had caused the lead group to halt, the others bunching up behind. Some men grumbled, others moved to the side and found a rock to sit on while they waited. Thomas moved along the ranks, curious what had caused the hold-up. He smiled when he saw what it was.

Yusuf had come to join them, bringing his four hundred men. The leader of the Malaka troops was discussing tactics, and when it was done, Yusuf started along the line. He stopped when he caught sight of Thomas, then came forward and embraced him, the force of the greeting testament to the boy who was now a man and a skilled leader.

"I'm glad you're with us, Thomas. Are there other physicians?"

"A few, no more than half a dozen. They will take up positions at the rear, so if you have any injured men who can walk send them back." He didn't have to say anything about men who were not capable of walking. Those would not last long in the howl of battle.

"You won't be at the rear, will you."

Thomas shook his head. He would have smiled, but already a familiar cold was settling through him. He patted the hilt of a knife to indicate he could look after himself.

"What are your orders?" he asked as they passed men starting to move downslope again.

"To protect the flanks. Why? Have you a better idea?"

"I'm not the general," Thomas said.

"No, but I trust your word above any man other than Olaf."

"Does he remain in Gharnatah?"

"My uncle sent him south." Yusuf pulled a face. "Though he stays in the city himself, afraid Muhammed will oust him if he leaves. Olaf has brought two hundred of his men and will attack the eastern flank."

In the faint light Thomas studied Yusuf, noting the strength in him, the certainty honed by the manner of fighting he had been undertaking in these hills, attack and withdraw, harry the enemy before slipping away. It was a tactic which could bring despair to a much larger force, and Thomas knew Yusuf was good at it. The fact he remained alive paid testament to that.

The Spanish were confident of their position on the flatter land north of the city, spread out for almost a mile, their presence sparked with fires and burning torches. It was clear they didn't expect an attack, certainly not one from the opposite direction to Malaka. Thomas was surprised — he had expected Fernando to be a better general and to set guards at a distance, to position men on the high ground above the passes to warn of approaching enemies. Perhaps he had and the men were all asleep, but no alarm was raised as the Moorish soldiers reached the low ground and spread out to either side.

There was no warning cry, everything had been arranged in advance. Men moved forward until they were among dozing Spanish soldiers, then turned and attacked. The first sound came as men screamed and died.

Thomas wasn't in the front rank but moved at the speed of the attackers ten ranks behind. He wore a heavy leather satchel over his shoulder and held a wickedly sharp knife in his right hand. He had debated whether to wear his chainmail jerkin and decided against, fearing he would look too much like a soldier. In the heat of battle he knew it would make no difference. Not that he cared, not at that moment, because the cold had filled him and he saw the world with a brittle reality that had saved his life many times before but stolen his humanity as well. He had hoped never to feel this way again but knew the hope was in vain. There was already too much violence in the world, and if the coldness meant he could protect those he loved he would welcome it again and again. He gave no thought to the men being attacked, nor Isabel and Fernando whose soldiers these were. They had come to destroy one of the great cities of al-Andalus. Besides, Thomas would not be doing the fighting, only offering comfort and treatment to those injured.

Chaos descended, and the night was filled with screams and shouts and the clash of metal on metal. Thomas held back, knowing the front ranks were not for him, for he couldn't be effective in the heart of battle. Instead he stood in place as men streamed past, some faces exultant with the joy of killing, others pale and grim with determination, a few showing nothing but fear and these, he knew, would be the first to die. Better to let the rage fill you and live than die whimpering. If you could. He knew killing was not for everyone.

The fighting was brief and fierce. Thomas treated those who could be treated and offered mercy to those who could not, and then a man staggered back from the melee clutching what remained of his arm. Blood spurted in time to his heartbeat from a deep slash that had almost severed it between wrist and elbow.

Thomas grabbed his jerkin and threw him to the ground, followed hard so his knee pressed into the upper arm to stem the flow of blood. The man screamed and tried to throw him off but Thomas was used to such objections and ignored him, the stronger and more determined of the two.

He made no move to ease the man's pain until he knew how serious the wound was, and whether he would die or not. He lifted his knee a little, allowing blood to flow again, watching as it jetted, thinking of a strategy. Then he decided to ignore the poppy liquor. Instead he swung a hard blow to the man's head, snapping it around and rendering him senseless, knowing the blow might kill him but not before loss of blood if he did nothing.

He took fine gut and a needle and drew back the edges of the wound. It was clean, muscle and tendon revealed as he wiped at the blood filling it. He found the main vessel and pinched it tight, leaning close in the dark to calculate if it was possible to re-join it, and deciding not. Instead, he doubled the upper vessel back on itself and stitched it. He waited a moment to see if the blood would burst through before adding more stitches, then he started to close the wound.

Half way through someone slammed into his back, knocking him to the ground. Thomas rolled away as a Moorish soldier fell hard, the life already leaving him. A Spanish soldier stood over him, grinning, before turning to Thomas, the grin growing wider.

As the man drew back to strike Thomas rose fast and buried his knife in the man's chest, knowing exactly where the heart lay. The soldier grunted as if punched and his knees gave way. Thomas ignored him — he was no longer a danger — and turned to finish closing the wound. The injured man was starting to come around and began to fight him off, and this time Thomas drew the cork on a phial of liquid and forced the contents into the man's mouth. It would take a while before it was effective, but Thomas was more than strong enough to finish his work and bandage the arm. He left the man where he lay and stood, ready for his next patient, suddenly aware that he was no longer surrounded by Moors but Spaniards. The attack had peaked and been rebuffed, and Thomas's companions were now fighting a retreat a hundred paces behind. For some reason none of the Spaniards took any notice of him, perhaps because he had not worn his chainmail.

Men jostled past, eager to pursue the fleeing Moors, the glint of triumph in their eyes. They had been taken by surprise, but fought off the attack, and now they would kill everyone they could. Except their leaders had a different plan. They had seen a Moorish retreat before, only to be ambushed in the narrow defiles, rocks rolled down on men, a hail of arrows descending.

Officers strode to the front, calling out, and slowly the blood lust faded. Men stood panting, stained swords in hands, heads down. One man looked up and stared at Thomas, a frown on his face, and it was obvious what he saw. A tall man dressed oddly, a dark Moorish *tagelmust* rolled at his neck. The man raised his sword and shouted.

Others turned, enough wildness remaining to hack him to pieces.

Thomas proffered the knife, wishing he had brought a sword, but it would have been too unwieldy.

"I am Thomas Berrington, friend to King Fernando!" He wondered if he should have used his new title of Sir.

Even as he shouted the words, in Spanish better than it once had been, he saw they fell on deaf ears. These

243

men had not yet finished killing, seeking revenge for fallen comrades.

"I can help your wounded." Thomas tried again, but already they were advancing, the bravest at the front, and he took one in the arm, not wanting to kill but slicing through the tendon so the sword fell from his hand. And then the others came, fast and eager.

Thomas stepped back, stepped again, and slammed into a figure behind who wrapped strong arms around him, lifting him from his feet.

A soldier came close, no hurry now. He circled the tip of his sword in front of Thomas's face, teasing with the promise of pain. Thomas kicked backward, connecting with a shin, but the pressure around his chest didn't slacken. He scanned the men, looking for officers, but if they were present they too wanted to see more blood spilled. One final conquest to end the attack.

The man with the sword came closer, using the tip to slice through Thomas's robe so it fell to the ground. Beneath he wore his usual shirt and breeches, no protection at all from what was about to come. He knew they would take his boots once he was dead. Good boots, supple leather. His father's boots that had been his since taking them from John Berrington's dead body, carrying them even though they were too big for him until he too had grown into a man, not even knowing why he kept them because he had hated the man. Hated him as a boy, hated him as a man, for what he had passed on to him. This urge to kill that engulfed what he regarded as his true soul.

He let it fill him now. They could kill him, of that he

was sure, but they would not do so without casualties on their part.

He stretched the fingers of his left hand, the only one he could use, until the tips brushed the end of a small dagger tucked into his belt. He eased it loose and without a moment's hesitation slammed it backwards into the belly of the man holding him. Even then his grip barely loosened until Thomas struck a second and third time.

As his feet landed on mud he darted to one side, the blade of the swordsman whistling through the space he had vacated. Thomas twisted and stuck the man in the side, not a killing wound but enough to discourage. By then others were coming, far too many to offer any hope at all, an entire army, three or four thousand strong. Thomas had faced heavy odds before but knew this was the end and wished he had thought to kiss Lubna before he left. An image of Will filled his mind, blond-haired and sturdy, easing his way into being a handsome man, a strong man.

Thomas took a breath and let it out in a long sigh.

So be it.

He struck, unaware that he moved like a dervish, that he moved like Jorge when he danced, his *tagelmust* swirling around his head, his feet and hands a blur. And then there came a moment of respite and Thomas stopped, breathing hard as Jorge had breathed hard, wondering why he was still alive. There came a clash of steel on steel and the men in front of him hesitated, fell back a pace, two.

Something knocked into him, and he went hard to his knees.

"Oh, for fuck's sake get on the horse or I'll let them kill you."

Thomas looked up at the figure of Yusuf astride a stallion that glowed moon-white in the darkness. He reached up but Yusuf was too high so Thomas stood, leaned for a moment against the heaving flank of the horse, then grabbed the saddle and pulled himself up behind Yusuf.

The shock among the Spaniards was starting to fade, and Yusuf handed Thomas his own sword before drawing another from its scabbard.

"Cowards, all of them." He grinned, slashing his sword through the air. Then he dug his heels into the horse's flanks and Thomas almost fell backwards over its rump before grabbing a handful of Yusuf's robe. Only as they raced away did he notice Yusuf's men riding alongside them, hard-faced Berbers who would follow their master into the gates of Hell.

TWENTY-SIX

Yusuf rode fast, recklessly, away from both Spanish and Moorish soldiers, into sharp-ridged hills. Thomas would have asked where they were going but needed to concentrate hard on simply holding on. Only when they descended into a small clearing and he saw a wooden cart waiting, and a body laid on the ground, did he understand. Yusuf hadn't been the only one from Gharnatah to fight tonight, but the other man was a shock. Thomas had always considered him invulnerable.

Thomas slid from behind Yusuf without a word and went to kneel over the figure that stared up at the sky. For a terrifying moment Thomas thought he was too late, but then the man's eyes flickered as he became aware of him and a grimace pulled his mouth down on one side.

"Apologise to my daughter," said Olaf Torvaldsson.

"Apologise yourself, for you will see her before noon."

"If I last that long."

Thomas knelt and examined a head wound. Bad

enough, but not fatal. Then he untied the leather jerkin and drew a sharp breath.

"Noon might be optimistic," said Olaf.

Thomas drew the jerkin farther apart, tracking the deep wound.

"A Spaniard?"

"A dead Spaniard. Now, anyway."

"You killed him?"

"What do you think?"

"How?"

"Did I kill him? With my axe, of course." Olaf smiled through his pain at the memory. "Took his head off."

"How did he do this to you? I have seen you fight, and you are invincible."

"Not anymore, it seems. I made the mistake of letting the fire take me." His eyes tracked Thomas's. "You know how it is. I have seen you in battle. You are like me. It is why I entrust my daughter to you."

"With me it is not the fire, but cold that takes me." Thomas wasn't sure why he said it, except he loved this man like a father, more than he had ever loved his own father.

"Each man has his own way. Beware of it, Thomas, for it makes a man believe himself invulnerable." He breathed softly for a moment, clear it pained at every inhalation. "I have been injured before, but fear this will be the last time."

"You forget who I am."

Thomas looked up to see Yusuf had come, together with a half-dozen hard-faced soldiers. He stood and watched as they lifted Olaf onto the bed of a cart. There was no horse, no donkey or mule. These men would draw their leader themselves. They raised him like he

248

weighed nothing at all, and Thomas wished al-Andalus had ten thousand more of their kind, for if it did this land might be saved.

"Would you have come to save me if Olaf hadn't been injured?" Thomas asked as he stood beside Yusuf.

"More than likely. You know how fond I am of you." He smiled. "Besides, there were only three or four thousand of them. If it had been eight..." He lifted a shoulder.

They both watched as the cart was led away.

Yusuf offered Thomas a horse, but he refused. Instead he ran to catch up with the cart and climbed onto its bed to kneel beside Olaf and start the work that might save him. He ignored the head wound as he stripped the big general's torso bare. He had a few instruments stowed in his pockets from the battle, but had lost his leather bag. He used what he had as best he could, examining the deep wound in Olaf's side, doing nothing until he was sure that doing something was the less dangerous choice.

"I'm sorry I have nothing for the pain. It's going to hurt a great deal."

"You forget who you talk to." Olaf bit his words short as Thomas started the examination. He tried to sit up, but Thomas held him down with one hand, knowing he couldn't have done so under normal circumstances.

"Lie still and I'll try to hurt you the least I can. It will be better when we get to the Infirmary."

"My men," said Olaf. "I have to tell them you mean me no harm if I call out."

"They know who I am." Thomas thought that might not be a good thing, but it also meant they knew of his skill. He might have worked on some of them in the past, for he had been in attendance at scores of battles and worked on hundreds of men, and if he had they no doubt hated him and were grateful in equal measure. Or more likely the hate outweighed the gratitude, but so be it. These men, Olaf's men, would not have stood at the back, but been in the front ranks. So yes, Thomas knew he would have treated at least some.

When Olaf screamed, the men came fast, only to be stilled by a stare from Thomas.

They travelled on, their path twisting to avoid Spanish scouts, until they came down to the walls of Malaka and entered the city.

"Will he live?" Lubna sat on a stone ledge, leaning forward, arms across her knees. She had come as soon as she received the message Thomas sent.

"He's strong. I've cleaned the wound and sealed the bleeding with a hot iron. Belia's potions will help if infection takes hold." He stared into Lubna's eyes. Thought of the child she carried. Another grandson or granddaughter for Olaf to spoil, and Thomas thought of how his face softened when the feared general bounced Will on his knee. Which reminded him he still had to find someone to continue training his son. A boy needed to know how to protect himself and, as he grew into a man, protect those he loved.

"He will stay with us," said Lubna.

"Of course."

"You were wise to bring us into the city before the Spanish came. Can we take him with us today?"

"He is better here for the moment. Let him sleep for now, there is enough poppy in his blood even for him."

"Then I will stay, too."

"We both stay," Thomas said. "I have arranged a room for us nearby. We can take turns to sit with him."

"I will do it. You are exhausted."

"It is nothing. I have also arranged for a nurse who will fetch us if there is any change."

"Is she good?"

Thomas considered a reply unnecessary.

"I sent Yusuf with Jorge to Diego's house," said Lubna. "It was hard to leave the other one, but you are right, we are safer inside the walls."

Thomas nodded, only half listening as his eyes grew heavy. The next time he opened them his neck was stiff and Jorge stood beside Yusuf with an expectation on his face.

"What?"

"I asked if you were coming home. Will misses you."

"Tomorrow," Thomas said. "When we bring Olaf." He glanced across to the man, who still slept. Lubna sat beside him, his big, gnarled hand in her small, soft one. "What are you doing here?"

"Lubna sent a message. Did you expect me not to come?"

"I don't know." But as he thought of it he realised Jorge and Olaf had become closer since events in Ixbilya almost two years before when the three of them had saved Belia from the Inquisition's dungeons. Olaf still thought Jorge too soft, too weak, but that was his opinion of almost all men. *No doubt including me,* Thomas thought. He glanced at the unglazed window to discover night had come again and wondered how long he had slept.

"Is it late?"

"Late enough to eat," said Jorge. "I was going to introduce Yusuf to al-Zaki's girls. The house is nearby."

"Why?"

"Why do you think?"

Thomas glanced at Yusuf. "Do you want to meet them?"

"It has been some time since I laid with a woman. And a man can stand only so much of war before wanting a beautiful woman."

"Four beautiful women," said Jorge. "Not counting his first wife."

"I thought there were six," Thomas said. "And are you sure they are willing?"

"Some have already left. That woman has driven them out. And yes, they are willing."

"I don't think I can manage four, let alone six," said Yusuf.

Thomas watched the exchange, wondering if he was still asleep and this was a dream.

"You are a prince, and they are in need of protection."

"I would never offer false hope," said Yusuf.

"But they would imagine it all the same."

"In that case we shouldn't go."

"Go find him a clean whore," said Lubna, from beside her father. She didn't bother turning around. "Two if you must."

"It is never too soon to begin selecting members of a harem," said Jorge to Yusuf. "You'll be Sultan one day and will need beautiful women to reflect your power."

Yusuf looked toward Thomas, a pleading in his eyes. "Can you tell him I only need to eat?"

"If it would do any good," Thomas said. "You know Jorge. Besides, you might enjoy yourself. They are all clean, all young, and yes, all more than willing I suspect."

Yusuf glanced toward Olaf. "Will he live?" Unknowingly echoing Lubna's words.

"He will."

"When will he wake?"

"Not until morning."

"I need to talk to him."

"I expect you do. And I think I know what about."

"What is your opinion of his answer?"

"I couldn't begin to work out how Olaf's mind works, other than he is fiercely loyal to whoever rules on the hill." Thomas waited for Yusuf to say something else, but he didn't. Eventually Jorge pulled him away, chattering, explaining the varying attractions of the women who had recently belonged to al-Zaki but were now in need of a new protector, if only from his ex-wife.

When they were gone, Thomas rose and touched Olaf's neck, searching for the pulse there, hard to find amongst the scars and muscle, but eventually it beat beneath his finger, strong and slow.

"Get some sleep," he said to Lubna. "I'll watch over him until dawn and then make arrangements to take him to Diego's house. Have the others come into the city yet?"

"They were doing so today. And I will stay, too."

"There's no need."

"*I* need to." She glanced at Thomas, her eyes devoid

of emotion, or emotion toward him at least, and he nodded and drew up a wooden stool. He closed his eyes.

When he woke again, dawn greyed the air and a mist hung in the empty street outside. Lubna's head rested on the bed, her breath lifting strands of dark hair as she breathed, and Olaf was awake.

Thomas stood, felt his pulse briefly before his hand was knocked aside.

"I will live, thanks to you."

"I am the decider of that, *Fa*."

Olaf tried to smile, gave up the attempt, perhaps the gesture too unfamiliar to come easily.

"Did you fix me?"

"As well as I could."

"Then I will live." He glanced at Lubna. Satisfied she continued to sleep he motioned Thomas close. "I have something to tell you."

"There are no secrets between us."

"Let us say I do not wish to wake her, then. When will I be well enough to return to Gharnatah?"

"Several weeks, perhaps longer."

"Then I need to tell you. What you decide to do is up to you. I will understand if you wish to do nothing, but you deserve to know."

"Know what?" Thomas leaned closer to Olaf, the scent of the soap they had used to clean his body sharp.

"I received a message a week ago while I still rode with al-Zagal." Olaf rested a moment, his eyes closed, then spoke again, his voice even softer. "We encountered the enemy early and were confident of teaching them a lesson, but they were ready for us. We were beaten. Badly beaten. Word got back to Muhammed. Word came back to us. The day after the news reached

Gharnatah he took al-Hamra. The city has a short memory. One defeat and they turn on their best hope and sit a fool on the throne."

Thomas waited, but the speech was over for the moment. A long speech for Olaf, who treated words like silver coins, too valuable to waste. Thomas knew what he wanted to ask, afraid of the answer that would come, but asked anyway.

"You have always told me you are the Sultan's man."

Olaf offered the smallest of nods. "Perhaps more so now. Fools need protection from themselves. But that is not all I need to tell you, merely the reason behind it."

Beside him Lubna shifted, and Thomas waited for her to settle. Outside in the street a store owner began to open shutters, talking to a passer-by in a language Thomas didn't understand. This was Malaka, after all.

He stared at Olaf, his eyes closed, and wondered if he had fallen into a doze.

But he had not.

"Muhammed has taken Helena. Taken her by force. That was the message I received. A message not to a general but a message to a father about his daughter. A message not altogether meant for me but, I believe, for you as well."

Thomas thought about Helena, Lubna's sister by a different mother. The exquisite Helena who had once shared his bed for half a year, and then, later, he had shared hers for a single night. Will was the result. At least, he hoped he might be; Helena continued to withhold that certainty from him.

"Did Muhammed send this message himself?"

"Possibly, I would not put such a thing beyond him."

Olaf's breathing grew faster and the muscles in his chest tightened.

"Where is the pain?"

The merest shake of his head. "It is not the kind you can cure. The messenger passed on other news, most likely thinking I needed to know it. Which I did, even if the hearing of it was hard. He is punishing her for loving you."

"Helena doesn't love me," Thomas said.

"More than she loves anyone else."

"It is years since she shared my bed. There is nothing between us anymore."

"But Muhammed does not know that, and sometimes I am not sure Helena does either. Do you deny Will is your son?"

"Sometimes I think he is, other times not."

"But you lay with her."

Thomas gave a brief nod. "Yes, I lay with her. But I had not lain with Lubna then. I would never betray her. I never loved Helena, but I do love Lubna."

"I know you do. But it is beside the point. Muhammed hurts Helena so he can punish you."

"Even though I don't know of it?"

"Retribution needs no reason for some men." Olaf's eyes opened, blue-grey like those of Helena, eyes that had seen everything a man could witness, both the good and bad, the blissful and horrific, and treated them all the same. "I would go plead for her. He might listen if I bend my knee and pledge allegiance. He will need someone like me, someone strong."

"There is no-one else like you," Thomas said.

"Which is why he might release my daughter. But I cannot go to him like this, weak." His eyes held

Thomas's, the question unasked, having no need to be asked.

"I can't go," Thomas said. "Not now, not yet."

"But later?"

Thomas stared at the man, as close to a father as any he had known, and he thought of Olaf's daughter, the blonde daughter, the woman who had once shared his house and his bed, and knew he didn't have an answer to the question.

TWENTY-SEVEN

The cart rattled along a cobbled street, Thomas guiding a mule as it drew its burden the short distance from the Infirmary to Diego's house where they now lived. Six Gomeres soldiers accompanied them, short, hard men with dark eyes that showed nothing. This was Malaka, a Moorish city of sorts, but the man they protected was Olaf Torvaldsson so no chances were to be taken. Thomas had been unsure whether Olaf would need extra protection or not, but had gone to where the Gomeres had made their camp below the Rabita fortress to ask their help, thinking of the killer who still roamed free in the city. It would not be taken lightly if he endangered al-Andalus's most famed general. Even the Gomeres captain, who had never before left his native North Africa, knew of Olaf's reputation and assigned these half dozen men.

Two of them roamed ahead, checking every side alley and doorway, their heads turning to scan for danger. Two more came behind. Yusuf had returned to the mountains and his men, to pick at the Spanish army, but promised to return once Olaf was strong enough to travel.

The streets were almost empty, which was why they were moving Olaf now, before traders set up their stalls. Despite the presence of the Spanish army beyond the city walls, life continued, but there was a brittle nature to it now, as if everyone walked on eggshells, waiting for the inevitable attack.

Lubna sat in the rear of the cart next to her father, who maintained a stoic silence through gritted teeth as the constant jostling aggravated the pain of his wounds.

Jorge walked beside Thomas, explaining in great detail the beauty and skill of each of the women, and how the night before he left Yusuf had managed to bed at least three before sleep, or more likely exhaustion, claimed him. He said nothing about his part in events, though Thomas was certain Belia didn't expect fidelity from him. She knew him better than that.

"Did you think Yusuf would really take any of those girls to be part of his harem?" Thomas asked when there came a brief break in the tale — caused more by Jorge's need to draw breath than that he had finished.

"Of course not, but they believed he might."

"Is it fair to let them think so?"

"Don't be so judgemental. It's not as if they're anything but willing. Yusuf is a fine-looking young man. Strong and virile. He is welcome after that husband of theirs."

"A husband who is dead, and whose killer we seek," Thomas said. "And what do you do while Yusuf is bedding these women? There are two older, good-looking women in that house as well, no doubt of much greater experience than those girls."

"I am doing nothing. Offering advice. I have spoken with them several times but they continue to tell the same tale they told us in Ballix. I even took Will with me one time. They made such a fuss of him he wants to go back."

"You took Will to that house? What were you thinking?"

"I was thinking if he saw how other people," Jorge glanced at Thomas, "how normal people live, it would do him good."

"That is hardly a normal household. Don't take him again."

Jorge smiled. "Now Yusuf is gone I have no excuse to visit, but you can't hide the truth of the world from Will."

"I can until he's older. Is that all you did when you went there?"

"I have Belia, and a man could want of no other. Besides, they have a lover of their own."

"They do?" Thomas said. "A man?"

"I haven't seen him yet, but the three of them make enough noise to wake the dead. I think he must be French because he calls out in a language I don't know."

Thomas smiled. He could have said it might be almost any language, for Jorge had only the two. This mysterious man might be speaking the language of China for all Jorge would be able to tell.

"Is Olaf going to live?" asked Jorge.

"I believe so."

"Good. I've grown to like him."

"And he you, I think."

"We live in strange times, do we not, when a Sultan's general and a Sultan's eunuch can become friends?"

The cart turned and the house revealed itself, substantial, taking up the entire end of the street. Two stories high, with the tops of trees showing above the roof, the city wall rising beyond the small garden behind. It was a fine house, but Thomas missed their previous home. He had liked the sense of freedom, but knew to have stayed would have been madness.

The Gomeres carried Olaf inside as if he weighed nothing. As they emerged, Thomas tried to offer them coin in exchange for their service but it was refused, and he knew better than to try a second time.

"Do any of you speak Arabic?" he asked.

Two of them nodded.

"Would either of you be willing to help train a boy in weapons?"

The other men turned the mule until the cart faced the right way for the return journey. The two glanced at each other. One of them shrugged and shook his head. The other considered the offer.

"What boy?"

"My son," Thomas said. "Olaf Torvaldsson's grandson."

The man grinned. "Is he as strong as the general?"

"He is a boy, but a strong boy."

"Sword? Bow?"

"And axe."

"I do not use the axe. It would have to be sword and bow. And riding, of course, as well as hands and feet." He stared hard at Thomas, almost a challenge. "Have you fought?"

"Yes."

The man looked him up and down, showing no indication whether he believed him or not. Thomas didn't

261

care if he did, only that he would train Will. He would take instruction better from a stranger, might one day need the level of skill this Gomeres could instil in him.

"If I offer to pay, will you refuse?"

"No. It is work you propose so of course you must pay me. How much is up to you. Whatever you think fair once you have seen what I can teach your son. Can I see him before I leave?"

Thomas led the way through the house, noting the man's companions didn't wait for him. They found Will playing with Diego in the rear courtyard. Not as extensive a playground as the hillside behind the other house had been, but enough for them to play-fight with wooden swords. It was Will who always wanted to fight, but Diego was a poor challenge. The sound of wood on wood clacked and echoed from the city wall at the far end of the courtyard. Thomas had had to stop Will from climbing it, but knew he probably did when he couldn't be seen. He would have done the same at his age.

Thomas stood beside the Gomeres, watching the man study Will and Diego.

"The short one is your son?"

"He is."

"Good, I can do something with him, but not the other. His name?"

"Will."

"Will." The sound was nothing like Thomas had spoken it. "He fights well. But then his opposition is not much, is he." He glanced at Thomas. "How hard can I be on him?"

"I would prefer you not to kill him."

"I will try, then." A hint of a smile touched the man's lips. "Yes, I will help you. I would like to start now, to see how much your son already knows. How good he might become. Truly he is grandson to Olaf Torvaldsson?"

"He is."

"Maybe you need not pay me anything at all, then."

"Then you can leave now."

The man turned to stare at Thomas, a sense of threat coming from him despite nothing seeming to have changed. And then he laughed.

"Good, I do not frighten you. That means your son will be strong, too, here where it counts." He tapped his skull. "Pay me, then. Pay me what you think." He turned away. "You, Will, come here."

Will stopped fighting and turned, though Thomas knew he had been aware of their presence since they arrived.

"I need to know your name," Thomas said.

"Of course. I am Usaden Hamid. I was born in the deep desert and learned to kill when I was little older than your son. I am Gomeres. There is nothing else you need to know."

Thomas turned away, leaving them to it.

Lubna was waiting for him inside, her face set, arms crossed. Thomas knew this had been coming, glad she had not waited and let her anger simmer. She met his eyes briefly then turned away. He followed, closing the door of their room behind him. Lubna continued to face away, staring out of the window to where Usaden was hitting Will with a stick. She cocked her head.

"What is that man doing to Will?"

"Saving his life. But that isn't what you want to say to me, so say it."

"You are going to abandon her? Did you think I

didn't hear what father told you? She is my sister. Would you have Muhammed abuse her, even kill her?"

"I cannot leave Malaka, you know that. I suspect the message was sent by Muhammed to lure me to Gharnatah. He will be ready if I go. Would you have me throw my life away for nothing?"

"Helena is nothing to you now?"

"You know she isn't, not in the way you are."

"She lived with you. Shared your bed. She carried Will for nine months. Does none of that mean anything?"

Thomas turned to one side, looking out to where Usaden was showing Will how to hold his wooden sword, how to strike at the weak parts of the body. Diego sat on a low wall, watching. His face showed no expression, but his body shifted in subtle ways, hands moving as he unconsciously copied Will's moves.

"I have a responsibility to you and the child you carry. To you and Will, to Jorge and Belia, and to your father as well, now. Yusuf, too."

"You talked to him before he left, didn't you?"

"Of course. Wouldn't it be the best solution for him to oust his brother? Imagine what it would be like to have someone young, someone intelligent and with sense ruling on the hill. A Sultan who could save something from this endless war."

"She is my sister."

"And you will be jealous if she comes to live under this roof. You know what she is like."

"She would want to lie with Yusuf when he returns, not you." Lubna showed a hint of a smile. "She always goes after the best-looking men."

"Yusuf is somewhere in the hills fighting until Olaf is recovered."

"Which will be weeks at least, more likely months." Lubna stared at him. "See, you shouldn't have brought me to the Infirmary if you didn't want me to know such things. I can treat father as well as you, you know I can. Go save my sister, Thomas." She laid a hand against his chest, and he could feel his heart beating beneath her touch.

"When Malaka falls we will have to leave. It can wait until then."

"Do you plan to take us back to Gharnatah?"

Thomas didn't reply, because he had no answer, not yet.

"Or are you going to accept the offers your other woman makes?"

She had no need to state who she meant. Thomas had made no secret of Isabel's overtures to him, no secret that they grew increasingly attractive as the years passed. This war would end in only one way, and it would be better to be on the side of the winner rather than the loser. But still he couldn't turn his back on al-Andalus.

Lubna withdrew her hand then used it to slap his face, hard. "You are hopeless, Thomas Berrington." She turned and walked from the room, her body tense with anger.

Thomas waited until his own anger abated then walked through the house to find Jorge watching Will receive his first lesson from Usaden. Sweat stood out on Will's chest and back. Usaden looked as if he had barely moved.

"Lubna thinks I should rescue Helena," Thomas said.

"Her anger has been simmering for a week now and she's convinced herself it's the right thing to do."

Jorge glanced at him. "Does she know you would have to bring her back here, to Malaka? She wouldn't be safe in Gharnatah, not even on the Albayzin."

"She must."

"Riding to Helena's rescue is exactly what Muhammed is hoping for."

"I know, but it's hard to turn my back on her."

"She is not your wife. Lubna is."

"Helena is Will's mother."

"In body only. She doesn't love him like Lubna does. She doesn't love you. Helena loves nobody but herself."

"And if Muhammed kills her?"

"He won't. Dead she can't draw you to him. Alive, mistreated, he hopes you will come to save her."

"When Olaf returns he will have to release her," Thomas said. "Won't he?"

Jorge raised a shoulder. "I'm not sure Muhammed respects Olaf as much as he should. He'll have his own people around him now. You know who they are. Faris al-Rashid and his companions, whispering false words in his ear. Tell me, why is that man damaging Will?"

Thomas wanted to discuss Helena's situation some more in the hope he could be persuaded, but he let it go for the moment because he knew there was little point. He had already made his decision, and Lubna would have to accept it.

"He's training him to survive," he said.

"Looks like a strange kind of training to me. I went to talk to Narjis again today. She told me the masters are afraid. After what happened to Izem Amreqan they expect someone else to be killed, and fear it will be them. Their deputies and clerks, too. They're all afraid. All except Ali Durdush, who tells them to get on with their trade."

"Amreqan might be the last. Almost two weeks have gone by and nothing has happened. Though that might be because the Spanish surround the city, and it's harder to come and go at will. We should go to the Alkhazabah now Olaf is recovering and see how secure this hoard of gold is. To warn whoever is tasked with protecting it."

Will came toward them, his face red with anger, and stamped past them both. Usaden followed, Diego trailing along beside him, Will's discarded wooden sword in his hand.

"You were hard on him," Thomas said.

"Not as hard as I will be."

"Then you will train him?"

Usaden nodded. "One day he will be a great fighter, but he is young still. He must learn to control his anger. It lets him down and clouds his judgement. Are you sure you want me to push him as hard as I must?"

"I can't do it myself. I love him too much."

"Then love him enough to let me make him invulnerable."

"No man is invulnerable, and certainly no boy."

Usaden laughed. "I will come every day if I can."

"I heard that some of your men take rooms in the city. We have a room here for you, if you will have it."

Usaden nodded. "I will ask if my captain will allow. I am sure he will when I tell him it is for Olaf Torvaldsson's grandson."

TWENTY-EIGHT

"I like the houses here," said Jorge as Thomas walked beside him through the district leading to the crenelated walls of the Alkhazabah — the first of two forts sitting on a hill that rose to overlook Malaka and the surrounding countryside.

"We already have a new house," Thomas said.

"Which I like well enough, but these are fine too, are they not?"

They were indeed, but Thomas was in no mood to indulge Jorge in a discussion over where they should live. But he agreed the houses were indeed some of the best in the entire city, surpassing even those beside the Ataranzana. The Malaka Guild possessed great wealth, but the Alkhazabah, and Rabita fort which loomed over it, was where true power lay. It made sense that the Guilds would store their riches here. It also made sense that Hamad al-Tagri, the governor of the city, would want it kept close. If he even knew it had been moved, that is. There was a distinct separation between the

Rabita and the rest of Malaka, as though they rarely communicated with each other.

Thomas's scribbled ten-day old note with its stamped seal gained them access through the outer entrance. This led to a paved area with high walls beyond, but the second door proved more problematic. The guards stationed there refused to admit them without higher authority, so they stood looking back the way they had come, trying to find a patch of shade.

"We should find somewhere to sit and drink," said Jorge.

"And miss our chance when someone comes?"

"I will not stand out here long. The sun is bad for my skin."

Thomas said nothing, trying to ignore Jorge's running commentary on how bad too much sun was, and how Belia's ointments kept his skin as smooth as it deserved to be. He was relieved when one of the guards called them over.

A grey-haired man of indeterminate but advanced years stood in the shade, as if he too had heard Jorge's theories on sunlight. Thomas noted that the man's eyes showed the first sign of cataracts, a condition easily corrected, but for which treatment was rarely sought.

"I am told you wish to access the inner chambers," the man said.

Thomas showed him the slip of paper. The man read it slowly before handing it back.

"This says to show you where the Malaka Guild's vault is."

"It does." Thomas received no response so had to prompt him. "Will you take us there?"

The man held his hand out again, and Thomas passed the paper across once more.

"I know Cesare Padvana, he was Izem's deputy. He is Master of Coin now?"

"He is."

"I heard what happened to Izem. Murderers outside the city walls and murderers within. I am glad to be old and will not need to worry myself much longer."

The man continued to stare at the paper, which shook slightly in his hand. News of Amreqan's murder had spread rapidly through the city and all would know of it by now. According to Narjis the other masters, their deputies and clerks, had taken to staying inside and increasing the number of their guards.

"Amreqan was murdered," Thomas said, "by someone who may have come here seeking access to the same place I do."

The man handed back the paper and turned away. "As you can see, entry to this place is not a matter of simply walking in. There are rules. Protections. Follow me. I am Kohen al-Farsi, Master of the Alkhazabah." He glanced at Thomas. "As far as I know, nobody has come seeking entrance other than the two of you. I know you, Thomas Berrington, but who is your friend?"

If al-Farsi knew him, why the show at the gate, Thomas wondered, *unless it was for the guards?*

"My companion is Jorge Olmos."

"A Spaniard?" Al-Farsi slowed before coming to a halt, a slow-motion procedure that took several paces. Light from a narrow lookout splashed against him, and he took a step away from it.

Thomas glanced through the slit, drawn as he always

was now to the dark stain of the Spanish army visible from this extra height.

"Not for a long time," he said. "He is a friend and can be trusted."

"The note names only you," said al-Farsi.

"I am happy to wait outside," said Jorge. "Or return to the house."

"We work together," Thomas said to al-Farsi. "And at the moment, I am working on behalf of the Malaka Guild. Please don't make this difficult for any of us. We are on the same side, and I expect even now the Spanish are selecting weak points in the city walls, deciding on where best to launch their next attack."

"Which is why I asked." But al-Farsi turned away and began to walk once more, the same gradual building of velocity until he attained a slow, swaying walk which he maintained as they climbed stone steps between high walls that turned and turned again, designed to slow the advance of an attacking force. They entered a wide courtyard planted with bushes and trees, the sound of water mixed with the cries of swallows. Al-Farsi slowed and sat on a bench, the burst of movement draining his meagre supply of energy. Thomas wondered if he was the right man for his position but admitted experience counted for more here than strength.

They had climbed above the level of the walls on the southern side, only the blue of the Mediterranean beyond. Spanish caravels and galleys waited at anchor, replacing the trade ships that had navigated these waters until recently. Trade would not begin again until the battle was done, perhaps not even then.

Al-Farsi too watched the intruders on the water before turning to Thomas. "The passages I brought you through are the only means of entrance to this court-yard. You will have noticed the stout oak doors, which can be closed in a moment and barred from within. They are not a permanent barrier but would take time some to break through, and then there is another, and another."

"That is interesting," Thomas said, "but is it of relevance to what I wish to see?"

"You need to know that the wealth of the Guild is protected. It is safe."

"I never doubted it."

Al-Farsi leaned forward, placed his hands on his knees, then tipped from the bench and tottered several paces while he straightened. Thomas felt his arm twitch, wanting to offer support, but stilled it with an effort of will knowing it wouldn't be welcome. Jorge showed no such restraint and took al-Farsi's arm and whispered something to him. The old man smiled and leaned against Jorge's strength.

"It is no distance now, but I thank you for your kindness." He took Jorge's arm, half leading the way toward a square tower with a single window that looked over the city. There was a door, then another. Not the series they had passed on the ascent, but if someone managed to get this far another dozen doors would prove little barrier.

Al-Farsi had keys and used them to open a stout oak door into a square tower.

"How many others have copies?" Thomas asked.

"There are three in total. One set is always in my possession. The other is with the captain of the guard. The third is sealed in the inner chambers of the fort."

"Durdush doesn't possess one? Nor the Master of Coin?"

"This place is my responsibility." Al-Farsi opened the door to reveal a chamber. The window that had been visible from outside was set high on one wall, sunlight splashing across the walls to provide illumination. Oil lamps were set in alcoves, not needed for now. Three sides were stacked to above a man's height with newly built crates, the scent of resin sharp in the air. The fourth wall also contained crates apart from where a set of steps led down. Thomas walked across and examined them.

"How many levels deep?"

"Seven beyond this one."

"All the same?"

Al-Farsi inclined his head, still leaning against Jorge, who stood like a sentinel beside him. "The lower levels were filled first, of course." He glanced around. "And this one will be filled soon."

"What happens then?"

"We ship the crates to a place of safety."

"Where?"

"That is none of your business, Thomas Berrington."

"How many times has this place been emptied?" He suspected that wasn't his business either.

"The last time was forty years ago. To my knowledge it has been filled and emptied five times in the past. This will be the sixth."

"But never before in a time of war?"

Al-Farsi seemed to consider a reply unnecessary.

Thomas looked around, trying to place a value on the wealth of the Malaka Guild, and failing. The numbers were simply too enormous to contemplate. He thought of the seemingly infinite cache of gold, silver, and jewels he and Jorge had liberated after the death of a merchant in Gharnatah, and it paled into insignificance.

"You say if the Spanish come there is an escape route?"

"On the lowest level. A tunnel that leads to the sea. The crates will be taken out that way to a waiting boat."

"What about the Spanish? They are unlikely to let any other vessel approach shore."

"It will be done when they are otherwise engaged. There is a plan in place and I am assured it will work."

"How many know of this plan?"

"All Guild Masters know of what we do, but not the entire plan, not the detail of it. Now I have told you and your companion, there are six, but even you do not know everything." Al-Farsi cocked his head and almost smiled. "You see, I honour your permission by revealing what we do."

"We are honoured indeed." There was sincerity in Jorge's voice, and Thomas saw it pleased al-Farsi, who had clearly taken a liking to him.

"As you should be. But I know of Thomas's reputation, otherwise I would not be so open with you. I heard you are a man who can be trusted."

Thomas was tempted to ask where this news had come from but knew it was irrelevant. Instead he stuck to the matter at hand and walked to one of the crates. Each was expertly cut and assembled, each the exact same dimensions. Not so small they would be unsuited for storing what lay within, not so large they could not be moved when necessary. He pushed at one but it offered no give at all — it was like trying to push a mountain. It would require several men and perhaps equipment to shift them.

"How long will it take to empty this tower? Not a matter of moments, I imagine. And how can anyone move these crates?"

"There are machines we use, pulleys, levers. Each was brought here, each can be moved. It will take a full day. That is how long the last emptying took, forty years ago, but we may be able to improve that if there are soldiers at the gates. Only so many men can work in here at once, as you can see. There is little room to spare, and the lower levels have even less."

"I take it the lower exit is locked?"

"And barred from this side. It would be impossible to gain entry that way."

"I would like to see for myself."

Al-Farsi seemed to consider the request before coming to a decision. "So long as you are happy to descend alone. All those steps are too much for an old man." He held out his keys and Thomas took them before glancing at Jorge, who nodded to indicate he would stay with al-Farsi.

The air cooled as Thomas descended, light fading until in the lowest chamber he could barely see. Someone had prepared for the eventuality, a lamp set in a stone alcove together with a flint and oiled cloth. He struck a spark, lit the cloth and transferred the flame to the lamp. When he raised it, he saw more crates stacked to the roofline. These were clearly older, their wood darkened by age, but still sound. A narrow walkway led between them to a barred door. It was narrow and low, with barely enough room for two men to drag each of the crates through.

Thomas unbarred the door and tested it, discovered he would also need a key, and tried each until one turned in the lock. He heard solid bolts withdraw, but once unlocked the door opened easily enough on well-oiled hinges. The passage was barely higher than the doorway, and Thomas had to bend to enter it. A scent of rot and salt-water greeted him as he made his way across a smooth floor where on wooden runners waited a cart of some kind. The walls of the tunnel were well-mortared, but water gathered on the cold stone and ran in rivulets to the ground. Part of the way in he stopped at a door set into one side of the tunnel. He glanced along to where another door sat at the end, obviously where the crates would be taken out to the shore. What was this second door for, he wondered? Curious, he tried the keys until one turned. He raised the lamp as he pushed through.

A second tunnel, wider than the one he had been in, ran away into darkness. Thomas walked forward. Less than a minute took him to a chamber where wheeled carts waited, ready to be used for transporting the boxes. More wooden rails ran across the floor. Water dripped from the roof, but each cart was covered with an oiled tarpaulin. The planning was impressive. He only hoped the reality would prove equally so. It would have been good to know how the Guild managed to keep the Spanish from simply sailing in and taking these riches once they were on the shore, but Kohen al-Farsi had been confident the plan would succeed.

At the far end of the chamber a second door, barred but without a lock, offered access to a continuation of the tunnel, which was wider here. Thomas assumed this was where the carts had been brought in, as it would be impossible to carry them down all the steps in the tower. He turned away and returned to the main passageway, making sure to lock and bar all the doors behind him. He smiled at the thought of leaving an unlocked door for someone to sneak in through and steal all of the wealth.

Once he had unlocked and removed the bars from the final door he hesitated, put his ear against the heavy wood, and listened. He heard the rhythmic wash of waves, a faint moan as wind caught a gap around the edge of the door, but nothing else. He knew there might be a score of men on the other side and he would never know. He considered whether it was more sensible to simply return to Jorge and al-Farsi, then berated himself for cowardice. If he saw anyone he could always duck back in quick enough and throw the bolts again. Thomas pushed softly on the door, opening it little more than a crack. Bright sunlight fell in, almost blinding him, and he waited for his eyes to adjust.

Dark sand and rock lay immediately beyond, and as he pushed it wider he was able to see in both directions. There was nobody close, but two hundred paces to the west a small group of men stood on the shoreline. They were too distant to make out who they were, or what they were doing, but it was unlikely they were Spanish. They were almost certainly men of the city come to try to catch fish, for food was growing scarcer by the day. He had even heard of people stripping leaves off the trees and boiling them into a thin soup, a dangerous practice at best.

Thomas walked out across the rough pebbles, relieved to be able to stand upright. He crossed the thirty paces to the waterline. Marks showed where rowboats had been pulled up, and he wondered if they had been practicing the removal of the crates, or were they from Spanish boats come to probe for weakness? The thought reminded him of Mandana's son, Pedro Guerrero, and he wondered if that was what he had been doing on the sea when his wife was attacked.

He turned around and looked back at the towering wall, over a hundred feet high and studded with slits for bowmen. The wall appeared to lean out toward him but he knew it was an illusion. He thought of what the Spanish had done at Ronda when they used powder to blow the door to the tunnels leading from the river to the town. Would they try the same here? The door was strong, but not strong enough to withstand that kind of force. Thomas would tell al-Farsi to set men on the top of the wall to look out for anyone bringing kegs ashore. A few tossed rocks, some arrows and hot pitch would be enough to discourage them. But he didn't expect an attack to come from this direction.

He saw it might be possible to spirit the crates away. To the east a cliff prevented anyone approaching from that direction. West the city wall extended almost to the shore. Thomas knew if it had been his plan he would have ships ready to attack the Spanish fleet, small as it was, to prevent their approach. There were enough trading boats in the harbour and riverside to do that. He judged the distance, trying to work out how long it would take to empty the tower. A whole day, al-Farsi had said. That would be too long. Then he realised it would only be a problem if the Spanish knew of what was going to happen, and almost certainly they did not. The Spanish ships wouldn't be expecting any danger from this direction. Their efforts, when the final attack came, would be concentrated where the Wadi al-Medina emptied into the sea. It appeared feasible, but as he stood on the shoreline Thomas was wondering why people had died, and whether it was connected to what was going to happen here. Izem Amreqan had been Master of Coin and would know all about what was planned — no doubt would have known even where the eventual destination was. Would he have shared that information with Zufar al-Zaki? If he had, for what purpose? Was that the reason both men were now dead? To hide the involvement of others? Woodville hardly seemed capable of such a plan, but he wouldn't have had to kill anyone himself. He had brought men with him from England, soldiers used to war, who were no doubt more than willing to follow orders for the amount of gold they would receive in return.

Thomas turned and walked along the base of the wall as he thought over the possibilities. He was looking for another entrance where the carts would have been taken through but found nothing before he reached the towering rock cliff on which the Alkhazabah and Rabita rested. Which meant the tunnel must rise into the Alkhazabah itself. As he considered the possibility, the more it made sense. Why risk two entries on the side of the sea, and bringing carts and men down through the protected fort itself would be much simpler. Thomas looked around, smelling salt water and dried weed, feeling the spray from waves on his face as the wind drove them to shore.

As he started back he believed Amreqan and the others had died to protect the secret of Woodville's involvement. Diego's father and mother were killed to ensure his father's suspicions did not gain a wider audience.

Thomas made his way back through the tunnel, taking care that each door was locked and barred, knowing al-Farsi would send someone down to check. If it was a conspiracy, how many others were privy to it? Would it go all the way to the top? Could Ali Durdush be involved? Was that the reason he had been meeting with Richard Woodville? The more Thomas thought it through the more it seemed possible. Someone within Malaka had made a deal with the Spanish in return for a portion of the riches.

It made more sense that Richard Woodville, a man in obvious need of a fortune to match his position, had come to Spain in search of the largest fortune in the known world. His story of seeking a bride for an English prince was little more than a useful excuse for his presence. Had he come to Spain with a plan, or only developed one when he found out about the gold? The only part that made no sense was Durdush himself. Was he involved or no more than a useful contact? And how could Woodville work his way into the trust of important men in Malaka well enough to be accepted as part of the conspiracy? Unless he had seeded the idea. Everyone knew that before long Malaka was doomed. Did some Guild Masters conspire together to enrich themselves once that came about? Still Thomas couldn't work out Woodville's involvement, and then a possibility came to him. The man was uncle to the King's wife. King Henry, who Thomas knew nothing of other than the rumour he was a calculating, clever man. Was he looking to enrich England? King's always needed money, and a lot of it. Yet still Thomas couldn't see how

Durdush would benefit from such a scheme when all he needed to do was steal the wealth for himself. He knew he would have to confront Durdush again, Woodville too if he could arrange another meeting somehow.

Thomas was almost at the top of the tower when he heard the first bark of cannon, and a moment later a distant crash as a ball landed within the city walls, followed closely by another, and he knew any opportunity to confront Woodville was now lost. The final assault had begun.

TWENTY-NINE

Thomas sent Jorge home with a message that he would follow within the hour, then walked through a panicked city to the Ataranzana. He wanted to confront Ali Durdush, to press him over what he knew, if anything, about a plot to steal the city's wealth.

With the fading of the afternoon the Spanish bombardment had slowed, only the occasional bark of a cannon breaking the calm that had descended on a population pushed beyond fear. A constant hum of ten thousand voices rose from beyond the wall, the rustle of men cleaning weapons, talking, cooking, fighting. The sound drifted into the city to form a background whisper, reminding everyone of what lay beyond, or what was still to come.

The Ataranzana cast long shadows from the final rays of the setting sun as Thomas approached. He glanced up, pleased to see several windows on the upper floor lit from within, but when he entered Ali Durdush's offices it was to be informed he was not there. He had been gone all day. Thomas pressed the clerk, but either he didn't know where his master was, or was unwilling to reveal the information. So instead he walked the length of the upper corridor to the office of Cesare Padvana, the new Master of Coin. Thomas was sure if his new theory was correct then Padvana must have information.

The man was still working. He glanced up, a flash of annoyance crossing his face before composing himself.

"Did you want something? I was about to leave." Padvana washed a hand across his face, pulled at his beard. "If it is more questions, my clerk is better able to provide answers." He indicated the papers scattered across his desk. "As you can see, I am still learning my new role."

Again the claim to know little, a claim Thomas now doubted.

"I have come from the Alkhazabah."

"Good for you." Padvana turned his attention to a ledger which lay open in front of him. Columns of tiny figures covered the pages, recording the minutiae of every transaction that took place in the city.

A sense of frustration built in Thomas as he watched the man. Like most of the Guild Masters he was arrogant and dismissive of those they considered their inferiors. Thomas stepped to the desk and swept it clear.

"What the–"

"Listen to me." Thomas leaned over the desk, his knuckles pressed against the smooth surface. He could feel a tremor passing through him. "Four people are dead, possibly more. One was your master. You know more than you're saying and you will tell me what it is, or I am going to pick you up and toss you through the window." It was a threat Padvana might doubt, but Thomas wasn't so sure he didn't mean it. He was exhausted, battling with frustration, and on the point of abandoning his task altogether so he could get on with his own life. Isabel had promised him sanctuary, a promise that looked more inviting by the hour.

Padvana rose to his feet, he too leaning across the desk until his face was inches from Thomas's. "I am no deputy anymore, Thomas Berrington, so take great care who you threaten."

He lifted his head a moment and shouted: "Guards! Here, now!"

Thomas smiled. "I saw no guards when I came in. They have better uses for their time these days. Go on, try calling louder. Here, let me help. *Guards! Guards!*" He used his full voice, already hoarse from too much talking, confident no-one would appear.

Padvana straightened, stepped back from the table. He looked right and left, craned his neck to see if anyone was coming along the corridor.

"What are you so afraid of revealing?" Thomas said. "That you are also involved in the plot to steal Malaka's wealth?"

"Plot?"

Thomas couldn't tell whether he spoke true or not, wishing once more he had brought Jorge, but even as he did so he knew Jorge was too soft for what he had come to do. He was willing to hurt, to inflict injury in order to find out what he needed to know. He considered himself a fool for not seeing it sooner. The spiriting away of the city's wealth to a single location. It might have been done several times before, as Kohen al-Farsi claimed, but never from a city under siege. Only someone over-confident, or stupid, would believe such a plan had any chance of success. Thomas didn't believe Padvana to be either, which only added to his suspicion.

"Yes, plot," he said. "If the city falls, the Guild will want its wealth protected, but you know as well as I that once the Spanish triumph, trade will continue as before. They are not stupid, they always retain those who make the wealth even if they enslave everyone else. Half the administrators in Ixbilya are Jews, even as the Catholic Church persecutes them."

"They will take our wealth," said Padvana. "Steal it all."

"And you will make more."

"There is so much of it!" Padvana's voice was a wail of horror.

"Which means there will be more again. Don't be a fool. Are you involved in the plot? Tell me now or you are no use to me at all. I will be a good friend to have when the Spanish enter the city, remember that. A good friend or a terrible enemy." Thomas reached across the desk. It was a stretch which almost toppled him but he caught Padvana's shirt and pulled him closer. "Are you involved? Who else?"

"There is no plot!"

"Don't take me for a fool. All these papers, the ledgers, you have been looking for something, haven't you. Was it your master then?"

"Let me go, you're hurting me."

Thomas hesitated, then unwound his grip. Padvana staggered back and dropped into the chair. His face was ashen and a twitch he was probably not even aware of tremored at the corner of his eyelid.

"I have had suspicions for some time, but could do nothing about them." His eyes rose to meet Thomas's. "How could I? He was my master, and I his deputy. How could I betray him? Besides, it seemed too audacious a plan to succeed."

"You could have told Durdush," Thomas said.

"No, I could not."

Thomas sat on the corner of the desk. "Because you suspect him too?"

Padvana nodded.

"Why?"

"They were always whispering in corners. Izem spent more and more time in Durdush's office. And then there were other meetings, with people not of the city."

"Was one called Woodville? An Englishman, like me?"

Padvana's gaze took in Thomas. "He is nothing like you. He is a gentleman."

"A gentleman in need of money. Who else?"

"I don't know, which is why I am studying the ledgers. There will be a clue in here somewhere. In Malaka nothing goes undocumented." He leaned over and picked up one of the discarded books. "Give me time, Thomas Berrington, and I will unmask the ring-leaders for you."

"Durdush?"

"If it is him. If he is involved in any way."

"Who do you know in his office? One of the clerks? They would know everything he does."

"And they would be fiercely loyal to him. No, the answer lies in the ledgers. Give me until morning and I will bring you names."

286

"You don't know where I live. I will return here at dawn."

"You live in Miguel Jiminez's house, it is common knowledge. I will come to you. It is too dangerous here, so close to power."

As he made his way toward Diego's house, Thomas wondered if he had made a mistake to believe Padvana's claim of innocence so readily, but knew it was also a test. If the man did not appear, it would confirm his guilt.

He was approaching the front door when a tall figure stepped from a side alley, his features obscured in the dark. Thomas reached for his belt only to discover he carried no weapon. They had had to leave them at the entrance to the Alkhazabah and he had forgotten to pick his up when they left, too distracted by the tumbling of his thoughts. He steeled himself for an attack, already planning his moves, when the figure passed through a wash of lamplight from a window and Thomas relaxed.

"What are you doing here?"

Yusuf smiled. "Olaf sent a message saying he was ready to leave."

Thomas shook his head even as he slapped Yusuf on the back, then he knew a slap was not enough and pulled him into an embrace, glad when it was returned, glad that some of the boy who used to worship him still remained.

"Whatever Olaf has said it's me who decides when he is fit enough to leave."

"He claims he is." Yusuf left his hand on Thomas's shoulder, the two of them standing in the night-washed street only a few paces from home.

"Then he claims wrong. He is Olaf Torvaldsson, so is already stronger than any three men, but knowing him he will want to return to battle immediately. I wouldn't have him die before he's ready."

"We need him. We need all the men we can get. We are losing this battle. Losing this war."

"Then come and tell Olaf you will oust your brother. You know my feelings on the matter. It's the only way anything can be saved." Thomas looked at Yusuf. "You have made a decision, haven't you?"

"I have."

"Do I need to ask what it is?"

"No."

When Yusuf told them of what he planned, Olaf was the first to speak.

"I have to return to Gharnatah." He spoke around a mouthful of meat. From the effort he made in chewing, Thomas suspected it was tough. Belia had managed to obtain a haunch of goat from a herder who had found his way through the Spanish and the wall.

"Ask your daughter if you're fit enough." Thomas knew he was a coward for not answering directly. "She spends more time with you than I do."

Olaf looked toward Lubna, who was forgoing the meat, using flatbread to wipe up some of the spiced sauce. "Thomas tells me I am too timid in my diagnosis. I would keep you another month at least."

Olaf turned back to Thomas and waited.

"You are not ready yet. Two weeks. I will decide in

288

two weeks." Even as he said it he knew Olaf would take it as a promise.

"I cannot wait that long. I will die of boredom. This idleness is driving me mad."

"I saw you with Usaden when I came home, helping to train Will. That was not idleness."

"I need distraction. Besides, a boy must learn the axe before the sword, and good as he is, Usaden does not know how to use one. He thinks it is to be gripped in the hand." Olaf shook his head at the foolishness of such a notion.

"So do I," Thomas said. "How else do you use one, with your feet?"

Olaf shook his head and popped another piece of meat into his mouth, started to speak around it. "Everyone knows you use a leather thong. An axe is too heavy to grip. Strike out—" and he demonstrated, his hand a blur until he winced and rubbed at his shoulder, "—and you only tire your arm and likely lose the axe. Have you not seen the leather strap tied to my axe when I fight?"

"I expect if I have I was too distracted trying to save my own life."

"Then come and watch tomorrow when I train Will and you will see how to use an axe." He smiled, a light in his eyes at the thought of battle. "With a strap, the axe has a life of its own. It moves itself. All I have to do is think about where I want it to go. Usually into a man's skull or his gut, I admit. So you see, I do not have to be fully restored in order to fight."

"Jorge tells me you have a new theory about the killings." It was clear Belia wanted to change the subject.

"I do, but I need to wait until morning before I can confirm it."

Belia ignored the prevarication and turned to Yusuf, wanting to know what he had been doing since he left them. Will, sitting beside Yusuf, leaned close, wanting to hear the details of every skirmish and battle.

When the meal was finished, Jorge took Yusuf out on some pretext, but Thomas knew they were going to al-Zaki's house and the women there. He couldn't blame Yusuf, nor Jorge, but was surprised when they re-appeared less than half an hour later.

"We were turned away." Outrage coloured Jorge's voice. "Gracia claimed all the girls had gone, but I saw two of them through a window. She lied to us. Why would she lie?"

"Perhaps she wants them for herself and her lover. Who knows." Thomas smiled. "Take him out again if you want, there are clean whores close to the Alkhaz-abah. If Olaf can't return to Gharnatah for a month, Yusuf will re-join his men tomorrow. Let him enjoy a woman while he can."

But they remained in the house for the moment, and later, when the women and children had gone to their beds, Thomas sat with Jorge, Olaf, and Yusuf, together with two flagons of wine, and tried to explain his thoughts. He found the words hard because he was only just beginning to work out what was happening himself.

At the end Yusuf said, "Why would this Durdush be involved? You say he is overall Master of the Guild?"

Thomas nodded, filling his cup again. He had lost count of how many he had drained already.

"Then surely he can simply take this wealth. It is his to control, is it not?"

"But the wealth doesn't belong to him, it belongs to all the individual Guilds."

"These are not normal times," said Yusuf. "If someone doesn't spirit this gold away then it falls to the Spanish. Gods, I would steal it myself if I knew how."

Thomas smiled. "I can probably help with that. I have some theories on the matter."

Jorge leaned forward. For once he had drunk less than Thomas, for once he had held his tongue until now while he listened. "Tell me again who you suspect."

"Woodville." Thomas held up a finger, then a second. "And ... someone else. Durdush, or Padvana, or ... or someone."

"I'm glad to see you have solved the mystery so eloquently. Why Woodville? The man is unlikeable, and English, but that is hardly sufficient reason to accuse him. Besides, is he clever enough?"

"He doesn't have to be clever, only to know others who are. He has the men he brought with him. He won't have dirtied his own hands with any killing when they can do it for him. Diego saw one of them strike the blow that killed al-Zaki. He said there were two men present, one taller. No doubt the other man was Woodville."

"And his companion, Danvers? He must be a part of it, too." Jorge shook his head. "Which is a pity, since I like the man, and he is handsome and, I suspect, willing."

Thomas frowned, more at the accusation than the observation. "It would make sense, but I've spoken with him and always thought him innocent, but how such can be if his master is involved is difficult to believe. So yes, he is likely involved as well, or being used without being aware he is."

"Danvers isn't stupid, but his master is. He would see through any attempt to keep something from him. Unless Woodville is being used by someone else. Do you think his story of a marriage arrangement is true?"

"I have no doubt he's here to discuss a pairing between one of Isabel's daughters and this English prince, but the man is in need of funds, and where better to find them than here in Malaka? It's even been parcelled up ready for him to take."

"Not all of it."

"He wouldn't need all of it. A dozen cases, even half a dozen. Damn, one would be more than he needs. It may be why he's in Malaka talking to Durdush. He claimed it was to foster trade with England, but even Diego could see through that. There can be no trade between England and Malaka once the city falls to the Spanish."

"Unless Spain and England are linked by marriage," said Jorge.

"I would like to talk to Danvers," Thomas said. "The two of us, you to decide if he speaks the truth or not, me to press him. If he is innocent, he might have some suspicion his master is not. If he is not innocent, or confirms Woodville is plotting, we can tell Durdush and let him worry about the Guild's gold. But how we talk to Danvers is a thing not clear to me. No doubt they reside amongst the Spanish while we are locked here inside the city walls. Perhaps Padvana will offer some clue in the morning."

Olaf had fallen asleep. Yusuf looked as if he was about to do the same. Now it was only Thomas and

Jorge, and Thomas knew he couldn't explain exactly why he believed what he did. Could Jorge be right, and his suspicions were based on nothing more than a dislike of Woodville? He needed to link the man to Amreqan and the Coin Guild. Which brought everything back to Cesare Padvana and what information he might bring in the morning.

THIRTY

It was the crash of falling masonry that woke Thomas. He leapt from the bed, on his feet even before his eyes were open. He stood, tense, but there were no cries, no screams. The missile had landed somewhere else in the city, only sounding loud in his dream.

Lubna rolled over, pulling the sheet across herself and mumbling. Thomas watched her for a moment, filled with wonder at the perfection of his wife, filled with a love that threatened to tumble him back into bed and tumble with her. Instead, he dressed and left the room, knowing he had kept her awake too long the night before with conversation and other amusements.

Olaf was already up, sitting at the long table, picking at the remnant of goat from the evening before. He glanced up and grimaced. "Am I really going to help Yusuf overthrow a Sultan?" Olaf shook his head as if in sorrow. "What have I become?"

"The saviour of al-Andalus." Thomas sat across from him and picked up a sliver of meat. It was no better than the night before, but he was hungrier now.

"What if becoming Sultan changes him? Muhammed wasn't so bad until he sat on the hill."

"Muhammed has always been bad. Yusuf isn't like his brother. We helped raise him, you and I, because his father didn't care. He wasn't in line to succeed as Sultan so Yusuf was left to his own devices. The boy has too sweet a soul for politics."

"He is no boy anymore, and I see nothing of the sweet in him anymore."

"You are right, Thomas, I have changed, and not for the better. It is what war does to a man. Not that there is a need to say such to either of you."

Thomas turned to see Yusuf in the doorway.

"How can anyone sleep through all this noise?" Yusuf picked up a piece of meat, sniffed it, and put it back. "And I do not have a sweet soul, Thomas. Not anymore. War has scourged it from me."

"You will find it again. I have to go out to question a man who was meant to come to me. I have a mind to go beat him about the head until he tells me what I want to know."

"Can I come?" asked Olaf. "I am of a mind to beat someone, too. Anyone will do. Does this beating concern the fanciful theory you told us of last night?"

"It does, but best you stay here. You, too." Thomas addressed the last to Yusuf, who was watching with interest. "I'll be back before the others are up. If I manage to find something better to eat — no, something edible — I'll bring it back with me."

The Ataranzana was almost deserted. With the Spanish blocking access from both sea and land there was no trade, and without trade the building was nothing more than a huge, empty shell. Some goods

295

remained in store, but people couldn't eat swords or carts or pots. Thomas felt the gnaw of hunger in his gut and wished he had forced himself to eat some of the goat, disgusting as it had been. Things would come to a worse pass yet, he was sure.

Durdush's office remained empty. It looked deserted, abandoned, a few papers scattered across the floor, shelves mostly empty, and Thomas wondered where the man had gone. He had been busy enough while Malaka thrived, was it not his duty now to steer it through more difficult times? Fernando and Isabel were people who could be dealt with, but on their own terms. Thomas had seen it at Ronda. Anger them and the city would suffer the consequences.

He went to the window and looked out at the stain of soldiers that stretched as far as the eye could see to the west. On the water, a dozen galleys rode a low swell, their oars shipped. They lacked sails, but because of that they were more manoeuvrable, not relying on a fickle wind. Watching them, Thomas realised two or three such galleys would be sufficient to move the cache of wealth stored in the Alkhazabah. Sufficient perhaps, but would they stand any chance of escape? It depended, he supposed, on the wind, its direction, and the determination of those manning the oars.

Another thought came to him. There was a Maritime Guild, concerned with operating and controlling the vast number of ships that sailed to and from Malaka. Its master would be a useful man to know when it came to transporting a vast quantity of gold and silver. He had no idea where those offices might lie, but Padvana would, and he intended to visit him next.

Nobody challenged him, because there was nobody

to do so, as he strode the length of the upper corridor to its far end. He glimpsed a lamp still burning on the desk, but there was no sign of Padvana. Had he left, or gone to join Durdush wherever he might be? Thomas almost didn't bother entering the office but, as he was about to turn away, he glimpsed something that stopped him cold. A hand showed from behind the desk, fingers curled as if trying to burrow into the wooden floor.

Padvana had been dead some time, several hours at least. Thomas knelt and felt the neck even as he knew it was pointless. The body was cooling, beginning to stiffen when Thomas palpated the jaw. In one corner papers had been piled to burn, the air acrid even though any smoke had now dispersed.

He sat back and stared at Padvana's body. Everything was slipping away from him. The Spanish were at the gates, the city was frightened, and someone planned to spirit away a wealth that would allow al-Andalus to fight for another decade. He knew he should give up his quest, for it was hopeless. He should return to Gharnatah alongside Olaf and Yusuf and help them remove Muhammed from the throne, help restore what could be restored.

He knew he ought to examine Padvana's body to discover how he was killed, but that too was pointless. What did it matter?

Thomas wondered if he would survive the coming assault. If they would all survive. And with the thought, he made a decision. Forget the deaths, forget the gold, forget Malaka — it was already lost. Let Woodville succeed in his plotting and enrich himself. He could buy himself new clothes. Thomas would go to Isabel and throw himself on her mercy. She would take him in, his family too. Some of them, in any case. Olaf and Yusuf would have to find their own path to freedom, but Thomas didn't doubt they could do so. The rest of them would seek Isabel's protection.

He felt lighter as he rose and descended to the street. He turned away from his new home and passed through a small gate to the sea's edge, looking for the fishermen he hoped might be there. They often came at dawn, and with luck would sell him some fish, octopus, whatever had been caught. Belia still had a little of the spice Narjis had given them and would make whatever he found edible if not succulent. But the shoreline was empty other than a galley pulled up in the distance beneath the towering wall of the Alkhazabah. Thomas wondered if they were moving the crates already, but it was no longer any of his concern. He cursed, his belly cramping with hunger as he started back toward Diego's house.

Spanish guns began their work once more, iron and stone balls flying overhead to crash into walls, roofs, streets, and squares. Most of the population huddled indoors, seeking a false safety. Few appeared on the streets, so when Thomas saw six men enter from a crossway ahead he assumed they were soldiers on their way to man the walls, until they turned toward him. He saw a short figure at their head, dressed in a leather jerkin, a wide-brimmed hat shading his face against the morning sun. They had come for him. Had they been watching the Ataranzana, expecting him to return, or was this meeting nothing but coincidence? It mattered little. All that mattered was their presence and intent.

Thomas touched his belt, found the hilt of a knife, but he carried no sword, and cursed his stupidity at leaving the house in a hurry. He watched as the men spread out to block the street. Beyond, a woman emerged through a doorway then turned back, slamming it behind her. The men were forty paces away. Thomas smiled and turned around.

Another six stood behind, even closer. Hard men, seasoned soldiers accustomed to battle and killing. Had Woodville used all of them in his plan, or only the short man in the hat? It mattered little. It mattered not at all. Thomas drew his knife and swung his arms. He had thought himself dead many times before, had fought unreasonable odds and managed to survive. He had no doubt he would survive this time, but knew it might prove difficult. He began to walk, hearing the men behind start to follow, saw the men ahead close the gap as he decided who he would kill first. The short man, obviously. It was clear he was their leader, despite his size. A half foot shorter than Thomas, but that meant nothing. Thomas had been smaller than that when he killed his first man. Size counted for nothing. A tall coward would always fall to a brave man with skill, however short they were. A dozen men. Another dozen men who would die today, and Thomas realised he had no idea how many he had killed over the years. More than a hundred, he was sure, but less than a thousand. It was not the kind of count most men kept.

The cold filled him as he yelled and sprinted toward the short man, who grinned, ready for him, sword in one hand, wicked knife gleaming in the other, but Thomas had faced better warriors in the past and the fight barely lasted seconds.

The man swung the sword, over-confident. Thomas ducked, swerved, then buried his knife in the man's side. It was not a killing blow, and as the man jerked away, the knife remained in his body and was pulled from Thomas's grasp.

No matter. He stepped back, twisted, and punched one of the others hard in the face before taking a sword from his limp hand. He sensed rather than saw the short man come at him again, but slower now. The knife had failed to kill him, but it had to be agony, and a hurt man couldn't help but slow down. Then Thomas remembered there were others behind him, alerted to the fact when some of those ahead stepped back as their companions readied to attack.

Thomas threw himself to one side, rolling away. Coming to his feet he placed his back against the city wall, facing the men, who took a moment to organise a fresh attack. It was the time that killed three of them.

Two figures appeared at the end of the street, one tall, the other a giant.

A battle axe hung from a leather thong on Olaf's wrist. Yusuf carried a sword in each hand and a smile on his face. They didn't rush, didn't cry out. Olaf began to swing the axe when he was twenty paces from the rear rank, barely touching the hilt. Instead he used its weight to swing it fast, the blade almost a blur, and Thomas saw what he had meant the night before. Will needed to learn how to fight this way. Olaf was a killing machine. His blade took a man in the back, and he went to his knees. The momentum of the axe carried it around in a wide curve before it struck a second time.

Thomas turned away and began to run as the short man dashed along the street, abandoning his companions to their fate. He was fast, but so was Thomas, despite the fire that started up in his lungs and the lead that filled his legs. The man ran back along the way Thomas had come, heading for the gate to the shore. Had he come from where the galley had been drawn up? Was this the start of their plan to steal the wealth of Malaka? If so it would come to nothing now.

Thomas almost caught him at the Ataranzana, and would have had a stray worker not come pushing a cart through the arches directly into his path. Thomas tried to swerve, but the man kept coming and he crashed into the side of the cart. Beyond he saw the short man glance back and double his effort, extending his lead. Thomas pushed away from the cart and set off once more.

Had the man turned east he might have escaped, but instead he went west. Whether he didn't know about the river, how wide and deep it was, Thomas had no idea, but he found him standing on the bank. He was removing his weapons and tossing them to the ground, knowing if he entered the water with them sheathed their weight would pull him to the bottom. He began to wade into the river, the bed sloping steeply so he floundered, arms thrashing, and Thomas smiled. He waited, knowing the man must either let the water to take him to his death or he had to return to shore. Except he was having trouble getting out of the river, so Thomas waded in to his chest and grabbed the man's jerkin and dragged him out. As he pulled him to the bank, Thomas caught the man and turned him onto his back, knelt on his arms and slapped his face.

Thomas spoke in English, rusty from disuse. "Who is your master? Tell me or you go back in the river, and this time you'll drown."

The man only laughed and spat salt water in Thomas's face.

THIRTY-ONE

"You should have killed him," said Olaf.

They stood on the street where the dozen men had ambushed Thomas. Three bodies had been taken away, the remnant of the attackers fleeing. Blood stained the cobbles. Under normal circumstances someone would already be there to clean it away, but these were not normal times.

"Dead he can't give any answers."

"But you no longer have him," Olaf pointed out. "We could have taken him with us to the house and asked him politely. And then when that failed, I could have persuaded him of his foolishness."

"I wouldn't stain Diego's house in that manner. He's locked up for now and I can question him again later. I'll even consider taking you with me next time, not that it will do much good. He simply stared at me. Didn't say a word. It was as if he knew he was invulnerable."

"Or doesn't care if he lives or dies," said Olaf. "Yes, take me next time and we will see how he fares."

Thomas turned to Yusuf. "Was I wrong? What would you have done?"

"I would have killed him, answers or not."

Thomas looked into Yusuf's eyes and saw the truth of his words, saw how much the boy he had thought he once knew so well had changed.

"I'll get a chance to try again, and when the Spanish come he'll be handed over as a murderer."

"Better ask your questions soon, then," said Yusuf.

Thomas started toward the house. "What made you come after me?"

"We didn't. Olaf was bored. I think he was looking for a fight, hoping some Spanish soldiers would try storming the walls. And then Diego came in and told us you were in danger. Jorge said he had done the same before and we should listen to him."

"How did you know where I would be?"

"We didn't, but Diego told us to come the way we did." Yusuf shook his head, his face serious. "I'm not sure I liked it when his prediction came true. It spooked me, I have to admit."

"He is strange, true enough," Thomas said. "That's twice he has saved my life now."

"You would have managed without us, I'm sure," said Yusuf. This time he smiled and Thomas saw it as a joke. "But it is lucky one of us was Olaf Torvaldsson, and I am no longer the boy who once sat on your knee."

"I noticed."

Will came skidding into the room as soon as they entered the house. He must have heard their voices. He leapt at Thomas, who plucked him from the air and swung him around.

"Where have you been, Pa?" Will clung to him. "Why are you all wet?"

"I fell in the river."

Will laughed and punched Thomas on the chest. "Silly Pa. I want to know how to swim. Diego can't swim. He told me I must learn."

"Why?"

Will shrugged.

"I'll teach you." Thomas watched Yusuf wander away into the main room as he carried Will the other way, climbing stairs to the room he shared with Lubna. He threw a laughing Will onto the empty bed and found clean clothes. He was tired, despite it not being noon yet, and lay beside Will, but his son kept asking questions and jumping on him so he sent him downstairs, sleep coming almost immediately, the sound of the city filtering away to nothing.

When he descended the stairs some hours later, Olaf and Yusuf had taken Will and Diego out, and Belia stood with her arms crossed over her chest and a scowl on her face.

"What have I done now?" Thomas asked.

"I told you I didn't want that man coming back here. And how does he know where we live?" She shook her head in anger, dark hair flying. "Take him to the Infirmary, I'll not have him here."

"Mandana?" Thomas said. "When did he come?"

"Now, a few moments since. He asked for Lubna but she refused to treat him. Do it and send him away. And no more, Thomas, this is the end of it."

"I'll tell him. Where is he?"

"In the courtyard. I told him he couldn't come inside. I won't have him tainting our house."

"You have the ointments?"

"Lucky for you that I do."

"No. Lucky for Mandana. I will end it today, I promise."

"Promises, that's all I ever get. I want action." But Belia turned away to fetch the lotions Thomas would need for Mandana.

He was waiting in the courtyard, talking to Jorge. Mandana offered a smile, or as close to a smile as he could raise. He offered one so infrequently his face had no doubt forgotten the art.

"Show me your arm." Thomas was abrupt, in no mood for small talk. He drew Mandana's sleeve up as the man held the stump of his left hand out. "Is there pain?"

"You ask me that every time, and my answer is the same every time."

"More than usual? Less?"

"It is better for your friend's cream, but there are good days and bad days."

Thomas poked at the mottled flesh with his fingers, wrapped his hand around the stump and squeezed. He watched Mandana's face for any reaction. There were times he wondered why he did this for him after what he had inflicted on so many people, but there appeared to have been a genuine change in the man over the last few years. He was still a killer, but now he killed only for a reason, and when ordered. Thomas wondered if the change was caused by Mandana being reconciled with his own son now. He appeared to comment on Will often enough to make it seem likely.

Thomas poured a little of the thick liquid into his

palm and applied it to the stump. He could feel a nub of bone sharp beneath the skin.

"Does it get hot or inflamed?"

"Not as much as it did. I told your friend she is a worker of miracles."

"Indeed she is. Are you with Fernando's forces?"

"I do his bidding, but my small band works away from the main army now, as well you know."

Thomas wasn't sure he knew the exact nature of the work. He recalled the few times he had seen Mandana and his men, the rump of those soldier-monks who remained with him, a small group now but deadly. He had glimpsed them once before the siege of Ronda. Again on a hillside beyond the dry river bed as Thomas made his way back from Auta fort.

Thomas finished applying the cream and wiped his hands in a cloth.

"Why did you move from that magnificent house on the hillside?" Mandana looked around at the room. "This place is fit enough for purpose, but it is just one more house among a thousand."

"It might have something to do with your friends surrounding Malaka."

Thomas noticed Jorge had gone to stare through the side door which led to the street, perhaps looking for Mandana's companions, perhaps searching for beautiful women.

"They are no threat to you. There are few among Fernando's army who are not aware of the relationship you have with him and the Queen. In particular the Queen. Is it not so?"

Thomas opened a small pot and poured the rest of the cream into it, encouraging the last reluctant drops with a wooden spill before stoppering the top. He handed the pot to Mandana.

"Use it the same as before. At least once a day, more if you can."

"I will see you again in forty days," said Mandana.

"No."

Mandana stared, his grey eyes cold, still the look of the wolf about him, but an old wolf now, a sick wolf. Thomas knew sick wolves were often the most dangerous.

"Your friend then, the exotic one. I would like her to rub lotion into my skin."

"No." It was Jorge who spoke without turning around.

Mandana stood and re-tied his robe, which had been laundered in the recent past. He looked almost respectable.

"How did you get into the city?" Thomas asked. "We are under siege, or hadn't you noticed?"

"I told them I was coming to see you, of course. Your name is known far and wide. The great Sir Thomas Berrington. And if I was refused there are other ways. You know there are."

A noise came from the street, laughter, shouts, and then the noise invaded the house and Thomas turned in time to scoop Will up as he ran toward him. His son clung to him, smelling of gunpowder and dust. Thomas looked at Olaf, who came in favouring his right side until he saw Mandana present and straightened up, refusing to show any hint of weakness in front of the man.

"We got meat, Pa," said Will. "*Morfar* got us meat."

"You took them too close to the wall, didn't you," Thomas said.

"They wanted to see the Spanish. And that's where you buy meat, close to the wall."

"You're a target, don't you realise that? Half the Spanish army know who you are, and every single man would take pride in bringing down the Sultan's great general."

"But they did not. We were outside no time at all, and see, I am home unharmed."

"This time. Don't take the boys again."

"They wanted to go. Besides, it does them good. A boy will become a man, and needs to know what becoming a man means." Olaf smiled and ruffled Diego's hair. "All except this one." He glanced toward Mandana. "I take it he is leaving?"

"He is."

Mandana nodded. Thomas accompanied him as far as the street, where he saw two robed men at the far end waiting for their master.

"I thank you, Thomas Berrington," said Mandana. "If there is anything I can do in return you need only ask. If it is in my power to grant, it will be done."

"I don't suppose you can stop this war, can you?" Thomas's mood had improved, a weight removed from him by capturing the killer, still curious as to who his master was, though he had a suspicion. He would go to question him again later and press to find out his master's name. He wanted a confirmation it was Woodville, though what good that would do he wasn't sure of. He wondered if he could go to Fernando and tell him what the man was plotting.

"I said something within my power," said Mandana.

"Have you seen your son recently? It is a hard thing to lose a wife."

"He still blames you for it, I'm afraid. I told him you would have done all you could, but sons do not often listen to a father's advice. I am sure you know that well enough." Mandana turned away, but Thomas called him back.

"One more question. Do you know of a man by the name of Woodville?"

Mandana laughed. "A countryman of yours, I believe. Yes, I have heard the name, but not met him. Why?"

"I wondered what had brought him to Spain."

"What brings all men to war? Money. Position. Power. A man can obtain all three if he fights well, and survives, of course."

"Woodville doesn't strike me as a man who fights well."

"He has a title, I understand, which means he will have others who perform the fighting for him, while he takes the majority of the spoils. I hear tell he has a companion who knows how to fight, and a small band of men he brought with him. It is the way of the world, you know it is, and nothing wrong with that. Is there anything else?"

"You're sure you haven't met him?"

Mandana shook his head. "I told you I have not."

"Or any of his men?"

"How would I know if I had? Do they wear some distinctive uniform?"

"No."

"Well, then." Mandana turned, and this time Thomas let him go. He watched as he greeted the two men, who glanced along the street to stare at Thomas before taking up position either side of their master.

Thomas's path to the Infirmary took him the same way Mandana had gone, but he saw no sign of him or his men. He became aware of the stink of gunpowder in the air. The sound of cannon fire had grown so frequent he had filtered it out, for to obsess on the noise could drive a man mad.

Lubna looked tired when he found her, hands already stained with blood, her clothes tainted with that and worse. As he approached, the soldier she was working on reared up from the table he was meant to be strapped to and swung a fist at her. Thomas moved fast, but not fast enough to prevent a blow which slammed into her chest and sent her to the floor. Then he was there, forcing the man down, pulling at the linen ties that someone had neglected to tie or knotted too quickly. It was not the soldier's fault, but even so Thomas made no attempt to be gentle and the man cried out.

Thomas turned to help Lubna but she was already on her feet, her face set with determination.

"Move away, I haven't finished with him yet." She tugged at the linen strips Thomas had tied and nodded, then picked up the thin tongs she had dropped and pushed them into the wound in the soldier's side. He screamed, but Lubna ignored the cry, as she ignored the struggling of his body. Her hand followed his movements to keep the instrument in place, then she grunted, squeezed hard, and drew out a round ball of iron. She dropped it into a bucket where it made a small splash. She turned away and crossed the crowded room to where a small brazier burned. Metal rods with wooden handles rested in glowing coals. She picked one up and returned. There was no hesitation as she thrust the iron into the wound in the soldier's side, and this time mercy came to throw him into a faint.

"You need to rest." Thomas caught her arm as she started to turn. "And I should check where he hit you."

"I am fine," said Lubna. She raised her gaze and stared at him. "And the baby is fine. There is too much work here. You would do better to help rather than examine a fit woman." She moved away in search of another patient, leaving the soldier's wound to be stitched by one of the helpers. Thomas watched for a moment, a thrill running through him. She had turned into a fine surgeon, and the softness he had feared would limit her ability was no longer present. He nodded to himself and went in search of someone he could help.

The next time there came a moment's respite he was surprised to discover night had fallen. Still the Spanish cannon barked, still wounded men, women, and children were brought in. Thomas went to where they arrived and took up his usual position as first man, filtering those who could be helped, turning aside those with minor injuries, ushering those who wouldn't live to a place where they could be cared for until their time came.

At some point Lubna brought him food and they ate standing in the courtyard, both barely awake, both knowing more work remained to be done. Lubna leaned against him and he saw how tired she was.

Became aware of how tired he was. He washed his hands at a trough, kissed her, and went back to work.

Dawn came, and with it a lessening in the numbers arriving at the Infirmary. Thomas found Lubna and had to almost drag her away.

"You don't have to do it all yourself," he said, surprised when she laughed. "What?"

"How many times have I said those same words to you?"

He scowled. "How many times have I listened to them?"

She held up a single finger, then folded it down to nestle between the others, and he laughed too.

The streets were cool in the grey morning light. A group of soldiers passed, Gomeres, and Thomas searched their ranks for Usaden but didn't see him. At the house, he allowed Lubna to wash first, then stood naked in the bedroom and tried to remove the stain of war from himself.

When he turned toward the bed, Lubna was almost asleep, but she turned her head to him, eyes still closed. "Go fetch Will, I'll sleep better if he's with us."

He nodded. She was right. His presence would help banish the memories both of them carried from their work that night. Diego was alone in the bed he usually shared with Will, the other one unused. Will wasn't with Olaf either, as he sometimes was, so Thomas slipped into Jorge's room.

Jorge grumbled and rolled to his side, but refused to wake. It was Belia who sat up, drawing the covers to hide her nakedness.

"Did you want something?"

"I was looking for Will."

"Why? Did you lose him?"

Thomas frowned, failing to understanding. "I left him here, and he's nowhere to be found. If he–"

"You sent a message for him to come to you. I thought it odd, but Yusuf said you knew the woman, as did he."

"What woman?" Thomas moved farther into the room. He stared through the window to avoid looking at Belia, half expecting to see Will standing in the street, but it was empty. "Who are you talking about?"

"The woman with the harem. Gracia — is that her name?"

Thomas let his breath out, unaware he had been holding it. "You let Will go into the night alone … with a stranger? With war raging? Are you mad?"

"I told you, he did not go on his own. That woman came, the wife of the dead man. The one who made the mistake of moving back into his house. She said you and Lubna were with her and would stay the night because her house is closer to the Infirmary. And that you wanted Will."

Thomas stared at Belia.

"Will knew her and went quite happily. Diego wanted to go too, but she told him he could not. Are you sure he isn't somewhere else in that house? Where did you and Lubna sleep?"

"We were never there. We've been at the Infirmary all day and night and came directly back here."

THIRTY-TWO

Thomas returned to their bedroom, but Lubna had already fallen into a deep sleep. He watched her for a moment, conflicted whether to wake her or not, then padded away on bare feet. Lubna didn't need to know what had happened until he had checked for himself, though he could see no innocent reason for Gracia taking him. He dressed quickly and woke Jorge instead, knowing he would need him.

As they made their way through almost empty streets, the bark of a lone cannon came. The crash of stone on stone followed a moment later as the corner of a house in the next street tilted, then clattered into the roadway to send up a billowing cloud of dust.

"He will be there, and we will bring him back," said Jorge.

"Did nobody think to question the woman? Why would we have sent for him in the middle of the night instead of walking the extra half mile to our own house?"

"Gracia said you wanted him with you, that you would sleep better with him at your side."

The explanation was so close to what Lubna had asked that Thomas saw how it might have persuaded them. But not why the two of them would have stayed at Gracia's house instead of walking the extra half mile home.

"What if we get there and the house is a pile of rubble? Damn al-Tagri — why doesn't he bow to the inevitable and surrender? Things will go worse for everyone the longer he continues this foolish stubbornness."

A group of people crossed the roadway ahead of them, a man with his two wives and five children. He carried one of the children, injured, in his arms. They disappeared toward the Infirmary without looking either way, for which Thomas was grateful. Had they asked for help he would have had to turn them down.

The house of Zufar al-Zaki appeared untouched, the turreted roof catching the rays of the rising sun. *This is the house where everything started*, Thomas thought, and a fear ran through him that it might be the place where everything came full circle with another death. He pushed the fear aside, but it came harder to him than it usually did because he couldn't bear the thought of losing Will. His chest hitched, and when Jorge turned to him, Thomas bit the inside of his cheek, his expression closed down.

The remnant of al-Zaki's harem were still asleep, but not for long. One glance at Thomas and the three women clustered toward Jorge, but for once he offered no better comfort and they milled together, clutching at one another.

"It's not you I want," Thomas said. "Where is Gracia?"

It took some time before any of them responded, and then the eldest was pushed forward.

"She went out."

"With my son?"

The woman frowned. "She left with a man. Is your son tall and good-looking?" She looked Thomas up and down and decided he might indeed be father to the man she had seen.

"He has four years, almost five. Did Gracia know the man she left with?"

A nod. "Yes. He has visited her before."

"What time did they go out?"

The woman's eyes searched a corner of the room before coming back to Thomas, but she wouldn't meet his gaze, staring at Jorge instead. "I was asleep but was woken by them arguing. I didn't want to go downstairs, so watched from the balcony."

"Arguing about what?"

"I don't know, they spoke Spanish. It looked like the man wanted Gracia to do something, and she was reluctant. In the end, he grabbed her arm and dragged her outside. I came downstairs when I was sure they were not coming back and looked through the window. I saw them at the end of the street."

"Going which way?" Thomas asked.

"Uhm ... that way?" She pointed, and Thomas had to work out the direction. It would have taken them to Diego's house if they walked far enough. Which they obviously had. He wished he had never brought his family into Malaka but kept them all on the hillside where they could have taken their chances with the

Spanish, but it was too late now and he had to deal with the consequences.

Will had been taken, that much was clear, and he believed he knew who else was involved other than Gracia.

"Did you hear a name? Anything?"

The spokeswoman shook her head. "But Olivia might know."

The name sparked a barely remembered memory, and it came slowly to Thomas that the woman spoke of Gracia's companion.

"Where is she?"

"I am here."

Thomas turned and saw her standing on the stairs. She wore a nightdress, one hand on the bannister. Thomas glanced at the young women still clustered around Jorge, then went to Olivia and grasped her arm. She cried out in alarm, but he dragged her up the stairs and then stopped, uncertain.

"Where is your room?"

"You are hurting me."

"And will hurt you more if you don't answer. Your room!"

She pointed with her free hand. Thomas pulled her inside and threw her to the bed. Olivia sprawled across the covers, eyes wide, and Thomas realised she feared he was about to rape her and took a step backwards.

"I have been told Gracia left with a man. Did you see him? Do you know him?"

Olivia shook her head. She was starting to regain her composure and sat up, arranging pillows behind herself and crossing her legs. "I woke when I heard your voice downstairs, but Gracia didn't disturb me if she left.

You're sure she has gone and isn't somewhere in the house?"

Thomas walked from the room and went to the top of the stairs. "Jorge!"

He waited until he appeared, one young woman still clinging to his arm.

"Ask them if the man knocked on the door or was Gracia expecting him." He returned to the room. "You expect me to believe you heard nothing and saw nothing?"

She smiled.

"But you know who the man is, don't you."

Thomas didn't know if he spoke the truth or not until he saw Olivia's smile fade. He crossed the room, hesitated, then sat at the foot of the bed, pleased when she didn't withdraw. Her eyes tracked his face, wary. From below the sound of the young women rose, a faint background chittering, and he knew if someone had come knocking on the door in the middle of the night it would have woken Olivia and Gracia both.

"She didn't mean for anyone to die," said Olivia, and a sudden fear ran through Thomas. He noted she had said *she* not *we*. Did that mean Olivia was nothing more than an innocent bystander? Except there could be no such thing, not if she knew of what was happening. Her duty would be to tell the authorities.

"Tell me how it started." Thomas tried to keep his voice soft, thinking of how Jorge might do this, and thought he almost succeeded.

"We needed money," she said. "What Zufar gave us couldn't feed a cat, let alone two women."

"What Zufar gave you? I don't understand. I thought he refused any divorce settlement."

Olivia smiled, a sly gesture. "Did you think he could give her up completely? Oh, those girls look pretty, but they lack the experience of two mature women." Once more the smile came.

Thomas thought she might have expected some show of shock from him, but if so she wasn't aware of what Jorge had shown him was possible between men and women, and more besides.

"He came to you ... where, in Ballix?"

"Always in Ballix. It wasn't as if we were whores. Not at the start. He left us small gifts. Sometimes very small gifts. As I said, not enough to live on. So really this is all his fault. Everything that happened is that man's fault."

"Why did Gracia allow him into your bed? He disrespected her by not honouring the divorce settlement. She told me she hated him. I believed her then, and I still believe her now."

"If she had not done so we would have starved."

"Who instigated these assignations? Zufar or Gracia?"

"Gracia went to him demanding money. She went without me, and when she came back she was different. I could tell something had happened. She had money but she wouldn't tell me how she had obtained it, not until later than night when we were in bed. Zufar had demanded sex. They fought. She told me he forced her, but I was never sure if that was the truth or not. But he gave her money again, later. Not much, guilt money no doubt. A month passed before she sent him a message telling him if he wanted he could lie with us both."

"How often did he..."

"Once a month, sometimes more. Whenever business took him to Ballix, or past it. Most routes east and north pass the town, and Zufar was much occupied with Guild business." Her eyes met Thomas, a challenge in them. "What he gave us each time he came was still not enough to live on."

"You could have worked."

"Gracia was used to a life of ease. Besides, if he was willing to pay us we were happy to service him." She smiled. "It rarely took long, not with the two of us working together. And then one day he brought a companion."

"The same man Gracia went with tonight?"

"I was asleep, I told you that."

"Of course you were. Who was the man Zufar brought to you?"

"His name was Woodville. Richard Woodville. A countryman of yours." Olivia tilted her head to one side. "Are you a skilled lover? Richard was exceptionally so. Are all Englishmen as skilled? He could–"

Thomas interrupted. "What did you tell him?" He had no wish to hear the details of what they did with Woodville. The man's presence only confirmed what he already knew. Woodville was here to enrich himself as well as forge a marriage.

"We didn't know it would end as it did."

"I'm sure you didn't. Your secret is out now, so tell me what you told him."

"Zufar liked to boast. About his wealth. About the wealth of the Guild. And then, when it was clear the Spanish were coming, about the untold riches that were being gathered in the Alkhazabah, and how he was going to take some portion of it for himself. He had a plan, though I never heard what it was, only that there was one."

Thomas stared at the headboard beside Olivia, trying to work out the connections, the significance, and failing.

"Explain to me. Assume I'm stupid."

Olivia's expression showed she didn't doubt it.

"Zufar brought Richard to us, introduced him. He made us a gift to the man. He thought he was being clever, but Richard talked too. He told us Zufar went to him with his plan to steal some of the Guild's gold when it was being moved. He said it was safe, and so simple to accomplish whoever meant to move the gold was a fool. But then Zufar got a letter from his clerk." She waved a hand. "Miguel something, he said, I have no other name. It threatened him."

"How do you know about the letter? Why would Zufar tell you of it?"

"Not Zufar, Richard. He was coming to us more and more often by then, and liked to impress us with how bad he was. It was him who told us Zufar had been sent a letter and was afraid they were about to be exposed, but that he had taken care of the matter."

"Did he say how?"

"No, only that they were safe now."

"Did he say what was in the letter?" Thomas was sure it would be the one Diego's father had written, making accusations against Izem Amreqan, unaware his own master was also part of the plot.

"Richard only said the letter threatened to expose them, that is all. He said Zufar had tried to calm the situation but failed. Richard said he had taken care of things. He boasted of it without saying how, but then Zufar died and we both knew. He had killed them to keep the plot from being exposed. We were afraid, but it was too late by then, so we kept quiet so he wouldn't kill us too. He had Izem Amreqan killed, I am sure. It was him the accusation had been made against, not Zufar, but they were all a part of it. Other than the man who wrote the letter, but he was silenced too." She laughed, but there was no trace of humour in the sound. "Richard was pleased because everyone thought the man had died of natural causes ... he hadn't realised this Miguel had talked with his wife, so she had to be taken care of. And then, of course, Zufar knew a secret and had to be silenced as well." She breathed out sharply and her face crumpled, as if only now realising the enormity of what they had done. When she looked up, unshed tears glistened in her eyes. "Are you going to kill me now?"

"Kill you? Why would I kill you?"

"Because Gracia said you are part of the plot. Two Englishman working together to steal Moorish gold." Her gaze flickered to a side cabinet, came back fast. "She has a letter I am to send to Ali Durdush if anything happens to her. She showed it to me. It names those involved, and your name is there."

"Woodville has Will," Thomas said. He walked fast beside Jorge as they made their way from al-Zaki's house. He had explained what Olivia had told him, explained what conclusions he had drawn from the information, and now they were almost home. "They'll have taken Will out of the city. Woodville will have made camp close to Isabel and Fernando, somewhere out there." He waved a hand in the vague direction of the city wall. "We can find him."

"Go into the Spanish camp?"

"Can you think of any other way to rescue my son?"

As they turned into the street, Thomas caught sight of a man kneeling in front of their door and broke into a run. The man heard the sound of his boots and turned, sprinting away fast. Thomas chased him as far as the alleys which wound against the western city wall next to the Ataranzana before deciding he had lost him for good. By the time he returned to the house, everyone was standing in the street outside.

"Did you find him?" Lubna's eyes were circled with dark bruises of exhaustion, but Thomas knew she wouldn't sleep until Will was returned to them.

"No, but I know who has taken him."

Lubna punched his chest. "So why are you not going after them? Why are you standing here?"

"Because we need to prepare."

"Will has been taken!" She screamed the words at him, her fists pummelling against him. "Our son has been taken."

Diego came to stand beside them, a hand reaching out to Lubna. "Will," he said.

"He's not here. Go back to bed and you will see him soon."

"A woman took him." Diego's expression appeared to have lost all the softness it usually possessed. Even his speech was clearer. "But it is all right, Thomas. He is unharmed. He will be safe until tomorrow."

Thomas turned toward Olaf. "Is Usaden inside?" The Gomeres had been lodging with them ever since they came to the city.

"As far as I know. I haven't seen him leave."

"Go fetch him, I need him to do something. You as well if you are willing."

"Of course I am willing." Olaf turned and went into the house.

"If it is fighting you want then I come too," said Yusuf. "For Will. For you. You know that, Thomas."

"What I plan will be fast and fierce and dangerous, and I dare not risk you among the Spanish. I have another task for you if you will do it. We all meet inside to make a plan, as soon as I've seen what that man was doing."

Thomas approached the smaller doorway he had seen the man kneeling at, cautious as he came closer. He had heard of the Spanish carrying small parcels of gunpowder armed with fuses. They would light them, then throw the entire thing into the enemy. But he could see nothing obvious as he knelt. Then he caught sight of the corner of a sheet of paper and reached for it.

He pulled out a note. A ransom note, of a kind. Written in English, which only confirmed Woodville had composed it, though there was no signature or seal, only the words scratched with a damaged nib so the ink had splashed and scattered around the lines.

We have your son. Stop looking into matters that are none of your concern and he will be returned to you safely in three days' time. Continue and he will be returned piece by piece.

THIRTY-THREE

"Get away from us!" Thomas pushed at the holy man al-Antiqamun, but he continued to prance around them. He reeked, both his body and the rags that clothed him. His hair was knotted, and Thomas tried to keep a distance between them, afraid of what might inhabit it.

"You go to kill Spanish, yes? I will help. I will curse them. I will call down Allah's holy fire on their heathen heads. Antiqamun come too, Thomas Berrington."

Thomas turned to Usaden, who stood impassive in front of the heavy Ataranzana gate. Behind him another score of Gomeres showed no more emotion than he did, not even the tell-tale tremor of fingers or tapping of toes normally seen before going into battle. These men were cut of sterner stuff than others.

"You explained what was needed?"

Usaden nodded.

"And they know they may not come back?"

Usaden smiled. "We will come back, all of us. We are Gomeres. And if we do not then we die willingly, for

325

your son. Besides, it will be an honour to see him fight." He glanced to where Olaf stood, an axe hanging from one hand, a shield gripped in the other. He had painted his face blue with a dye Belia had prepared for him, the whites of his eyes standing out in the darkness.

Hours had passed before they were ready. Lubna had disappeared, still angry at Thomas for not dashing to Will's immediate rescue.

"Is he recovered enough?" Usaden leaned close so no-one else could hear.

"He claims he is."

"But you are the physician."

"And he is Olaf Torvaldsson." Thomas didn't believe any other explanation was needed. He had seen how fearsome Olaf could be when he attacked the men in the street. He glanced at the sky, full dark now, the moon dipping toward the western horizon. "It is time to go."

"Yes. It is time." Usaden waved a hand and four of the Gomeres released the heavy boards holding the gate shut, but they didn't swing it wide yet. Instead it allowed them to open a smaller door. The men stepped through without a sound, without looking back.

Thomas glanced at Jorge and saw his hand clenched at his chest. He touched his shoulder but said nothing, and Jorge nodded. He would do this for love. Love of Will, love of Lubna, and love of Thomas, who wondered at what exact moment the two of them had become so close. It had crept up so slowly he could identify no particular moment in time, only the accumulation of days, months, and years that had brought a realisation of how much they relied on each other. They had become inseparable. Brothers.

He stepped away and followed the Gomeres, knowing Jorge would be right behind.

Beyond the door a wide wooden bridge arched above the Wadi al-Medina to where a second gate lay, built into a stone tower. The bridge was empty, their boots sounding too loud as they crossed it. At the far side half a dozen guards stood sentry, but at the approach of the Gomeres they began the process of unlatching a doorway like the one they had already passed through.

"What is happening beyond?" Usaden asked.

"There are a few men, but not many. Now and then someone tries to raise a ladder and we fire arrows at them. Go through fast and go through hard. May Allah be with you."

Usaden glanced at his companions, but his gaze rested longer on Thomas and Jorge.

"You are sure of this?"

"Of course," Thomas said.

"We will try to give you an hour, but more likely it will be less."

"A quarter hour will suffice. Once we are among them we'll be safe enough." He and Jorge had dressed as Spanish soldiers, picking out the clothes from a stack taken from dead attackers. Thomas's outfit was tight, Jorge's even more so, but Belia had unpicked the seams and made them a little more comfortable. Thomas had thought the day would pass in an agony of impatience, but it seemed to have flown by in an instant so much needed to be done.

Usaden turned away and nodded to the sentries. As the door was pulled open they ran through. Other men might shout and scream to frighten the enemy. The Gomeres ran in silence, their swords doing all the talking needed.

A group of Spanish sat on the banks of the river, getting to their feet only slowly, some not even rising to their knees before sharp steel stole their lives.

Thomas and Jorge followed at the rear, deliberately hanging back.

Olaf walked rather than ran, his axe whistling about his head at the end of its leather strap, his shield clattering as Spanish swords swung at him. He was unhurried, a bringer of mayhem in the darkness. A Northman.

Al-Antiqamun stood amongst the confusion, arms held aloft as he called down Allah's fire on the heathens. It was even possible that for him flames did fill the sky. For some reason, nobody tried to kill him.

Thomas grinned, but it was a rictus of anger. He wanted to join the others, to stab and cut and wound, but knew he couldn't indulge himself. Later, perhaps, once they had freed Will. Show the boy what war was really about. A lesson that might cure some of his aggression, or might not. A brief memory came to Thomas of his first experience of battle, and how he had pissed himself in fear. But that had been long ago and far away, and he had learned since to love the chaos of war. Except tonight he turned his back on the melee.

He parried a thrust from a Spaniard and ran past him, trusting Jorge would be close behind. South along the river bank until they came to dark volcanic sand, then west, the sound of waves on their left.

Thomas stopped after a quarter mile, trying to drag breath into his lungs. Beside him Jorge did the same. The Spanish camp slept. From a distance of three or four hundred paces came the sound of metal on metal and the screams of dying men, ignored by those asleep in tents or laid on the ground around fires that had burned to little more than embers. Such attacks were common on both sides, and the army knew to ignore everything other than the orders of their King. Which is what Thomas was relying on. He started off once more, working his way through the sleeping men, the pair of them nothing more than two soldiers returning from the latrine pits or the whores who would have set up camp nearby.

He picked his way carefully, moving west, always west, until they were almost at the rear of the camp of over ten thousand men, knowing that the tents of the nobles would lie as far from the city wall as possible. Somewhere close to here, Fernando slept, or sat awake making plans. Thomas wondered if Isabel had joined him. He knew she was not afraid of the field of battle, and that her presence improved the morale of her soldiers far more than did her husband's.

"I take it you have a plan," said Jorge.

"Wherever they've taken him will be close to Woodville." Thomas's eyes scanned a darkness lit by the glow of fires, one or two lamps raised on poles illuminating grey canvas.

"Why would he keep him so close?"

"Because it's what I would do. It gives him control, and power."

Jorge shook his head. "I still don't see it. He is a friend to Fernando, an important man. His niece is married to the English King. Why risk all of that?"

"He has titles, but my father always said a title doesn't put food on the table. He needs money. He needs the wealth of Malaka, or at least a part of it. That's what all this is about. The killings to silence men. He intends to steal the Guild's gold."

"Not possible," said Jorge. "You saw the tower it's held in, the way it's guarded day and night, and the escape tunnel. If he thinks he can get his hands on that he's a bigger fool than I already take him for."

"It can be done."

Jorge laughed, hand over his mouth to cover the sound. "Believe what you will. So where will we find Woodville?"

Thomas nodded to where a large tent stood apart from the others. "That will be Isabel and Fernando. Woodville will be close. There ... or there ..." He pointed to other fine tents, each with banners snapping in a strong breeze that carried the sharp odour of rotting fish. The army would need to net vast quantities to feed themselves, and the waste must be somewhere nearby.

As he surveyed the shadowed camp, the sound of a man's shout carried clear through the night. A familiar voice, and then a familiar figure. Al-Antiqamun ran ahead of a group of soldiers, his tattered robes fluttering behind. He might have escaped, if that indeed was his intention, but another group intercepted his path and he ran straight into them.

"Madman," said Jorge. "If he's not careful he'll wake the whole camp and we'll be captured too."

"Fernando will free us if we are." Thomas watched a scuffle as the soldiers tried to hold onto al-Antiqamun without getting any closer than they had to, which was not a simple task. A conversation appeared to be taking place, and after several minutes four men led al-Antiqamun away toward one of the finer tents.

"Where are they taking him?" said Jorge. "That's not Fernando's tent."

"It's not. But it might be Woodville's." Thomas took a few steps into the camp. Men had woken but were beginning to settle again now, soldiers able to sleep at any time. Thomas followed narrow trails that wound through camp fires and sleeping men, the stench of unwashed bodies mixing with the smoke. A crescent of the low-hanging moon offered barely enough light to pick a way through.

Al-Antiqamun was being dragged through the entrance of the tent and Thomas moved faster. He arrived at one side and leaned close, listening for voices within. He recognised one only slowly, because al-Antiqamun was speaking in Spanish, a skill he had never shown before.

"... have news for their graces," said al-Antiqamun. "There is a way to gain entrance to the city, a place where a thousand men might pass undetected. And I will tell only the King."

"The King is busy. Tell me and I will pass your message on."

"Ask these men to loose me first."

"I won't do that."

"Then I cannot tell you what I know. It is a shame. This siege could end tomorrow."

The soldier laughed. "It ends tomorrow anyway, madman."

Jorge pulled at Thomas's sleeve, but he jerked his arm away.

"He's not your killer," Jorge whispered, his mouth against Thomas's ear.

"Let's wait a little longer and see what happens." Thomas stepped away from the tent, unwilling to continue their conversation in whispers. He walked two dozen paces, a dozen more, then stopped beside another fine tent from which came no sound.

"Have you forgotten your son so easily?" said Jorge.

"Diego said he wouldn't be harmed tonight."

"Diego? You put too much faith in that boy's mysterious powers. It's not like you."

"Has he been wrong yet?"

"One earth shaking and a ring, some trick with dice, and the ring was likely nothing more than some shiny thing he wanted. You know who we seek isn't afraid to cut, or take a life."

"Will is five years old," Thomas said, as if that fact alone offered protection, but even as he spoke he knew whoever had taken his son wouldn't care if he was five months old. Yet he also believed Diego, but didn't know why.

He started walking again, away from where al-Antiqamun was pleading his case. Except as he began to pick his way toward the other well-appointed tent, shouts came from behind and he turned back.

Al-Antiqamun came sprinting from the entrance of the tent, robes once more flying. Without hesitation he headed directly toward the largest tent on this side of the gathered army. His poor excuses for captors came out behind, one of them clutching his arm, and even in the dark Thomas saw blood trailing from the man's fingers.

Al-Antiqamun reached the tent and tossed aside a

sleepy guard who stood at the entrance. Thomas began to run, back the way they had come, uncaring if Jorge chose to accompany him or not. If al-Antiqamun posed a threat to Isabel or Fernando he had to be stopped. It was a clever plan, and showed more cunning that he would have given the madman credit for.

He reached the entrance before the Spanish soldiers, who came more slowly, and dashed inside. Thomas cried out. A well-dressed woman stood with her back to him and at first he took her for Isabel, the man beside her Fernando. Then he saw the woman's hair was dark, curling and long, and the man was taller than the Spanish King. Not that al-Antiqamun knew that. His momentum carried him at the man, a knife raised above his head.

He slashed out with more intent than purpose and landed a blow that parted the fine cloth on the man's chest, but drew only a shallow wound before Thomas reached them. He leapt at al-Antiqamun, landed on his back and wrapped his legs around him, grasping his wrist as the knife began to descend again.

The dark-haired woman screamed. The well-dressed noble cursed and clutched a hand to his chest, the pain of the wound hiding the fact it was not life threatening.

Thomas twisted al-Antiqamun's wrist to dislodge the knife. He released his legs and regained his feet, spun the man around and punched him hard on the side of the head.

Al-Antiqamun laughed, and then the soldiers arrived.

Thomas stepped back so they could arrest the man again, but instead two of them drew their swords and slashed at the mad preacher until he dropped to his knees. One of them stepped close, placed the tip of his bloodied sword against al-Antiqamun's shoulder and pressed down.

Arms grasped Thomas, one to either side, and the man who had delivered the killing blow turned to him, a smile on his face.

THIRTY-FOUR

"This man is Thomas Berrington, friend to your King!" Jorge stood inside the entrance to the tent, as if unwilling to commit himself in case the soldiers turned on him too. Not that he would stand much of a chance if they did, wherever he stood.

"And I'm the Pope," said the soldier with the bloodied sword. He took another step toward Thomas, who had relaxed so that those who held him had in turn relaxed their own grip.

"In that case, your holiness, you will no doubt show him mercy."

"The mercy of a blade." The man turned the tip of his sword, exploring the places he might strike. Here ... or here? Wherever he chose it would be a killing blow, Thomas had no doubt.

The dark-haired woman came close, stepping between Thomas and the soldier. "This man is innocent. He saved the life of Don Alvaro, and no doubt my life as well." She glanced toward Thomas, dark eyes alive with something, the excitement of death, the joy of contin-

uing to draw breath. "Let him loose, for the man is a
hero and should be rewarded."

Just what I need, thought Thomas, *an admirer.* He
tested the grip of those holding him, but served only to
remind them he was meant to be held prisoner.

"I have heard mention of your name, sir," said the
woman. "Sir Thomas, they call you, the King and
Queen. I hear you are friend to the English King Henry,
and an important man in your country." Her voice, until
now soft, hardened into a tone of command, someone
used to being obeyed. "Now unhand him!"

Thomas thought she had confused him with
Woodville, but it didn't matter because miraculously the
men released their hold.

Thomas shook his shoulders, stared into the eyes of
the man who had been ready to spit him. The soldier
took a step back and glanced at his sword, as if seeing it
for the first time. He shook his head and sheathed the
weapon. He looked toward Jorge, who had come a few
more paces inside.

"Is it true he is friend to King Fernando?"

Jorge nodded. "And the Queen. But we will make no
mention of this matter, for you did well to kill the
madman. That is all anyone needs to know."

"No, it is not," Thomas said. He stared at the man in
front of him. "I seek another Englishman, one by the
name of Woodville. Do you know where he is?"

"The name only," said the soldier, "but not where he
makes his camp." His companions moved past him,
picked up the body of al-Antiqamun, and dragged it
away.

"I know of who you speak." The woman came close
and touched Thomas's arm. She glanced toward Jorge,

back to Thomas, as if trying to make a decision between them. For once, against all past experience, she chose Thomas.

This is all I need, he thought, hoping Jorge would turn up his charm and distract her. Her companion had unbuttoned his vest and shirt to examine the slash across his chest.

"I am bleeding!"

Thomas went to him and pulled at the edges of the wound. "It is shallow, and clean. Find untainted water and wash it well, then leave the wound uncovered until morning. If it begins to itch or turn red, wash it again and keep the wound open."

"And if it becomes worse?"

"I would normally tell you to send a message for me, but under the current circumstances that might prove difficult."

"You are friend to Fernando and Isabel, are you not? That is what your companion said. So why can I not send a message?"

"Because I live on the other side of the city walls."

"You are a heathen?" The woman came closer, this new information only serving to increase Thomas's attraction.

"I am nothing," Thomas said. "Now, if you will show me where Woodville has set his camp I need to talk with him." He preferred not to mention the true purpose behind their presence.

She glanced at her companion, who continued to press and prod at his wound, then turned back. "I will take you. Both of you." A hint of a smile crossed pretty lips before she turned away.

"Nobles," said Jorge as he fell into step beside

Thomas. "Sometimes I wonder what is going to become of the world."

"I think we already know what is going to become of the world. Nothing good."

The woman led them toward a large tent, not as big as the one she had been in, but substantial. Thomas caught her wrist and drew her to a halt.

"That is far enough. My thanks."

"I know Richard, it is no trouble to take you inside."

"I know him, too," Thomas said. "Please, I wish to surprise him. Return to your companion and remind him to clean the wound."

When they moved away, the woman stayed where she was.

"What if Will isn't here?" asked Jorge.

"He won't be, this is too open. He would be heard if he cried out." Thomas angled toward the side of the tent where the rear backed onto open country. What had once been fields of crops now lay scorched and blackened, the stink of their burning thick in the air. "But Woodville will know where he is."

"Why are you so sure? Because Gracia's lover told you? I wouldn't trust the word of either of them."

"I believe it because he is here. I don't know the man, but I know his type. Why would an English Earl make the dangerous journey to Spain unless he seeks something?"

"He is already an important man. I don't understand it. We should be looking for the true culprit, not this popinjay."

Thomas almost laughed at the words, coming from Jorge.

"The man has status, but he lacks the wealth to

support it. He wants all or part of the Guild's gold and is willing to kill to get it."

"But not kill with his own hands," said Jorge.

"Of course not. He is an Earl. He will have someone to do the killing for him. You remember his men we saw making camp near Auta Fort? Soldiers, mercenaries brought from England. Whether he came with a purpose in mind or not doesn't matter. He has found a purpose now, but made a mistake in taking my son."

Thomas halted close to the rear canvas wall. The wind from the sea caused it to billow, a shiver running through it. "Here, I think." He drew a knife, short but sharp, and punched a hole at head height. He used both hands to pull the blade down, sawing to part the heavy canvas.

A pale yellow light greeted him, a stale smell, and he pushed into a chamber larger than expected. The light came from a lamp hanging from a wooden support which held up the roof. A wide bed occupied one side of the chamber, and Richard Woodville lay turned away from them, fast asleep.

Thomas crept close and leaned over the man. Beyond him a second pillow showed an indentation, the covers disturbed where someone had lain beside him, but whoever it was had gone. Unless they had only gone outside to relieve themselves. Thomas reached over and felt the pillow, but it was cool.

Woodville stirred, rolled onto his back, mumbling.

Thomas placed a hand over Woodville's mouth and held the knife so he would see it as soon as his eyes opened, which they did almost at once. They darted between the two men and he struggled, but Jorge came and held him down.

"I have a question." Thomas kept his voice low. He was sure at least one guard would be standing at the entrance to the tent, possibly more. Even if they didn't, a hundred soldiers were within earshot. "Answer me true and you can return to your dreams. Mislead me, or lie, and I will find a use for this blade. My companion is able to detect a lie when he hears one, trust me. I am going to remove my hand now. Cry out and it will be the last sound you make. Trust me on that, too."

Thomas withdrew his hand, ready to press it back if Woodville made a sound.

The man lay there, breathing hard.

Thomas reached inside his robe with his free hand and closed his fist around the ring Diego once possessed. He had returned to his room at the last minute before they left to retrieve it. He withdrew his hand but kept it closed around the ring for the moment.

"You can release him now," Thomas said to Jorge. "You are not going to fight back, are you, Richard?" He deliberately used the man's first name, knowing it would annoy him. Despite leaving England over thirty years before he knew the ways of the nobility well enough to be able to insult one.

"I will have you killed for this," said Woodville.

"You will try, I am sure, but you should know I am a difficult man to kill. Now, one question to begin with."

"Ask it." Woodville's eyes darted between them, around the tent, but there was nothing there to help him, and it was clear he was afraid to call out with a knife at his throat.

Thomas opened his hand so the ring caught the lamplight. "This is yours, is it not?"

Woodville stared at the ring, his expression the only

answer needed, even though when he spoke he said, "I have never seen it before in my life."

"I am disappointed in you, an English gentleman, lying in such a manner. I know it is yours. A gift from your sister, Elizabeth, wife to your last king. The inscription makes it clear."

Woodville's expression changed, as much to do with the threat of violence coming from Thomas as any words. "Where did you get it? I have not seen the ring in months. I believed it lost, at home."

"You expect me to believe that?" Thomas leaned close so his face was inches from Woodville's. "You lost it when you killed Zufar al-Zaki. Tell me, what have you done with my son?"

A look of confusion crossed Woodville's face. "What nonsense is this? Your son? I did not even know you had a son, nor a wife. Not even a dog, unless this is your loyal hound beside you."

Jorge smiled.

"Where is Will?"

"Who?"

"I can use this knife to end your miserable existence unless you tell me, and am content to take my time over it, just like your own dog does."

Woodville tried to sit up, but Thomas laid a hand on his shoulder.

"When you start making sense I might be able to answer you."

Thomas glanced at Jorge, a sudden uncertainty coming to him. Jorge shook his head. "He knows of what you speak. Cut him."

Thomas smiled, saw the colour drain from Woodville's face. The knife flashed and a line of red bloomed on the man's arm. He cried out, clutching the wound to his chest.

"I'm still waiting," Thomas said, "but my patience is beginning to wear thin."

"I know nothing of what you are saying. I came here to arrange a marriage between two countries, nothing more."

The knife darted again and blood welled on the other arm.

"Stop it! Stop this foolishness now."

Thomas's uncertainty grew. He knew enough about men to tell when they were lying and when not. He glanced at Jorge, who knew such things even better.

"Is it him or is it not?"

Jorge shook his head. "You told me Gracia said it was him."

"Who is Gracia?"

"Al-Zaki's wife."

"And who is al-Zaki? Make sense, man, or kill me now and be done with it."

Thomas sat on the bed beside Woodville. Jorge came and sat on the other side. He stretched his legs out.

"This is a fine bed." He patted the mattress stuffed with feathers, leaned over and sniffed at the pillow on his side of the bed, a brief frown marking his brow. "Who has lain beside you? Not a woman. Is your companion Danvers?" Jorge smiled. "He is handsome enough, I give him that, and I am certainly no man to judge another over his preferences. What does he know of this business?"

"You are as mad as your master."

"Oh, I have no master," said Jorge. He reached out and ran a finger along Woodville's jawline, up into his hair. "Now tell Thomas what he wants to know before he loses patience. I should warn you he is not a patient man."

"I don't *know* what he wants." Woodville's voice was a wail of anguish. "Yes, Edward laid beside me, but he rose and left hours since. I am sure you have shared a bed with your master, too. It means nothing. Nothing at all."

Jorge sniffed the air like a hound, moving his lips. He smiled. "Do not pretend to a man who knows the scent of sex as well as I do. Tell Thomas where you have taken his son."

Woodville tried to sit up, but Thomas held him down with one hand.

"I know nothing of your son, nothing of any killings. I tell you again, I am here on behalf of my king." He glanced at Thomas's hand. "Yes, that ring is mine, but I told you I have not seen it for months." His eyes narrowed. "Perhaps Edward stole it. Yes, that must be it, Edward stole my ring. It is him you seek."

Thomas rose and walked into the chamber. He waited for Jorge to join him but made sure to keep an eye on Woodville, who remained lying on the bed, too afraid to attempt escape. What he said made a kind of sense. The man was a weakling and a coward. Danvers was not, but he had always appeared too amenable to have carried out the killings.

"Do you believe him?" he asked Jorge, keeping his voice low.

"As far as I can tell he speaks the truth. He is not clever enough to make up such an outrageous lie."

"Danvers is an Englishman, too, and they are of similar appearance. What if he told them he was his master? Would it not make sense if he planned theft and murder? Olivia told me the man who laid with them was a skilled lover." Another glance toward Woodville. "That is not him."

"No, it isn't, but Danvers ... yes, he could be. He is a little like me, but has all his manhood intact."

Thomas stared at Woodville. He saw the weakness of the man, lying there awaiting his fate. Most others would at least attempt an escape, or to fight. He looked around. Woodville didn't even have a weapon nearby.

Thomas approached the bed. "Where has Danvers taken my son?"

"He tells me nothing, disappears at all times of the day and night. He was gone all day yesterday and only returned at midnight, and now he is gone again."

"Where?"

Woodville seemed to collapse, any remaining resistance broken. "Yesterday he rode west, returned from that direction. I do not know where he went, but that is the direction you seek. There is nothing left there, Fernando has burned the land as far as the eye can see."

Thomas stared at Woodville. Smiled when the man pulled away as he saw the intention in Thomas's eyes. And it was true, Thomas wanted to kill him. He was trying to decide how much truth lay in the man's words. If he thought Woodville was involved he could not allow him to live, not after Will had been taken. But he wasn't sure. He glanced at Jorge, who no doubt knew what he was thinking and offered a tiny shake of the head.

Thomas slid his knife back into its scabbard and stood. He dropped Woodville's ring on the bed.

"If you tell me wrong I will return and make you eat that. And then I will cut it out of you."

"I speak the truth. One Englishman to another, Sir Thomas."

Thomas's fingers twitched.

* * *

"I thought you were going to kill him when he said that," said Jorge.

"He's too big a fool to die over a few words."

They were a quarter mile from the rear of the Spanish camp, following a wide roadway, well paved, that led like a taut string into the distance. To either side lay burned crops and the ruins of shacks and houses that had once dotted this landscape. A low mist rose no higher than their knees, parting like water as they walked. Through the darkness the shape of a single farmhouse lay outlined against the far hills. It was the only building left standing in the burned landscape.

"What do we do when we get there?"

"Watch. It will be light soon. We find somewhere to hide and see the lie of the land, and then when we're sure, we take Will and kill them all."

"I will leave the killing to you, if you don't mind. I don't have the same taste for it as you."

Thomas glanced at Jorge. "It's not something I do lightly, but there comes a time when men must be punished for the evil they inflict on others. You will be with me, though, won't you?"

"Of course. I will always be with you."

THIRTY-FIVE

Thomas pressed his back against the rough stone of the farmhouse. His nose stung from the acrid smoke that continued to taint the air, but the house itself appeared unharmed. To his right a window was propped half open, casting a narrow arc of light across the ground beyond. The mist had risen, cloaking the burned land with a silver carpet. Thomas listened for voices, for some clue his son was held captive within. He knew, of course, he could simply storm inside and kill anyone he met, but what if Will wasn't here? And if he was, someone might be holding a knife to his throat. Thomas didn't doubt, if that was the case, whoever held it would not hesitate to kill his son. So he waited until he knew more. Jorge remained hidden on the far side of the roadway, crouching behind a stack of blackened straw.

Thomas drew his sword, a thrumming impatience building within. Will had been held captive for almost a full day now, and he wondered how he fared. Was he afraid? Or was he — and the thought came even though he didn't want it to — already dead? It wasn't a possibility he was willing to acknowledge.

Thomas tensed, readying himself to burst through the door, when there came the sound of a rapidly approaching horse. At first he couldn't place from which direction it came and hesitated, then he caught movement in the growing light, a shadow within the low-lying mist, and he stepped back out of sight. He glanced toward Jorge, relieved he couldn't see him, which meant the rider wouldn't either.

Thomas stepped carefully along the side of the house in search of another window where he could listen. On the far side, he found what he was looking for, as well as a hatch set into the ground which must offer access to a cellar of some kind. He tested the doors and found them unlocked. Carefully he raised them and propped them open.

The horse pulled up and there came the sound of people moving from the house onto the roadway.

"It is now, today," said a voice in rough Spanish. "I want you with me, all of you."

Thomas wondered why English was not used until he heard Gracia's voice. "And the boy?"

"He's no use to us anymore. Kill him. Leave the body as a warning. Berrington should have been more careful."

"You said nothing of killing," said Gracia.

"He's a dangerous man." A different voice. Thomas was frantically trying to work out how many he would have to fight, how many he would have to kill, all reluctance stripped from him now. They had kidnapped Will, used him as a tool, and would now discard him.

"Don't worry about Berrington — he will be dead

soon, his family with him, and by sunset we will all be rich beyond the dreams of man. Now go kill the boy, then follow me."

Thomas dropped through the cellar hatch and crouched. He found himself in a small space, a dim lamp swinging from the beam of the floor above. Will sat on a filthy blanket in one corner, a knife in his hand and cold determination on his face. Thomas gave a grin at the sight of his son ready to fight. Of course he would be ready to fight.

He scooped him up and kissed his face, then set him down again. He expected someone to come into the cellar, but nobody appeared. Perhaps they were still gloating over the coming together of their plan, though he thought Gracia had sounded more unsure about the way events had turned out.

He went to one knee. "How many?"

Will held up a hand, fingers spread. Five. Plus the man who had just arrived. Danvers, if Thomas was not mistaken. The man who was behind everything. Not Woodville, but the companion turned master.

Thomas picked Will up and lifted him through the broken hatch, set his feet on the blackened earth.

"Go to the front and show yourself. Jorge is there, he will take you away from here."

"Pa come."

"Not yet. I'll follow as soon as I can."

Will stared down at his father, his mouth set, the knife still held in his small hand. He took a step toward the open hatch. "Pa stay, Will stay."

Thomas pushed him. "Go. Go now. This is important. Ma needs you to keep her safe. Do what I say."

Thomas thought his son would resist again, but

instead, after a moment he turned and ran around the side of the house. Thomas could only hope Jorge was watching and would know what to do.

Still nobody had descended the stairs, and then he realised why as Will gave a cry, followed instantly by a man's curse. There came more shouting from the front of the house, then the clatter of a horse moving away at speed.

Thomas scrambled out of the cellar the way he had come to find himself confronted by four men. There was no Gracia. No Danvers. One of the men was familiar and grinned at him, waving his sword in a pointless show of bravura. Someone had released the man Thomas had handed over to the authorities, but he wouldn't be spared a second time.

Thomas looked around for Will but couldn't see him. That was good. He didn't want him to witness what was about to happen. He saw one of the men nursing his arm, beads of blood dripping through his fingers, and Thomas knew his son had done that. Will was so much like him, and an exultation rose through him, a need to release a tension he had held in check for too long.

He struck without warning. No more mercy. He took the first man in the throat, then turned to the others. Two stepped away, turned to run, but they only delayed the inevitable. It took Thomas less than five minutes, and when he was done he searched the house, but there was no sign of Gracia. He started alone down the road, leaving four bodies behind and a hunger inside to kill more.

Thomas caught up with Jorge halfway to the Spanish camp. He carried Will in his arms, which slowed him, but as Thomas fell into step he heard how they had hidden while the mounted man swept past.

"Was he alone?" Even as Thomas asked the question, thoughts tumbled through his mind, trying to make sense of the new information he had overheard.

"I couldn't tell, he passed at full gallop."

"Gracia wasn't at the house."

"How many were there?" asked Jorge.

"Four."

"How many did you leave alive?"

Thomas ignored the question, believing an answer unnecessary. "The horseman was Danvers. Are you sure there was no-one with him?"

It was Will who answered. "The woman." He clung to Jorge as they walked, head turning between the two of them. "The woman who took me." He laughed. "She was hanging on." He flailed his arms in copy of what he had seen. "She said I was not to worry. I was safe with her."

"Danvers is controlling all of this," Thomas said. "What I don't know is whether Woodville is involved or has only been used."

"He's being used," said Jorge.

"I'm not so sure. A man will do much for love, even that of another man."

"There's no even about it. But you're right, except in this case Woodville is a man who has no great love of sex."

"What is sex?" asked Will. "Like money?"

Jorge laughed and handed him across to Thomas. "Something like, yes, but more powerful."

"Danvers said something I could scarcely believe. He said my entire household is in danger." They increased their pace now Thomas carried Will. He held his son's body against his chest, the touch calming the violence in his soul. "Does he know who we have in our household? Danvers said I'm in danger, my family is in danger ... but Olaf, Yusuf, and Usaden. Gods, those three are enough to stop an army. And Danvers has four less men now. How many did we see camped at Auta fort — a dozen, was it? One is locked away, Olaf and Yusuf killed three. That leaves him with only four men. Four men against me, Olaf, Yusuf, and Usaden? They stand no chance."

"Unless he has access to others," said Jorge. "Fighting men are cheap in times of war, ready to turn a small profit for the kind of work they are good at."

"That could mean someone else is involved, and I have an idea who it might be."

The day had almost fully arrived. Long shadows fell across the ground as men rose and gathered into groups. Horses were saddled. From close to the city walls the deep cough of cannon sounded, the barrage a constant now. The wind had stilled to almost nothing and smoke hung in the air as fires were stamped into coals. Thomas made his way toward a pristine white tent where long banners flew, but before they reached it he saw Fernando astride a glistening black stallion, men around him. And then Thomas stopped. One of the men was Ali Durdush, and they were talking, heads close together, before Fernando grasped the Guild Master's arm and allowed him to ride toward the city. Thomas cried out, but the distance was too great to allow his voice to carry.

He thrust Will into Jorge's arms. "Take him home, gather everyone together, and take them to the Alkhazabah, it will be the last place to fall. I will meet you there. Take them as far and as deep you can, even into the Rabita if the gates are open, they will be even safer there."

"Where are you going?"

"Durdush has sold Malaka to the Spanish. No doubt the city gates are thrown wide by now. Run, Jorge, steal a horse, do whatever you can, but get there first before the house is attacked. This army is in no mood for mercy."

"And you? Come with us, Thomas. Nobody can kill you and I will feel safer if you are at my side."

"I have to speak with Isabel. I can think of nothing else that might save us all." He shook his head. "I can think of nothing." He pushed at Jorge. "Go. Here!" He swung to one side and grabbed the reins of a horse as it came past, tugged on them and hauled the rider to the ground.

Jorge swung into the saddle like a man used to riding, and Thomas smiled at how his friend had changed so much. He handed Will up to him then slapped the horse's rump hard before either could object. It took off at a run, Jorge bouncing wildly, Will clutched safe in front of him.

"Hey, what–" The man rose to his feet, then went down again as Thomas punched him.

A group of grey-robed men approached Fernando, Mandana at their head, his son beside him, and there was a hurried conversation. It was as Thomas feared. Danvers needed men, and Mandana had them. They had both been in Malaka the last months, and now the coincidence of such seemed too great. Thomas scanned the melee but there was no sight of Danvers. Had he returned to Woodville to break the last ties with his past? Thomas considered making his way there, then decided he owed Woodville nothing.

He pushed through the crowd; soldiers, women, cooks, and squires, men in command and men taking commands. He was almost close enough to Fernando to call out when the King spurred his mount and rode away at speed. The robed figures remained, Mandana's skeletal form perched on too small a horse. Pedro Guerrero sat upright on a larger mount. Mandana saw Thomas and grinned, leaned over and said something to his son. He pointed and they both pushed toward him.

Thomas backed away, turned and ran, trusting agility over size. He believed he could take them both, but not when the rest of the Spanish army lay all around.

The entrance to the royal tent was well-guarded, so he waited until everyone was looking east, watching as the army gathered its strength for the final onslaught. When it was safe he slipped around the side of the tent and used his knife to make an opening in the canvas. A slight figure turned fast. The three women attending her stepped between their Queen and the intruder.

"Isabel," Thomas said.

She stared at him, her face paling.

"I was told you were dead!" She let a ragged laugh loose. "I should have known better. Praise God you live, Thomas."

For the first time he noticed how she was dressed, or partly dressed. Her legs were encased in bright steel armour, finely etched patterns cut into its surface. One arm was similarly encased, but an attendant held the breast plate in her hands and Isabel, Queen of Castile, stood in little more than a thin shift in front of a man who was not her husband.

The woman who held the breast plate ran at him, swinging it wildly toward his head. Thomas caught it in one hand and slid his other arm around her waist, held her against him as he approached Isabel. Another of the women turned and fled, no doubt to fetch guards.

"Tell them you know me," Thomas said. He released the woman and handed the breast plate back to her, then turned his back. "Cover the Queen."

Four guards burst into the chamber and came to an abrupt halt. They half turned, unable to gaze on Isabel, but aware of the intruder. They shuffled in his direction, heads averted from their Queen.

"Leave him!" Isabel's voice carried a sharp command and the men halted, uncertain. "I know Sir Thomas. He is a friend."

Still the men were unsure. A friend was one thing, but a friend in the company of their half-dressed ruler?

Isabel waved a hand. "All of you, leave now. Thomas, come closer, and turn around. You have seen me in childbirth, I am sure my dugs are no mystery to you. You would not be here without good reason."

Thomas watched as the guards drifted one by one from the chamber. The last man glanced back at him and Thomas saw a fierce hatred in his eyes. He turned to look at Isabel, unconcerned. He had more than enough enemies already, what was one more?

"What is happening?" he asked. "I saw Durdush with Fernando. Has he surrendered the city?"

Isabel held her arms out and the women continued

to dress her in the suit of armour. He could see they wanted to cover her chest, but despite what she had said her breasts did not show, only the swell of them beneath the thin shift. It was necessary to clamp the armour together in a specific order, the breast-plate the last item. They fussed around the Queen, clipping and tying and fussing some more.

"Malaka falls," said Isabel. "Fernando rides to accept their surrender. All except your fool of a governor, but he can rot in that fort until doomsday for all we care."

"And Durdush?" Thomas looked around, found a chair, and sat. Another breaking of protocol, but he was tired. His bones ached, and he wondered how much longer he could keep going.

"It is he who surrendered to Fernando. He does not want to see Malaka destroyed, but my husband is in no mood for mercy, not after the resistance they have shown."

"Durdush returned to the city," Thomas said.

"Did he? I leave such matters to the King. Is that all you came here for? You took a great risk for so little information."

Finally the women were ready to attach the breast plate. Isabel held her arms out from her body as they laid it against her and threw more catches, tied more ties. One of them brought a simple helmet, etched with the same marks that adorned the rest of the armour, but Isabel waved it away.

"Leave us, I will call you when I am ready."

The women looked at each other.

"I said leave us!" Isabel's voice was sharp, an unmistakeable power in it that sent the women scurrying away.

"There, that is better," said Isabel. "Just you and I, Thomas. Bring me a chair so I may rest a moment. I do not think I can move far enough on my own."

He rose and brought a wide, padded chair and held her arm as she eased herself into it.

"Now bring another so you can face me while we talk. Tell me what you are afraid of." She smiled, but there was no hint of cheer in it. "I see it in your face and eyes. You are afraid, and you are here. What can I do?"

"I saw Mandana with Fernando," Thomas said. "His son was with him. Do you know what task has been set them?"

"Fernando thinks I don't know of his dalliance with the man, but I know everything." She frowned. "I did not know about a son. Are you sure?"

"Quite sure. What are they tasked with?"

"There are men who wish to strip Malaka of every last coin and jewel, in war there always is. Fernando sends Mandana to stop them."

"So he may take the gold for himself," Thomas said.

"I will allow your impertinence because I know you are afraid, but there is no need for fear. Mandana has been sent to watch out for your family, too. You have your wife and friends in the city. They are to be protected." She leaned forward. The joints of her armour grated together and she winced. "Did you think I would not watch out for you, Thomas?" She held out a hand, hers small and pale, waiting for him to respond. Thomas stared at it. Eventually he reached out and took hers, aware of how much protocol he was breaking, but Isabel gripped his fingers tight.

"We are friends, you and I, are we not? Good friends." A smile. "I will do all in my power to keep you safe, for I have not finished with you yet. Come to me, Thomas, take my offer of a place beside me, for your world is ending. You know it is. Soon, next year, your al-Andalus will be gone. Come to me now and help me build a new Spain to match the power of England and France."

He stared at her hand, feeling a tremor run through her, knowing she would feel the same from him. He thought about all she had said, both now and over the years he had known her. The offers. The friendship. And more. He knew the world he loved was ending. Knew it had no place for him anymore.

He looked up and met her eyes.

"Yes. When this is done I will come to you."

Isabel smiled.

THIRTY-SIX

Isabel gave Thomas a horse so he could reach Malaka faster, but he abandoned it almost at once. The press of other mounts, of men and equipment, was too great. He continued on foot, trying to slip past bodies and often failing so progress was slower than he wanted. When he had sent Jorge back for the others he hadn't expected the attack to come so soon, or so violently. The entire Spanish army was attempting to enter Malaka, some directly through the Ataranzana gate, others splitting northward for the Antequera gate and others which lay beyond. Only the Rabita and Alkhazabah would remain as places of refuge. At least for now.

The throng grew ever thicker, and Thomas saw why. Ahead lay the fortified bridge, a bottleneck for the thousands trying to enter the city through gates that had been opened to allow the Spanish access. As they forced their way across, some men were pushed over the sides into the slow flowing river. Most, heavily armed, sank like stones. Others fought for a while only to disappear more slowly. Only the lightly armed managed to reach the far bank, carried two hundred paces south of the bridge before they could leave the water.

Thomas looked north, trying to see over the heaving mass of men. That direction was no better. He pushed his way to the south, pulling his weapons free and dropping them on the ground. He discarded the leather jerkin that was meant to disguise him as a Spaniard, removed everything he could until he wore only linen shirt and trousers. The crowd began to thin as he approached the river, people moving with him now as they tried to reach the bridge. Thomas came to the edge of the river and hesitated. Even slow-flowing the current was relentless. He saw men attempting to reach the far bank, most of them failing only to disappear beneath the surface. Their bodies would wash up along the shoreline for days, or become food for the fish of the bay.

Thomas hated the water. It had not always been so. As a boy he had leapt into the deep pools of the Lugge, which flowed swift through his father's fields, and allowed the river to carry him where it would. And then he had been taken across the sea in a fragile ship and lost his love of water. But he knew he could swim well enough for what was needed this day.

He leapt now as he had leapt into the Lugge, a longer drop this time, the water embracing him like a lover as it closed over his head. Thomas used his arms and legs, grasping for the surface. He broke through and knew, had he not discarded everything, he would be lying on the river bed by now.

He orientated himself. The current had already

carried him a score of paces south and he felt it pushing against him as he began to stroke toward the far bank. It was no great distance. He would have laughed at the task as a boy, and that boy would have laughed at the grown man who now made such hard work of it. For a moment Thomas thought he saw himself as a twelve years old, standing on the far bank laughing. A moment of raw fear ran through him at the notion that what he saw was his own death. He increased his effort, almost halfway across, and then the far bank was closer than the one behind.

His feet caught in weeds and he sank beneath the surface. He kicked, freed himself, and put in one last effort. The next time his foot caught it was on mud, and he reached for the reeds lining the bank and pulled himself clear of the water. It cascaded from him as he walked toward the arched doors of the Ataranzana, their gates thrown wide to allow the invaders entry. He cursed Ali Durdush and vowed he would find the man and punish his treachery. He saw a dead Spaniard washed up on the bank and took his knife.

Within the Ataranzana, soldiers moved in chaotic patterns, and Thomas realised there was no-one in charge anymore. Commanders had turned as feral as their men, seeking murder, rape, and plunder. It was what they had come to war for.

In an alcove Thomas saw a man mounting a woman, her bloodied face turned aside, and he detoured to slide the stolen knife into the soldier's neck and toss his body from her. She lay stupefied as Thomas moved on, knowing it would only be moments before someone else took the dead man's place, but he couldn't save everyone. Couldn't save even one, it seemed, but he had others who needed his protection more.

Around him chaos reigned, and fear weakened him. How could his family survive such madness? He only hoped Jorge had been in time to take them to the relative safety of the Alkhazabah. There would other women, other soldiers, and he tried to make himself invisible, a tall man in wet clothes, his feet lacking boots. Only those he loved mattered now.

He reached Diego's house, hoping to find it empty and relieved when it was. Empty of who he sought, though not of others. Half a dozen Spaniards sat in chairs, jugs of wine cradled against their chests. They had piled Thomas's papers and books in the fireplace and lit them despite the heat of the day. It was mindless destruction, but that was what they had come for as much as the plunder. Thomas watched the men a moment, turning away when one of them noticed him and began to rise. There would be enough death in the city today without adding to it. There was nothing for him in the house anymore.

He passed the workshop of Narjis al-Ishraq, the Mistress of Spice, and saw the door broken to lie in the street. The screams of women came from inside, but he continued on. He hoped that most of her girls had already escaped, but if not there was nothing he could do. Thomas's world had shrunk to the eye of a needle. Lubna. Jorge and Belia. Olaf and Yusuf. Will and Diego. Nothing else mattered.

At the Infirmary soldiers had dragged physicians and nurses outside. Some had been killed, others defiled. A few wandered the wide street, not knowing what to do or where to go. Thomas ignored them. His destination was closer. Only a quarter mile more.

Shouting came from an alley and a score of Gomeres ran out and turned, forming a barrier as a hundred Spaniards attacked without hesitation. He scanned the Gomeres for Usaden but didn't see him. He hoped the man lived. He grimaced as the two forces clashed, almost sorry for the Spaniards who had no doubt thought the Gomeres easy prey.

The stench of powder, of burning and blood filled the air. Tatters of smoke rose from buildings. The bodies of men, women, and children lay on every corner. In a small square a commander had organised his men and they were dragging anything of worth from the surrounding houses and piling it onto an already large cache.

Thomas reached the old Roman amphitheatre. There were soldiers here, but the majority of the Spanish had not reached this far yet. He passed through an open metal gate, wondering where all the guards had gone. He stopped to catch his breath at the next barrier, a heavy doorway that resisted his efforts to open it. He hammered on the wood, wishing he had taken weapons from one of the dead soldiers. All he had was the short knife he had stolen at the Ataranzana, and he counted himself fortunate he hadn't needed to use it.

He hammered at the door again, sure someone must hear him on the other side. A group of Spaniards entered the wide square fronting the Alkhazabah, but they ignored him, drunk on stolen wine and killing. Thomas scanned their number anyway, looking for the man he sought, though not expecting to find him. Danvers. Woodville's lover. If he found the man he promised himself he would take his time killing him. Let him know how his victims had felt, even if Danvers had not taken their lives himself. He hammered on the door again. This time the sound attracted the attention of some of the soldiers, who turned and called out insults and threats. A group of half a dozen started forward at a fast walk, weaving only slightly.

Thomas watched them come and prepared himself.

There were six, well-armed but drunk.

And then a hoarse voice called out as a new group came into the square, a tall man at their head, his companions dressed in grey robes over clothing designed for war.

"Leave that man, he is mine!" shouted Mandana.

His group were larger, a score at least, and they pushed past the six soldiers until they stood in front of Thomas. His gaze swept across them, a sense of dread settling through him. A half dozen he could have defeated, perhaps, but not this many. He knew how well-trained Mandana's men were, how fanatic their devotion to both him and their God. And then he saw, standing at the rear, Pedro Guerrero. His eyes blazed, locked on Thomas, and he knew the man still carried a hatred and blamed him for the death of his wife.

Thomas held his arms wide. He dropped the knife from his grasp and Mandana laughed.

"We are not here to kill you, Berrington. There are more important matters to attend to inside these walls. Fernando has sent me to take the fortress on the hill. He also mentioned I should protect your family if I could."

Thomas frowned. Was what Isabel had told him the truth, then? He could scarce believe it.

"Why?"

"Because he is my King and has asked it. Besides, this madness will end by the morrow and then my true work will begin. Priests are already tearing out the inside of the mosque so they can erect an altar. The King and Queen will come to attend the first speaking of Christian prayers in this city for half a millennium." Mandana stepped past Thomas, reached up with his good hand, and hammered the hilt of a sword on the door.

"Call out to them," he said. "They will admit you, like they have admitted your friends."

"If there is anyone there." Thomas glanced across the gathered men, but Guerrero had gone, together with half of their force. For a moment he wondered if the man had ever been there, or had it been nothing more than his own mind conjuring phantoms from his dread.

Mandana stepped back and looked up at the walls. He turned to one of his men. "Go see if you can find ladders. There will be some outside the city walls, which are..." He looked at Thomas, who pointed.

"That way will be closest. Three hundred paces and you will find a gate, no doubt thrown wide like all the others." He pushed past Mandana and found a section of low wall to sit on. He tried to remember the last time he had slept and couldn't. Exhaustion washed over him in waves and he gave a start, unsure if he had slept or not as Mandana came to stand in front of him.

"Tell me, why do you really want to enter these walls? Not to protect my family, I am sure. Is it the gold? If so it's already being taken somewhere you can't reach it."

The men Mandana had sent returned carrying three

roughly fashioned ladders. They lifted them against the walls where they reached above the parapet.

Thomas rose and stood close to Mandana. "I'm still not sure I trust you. Allow me an hour before you follow, and then I will help you. I know a man who can give you access to the Rabita, but there will be soldiers there."

Mandana's pale eyes studied Thomas. "I am used to soldiers fighting against me and I am still here. My men are well trained." He nodded. "Not an hour, I will allow you half that, and then we come. Find your man so we can move quickly."

Thomas glanced at the ladders. One man had already ascended to the walkway at the top of the wall, another was climbing up. "Call your men back. Or leave them there if you wish. But give me time."

Mandana washed a hand across his face, the skin of both face and hand stained dark with dirt. "Not for you, but for your son, Berrington. A man must love his son, must he not?"

Thomas hesitated, trying to see beyond Mandana's eyes into his soul. Could he trust him or not? The man was a master of subterfuge, but these last years he had seemed to soften, had come to him for his help, and Belia's potions. Did that mean anything, or nothing? He didn't know, but he did know the man had changed. He looked across the soldiers but still saw no sign of Guerrero and was convinced he had never been there. A mirage. A ghost of fear.

Thomas ran to the ladder, climbing fast. A soldier at the top drew his sword, but Mandana called out and he sheathed it again. Thomas looked down, but already Mandana was leading his men away, forming them into ranks as Moorish soldiers came from roadways into the wide square. Now it was Mandana about to protect the entrance of the Alkhazabah.

Thomas turned away and ran along the narrow walkway to where a set of steps took him down to the inner sanctum. There were three more doors he had to pass through, but they were also three doors protecting those he loved.

THIRTY-SEVEN

Within the Alkhazabah it was almost possible to forget that a battle raged in the city beyond its walls. There were few guards, but those he came across Thomas tried to persuade to follow him. Only a third of them did, but by the time he penetrated to the inner chambers he had half a dozen men with him. He climbed through narrow pathways with high walls which were designed to slow attackers, turning and turning again on themselves. As he ascended to the inner chambers, he made sure to bar each door behind with the solid oak bars standing ready beside each. He passed people carrying valuables in a vain attempt to save something from the Spanish. The Alkhazabah boasted three layers of high walls, but everyone knew they would eventually be breached. Thomas almost missed finding Jorge and the others because they were not where he had told them to go.

He turned into a large courtyard where a pool of still water ran from one side to the other. Dark yews scented the air with their sap. Lubna and Belia sat on a stone bench, staring across the wall to the distant sea, as if it offered a promise of freedom. Thomas could barely stop himself from punching Jorge.

"Why are you here? I told you to take them to the chambers beyond the store tower, into the Rabita if you could."

"There are stout walls between us and the chaos out there," said Jorge. "Would you have me subject them to darkness and misery when they are safe here?"

"Mandana is coming," Thomas said, unsure if that was a threat or not. Isabel had told him he had been sent to protect his family, but still he couldn't bring himself to fully trust the man.

"Both Olaf and Yusuf are here, plus Usaden. And me, of course. We are a match for any score of men, if not more."

"Olaf is not fully recovered." Even as he said the words Thomas recalled the sight of him striding into the midst of the Spanish soldiers, axe swinging.

"I would still back him against a dozen men."

"As would I. But our work this day isn't done yet. Danvers has a plan to steal the gold, and I think I know how he means to do it. I need you all with me. The women and children must go farther. You have to take them where I asked."

Yusuf came to stand close, Olaf a few feet away. Usaden remained with the women, a sword in one hand. His expression alone was enough to kill most men.

"I won't leave the women unguarded," said Yusuf.

Thomas knew he meant Lubna. Yusuf had developed far too great an interest in her, perhaps seeing there all the attributes a Sultan would need in a wife.

"I brought a few men with me, and there are others, all looking for someone to command them. Go find others and give them orders they can follow."

"I stay here." Yusuf's face was set firm. Thomas knew he didn't have time to persuade him if he wanted to stop Danvers' plan, nor the strength to drag him away unwillingly.

He gave a curt nod. "Very well. Keep Olaf with you then, I can manage what I need to do with Jorge."

"I come with you," said Olaf. "How can I face my daughters if you get yourself killed? I know you, Thomas. You are headstrong."

Headstrong? This coming from Olaf. Thomas shook his head.

"Usaden then, and whatever soldiers you can find. Take everyone to the safety of the inner chambers and protect them."

Yusuf laughed. "If my brother and father could hear you issuing me orders they would take your head." He stepped close and embraced Thomas, kissed both cheeks, then held his face in his hands and kissed his mouth. "I will care for them as if they are my own. Which they are, in here." He slapped his chest. "I would rather call you father than the one I have. Here, you have come to a fight without a proper weapon, take this." Yusuf wore two swords. He drew the one on his left, a blade of exquisite beauty obviously crafted especially for a prince of the ruling dynasty. For a moment Thomas thought of refusing, then reached out and took the hilt. Yusuf was right, he had come here with nothing more than a stolen knife and might need a weapon before the day was finished.

He went to the small group gathered in the shade

beneath the stand of yews. Here in the courtyard, with a view over the walls to the sea, it was easy to believe they were safe, but a battle was being fought nearby. He embraced Lubna and kissed her, placed his hand over the swell of her belly until he felt their child move, then kissed her again. She clung to him.

"Stay with us, Thomas. Forget the killings, forget this plot. Stay with me and Will."

"You know I can't. Not now. Do you expect me to turn away from those guilty of murder?"

"I do not care. All I care about is you and those I love. What does it matter if they escape? You cannot heal the entire world. This wealth you protect is not yours. Let it go."

Thomas pulled free of her arms, pushed at her as she came after him, his heart breaking when he saw the tears that streaked her face.

"You are safe here. Go with Yusuf. And you know me, I always return. We will celebrate tonight and laugh over our fears." He turned and walked away, but Will came running after him and clutched at his legs. Thomas lifted him, inhaling his scent before setting him on his feet and going to one knee so he was level with his son. "I have an important job for you." He waited until Will nodded. "Look after Ma and the others. Can you do that?"

Will gave another nod. Thomas handed him the knife he had taken from the dead Spaniard, and Will stared at it, then took it, determination on his young face. Thomas hugged him, then pushed him away, watching as his son wiped an angry arm across his face. He stared up at Thomas as if trying to inhale a memory that might last forever.

"Don't go, Pa. Diego says you can't go."

Thomas touched Will's head, ruffled his hair. "I have to." He slapped his chest. "I'm like *morfar* — nobody can kill either of us."

"But they might kill us. Diego told me they might kill us."

Thomas looked past Will to where Diego knelt in the shade of the Yews. He had the set of dice he had been given and threw them over and over again, each throw tumbling before coming to rest with two threes uppermost. It was a clever trick but meant nothing, certainly didn't mean Diego had the gift of prophecy.

Thomas went to one knee and held Will's shoulders. "Diego sees things that aren't there, you know that. I *have* to go. You're safe here. Usaden is with you, and Yusuf. Do you think anyone can get past those two?" He embraced Will one last time and rose, turned away quickly before the boy could make any further objection. Thomas knew he had already spent too long here.

He felt a sense of freedom, of completion, as he joined Olaf and Jorge. Three of them would be enough in the tunnel to the beach. Enough to punish guilty men who believed they were about to escape with the wealth of a city. He rose and led the way to the tower that stood higher than the rest of the fort, hoping he would be in time, and that his theory was right.

The body of Kohen al-Farsi, Master of the Alkhazabah, lay at the foot of the steps that led down to the lower chambers. Thomas knelt at his side but found no wound other than a dark bruise to his forehead where he had hit the stone on his way down. He checked for a pulse but it had stilled. His hand was clutched around the keys which had been used to open the tower, and Thomas took them. He had promised Mandana he could offer an easy way into the Rabita, and the keys would do that.

"Where are the guards?" said Jorge.

"Their job is done — there's no gold left here anymore." Thomas rose to his feet. He went to the entrance of the top chamber and looked in. The stone floor was empty, but marks in the dust showed where crates had once stood, other marks where they had been moved. A sturdy pulley system showed where they had been lowered to the base of the tower, the ropes still swinging. "The guards have taken the crates down to the tunnel. Which is where we need to be. It was always going to be on this day. The day the Spanish entered the city."

He started down the steps, which turned and turned, descending ever deeper. Each chamber they passed lay emptied of the wealth that had once been stored there.

"Gods, how much value was here?" asked Olaf, seeing the chambers for the first time.

"No man will ever know. More gold than anyone can imagine. More riches, I suspect, than even the Malaka Guild knows. Each of these rooms was filled with crates. Each crate held enough wealth to last a king a century, and there were ... I don't know how many."

"We have passed six floors so far," said Jorge, "and we are nearing the bottom, so eight in total. How many crates in each?"

"Does it matter?" Thomas snapped.

"I was curious, that is all."

They reached the lowest level, which also lay empty. In the far wall the stout door Thomas had used before stood open, a strong draught greeting them. He ducked his head to enter, knowing Olaf would find it difficult, but the old general made no comment as he followed in the rear.

The tunnel was dark, without light of any kind, but a faint illumination came from far ahead, growing as they walked, and the sound of waves breaking on rocks came to them. They passed the door to the side chamber and Thomas pushed against it in passing, relieved to find it held firm. For a moment, he had feared more men might emerge to block their escape route.

Thomas held up a hand as the exit approached, went on hands and knees and crawled forward. He sighted five men, all with their backs turned. One of them was tall, and when he turned Thomas saw it was Woodville, who must have been telling the truth when he said he was negotiating on behalf of Fernando — though why the King would trust an Englishman was a mystery.

"We agreed the share in advance," said Ali Durdush, speaking in stilted Spanish. "Thirty crates for the King, the remainder for the city."

"Don't you mean the remainder for you?"

"I am the city now," said Durdush.

"We should kill them all now." Olaf knelt beside Thomas, his teeth showing white in the dimness.

Thomas looked beyond the small group. Four crates remained beyond the tunnel. The rest were either being carried, or had been carried, to waiting galleys which were pulled up on the beach. There were four, because three would not have been enough. No wonder men had died for this knowledge.

"Danvers isn't here."

"Who is Danvers?" asked Olaf. "Is he Spanish? I am in the mood to kill more Spanish."

"These aren't the men I seek," Thomas said, moving back into the tunnel. Olaf and Jorge stayed close to the entrance, Olaf out of the need for mayhem, Jorge from curiosity.

"They're arguing," said Jorge, and Thomas came closer again. Durdush was standing close to a clerk Thomas had not seen before. It was he who was doing the shouting.

"Where are they!" The clerk stepped close to Durdush, unafraid of his status. They had switched to speaking Arabic, and Woodville stood to one side, a frown on his face, his own position threatened.

"Every crate has been brought out."

"Didn't you think to count them? There are two missing."

"We brought every crate out. It was not our job to count them. Is that not your job as senior clerk to the Coin Guild?" Durdush pushed closer to the man, using his bulk as a threat. "Why would we think to do so? Have them counted again. How many should there be?"

"Sixty-four, and I make only sixty-two." The clerk started across the black sand toward the galleys where loading continued, each crate lifted on a pulley to be swung aboard. Before he reached it, another galley rounded the headland and pulled hard for the shore. Standing at the prow, ready to be the first to jump to the beach, was Fernando. Thomas guessed he had not trusted the exchange of crates to either Woodville or Durdush.

"There's nothing for us here," Thomas said, moving

back inside once more, and this time the other two followed. He only went as far as the side tunnel before stopping and trying the keys he had taken from al-Farsi. One of them released the lock and he pushed the door open a crack, just enough to peer beyond, but all he saw was darkness.

"We should go back to the others," said Jorge. "Mandana will be in the Alkhazabah by now."

"And has been told to protect my family. Danvers is this way, with two crates of gold." Thomas pushed the door open and stepped through, uncaring if the others followed or not. He ran his hand along the roofline, knowing there were no obstructions ahead, trusting to memory.

After he had gone sixty paces, the depth of darkness changed. Another forty and he could make out the shape of the tunnel where it opened into the chamber he had found on his first visit. From behind he heard the others start to follow, a curse from Jorge as he banged his head on the roof.

A candle guttered on a shelf in the chamber, its meagre light almost blinding after the passage through the tunnel. There were no crates and no people. Thomas took the candle and went on, into the passage on the far side he had not explored the last time he came here.

As he suspected, the tunnel began to slope upward. Wooden rails continued to run along the floor, marks on them showing that something had been dragged along them recently. The passage curved back on itself, still rising, then curved again.

"How much farther?" Jorge was right behind Thomas now.

"I've no idea. We must be getting close to the surface by now." He stopped, listening, but heard nothing, the silence as dense as the darkness would be without the candle. He started off again, moving faster, a fear growing that Danvers might escape justice altogether.

Another curve and then light appeared ahead, a sliver of blue sky, the dark green shadow of a yew, and Thomas dropped the candle and began to run. He came out into a small courtyard. Nine men stood around two wooden crates, trying to work out how to carry them up a set of a dozen steps. One of the men was taller than the others, unmistakeable as Danvers. He was speaking Spanish better than his master as he tried to cajole the mercenary soldiers into following some kind of plan. He didn't hear Thomas, nor Jorge when he joined them, but as Olaf emerged the big general let out a roar and launched himself at the group.

Two of the soldiers ran immediately. Another fell to Olaf's axe before he had even drawn his sword. And then the others were defending themselves.

Thomas had eyes only for Danvers. He saw the man step back, saw him look to where the crates sat on the cobbles, taunting him with their closeness, then he turned and ran up the steps.

Thomas ignored the others, pushing one man aside as he came at him. He knew Olaf could handle them on his own, even if Jorge tried to help. He ignored the fire in his legs and the ache in his lungs as he gained on Danvers. The steps, like all those in the Alkhazabah, turned several times. Danvers was unfamiliar with their layout. Thomas caught up with him as they careered into a small courtyard deep inside the fort. He grabbed at Danvers, who stumbled to his knees. But he was fast.

Even as Thomas loomed over him he rolled, a sword appearing in his hand. He struck out, almost taking Thomas in the thigh, but Thomas managed to leap aside at the last moment. It gave Danvers time to regain his feet. This time he didn't run but faced Thomas, who drew the sword Yusuf had given him. He hoped it worked as well as it looked.

Danvers' eyes flickered to where the steps entered the courtyard, came back to Thomas.

"There are two crates. Enough for a hundred men, let alone the pair of us." He offered a smile, the same charisma that clung to the man still present, but Thomas saw it now as nothing more than a mask hiding the truth of what lay in Danvers' soul. "I will even call my dogs off if we come to an arrangement.."

"What dogs?" Thomas took a step closer. "If you mean Richard, he is on the beach haggling for the funds to take him home. As for your men, I believe I killed them all at the farmhouse."

"Which is why I sent others. Richard is useful, and he has the contacts I could not possibly broker. There was a man, a priest's son, who was more than willing to kill your entire family for remarkably little in return. He mentioned something about revenge."

"Priest's son?"

Danvers smiled and nodded. "I believe you know the priest. Old man, one hand. Not long for this world, I would say. But his son ... you know him too, and he knows you. Pedro Guerrero. Spanish, but an interesting man all the same. He bears no love for you, Thomas Berrington, no love at all." Danvers cocked his head to one side. "So do we have a deal? The gold in exchange for all your lives?"

"We have no deal."

Thomas thought it would be hard, that they would need to fight, to test each other, for he calculated Danvers had seen much of war, but in the end it was easy. Too easy, with no sense of satisfaction.

Danvers had expected Thomas's answer and struck first. Thomas stepped to one side, bent at the knee, and slid Yusuf's wondrous sword into the space between two ribs. Danvers looked down in surprise, then fell backwards, Thomas's blade coming free as easily as it had entered. He lay on his back, eyes wide, life already gone, and Thomas wanted to strike at him again and again. Instead he ran back to where he found Olaf standing with blood on his face, all of the soldiers scattered around him, not a single body intact.

"Quickly, now," Thomas said, "Danvers has sent men against the others."

THIRTY-EIGHT

When they had descended into the tower, the Alkhaz-abah had been almost deserted, its inhabitants taking shelter in the deepest cellars and rooms, in the places Thomas had told his family to go. Now Spanish soldiers barred their way, but not for long as Olaf tossed them aside. He took care not to injure any, his blood-lust sated for the moment.

Thomas was afraid the others had ignored him, or been too slow, so he ran toward the courtyard where he had left them. Spanish soldiers and mercenaries from a dozen lands lay even thicker between him and his destination, but he ignored them, and they in turn ignored him, perhaps thinking he was one of their own. One more man in search of plunder. He heard a clash of weapons behind and knew Olaf had found another fight. He was holding men back from ascending the passageways designed to resist invasion. One man like Olaf would be enough to resist an army in their confined space.

When Thomas reached the courtyard he felt a wash

of relief when he saw no-one standing there, then discovered the reason for it. A clutch of bodies lay close together in the shade cast beneath scented yews.

"Lock the gates," Thomas ordered as Olaf and Jorge came in behind him. Olaf obeyed, but Jorge ran past to throw himself on the ground beside a crumpled figure. He turned the body over and gave a great cry that rent the air.

"I am here, my love." Belia stepped from behind the cover of the trees and went to her knees beside Jorge.

Thomas stared at them. At the figure they knelt over. His feet refused to move. He didn't want to see what they saw. Then Will was there on sturdy legs. In his hand he held the knife Thomas had given him. It dripped blood on to the cobbles.

"I stuck him, Pa," he said, but his face showed no colour, and there was nothing of triumph in his words. "Madana — Will stuck him good. But he–" The boy looked toward the trees then broke down, falling to the ground. It was the spur Thomas needed to make him move. He scooped Will into his arms and carried him to the others, knowing what he would see but hoping the body might by some miracle belong to someone else.

Thomas glanced into the shade beneath the trees. Another figure lay there. Diego, with a sword in his hand. Like Will's the blade was stained, and Thomas could scarce comprehend the fear he must have felt, and his bravery at confronting their attackers. It was obvious he had tried to defend the others. Had he not done so he might well have been ignored, but Diego had accepted them all as his family and perished as a result.

Yusuf, the heir to Gharnatah lay, on his back in the courtyard, bloodied sword in one hand, knife in the other. He was surrounded by a dozen dead Spaniards. Thomas gave no heed to the other bodies. They were nothing, not of his family. Some were Mandana's men, but Mandana was not among them. Others were Spanish soldiers recruited on the journey through Malaka. Over a score of men, and Thomas knew Yusuf and Usaden would have been responsible for most of their deaths. He glanced around, but there was no sign of Usaden, and he imagined his body must lie concealed somewhere out of sight.

He glanced at Yusuf again as he passed. The last hope for al-Andalus. Thomas knew he had died protecting Lubna. Had sacrificed his own life for the love of her. For it was Lubna that Jorge and Belia knelt over. They lifted her upper body, and Thomas felt his heart begin to beat again as he saw her eyes open. He threw himself to the ground and gripped her hand. It was slick with blood and he tore at her robe, despair filling him as he surveyed the damage done to her.

"Save …" Lubna's voice was barely a whisper.

Thomas leaned close, hands touching, finding wound after wound. He had come here almost naked, without his instruments, though he could see the only instrument that would save Lubna was a miracle. She was beyond anything even the famed Thomas Berrington could perform, and he cursed to the sky, a loud wailing that he hoped would pierce the hearts of whatever Gods sat above.

Lubna lifted a hand and gripped his shirt, pulling him close so his ear lay against the lips he had kissed so often.

"Save our child, Thomas … you cannot save me … but you can save our child."

Her head fell back and her eyes closed, exhausted by the effort of speaking.

Thomas placed his fingers to her neck. Lubna's heart still beat, faint and fast, but she lived yet, and he knew he couldn't hasten her passing despite what she had asked him to do. He shook his head, trying to clear the agony from it, trying to ignore his guilt at leaving her here. All the wealth of the Guild, all the wealth of the world, was nothing compared to Lubna, and he knew he would carry this pain forever, would always regret what he had done instead of being with her, even as he knew it would have meant his own body lying in the courtyard. What was the point of living if she was not at his side?

Olaf stood with his back to the thick wooden gates. They were barred with planks but shuddered at each blow from the other side. Olaf remained as firm as oak, as strong as ever. A figure appeared from the far side of the courtyard and Thomas tensed, expecting more soldiers, but it was Usaden, a pair of bloodied swords in his hands. He glanced at Lubna, at Thomas.

"They have gone deeper. If they return you will have to fight." He stopped beside Thomas. "The man who struck her has gone. I chased, but could not find him." He stared down at Lubna for a moment, then shook himself and went to join Olaf at the gates.

Jorge held Belia in his arms, while she in turn held Will, who stared at Lubna and Thomas with shock on his face.

"Ma," he said, trying to tug free of Belia's arms but unable to do so.

"Is she?" said Jorge.

Thomas shook his head. "Not yet."

"Then save her. You can save anyone, so save her."

"I can't work miracles." He held Lubna's hand, hoping she felt his touch, wanting it to be the last thing she knew before departing this life and going to her God. For go she would, he was sure. Her faith protected her, and for a moment Thomas wondered if that was the difference between those who believed and those, like himself, who believed in nothing. Was it that belief which carried them to heaven?

Lubna made a sound, but her eyes remained closed.

Thomas saw the child within her turn, the shape of an elbow, a knee. Boy or girl? He didn't know, nobody could know despite what the midwives claimed. He didn't want to know. He traced Lubna's belly and found no wound there, so she was right, the child could be saved, but only by ending her own life the sooner. And he couldn't do that. He couldn't end her life a single second before her due. He thought of Guerrero's wife brought in all those weeks ago, when Thomas's own life had still been whole. There had been no hesitation that day. But he couldn't do the same to Lubna. It was the logical choice, for he knew there was no saving her, yet still he couldn't do it. Given the same choice a thousand times over he would make the same decision. So he waited, stroking her face and kissing her lips. Let her pass in peace, he thought, let her pass without pain.

His mind went forward, thinking of where she would want to lie. He knew it would have to be done today, as her religion demanded. He would build the pyre himself, alone if the others would allow it. But even as the thought came to him he knew Olaf wouldn't allow him to do so, nor Jorge. And why should they, for did they not love Lubna as much as he did?

Lubna's chest shuddered as she fought for breath.

It would be a mercy to do as he had done so often and bring an end to her suffering, but he could not. He had always been cold. Brutal, even. But never with her. He could never be anything but loving with her.

She is too strong, he thought. *She will fight to the very end.* Strong, but not strong enough to escape what was coming for her. He glanced up as Belia knelt on the other side of Lubna. Her fingers reached out and touched Lubna's neck, pushed dark hair from her face. Her hand went to Lubna's swollen belly and laid there as the child moved within, a sense of urgency in the movement now.

"You have to bring it out," said Belia.

"Not while she lives."

"It will be too late then." She turned. "Jorge, bring me a blade."

"No!" Thomas struck out. He caught Belia on the side of the face and she fell backward. Then Jorge was on him, punching Thomas in turn, who took the blows without feeling them. Olaf came, wrapping his arms around Jorge and tossing him aside. He returned and stood over his daughter, watching, all his great strength futile.

A crash sounded and the last door into the courtyard flew open. Spanish soldiers streamed in. Usaden's blades flashed and men fell back, then all at once the fighting stilled as Fernando walked in amongst his troops. He glanced at Thomas, at who he knelt over.

"These people are to be left alone," he ordered. He came to Thomas, but there were no words. Instead he laid a hand on his shoulder, then moved on, passing through the courtyard and beyond as he led his men deeper into the fortress.

Lubna coughed, blood staining her lips. Thomas wiped it away and she kissed his fingertips. Her lips moved, and Thomas leaned close.

"My love…"

He kissed her brow.

And then she spoke her last words, spoke them to him alone.

Her chest rose one more time, fell and lay still.

Belia pulled herself to her knees, a growing bruise on her face. She looked at Olaf. "Take him away from here, for he cannot see what I must do now."

Olaf bent and wrapped his arms around Thomas. He fought to escape, but there was no breaking the iron grip. He was carried to the far side of the courtyard so did not see as Belia took Jorge's knife and used it to release the life still held within Lubna. But Thomas did hear when a newborn let forth a wail to match his own as he threw back his head and howled at the sky.

THIRTY-NINE

It was a high peak. A place where eagles soared. South, the bright sea glittered. In the far distance clouds rose in towers marking where the coast of Africa lay. North, mountains ran away as far as the eye could see. West lay Malaka, spires of smoke rising into the air, the ground around it dark with moving soldiers. The city had fallen after a ferocious battle, and now the Spanish were attempting to rebuild it. Most of the population had been enslaved, but the rich, like Durdush, were allowed to escape with their families and goods. Thomas had heard nothing of Woodville since he saw him at the beach. He wondered if he had managed to obtain a small portion of what had been spirited away that day, but he did not think of it much. His own world had been destroyed. He would need to rebuild it in a new way, once this final task he had set himself was done.

Thomas took a burning torch from where it lay in a small fire and walked to the pyre they had all built. He took a breath, feeling his chest shudder, but he had no tears left. He was empty of everything but pain. He thrust the torch into the dry kindling and stepped back, but not far. The roaring heat burned his hair and skin, but he wanted to feel it, to experience Lubna's ascension.

Then the others came, tossing their own torches after his. Jorge. Belia. Olaf. Will.

His new daughter lay against Belia's breasts, trying in vain to suckle. They had found a wet-nurse, but the woman remained below in the city. She was not of their family, and this moment was only for family.

Will came and took Thomas's hand, and he stepped back to protect the boy from the heat.

Flames rose. Wood crackled. Smoke curled into the air, carrying Lubna's soul to wherever its next home would be. Diego's body lay in the Christian burial ground with his mother and father. Yusuf's had been sent to Gharnatah where it would be interred with all the ceremony due a prince.

They stayed on the hillside, all of them, until the flames died down. They gathered Lubna's ashes, the nuggets of unburned bone, and placed them in a stone box. And then, as the sun touched the western horizon, Thomas turned away. He passed Will to Jorge.

"Take care of him. Take care of them both."

"You take care of him."

Thomas shook his head. "If I don't come back you must promise to raise him to be strong and make up his own mind. My daughter too."

"She has a name," said Jorge. "Use it. Amal. It was gifted her by Lubna. She would want you to use the name."

Thomas recalled Lubna's last words to him in the moments before her final breath. The gift of a name for their child. Jorge was right, he must use it.

"Look after Amal, then. And if I don't return, raise her as your own. You told me Belia wants children, then I gift you both of mine. Ask Usaden to accompany you when you leave Malaka. You will need someone strong when I'm no longer there."

"You will return," said Jorge, but Thomas knew it was more a hope than expectation. He turned and walked away. He had men to kill, and a coldness in his heart he hoped would never soften until the last of them could do no more harm.

Usaden was waiting for Thomas as he descended the hillside. He fell into step beside him.

"You are sure of the men who did this?" Thomas asked, not looking at the Gomeres, who had grown to become a friend.

"The son of the greybeard," said Usaden. "Yes, I am sure. I saw it with my own eyes. Will struck the father, but his son struck Lubna." They walked for a time in silence, shadows growing around them. After a time Usaden said, "I could not stop it, could not reach them. We will kill them slowly."

"I will kill them slowly," Thomas said. "I have a more important task for you. Look after those who live. Continue to train Will. He needs to be strong enough to survive in this world."

"I would rather be with you."

"And I would rather you be with them."

Thomas walked on after Usaden stopped. He didn't look back, but knew the man would stand still as a statue until he could no longer see him. And then he would do what had been asked.

As would Thomas.

HISTORICAL NOTE

For the purposes of fiction I have greatly compressed the timescale of events in 1487 that led to the fall of Malaga. Spanish troops arrived at the walls of Velez-Malaga on April 16th, blockading the mouth of the Wadi al-Cuevo. The fighting was sporadic until Velez surrendered on May 2nd, leaving Fernando and his troops to move against their main target of Malaga.

The subsequent siege and blockade was one of the longest and most vicious of the entire war against the Moors, trying the patience and stamina of both Fernando and Isabel. It began on May 7th and continued until the city surrendered on August 18th, a period of over three months. Hamid al-Tagri retreated to the Gibalfaro fort (then called the Rabita), from the safety of which he refused to surrender. However, he had no option but to admit defeat two days after the city fell.

Such an extended siege would make the timescale of *The Fortunate Dead* unwieldy and severely impact

Thomas's investigation, and so I have deliberately compressed both the time period and events that occurred.

What is known as recorded fact is that the citizens of Malaga took to eating whatever food they could: horses, mules, dogs, birds, even leaves from the many trees. It is also hinted at that Yusuf, the younger brother of Muhammed XII, did indeed conduct guerrilla raids on the Spanish with a small band of men and lost his life during the final chaotic fighting in Malaga.

Yusuf's uncle, al-Zagal, brought a large Moorish force from Granada to attack the Spanish but was ambushed in the dark, with many of his men killed and others fleeing for their lives. While he was attempting to relieve Malaga, his other nephew and elder brother to Yusuf, Abu Abdullah, Muhammed XII, launched a coup and replaced him in the Alhambra, cementing a hold on power that would last until January 1st 1492. But those events lie in the future for my characters.

An earthquake was recorded as occurring on April 14th, 1497 — far too cataclysmic an event to ignore while writing this book. A day or two later, torrential rain washed away sections of mountainside already weakened by the shaking of the earth, and flooded the streets of Malaga. Having spent time in Spain during the occasional torrential downpours, it has given me a small inkling of what this must have been like, and much of the description of the rain and its aftermath comes from personal experience.

I created the structure of the Malaga Guild for the purpose of this story. Medieval Guilds were present throughout Europe, North Africa, and the Middle East at this time, and were well-established. It seems unlikely

that some form of organisation to control the significant trade flowing through the city would not be in
place.

Various online sources indicate, though with no
great certainty, that Isabel and Fernando resided at Auta
Fort to the north of the small town of Riogordo during
the siege of Velez-Malaga, before moving their headquarters closer to Malaga. If it ever existed, Auta Fort
no longer shows as even a pile of stones, and the references to it are vague, although more certain indications
are that the Spanish King and Queen did make the
Riogordo area their base for a period of time before the
main assault on Malaga. As I own a small house in this
area, I have indulged myself by bringing Thomas
Berrington and Jorge past my own front door on their
way to and from Riogordo.

For the purpose of this story I have taken liberties
with some horticultural timings. Around the town of
Riogordo the almonds are in blossom during early
February, not April, but the sight of them is so
wonderful I had to include reference to them. Please
forgive me, and if you ever have the chance to visit the
Axarquia region early in the year you will see what I
mean — waves of grey-pink almond blossom coat the
hillsides. However, wild asparagus can be picked for
most of the year and is both abundant, if you know
where to look, and delicious.

The present town of Velez-Malaga now sits over a
mile inland from the sea, but this is a result of long
work to recover land for agricultural use, in particular
the growing of sugar cane which was once a major crop
of Andalusia, since fallen into obscurity. At the time I
write about, the Mediterranean lapped at the edges of

Velez-Malaga, and the dry riverbeds that now criss-cross the area would have had a more regular supply of water flowing through them.

As ever, my thanks go to the viking sisters (who berated me in no small manner that viking is a verb, *not* a noun) who provided invaluable advice on how a Northman would use an axe. The reference to a leather thong came directly from Gee, with any mistake or misuse my own. They also explained how the different Northern countries had their own unique roles to play. Norwegians were the explorers. The Danes were traders. And the Swedish were the warriors and mercenaries.

Finally, I spent sleepless nights over whether someone should survive this book (I mention no name in case you happen to read this note before the book itself). I had planned their demise at the outset, but as the moment of writing those final scenes approached they became harder and harder. I did not want to lose this character, who has become as much a real person to me as those I know, but it was necessary for the continuation of Thomas's story, however much it must have hurt him too.

Finally, my thanks to Thomas Shepherd for the map of Malaga as it would look in 1487, based on a version that can be found in Malaga Museum. Thomas has also produced an even more detailed map of Granada at the same time period, and a drawing of Thomas's house in the Albayzin. You can find higher resolution images of both maps and Thomas's house on my website, here.

Book 7 of Thomas's adventures, *A Promise of Pain*, takes him into the Moorish hinterland of the Axarquia and Alpujarras in search of revenge. It will be released within a few months of *The Fortunate Dead*.

My apologies for any anguish I have given my readers. Just remember — in fiction, as in life, nobody is safe.

REFERENCES

Apart from my usual sources, the following have been invaluable in writing *The Fortunate Dead*:

William Hickling Prescott: *The History of the Reign of Ferdinand and Isabella the Catholic – Volume 2.*

The Return of the Guilds: Towards a Global History of the Guilds in Pre-industrial Times: v. 1: Edited by Jan Lucassen, Tine de Moor, Jan Luiten van Zanden.

Granada 1492, The twilight of Moorish Spain and *The Moors, The Islamic West 7th-15th Centuries AD.* Written by David Nicolle, illustrated by Angus McBride. These two books (and others in the series) might be mistaken for school texts for children. But delve inside and there is a wealth of detail and meticulous research, as well as wonderful drawings and campaign maps. Both are highly recommended for an overview of the period I write about.

PLACE NAMES

For many of the Spanish cities and towns which lay beyond the boundary of Andalusia the current Spanish name has been used, except where the town had a significant Moorish past, such as Cordoba and Seville.

I have conducted research on the naming of places within Andalusia but have taken a few liberties to make the names easier to pronounce for a modern day audience. Where I have been unable to find reference to the Moorish name of a place I have made one up.

---

al-Andalus ... Andalusia
al-Mariyya ... Almeria
Gharnatah ... Granada
Ixbilya ... Sevilla
Malaka ... Malaga
Randonda ... Ronda
Qurtuba ... Cordoba
Sholayr ... Sierra Nevada mountains

ABOUT THE AUTHOR

David Penny is the author of the Thomas Berrington Historical Mysteries set in Moorish Spain at the end of the 15th Century. He is currently working on the next book in the series.

Find out more about David Penny
www.davidpenny.com

Printed in Great Britain
by Amazon

JULIE MOORE

Oxford Academic Vocabulary Practice

UPPER-INTERMEDIATE | B2–C1

OXFORD

UNIVERSITY PRESS

ACKNOWLEDGEMENTS

*The authors and publisher are grateful to those who have given permission to
reproduce the following extracts and adaptations of copyright material:* p.12
Extracts from http://blog.oxforddictionaries.com/author/oxford-dictionaries/,
by permission of Oxford University Press. p.16 Extracts from *Making Sense:
A Student's Guide to Research and Writing (Eighth Edition)* by Margot Northey
and Joan McKibbin © Oxford University Press Canada, 2015. Reproduced
by permission of Oxford University Press. p.18 Extract from *IB Psychology:
Course Companion* by John Crane and Jette Hannibal (Oxford University
Press, 2009), © Oxford University Press, 2009. Reproduced by permission of
Oxford University Press. pp.22, 42 Extract from *Making Sense: A Student's Guide
to Research and Writing; Life Sciences (Second Edition)* by Margot Northey and
Patrick von Aderkas © Oxford University Press Canada, 2015. Reproduced by
permission of Oxford University Press. p.24 Extracts from 'Earth Structure'
from *The Oxford Companion to the Earth*, edited by Paul L. Hancock and Brian J.
Skinner (Oxford University Press, 2003). By permission of Oxford University
Press. p.25 Definitions from *A Dictionary of Human Geography* by Noel Castree,
Rob Kitchin and Alisdair Rogers (Oxford University Press, 2013). Reproduced
by permission of Oxford University Press. p.29 Extracts from 'Moravian
Missions' by Carol Brice-Bennett, from *The Oxford Companion to Canadian
History* edited by Gerald Hallowell (Oxford University Press, 2004). By
permission of Oxford University Press. pp.29, 89 Definitions from *A Dictionary
of Business and Management 5e* edited by Jonathan Law (Oxford University
Press, 2009). Reproduced by permission of Oxford University Press. p.31
Extracts from 'Population Levels and Trends' from *The Oxford Companion
to Family and Local History (Second Edition)* by David Hey and edited by David
Hey (Oxford University Press, 2008). By permission of Oxford University
Press. p.31 Definitions from *A Dictionary of Economics (Fourth Edition)* by John
Black, Nigar Hashimzade and Gareth Myles (Oxford University Press, 2012).
Reproduced by permission of Oxford University Press. p.45 Extracts from
'Genetics of Behaviour' by William J. Connolly, from *The Oxford Companion to
the Mind (Second Edition)* edited by David Hey (Oxford University Press, 2004).
By permission of Oxford University Press. p.47 Extracts from *Making Sense:
Engineering and the Technical Sciences (Fourth Edition); A Student's Guide to Research
and Writing* by Margot Northey and Judi Jewinski, © Oxford University Press
Canada, 2012. Reproduced by permission of Oxford University Press. pp.48,
52, 53 Extracts from *Writing Critically: Key Skills for Post-Secondary Success* by
Mark Feltham, Wm. Paul Meahan and Whitney Hoth, © Oxford University
Press Canada, 2015. Reproduced by permission of Oxford University Press.
p.54 Extracts from 'Language Policy' from *The Oxford Companion to Politics of the
World (Second Edition)*, edited by Joel Krieger (Oxford University Press, 2004).
By permission of Oxford University Press. p.55 Extract from *A–Z of Plastic
Surgery* by Andrew Hodges (Oxford University Press, 2009). By permission of
Oxford University Press. p.55 Extracts from 'Declaration of Independence'
by William M. Wiecek, from *The Oxford Companion to the Supreme Court of the
United States (Second Edition)* edited by Kermit L. Hall (Oxford University Press,

2005). By permission of Oxford University Press. p.36 Definition from *A
Dictionary of Sociology (Fourth Edition)* edited by John Scott (Oxford University
Press, 2014). By permission of Oxford University Press. p.62 Definition
from *A Dictionary of Environment and Conservation (Second Edition)* by Chris
Park and Michael Allaby (Oxford University Press, 2013). By permission
of Oxford University Press. p.74 Extracts from 'Negative Attitudes Toward
Physical Activity: Measurement and Role in Predicting Physical Activity
Levels Among Preadolescents' by Timothy D. Nelson, Eric R. Benson and
Chad D. Jensen, *Journal of Pediatric Psychology* Volume 35 (1), 2010. Reproduced
by permission of Oxford University Press. p.78 Extracts from 'Smoking'
from *The Oxford Companion to the Body* by Colin Blakemore and Sheila Jennett
(Oxford University Press, 2003). By permission of Oxford University Press.
p.87 Extracts from *Statistics: A Very Short Introduction* by David J. Hand (David
J. Hand, 2008). By permission of Oxford University Press. p.88 Extracts
from 'Energy Systems' by Frank N. Laird and Edward J. Woodhouse, from
Science, Technology and Society, edited by Sal Restivo (Oxford University Press,
2006). By permission of Oxford University Press. p.89 Definition from *A
Dictionary of Computing (Sixth Edition)* by John Daintith and Edmund Wright
(Oxford University Press, 2008). By permission of Oxford University Press.
p.90 Definition from *Concise Medical Dictionary (Eighth Edition)* by Elizabeth A.
Martin (Oxford University Press, 2010). By permission of Oxford University
Press. p.93 Extracts from *The International Business Environment* by Leslie
Hamilton and Philip Webster (Oxford University Press, 2009). By permission
of Oxford University Press. p.94 Definition from *A Dictionary of Contemporary
World History (Third Edition)* by Jan Palmowski (Oxford University Press, 2008).
By permission of Oxford University Press. p.95 Extracts from 'legal practice,
styles and skills of' by Carrie Menkel Meadow, from *The New Oxford Companion
to Law* edited by Peter Cane and Joanne Conaghan (Oxford University Press,
2008). By permission of Oxford University Press. p.98 Definitions from *A
Dictionary of Human Resource Management (Second Revised Edition)* by Edmund
Heery and Mike Noon (Oxford University Press, 2008). By permission of
Oxford University Press. pp.100, 101 Extract from *Political Economy: The Contest
of Economic Ideas (Third Edition)*, by Frank Stilwell (Frank Stillwell, 2012). By
permission of Oxford University Press. p.86 Definition from *A Dictionary
of Weights, Measures, and Units* by Donald Fenna (Donald Fenna, 2002). By
permission of Oxford University Press. p.7 Extracts from 'How To Get A Phd:
a handbook for students and their supervisors' by Estelle M. Philips and Derek S.
Pugh, © Phillips and Pugh, 2010. Reproduced with the kind permission of
Open University Press. All rights reserved. p.38 Map '7.14 Population Density
– June 2010' from 'Geographic distribution of the population' by Australian
Bureau of Statistics (ABS), included within '1301.0 – Year Book Australia,
2012' by ABS, Canberra, 24 May 2012 © Commonwealth of Australia.
Released under the Creative Commons licence – Attribution 2.5 Australia,
http://creativecommons.org/licenses/by/2.5/au/.

Sources: p.15 http://www.wildlifeonline.me.uk/hedgehogs.html. p.14 http://
www.cdc.gov/nchs/data/nhsr/nhsr010.pdf. p.15 http://www.metoffice.gov.
uk/holiday-weather/asia/thailand/bangkok. p.48 'Reducing consumption of
sugar-sweetened beverages to reduce the risk of childhood overweight and
obesity: Biological, behavioural and contextual rationale' by Tim Lobstein,
www.who.int, September 2014.

Illustrations by: Oxford Designers and Illustrators: pp: 14, 15 (rainfall chart),
23, 24, 30, 38 (pool, map).

*We would like to thank the following for their kind permission to reproduce
photographs:* Alamy Stock Photo pp.6 (university graduate/Mark Phillips),
18 (diabetes information/BSIP SA), 22 (business structure/Zoonar GmbH,
Ivan Ryabokon), 26 (warehouse operative/Juice Images), 31 (Floyd Burroughs
and children on porch/Everett Collection Historical), 32 (female workers at
spinning mill/Arterra Picture Library), 36 (Asian family/Corbis Premium),
45 (twin girls with lollipops/Judith Thomandl, imageBROKER), 47 (vector
of pencil and illustration/Vik_Y), 51 (Mozambique forest/Mike Goldwater),
56 (consumer food information/Steven May), 56 (Apple iTunes screenshot/
NetPics), 83 (traffic in sandstorm/B.O'Kane), 92 (girls school Gambia/Finnbarr
Webster), 98 (call centre employees/Blaize Pascall), 103 (satelite dishes
rooftops/Kirsten Holst, Gallo Images); Getty Images pp.43 (steel workers/
Monty Rakusen), 64 (colleagues discussing/Portra Images), 90 (doctor and
patient/Ariel Skelley); Shutterstock pp.8 (science students/wavebreakmedia),
10 (archaeology students/thomas koch), 12 (pencil/MOSO IMAGE),
15 (diagram of air circulation/Slavo Valigursky), 16 (scientist in laboratory/
Alexander Raths), 24 (Earth structure/Webspark), 35 (Vietnamese woman
on phone/Seree Tansrisawat), 38 (frozen fruit and vegetables/Africa Studio),
39 (fresh fish/Skynavin), 48 (male student/Jasminko Ibrakovic), 55 (American
constitution and flag/danielfela), 56 (woman at market/Goran Bogicevic),
62 (cooling towers/Jaromir Chalabala), 68 (DNA molecules/Mirexon), 70 (blue
electric board/Family Business), 72 (turtle/David Evison), 76 (motorcycle taxi/
TonyV3112), 78 (no smoking sign/maodoltee), 87 (blood pressure meter/
David Orcea), 88 (wind turbines/stocknadia), 94 (EU flag/Julinzy), 100 (Sale
signs/Andy Dean Photography).

Cover photographs: Shutterstock; (coral/antos777), (student/wavebreakmedia),
(molecule model/alice-photo), (Stock market display/Kanok Sulaiman).
Back cover photograph: Oxford University Press building/David Fisher

*The publisher would like to thank the following people for their advice and assistance
in developing the material for this series:* Elif Barbaros (Erciyes University),
Kenneth Anderson (Edinburgh University), Alison Macaulay, Fatos Eskicirak
(Bahçeşehir University), Ros Gallacher (University of Strathclyde), Ilkay
Gökçe (Ege University SFL, Izmir), Anne Kelly, University of Strathclyde,
Mümin Şen (Yıldırım Beyazıt University), Libor Stepanek (Masaryk
University, Brno) and Irmak Çiçek Yücel (Bosphorus University, Istanbul).

Contents

Introduction

Who is this book for?

Oxford Academic Vocabulary Practice is designed for anyone who is studying, or plans to study, at college or university level in English. It aims to help you build your knowledge of academic vocabulary and, through practice, give you the confidence to use this language in your own writing.

What vocabulary is included?

The book mostly focuses on vocabulary which will be useful to students of any academic subject. The last section (Units 37–45) deals with language which is particularly relevant to different disciplines (business, law, medicine, etc.), but it doesn't include highly specialized subject vocabulary.

The book contains vocabulary that students at university level might need to use in their own writing; thus the focus is on *productive* vocabulary rather than *receptive* vocabulary (which you might need to understand when reading).

The keywords include many items from the *Academic Word List* (AWL); these are highlighted using the AWL symbol AWL . The choice of AWL items is based on those which are most useful for productive purposes, and doesn't include AWL items that are less frequent in student writing.

The research for the book was also heavily informed by the *Oxford Corpus of Academic English*. This was used to check the frequency and usage of words, and also provided many of the examples in the activities.

How is the book organized?

The book is divided into 45 main units and five review units. These are organized into broad sections focusing on academic study, describing basic concepts and relationships, and expressing evaluation. There are also sections that explore key concepts and skills in understanding how to learn and use academic vocabulary and common functions in academic writing.

Each review unit starts with a longer piece of student writing that shows vocabulary and features from the preceding set of units in an authentic academic writing context (e.g. a report, a critique, a case study). There are also activities to revise and practise a mix of vocabulary from the units.

At the back of the book you will find:
- a list of the language and academic terms used in the book

- a list of common academic collocations (e.g. *conduct research*)
- a list of dependent prepositions used with the keywords in the book (e.g. *react to, source of*)
- a list of affixes: prefixes (e.g. *un-, re-*) and suffixes (e.g. *-ization, -ment*)
- a glossary giving definitions of all the keywords in the book, based on the *Oxford Learner's Dictionary of Academic English*. It also contains information about pronunciation and word families.
- an answer key for all the exercises

Using the book

The book can be used either for self-study or in class. The glossary and other reference lists at the back of the book make it ideal for independent study. Alternatively, many of the texts could form the basis for discussion and further comprehension activities in class, and some units end with a writing task which is also suitable for a classroom context. The units are designed to be independent, so you can either work through the units in order or choose units that are most interesting to you.

Each unit starts with a list of around 15 keywords or phrases to learn. The units are divided into two or three sections. Each section starts by showing how the vocabulary is used in context. There are a variety of text types, including authentic academic texts and extracts from writing by university-level students. There are a number of questions to help you think about how the vocabulary is used in the text. This is then followed by activities which focus on the meaning and usage of the keywords. You can find answers to all the exercises in the back of the book. Some units end with a more open writing task. This gives you the opportunity to practise using the vocabulary in a short piece of writing.

Although each unit contains highlighted keywords, many of these words are repeated and recycled in other units. This means that as you work through the units, you will gradually begin to understand better how these words are used and get plenty of practice in using them yourself.

Abbreviations used in the book

adj	adjective	sb	somebody
adv	adverb	sth	something
AWL	*Academic Word List*	v	verb
n	noun	WF	word family

1 University study

Words to learn

academic AWL	degree	graduate (n)	research proposal
assessment AWL	discipline	lecture AWL	seminar
assignment AWL	dissertation	PhD	submit AWL
coursework	graduate (v)	project AWL	supervisor

Talking about undergraduate study

A When you start your university studies, you are an undergraduate. You study for your first **degree** or Bachelor's degree.

When you complete your degree, you **graduate**, usually at a graduation ceremony, and you become a **graduate**. You normally receive a BA (Bachelor of Arts) or a BSc (Bachelor of Science), depending on your **discipline**.

Usage note regional differences

The education systems in different countries can be organized quite differently. Be aware of differences in the language used to describe the system and the way people study.

For example, in the US, you can say that someone **graduates** from high school, but in the UK, you typically only **graduate** when you finish your first degree at university.

1 Put these events in a logical order. Some events typically happen at the same time.

▶ EXAMPLE: You are an undergraduate. _1_

1 You go to your graduation ceremony. _
2 You graduate from university. _
3 You study for your first degree. _
4 You successfully complete your degree. _
5 You receive your BA or BSc. _

2 a Complete the sentences using words from the box.

graduate graduated graduates graduation undergraduates

1 I _____ from Nanyang Technological University with a degree in communication studies last year. __

2 We're having problems recruiting science _____ to become teachers because of the low pay. __

3 Many first-year _____ are living away from home for the first time. __

4 A high percentage of students from the course find a job immediately after _____ . __

5 Many students now _____ with high levels of debt. __

b Mark each of the keywords in 2a as a noun (n) or a verb (v).

Talking about postgraduate study

B If you go on to do a master's degree, you usually start off with a taught programme of **lectures** and **seminars**. You have to do a lot of reading and you probably have to complete **assignments** or **coursework** which you **submit** to your tutor for **assessment**. At the end of your master's, you typically write a **dissertation**.

"Planning a dissertation and the notion of the dissertation itself is a daunting prospect. However, I realized that the fact that I had never previously completed a **project** of this scale and did not know where to begin were the reasons why I felt overwhelmed. By attending every lecture and completing the seminar tasks, I built up my knowledge. The project then seemed achievable."

Source: student reflective report

3 Match the words in the box to their descriptions.

assignment   coursework   dissertation   project   task

1 a long piece of writing on a particular subject written for a university degree _____
2 work that students do during a course of study, not in exams _____
3 a piece of work which involves several parts, e.g. reading, research, writing a report, preparing a presentation, etc. _____
4 a short activity, such as reading something or completing an exercise, which may be one part of a larger piece of work _____
5 a piece of work a student is asked to complete and submit as part of course, for example, an essay or a report _____

C Doing a PhD

At undergraduate level, everything is generally organized for the student. When you undertake a **PhD** though, you have to take responsibility for managing your own learning. Of course, you will get help from your **supervisor**, from other **academics** in the department and from your fellow students, but ultimately, it's down to you to develop your **research proposal**, to decide what's required and to carry it out.

The overall university framework for research students ensures that they all progress through their studies in a similar way, but there are differences between disciplines. In the sciences, supervisors are often managing a laboratory, and as a PhD student, you may be recruited to work on a project as part of a larger research team. In contrast, in the humanities and social sciences, students often come up with their own research topic and the role of the supervisor is just to offer general advice and supervision.

4 Do the pairs of words have a similar meaning (S) or a different meaning (D)?

1 a PhD student – a postgraduate student __
2 a supervisor – a lecturer __
3 an academic – a student __
4 a research proposal – a research project __
5 a discipline – a subject __

5 a Find verbs in the texts in this unit which collocate with the nouns in the table. Use the glossary on pp.129–144 to help you if necessary.

Verb	Noun
study for	a degree
1 _____	a degree
complete	coursework, an assignment
2 _____	coursework, an assignment

Verb	Noun
3 _____	a lecture, a seminar
4 _____	a dissertation
5 _____	a PhD
6 _____	a research proposal

b Complete the sentences using the correct form of verbs from the table in 5a. Sometimes more than one option is possible and some verbs are used more than once.

▶ EXAMPLE: He _completed_ his law **degree** in 2005 and graduated from the University of Melbourne.
1 Some students _____ their **assignments** online, but also give their tutor a hard copy as backup.
2 Students need to manage their time to _____ all their **coursework** before the deadline.
3 Students are expected to _____ at least 80% of **lectures**.
4 He's currently _____ his **dissertation** on contemporary South African cinema.
5 Students participate in group discussions to help them _____ a **research proposal**.
6 The department welcomes applications from students who wish to _____ a **PhD** in classics.

6 Write a short paragraph describing your own past, present or planned studies. Try to use some of the vocabulary in this unit. Think carefully about which verbs to use with different nouns, e.g. _complete a project_.

2 Academic disciplines 1

Words to learn

applied sciences	earth sciences	environmental **AWL**	natural sciences
biology	ecology	geology	physical science
chemistry	electronics	life sciences	physics
civil engineering	engineering	mechanical	technological **AWL**

Natural sciences

A Studying on one of our **natural sciences** programmes will give you the opportunity to explore solutions to some of the key challenges facing our modern world, from an ageing population to climate change. You can choose to specialize in any of the following areas:

Physical sciences: with a focus on the forces that govern our natural world through the study of **physics** and **chemistry**.

Earth sciences: not only the traditional disciplines of geography and **geology**, but also developing areas such as **environmental** science and **ecology**.

Life sciences: the study of living organisms through **biology**, zoology and botany, as well as interdisciplinary areas like biochemistry and biomechanics.

1 Complete the table. Use the glossary on pp.129–144 to help you if necessary.

Discipline	Adjective	Person
science	scientific	scientist
physics	1 _____	2 _____
3 _____	chemical	4 _____
geology	5 _____	geologist
6 _____	ecological	7 _____
8 _____	9 _____	biologist

2 Complete the sentences using words from the table.

1 The devices are used by _____ to measure tiny movements in the rock.
2 Ageing, like other _____ processes, is determined by genetic factors that are established before birth.
3 Quantum mechanics is the branch of _____ that deals with ultra-small-scale atomic particles.
4 In recent decades, the _____ community has made great progress in understanding how the climate works.
5 Some _____ predict a loss of between 30 and 50% of the world's animal species in the next century.
6 The heat triggers a _____ reaction that turns the polymers into a hard, incredibly strong structure.

Engineering and applied sciences

B The faculty of **engineering** and computing is divided into four departments which are all committed to advancing knowledge and **technological** innovation in the **applied sciences**:

- Mechanical engineering
- Electronics and electrical engineering
- Civil engineering and architecture
- Computer science

3 Choose the best word to complete the sentences.

1 The vehicle is the result of seven years' work by a team of *engineering / engineers* and designers.
2 The *applied / mechanical* sciences are concerned with using scientific knowledge to solve practical problems.
3 Moving pictures were a *technology / technological* breakthrough of the late 19th century.
4 *Civil / Mechanical* engineering deals with the design and construction of the built environment: roads, bridges, etc.
5 First-year *computer science / electronics* students focus on the basic techniques of circuit design.

4 Cross out the word in each group that does not form a strong collocation. Use the list of collocations on pp.107–110 to help you if necessary.

▶ EXAMPLE: civil/mechanical/~~physical~~ engineering
1 applied/civil/environmental science
2 computer/natural/information technology
3 environmental impact/science/geology
4 interdisciplinary chemistry/research/team
5 physical sciences/forces/technology
6 marine/human/geological biology

> **Usage note** perspective expressions
>
> In academic writing, we often need to talk about our **perspective** on a topic. Are we looking at an issue from a scientific perspective, a legal perspective or an economic perspective, for example? There are number of useful expressions you can use to introduce perspective:
> - *From an* engineering **viewpoint/standpoint** …
> - *In terms of* the environment/economic policy …
> - *In* engineering/economic **terms** …
> - *Historically/Politically* **speaking** …
> - *From a* scientific/economic **perspective** …

5 Match the sentence halves.

1 In geological terms,
2 From a scientific perspective,
3 In terms of technology,
4 From an engineering viewpoint,
5 Ecologically speaking,

a these results are promising, but a reliable treatment for patients could still be a long way off.
b constructing such a platform should be relatively straightforward.
c these birds are important for the environment because they're at the top of the food chain.
d we have seen most investment in systems to track and report on customer usage.
e 'gradual' means over several million years.

6 Write a short paragraph (three or four sentences) describing how one of the following areas of life has been influenced by science in recent years. Try to use some of the words and expressions from this unit.

- Transport
- Communication
- Health
- Energy and power

3 Academic disciplines 2

Words to learn

ancient	commerce	international relations	political
anthropology	creative AWL	legal AWL	psychology AWL
archaeology	cultural AWL	literature	social
civilization	economic AWL	management	

Arts and humanities

A I'm studying for a degree in English literature. As well as reading the great literary works from the past, we study contemporary novels and poetry. I'm also doing a course in creative writing, where I'm working on a series of short stories.

I did my first degree in ancient history and I was particularly interested in ancient Greek civilization. So now I'm doing an MA in archaeology and I'm hoping to get some experience working on an archaeological site in Crete as part of my master's research.

I studied anthropology at university, which is concerned with the different social and cultural norms and traditions of people around the world. Now I'm doing my PhD, working with nomadic peoples in Mongolia. They're really fascinating from an anthropological perspective and they've been incredibly friendly and welcoming during my fieldwork, too.

1 a Choose the best words to complete the sentences.

1 *Societies / Social* vary enormously in how they organize themselves, their *culture / cultural* practices, as well as their religious, political and economic arrangements.

2 Our students spend four weeks doing fieldwork at Berkeley Castle, excavating the remains of a Roman settlement alongside professional *archaeologists / archaeology*.

3 The department offers the opportunity to study the *literary / literature*, art and culture of Greek and Roman *civilians / civilizations* and their impact through the ages.

4 The first year focuses on different *literature / literary* genres including novels, poetry and drama.

b Which of these disciplines do each of the statements in 1a refer to?

ancient history   anthropology   archaeology   literature

1 _____   2 _____   3 _____   4 _____

2 a Match the adjectives, 1–5, to the sets of nouns they collocate with, a–e. Use the glossary on pp.129–144 to help you if necessary.

1 ancient
2 literary
3 anthropological
4 archaeological
5 cultural

a site/evidence/remains
b tradition/norms/diversity
c history/times/civilization
d work/genre/criticism
e study/fieldwork/perspective

b Complete the sentences using the best noun from 2a.

1 In ancient _____, the warrior caste of Japan practised meditation to become better fighters.

2 Some anthropological _____ are entirely based on interviews with community members.

3 Film adaptations can open up new audiences for great literary _____.

4 The existence of three official languages reflects the country's cultural _____.

5 Evidence from archaeological _____ across New England indicates that population sizes grew rapidly.

Social sciences

B

The thing I enjoyed most about my studies was the mix of areas it covered. As well as studying economic theory, we looked at how trade and commerce actually work in a modern globalized world. Through a number of case studies, we looked at the structure of multinational corporations and examined some of the key concepts in business management. I think my favourite part of the course was business psychology, which is a really fascinating area.

Studying on a course in international relations, you get to meet a really interesting mix of students from different backgrounds. The master's programme involves looking at not just the political relationships between countries, but also how economic, environmental, legal and sociocultural issues affect the way countries interact.

3 Complete the table. Use the glossary on pp.129–144 to help you if necessary.

Field	Adjective	Adverb	Person
commerce	*commercial*	*commercially*	-
1 _____	economic	2 _____	economist
3 _____	legal	legally	4 _____
management	managerial	5 _____	6 _____
politics	7 _____	8 _____	politician
9 _____	psychological	psychologically	10 _____

4 Complete the text with words from the table.

When a company decides to move into a new market, of course the venture has to be ¹_____ viable and likely to make a profit for the parent company, but ²_____ isn't the only factor to consider. There will be ³_____ regulations that they have to abide by which may be different from country to country. They may even come up against ⁴_____ opposition to foreign investment where a government is trying to encourage local businesses to develop. Then they have to adapt to the local culture. The ⁵_____ of work and doing business can vary greatly between countries, and it is important to adopt a ⁶_____ style which takes account of the beliefs and attitudes of local employees.

5 Complete the extracts from student essays using the correct form of the word in brackets.

In western ¹_____ (social) at least, education is considered a necessity which should be available to every child. Although much education is government funded, education also has the potential for ²_____ (commerce) gain. This makes it a ³_____ (politics) sensitive issue.

The concept of childhood is not consistent across ⁴_____ (culture). For the purposes of this essay, I will be taking the ⁵_____ (law) definition of childhood. There is no single ⁶_____ (law) that defines the age that one is a child within the UK, but the UNCRC (1989) states that a child is "... every human being below the age of eighteen".

4 Structuring an assignment

Words to learn

abstract AWL	bibliography	introduction	outline
acknowledge AWL	conclusion AWL	journal AWL	reference
appendix (plural:	draft AWL	limitation	theme AWL
appendices) AWL	heading	literature review	thesis AWL

Organizing an essay

A At this point, you have finished with your research, and have collected all the material needed to write the essay. However, before you begin you should take a moment to step back and re-evaluate the essay question or topic. Consider your approach to the question, the main **themes** or ideas that are emerging, the arguments you can pursue, and the kind of evidence that you need.

Another important step is **outlining** the structure of the paper. You are probably aware that an essay needs an introductory paragraph, a main section, and a **conclusion**, but that basic format should be expanded upon in your specific essay plan. Think about creating an **outline** of **headings** for the main section based on the different **themes** you plan to touch on. You might also consider adding **draft** notes under these headings to help you once you begin writing.

Source: Oxford Dictionaries. (2015). *4 things to do before you start writing an essay.* OxfordWords blog.

1 **Complete the student notes about organizing material for an essay based on the advice in text A.**

1 Research the topic and collect material, then _____ the structure of the essay.
2 Create an _____ with an _____ paragraph, a main section and a _____ .
3 Use _____ within the main section for each different _____ you plan to write about.
4 Add _____ notes under each heading.

2 a **Complete the parts of speech of the highlighted words: noun, verb, adjective or adverb. Use the glossary on pp.129–144 to help you if necessary.**

▶ EXAMPLE: **outline** the structure *verb*; create an **outline** *noun*

1 in your **introduction** *noun*; an **introductory** paragraph _____
2 the main **themes** _____; the essay is organized **thematically** _____
3 in the **conclusion** _____; he **concluded** with suggestions for further research _____
4 use **headings** for each section _____; the first section is **headed** 'background' _____

b **Choose the best word form to complete the advice.**

1 Spend some time *outline / outlining* your ideas and organizing your main points into an appropriate structure.
2 In your *introduction / introductory*, make sure you set out the main idea that you will develop in your essay.
3 You could organize your main section *thematic / thematically*, dealing with one key *thematic / theme* in each paragraph.
4 If a section is *headed / heading* 'historical background', for example, then make sure your notes all relate to the past and not the present situation.
5 Typically, you should *conclude / conclusion* your essay with an answer to the overall question posed in the introduction.

3 Find verbs in text A that are used with the highlighted nouns below. Complete the sentences with the correct form of the verbs.

1 You should draw on evidence from a variety of sources and identify important **themes** that _____ .

2 Before you start writing, you need to _____ an **outline** to help you organize your ideas.

3 _____ **draft** notes under each heading, but be brief at this stage.

4 The article _____ on a number of key **themes** within international development in this region.

5 Write a plan that _____ the overall **structure** of the project.

Organization of an academic paper

B Academic disciplines have different guidelines for organizing an academic paper. However, most papers, whether they are student assignments or in an academic **journal**, conform to a basic format.

Abstract: An **abstract** is a short summary of the entire paper, including both the aims and the conclusions. It helps the reader decide whether or not they want to read the paper.

Introduction and background: Most **introductions** describe the general topic area and then focus on the main point of the paper: the research question or the writer's **thesis**. This section also gives background to the topic. It often includes a **literature review**, which describes previous research that is relevant to the main point of the paper.

Methodology and results: In a paper based on primary research, these sections give a detailed description of the design of the experiment and the results obtained.

Discussion: This is the key section of the paper where the writer sets out their main thesis or claim. It should include a detailed and well-supported argument and discussion of the issue. In a paper based on research, it gives an interpretation of the results.

Conclusion: The conclusion should be more than just a summary of the paper. It should show why the main ideas are significant and what implications they might have. It might also **acknowledge** any **limitations** of the paper, such as a small sample size, and outline possible further areas for research.

References: Sometimes also called a **bibliography**, this section contains a detailed list of all the sources used in the paper. The reader can also use these **references** to find more information on the topic.

Appendices: Detailed data that are too lengthy to include in the main part of the paper can be included in an **appendix** at the end.

4 In which section of an academic paper would you find the following information? More than one section may be relevant.

1 What did the researcher find during their experiment? _____

2 Which other academic papers or books can you read to find out more? _____

3 How might the research affect people or the world we live in? _____

4 Is the paper interesting or relevant to you and worth reading? _____

5 How was the research conducted? _____

6 What is the writer's stance or viewpoint? _____

7 Which things was the writer unable to include in this research/paper? _____

8 What are the writer's detailed arguments? _____

5 Choose the best word to complete the sentences.

1 Employees participated in one-hour interviews. (See *appendix / bibliography* for transcripts.)

2 One of the *acknowledgements / limitations* of our study is the small sample size of some categories.

3 The central *interpretation / thesis* of the paper is that space exploration is best left to robots rather than humans.

4 Section II presents *background / a literature review* of previous studies on charitable giving.

5 After scanning titles and *abstracts / discussions,* we found 47 trials that seemed to evaluate this specific treatment.

6 Details of the trials were published in a medical *journal / source*.

5 Describing visual data

Words to learn

arrow	diagram	illustrate AWL	plot
axis	distribution AWL	key	segment
bar chart	figure	label AWL	visual AWL
curve	graph	pie chart	

Graphs

A Figure 1 is a **graph** showing the **distribution** of heights of men and women. Height in centimetres is **plotted** along the horizontal **axis** and the percentage of people at each height is shown on the vertical axis. The resulting **curves** indicate that the most frequent height for women in this sample is around 162 cm and for men, 176 cm.

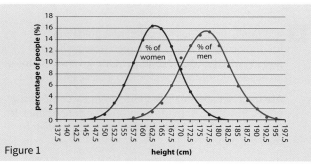

Figure 1

1 Complete the sentences using words from the box.

> axis curve distribution figure graph plot

1 After you have collected your data, you need to _____ the results on a _____ .
2 The numbers along the horizontal _____ show the height in centimetres.
3 The shape of the _____ shows you the _____ of the data across the whole sample.
4 In a piece of writing, each graph, chart or diagram is called a _____ and is given a number.

2 a Find verbs in text A that are used with the nouns *graph* and *curve*.

1 graph _____ 2 curve _____

b Match the sentence halves to make more collocations with *graph* and *curve*.

1 The second graph clearly
2 The purpose of plotting
3 The solid curve
4 The results produce

a a graph is to make the relationship between two sets of variables clearer.
b illustrates the dramatic differences between incomes in rural and urban areas.
c represents the average wage in urban areas.
d a bell-shaped curve known as a normal distribution.

Charts

B Representing statistics and other data in **visual** form can make detailed information more immediately accessible to your reader. For example, you could show the proportions of different foods consumed by a particular animal as a **pie chart**, where each **segment** represents a type of food.

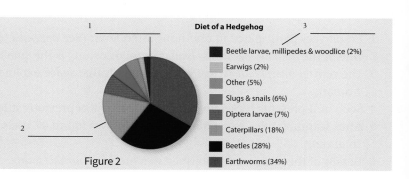

Diet of a Hedgehog

■ Beetle larvae, millipedes & woodlice (2%)
■ Earwigs (2%)
■ Other (5%)
■ Slugs & snails (6%)
■ Diptera larvae (7%)
■ Caterpillars (18%)
■ Beetles (28%)
■ Earthworms (34%)

Figure 2

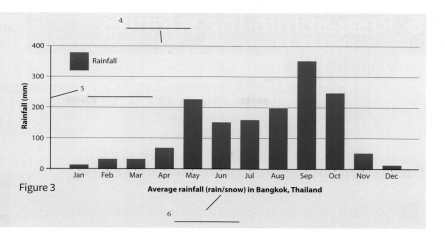

Or you could show average rainfall in an area as a **bar chart**, where each bar indicates the amount of rain in each month. It is important to **label** any **visual** data clearly so that the reader understands exactly what it shows. You may need to include a **key** to show what each part of the chart represents. In an academic paper, each graph or chart is usually labelled Figure 1, 2, 3, etc. for easy reference.

Figure 3

4 _____

Rainfall

5 _____

Average rainfall (rain/snow) in Bangkok, Thailand

6 _____

3 **Label the two diagrams in text B using words from the box.**

axis   bar chart   key   label   pie chart   segment

4 **Complete the sentences using the correct form of the keywords from text B.**

1 Figure 2 is a _____ showing the typical diet of a hedgehog.
2 In Figure 2, the _____ shows what the different colours in the chart represent.
3 The red _____ shows the percentage of earthworms in the animal's diet.
4 The _____ in Figure 3 shows rainfall patterns in millimetres through the year.
5 The horizontal axis is clearly _____ with the months of the year.
6 By showing the information in a _____ form, it is easy for the reader to identify the times of year with the heaviest rainfall at a glance.

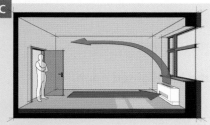

Figure 4

The **diagram** in Figure 4 **illustrates** the flow of hot and cold air in a room with an air-conditioning unit mounted on the wall. The red **arrow** indicates the flow of hot air into the room and the blue arrow represents cooled air from the unit.

5 **Choose the best word to complete the sentences.**

1 Draw a *graph / diagram / bar chart* to show the layout of the buildings.
2 The figures for the past ten years can be *illustrated / distributed / plotted* on a graph to show the trend.
3 The red *axis / arrow / label* indicates the direction in which the aircraft is travelling
4 Each *key / segment / axis* in the chart represents a different type of physical activity.
5 The results of the survey are shown in *Figure / Diagram / Chart* 5.2.
6 A sequence of coloured pictures is used to *illustrate / indicate / reference* the different stages of the butterfly's development *visually / horizontally / representatively*.

6 **Complete these sentences so they are true about Figures 1–4 in this unit.**

▶ EXAMPLE: The horizontal axis in Figure 1 _shows height in centimetres_.

1 The green curve in Figure 1 _____ .

2 The key in Figure 2 _____ .
3 Each bar in Figure 3 _____ .
4 The arrows in Figure 4 _____ .

7 **Find a graph, chart or diagram in your subject area (in a textbook or online) and write three or four sentences to describe it using words from this unit.**

6 Research in the sciences

Words to learn

analyse AWL	equipment AWL	method AWL	unit
calculation	format AWL	perform	yield
carry out	interpret AWL	set up	
conduct AWL	material	statistical AWL	

Describing an experiment

A Students in the sciences are often asked to report formally on the results of scientific experiments. Although lab reports generally conform to a basic format, each discipline has slightly different requirements. You must conduct your experiment as objectively as possible and present the results in such a way that anyone who reads your report or attempts to duplicate your procedure will be likely to reach the same conclusions that you did.

Materials and methods:
The materials section of a lab report should contain a description of the materials and equipment you used and some explanation of how the experiment was set up.
The method section is a step-by-step description of how you carried out the experiment, with the procedures described in the order in which you actually performed them.
Although you should be concise in your description of the experimental method, make sure that you don't omit essential details. If you heated a test tube, for example, you must report what temperature it was heated to and for how long. Readers must know exactly what controls to apply if they try to perform the experiment themselves.

Source: Northey, M. & McKibbin, J. (2015). *Making Sense: A Student's Guide to Research and Writing.* Ontario: Oxford University Press.

Usage note *conduct, carry out* and *perform*

These verbs can all be used to talk about doing research. **Conduct** and **carry out** are the most general words; you can 'conduct' or 'carry out' research, an experiment, a study, an analysis or a test. **Conduct** is slightly more formal than **carry out**.
Perform is typically used to talk about doing a specific task rather than a whole research project.
• *Statistical analyses/Blood tests were performed.*

1 Match the sentence halves. Think about both meaning and the highlighted noun + verb collocations.

1 To date, much less research
2 Use a diagram to illustrate how you set up
3 The collision test
4 Care should be taken when using
5 All experiments in this study

a electrical equipment in the laboratory, especially close to water.
b were carried out under carefully controlled conditions.
c has been conducted into the effects of temperature on these processes.
d the equipment for the experiment.
e was performed using a passenger car of 9500 kg mass.

Results and discussion

B The *results* section is the section of most interest to scientists, and they depend on its accuracy. It usually contains a mix of data and description. It will also likely contain some statistical calculations.

You should pay special attention to the units of any quantities; to omit or misuse them is a serious scientific mistake. Taking care to include all units will also reveal mistakes in your calculations. If your units don't cancel properly to yield the result you expect, you will know you have made an error.

The *discussion* section of the lab report allows you the greatest freedom, since it is here that you analyse and interpret the test results and comment on their significance. You should show how the test produced its outcomes – whether expected or unexpected – and discuss how these elements influenced the results.

Source: Northey, M. & McKibbin, J. (2015). *Making Sense: A Student's Guide to Research and Writing.* Ontario: Oxford University Press.

2 Complete the diagrams using the words in the box.

equipment   materials   methods   statistical calculations   units

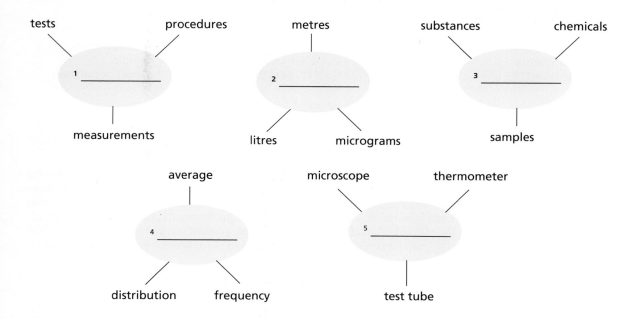

tests   procedures   metres   substances   chemicals

1 _____   2 _____   3 _____

measurements   litres   micrograms   samples

average   microscope   thermometer

4 _____   5 _____

distribution   frequency   test tube

3 Complete the table. Use the glossary on pp.129–144 to help you if necessary.

Noun	Verb	Adjective
1 _____	-	statistical
calculation	2 _____	-
3 _____	analyse	4 _____
5 _____	interpret	-

4 Complete the sentences using the correct form of words from the table.

1 Using the values from this test, we can _____ the rate of the reaction under any specified conditions.

2 The _____ tests showed no significant difference between the effectiveness of the two substances.

3 A range of _____ techniques has made it possible to date land surfaces very accurately.

4 We cannot be sure that this _____ of the genetic data is correct, and others are certainly possible.

5 The results _____ with the aid of statistical software.

5 a Complete the statements using the correct form of the verbs from the box.

analyse   conduct   interpret   set up   yield

1 The experiment _____ a set of data.

2 The researcher _____ the results and writes a report.

3 The researcher _____ the experiment following a set of procedures.

4 The researcher _____ the equipment for an experiment.

5 The researcher _____ the data using statistical calculations.

b Put the steps in 5a into a logical order.

_____

7 Research in social sciences

Words to learn

aim	consent AWL	finding	procedure AWL
biased AWL	data AWL	flaw	representative
confidential	distortion AWL	investigate AWL	sample
confirm AWL	ethical AWL	participant AWL	target population

Understanding the research process

A Aim, procedure, findings

The **aim** is the purpose of a study. An aim indicates which behaviour or mental process will be studied. The group whose behaviour the researcher wishes to **investigate** is called the **target population**. After identifying the aim, the researcher will plan a **procedure**. This is the step-by-step process used by the researcher to carry out the study.

The **findings** state how the researcher interpreted the **data** that were collected. Research findings are always open to discussion and debate. Maybe the researcher has interpreted the results in a way that is **biased**, or perhaps there were **flaws** in the procedure. If other research studies **confirm** the findings, the study is more credible.

Source: Crane, J. & Hannibal, J. (2009). *IB Psychology: Course Companion.* Oxford: Oxford University Press. p.17.

1 Put the steps in the research process in a logical order.

1 Interpret the data _____
2 Decide on the aim of the study _____
3 Plan the procedure _____
4 Identify the target population _____
5 Write up the findings _____
6 Carry out the study _____
7 Collect the data _____

2 Choose the best word to complete the sentences.

1 The aim of this study is to *identify / investigate* the relative effectiveness of these two methods.
2 The experimental *population / procedure* was divided into four steps.
3 The available *data / research* indicate that consumer spending has declined.
4 The researcher has to collect, analyse and then *interpret / confirm* the data.
5 She published her *data / findings* in the Journal of Public Policy Research.
6 Reviewers have highlighted a number of *flaws / bias* in the design of the study.
7 Our data *confirms / interprets* the findings of previous studies.
8 Using only university students as participants in a study can easily lead to *credible / biased* results.

Participants

B

People who take part in a psychological study are called **participants**. Normally, psychologists define a target population – that is, a specific group of people whom they are interested in for their study. The nature of the group of participants, what psychologists call the **sample**, is very important in determining the usefulness of a piece of research.

The goal in sampling is to obtain a sample that is **representative** of the target population. In psychological research it is not possible to test the whole population. Researchers often try to obtain a sample that represents a population – that is, a representative sample.

The size of a sample matters if it is to be representative. Small groups are more open to **distortions** than large ones. In a small group, each individual has quite a lot of influence on the overall result.

Source: Crane, J. & Hannibal, J. (2009).
IB Psychology: Course Companion.
Oxford: Oxford University Press. pp.18–19.

3 Complete the table.

Verb	Noun	Adjective
1 _____	participation, 2 _____	participatory
3 _____	sample, sampling	-
represent	representation, representative	4 _____
distort	5 _____	distorted

4 Complete the text using words from the table.

When you're looking for people to ¹_____ in a study, it's often easiest to ask other students. The problem though is that your ²_____ may not be very ³_____ of your target population; it will only contain young, relatively well-educated people, probably from a fairly narrow socio-economic background. This can ⁴_____ the results and mean that you can't generalize about your findings. To avoid this type of ⁵_____ , you need to include ⁶_____ who ⁷_____ a wider range of ages, backgrounds, etc.

Research ethics

C Another important consideration in research is that participants should be treated in an **ethical** manner. Psychologists now agree to follow certain ethical standards in order to avoid harming participants.

- Informed **consent**: Participants must be informed about the nature of the study and agree to participate.
- **Confidentiality**: All the information that is obtained in a study must be **confidential**.

Source: Crane, J. & Hannibal, J. (2009). *IB Psychology: Course Companion.* Oxford: Oxford University Press. pp.21–22.

5 Match the sentence halves.

1 Any research project must follow
2 It is important to maintain the confidentiality
3 A person can only give
4 All interviewees were assured
5 Research ethics rules

a informed consent if they fully understand the nature of the study.
b the university's ethical guidelines.
c that their responses would remain confidential.
d apply to all participants in a study.
e of any personal information provided.

6 Rewrite the sentences replacing the highlighted words with a word from the box. Make any other changes necessary.

~~aim~~ biased confirm distortion flawed participant target population

▶ EXAMPLE: Set out clearly why you are conducting _the aims of_ a piece of research.
1 The people who take part _____ should be properly informed about the exact procedures.
2 When choosing a sample, consider how well it reflects the whole group of people you are interested in _____.
3 A small sample can lead to data which isn't representative _____ because one individual can heavily influence the results.
4 It is important to analyse and interpret your data in an objective way to avoid findings that unfairly favour a particular point of view _____.
5 If a study is not carried out carefully _____, the results will not be viewed as credible.
6 A piece of research will carry more weight if other studies obtain similar _____ results.

Student writing: a reflective report

Reflective writing asks students to think critically about the course and themselves as learners. You may be asked to reflect on an experience such as a field trip, on specific aspects of tasks, such as how you chose a topic, or on your course as a whole. The writing may be a task on its own or a final section to an assignment such as a research report. You will need to show evidence that you are developing relevant skills and attitudes, that you can question your initial assumptions, and that you can connect theory and practice.

Source: (2014). Oxford Academic Writing Tutor *Oxford Learner's Dictionary of Academic English*. Oxford: Oxford University Press. p.AWT20.

A As a student studying for a master's in education, I have a particular interest in the student experience of education at tertiary level. I completed my undergraduate studies at a US university where I **graduated** with a BA in education. I came to the UK to pursue my studies on a taught MA programme. During my first few weeks, I experienced a real 'culture shock', not just at living in a new country, but also because of what I realized is a very different approach to university education.

B One of the significant differences is the degree of specialization within the two systems. In the US, undergraduate students take a broad range of subjects in their first one or two years, with an emphasis on developing a range of knowledge. So it's not uncommon to choose courses from a mix of **disciplines**, even combining arts or social science subjects with **natural sciences** or engineering. It's only later that you choose your 'major', or main subject. In the UK, by contrast, students specialize very early on, selecting a specific discipline right from the start and exploring that field in depth over the course of their three or four years of undergraduate study. This means that students come out at the end of their **degree** with a more detailed knowledge of their chosen area.

C The second thing I noticed was the degree of independence required of students. When I started my MA programme, it seemed as if I didn't have much work to do. During my first degree, we were given a set reading text or an **assignment** to complete after almost every class. My master's programme though, consists mainly of **lectures** and **seminars** with apparently very little homework. We have only one assignment per course to be **submitted** at the end of term, and a final exam. I soon realized however, that instead of setting specific homework tasks, my tutors were expecting students to do a lot of extra work independently – going to the library and reading around the subject for ourselves.

D Increasing numbers of international students are moving around the world to study, and the US and the UK are the top two destinations (British Council, 2014). With this and my own experiences as a student in these two very different academic cultures in mind, I decided to focus on differing student experiences of higher education as the topic of my master's **dissertation**.

E I plan to **conduct** a study to investigate the experiences of international students at both UK and US universities. I will select a **sample** of students from the two **target populations** initially to complete questionnaires. Then I hope to follow up with one-to-one interviews, conducted either face-to-face or via Skype. Of course, I have to **acknowledge** the **limitations** of my research: a small sample will not necessarily be **representative** of such a huge student body. Nevertheless, I hope that my **findings** can still contribute to a better understanding of student experiences in a globalized educational context.

1 What is the writer of the text reflecting on?

_____

2 Match the headings, 1–6, to the sections of the text, B–E. Two headings are not needed.

1 The wider context _____
2 Degree of student independence _____
3 Undergraduate and postgraduate study _____
4 Initial research outline _____
5 Research aims and thesis statement _____
6 Degree of specialization _____

Focus on collocation

3 Complete the sentences using the correct form of the verbs in the box. Some verbs are used more than once. Look back at the previous units or use the list of collocations on pp.107–110 to help you if necessary.

> acknowledge   collect   complete   conduct   emerge   graduate   illustrate   study   submit

1 Although I _____ with a **BSc** in engineering, I chose to _____ **business management** at master's level.
2 Students on the master's programme typically _____ a small-scale research **project** starting at the end of the second term, and they have to _____ their **dissertation** at the start of October.
3 All the participants in the study were asked to _____ a short **questionnaire**. We then _____ face-to-face **interviews**.
4 In the methods section, you need to describe how you _____ your **data** or how you _____ your **experiment**.
5 Using **graphs** and charts to _____ your results can help your reader to understand the data.
6 The discussion section is where you write about the key **themes** that _____ from your research.
7 In your conclusion, you often _____ any **limitations** of your study, for example limited time or resources.

4 Complete the extract using one preposition (*in*, *at*, *of*, etc.) in each gap. Look back at previous units or use the list of dependent prepositions on pp.111–113 to help you if necessary.

Of course, most students go to university with the aim [1]_____ getting a qualification at the end of their studies. They hope to graduate [2]_____ a degree [3]_____ history or engineering or whatever. But is the role of higher education just to produce graduates with a detailed knowledge of their discipline? Or should the experience of participating [4]_____ an academic degree programme teach you more general skills, such as critical thinking, time management and the ability to work as part of a team? If so, then there are clearly implications [5]_____ this shift of emphasis [6]_____ university assessment procedures. We need to consider whether the grades for assignments and exams are really representative [7]_____ a student's skills, or whether they just reflect the ability to absorb information. The limitations [8]_____ the current approach to assessment are clear, but finding a way of effectively testing how a student's skills develop may be more difficult.

Focus on word families

5 Complete the sentences with the best form of the word in capitals. Use the glossary on pp.129–144 to help you if necessary.

1 Late _____ of assignments will result in marks being deducted. SUBMIT
2 It is difficult to argue that the views expressed in such small survey are _____ of all young people. REPRESENT
3 Many students only have a vague idea of what they hope to do after _____ . GRADUATE
4 Formal exams are still an important part of the university _____ system. ASSESS
5 Researchers _____ to conduct a small-scale pilot study initially. PROPOSAL
6 Participants, who were evenly _____ across gender, ranged in age from four to 16 years. DISTRIBUTION
7 It seems reasonable to _____ that the regulations have improved working conditions. CONCLUSION
8 Students' motivation to achieve _____ can come from a number of sources. ACADEMIC

Words to learn

category AWL	criterion AWL	item AWL	sector AWL
characterize	divide into	level	selection AWL
class	feature AWL	overlap AWL	status AWL
classify	hierarchy AWL	rank	system

Classifying

A Classifying means **dividing** something **into** its separate parts according to a given principle of **selection**. The principle or **criterion** may vary. You could classify crops, for example, according to how they grow (above or below the ground), how long they take to mature, or what climatic conditions they require. If you are organizing your essay by a **system** of **classification**, remember the following guidelines:

- You must account for all members of a **class**. If any are left over, you need to alter some **categories** or add more.

- You can divide categories into subcategories. You should consider using subcategories if there are significant differences within a category.

- You should include at least two **items** in each subcategory.

Source: Northey & von Aderkas. (2015). *Making Sense in the Life Sciences: A Student's Guide to Research and Writing.* Ontario: Oxford University Press.

1 Complete the sentences using the correct form of the highlighted keywords from text A.

▶ EXAMPLE: Applying the <u>selection</u> criteria resulted in a list of 423 small businesses that formed our sample.

1 Crime can be _____ two types: crimes with victims and victimless crimes.

2 The habitat is mapped as a grid where each square is _____ according to habitat type.

3 One _____ of proteins, known as enzymes, acts to regulate the biochemical functions essential to life.

4 Figure 6.8 lists the major _____ of products and services sold, according to the company's website.

5 Ensure that there are the same number of _____ on each list.

6 Participants who met the study inclusion _____ received a written consent form.

7 A standardized _____ for describing soil types has been developed.

8 The World Health Organization publishes an international _____ of diseases (ICD).

Types of classification

B A **hierarchy** is a system of classifying items or individuals in terms of their relative importance or **status**. A hierarchy is often represented as a pyramid with a small number of very important items or individuals at the top and the least important forming the lowest **level**. For example, the people in an organization often fit into a hierarchical structure, with the CEO and the board of directors at the top and the lowest-**ranked**, and probably lowest-paid, workers at the bottom.

[1] a _____ structure

[2] the lowest _____

C Areas of human activity, for example within an economy, are often divided into **sectors**. Businesses that have similar **features**, for example those which produce goods, could be grouped together as the 'manufacturing sector'. Sometimes these sectors can **overlap**. So a company that has factories making consumer goods could be **characterized** as part of the manufacturing sector. However, if that same firm also owns shops in which it sells its goods, it may be classified as part of the 'retail sector' as well.

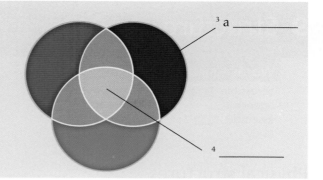

³ a _____

4 _____

2 Complete the labels on the diagrams in texts B and C using words from the box.

> hierarchical level overlap sector

3 Match the sentence halves.

1 Increasing costs within the public health care
2 Someone's position in a social
3 In general, non-manual, office-based occupations rank
4 Study participants were grouped
5 In marketing, the term 'social grade' refers to a system

a sector remain a serious issue.
b higher than manual occupations.
c into five categories by occupation.
d of classification of consumers based on their socio-economic group.
e hierarchy is generally measured by education, income or occupation.

4 Do these pairs of words have a similar meaning (S) or a different meaning (D)?

1 rank – status __
2 classify – categorize __
3 divide into – select __
4 criteria – principle __

5 feature – characteristic __
6 item – level __
7 class – category __
8 overlap – division __

5 Rewrite the sentences replacing the highlighted word or expression with the correct form of a keyword from this unit.

▶ EXAMPLE: The activities were put in order _ranked_ according to how much physical energy they required.
1 All the words and phrases were divided into four groups, with four to eight things _____ in each category.
2 We used the following criteria to choose _____ participants for the study.
3 There are clearly some things in common _____ between the banking and accounting sectors.
4 Depending on the aim of the study, it might be appropriate to put people together _____ by age, by gender or by occupation.
5 The most striking thing about _____ this group of insects is their ability to change colour to match their environment.

6 Describe a system of classification in one of the areas below or an area that you are interested in.

• Chemical elements
• Jobs and professions

• Industries or parts of the economy
• Files stored on your computer

▶ EXAMPLE: The economy can be divided into the public and private sectors. The public sector consists of organizations owned and run by the government, such as schools and health services.

9 Structure

Words to learn

accessible AWL	composition	framework AWL	layer AWL
agency	consist of AWL	independent	property
assembly AWL	core AWL	interior	structure AWL
body	expose AWL	internal AWL	vehicle AWL

Physical structures

A Earth structure

The **interior** of the Earth is inaccessible; all that we know about it has to be deduced from our knowledge of the rocks **accessible** to us and from the shape and physical **properties** of the Earth as a whole.

The Earth is, in the broadest sense, a series of concentric spherical shells, each shell having distinct physical or chemical properties. The outermost, and thinnest, shell is the crust. Then, descending into the interior, the next shell is the mantle, which extends to a depth of 2891 km. Finally at the centre of the Earth is the **core**.

The rocks **exposed** at the surface of the Earth are part of the crust. The crust is a thin **layer** of silica-rich rocks. The crust that makes up the continents differs in origin, **structure** and **composition** from the crust beneath the oceans.

Source: Hancock, P.L. & Skinner, B.J. (eds.). (2000). *The Oxford Companion to the Earth.* Oxford: Oxford University Press.

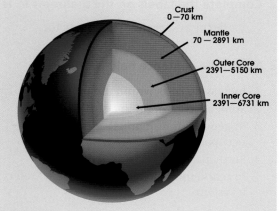

Crust
0—70 km

Mantle
70 — 2891 km

Outer Core
2391—5150 km

Inner Core
2391—6731 km

Glossary
concentric (*adj*): Concentric circles are arranged one inside the other with the same centre.
spherical (*adj*): shaped like a sphere or a ball; round

---

1 Choose the best word to complete the descriptions of the diagram.

1 The diagram shows a cross section of the *origin / interior* of a spherical object.
2 The object is composed of *layers / properties* which are represented by coloured rings.
3 The innermost part or the *core / surface* of the object is shown as very dark blue, almost black.
4 The red layer represents the surface of the object which is *exposed / inaccessible* to air and light.

2 Complete the headings using words from the box.

accessible	composition	core	layers	properties	~~structure~~

▶ EXAMPLE: The <u>structure</u> of an atom: An atom consists of electrons surrounding a nucleus that contains neutrons and protons.

1 The _____ of the atmosphere: The atmosphere is made up of 80% nitrogen and 20% oxygen.
2 The _____ of water: Water sticks to itself (cohesion) and it also sticks very well to other things (adhesion).
3 The _____ of the reactor: The central part of a nuclear reactor is where the reaction takes place.
4 The _____ of soil: A sample from the river bed shows very clearly the different soil types one on top of the other.
5 The _____ areas: Only certain parts of the volcano can be reached by researchers, others are too dangerous.

The structure of organizations

B United Nations

An international organization founded in 1945 in the wake of the Second World War as a **vehicle** to try and maintain international peace and security, develop friendly relations among nations, and promote social progress, better living standards, and human rights. Initially **consisting of** 51 member countries, it now has 193 members, and its main headquarters are located in New York. There are six main UN **bodies** to which a range of **agencies**, bodies, and committees report. The General **Assembly** is the main deliberative organ of the UN and is **composed of** representatives of all member states.

Source: Castree, N., Kitchin, R. & Rogers, A. (2013). *A Dictionary of Human Geography*. Oxford: Oxford University Press.

Glossary
deliberative organ (*n*): the part of the organization that discusses and makes decisions

C The International Criminal Court (ICC) was set up in 2002 to investigate human rights violations committed by individuals. Its remit is to act as a court of last resort in situations where cases cannot be brought under national law. The court has to operate within its own **internal** legal **framework** in such a way as to abide by internationally recognized human rights law. Although it is technically **independent** of the UN, the UN was instrumental in its creation and the two organizations maintain strong links.

Glossary
remit (*n*): the area of activity over which someone has authority, control or influence

3 Choose the best word to complete the sentences. In some cases, both words are possible.

1 Representatives of four international *agencies / bodies,* including the EU, participated in the discussions
2 Are such regulations an effective *vehicle / agency* for reducing greenhouse gas emissions?
3 A limited company must have an audit committee that *is comprised of / consists of* independent members.
4 Businesses that are owned by private individuals and *organizations / bodies* are part of the private sector.
5 The Commission continues to struggle to enhance its *internal / interior* management processes.
6 This established a broad regulatory *framework / structure* for setting environmental standards.

Usage note

If the everyday meaning of a word doesn't fit in a particular context, check whether there is a specialist academic sense.

• **body**
1 (of a person/animal)
   • *the human body*
2 (official group of people working together)
   • *professional bodies, such as the Law Society*
• **vehicle**
1 (car, truck, etc.)
   • *cars and commercial vehicles*
2 (sth used as a way of achieving a goal)
   • *Economic growth offered the best vehicle for solving social problems.*

4 Choose one word from the box to complete each pair of sentences. You may need to change the form of the word in some cases.

assembly   body   property   vehicle

1 a The company was in control of the land and all _____ on it.
  b The tests detected significant changes in the physical _____ of the materials.
2 a Almost all the mothers in the study believed that parents were the main _____ for influencing healthy eating.
  b The President announced tough targets for new fuel-efficient _____ to cut pollution.
3 a The World Trade Organization is an international _____ , the purpose of which is to promote free trade.
  b Other measures included the child's _____ weight at six and 18 months.
4 a It is not easy to insert quickly; _____ of its components requires several steps in the correct sequence.
  b In 2007, the national _____ approved the nationalization of various oil and gas projects.

Words to learn

continuous	frequent	potential AWL	projection AWL
following	initial AWL	preceding	sequence AWL
forecast	interval AWL	preliminary AWL	subsequently AWL
forthcoming AWL	period AWL	prior to	ultimately AWL

Forecast and frequency

A As our product is aiming to enter a large consumer market, **continuous** production will be needed in order to meet the **potential** demand. Consequently, we are looking to receive bulk supplies of components from the suppliers at weekly **intervals** based on **forecast** sales **projections**.

Once the product has passed its **initial** launch **period** and sales become more consistent, we will be able to re-evaluate the amount of supplies needed to match the demand and **subsequently** make any changes to the supply process, such as having less **frequent** deliveries of higher volume, or vice versa.

Source: student report

1 Complete the paraphrases using keywords from text A.

▶ EXAMPLE: How many people do we expect to attend based on previous events?
What are the projections for attendance based on previous events?

1 How many days are there between each measurement?
What is the _____ between each measurement?

2 Water flows into the system non-stop.
There is a _____ flow of water into the system.

3 Breakdowns are quite common due to the difficult conditions.
There are _____ breakdowns due to the difficult conditions.

4 A risk assessment has to consider all problems that might happen.
A risk assessment has to consider all _____ problems.

5 The findings from the first stage of the trials are promising.
The _____ findings from the trials are promising.

6 Income has risen much faster than the predicted growth rate.
Income has risen much faster than the _____ growth rate.

7 The amount of time needed to train someone depends on their previous experience.
The training _____ depends on someone's previous experience.

2 Choose the best word to complete the sentences.

1 Make a plan for dealing with *potential / potentially* problems from the start.
2 The campaign will *initial / initially* focus only on the European market.
3 Recently the airline increased its flight *frequency / frequently* from two to four flights per week.
4 The human body is involved in a *continuous / continuously* process of repair.
5 Longer-term *projected / projections*, however, are much less certain.

Sequence

B Good market research is essential **prior to** launching a new product.

The **preliminary** sales projections were promising.

The **following** section details the **sequence** of events in the production process.

Some details will be further refined during **forthcoming** testing.

We will re-evaluate the situation and **subsequently** make any changes to the supply process.

As discussed in the **preceding** section, demand for the product was established via market research.

Ultimately, the sustained success of the product will depend on a number of factors.

> **Usage note** sequence in a text
>
> In a longer piece of writing, you sometimes need to refer back or forward to other sections.
> * As noted **in the previous section**, …
> * The framework outlined **in the preceding section**…
> * **The following sections** describe the data collected from the experiment.
> * Possible reasons for this will be discussed **in a later section**.
>
> To refer to figures and diagrams on the same page, you can use:
> * The model adopts a two-stage approach, illustrated **in Figure 3.5 above**.
> * **The table below** shows the average scores for…

3 Which of these words from text B refer to something that happens before something else or at the beginning (B), and which describe something happening after or in the future (A)?

1 prior to __   3 following __   5 subsequently __   7 ultimately __
2 preliminary __   4 forthcoming __   6 preceding __

4 Complete the sentences using keywords from text B.

1 The results of the study will be published in a _____ article.
2 A _____ analysis was conducted to determine if the sample needed to be divided into subcategories.
3 For the 12 hours _____ surgery, patients are not allowed to eat or drink.
4 None of the participants had been admitted to hospital within the _____ 12 months.
5 Several of the volunteers on the programme _____ became paid welfare workers.
6 Figure 3.2 illustrates the typical _____ of steps involved in the construction process.
7 It is hoped that this research will _____ lead to successful treatments for the condition.
8 This question will be addressed in the _____ sections.

5 Put the steps into a logical order. Use the highlighted words to help you.

▶ EXAMPLE: First of all, we conducted a small-scale pilot study prior to embarking on the main research project. _1_

1 During the pilot study, we encountered a number of problems, so subsequently we adjusted our methodology. __
2 These samples were collected at intervals of 10–12 days. __
3 The full findings of our research will be presented at a forthcoming conference. __
4 Then the main research project began in May. __
5 Over the following months, we collected over 50 samples. __
6 Finally, when all the samples were collected, we analysed the data. __
7 During this period, weather conditions were continuously monitored for any changes that might affect the results. __

Words to learn

abandon AWL	eliminate AWL	initiate AWL	terminate AWL
arise	emerge AWL	introduce	undertake AWL
cease AWL	establish AWL	permanent	
commence AWL	found AWL	suspend AWL	

Starting

A 1 The contractor is required to obtain a licence before **commencing** work. The defendant failed to do so in this case.

2 Among his many different ventures, Thomas Edison **founded** the General Electric Company in the late 19th century.

3 New problems **emerged**, however, as a result of the reforms, in particular the need for a more transparent mechanism for dealing with complaints.

4 The report's recommendations concerning policing methods and training were largely accepted by the government of the time. However, due to the political climate, only limited steps were taken to **initiate** changes.

a According to Woods (2002), little action was taken to **introduce** changes as a result of the report.

b Jones (2010) reports that further problems **arose** in the wake of the changes.

c The regulations state that the contractor must obtain a licence before **undertaking** the work.

d The company was **established** at the end of the 19th century.

1 Match the extracts from academic texts, 1–4, to the student citations that paraphrase them, a–d.

1 _____ 2 _____ 3 _____ 4 _____

2 Match the pairs of verbs from the extracts in A (1–4, a–d) to the sets of nouns they collocate with in the table.

1 _____ , _____	a company, an institution, an organization
problems, issues, differences	2 _____ , _____
3 _____ , _____	study, work, training
4 _____ , _____	a change, a policy, reform

3 Complete the sentences using the correct form of keywords from the extracts in A. More than one option may be possible.

1 These methods will allow the company to gain data that it can use to improve any areas where problems _____ .

2 Women have always worked, but it is the forms of work that they _____ that has changed.

3 Comparing the findings from this group to the total sample, two notable differences _____ .

4 Prior to _____ this study, we had carried out a pilot study to test the methods.

5 The following questions were posted to _____ the discussion within the focus group.

6 The Red Cross is a non-governmental organization _____ by Henri Dunant to aid the victims of armed conflict.

7 1908 saw the implementation of the first Children's Act which _____ juvenile courts and _____ the registration of foster families.

Finishing

Glossary
Inuit (*n*): a race of people from northern Canada and parts of Greenland and Alaska
missionary (*n*): a person who goes to a foreign country to teach the people there about Christianity

C *laying off*

Suspending or terminating the employment of workers because there is no work for them to do. If the laying off involves a **permanent** termination of employment, redundancy payments will be involved.

Source: Law, J. (ed.). (2009). *A Dictionary of Business and Management.* (5 ed.). Oxford: Oxford University Press.

4 Answer the questions about texts B and C.

1 What was the effect of the missionaries setting up trading stores in northern Labrador? _____
2 How were the Inuit influenced by the Christian religious movement of 1804? _____
3 Why are workers usually laid off? _____
4 When do laid-off workers receive a redundancy payment? _____

5 Find the relevant sections in texts B and C that match the paraphrases 1–4. Then replace the highlighted words below with a form of a verb from text B or C.

▶ EXAMPLE: Over time, the Inuit stopped *ceased* travelling south to trade.
1 The network by which the people from the north traded goods disappeared _____.
2 Inuit people were initially reluctant to give up _____ their traditional beliefs.
3 Work may be halted _____ for a temporary period.
4 When a worker's job is ended _____ completely, they may receive compensation.

6 Complete the sentences using the correct form of the word in capitals. Use the glossary on pp.129–144 to help you if necessary.

▶ EXAMPLE: Managers may be involved in the recruitment of workers and the *termination* of contracts. TERMINATE
1 Organizational change is often closely linked to the _____ of new technology. INTRODUCE
2 These are the most significant reforms since the _____ of the national health care system. ESTABLISH
3 There was a complete _____ of diplomatic relations between the two countries. SUSPEND
4 Now we are seeing the _____ of megacities all over the world. EMERGE
5 He reaffirmed the commitment of the United Nations to the _____ of racial discrimination. ELIMINATE
6 Throughout the 18th and 19th centuries, these ideas led to the _____ of schools, hospitals and police forces. FOUND
7 Smoking _____ campaigns can have benefits throughout the age range. CEASE

7 Write a short paragraph (three or four sentences) describing the start or the end of something. Use one of the ideas below or your own. Try to use words from this unit.

• The start of an organization or company
• A tradition/practice that no longer happens
• The setting up of a system
• A historical event

12 Trends

Words to learn

adjust AWL	downturn	range AWL	successive AWL
collapse AWL	dramatic AWL	rate	trend AWL
decline AWL	fluctuate AWL	stabilize AWL	underlying AWL
demographic	maintain AWL	steadily	

Describing statistics

A Figure 1 illustrates a typical pattern of weight loss and gain for one of the dieters featured in the study. It shows how there are **dramatic fluctuations** in their weight as they embark on **successive** diet regimes. With each attempt, they initially lose weight, then their weight **stabilizes** for a period. However, as they struggle to **maintain** the diet, they regain the weight lost. What is perhaps most striking though, is that rather than simply **fluctuating** within a fixed **range**, the **underlying trend** is **steadily** upwards over time.

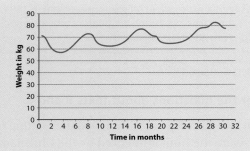

Figure 1

1 Complete the paraphrases with words from the box that have a similar meaning to the highlighted phrase.

> dramatic   fluctuated   maintain   range   stabilized   ~~steadily~~   successive   underlying

▶ EXAMPLE: The temperature continued to increase at roughly the same rate – it increased _steadily_.

1 The price of coffee on the world market has gone up and down a lot in recent months – the price has _____ .

2 The age of the participants was between 21 and 54 – they were within the age _____ 21 to 54.

3 During the rainy season there is a sudden and significant rise in the number of cases – there is a _____ rise.

4 After a period of instability, the value of the currency has been more or less the same for a period of time – the value has _____ .

5 Unemployment is affected by seasonal factors, but ignoring these variations, the trend is downwards – the _____ trend is downwards.

6 Staff are required to continue to reach high professional standards – they must _____ high standards.

7 Worldwide cocoa production fell in 2008 for the fourth year in a row – it fell in four _____ years.

2 Complete the text using the correct form of words in the box to describe the graph in Figure 2. Add any other words as needed.

> ~~dramatically~~   fluctuate   range   stabilize   steadily   trend

Through most of the second half of the 20th century, global oil production increased _dramatically_. After a period of instability during the 1970s, production [1]_____ in the early 1980s, then it [2]_____ . The amount of oil produced [3]_____ over the next three decades, but it remained [4]_____ 50 to 70 million barrels a day until 2004. Throughout this period though, [5]_____ was upwards.

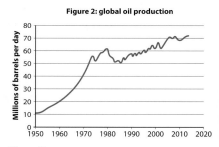

Figure 2: global oil production

Figure 2

Social and economic trends

B Interest in the study of demographic trends began in an informed way in the late 17th century. The first national census to be taken in Britain was that of 1801. The population of England and Wales was counted at 8.9 million, which is usually adjusted for under-recording to 9.2 million. The second decade of the 19th century experienced the fastest rate of growth. By 1851 the population of England and Wales had almost doubled to 17.9 million, and by 1911 it had doubled again to 36.1 million. The 20th century saw slower rates of growth.

Source: Hey, D. (ed.). (2008). *The Oxford Companion to Family and Local History*. Oxford: Oxford University Press.

Glossary
census (*n*): an official count of the population

C The Great Depression was a worldwide economic downturn beginning in the late 1920s and lasting until the mid-1930s. In the US the Great Depression began on 29 October 1929 with the stock market collapse. The effect of the Great Depression was to reduce international trade and national incomes. Farming was particularly badly hit with large declines in agricultural product prices.

Source: Black, J., Hashimzade, N. & Myles, G. (2012). *A Dictionary of Economics*. Oxford: Oxford University Press.

3 According to texts B and C, which of these things increased (I) and which decreased (D)?

1 The rate of population growth in Britain during the 19th century. __
2 The value of shares on the US stock market after October 1929. __
3 International trade during the Great Depression. __
4 The price of agricultural products during the 1920s and 30s. __

4 Match the beginning of each sentence, 1–6, to two possible endings, a–l.

1 The annual **rate**
2 **Demographic**
3 The global **economic**
4 Following the **collapse**
5 After **adjusting**
6 There was a **decline**

a of the property market, many home-owners were unable to sell.
b trends have led to a shortage of key workers in some areas.
c in the number of women elected to parliament.
d for age, sex and occupational status, the associations remained significant.
e of communism, the societies of Eastern Europe underwent economic transition.
f depression of the 1930s strongly affected Arizona.
g in demand for imported goods.
h of growth of car production stood at 40% in March.
i information, such as gender, age, and occupation was gathered.
j downturn in 2008 affected China's export markets badly.
k of inflation fell to 2.5% in September.
l for socio-economic factors, the studies still show systematic variations.

5 Complete the sentences using the best preposition (*of, in,* etc.). Use the list of dependent prepositions on pp.111–113 to help you if necessary.

1 Greater **fluctuations** _____ sea levels will particularly affect coastal communities.
2 All results fell _____ the normal **range** for this age group.
3 The island is experiencing a long-term **decline** _____ the number of visitors.
4 Even after **adjusting** _____ age, there were significant differences between the four groups.
5 These economies experienced high **rates** _____ economic growth.
6 The **downturn** _____ the housing market has affected all those firms involved in this sector.

13 Change

Words to learn

adapt AWL
amend AWL
evolve AWL
expand AWL

implement AWL
in response to
migrate AWL
modification AWL

re-evaluate
replace
shape
shift AWL

substitute AWL
transform AWL
transition AWL
upheaval

Gradual change

A Household-work strategies were shaped by the onset of the industrial revolution and the changing structure of the family. The expansion of industry led to mass urbanization as new opportunities caused huge numbers to migrate from rural communities into urban areas.

Contemporary family structures evolved in response to industrialization, science, and technology. With the development of specialized wage labour, work moved beyond the reach of the family unit and led to the redefinition of family relationships. Urbanization produced a shift from the more nuclear families that had previously existed, to more extended family forms in towns and cities.

Source: student essay

1 Match the definitions to keywords from text A.

▶ EXAMPLE: to change gradually because of circumstances _evolve_

1 the growth of something in terms of size _____
2 to affect the way something happens _____
3 a gradual change from one thing to another _____
4 to move from one place to go and live and/or work in another _____
5 because of something that happens _____

2 Complete the table. Use the glossary on pp.129–144 to help you if necessary.

Noun	Verb	Noun	Verb
shape	shape	response	3 _____
expansion	1 _____	4 _____	migrate
2 _____	evolve	shift	5 _____

3 Complete the sentences using the best form of a word from the table. More than one option may be possible.

1 Research in molecular biology gradually _____ from the analysis of single genes to the analysis of whole genomes.
2 The rapid _____ of higher education in the region has highlighted an increased need for good-quality teaching.
3 Organizations and companies that _____ quickly to change are successful.
4 The paper looks at the role of science and scientists in _____ public policy in a range of areas.
5 Founded in 1978, the business _____ slowly from a small contracting company to an established leader in its industry.

Planned changes

B With the globalization of the automotive industry, organizations have had to **re-evaluate** their strategies to **adapt** to changing demands. Previously, local manufacturers predominantly built and supplied vehicles for national markets. Increasingly now, this model is being **replaced** by global component suppliers who deliver components around the world where they are instead simply assembled. This **transition** has, of course, meant major **upheavals** for many of those employed in the industry. As changes have been **implemented**, the nature of some roles has been completely **transformed**.

C When an order is processed, any **modifications** to the order, for example for one product being **substituted** for another, have to be logged on the system so that the delivery note can be **amended** to show the changes clearly.

4 Group the words in the box according to their general meaning.

adapt   amend   modify   replace   substitute   transform   upheaval

To make a small change to something	(To make) a big change to something	To exchange one thing for another
adapt ¹ _____ ² _____	³ _____ ⁴ _____	⁵ _____ ⁶ _____

5 a Match the sentence halves. Focus especially on the collocations with the highlighted keywords. Use the list of collocations on pp.107–110 to help you if necessary.

1 After initial testing, a number of **modifications**
2 Such support services are aimed at students making
3 The board will meet again in six months to **re-evaluate**
4 Successive governments have promised to **amend**
5 He was given the task of **implementing**
6 The novel is set against the social and political
7 Technology continues to **transform**

   a the way we do business.
   b the situation and decide whether further action is necessary.
   c were made to the design.
   d the **transition** from high school to college.
   e **upheavals** of the 1960s.
   f the laws surrounding libel.
   g the changes and overseeing their success.

b Underline the key collocation(s) that goes with the highlighted word in each completed sentence in 5a.

   ▶ EXAMPLE: After initial testing, a number of **modifications** <u>were made</u> …

6 Write one sentence describing something that has changed in each of the following ways in recent years. Use the highlighted word in your answer.

• Something that has **expanded**
• Something (or someone) that has had to **adapt** to changes
• An **upheaval**
• Something that has changed **in response to** an event or situation
• Something that has been **replaced**
• A **shift** from one thing to something (slightly) different

   ▶ EXAMPLE: _The budget airline industry has expanded rapidly over the past decade._

Words to learn

communications AWL	deprived	located AWL	regenerate
community AWL	facilities AWL	nationwide	remote
confined to AWL	infrastructure AWL	network AWL	route AWL
construct AWL	isolated AWL	property	widespread AWL

Urban areas

A Within this area, there is a need for quality and affordable housing. A recent **nationwide** house and condition survey to check that **properties** have a good standard of repair and modern **facilities** highlighted that 32,000 dwellings in the city did not meet the decent homes standard. In addition, 35% of all residents fall into the most **deprived** 20% nationally, which has been linked to poor health status. Consequently, both deprivation and poor quality housing are major sources of health inequality.

To attempt to address these issues, a new housing policy has been developed. The aim of the policy is to increase housing provision through the building of several mixed tenure social tower blocks within deprived areas of the city. The main objectives are to provide safe and affordable housing, establish socially cohesive local **communities** and **regenerate** currently deprived areas. Tower blocks are proposed as they offer the opportunity to **construct** a large number of homes within a relatively small space.

Source: student essay

Glossary

mixed tenure: having a mix of different people living somewhere

socially cohesive: with people from different social groups living well together

Usage note *-wide*

The suffix **-wide** describes something that happens or exists across a whole area. There are several common words ending in **-wide** – 'worldwide', 'nationwide', 'countrywide' – and it can be adapted to talk about other areas – 'regionwide', 'citywide', etc.
For more about prefixes and suffixes see Unit 30 and the list on p.114.

1 Find six words in text A that refer to buildings where people live, and divide them into two groups: formal words and more neutral, everyday words.

Formal	Neutral
1 _____	4 _____
2 _____	5 _____
3 _____	6 _____

2 Rewrite the sentences, replacing the highlighted words with keywords from text A.

1 After a successful pilot study, the scheme is soon to be extended to the whole country _____.
2 Several houses and apartments _____ near to the river are regularly affected by flooding.
3 Major sporting events like the Olympics have been used to improve _____ neglected urban areas.
4 The company provides excellent places to take part in sport, places to eat, etc. _____ for its employees.
5 It is important for planners to consult all stakeholders, including the people who live in the area _____.
6 The school takes children from many of the city's poorest _____ neighbourhoods.

Usage note sensitive language

When talking about sensitive topics, it is important to choose appropriate vocabulary that will not cause offence. For example, when talking about people who have less money than others, instead of describing them as **poor**, which has a strongly negative meaning, you could say they are **deprived** or **disadvantaged**. When you are reading about a topic, take note of the vocabulary used by other academic writers.

3 Complete the extracts using words from the box. Some words are not needed.

| constructing | deprivation | deprived | facilities | home | properties | regeneration |

Arguably, the first large-scale ¹_____ of an existing urban area was undertaken by Georges-Eugène Haussmann in Paris between 1852 and 1870, in which a large part of medieval Paris was cleared to create a more modern layout, including better road networks and ²_____ such as public parks and monuments.

The major wave of renewal in Western Europe and North America took place from the 1950s onwards. It centred on slum clearance in ³_____ neighbourhoods, demolishing substandard and overcrowded ⁴_____ and in their place ⁵_____ more modern public housing projects.

Rural areas

B Unemployment is a particular issue for those living in isolated rural communities. Those not located on major public transport routes find themselves confined to the local area, often with limited employment opportunities.

C Communications are often seen as key to the development of the rural economy. It has been suggested that mobile phones are more appropriate for providing services to rural areas than fixed lines because of lower infrastructure costs and easier delivery. As mobile networks become more widespread, coverage is improving in even the remotest areas and costs are also coming down.

4 Are the statements true (T) or false (F)?

1 If a problem is widespread, it is confined to a specific area. __
2 An isolated community has good transport links to other towns and cities. __
3 Airlines fly different routes between major cities. __
4 A remote location is a long way from population centres. __
5 A country's infrastructure includes roads, railways, the electricity grid, water system and communications network. __

5 a Match each word, 1–8, with a word which has a similar meaning, a–h.

1 confined	a common
2 deprived	b house
3 isolated	c limited
4 located	d nationwide
5 nationally	e poor
6 property	f renewal
7 regeneration	g remote
8 widespread	h situated

b Choose the best synonym to complete the sentences.

1 At that time, foreign nationals did not have the right to own land or *property / houses*.
2 Pollution above these levels can have a *common / widespread* effect on the general population.
3 Older people can become socially *isolated / remote*, with little contact beyond their immediate family.
4 There were further negotiations over the *regeneration / renewal* of the contract after a period of two years.

6 Describe the following in your own country. Write one to three sentences about each one using vocabulary from this unit.

- The location of the capital city
- An isolated community
- The transport network
- A typical property in an urban area
- An area that has been regenerated

15 People

Words to learn

class	immigrant AWL	minority AWL	relationship
discrimination AWL	inheritance	occupation AWL	sibling
ethnic AWL	integrate AWL	partner AWL	spouse
generation AWL	marital	related to	status AWL

Family relationships

A Kinship is one of the main organizing principles of human society, and kinship systems have been extensively studied by social anthropologists. Kinship systems establish **relationships** between individuals and groups on the model of biological relationships between parents and children, between **siblings**, and between **marital partners**. The relationships between parents and children (and by extension between grandparents and grandchildren) determine modes of **inheritance** as well as the overall political relationships between **generations**.

Source: Scott, J. (ed.). (2014). *A Dictionary of Sociology.* (4 ed.). Oxford: Oxford University Press.

1 Find keywords in text A that are more formal terms for:

1 brothers and sisters _____
2 husband and wife _____
3 family members of roughly the same age _____
4 receiving money or property from parents or grandparents when they die _____

B A kinship system shows the ways in which family members, such as **spouses**, siblings and different generations, are **related to** each other (Scott, 2014).

C According to Scott (2014), the way in which property is **inherited** by younger generations from parents or grandparents is determined by the relationships between family members within a particular culture.

2 Read texts B and C. Match the words and phrases below to words and phrases from text A.

1 spouses _____
2 ways in which family members are related _____
3 the way in which property is inherited _____

3 Choose the best words to complete the sentences.

1 Typically, the youngest child may be less independent than their older *spouses / siblings*.
2 He is the fourth *generation / inheritance* of his family to run the business.
3 The case study explores *relationships between / related to* step-siblings in a family where parents have remarried.
4 A family member, usually the eldest son, *inheritance / inherits* the land and any property built on it.
5 The survey found that women living with a *relationship / partner* took responsibility for most of the childcare.
6 Although they share the same name, they are not *relationship between / related to* each other.
7 In old age, it is common for *marital relationships / spouses* to care for each other.

Social groups

D The social **status** of an individual is determined by factors such as their age, gender and **occupation**. In societies with a strong **class** structure, a person's family background influences their position in the social hierarchy. The **ethnic** background of an individual may also affect their social standing. **Minority** groups, such as recent **immigrants**, may experience **discrimination** and find it difficult to **integrate** into the wider society.

4 Match the sentence halves. Use the list of collocations on pp.107–110 to help you if necessary.

1 In the survey, slightly more women reported experiencing
2 The research found that ethnic
3 The audience represents a varied demographic in terms of social
4 The link between life chances and social
5 During the 1990s, there was a large influx
6 An employee in a professional

    a of **immigrants** from Turkey and Egypt.
    b **status**, age and gender.
    c age **discrimination** at work than men.
    d **minority** students are more likely to leave high school early.
    e **occupation** is five times more likely to receive training than an unskilled employee.
    f **class** is more complicated than the simple link between health and income.

5 Complete the sentences using the best preposition (*in*, *at*, *of*, etc.). Use the list of dependent prepositions on pp.111–113 to help you if necessary.

1 Children of first-generation immigrants generally **integrate** _____ the host society more easily than their parents.
2 The two characters are distantly **related** _____ each other; they share the same grandmother.
3 The report found widespread **discrimination** _____ people with mental health problems.
4 Factors such as changes in the role and **status** _____ women in society contribute to shifts in marriage patterns.
5 Social capital refers to **relationships** _____ individuals which are based on trust rather than contract and payment.

6 Tick the words which can be used to refer to an individual.

a partner __   c immigrant __   e sibling __   g generation __
b ethnic __   d family member __   f spouse __   h minority __

7 Find nine noun phrases using words in the box. Some words are used more than once.

| class ethnic first future generation group ~~marital~~ minority partner social ~~status~~ |

▶ EXAMPLE: _marital status_

1 _____   4 _____   7 _____
2 _____   5 _____   8 _____
3 _____   6 _____   9 _____

8 Write a short paragraph (three or four sentences) about one of the following topics from the perspective of your own country or culture. Use vocabulary from this unit.

• Family structure and relationships between generations
• The factors which determine an individual's social status
• Minority groups and their position in society

Words to learn

accumulate AWL	dimension AWL	minimal AWL	scope AWL
adequate AWL	exceed AWL	predominant AWL	sole AWL
comprise AWL	lack	proportion AWL	trace AWL
density	maximum AWL	range AWL	volume AWL

Describing size and range

A This raises an important point, as there is such a diverse range of schemes and initiatives operating at a national and regional level that it becomes difficult to isolate the effectiveness of each one.

B There are different levels of deafness and hearing loss; however, it is not within the scope of this essay to consider all of these levels. Therefore, this essay will mainly focus on people who are born with severe or profound deafness.

C Nolan and Marginson (1990) contend that in other economies such as Sweden and Germany where union density and the proportion of the workforce covered by collective agreements is higher than in Britain, so is labour productivity.

D The rate of cooling of a particular food product will depend on its physical dimensions, such as volume and density.

1 Use the glossary on pp.129–144 to find the correct meanings of *density* in texts C and D.

Figure 1

2 Complete the descriptions of Figures 1 and 2 using keywords from texts A–D.

1 If the _____ of a swimming pool in Figure 1 are 10 m long by 5 m wide and 1.5 m deep, then the _____ of water it holds is approximately 75,000 litres.

2 As a country with large unpopulated areas, the _____ of the population in Australia is just three people per square kilometre. A large _____ of the population, 89%, live in urban areas, mostly located around the coast.

Figure 2

Australian Bureau of Statistics (ABS), June 2010

3 Complete the sentences using keywords from texts A–D.

1 The term 'public sector' covers a very wide _____ of activities around the provision of government services.

2 The machine gauges the coin's weight and _____ very quickly to determine its value.

3 A large _____ of the population, especially urban residents, speak English.

4 Since the 1960s, large _____ of river water have been diverted for agriculture.

5 The areas with the highest _____ of palms, up to 7,000 trees per hectare, are Para and Amapa.

6 Whether this could be maintained would need a longer-term assessment, which was beyond the _____ of this study.

Describing large and small quantities

E The poverty faced by children from working-class families is exacerbated by the need for both parents to work and a **lack** of affordable childcare. This situation is even more acute in single-parent households where the **sole** carer struggles to earn enough to cover childcare costs.

F Most fish and shellfish contain **traces** of mercury, which occurs naturally in the oceans. In most cases, the amounts are **minimal** and pose little risk to human health. However, in larger fish, levels of mercury can **accumulate** over time.

G The factory was still a significant source of pollution. According to studies, the levels of heavy metals in the air, soil and water in the area far **exceeded** the **maximum** permitted levels.

H A diet which **comprises** plenty of fruits and vegetables, whole grains as the main form of carbohydrate, unsaturated fats as the **predominant** form of dietary fat, and **adequate** fatty acids can offer significant protection against coronary heart disease.

4 **Read texts E–H. Do the texts describe large quantities (L) or small quantities (S)?**

1 Text E: __   2 Text F: __   3 Text G: __   4 Text H: __

5 **Rewrite the sentences replacing the highlighted words with keywords from texts E–H.**

▶ EXAMPLE: The lowest-risk group is made up of <u>comprises</u> those patients with no recorded risk factors.
1 Decision-makers do not have enough _____ information about all the relevant factors.
2 Emissions from the power plant went over _____ safe legal limits.
3 The coolant water may contain tiny amounts _____ of mildly radioactive elements.
4 The petrol-powered internal combustion engine is the most common _____ type of vehicle engine.
5 Some chemicals are not toxic below a certain level but produce elevated risk as they build up _____ in the atmosphere.
6 For these communities, fishing is their only _____ source of income.
7 Advertising needs to reach the largest _____ number of customers within a given market.
8 The programme was withdrawn because there wasn't any _____ funding.
9 Traditional fishing methods had only a very small _____ impact on the marine ecology.

6 **Complete the sentences using the best form of the nouns in the box. Think about the meaning and the form of the noun.**

> acid body option paper people substance
> traffic understanding

1 Saturn is approximately 75% hydrogen and 25% helium with **traces of** other _____ , such as methane.
2 This issue is beyond the **scope of** the current _____ .
3 Over the next 20 years there will be a dramatic increase in the **proportion of** _____ aged over 55.
4 The above trend has resulted in an increase in the **volume of** _____ along major highways.
5 The survey highlighted a **lack of** _____ about the role of carbohydrates in the diet.
6 Advances have been made in the development of targeted therapies, resulting in a wider **range of** _____ for patients.
7 We measured the **dimensions of** the _____ of 53 dolphins.
8 If there is an **excess of** _____ in the solution, then the pH will typically be in the range of 2.5 to 1.0.

> **Usage note**
>
> Expressions of quantity are typically followed by a particular type of noun: countable or uncountable, singular or plural.
> • a **range** of schemes
> • a **proportion** of the workforce/ patients
> • the **dimensions** of the device
> • the **scope** of the study
> • the **volume** of water/exports
> • **traces** of DNA/chemicals
> • a **lack** of evidence/resources
> • an **excess** of males/nitrogen

Student writing: explanations

Writing an explanation allows you to demonstrate your understanding of a particular subject area. An explanation may be a short assignment in its own right or it might form part of a longer piece of writing. You might be asked to describe a process or a technique or to explain how something is structured or classified. Alternatively, you may have to write an explanation of a particular model or a theory. An explanation should not just be copied from a textbook, but should be written in your own words. It should be clearly structured and include the relevant information and degree of detail asked for in the question.

A Egan's three-stage model of counselling

Counselling aims to enable clients to help themselves to reach a more satisfying level of living (Sutton and Stewart, 2002). Sanders (2002) argues that Rogers and Egan helped develop the notion that counselling is a skilled practice. Rogers categorized six core conditions that counsellors need to provide in order for client self-healing to commence. Egan incorporated Rogers' core conditions into his set of counselling skills, which are divided into three stages.

Stage one aims to build up a rapport between counsellor and client during their initial meetings. This helps to create a trusting relationship, which allows the client to explore whatever it is they feel able to explore (Sanders, 2002).

Stage two of Egan's model aims to enable the client to view their life from different perspectives.

[The writer goes on to explain the five skills that a counsellor can use.]

Stage three completes Egan's three-stage model. This stage encourages the client and the counsellor to collaborate and consider possible plans of action, and to evaluate the risks and outcomes of these actions (Sanders, 2002). This will hopefully enable the client to progress in a positive and resourceful way. It must be noted here that each of the stages are not used in isolation, but can be completed simultaneously and repeated in response to the client's needs.

1 Complete the diagram illustrating Egan's three-stage model using keywords from text A.

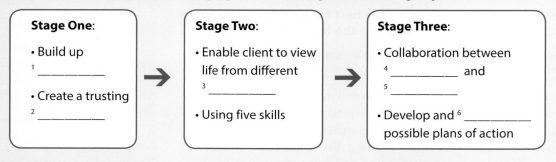

Stage One:
- Build up
  1 _____
- Create a trusting
  2 _____

Stage Two:
- Enable client to view life from different
  3 _____
- Using five skills

Stage Three:
- Collaboration between
  4 _____ and
  5 _____
- Develop and 6 _____ possible plans of action

2 Read text A. Mark the statements true (T) or false (F) according to the text.

1 Counselling aims to improve clients' level of satisfaction with their lives. __
2 Egan developed a classification that includes six core conditions that counsellors need to provide. __
3 Egan's model of counselling skills is divided into three stages. __
4 During the initial stage, the focus is on building the relationship between client and counsellor. __
5 Stage two involves the client viewing their life from five different perspectives. __
6 During the final stage, counsellor and client create a plan of action together. __
7 Each of the stages must be followed separately and in the correct order. __
8 The counselling process may go through each stage more than once if necessary. __

Focus on collocation

3 a Match the adjectives, 1–6, to the nouns, a–f, to form noun phrases. Look back at Units 8–16 or use the list of collocations on pp.107–111 to help you if necessary.

1 demographic _	4 physical _	a community	d upheaval
2 manufacturing _	5 local _	b properties	e sector
3 economic _	6 political _	c trend	f downturn

b Complete the explanations using an appropriate form of words from the box. Not all the words are needed. Think about both meaning and collocation.

> compose do dramatic introduce make nationwide preceding re-evaluate response strong thin widespread

The ¹_____ increase in the proportion of the population aged over 60 in many developed countries means that governments are being forced to ²_____ the situation regarding pensions and other state benefits. Inevitably, reforms are being ³_____ in many countries in ⁴_____ to this shift, such as increasing the retirement age. As a consequence, individuals may have to rethink how and when they ⁵_____ the transition from work to retirement.

Plywood is ⁶_____ of three or more ⁷_____ layers of wood glued together. The grain of each layer is at right angles to the ⁸_____ layer in order to give the material greater strength. Light in weight and capable of being bent into curved forms, it has ⁹_____ uses in construction and furniture-making.

c For each explanation, identify what is being explained and match it to a noun phrase from 3a.

1 _____   2 _____

Focus on word families

4 Rewrite the sentences using the form of the highlighted word shown in brackets. Make any other changes necessary. Use the glossary on pp.129–144 to help you.

▶ EXAMPLE: In the second quarter, there was a **dramatic** rise in the rate of inflation.
In the second quarter, _the rate of inflation rose dramatically_. (*adverb*)

1 The school has been on the same site since it was **established** in 1586.
The school has been on the same site since _____. (*noun*)

2 After the accident, the company ordered the **suspension** of all operations at the plant.
After the accident, the company _____. (*verb*)

3 The study aims to investigate how **frequent** such extreme weather events are.
The study aims to investigate _____. (*noun*)

4 During triage, patients are **categorized** according to their level of need.
During triage, patients are _____. (*noun*)

5 **Initially**, employees tend to be resistant to new working practices.
During the _____. (*adjective*)

6 Existing models do not provide an **adequate** explanation for this gap.
Existing models do not _____. (*adverb*)

7 During testing, the design was **modified** significantly in a number of ways.
During testing, a number of _____. (*noun*)

8 Some species **adapt** more easily to changing environmental conditions than others.
Some species _____. (*adjective*)

Words to learn

coincidence AWL	correlation	lead to	product of
condition of	direct	motivation AWL	repercussion
consequence AWL	ensure AWL	play a part in	result from
contribute AWL	factor AWL	priority AWL	

Describing causes and effects

A A cause-or-effect analysis is really a particular kind of process discussion in which you explain how certain events have **led to** or **resulted from** other events. Usually you are explaining why something happened. When exploring causes and effects, always avoid oversimplifying relationships. If you are tracing causes, distinguish between a **direct** cause and a **contributing** cause, between what is a **condition of** something happening and what is merely a **correlation** or **coincidence**. There are many examples of spurious relationships: for instance, if you found that since 1980, carbon dioxide levels have increased and obesity levels have also increased, you cannot jump to the conclusion that increases in obesity cause increases in CO_2. Similarly, you must be sure that the result you identify is a genuine **product of** the event or action.

Source: Northey, M. & von Aderkas, P. (2015). *Making Sense in the Life Sciences: A Student's Guide to Writing and Research.* Ontario: Oxford University Press. p.49.

1 **Match the terms, 1–4, to the examples, a–d. Use the glossary on pp.129–144 to help you if necessary.**

1 a direct cause
2 a contributing cause
3 a correlation
4 a coincidence

a There is probably no connection at all between the increase in obesity and the rise in carbon dioxide levels.
b As far back as the 1970s, experts established that smoking can lead to lung cancer.
c Obesity is widely recognized as one of the factors giving individuals an increased risk of heart disease.
d Many studies have shown a link between low income and poor health, but the exact relationship is complex.

2 **Identify the cause (C) and the effect (E) in each sentence.**

▶ EXAMPLE: The programme (C) **led to** greater levels of awareness (E) regarding the benefits of consuming fruit and vegetables.

1 Expertise (__) is a **product of** years of experience within a particular domain (__).
2 A number of factors (__) **contributed to** the development and growth of Silicon Valley (__).
3 Several new policies (__) **resulted from** the report (__).
4 For newly industrializing nations, education (__) is frequently seen as a **condition of** economic development (__).

Talking about reasons and implications

B While there are socially affected **factors** such as sex or age that come into play with respect to the strategies that specific learners use, **motivation** must also **play a part in** whether an individual is a good language learner.

C A project manager faces a significant challenge when deciding between alternative project proposals, and the **repercussions** of choosing the wrong proposal can be serious. Thus, to **ensure** that they select the most viable projects, many managers develop **priority** systems: guidelines for balancing the opportunities and costs entailed by each alternative.

D The study found that the occupational histories of men expose them to work-related ill health, which has consequences for life expectancy and chronic disease in old age. These findings have implications for future research and for public health practice.

3 Read texts B–D, then match statements 1–5 with statements a–e.

1 Factors that might affect which strategies learners use.
2 An individual language learner's motivation.
3 The repercussions of choosing the wrong proposal.
4 The consequences of work-related ill health.
5 The implications of work-related ill health for public health practice.

a A shorter life and poor health in retirement.
b More health care resources may be needed to treat this group of people.
c To get a better job or to communicate with family abroad.
d The company may lose money and the manager may lose her job.
e How old they are and whether they are male or female.

4 Some words are followed by different prepositions depending on the context. Complete the sentences using the best preposition (*in*, *from*, *for*, etc.). Check the list of dependent prepositions on p.111–113.

1 The virus spread to 28 countries, infecting 8,096 people and resulting _____ 774 deaths.
2 Company directors must consider the likely consequences _____ their decisions in the long term.
3 This finding has major implications _____ the design of future clinical studies.
4 They found only a modest correlation _____ brain size and scores on mental tests.
5 The outcome of this case has potential repercussions _____ policy-makers.

5 Complete the sentences using keywords from this unit. Add any other words needed. More than one option may be possible.

▶ EXAMPLE: Obesity is often cited as *a contributing cause of* medical conditions such as stroke and heart disease.

1 The study found _____ between the quantity of urban green space and the perception of health.
2 Qualitative research methods, such as interviews, are used to uncover underlying _____ people's behaviour.
3 It is possible that the variation in the results _____ differences in the measuring techniques used.
4 The media has a role to play in holding businesses to account for _____ their actions.
5 Families, schools, neighbourhoods and workplaces all _____ forming an individual's values.
6 Time management involves ranking tasks in order of _____ .
7 An effective regulatory regime is essential _____ companies follow the safety guidelines.

6 Describe one or more of the cause and effect relationships below, using words from this unit. Write two to four sentences for each, including information about possible motivations and/or implications where relevant.

- Human activity → loss of wildlife
- Advances in medicine → increased life expectancy

- Modern communications technology → English as a world language
- Supply/demand → price of goods

18 Compare and contrast

Words to learn

alike	common	differentiate	identical AWL
alternative AWL	conflicting AWL	between AWL	on the contrary
analogy AWL	contradict AWL	distinctly AWL	similarity AWL
as opposed to	conversely AWL	dissimilar AWL	variation AWL

Contrast

A Recently, a study revealed that the traditional mechanism of unions and employee participation in problem-solving produced lower absenteeism (Colvin *et al.*, 2005). **Conversely**, Mefford's study (1986) found that unionization increased absenteeism.

B A recent study by Colvin *et al.* (2005) showed that traditional communications mechanisms through unions and other forms of employee participation resulted in lower absenteeism. This apparently **contradicts** Mefford's study (1986), which found that unionization increased absenteeism.

C Different studies have offered **alternative** perspectives on the relationship between unionization and absenteeism. Mefford (1986) found that traditional union mechanisms increased absenteeism, whereas Colvin *et al.* (2005) suggest that, **on the contrary**, unionization actually lowers absenteeism.

D In the literature, there is apparently **conflicting** evidence regarding the relationship between unionization and employee absenteeism (Mefford, 1986, Colvin *et al.*, 2005). To understand this **variation**, it is important to **differentiate between** studies carried out in **distinctly** different contexts.

Glossary

absenteeism (*n*): when workers are away from work, often without a good reason
unionization (*n*): the situation in which a large part of a workforce is a member of a trade union

1 Texts A–D paraphrase roughly the same ideas. Read the texts and answer the questions.

1 Which study found that union members were *more* likely to be absent from work? _____

2 Which study found that union members were *less* likely to be absent? _____

2 Is the highlighted word or phrase appropriate in each context? If it is, put a tick. If not, write a word that correctly expresses the relationship between the ideas.

1 If there is a rise in the price of raw materials then a manufacturer's profit rate will fall. **Conversely**, if it is able to find a cheaper supplier of materials, then its profit rate will rise. _____

2 Modern communications technology has improved productivity in many ways. **On the contrary**, it creates its own stresses for employees who feel pressured to take work home. _____

3 Small fire stations can be spread evenly across a region. A **contradictory** approach is to focus resources into fewer large stations located in areas of highest risk, such as urban centres. _____

4 The scene was confused and witnesses gave **conflicting** accounts of what had happened. _____

3 Choose the best form of the word or phrase to complete the sentences.

1 *Conflicting* / *Conflict with* results may arise if samples are taken from different populations.

2 New questions posed from different points of view can sometimes lead to *alternative* / *alternatively* interpretations of the same data.

3 In cases where there is limited or *contradicted* / *contradictory* evidence it may not be possible to draw firm conclusions.

4 This new system needs to be implemented weekly *as opposed to* / *the opposite of* once per month.

5 There is significant *variety* / *variation* in the length of maternity leave between countries.

6 Shakespeare's sonnets are generally recognized as falling into three *distinctly* / *distinct* groups.

Comparisons

The effects of genes vary with differences in the environment in which the organism develops and lives. This can be appreciated by an **analogy**. The taste, texture, and quality of a cake can be modified by changing both the ingredients and the way it is cooked, but it is not always easy to tell what has been changed by eating the cake. Much recent research in behaviour genetics has sought to identify the contributions of genetic and environmental factors in order to determine the causes of differences in behaviour.

Twin studies are probably the best-known method of studying the genetical basis of behaviour. Twins are either **identical** (monozygotic, MZ) or fraternal (dizygotic, DZ). MZ twins are derived from the splitting of a single fertilized egg, whereas DZ twins derive from the fertilization of two eggs. DZ twins are no more genetically **alike** than ordinary siblings, but since they share a **common** prenatal environment and usually grow up together they tend to be more alike than siblings born at different times. Differences within MZ pairs arise only from environmental origins, whereas differences between DZ pairs are a consequence of genetic and environmental factors. Observations on MZ twins reared apart and hence in **dissimilar** environments provide information on the differentiating effects of the environment. In general, the results of such investigations show that family environments can vary greatly without obscuring the basic **similarities** between MZ twins.

Source: Connolly, K. J. (1987). Genetics of Behaviour. In Gregory, R. L. (ed.). (2004). *The Oxford Companion to the Mind*. (2 ed.). Oxford: Oxford University Press.

Glossary
prenatal (*adj*): before birth
obscure (*v*): to cover something or make it difficult to see

4 Read text E and answer the questions.

1 Which type of twins are more alike: MZ or DZ? _____
2 Which factors cause differences between MZ twins and between DZ twins? _____

5 Complete the sentences using keywords from text E.

1 The globalization of trade implies that patterns of consumption become more _____ in different countries.
2 While the research process may differ, the approach adopted will always share a number of _____ features.
3 Even chickens kept in _____ conditions and fed the same food will vary in weight due to all the other factors.
4 She asks whether discrimination comes from a natural distrust of people who are _____ to ourselves.
5 Using the _____ of a computer, the brain is the hardware and the mind is the computer's software.
6 There are _____ between the very old and the very young in that both are more vulnerable to illness.

6 Rewrite the sentences using the words in capitals. Make any other changes necessary.

1 Levels of pay across the country are very different. VARY

_____

2 The methods and procedures used for both experiments were exactly alike. IDENTICAL

_____

3 The two organizations share a number of common characteristics. SIMILARITY

_____

4 The evidence from the second study seems to contradict the first. CONFLICTING

_____

5 Neither this study nor others examining this approach have demonstrated any serious harm to patients. Results seem to suggest instead that in general it improves the quality of care. CONTRARY

_____

19 Problem and solution

Words to learn

account for	constraint AWL	impairment	recur
adverse	contingency	impose on AWL	requirement AWL
aid AWL	criteria AWL	limitation	resolve AWL
barrier	detect AWL	random AWL	

Identifying problems and solutions

A Random spot checks on deliveries and at various stages of the manufacturing process give a chance for any problems to be detected. If a problem were to arise with a delivery of components, the company can use the technology to track the item back to the location, date, and even time of production of the components and resolve any issues with the supplier, ensuring the problem does not recur.

B Next, I was able to think about the overall project scope. This is a key step in aiding the potential success of a project; as confirmed by Larson & Gray (2011), 'a poorly defined scope is the most frequently cited barrier to project success.'

C The individual will fall into the category of a disabled worker if she has an impairment which has 'a long-term adverse effect on her ability to carry out normal day-to-day activities'.

1 a Match the extracts from student writing, A–C, to the type of writing described.

1 a law essay about discrimination
2 an engineering proposal
3 a reflective report about study skills

b Now match the extracts, A–C, to the type of problem described.

1 maintaining quality control
2 defining a person's physical abilities
3 avoiding possible problems with an approach

Usage note *problem* or *issue*

Problem and **issue** can often be used to describe exactly the same situation.
  • *A **problem** arose with the tracking software, but the **issue** was quickly resolved.*
Typically though, a **problem** is a specific event or situation that can be identified and possibly fixed.
  • *Air travel poses particular **problems** for medical equipment, for example, it may be affected by changes in air pressure.*
An **issue** is often a more complex set of circumstances that doesn't have a simple solution.
  • *There are ethical **issues** to be considered.*

---

2 a Do the highlighted words have a similar meaning (S) or a different meaning (D)?

1 A prevention programme aims to find / detect and treat problems early. __
2 Brain imaging is now commonly used to aid / help diagnosis. __
3 It is important to find a new solution that will prevent the problem recurring / arising. __
4 The questions were presented in random / unplanned order. __
5 The cost of coaching and equipment is a barrier / an aid to participation in sport for some groups. __
6 This treatment is slightly less effective, but has far fewer adverse / negative effects for the patient. __
7 It is not surprising that physical impairment is / barriers are associated with low levels of employment. __
8 There are always pressures to pose / resolve problems quickly so that time will not be lost. __

b Check your answers. In sentences where the two words have a different meaning, identify which word fits better in the context.

A problem statement

D If you are writing a proposal, your reader might find it useful if you present a short summary of the problem, along with a discussion of the **constraints** (the **limitations imposed on** the solution) and the **criteria** (the features or characteristics required of the solution).

If you are preparing a problem-solution proposal, you will include all the specifics of your timelines and budgets in addition to your objectives and the procedures you expect to follow. Remember that a proposal is written before a project is undertaken; you look efficient if you **account for** as many **contingencies** as possible. On the other hand, a final project report is submitted after all the work has been completed, whether or not things took place according to plan. Part of your discussion in a final project report will consider how well the results met the original **requirements** set out in the proposal.

Source: Northey, M. and Jewinski, J. (2012). *Making Sense in Engineering and the Technical Sciences: A Student's Guide to Research and Writing.* (4 ed.). Ontario: Oxford University Press. pp.56–57.

3 Match the words in the box to the definitions.

> account for   constraint   contingency   criteria   impose on   limitation   requirements

1 something that restricts how you can go about solving a problem _____ / _____
2 a set of things that you need to include in your proposal _____ / _____
3 an event that may happen but that is not certain to happen _____
4 to consider how to deal with something in advance _____
5 to give someone rules that they must work within _____

4 Complete the sentences using highlighted words from text D. More than one option may be possible.

1 To operate in cold climates, the design must _____ the effects of cold on the materials used.
2 Strategic planning involves looking at a range of _____ that the organization might have to face in the future.
3 If time _____ are a concern, steps two and three can be carried out together.
4 The construction must meet strict performance _____ for energy and water consumption.
5 Slow broadband speeds in some parts of the world _____ limitations on the design of websites.

5 Complete the sentences with collocations from texts A–D.

1 Some of these chemicals can have **adverse** _____ on plants and animals that come into contact with them.
2 The size and nature of your sample are likely to **impose** _____ on the kinds of analysis techniques you can use.
3 Services must be designed to **meet** customer _____ effectively.
4 Although the child's behavioural **issues** initially seem to have been _____ through extra support, **problems** _____ when he started high school.

6 Write a short paragraph (three or four sentences) describing one of the problems below and possible solutions, or choose a problem from your own discipline. Try to use some of the words from this unit.

- Controlling hospital infections
- Teaching mixed-ability classes
- Designing a low-energy home

20 Evidence

Words to learn

claim   establish AWL   reject AWL   source AWL
collect   evidence AWL   relevant AWL   sufficient AWL
compile AWL   factual   rely on AWL   support
comprehensive AWL   primary AWL   secondary   unsupported

Supporting evidence

A Arguments frequently include factual claims. A fact can be defined as something which can be objectively confirmed or measured, often an object but sometimes an event or action. For instance, Louise Zacarias in *Students Need a Gap Year* makes this factual claim:

> "Currently, more than 50 per cent of all incoming students to Canadian universities are unprepared to manage the stress levels they encounter."

If you came on this sentence all by itself in an argument, it would be an unsupported claim. If someone makes a statement like this, he or she must provide information about the source of this knowledge.

If a factual claim like the one above is unsupported, it does not mean the claim is false. It may be true, but you have no way of knowing unless you can consult the evidence yourself, or at least have the possibility of doing so. Any argument that relies on unsupported factual claims is a weak argument, and critical, reasonable decision-makers will reject any recommendations made on that basis until the writer or speaker supports the claim with factual evidence.

Source: Feltham, M., Hoth, W. & Meahan, P. (2015). *Writing Critically: Key Skills for Post-Secondary Success.* Ontario: Oxford University Press. p.50.

1 Read text A. Mark the statements true (T) or false (F).

1 A claim is a fact that can be confirmed or measured. __
2 Factual information can be about an object, an event or an action. __
3 An unsupported claim does not give a source for the information. __
4 An argument that relies on evidence is weak. __
5 A critical academic reader does not agree with the writer's arguments. __
6 You might reject an argument because it does not have enough evidence to support it. __

2 Complete the statements using words from the box.

claims   evidence   factual   reject   rely   source

1 Supporting _____ includes the examples and facts that a writer uses to support an argument.
2 In order to build a strong argument, you must provide the _____ of your information.
3 Your essay should not _____ entirely on evidence from a single source.
4 You should _____ an argument that is based on unsupported _____ .
5 _____ evidence can be demonstrated through statistics, data or other forms of proof.

3 Match the descriptions, 1–4, to extracts a–d from a student essay.

1 supporting evidence
2 an argument based on evidence
3 evidence from a cited source
4 an unsupported claim

a High consumption of sugary drinks is causing obesity among children.
b Medical experts have identified sugary drinks as one of the major contributing factors in increasing levels of obesity.
c According to the World Health Organization (2014), surveys show that children in countries as diverse as Ghana, Kuwait and Mexico are consuming more than one sugary drink per day.
d The evidence above points to high consumption of sugary drinks as a major factor in increasing levels of childhood obesity worldwide. It seems clear that global action needs to be taken to prevent this issue escalating.

Collecting evidence

B Academic writing is always based on evidence. This may be **primary** data which you **collect** yourself from experiments, surveys and other forms of research, or it could be **secondary** data which you **compile** from written sources. Whatever the sources of your data, there are several key points to bear in mind:

- You need to find **sufficient** data to support your arguments. The number of sources you draw on will depend partly on the scope of your task. A short essay might be based on a handful of sources, whereas a longer project might involve a **comprehensive** review of the available literature.

- All the evidence you cite should be directly **relevant** to your argument.

- Evidence should be from **reliable** sources, such as academic books and peer-reviewed journals. You should beware of using data when you cannot **establish** the exact source. This is particularly important when you are searching online.

4 **Group the keywords in text B into three categories.**

Finding evidence	Types of evidence	Evaluating evidence
collect ¹ _____ 2 _____	primary ³ _____	sufficient ⁴ _____ 5 _____ 6 _____

5 **Rewrite the sentences replacing the highlighted words with keywords from text B. Make any other changes necessary.**

1 When you start researching your topic, make _____ a list of possible sources of information.
2 When you are putting together _____ evidence for a piece of work, keep a record of all sources.
3 It is important to find out _____ the source of any data you find online.
4 Information found online can't always be trusted _____, especially if the source isn't given.
5 Check that all the evidence you cite is directly connected to _____ the topic of your essay.
6 If you cannot find enough _____ evidence to support a particular point, you may have to review your arguments.
7 Textbooks can often provide a thorough and detailed _____ review of the research in an area.
8 If you read about a piece of research in a source which is reporting someone else's work _____, then it is good practice to try and read the original source _____ wherever possible.

6 **Evaluate the claims about the challenges and benefits of learning English. Note down one or two points about each claim.**

▶ EXAMPLE: English is the most popular second language globally.
   This claim may be true, but it isn't supported by any evidence from sources.

- Experts claim that to understand a text in English, a reader needs to know 95% of the words in it.
- According to a report by the British Council and Oxford University (2014), an increasing number of universities worldwide are using English as the 'academic lingua franca', making it a key skill for students in many countries.
- Mandarin Chinese is the most widely spoken language in the world, accounting for around 14.1% of the world's population (Worldfacts.com).
- Universities around the world can only successfully make the transition to teaching through the medium of English if they provide enough language support for students.

21 Theory and concepts

Words to learn

abstract AWL   concept AWL   hypothesis AWL   phenomenon AWL
assumption AWL   context AWL   infer AWL   real-world
base upon   define AWL   metaphorical   scenario AWL
circumstance AWL   generalization   model   theory AWL

Talking about theories

A In the late 1970s Argyris and Schon developed a **theory** of organizational learning which they referred to as 'single loop learning' and 'double loop learning'. The distinction between the two **models** is that the former involves the detection and correction of errors concerning only the actions that a company executes. The latter involves looking at problems in further depth and questioning the **assumptions** or goals that a company **bases** its policy **upon**.

B The lack of women represented in higher positions in employment was typified by the **concept** of a **metaphorical** 'Glass Ceiling' that began to be debated in the 1980s. Evetts (1994: 6) **defines** the Glass Ceiling as "…a barrier so subtle that it is transparent, yet so strong that it prevents women and minorities from moving up the management hierarchy".

C The Affective Filter Hypothesis was made famous by Krashen (Walters and Frei 2007:41-42). This **hypothesis** suggests that if the student is contented and feels comfortable within the classroom environment, their 'Affective Filter' is lowered. This enables learning to become more successful.

Source: student writing

1 Match the key ideas, 1–4, from texts A–C to their descriptions, a–d.

1 Organizational learning
2 Single loop learning
3 The Glass Ceiling
4 The Affective Filter

a a model of a process
b a hypothesis
c a metaphorical concept
d a general theory

2 Match the sentence halves.

1 Ansoff focused on strategic decisions, which he **defines**
2 In the aftermath of the Second World War, the **concept**
3 The analysis is **based**
4 Carter argues that the **metaphorical**
5 Charles Darwin developed the modern **theory**
6 Suppose we want to develop a **model**
7 It is easy for managers to make too many **assumptions**
8 These findings support our **hypothesis**

a 'melting pot' does indeed characterize much American culture.
b as "decisions on what kind of business the firm should seek to be in".
c about what employees already know and can do.
d of evolution in the 19th century.
e to predict graduates' salaries, based on data about subjects studied and examination scores.
f that geographical distance affects the patterns of communication in relationships.
g upon data from a survey that examines health and interpersonal connections among older Americans.
h of human rights began to be recognized at an international level.

3 **Cross out one word in each set which doesn't collocate with the highlighted word. Use the list of collocations on pp.107–110 to help you if necessary.**

▶ EXAMPLE: develop/~~make~~/test a **theory**

1 develop/make/question an **assumption**
2 a key/practical/theoretical **concept**

3 a(n) alternative/factual/working **hypothesis**
4 **define** a group/theory/term

Talking about general ideas

D Typically, academic writing focuses on **abstract** concepts. It describes processes, such as photosynthesis or learning a language, or **phenomena**, like earthquakes or globalization. It examines the components involved, the **context** in which something occurs and the **circumstances** necessary for it to happen.

A lot of academic work involves observing and examining a particular situation in detail, not just to understand that particular context, case or event, but so as to make **generalizations**. General patterns and relationships can be **inferred** from the data and then these can be applied to different times, places or events to predict what will happen in a given **scenario**.

For example, ecologists might observe that intensive logging in one area leads to an increase in landslides. By analysing the processes at work, they develop a model for how the removal of trees from an area destabilizes the soil and increases the risk of landslides. This **theoretical** knowledge, of course, then has **real-world** implications and can be applied to other contexts to help predict and possibly prevent similar events.

4 **Match the descriptions, 1–6, to the examples, a–f.**

1 the **circumstances** directly leading up to an event
2 a **theoretical scenario**
3 a **real-world example**
4 the wider **context** within which an event happens
5 a natural **phenomenon**
6 a **generalization**

   a landslide (a mass of earth and rock that falls down the slope of a hill or mountain)
   b When the trees were cut down, because the soil was quite shallow and no longer held together by the tree roots, as soon as there were heavy rains, the soil began to be washed down the hill and this led to landslides.
   c Any area of naturally occurring forest, especially on a hillside, that is cleared becomes prone to soil erosion and eventually landslides.
   d This area of forest is in a region where local people are very poor and they need to clear land to grow crops to provide food for their families. There are few government controls on land use.
   e Imagine a very large area of forest was cleared in an area above a heavily populated settlement. Given heavy rainfall, major landslides could be triggered, potentially causing serious damage and loss of life.
   f In 2014, more than 130 people were killed and 44 homes were destroyed in landslides in India.

5 **Complete the sentences using the best form of the word in capitals. Use the glossary on pp.129–144 to help you if necessary.**

1 This article develops a _____ model of urban development. THEORY
2 The glossary provides _____ of the key terms used in the book. DEFINE
3 The authors _____ that these differences would decrease when groups were matched by age and education. HYPOTHESIS
4 To use a theatrical _____ , in a successful society the actors do not just read through their parts. METAPHORICAL
5 It is not possible to _____ from such a small-scale study. GENERALIZATION

22 Critical thinking

Words to learn

analysis AWL	critical	objective AWL	recognize
assessment AWL	evaluate AWL	put forward	response AWL
convince AWL	ignore AWL	question	stance
credible	logical AWL	reaction AWL	

Critical thinking

A In both school and the workplace, **critical** thinking skills are some of the most important skills you can have. When you think critically, you are looking for potential problems and flaws in arguments – for example, lack of evidence. If this definition sounds negative, you can think of critical thinking as a method for testing arguments to make sure they work, and if they don't work, it's a method for improving them.

Source: Feltham, M., Hoth, W., Meahan, P. (2015). *Writing Critically: Key Skills for Post-Secondary Success.* Ontario: Oxford University Press. p.47.

Usage note *critical*

In everyday usage, if someone is **critical of** an idea, they find faults or problems with it. This sense of **critical** is used in academic writing to talk about people's opinions and reactions.
• *Kennedy became increasingly* **critical of** *the administration's policies.*
However, if a student or an academic is **critical**, we mean that they look carefully and objectively at an argument (or piece of information) in order to make judgements about its good/bad qualities.

B What does critical thinking involve?
"When you **evaluate** an argument, you make an **assessment** of how **credible** it is. You need to ask critical questions. Are the claims **logical** and reasonable? Is there sufficient evidence to support the main points in the argument? You should **question** any points that are not supported by reliable evidence."

1 Do the highlighted words have a similar meaning (S) or a different meaning (D)?

1 Critical thinking involves **evaluating/assessing** the strength of an argument. __
2 This seems like a **critical/logical** analysis of the situation based on the evidence available. __
3 The paper **challenges/questions** the assumption that technology always improves efficiency. __
4 No **credible/reliable** evidence exists to support the view that people's political behaviour can be explained by their race. __
5 While these are potentially useful techniques, there has been little **critical/negative** appraisal of their effectiveness. __

2 a Find words in texts A and B that collocate with words 1–4. The part of speech is given to help you.

▶ EXAMPLE: evaluate <u>an argument</u> (*noun*)
1 **question** _____ (*noun*)   2 _____ an **assessment** (*verb*)
3 **critical** _____ / _____ (*nouns*)   4 a **credible** _____ (*noun*)

b Match the sets of collocates to the highlighted words in 2a. Use the list of collocations on pp.107–110 to help you if necessary.

1 offer, provide, give a(n) _____
2 a _____ analysis, approach, review
3 _____ the impact, effectiveness
4 a _____ source, account, piece of evidence
5 _____ an assumption, a view, an idea

c Complete the sentences using words from 2a and 2b.

1 Different experts made conflicting _____ of the evidence presented.
2 Murray's book offers a _____ analysis of the key points surrounding this issue.
3 Psychologists _____ the idea that the brain could not process more than one signal at a time.
4 It may be too early to _____ the long-term impact of these reforms.
5 This research provides _____ evidence that mass media can encourage political participation.

Critical analysis and response

C Critical analysis involves breaking down a complex situation, problem or text into its component pieces.

The combination of critical thinking and critical analysis is essential to producing a critical response, which is your reaction to an argument and to its various main and supporting points.

Source: Feltham, M., Hoth, W. & Meahan, P. (2015). *Writing Critically: Key Skills for Post-Secondary Success*. Ontario: Oxford University Press. pp.47–48.

D How can you be a more critical reader?
"It's difficult for any writer to be completely objective. In fact, any good academic writer will take a stance and put forward an argument. They want to convince you that their argument is the strongest. As a critical reader, you need to recognize what it is the writer is trying to make you believe and identify any examples of clear bias. In particular, look out for any evidence they have ignored which may be relevant."

Usage note *reaction, response* or *reply*
These words all describe something you do or say as a result of something that has happened.
A **reply** is something you say or write in answer to a question:
- *In reply to a question from the audience, he explained …*
A **response** is something you decide to say or do, usually after thinking about it:
- *Participants' responses to the interview topics were recorded.*
- *One response to the problem …*
A **reaction** is typically the first thing you feel, say or do without thinking about it:
- *The announcement provoked an initial reaction of surprise and concern.*

3 Choose the best word to complete the sentences.

1 The Appeal Court took the same *analysis / stance* and the case was rejected.
2 There was a large-scale campaign to *convince / recognize* the public that the vaccine was safe.
3 The experiments used *convincing / objective* measures of performance, such as reaction time.
4 The initial government *reaction / reply* was to dismiss the claims.
5 In general, the students gave the interviewer their full attention and provided considered *reactions / responses*.
6 Two major arguments have been *recognized / put forward* to account for this variation.
7 A thorough analysis cannot simply *ignore / recognize* data that does not fit with the hypothesis.
8 It is important, however, to *react / recognize* the subtle differences between the two approaches.

4 Complete the sentences using the best form of the word in capitals. Add any prepositions that are needed. Use the glossary on pp.129–144 and the list of dependent prepositions on pp.111–113 to help you.

▶ EXAMPLE: More rigorous *evaluation of* these programmes is clearly needed. EVALUATE
1 Reliability and validity are important criteria when _____ the quality of research. ASSESSMENT
2 Knowledge develops because individuals _____ the same information in different ways. REACTION
3 In the study, we _____ data from a sample of girls who attended seven different schools. ANALYSIS
4 There is growing _____ the need to integrate human rights into corporate policies. RECOGNIZE
5 Companies have to _____ changes in patterns of consumer behaviour. RESPONSE

23 Belief and opinion

Words to learn

advocate AWL	further	opponent	reluctant AWL
ambiguous AWL	ideology AWL	perception AWL	supporter
cause	interest	pressure	symbolic AWL
controversial AWL	lobby group	reformer	

Political beliefs

A **Language policy**

Like all other public policy making, language policy is the result of **perception** of problems and the organization of **interests** with demands for government action. **Supporters** believe that communication problems of classes, ethnic groups, newly independent states, genders, age categories, or regions can be resolved by a language policy such as a mass literacy campaign, bilingual language education, officialization of one or more languages, or **symbolic** recognition as a national language. **Ideologies** of liberation, equality, social change, democracy, nationalism, and pluralism transform demands to solve narrowly defined communication problems into a program to change the society and political system.

Source: Weinstein, B. (2004). *Language Policy*. In Krieger, J. (ed.). *The Oxford Companion to Politics of the World*. (2 ed.). Oxford: Oxford University Press.

B According to Weinstein (2004), language policy may be the result of **pressure** on government from **lobby groups** who **perceive** that language is the root **cause** of some wider issue. Thus, what seems to be a simple issue around language is used to **further** a social or political **cause**.

Glossary
officialization (*n*): the process of making something official

1 Identify words or phrases in text A with a similar meaning to the phrases from text B.

1 pressure on government _____
2 lobby groups _____
3 perceive that _____
4 a social or political cause _____

2 Tick the correct meaning of the words according to their use in texts A or B.

1 interest   a (*noun*) people with a connection to something that affects their attitude to it __
           b (*noun*) an activity or a subject that you enjoy __
2 pressure a (*noun*) the force with which something presses against something __
           b (*noun*) the action of making someone feel that it is necessary to do something __
3 further   a (*adj*) additional, extra __
           b (*verb*) to help the progress of something __
4 cause   a (*noun*) a person or thing that makes something happen __
           b (*noun*) an idea that people support or fight for __

3 Complete the sentences using keywords from texts A or B. More than one option may be possible.

1 The role of the president is largely _____ nowadays, holding no real power.
2 Social media has been used very effectively to _____ the goals of the movement.
3 Powerful business _____ campaigned against the new regulations.
4 Ministers are thought to have put _____ on broadcasters not to show the footage.
5 The government came into conflict with both consumer and environmental _____ over the issue.
6 The public _____ of risk can be quite at odds with expert advice, whether it's the fear of crime or the latest health scare.
7 The need for urban planning is widely acknowledged by people regardless of their political _____ .
8 The _____ of different political parties are often clustered geographically.

Controversy

C The management of burn blisters is **controversial**. Some **advocate** leaving blisters intact to provide sterile wound coverage. However, blisters are rich in prostaglandins which may increase wound depth.

Source: Hodges, A. (2008). *A–Z of Plastic Surgery*. Oxford: Oxford University Press.

D The constitutional and legal status of the Declaration of Independence is curiously **ambiguous**. John Hancock and James Madison both considered it to be, in Madison's words, "the fundamental Act of Union of these States". Yet lawyers generally, and the Supreme Court in particular, have been **reluctant** to treat the Declaration as part of American organic law. **Reformers** insisted that the Declaration was part of the constitutional order, while their **opponents**, including John C. Calhoun, denigrated its authority and validity.

Source: Weicek, W. M. (2015). In Hall, K. L. (ed.). *The Oxford Companion to the Supreme Court of the United States*. (2 ed.). Oxford: Oxford University Press.

Glossary
prostaglandin (*n*): a substance produced in the body which affects how the body works
denigrate (*v*): to say that something does not have any value

4 According to texts C and D, what do people disagree about? Tick the best two options.

a Whether or not it is better to cover burn blisters to keep them clean. __
b Whether or not it is better to leave the skin covering burn blisters unbroken. __
c Whether the US Declaration of Independence is a basic part of the law and constitution. __
d Whether the US Constitution should be reformed. __

5 Rewrite the sentences, replacing the highlighted words with keywords from texts C and D. Make any changes necessary.

1 Those against _____ the changes claim that they impose unnecessary extra costs on business.
2 The report recommends _____ an individualized approach to care that takes each patient's specific needs into account.
3 Those who want change _____ argue that the current voting system is unfair.
4 The exact role of diet in reducing the risk of cancer remains not completely clear _____.
5 Employees are often not very willing _____ to accept changes to their working conditions.
6 Immigration is an issue over which there is a lot of disagreement _____ across Europe.

6 Complete the table. Use the glossary on pp.129–144 to help you if necessary.

Verb	Person
1 _____	supporter
2 _____	lobby group, lobbyist
advocate	3 _____
4 _____	reformer
5 _____	opponent

7 Complete the sentences with the best form of a word from the table. More than one option may be possible.

1 Some people strongly _____ the death penalty, even for those convicted of murder.
2 Although he wasn't a political activist, Cole was a steadfast _____ of the civil rights movement.
3 The 2009 report _____ the creation of global emissions regulations for greenhouse gases.
4 The internet allows individuals to set up campaigns _____ for social or political change.
5 Betty Friedan was a social _____ and influential figure in the American movement for women's rights.

24 Positive evaluation

Words to learn

accept	feasible	promote AWL	straightforward AWL
awareness AWL	flexible AWL	realistic	strengthen
coherent AWL	goal AWL	robust	valid AWL
compelling	positive AWL	statistically significant	

Evaluating a programme

A To date, the most comprehensive evaluation of the 5-A-DAY programme was completed by Bremner et al. (2006), evaluating 66 groups promoting the 5-A-DAY message. The evaluation reported several positives, including each group forming successful partnerships with local organizations such as schools, councils and businesses. Although the evaluation highlighted that participants in the programme areas did not demonstrate a statistically significant improvement in fruit and vegetable consumption compared to control groups, it did highlight that the programme led to greater levels of awareness regarding the benefits of consuming fruit and vegetables.

Source: student essay

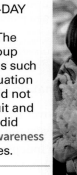

1 Read text A and answer the questions.

1 What do you think the 5-A-DAY programme aimed to do? _____
2 In what two ways was it successful? _____
3 What did it fail to achieve? _____

2 a Match the words in the box to the definitions.

> important   significant   statistically significant

1 great enough to have an effect or to be noticed, especially one that can be measured _____
2 valuable or having a great effect on people or things _____
3 giving results that are different from what would be expected from a randomly chosen situation
_____

b Complete the sentences using words from 2a.

1 Work is a very _____ aspect of people's lives, providing not only income but also a sense of identity.
2 Genetic factors are known to play a(n) _____ role in the development of the condition.
3 We found a(n) _____ increase in size over the period of the study.

3 Choose the correct form of the words to complete the sentences. Use the glossary on pp.129–144 to help you if necessary.

1 In order to begin to solve a problem, we must first become *aware / awareness* of it.
2 According to Vygotsky, peer-assisted learning activities *promote / promotion* cognitive development.
3 Several case studies suggest that at least some polluters respond *positive / positively* to complaints.
4 Occupational health management should focus on raising *aware / awareness* of the risks of prolonged driving.
5 There is considerable debate regarding *positive / the positives* and negatives of sun exposure.

Evaluating an argument

B There is currently no single method used for measuring physical activity. There are **valid** arguments for a number of different methods.

C This new evidence further **strengthens** the argument that …

D The court **accepted** this argument and the company's appeal was upheld.

E The paper presents a strong and **coherent** argument in favour of tighter controls.

F A further **compelling** argument for international cooperation arises from a desire to encourage best practice.

4 **Match the words from the box to a word with an opposite meaning.**

confused   dismiss   incoherent   invalid   reject   unconvincing   undermine   weak

1 valid: _____
2 strengthen: _____
3 accept: _____ / _____

4 coherent: _____ / _____
5 compelling: _____ / _____

5 **Choose the best word to complete the sentences.**

1 The paper lacks a *coherent / compelling* argument, jumping from one idea to the next without any clear links.
2 Whether you *accept / strengthen* or reject an argument should be based on the strength of the evidence.
3 This argument is only *compelling / valid* if we accept the premise that these characteristics are completely genetic.
4 The risk of accidents is one of the most *coherent / compelling* arguments against nuclear power.

Evaluating a solution

G When approaching an engineering problem, it is important to set yourself **realistic goals**. Consider what you can achieve within the time and resources you have available. Carefully evaluate your design at each stage:

- Is the solution **feasible**? Look carefully at any constraints, such as the physical space you have to work within.
- Is your design **robust**? Ensure you carry out adequate testing to identify and address any weaknesses.
- Is the end product **straightforward** to use? Always keep the user in mind during the design process.
- Is the solution **flexible**? A good design can be adapted to work in different contexts or for different clients.

6 **Complete the statements using keywords from text G.**

1 This approach could be used in a number of different situations – it's _____ .
2 The project has goals which are not too ambitious – they're _____ .
3 The design did not fail under test conditions – it's _____ .
4 The design is likely to work because it takes account of all the practical constraints – it's _____ .
5 The final design is simple to use – it's _____ .

7 **Match the beginnings of the sentences with two possible endings. Use the list of collocations on pp.107–110 to help you if necessary.**

1 Overall, there is a lack of a **coherent**
2 The report includes a **comprehensive**
3 This may be the only **feasible**
4 There are **compelling**

a review of research in this area.
b arguments on both sides of the debate.
c argument, with no links between each claim.
d framework for teachers to work within.
e solution given the constraints of time.
f list of products containing these chemicals.
g reasons in favour of greater regulation.
h option to control the issue in many cases.

Words to learn

defect	inconsistent AWL	persist AWL	undermine
discourage	inequality	pose AWL	unnecessary
error AWL	misleading	restrict AWL	unproductive
failure	omission	shortcoming	unsustainable AWL

Negative prefixes

> **A** Addison and Hirsch (1989) contend that there are too many statistical **shortcomings** in the testing procedures used in many of the studies and results have proved to be **inconsistent**.

> **C** It has become clear that 'conventional' food systems are **unsustainable**, and so there is a need for all actors in the production-consumption process to think about the consequences of food provision.

> **B** It is argued that unions may promote more restrictive work practices, **discourage** investment in new technology, and insist on pay for **unnecessary** or **unproductive** labour in order to protect the job security of their members.

> **D** Truman (1996) argues that: 'whilst the **inequality** in wages is stark, these figures may be **misleading** since the nature of the labour market means it is not possible to make direct comparisons between men's work and women's work.'

Source: student essays

1 Complete the comments using keywords from texts A–D.

> EXAMPLE: Some young people don't apply for university because they think the fees are too high. The high fees _discourage_ them.

1 The advertised price of some flights doesn't include taxes and other hidden costs. It's _____ .
2 Delays were caused by factors which could easily have been avoided. They were _____ .
3 The way the rules are applied varies greatly in different areas. It's _____ .
4 Fishing at the current rate cannot continue in the long term as fish stocks diminish. It's _____ .
5 Current working practices mean employees waste a lot of time. They're _____ .

2 Match the words in the box to the appropriate prefix in the table to give a negative meaning. Use the glossary on pp.129–144 to help you if necessary.

> adequate   advantage   agree   equal   ~~important~~   interpret
> organized   realistic   reliable   significant   understand   use   valid

un-	in-	dis-	mis-
important 1 _____	4 _____	7 _____	10 _____
2 _____ 3 _____	5 _____	8 _____	11 _____
	6 _____	9 _____	12 _____

3 Find a word with a negative meaning from exercises 1 and 2 that means the same as the highlighted words.

1 Always ensure that other laboratory users are not exposed to risks that are not necessary. _____
2 The distribution of wealth in a way which is not equal remains a problem in the country. _____
3 Precautions should be taken to avoid data not being used in an appropriate way. _____
4 Research found that the social care system was not well organized and was slow to respond to problems. _____
5 An increase in workers on short-term contracts does not encourage firms to invest in staff training. _____

Describing problems and weaknesses

E A product should be recalled when a **defect** is serious enough to **pose** a danger to users.

F In a major health emergency, the **omission** of any one group or the **failure** of one group to implement emergency procedures correctly could **undermine** the effectiveness of the control strategy.

G One of the **shortcomings** of this type of scanning equipment is that its use is **restricted** to studying the external surface of an object.

H Despite attempts to improve the system for collecting patient data, major **errors** in the reporting of key information still **persist**.

4 Match the sentence halves.

1 Rigorous testing is essential to identify any **defects**
2 One of the **shortcomings** of the current system
3 The report was critical of the organization's **failure**
4 The introduction of foreign species may **pose**
5 If the problem **persists** after several days,
6 There is a methodological problem **undermining**
7 The services are currently **restricted**

a the credibility of test results of this kind.
b is the length of time taken to deal with cases.
c to a few major cities.
d seek medical advice.
e a threat to established native ecosystems.
f to provide adequate training for all employees.
g which may cause a part to fail suddenly.

5 a Match the verb + noun collocations used in texts A–H.

1 pose
2 undermine
3 discourage
4 restrict

a the use
b investment
c a danger
d the effectiveness

b Match the nouns in the box that collocate with the verbs. Use the list of collocations on pp.107–110 to help you if necessary.

access   confidence   credibility   movement   participation   problem   smoking   threat

1 pose a _____ / _____
2 undermine _____ / _____
3 discourage _____ / _____
4 restrict _____ / _____

c Complete the sentences using the correct form of one of the verbs in 5a.

1 The software allows parents to _____ access to certain websites.
2 Widespread corruption _____ confidence in public institutions.
3 The negative presentation of politicians in the media _____ participation in the political process.
4 The conference discussed the threat _____ to the region's security by organized crime.

6 Write one or two sentences giving a negative evaluation of one of the topics below. Remember to give objective criticisms, not just subjective, personal opinions. Try to use some of the keywords from this unit.

- An approach to solving a problem, such as cutting traffic or reducing disease
- An old theory or method of doing something that has now been replaced by new ideas

▶ EXAMPLE: *Banning cars from city centre areas may reduce traffic congestion, but it also poses a threat to retail businesses because it discourages shoppers from coming into the city.*

Student writing: critical evaluation

Almost all student writing in any discipline will involve an element of critical evaluation. The purpose of critical evaluation is to show your ability to assess the merits of an academic text. Evaluation involves highlighting the positive and negative aspects of the focus of your discussion. It is part of constructing a viewpoint or an argument which is objective and informed by further reading or experimental study.

Source: (2014). *Oxford Learner's Dictionary of Academic English.* Oxford: Oxford University Press. Oxford Academic Writing Tutor.

Introduction:

The **sustainability** of the global food system has been at the centre of much debate in recent years. It has been argued that Alternative Food Networks (AFNs) are more sustainable than the 'conventional' industrialized, intensive farming methods. Furthermore, this emergence can be seen **as a result of** concerns surrounding the **consequences** of modern food production and consumption. However, to simply equate sustainability of the global food system with AFNs should be met with caution, as this **ignores** the actual nature of the system in different contexts. Moreover, the **definitions** of some of these terms need proper consideration to fully understand both what the **concept** of sustainability is, and whether such 'alternatives' meet its **criteria**. This report will critically analyse such issues by first understanding how and why sustainability is applicable to the global food system. Secondly, it will assess the nature and implications of AFNs, and thirdly, the **credibility** of foods labelled as 'local' and 'quality' will be examined.

Sustainability and food:

As stated in the United Nation's Brundtland report, 'Sustainable development is development that meets the needs of the present without compromising the ability of future generations to meet their own needs' (UN, 1987). In the context of food systems, meeting 'need' involves the production and consumption of food. The link to sustainability is thus obvious, as the ability to continue to produce food is a key component of human existence. Yet policies that **support** intensive farming seem to have been short-sighted: mass producing food to the detriment of the environment and animal and even human health. Growing concern for the long-term sustainability of such 'conventional' systems has **led to** an increasing interest in '**alternative**' methods (Tansey and Worsley, 2000). However, the sustainable fulfilment of 'need' is not necessarily accomplished simply by **rejecting** conventional methods. AFNs will now be assessed within this context to establish their **feasibility**.

[The writer goes on to explain more about 'AFNs and local food production' and 'Quality and consistency in AFNs' ...]

Conclusion:

This review has critically examined some of the key aspects of AFNs in order to **evaluate** their sustainability. AFNs can be seen as an 'alternative' to 'conventional' methods of food production-consumption, but in reality, the situation is far more complex. What emerges clearly, however, is a theme of 'reconnection' through the creation of shorter supply chains that benefit the land and people. However, the concept of 'local' is somewhat **ambiguous**, and ensuring **consistency** can be difficult. Furthermore, AFNs rely heavily on ethical and moral **priorities**, meaning that many **advocates** of AFNs are those able to afford this luxury. While a transition to AFNs may be economically difficult for less wealthy people and places, 'conventional' food systems are clearly **unsustainable**, and so there is a need for all actors in the production-consumption process to consider gradually incorporating the principles of AFNs into mainstream food networks.

1 Overall, is the writer of the essay for or against the idea of Alternative Food Networks?

2 Are ideas from the text positive evaluations of AFNs (P) or negative (N)?

1 AFNs are more sustainable than conventional methods because they do less harm to the environment. __

2 AFNs provide a closer connection between consumers and food production. __

3 Food labelling within AFNs is not always reliable. __

4 Currently, food produced by AFNs is relatively expensive and not accessible to everyone. __

Focus on evaluation

3 Mark the pairs of words similar in meaning (S) or roughly opposite (O).

1 sustainable – unsustainable __
2 support – advocate __
3 ambiguous – evident __

4 consistent – reliable __
5 assess – evaluate __
6 alternative – conventional __

4 a Read the two critical evaluations in 4b below. Decide whether each one is largely positive (P) or negative (N).

1 __   2 __

b Complete the evaluations using the correct form of words from the box. Look back at Units 17–25 or use the glossary on pp.129–144 to help you if necessary.

adverse   barrier   consequence   persistent   pose   promoting
reliable   response   restrict   scenario   similarly

1 Hunger and malnutrition are _____ and widespread problems in many developing countries. The effects of global climate change can quickly exacerbate these problems and _____ economic growth. _____ weather conditions, such as floods and droughts, which _____ significant threats to agricultural production, are likely to increase in the near future as the climate changes. As a _____ , lost agricultural production and vulnerability to disease can become a substantial _____ to these countries' ability to feed themselves.

2 Industrial clusters have historically been viewed in terms of _____ economic development. The Harare clusters are different in that they are specifically a _____ to a pressing social and environmental health issue: the need for clean drinking water in the city. _____ , businesses also need _____ water supplies for industrial processes. Firms in the clusters try to achieve a win-win _____ , where activities that are good for the wider community, such as improved quality of and access to water, are also good for business.

Glossary
exacerbate (*v*): to make something worse
cluster (*n*): a group of things of the same type that are found close together

Focus on collocation

5 Choose the best verb to complete the sentences. Look back at Units 17–25 or use the list of collocations on pp.107–110 to help you if necessary.

1 The model *meets / makes / provides* some important assumptions.
2 Stanford University has *made / played / posed* a large part in the creation of Silicon Valley.
3 Different problems can *arise / pose / resolve* as a consequence of the same disease.
4 The clinician and patient should *impose / set / meet* long-term goals before starting therapy.
5 The findings presented *play / provide / make* clear support for our hypothesis.

6 Complete the sentences using the best preposition in each gap. Look back at Units 17–25 or use the list of dependent prepositions on pp.111–113 to help you if necessary.

1 Factors that may contribute _____ the development of diabetes include environment or genetics.
2 We cannot infer a direct causal relationship _____ these results.
3 Such policies do not differentiate _____ different types of crimes.
4 Some countries have imposed restrictions _____ television advertising of products to children.
5 Schools are _____ increasing pressure to lift levels of achievement.

26 Word families

Words to learn

assistance AWL   intervene AWL   pursuit AWL   voluntary AWL
attainable AWL   mental AWL   regulation AWL
commitment AWL   neutral AWL   restore AWL
emission   physical AWL   specify AWL

Flexibility and paraphrasing

A Kyoto Protocol: An international agreement that sets limits on the **emission** of greenhouse gases into the atmosphere, in order to reduce the threat of global warming by air pollution. The protocol **specifies** targets and deadlines for the level of emission reductions. Under the Kyoto Protocol, rich industrial developed countries agreed to reduce their emissions of greenhouse gases by an average of 5.2% by 2010. Developing countries were not set formal emission limits, partly because to do so would unfairly inhibit their **pursuit** of economic growth.

B **voluntary commitment**: The formal name, under the Kyoto Protocol, for any actions that a government or organization takes to reduce pollution emissions on a voluntary basis, outside what is required by **regulations**.

Source: Park, C. & Allaby, M. (2013). *A Dictionary of Environment and Conservation*. (2 ed.). Oxford: Oxford University Press.

Usage note using word families

Word families are the different parts of speech of a word (noun, verb, adjective, adverb). Using them can help you to find the best way to express an idea and paraphrase ideas from a source.

Word families are shown for each word in the glossary on pp.129–144.

1 Complete the paraphrases of ideas in texts A and B using the best form of a word from the box. Use the glossary on pp.129–144 to help you if necessary.

> commitment   emission   pursuit   reduce   regulations   specify   voluntary

1 The Kyoto Protocol aims to reduce the level of greenhouse gases that are _____ into the atmosphere.
2 The protocol sets out _____ targets for the reduction of emissions.
3 Developed countries agreed to an average _____ of 5.2% by 2010.
4 No formal limits were set for developing countries to allow them to _____ economic growth.
5 Governments can also _____ _____ to extra initiatives outside of the _____ framework.

2 Complete the sentences using the best form of the word in capitals.

1 The groups are typically run by unpaid _____ from the local community. VOLUNTARY
2 As the surface temperature rises, it _____ thermal radiation. EMISSION
3 This enables participants to act together more effectively to _____ shared objectives. PURSUIT
4 Many professions have adopted a code of practice to _____ their activities. REGULATION
5 These programmes should be _____ targeted at less experienced and younger teachers. SPECIFY
6 Suppose the state imposed heavy taxes on the profits of firms that _____ the environment. POLLUTION
7 All contracts must satisfy certain legal _____ if they are to be valid. REQUIRE
8 It is important to encourage individuals to _____ to an agreed plan of action. COMMITMENT

Word formation

C	The right to health is enshrined in international law. The International Covenant of Economic, Social and Cultural Rights (ICESCR) requires states to recognize the right of everyone to the enjoyment of the highest **attainable** standard of **physical** and **mental** health.

D	The International Committee of the Red Cross (ICRC) describes itself as an impartial, **neutral** and independent organization whose humanitarian mission is to protect victims of armed conflict and other violent situations and to provide them with **assistance**. Protection work typically involves visiting people deprived of their liberty, **intervening** during hostilities on behalf of civilian victims and **restoring** family links between people separated by war. Assistance entails the provision of humanitarian aid.

3 Put the suffixes in the wordbox into the 'Ending' column in the table according to their typical part of speech. Then complete the 'Examples' column with examples of words with each suffix that appear in this unit.

-able -al -ally -ate -ify -ize -ly -ment -sion -tion

Part of speech	Ending	Examples
noun	_-ment_	enjoyment, 7 _____
	1 _____	8 _____
	2 _____	9 _____
adjective	_-al_	mental, 10 _____
	3 _____	11 _____
verb	_-ate_	regulate, 12 _____
	4 _____	13 _____
	5 _____	14 _____
adverb	_-ally_	typically, 15 _____
	6 _____	16 _____

Usage note word formation

Being familiar with the common **suffixes**, or word endings, used to form different parts of speech can help you to recognize and remember different members of a word family.

-*ment* (= nouns): *enjoyment*
-*ate* (= verbs): *regulate*
-*al* (= adjectives): *mental*
-*ally* (= adverbs): *typically*

Some words have more than one noun or adjective form with different suffixes and meanings:
• *assistance (n) – assistant (n);*
• *pollution (n) – pollutant (n) – polluter (n);*
• *developed (adj) – developing (adj).*

Some words don't follow a typical pattern and have to be learnt individually:
• *legal (adj) – legislation (n) – law (n).*
For more about suffixes, see Unit 30 and the list of affixes on p.114.

4 Complete the paraphrases using the form shown in brackets of the highlighted word.

▶ EXAMPLE: Only the most serious cases require the **intervention** of senior management.
Senior management only need _to intervene in the most serious cases_. (*verb*)

1 Researchers were present to offer the children **assistance** with completion of the questionnaires.
Researchers were present to _____. (*verb*)

2 Algeria became an **independent** country in 1962.
In 1962, Algeria _____. (*noun*)

3 The workplace must be easily accessible to **physically** disabled employees.
There must be easy access to the workplace for employees with a _____. (*adjective*)

4 The **restoration** of business confidence is essential to encourage economic growth.
In order to encourage economic growth, it is essential to _____. (*verb*)

5 There is a lack of support for young people suffering from **mental** illness.
There is a lack of support for young people who _____. (*adverb*)

6 The guidelines set out **specific** limits on how long samples can be retained.
The guidelines _____. (*verb*)

7 According to the constitution, the president is obliged to remain politically **neutral**.
According to the constitution, the president is obliged to maintain _____. (*noun*)

Words to learn

attitude AWL
attribute AWL
benchmarking
concentration AWL

cooperation AWL
coordination AWL
correspondence AWL
diversity AWL

formation
incidence AWL
insight AWL
occurrence AWL

practice
protective
systematic

Countable and uncountable nouns

A A 'metallogenic province' is a geographical area which is characterized by the occurrence of high concentrations of mineral deposits of the same type. The causes of the formation of metallogenic provinces are not clear.

B Culture is a set of values and expectations which serves as a filter for one's perception of the surrounding environment, guiding behaviour and social interaction. Project teams with high national diversity demonstrate divergent preferences for social interaction norms. These can create difficulties in tasks which require high degrees of coordination and cooperation.

Usage note countable and uncountable nouns

Uncountable nouns which describe abstract concepts and processes are common in academic writing:
   diversity, coordination, cooperation.

These nouns do not have a plural form and are used with a singular verb form. Other nouns can be either countable (C) or uncountable (U) depending on their context and meaning:
- *the **occurrence** (U) of high **concentrations** (C) of mineral deposits*
- *Earthquakes are regular **occurrences** (C) in some parts of the world.*
- *There has been greater **concentration** (U) on basic maths and literacy.*

1 Are the nouns from texts A and B used in a countable (C) or uncountable (U) sense?

1 area __
2 formation __
3 culture __

4 perception __
5 behaviour __
6 diversity __

7 preference __
8 degree __

2 a Complete the sentences using the correct form of the nouns in the box.

concentration   cooperation   ~~coordination~~   diversity   formation   occurrence   preference

▶ EXAMPLE: Better *coordination* between different service providers (*leads*) *lead to* to fewer delays.

1 A strong _____ for sweet foods *was / were* observed in both groups.

2 Intergovernmental _____ *has / have* always had a significant influence on the EU's development.

3 Geological _____ with sufficient porosity and permeability to supply water *is / are* classified as aquifers.

4 Thus, greater _____ *increases / increase* tolerance as a result of more exposure to other ethnic groups.

5 Relatively high _____ of metals such as copper, nickel and lead *was / were* found in the waste water.

6 The _____ of chronic disease in a family often *has / have* far-reaching effects.

b Choose the correct form of the verbs in the sentences in 2a.

Noun phrases

C The difference in the **incidence** of cardiovascular disease between younger men and women could be **attributed** to a possible **protective** effect of endogenous oestrogens (female hormones).

D Overall, there seems to be a **correspondence** between the client base of a consulting company and the **attitude** toward **benchmarking** as an appropriate method for identifying best **practices**. Larger companies are engaged in many projects for many clients and therefore seem to be in a better position to carry out **systematic** comparisons of practices. The client base of smaller consultancies, however, is too small to make effective use of such **insights**.

Usage note

Academic writing contains a higher proportion of nouns than general spoken English. Nouns and noun phrases are used to express complex, detailed information in a concise way. Compare the example below to the single sentence in text C.

More younger men than women suffer from cardiovascular disease. Endogenous oestrogens may possibly help to protect women from the disease. This could be a reason why men and women are affected differently.

Text C: **The difference in the incidence of cardiovascular disease between younger men and women** *could be attributed to* **a possible protective effect of endogenous oestrogens** *(female hormones).*

---

3 Read texts C and D. Mark the statements true (T) or false (F) according to the texts.

1 More younger women suffer from cardiovascular disease than men in the same age group. __
2 Female hormones may help protect against cardiovascular disease. __
3 Smaller consulting companies are more likely to systematically compare the working practices of the companies they work with. __

4 Put the words in the best order to form noun phrases.

▶ EXAMPLE: cardiovascular disease / an investigation / in / of men and women / into / the incidence
an investigation into the incidence of cardiovascular disease in men and women
1 of / systematic benchmarking / a correspondence / the use / between / company size and
2 parents and teachers / the attitudes / differences / between / of / toward / classroom discipline
3 as a family / of / the traditional practice / together / cooking and eating
4 evaluating / computer games / children / a suitable method / for / the effects / of / on

5 a Complete the sentences using the correct preposition(s). Use the list of dependent prepositions on p.111–113 to help you if necessary.

▶ EXAMPLE: A systematic comparison _of_ the results of previous studies (*has*)/ *have* highlighted two significant patterns.
1 The occurrence _____ significant life events such as unemployment or severe illness *was / were* identified within the sample group.
2 The attitude _____ directors _____ risk clearly *influence / influences* decisions that affect the success of the business.
3 Over time, the interactions _____ individuals within a particular context *develop / develops* into strong networks.
4 An individual's perception _____ the impact _____ their condition _____ their day-to-day life *is / are* dependent on a number of factors.
5 A high degree _____ cooperation _____ national courts and the Court of Justice *is / are* required to ensure uniform application of law.
6 Differences _____ the size of similar species in different locations *is / are* often attributed to the availability of food.

b Underline the main noun in each noun phrase in the sentences in 5a.

c Choose the correct verb form to complete the sentences in 5a.

Words to learn

acquire AWL	employ	gain	utilize AWL
conform to	end up	obtain AWL	
deduce AWL	exclude AWL	recover AWL	
dispose of AWL	exploit AWL	retain AWL	

General and specific verbs

A Would the same results have been **obtained** if the research had been conducted at different points in the year?

B In order for users to better **exploit** this new technology, we need a means of sharing the range of useful strategies expert users are known to **employ** to perform different tasks.

C Large firms in general are able to **utilize** resources in order to **acquire** and process information relating to their market environment. They can then use this information to **gain** an advantage over their competitors.

D Even within the new, more regulated system, individual managers **retain** some flexibility in how they implement the policy within their department.

1 Read texts A–D and complete the table using verbs from the texts.

Basic verb	More formal, academic verb
use	1 _____ + resources, technology, an approach
	2 _____ + a method, a strategy, a technique
	exploit + an opportunity, resources, technology
get	3 _____ + results, information, data
	4 _____ + knowledge, skills, information
	5 _____ + access, insight, an advantage
do	6 _____ + a study, research, an interview
	7 _____ + a task, a function, a test
	implement + a policy, a strategy, a change

Usage note

A number of basic verbs – **do, make, get, put, use**, etc. – do not have clear, precise meanings. For this reason, academic writers tend to avoid them and choose verbs with a more specific meaning.
Rather informal:
- *Researchers first **do** a small pilot study.*
- *Machines are now able to **do** these tasks.*

More academic:
- *Researchers first **conduct** a small pilot study.*
- *Machines are now able to **perform** these tasks.*

2 Rewrite the sentences replacing the highlighted words with one of the more formal verbs in exercise 1. Make any other changes necessary. More than one option may be possible.

▶ EXAMPLE: Adaptable species will quickly grow or reproduce to make the most of opportunities where there is no competition. _exploit_

1 Trainees typically spend up to five months in the Commission getting work experience. _____

2 In recent years, the government has had economic policies favouring foreign investors. _____

3 Are leaders born or can individuals get the skills of leadership? _____

4 Despite great progress, the available technology has not been fully used in some areas. _____

5 Unauthorized access to such a database may be secured by dishonestly getting password details. _____

6 The following two designs do exactly the same functions but have different physical features. _____

Phrasal verbs in academic writing

E Twenty-two of the 50 candidates put forward for selection were **excluded** on the grounds that they had insufficient experience or lacked the required qualifications.

F All equipment is required to **conform to** strict quality standards. Where manufacturing defects directly result in problems, the consumer can **recover** the cost of any repairs.

G As it became possible to **deduce** the function of individual genes, the next step was to extend this study to entire genomes and to establish how all of the genes within an organism operate together as a unified whole.

H If it comes to light that a clothing company **disposes of** 500 coats with slight imperfections while, at the same time, refugees are freezing in the cold, the company could very well **end up** facing a major public relations challenge.

Usage note

Phrasal verbs are less common in academic writing than in general English because they are often vague and potentially ambiguous. However, some phrasal verbs are used:
- *Twenty-two of the 50 candidates **put forward** for selection …*
- *All equipment is required to **conform to** strict quality standards …*

3 Find five examples of phrasal verbs in texts E–H.

_____ _____ _____ _____ _____

**4 Complete the sentences using a preposition in each gap.
Use the glossary on pp.129–144 help you if necessary.**

▶ EXAMPLE: The government failed to conform _to_ the requirements of international human rights law.
1 Freud puts _____ a set of startling new claims.
2 In Germany, reunification resulted _____ a dramatic increase in east-to-west migration.
3 The questionnaire consists _____ 25 true-or-false items.
4 Brady carried _____ a series of experiments with small vertebrates.
5 The loss of tropical forest leads _____ local climatic change.
6 The waste had been illegally dumped rather than being disposed _____ properly.
7 Our study is partly based _____ survey data.

5 Find single-word verbs in texts E–H that have a similar meaning to the phrasal verbs.

1 get back _____ 2 find out _____ 3 rule out _____ 4 work out _____

6 Rewrite the sentences, replacing the phrasal verbs with more formal verbs from the box. Use the glossary on pp.129–144 to help you if necessary.

compile   deduce   establish   exclude   fluctuate   monitor   resolve   undergo

▶ EXAMPLE: Further studies are needed to find out _establish_ how lasting such effects could be.
1 Analysis of plant fossils can be used to work out _____ ancient levels of atmospheric O_2.
2 Further experimentation may help to sort out _____ this problem.
3 The number of cases each year was relatively small, and rates went up and down _____ considerably as a result.
4 Of course, we cannot rule out _____ the possibility that other factors may have contributed to this result.
5 Patients going through _____ surgery are at risk of developing blood clots.
6 It is during visits to the clinic that babies were weighed to check up on _____ their progress.
7 Early in the 16th century, parish priests in London put together _____ weekly lists of deaths from plague.

Words to learn

allocation AWL	come into contact	derive AWL	parallel AWL
alteration AWL	with AWL	interaction AWL	responsible
capable AWL	compatible AWL	in terms of	transfer AWL
	convert AWL	nature	

Prepositions with nouns, verbs and adjectives

A There are several reasons why it is important to identify the **nature** of soot from combustion processes. Epidemiological data have shown clearly that long-term breathing of air polluted with smoke **derived** from certain sources can have serious adverse effects on human respiratory and cardiac systems. What is not clear, however, is exactly which elements are most **responsible** for the ensuing health problems.

B First formulated in the 1950s, the somatic mutation theory explains aging as a gradual accumulation of random **alterations** to the DNA in the cells of our body. This theory is **compatible** with the other major theory of aging: the free-radical theory of aging. Whereas the latter provides a logical explanation for where most of life's wear and tear comes from, the somatic mutation theory also explains how this can result in physical decline and increased disease.

Glossary
soot (*n*): black powder that is produced when wood, coal, etc. is burnt
combustion (*n*): the process of burning sth
epidemiological (*adj*): to do with the branch of medicine that deals with the spread and control of diseases
mutation (*n*): a process in which the genetic material of a person changes in structure

1 Read texts A and B. Mark the statements true (T) or false (F).

1 Breathing smoke from certain sources can have a harmful effect on human health. __
2 Research has identified which types of smoke are most harmful. __
3 The two theories mentioned in text B offer conflicting explanations for the aging process. __

2 Find the prepositions that are used with these words in texts A and B.

1 nature _____
2 effect _____
3 accumulation _____
4 alteration _____
5 theory _____
6 explanation _____
7 pollute sth _____
8 derive _____
9 responsible _____
10 compatible _____

Usage note preposition choice
The choice of preposition after nouns, verbs or adjectives can sometimes change the meaning.
For more information about prepositions, see the list of **dependent prepositions** on pp.111–113.

3 In each of the sentences there is a preposition missing. Insert the correct preposition to follow the highlighted word. The preposition may not always come directly after the word.

► EXAMPLE: The evidence to date **derives** largely *from* laboratory studies.
1 The paper defines the key risk factors **responsible** the development of the condition.
2 The exact **nature** this process is unclear.
3 Several explanations have been **put forward** the existence of these gaps.
4 Any **alterations** made the terms of the contract must be agreed by both parties.
5 Any such agreement between airlines must be **compatible** competition rules.
6 From one perspective, education can be viewed simply as the **accumulation** knowledge.

Common preposition patterns

C The book describes the scientific and technological principles behind how energy is generated and how it can be **converted** from one form to another. It also explores the consequences of energy use for the environment **in terms of** creating pollution and contributing to climate change and the implications of this for policymakers.

D The paper draws **parallels** between the global depression of the 1930s and the recent economic crisis. It asks what can be learnt about the impact of such events on the global financial infrastructure and focuses in particular on the **interaction** between events and institutions.

E This article looks at different means of **transferring** patient information between clinical settings, for example from a family doctor to a hospital clinic. It describes case studies in which patients **come into contact with** a number of different practitioners, and assesses the repercussions of accurate information transfer for continuity of care.

F The lecture explored how all organisms have to balance the **allocation** of resources to growth and reproduction. A long-lived species may mature slowly and delay reproduction until conditions are favourable, whereas those living in unpredictable habitats need to be **capable** of acting quickly to exploit brief periods of plenty.

Usage note patterns of prepositions
- change/transition/shift **from** A **to** B:
  *how it can be **converted from** one form **to** another*
- the effect/impact **of** (an event) **on** sb/sth:
  *the **impact of** such events **on** the global financial infrastructure*
- the allocation/distribution/provision **of** sth **to** sb/sth:
  *the **allocation of** resources **to** growth and reproduction*
- connection/relationship/parallel **between** A **and** B:
  *the **interaction between** events **and** institutions.*
- but, A has a connection **with** B:
  *patients come into **contact with** a number of different practitioners.*
- noun/adjective + preposition combinations are typically followed by a verb in the **-ing** form:
  ***in terms of** creating pollution; **capable of** acting quickly*

4 Choose the best option to complete each sentence.

1 The same standards apply to any staff who come into direct contact *between / with* customers.
2 We examine the impact of globalization *for / on* higher education.
3 They found that a questionnaire was as effective as a medical examination in terms of *assess / assessing* fitness.
4 New technologies have changed the way young people interact *between / with* each other.
5 There may have been errors in the transfer of data from the questionnaires *to / with* the database.
6 Most other planets do not have an atmosphere that is capable *to support / of supporting* life.

5 Complete the sentences using the best preposition in each gap. Use the list of dependent prepositions on pp.111–113 to help you if necessary.

1 It is important to account for the correlation _____ age and physical health.
2 Evidence _____ the current study provides support _____ this hypothesis.
3 Two genes were identified as having an association _____ the control of eating behaviour.
4 The sample was representative _____ the Finnish working-age population _____ terms _____ age and gender.
5 Figure 17 is a typical example _____ a page generated by a search engine _____ response _____ a user query.
6 The study investigates the impact _____ work _____ health among older workers and the implications _____ this _____ health services in the future.

30 Affixes

Words to learn

accountable	automation AWL	equivalent AWL	uniform AWL
active	ceaseless	reinforce AWL	visible AWL
adulthood AWL	employee	transportation AWL	

Prefixes

A While total consistency is impossible, there are ways to reduce inconsistencies. One involves the design of the service in such a way as to make it as **uniform** as possible. This might be accomplished via **automation** where possible or by training personnel to follow strictly controlled guidelines.

B Japan is in the midst of a profound transformation. The country's population has begun to shrink and it is projected that the population will continue to decline at a rate of approximately 800,000 people per year. This is **equivalent** to losing a city the size of Niigata annually.

Usage note affixes

Prefixes (at the beginning of words) and suffixes (at the end of words) can help you understand and remember words.
For a list of **affixes** and their meanings, see p.114.

C Digital systems have dramatically changed our lives and the digital revolution is driven by microelectronics. Digital circuits exist in almost every electrical appliance we use in our homes, in the vehicles and **transportation** systems we use to travel and in the telephones we use to communicate.

D The student website includes interactive quizzes and games, as well as audio and video clips which **reinforce** themes raised in the programme itself.

1 a Match the highlighted prefixes in the words from texts A–D to their meanings.

▶ EXAMPLE: across; beyond: ———————   a **transportation**
1 equal; equally: b **automation**
2 one; having one: c **equivalent**
3 again: d **interactive**
4 by itself; without a person to operate it: e **microelectronics**
5 over a long distance: f **reinforce**
6 small; on a small scale: g **telephone**
7 between; from one to another: h **uniform**

b Complete the sentences using an appropriate form of a word from 1a.

1 Samples are taken at a(n) _____ rate of two samples per second.
2 The app allows students to create bibliographic records _____ to the manual form of index cards.
3 Training is a(n) _____ process that requires input from both the trainee and the employer.
4 Manufacturing facilities are located near the source of raw materials to minimize _____ costs.
5 Workload growth has been managed by increasing levels of _____ , rather than by increasing staff numbers.

2 Complete the highlighted words using prefixes from exercise 1.

▸ EXAMPLE: These issues cross national borders, so _unílateral_ action by a single state is ineffective.

1 The justice system strives to achieve fair and _____table treatment of all citizens.
2 Interviewers need good _____personal skills to develop a relationship with respondents.
3 In contrast to bacteria and other _____organisms, fungi can be very large in size.
4 The global economy is, of course, dependent on modern _____communications.
5 Financial _____actions between countries are recorded in the balance of payments.

Suffixes

E A sample of gas exerts a pressure on the walls of its container because the molecules of gas are in **ceaseless**, random motion and exert a force when they strike the walls.

G Employees who sought to make those in power more **visible** and **accountable** through the persistent demand for more information and the questioning of decisions were relatively more effective in achieving change.

F Most studies have focused on children, and comparable data for individuals as they progress into **adulthood** are scarce.

H There is up to a fourfold difference in blood requirement between resting and **active** muscle.

3 a Match the meanings, 1–5, to the highlighted suffixes in a–e.

1 a person or thing that does something
2 multiplied by
3 a person affected by an action
4 possible to
5 a state, at a particular period of time

a a fourfold difference
b more visible and accountable
c progress into adulthood
d the walls of its container
e employees

b Identify the part of speech of the highlighted words in 3a.

4 Choose the best option to complete the sentences.

1 The steel plant remains the major _employee / employer_ in the area.
2 Microorganisms are measured in micrometres, and are frequently _visible / invisible_ to the human eye.
3 These data fail to _account / be accountable_ for the large numbers of migrants living in the city.
4 Organizations can take _active / action_ to reduce the causes of stress in the workplace.
5 Risk factors for chronic disease and ill health can be identified in early _adults / adulthood_.

5 Complete the sentences using the best form of the word in capitals. You may need to add a prefix or a suffix.

1 Always wear a suitable laboratory coat, protective goggles, and _____ gloves. DISPOSE
2 European car _____ have to change their specifications to sell to the USA. MANUFACTURE
3 Air accident investigators rely on information from the black box flight recorder to _____ events. CONSTRUCT
4 Where patients do not speak English, an _____ may be needed. INTERPRET
5 The almost _____ availability of information via the internet poses its own problems. LIMIT
6 Sixty-four per cent of the _____ mentioned using instant messaging services. INTERVIEW
7 In this situation, information from the patient may be _____ and should be checked with hospital records. RELY
8 Greater interdependence implies a more _____ relationship between states. COOPERATE

31 Collocation

Words to learn

commission AWL	execute	phase AWL	quantitative
consult AWL	incentive AWL	observation	violate AWL
distinction AWL	instruction AWL	qualitative AWL	

Types of collocation

A Tourism can provide a strong **incentive** for wildlife conservation. A report **commissioned** by WWF found that Kenya's economy earns US$250 million from tourism a year and that the Kenyan Wildlife Service benefits directly from tourist income by about US$18 million annually.

B Research methods programmes typically make a **distinction** between **qualitative** and **quantitative** methods. In reality, however, the two often overlap. A biologist researching the nesting behaviour of sea turtles, for example, might collect quantitative data about the time that turtles come up onto a beach, the number of eggs they lay, etc., but they might also make **observations** about the animals' behaviour and about the attitudes of local people towards the turtles: qualitative data. Both approaches will contribute to their final report.

1 Complete the 'Collocation' column in the table using collocations from texts A and B. Then complete the 'Collocation type' column by identifying the types of collocation.

Collocation	Collocation type
1 _____ + a report	verb + 2 _____
3 _____ + an incentive	
4 _____ + a distinction	
a 5 _____ + incentive	adjective + 6 _____
qualitative/quantitative + 7 _____ / _____	
benefit + 8 _____	verb + adverb

Usage note *make* and *do*

Although academic writers often avoid general verbs like **make** and **do** (see Unit 28), some strong collocations with these verbs are common in academic writing.
make + a distinction, observation, decision, contribution:
 • *make* a distinction *between*…
do + work, business, research, harm, damage:
 • the **work done** by Turing and his colleagues
For more about **collocations**, see pp.107–110.

2 Choose the best word to complete the sentences. Use the list of collocations on pp.107–110 to help you if necessary.

▶ EXAMPLE: Petras and Morley (*make*)/ *provide* a **distinction** between the regime and the state.
1 The figures are from a **report** *commissioned* / *provided* by the International Council for Science.
2 International trade is likely to **benefit** *directly* / *strongly* from more transnational connections.
3 Farmers have a *general* / *strong* **incentive** to clear land in order to claim government subsidies.
4 A failure of food safety control can *do* / *make* serious **damage** to the reputation of a business.
5 The research was aimed at understanding customers' motivations and used focus groups and other *qualitative* / *quantitative* research **methods**.
6 Helmholtz *did* / *made* important **contributions** in all major fields of science.

Collocations in academic disciplines

C
  i   A number of issues arose during the initial **phase** of the study.
  ii All these elements are in the gas phase on account of the very high temperatures.

D
  i   It is important to ensure that participants understand and follow the **instructions** carefully.
  ii Some processors have multiple processing units and **execute** instructions in parallel.

E
  i   It is, of course, possible to find anomalies: examples which **violate** the normal rules.
  ii The applicant could reasonably claim that his removal from the country would violate Article 2 of the Convention.

F
  i   There is evidence that about one in five people experiencing an episode of back pain will **consult** a primary care physician.
  ii Students are recommended to consult the references for additional reading.

Usage note collocations in academic disciplines

Some collocations are largely used within specific academic disciplines:
  • *the **gas phase*** (chemistry/science)
  • ***violate Article 2*** (law)
When you are reading texts in your own discipline, make a note of frequent collocations.

3 a Match the texts, C–F, to the disciplines in the box. Write 'any' for texts which could come from almost any discipline.

  chemistry   computer science   law   medicine

1 C i *any*   ii _____   3 E i _____   ii _____
2 D i _____   ii _____   4 F i _____   ii _____

b Identify the different collocations used with the words below in each pair of extracts.

1 the i _____ ii _____ phase   3 violate a(n) i _____ ii _____
2 i _____ ii _____ instructions   4 consult a i _____ ii _____

4 a Do you think the highlighted collocations are typically used in a specific discipline (SD) or can they be used across a range of academic disciplines (any)?

1 During an **early phase** of the study, the project team consulted extensively with the local community. __
2 Thus, the denial of freedom of movement in this context **violates** the **Convention**. __
3 It is generally not possible for the patient to see a specialist without first **consulting** a **general practitioner**. __
4 The **instructions given** to respondents are an important part of reducing possible errors. __
5 The next step involves finalizing and **executing** the research **plan**. __
6 The new cable and satellite television channels were **commissioning** very little new **work**. __
7 Hubble's **astronomical observations** revealed that the universe contains galaxies which on average are moving apart from one another. __

b For each of the examples in 4a that are from a specific discipline, identify the discipline area (e.g. science, law, etc.).

5 a Use an academic search engine (such as Google Scholar) or a university library search facility to search for examples of the words below. Identify two or three common collocations that you find.

1 principle (*noun*)   2 analysis (*noun*)   3 conduct (*verb*)   4 complex (*adj*)

b Which of the collocations are common across academic disciplines and which are specific?

▶ EXAMPLE: *basic principle (general), legal principle (law)*

32 Synonyms

Words to learn

associated with   corporation AWL   premise   with regard to
challenging AWL   drawback   revenue AWL
considerable AWL   panel AWL   salary

Avoiding repetition and creating cohesion

A Based on the premise that positive and negative attitudes toward physical activity each have an effect on children's physical activity, individuals can be categorized along both dimensions, creating a typology of attitudes (i.e. High Positive/High Negative, Low Positive/High Negative, High Positive/Low Negative, Low Positive/Low Negative). Using these categorizations, predictions can be made for the four groups with regard to physical activity. Individuals who have high positives and low negatives might be considered likely exercisers because they perceive significant advantages associated with physical activity but few disadvantages. Conversely, those with low positives and high negatives may be considered unlikely exercisers because they perceive few benefits and many costs. Individuals reporting high levels of both positive and negative may be considered ambivalent because they recognize benefits to exercise but also acknowledge considerable drawbacks.

Source: Nelson, T., Benson, E. & Jenson, C. (2010). Negative Attitudes Toward Physical Activity: Measurement and Role in Predicting Physical Activity Levels Among Preadolescents. *Journal of Pediatric Psychology.* Oxford: Oxford University Press. 35(1). pp.89–98.

Usage note synonyms in a text

Notice how the writer uses the highlighted synonyms, **positives**, **advantages** and **benefits**, to refer to the same idea in text A. Using synonyms in your writing does two things:

• creates cohesion in your text by linking ideas together in a way that is easy to follow
• avoids repetition of the same word or phrase and makes the text more interesting for the reader.

1 Read text A and match the three groups, 1–3, according to their attitude towards exercise and their likely behaviour, a–c.

1 strong positive feelings about exercise and few negative feelings
2 strong negative feelings about exercise and few positive feelings
3 both strong positive and strong negative feelings about exercise

a unlikely to exercise
b no clear effect
c likely to exercise

2 Complete these sets of synonyms from text A.

▶ EXAMPLE: positives / advantages / <u>benefits</u>
1 negatives / disadvantages / _____ / _____
2 physical activity / _____
3 significant / many / _____
4 perceive / _____ / _____

3 Tick the options which have a similar meaning to the highlighted phrase in the extracts from text A. Use the glossary on pp.129–144 to help you if necessary.

1 **Based on the premise that** positive and negative attitudes toward physical activity each have an effect on children's physical activity …
a Starting from the assumption that __   b Based on the idea that __   c Given that __

2 Predictions can be made for the four groups **with regard to** physical activity.
a regarding __   b connected with __   c in terms of __

3 They perceive significant advantages **associated with** physical activity.
a when it comes to __   b in association with __   c connected with __

4 **Conversely**, those with low positives and high negatives may be considered unlikely exercisers.
a As opposed to __   b In contrast __   c On the contrary __

Understanding differences between synonyms

B
i Revenues generated through fuel taxes can be used to subsidize cleaner forms of transport.
ii Arts organizations will typically generate income through a number of streams: ticket sales, government subsidy, private donations, and business sponsorship.
iii Over the same period, the average salary of a CEO employed in a large corporation has risen dramatically.

C
i Prior to his academic career, he enjoyed a successful commercial career with a variety of international organizations.
ii Many of the largest corporations are household names, familiar to people everywhere in the world.
iii An intergovernmental panel of experts was established to review the issues.

D
i For most firms, setting prices is a difficult task which involves both scientific analysis and trial and error.
ii These workers are mostly interested in challenging work which requires considerable creativity and initiative.
iii One of the toughest jobs in the business world is turning around a failing company.

4 Match the sets of synonyms 1–3 from texts B–D to the best general definitions, a–c.

1 revenue – income – salary
2 organization – corporation – panel
3 difficult – challenging – tough

a a group of people working together
b money earned
c not easy and requiring a lot of effort

5 Complete these notes from the *Oxford Learner's Dictionary of Academic English* using words from exercise 4. Some words are used more than once.

1 _____ and _____ may each refer to money that an organization receives, for example from the sale of goods or services, but _____ may also mean the money a person earns from their job.

2 A _____ task, problem or situation is difficult to deal with; the word can be used in an approving way to describe something that is difficult but which you hope to achieve or overcome.

3 Multinational and _____ are both used to mean a company that operates in more than one country. _____ can be used to mean a company that exists to make a profit, or a non-profit group.

> **Usage note** differences between synonyms
>
> Synonyms may have a similar meaning, but they typically differ in some ways.
>
> • Context: they may be used to talk about different people, contexts or things: **revenue** = money earned by a company or a government, **salary** = money earned by an individual
>
> • Range: one word may be quite general, whereas a synonym might be more specific: an **organization** = any organized group, a **corporation** = a commercial company
>
> • Register: they may be appropriate in different styles of writing: formal/informal, general/specialist, etc.

6 Choose the best synonym to complete each sentence.

1 Profit is what remains of total sales *revenues / salaries* after all costs of production have been paid.
2 All applications should be reviewed by a review *panel / organization* prior to an official decision.
3 Consciousness is probably the most *challenging / tough* subject of psychological research.
4 Women were banned from attending political meetings or joining political *corporations / organizations* after 1850 in France, Germany, and Austria.
5 Gardiner *et al.* (2002) have presented *considerable / many* evidence contradicting this account.
6 Outside the city, lower population densities increase the *cost / drawback* per passenger kilometre of public transport.
7 In giving feedback, we always highlight the *positives / advantages* as well as any lessons learnt.

Words to learn

allegedly	arguably	primarily AWL	so-called AWL	theoretically AWL
apparent AWL	in principle AWL	principal AWL	somewhat AWL	to some extent
approximately AWL	on average	seemingly	supposedly	typically

Expressing ideas accurately

A
a Women live longer than men.
b Women **typically** live longer than men.

a The region has equal numbers of speakers of both languages.
b The region has **approximately** equal numbers of speakers of both languages.

a All of these concerns have now been addressed.
b All of these concerns have **to some extent** now been addressed.

a The gains using this alternative approach are reduced.
b The gains using this alternative approach are **somewhat** reduced.

a The reason women earn less than men is that they work in different kinds of jobs.
b The **principal** reason women earn less than men is that they tend to work in different kinds of jobs.

a Americans buy more than 50 new garments each year.
b Americans buy, **on average**, more than 50 new garments each year.

a This rise in male mortality during adolescence is due to risky behaviour.
b This rise in male mortality during adolescence is **primarily** due to risky behaviour.

Usage note being accurate

Academic writers use certain words and expressions, known as **hedging**, to ensure that what they say is accurate. Sometimes this language shows that a claim is not completely true in every situation. For example, if you state 'Women live longer than men', readers will respond that some men live longer than some women. It would be more accurate to say:

- *Women **typically** live longer than men. **On average**, women live longer than men.*

Hedging is also used to express the degree to which something applies:

- ***Approximately** half of those surveyed (48.5%) … (= not exactly half)*
- *Our findings suggest that improved teamwork **could to some extent** solve this issue. (= not completely)*

Although hedging language can seem less confident, it actually makes your argument stronger. By showing that you have thought about all the details, it is more difficult to criticize your argument.

1 How does the addition of the highlighted words in text A affect the meaning?

2 Complete the sentences using keywords from text A. Sometimes more than one option is possible.

1 Consumers' decisions regarding how much to spend will be limited, _____ , by their income.
2 The number of medical lawsuits in Japan has _____ doubled in the last ten years.
3 Onset of the disease _____ occurs in late adolescence.
4 Sociobiologists are _____ concerned with the interactions between individuals within animal groups.
5 In the countries studied, registering property takes 100 days _____ .
6 The application process has been _____ simplified in recent years.
7 In Asia, habitat loss has been the _____ cause of decline in both species.

Expressing stance

B The move to online music downloads is **arguably** the biggest shake-up the music business has ever seen. It initially led to an explosion of **so-called** music piracy: the illegal sharing of music files online.

C Industrial waste was dumped directly into the river in **apparent** disregard of environmental regulations. Subsequently, dozens of local residents have been hospitalized with symptoms **allegedly** caused by the resulting pollution.

D Although, **in principle**, privacy is valued and protected in society, in many respects, children's privacy is increasingly restricted. Controls **supposedly** designed to keep children safe online are seen by many young people as just another intrusion on their privacy.

E This new approach is not without its critics. More traditional education-to-work programmes **seemingly** teach more practical skills that, **theoretically**, better prepare young, unemployed people for the labour market.

Usage note expressing stance

Academic writers use hedging to show what they think about a claim: to express their stance.

- *This raises an **apparent** contradiction.* (= It seems to be a contradiction, but it may not be.)
- *Participation in the plan was **supposedly** open to all the countries.* (= This is true in theory, but I know it isn't completely true in practice.)
- *He studied the cultures of **so-called** primitive peoples.* (= The label 'primitive' has been used, but I disagree with its use.)

---

3 Match the statements, 1–6, to the writer's stance, a–f.

1 Damage to one part of the brain often results in **seemingly** random patterns of impairment.
2 There is no reason why, **in principle**, quality should be higher in one factory than in the other.
3 The study looks at the effects of our **so-called** '24-hour culture' on health.
4 Such a heavy focus on testing in education **arguably** leaves little space for encouraging creativity.
5 The company was criticized in the media for **allegedly** mistreating staff in its factories.
   a This should be possible, but in reality, there may be problems.
   b This has been stated as a fact, but no proof has been given that it's true.
   c This is the term used to describe this idea, but I don't think it's accurate.
   d There doesn't seem to be a logical pattern, but there may be one we haven't found yet.
   e This is a view I believe can be supported by good arguments.

4 Do these words and expressions have a similar (S) or different (D) meaning?

1 so-called – arguably __
2 in principle – theoretically __
3 supposedly – allegedly __
4 apparent – so-called __

5 Choose the best word or expression to complete the sentences.

1 The participants in this sample exhibited the *typical / typically* pattern of age differences.
2 Some visiting lecturers were surprised by the students' *seeming / seemingly* lack of respect for authority.
3 Plant growth is *primary / primarily* dependent on conditions such as temperature and rainfall.
4 The regime was investigated for *alleged / allegedly* abuses of human rights.

6 Add one or more hedging words or expressions from this unit to each statement to make it more accurate or to express a clear stance. More than one option may be possible.

1 Dietary habits are established in childhood.
2 In India, 30% of the population is under the age of 14.
3 A great deal of criminal activity is conducted via the 'dark web': a part of the World Wide Web which is not available via conventional browsers.
4 Although men and women have equal political rights in many countries, men still dominate in parliaments around the world.

34 Emphasis

Words to learn

crucial AWL	fundamentally AWL	overwhelming	undeniably
dominate AWL	greatly	seriously	undoubtedly
enormously AWL	imperative	severely	
entirely	inevitable AWL	unavoidable	

Degree adverbs

A In a number of ways, business-to-business (B2B) marketing is **fundamentally** different from the marketing of consumer goods because organizational buyers do not consume the products themselves.

B The participants in the study were all **severely** disabled and depended **entirely** on carers for many of their basic, day-to-day needs.

C Secure ownership of land is foremost, since insecurity can **seriously** undermine the farmer's ability to earn a sustainable livelihood.

D Nicotine found in tobacco is habit-forming, indeed it can be described as addictive. However, individual tobacco addicts vary **enormously** in their level of dependence. Programmes to stop people smoking are now being offered and the number of places in which smoking in public is acceptable has **greatly** reduced.

Source: Cuthbert, A. (2001). Smoking. In Blakemore, C. & Jennett, S. (eds.). *The Oxford Companion to the Body.* Ontario: Oxford University Press.

1 Match the keywords in texts A–D to the definitions. Some of the words are synonyms and match the same definition.

1 in an important and basic way _____

2 to a significant degree _____ / _____

3 in every way possible _____

4 very much; to a large degree _____ / _____

2 Put the adverbs in capitals in the correct place in the sentences.

▶ EXAMPLE: Politicians argue that minor reforms will not fix a law that is *fundamentally* flawed. FUNDAMENTALLY

1 Bias from inaccurate instruments can result in misleading results. SERIOUSLY

2 The migration of workers to large cities has increased the urban population. GREATLY

3 These brands benefitted from the growing popularity of physical fitness. ENORMOUSLY

4 In this group of patients, short-term memory is impaired. SEVERELY

5 Several of the studies rely on evidence from interviews with managers. ENTIRELY

Usage note *adverb patterns*

Degree adverbs are used with particular adjectives or verbs to show how significant something is.

adverb + adjective:
- *enormously + popular, influential, important, successful*
- *entirely + different, new, clear, dependent*
- *fundamentally + different, important, flawed, similar*
- *seriously + ill, wrong, misleading, deficient*
- *severely + disabled, ill, constrained, limited*

verb + adverb:
- *vary, benefit, increase, differ + enormously*
- *depend, rely, focus + entirely + on sth*
- *vary, differ, contribute, benefit + greatly*

adverb + verb:
- *entirely + eliminate, ignore + sth*
- *fundamentally + change, alter, affect + sth*
- *greatly + increase, reduce, influence, enhance (+ sth)*
- *seriously + affect, undermine, damage + sth*
- *severely + limit, affect, restrict, impair + sth*

Adding emphasis

E The **overwhelming** majority of voluntary organizations are very small and rely in no small measure on the time and resources of their volunteers.

F Some commentators have questioned the economic benefits of this technology. Our results confirm that the technology is **undeniably** useful, although in some cases the gains have been exaggerated somewhat.

G As this is a treatable condition, it is **imperative** that clinical staff act in the patients' best interest and encourage them to stay for treatment.

H Resistance to change is often an **inevitable** consequence when people's work patterns are disrupted. Change management techniques are designed to help overcome this resistance.

1 Guidelines explain that it is **crucial** for staff to encourage patients to continue with treatment.

2 Some degree of resistance to changes in working patterns is **unavoidable**.

3 Despite criticisms, research has shown that this technology **undoubtedly** brings benefits.

4 The voluntary sector is **dominated** by small organizations.

3 Match the student paraphrases, 1–4, to the texts, E–H.

1 _____ 2 _____ 3 _____ 4 _____

4 Match the sentence halves.

1 Enzyme reactions account for the **overwhelming**
2 If there is an outbreak of the disease, it is **imperative**
3 Social and emotional skills are **crucial**
4 Increased global competition is an **inevitable**
5 The foundation provides an **undeniably**

a consequence of the opening up of international markets.
b for child development and well-being.
c majority of all biochemical reactions.
d useful resource for young filmmakers.
e that it is contained quickly.

5 Choose the best form of the word to complete the sentences.

1 There are some *fundamental / fundamentally* differences between the two approaches.
2 Reports indicate that those arrested were *overwhelmingly / overwhelming* male in the age range 25 to 35.
3 Historical accounts of this development have focused *entirely / entire* on domestic factors.
4 Even in *severe / severely* cases, the problem usually diminishes as the child grows older.
5 An increase in simple, repetitive tasks may be an *inevitable / inevitably* result of modern technology.
6 In most processes, a certain level of waste is *unavoidable / unavoidably*.

6 Add an appropriate adjective or adverb from the unit to the sentences to add emphasis. Several options may be possible.

1 Individuals differ in their response to the same event.
2 Coastal populations are likely to be affected by the impacts of climate change.
3 A period of extreme dry weather contributed to food shortages in the region.
4 The role of informal carers is important in providing care for growing numbers of older adults.
5 Shareholders voted in favour of the proposal.

Words to learn

argue
cite AWL
comment AWL
critique

ellipsis
footnote
maintain AWL
note

paraphrase
quotation marks
quote AWL
refer to

suggest
summarize AWL
with reference to

Types of citation

A In academic writing, it is necessary to support your points by **referring to** or **citing** other authors. This is done in your text through a citation. Any in-text citation must be accompanied by a full reference in the bibliography. The bibliography provides all the additional details (the title, author, publisher, etc.) a reader would need to read the source for themselves.

The format of an in-text citation and the bibliography is determined by the citation style. The citation style determines the referencing system you will adopt. There are two systems – the author-date system and the **footnote** system.

Material from sources can be reported in several ways, including:

Quoting. This means repeating the language from the source exactly.

- Use **quotation marks** at the beginning and end of the quotation.
- If any words have been left out, replace them with an **ellipsis** (three dots separated by spaces).

Paraphrasing. This means taking an idea from a source and expressing it in your own words.

Source: (2014). *Oxford Learner's Dictionary of Academic English.* Oxford: Oxford University Press.

1 a Answer the questions about the extracts.

1 Which of the extract(s) include a quotation? _____
2 Which extract(s) include a paraphrase? _____

1 _____
2 _____
3 _____

i According to Schultheiss and Cheng (2012), 'Certain types of food … have typical distributions patterns'.

ii Schultheiss and Cheng (2012) explain that nectar from flowers usually comes in patches as one plant often has several flowers.

iii Flowers and fruit provide a renewable source of food allowing an animal to return to the same source time and again.[4]

4 _____

[4] Schultheiss, P. and Cheng, K. (2012). Finding food: outbound searching behavior in the Australian desert ant *Melophorus bagoti. Behavioral Ecology.* [Online]. 24 (1). pp.128–135.

b Complete the labels using words from the box.

ellipsis   footnote   in-text citation   quotation marks

2 Choose the best word to complete the guidelines.

1 Whenever you *quote / refer* to ideas from other authors, you must acknowledge the source.
2 When the exact wording is important, you can *paraphrase / quote* directly from the source text.
3 Even if you use your own words to *paraphrase / quote* an idea from a source, still include an in-text citation.
4 All the sources you have *cited / referred* in your essay should be detailed in your bibliography.

Reporting language

B Macdowall *et al.* (2006) **note** the importance of assessing the position and influence of key stakeholders.

Bonneyfoy *et al.* (2004) **suggest** that a housing policy requires several stakeholders to be involved. Initially, this could present a challenge in itself as Taylor *et al.* (2003) **comment** that each stakeholder will have different viewpoints.

C The healthy-eating guidelines (Department of Health, 2005) **summarize** the food and nutrition related topics from the original report.

D Based on a comparison between unionized and non-unionized plants, Metcalf (1986) **maintained** that unions have a negative impact on productivity and the economy. In a **critique** of his work, Nolan and Marginson (1990) **argue** that "despite the popular prejudice that unions are bad for performance, serious academic inquiry has failed to provide hard facts that would support this position".

E **With reference to** the United Nation's Millennium Development Goals (MDGs), there is now a strong emphasis in international development on addressing gender inequality, the AIDS epidemic and wider sustainable development issues (United Nations, 2008).

Source: student essays

3 Underline examples in texts B–D of the following:

1 quotation
2 paraphrase
3 in-text citations
4 reporting verbs

> **Usage note** reporting verbs
>
> Verb + **that** clause:
> · *Metcalf maintained that unions have* …
> Verb + object:
> · *Macdowall* et al. *note the importance of* …
> Some reporting verbs can be followed by either of these structures, some are only (or typically) used with one of them. Make a note of how reporting verbs you come across are used.
>
> | | |
> |---|---|
> | *argue that* … | *argue the case/a point/the merits of* |
> | *note that* … | *note the difference/the importance/an increase* |
> | *suggest that* … | *suggest an approach/link/a need* |
> | *maintain that* … | *summarize the results/the findings/the data* |

4 Match the sentence halves. Think about collocation, meaning and grammar.

1 The article **summarizes**	a that the contract was valid and legally binding.
2 These studies **suggest**	b a marked increase in the frequency of outbreaks.
3 Prosecutors **maintained**	c the findings from studies from several different countries.
4 Wilson has **argued**	d the case for interpreting books in their historical context.
5 Dessens (1990) **noted**	e a complex link between climate and ecosystem response.

5 Match the extracts 1–4 from academic texts to the descriptions, a–d.

1 These data highlight a broad trend of growth in co-authorship of scientific papers.
2 The methods were flawed due to an incomplete understanding of the nature of earthquake waves.
3 The results indicate a possible causal relationship between supervisor support and work ability.
4 The views of teachers and academics were clearly not reflected in the final government report.

  a The writer **suggests** a link.
  b This is a **critique** of another study.
  c The writer is **summarizing** the findings.
  d The writer **maintains** that something is the case; showing a clear stance.

6 a Find at least three or four examples of citation in texts from your own discipline. Identify and make a note of the reporting verbs, collocations and structures used.

▶ EXAMPLE: Curtis and Steed (1980) suggested three reasons for this growing regionalization.
suggest + a reason for sth

Words to learn

a case in point
albeit `AWL`
for instance `AWL`
hence `AWL`

in other words
namely
nevertheless `AWL`
nonetheless `AWL`

respectively
the former
the latter
thereby `AWL`

whereby `AWL`
via `AWL`

Expressing connections

A The growing number of people working remotely from home are able to maintain relationships with colleagues, **albeit** indirectly, **via** social media networks.

B To reduce capital investment, the flexibility of a manufacturing system is an important factor in the design. **Nonetheless**, there are some manufacturing systems that are dedicated to one product because of the high-value nature of the product.

C The translation of Shakespearean texts into other languages is part of the process **whereby** Shakespeare has been received in non-English-speaking countries. Translators adapt texts to the tastes and expectations of different cultures. **Hence** such translations have not only linguistic, but also cultural and even political dimensions.

D Despite major damage, tree cover regenerates rapidly after a hurricane, **thereby** helping to reduce impacts on the soil below. **Nevertheless**, some signs of hurricane impact are present for decades.

1 Read texts A–D and answer the questions.

1 How do homeworkers maintain contact with colleagues?_____
2 Is this the same as having face-to-face contact in the office?_____
3 Is flexibility always the most important factor in designing a manufacturing system?_____
4 What role does translation play in how people in non-English-speaking countries view Shakespeare?_____
5 Why do translations have cultural and political dimensions?_____
6 What helps to reduce the impact of a hurricane on soil?_____
7 Does the regeneration of tree cover immediately reverse the effects of a hurricane?_____

2 Choose the best keyword from texts A–D to link the ideas in sentences 1–6. Sometimes more than one option is possible.

▶ EXAMPLE: Although visitors from some countries do not need a visa, they are, _nonetheless_, required to complete a landing card on arrival.

1 Access to the system may be restricted _____ the use of passwords.
2 At low levels of employment, incomes are low and _____ spending by consumers is restricted.
3 There are far fewer refugees in this region than elsewhere, but it is _____ a significant issue locally.
4 Population aging is occurring in most countries around the world, _____ at different rates.
5 Fatigue is the process _____ damage, caused by repetitive use over time, results in a mechanical failure.
6 Technology can provide a means for employers to speed up work, _____ reducing labour costs.

Examples and restatement

E The use of online resources in the classroom may not be practical in all contexts, **for instance**, in areas with poor broadband connectivity.

F Some of the effects of climate fluctuation are very surprising. **A case in point** is the increase in traffic accidents associated with more frequent dust storms.

G Table 8.2 suggests that health care expenditure per head of the population has very little direct impact on two of the indicators of the state of a nation's health, **namely** infant mortality rates and life expectancy.

H Once all the data are collected, the challenge is to piece them together in a way that reveals general themes. It can sometimes be difficult, **in other words**, to see the bigger picture.

I The study looked at two different approaches to road safety awareness: campaigns targeted at the whole population and at high-risk groups **respectively**. **The former** feature various different aspects of road safety, whereas **the latter** are focused more specifically on speed awareness, the major cause of accidents among male drivers aged 18 to 25.

3 Read texts E–I. Answer the questions.

1 Which two words or expressions introduce more information about a previous idea?_____
2 Which two words or expressions introduce an example?_____
3 What do **the former** and **the latter** refer to in text I? _____

4 Choose the best word or expression to complete the sentences.

1 In every known culture, humans exhibit emotions through the same means, *namely / respectively* facial expressions.
2 The internet has not affected all business sectors to such a degree. The construction industry is *the latter / a case in point*.
3 The traditional distinction between science and technology sees *respectively / the former* as being concerned with basic research and *the later / the latter* with applied research.
4 Some reactions are much slower. *For instance / A case in point*, the reaction to produce ethyl ethanoate usually takes several days.

> **Usage note** *instance* and *case*
> These two keywords are used in a number of common expressions to refer to particular examples.
> • *People changing their behaviour because they know they are being observed is **an instance** of the 'reactive effect'.*
> • *The whales migrate long distances; **in one instance**, a tagged animal travelled 9,800 kilometres.*
> • ***In some cases**, the orders arrived late, **in other cases**, the goods were damaged in transit.*
> • *India has long histories of records in some languages, going back about 3,000 years **in the case of** Sanskrit.*

5 Complete the sentences using an appropriate expression including the word in capitals. More than one option may be possible.

▶ EXAMPLE: <u>In some cases</u> , medication may cause adverse side effects. CASE
1 Heavy storms tend to be a feature of La Niña years. The flood of February 1996 is _____ . CASE
2 The research was explained to all participants and informed consent was obtained _____ . CASE
3 A company can branch out into new product areas. _____ , British clothing designer Paul Smith has successfully extended his brand into perfumes. INSTANCE
4 The range of options appears in a drop-down menu, _____ a list of years. CASE
5 Many of his films have been censored and _____ even banned altogether. INSTANCE

Student writing: conclusions

The conclusion of an essay often summarizes the main points, but it should not just repeat them. It shows how the arguments relate to each other and back to the thesis statement. It also draws wider conclusions such as implications of the ideas discussed, practical applications, predictions for the future, and suggestions for further research. The conclusion may also acknowledge any limitations of the essay, for example, points that were not discussed.

Source: de Chazal, E. & Moore, J. (2013). *Oxford EAP: Advanced/C1*. Oxford: Oxford University Press.

A In conclusion, this essay has considered a variety of different approaches via which a child who is deaf may acquire language. Although to some extent all children develop differently, which makes it difficult to generalize about the best approach[1], it seems that learning to communicate orally is typically a laborious process and often has disappointing results for many children who are severely or profoundly deaf. Thus, it seems that sign language is a more natural choice of communication. This has implications for both parents and the education system.[2] Lewis (1987) argues that[3] signing should be encouraged; hence, parents may consider learning a natural sign language. The child should also have the opportunity to be immersed in a community of other people who are deaf, such as a school, so that they have the ability to interact with other sign language users. This not only enables a child to develop a language, but crucially also helps them to develop cognitively and emotionally as they have a means of expression (Bavelier *et al.*, 2003)[3].

Although some parents may be concerned that learning a sign language will isolate their child from the community of hearing people, Mayberry *et al.* (2002) suggest that[3] the acquisition of a sign language could facilitate the acquisition of a spoken language. It is also important to consider that if a child fails to learn a spoken language and has little exposure to a sign language, they may become victims of the 'critical period', the time during childhood most associated with successful language development, and are thereby not able to become proficient in any language at all[2] (Pinker, 1994)[3]. Thus, to reduce the risk of this happening, Bavelier *et al.* (2003) propose that[3] there should be a bilingual approach, whereby students use full natural signing for part of the day and are taught oral and literacy skills for the other part. This approach may help children who are deaf to reach their full potential.

Glossary
laborious (*adj*): taking a lot of time and effort

1 Read text A. Match the words in the box to the highlighted parts of the conclusion marked 1–3.

> acknowledging limitations   citations   implications

1 _____   2 _____   3 _____

2 Identify one or two sentences which summarize the writer's overall stance on the topic. Which approach do they support?

Focus on collocation

3 Find words in the text to complete these collocations.

1 acquire + _____ (*noun*)
2 a laborious + _____ (*noun*)
3 _____ / _____ (*adverb*) + deaf
4 _____ (*verb*) + implications for sb

5 _____ (*verb*) + the opportunity to do sth
6 a _____ (*noun*) + of expression
7 reduce + the _____ (*noun*)
8 _____ (*verb*) + your (full) potential

4 **Complete the sentences using an appropriate word from the box. Not all the words are needed. Look back at Units 26–36 or use the list of collocations on pp.107–110 to help you if necessary.**

| challenging   enormously   exploit   fundamentally   gain   seriously   sustain |

1 They provide an account of how entrepreneurs discover and _____ market **opportunities**.
2 Developing global company standards can be a very _____ **task**.
3 Your institution can give you a user name and password to _____ **access** to these databases.
4 This perspective is _____ **different** from earlier models.
5 Over the decades, three changes occurred that _____ **undermined** the system.

5 **Complete the sentences by writing the missing preposition in the correct place. Look back at previous units or use the list of dependent prepositions on pp.111–113 to help you if necessary.**

▶ EXAMPLE: All governments exercise some degree *of* control over the monetary systems.
1 The findings revealed insights the relationships between different environmental indicators.
2 The long working hours of MPs are not always compatible family responsibilities.
3 This method of sampling is not systematic terms of spatial distribution.
4 'Pharmacokinetics' refers the processes involved in the delivery of a drug to its target site.
5 They should be assessed separately since the relevant variables are different each case.
6 However, transferring knowledge individuals to the wider organization presents practical challenges.

Focus on synonyms

6 a **Complete the table with words from the box to form sets of synonyms or near synonyms.**

| adapt   attain   difference   existence   in terms of   incidence   modify   obtain   somewhat   to some extent   variation   with reference to |

A	B	C
acquire	1 _____	2 _____
occurrence	3 _____	4 _____
alter	5 _____	6 _____
diversity	7 _____	8 _____
in many respects	9 _____	10 _____
with regard to	11 _____	12 _____

b **Choose the best option to complete the sentences.**

1 A feature of globalization is the *existence / occurrence* of groups of customers with similar needs spread across different countries.
2 This group had *a somewhat / in many respects a* larger percentage of women (54% versus 47% men).
3 The article provides a brief overview of the topic *with reference to / in terms of* a number of key studies.
4 Within a species, some individuals *adapt / modify* to exploit different parts of the available resources.
5 The success of the plan will depend upon a collaborative approach to *attain / acquire* goals in the short and long term.
6 Interestingly, there were no *differences / diversity* between boys and girls in terms of the factors measured.

Words to learn

deviation AWL	mean	square	variability AWL
digit	measure	square root	whole number
equal to	multiply	sum of AWL	
formula (plural:	record	symbol AWL	
formulae) AWL	round to	value	

Formulae and calculations

A Standard **deviation** (symbol SD or σ) is a **measure** of the **variability** in a set of numbers, **equal to** the **square root** of the variance. The deviation for each number is the difference between it and the mean **value** for the set.

Source: Fenna, D. (2004). *A Dictionary of Weights, Measures, and Units.* Oxford: Oxford University Press.

$$SD = \sqrt{\frac{\Sigma\,(x-\bar{x})^2}{N-1}}$$

The **formula** for standard deviation (SD) where:

Σ (pronounced *sigma*) means '**sum of**'

x = each value

$\bar{x}$ (pronounced *x-bar*) = the **mean** or average of all the values

N = the number of values in the data set

Usage note *variation, variability* and *variance*

Variation is a change or difference, especially in the amount or difference of something. It can be a countable noun to talk about individual changes or an uncountable noun to talk about differences in general:

• *the impact of variations in class size; There is enormous variation between individuals.*

Variability (uncountable) is the fact of something being likely to vary:

• *The data show considerable variability.*

Variance is a statistical measure of how much variation there is among the values in a set of data. In statistics, **deviation** is the amount by which a single number varies from a fixed value.

1 **Complete the explanations using words from the box.**

equal to   formula   mean   squared   sum of   symbol

The ¹_____ for calculating the area of a circle is: area = πr² (pronounced **pi** r ²_____), where the ³_____ π represents a value ⁴_____ 3.1415 and r is the radius of the circle. To find the ⁵_____ or average of a set of numbers, calculate the ⁶_____ all the numbers in the set and then divide it by the number of values in the set.

2 **Complete the statements using the correct preposition (*in, of, to*, etc.). Use the list of dependent prepositions on pp.111–113 to help you if necessary.**

1 Calculate the sum _____ all the known distances.
2 The formula _____ Body Mass Index is weight in kilograms divided by height in metres squared.
3 The speed of a tsunami wave is proportional to the square root _____ the depth of the ocean.
4 The Richter scale is a widely used measure _____ earthquake magnitude.
5 This yields a prediction for each household equal _____ 1.219 tons of carbon dioxide emissions.
6 There was substantial variability _____ the number of patients seen per doctor.
7 We have observed much larger deviations _____ the norm than would be predicted by standard statistical analysis.

Statistical accuracy and error

B Data may be incorrect in any number of ways and for any number of reasons. At a low level, mistakes are often made in reading instruments or **recording** values. For example, a common tendency in reading instruments is subconsciously to **round to** the nearest **whole number**. Distributions of blood pressure measurements recorded using old-fashioned (non-electronic) instruments show a clear tendency for more values to be recorded at 60, 70, and 80 than at neighbouring values, such as 69 or 72. As far as recording errors go, **digits** may be transposed (28 instead of 82); the handwritten digit 7 may be mistaken for 1; data may be accidentally put in the wrong column on a form, so accidentally **multiplying** values by 10; and so on.

Source: Hand, D. (2008). *Statistics: A Very Short Introduction.* Oxford: Oxford University Press.

Usage note *rounding*

Sometimes, if a value is expressed as a fraction (18.9, 2.316, etc.), you **round** it **to** a whole number for simplicity. Typically, if the fraction is less than 0.5, you **round** the number **down**. So 2.316 becomes 2.
If the fraction is greater than 0.5, you **round** the number **up**. So 18.9 becomes 19.

3 Complete the descriptions of the errors.

Actual value	Recorded value	Error
10.86	11	The measurement was [1] _____ to the nearest _____ .
125.45	125	The number was rounded [2] _____ .
276	267	The [3] _____ were accidentally transposed.
120	1200	The value was [4] _____ ten.
25.9186	25.986	There was a mistake in [5] _____ the value.

4 Match the numbers in the box to the words. Some numbers match more than one word.

> 12.876   4   6.75   75   9

1 value: _____
2 whole number: _____
3 digit: _____

5 Choose the correct word to complete the sentences.

1 The basic *formula* / *symbol* for the area of a triangle is area = ½ x base x height.
2 The figures were rounded up or down to the nearest whole *digit* / *number*.
3 Estimates of the mean yield per unit area were *equalled* / *multiplied* by the total areas of the relevant rice fields.
4 Students are eligible for the classes only if their IQ scores are *equal* / *sum* to or above 130.
5 Small *deviations* / *variability* from the exact values are expected.
6 Monitoring devices can *record* / *round* the temperature of vaccine shipments.
7 An alternative *measure* / *value* of engine performance is thermal efficiency.
8 How important are genes in explaining the *variability* / *variance* among people in their risk for developing these disorders?

Words to learn

capacity AWL	function AWL	model	renewable
conventional AWL	generate AWL	nuclear AWL	specification AWL
demonstrate AWL	hybrid	performance	technique AWL
energy AWL	install	prototype	

Energy systems

A The contemporary **energy** system has two basic components, electricity and fluid fuels. In the year 2000, the world had a total **installed** electrical **capacity** of 3,365 gigawatts (billions of watts), producing nearly 14 trillion kilowatt hours (kWh). The United States consumes about a quarter of the total. This is supplied by some 100,000 electric power plants and 10 million miles of power lines. Coal-fired power plants account for about 38 per cent of electricity generation in the United States, followed by natural gas, oil, **nuclear**, and hydro power.

Alternative energy advocates long have believed that **renewable** energy from sun, wind, and biomass could supply the planet's needs. Electricity **generated** by wind turbines is now the largest renewable source, with installed capacity of 31,000 megawatts in 2002, equivalent to about 31 large coal or nuclear power plants.

If the price of renewables drops while gas and oil become more costly, market choices may begin to replace fossil fuels with renewables. However, modifying systems is more complex than simply unplugging one technology and plugging in another as prices change. Social preferences also shape energy outcomes. Very efficient compact fluorescent light bulbs are cheaper overall than **conventional** bulbs but have not been widely embraced. **Hybrid** cars have not flown off US car lots, despite their equivalent **performance** to other small cars and despite excellent ratings from automotive experts.

Source: Laird, F. & Woodhouse, E. (2005). In Restivo, S. (ed.). *Science, Technology, and Society.* Oxford: Oxford University Press.

Glossary
fluorescent light bulb (*n*): A compact fluorescent light bulb contains a small glass tube filled with gas and coated with a substance that produces visible light when an electric current is passed through it.

1 Read text A. Are the types of energy production or usage conventional (C) or alternative (A)?

1 coal-fired power plants __
2 nuclear power __
3 renewable energy __
4 wind turbines __
5 fluorescent light bulbs __
6 hybrid cars __

2 a Complete the text using words from the box.

energy   generate   install   renewable

The company supplies solar-powered generators to remote rural communities. The equipment is easy to ¹_____ and can ²_____ power in locations without access to the mains power grid. By using ³_____ from a ⁴_____ source, sunlight, they are also much cleaner than petrol generators.

b Now complete the second text in the same way.

capacity   conventional   hybrid   performance

The ¹_____ of electric cars now matches that of many other road vehicles. They are still limited, however, by their battery ²_____ , which means that most commercially-available electric cars need to stop after around 150 km to recharge. ³_____ vehicles overcome this problem by combining both electrical power and a ⁴_____ petrol-driven engine.

3 Use the negative form of the words in the box to complete the sentences. Choose the correct prefix (*de-*, *in-*, *mis-*, *non-*, *un-*). Use the glossary on pp.129–144 to help you if necessary.

> conventional   install   renewable

1 His _____ approach to product design initially encountered widespread scepticism.
2 Users should be able to _____ the software easily if they no longer need it.
3 There is only a fixed amount of oil and other _____ mineral resources available.

The design process

B prototype: A pre-production model developed to evaluate the feasibility of new ideas, materials, technology, and design techniques as part of new product development. In addition to the technological evaluation, consumer clinics may be used to establish the opinion of potential customers on the acceptability of the product.

Source: Law, J. (2009). *A Dictionary of Business and Management.* (5 ed.). Oxford: Oxford University Press.

C performance testing: The specification for a system will usually have some requirements for how well the system should perform certain functions. Thus while functional testing will, for example, demonstrate that the sum and average of a set of numbers will be calculated, performance testing will concentrate on how well the calculation is done (speed, accuracy, range, etc.).

Source: Daintith, J. & Wright, E. (2008). *A Dictionary of Computing.* (6 ed.). Oxford: Oxford University Press.

4 Complete the text using words from the box.

> demonstrate   functions   model   prototype   specifications   techniques

Students develop a ¹_____ : typically a full-scale working ²_____ of the product. This gives them the opportunity to ³_____ the range of ⁴_____ they have learnt during the course. They also go through a process of testing their design to check whether the product meets their design ⁵_____ . Does it perform the required ⁶_____ effectively? Does it have any faults or problems that can be improved?

5 a Complete the table with the correct forms. Use the glossary on pp.129–144 if necessary.

Verb	Noun	Verb	Noun
generate	generation	3 _____	specification
install	1 _____	4 _____	function
2 _____	performance	demonstrate	5 _____

b Complete the sentences using words from the table in an appropriate form.

1 The introduction of new technology requires both the training of staff and the _____ of relevant equipment.
2 It is important to _____ the time period required for the process.
3 We show how electrochemical reactions can _____ electric power directly.
4 Figure 3 illustrates a computerized fuel injection system that improves the _____ of an engine.
5 For devices to _____ effectively, it is also desirable to achieve room temperature operation.

6 Write a short paragraph (three or four sentences) describing a recent innovation in science or technology. Use one of the ideas below or your own. Try to use vocabulary from this unit.

- A new way of manufacturing something, e.g. using new materials, 3D printing, etc.
- An innovation in transport, e.g. solar-powered flight, driverless cars, etc.
- A new way for people to interact with computers, e.g. voice recognition, robots, etc.

39 Medicine

Words to learn

administer	disorder	monitor AWL	therapeutic
chronic	examination	stabilize AWL	transmit AWL
contract AWL	exhibit AWL	symptom	undergo AWL
diagnosis	infectious	terminal AWL	

Diagnosis

A **diagnosis**: the process of determining the nature of a **disorder** by considering the patient's signs and **symptoms**, medical background, and – when necessary – results of laboratory tests and X-ray **examinations**. Unlike **therapeutic** procedures, diagnostic processes usually do not directly benefit the patient in terms of treatment.

Source: (2010). *Concise Medical Dictionary*. (8 ed.). Oxford: Oxford University Press.

B When dealing with potentially serious **infectious** diseases, it is important to consider:
- whether the symptoms the patient is **exhibiting** could have other causes
- how the patient may have **contracted** the disease
- whether the patient could have **transmitted** the disease to others.

1 Read the texts. Mark the sentences true (T) or false (F).

1 The process of diagnosis involves treatment. __
2 Therapeutic procedures help a patient to recover from an illness or injury. __
3 A symptom is the cause of a medical condition. __
4 An examination helps to find out more details about a patient's illness or injury. __
5 An infectious disease can be transmitted from one person to another. __
6 When someone contracts a disease, they no longer exhibit any symptoms. __

2 Complete the sets of sentences using the correct form of the keywords.

1 diagnosis – diagnostic – diagnose
  a The patient was _____ with a rare blood disorder.
  b An ECG test will help in making the correct _____ .
  c A simple _____ test is available for malaria.
2 examine – examination
  a If you are also going to _____ the patient, make sure you have all the right equipment before you start.
  b On clinical _____ , the patient had a raised blood pressure.
3 therapy – therapeutic – therapist
  a A specialist speech and language _____ may also be able to provide assistance.
  b The patient has been receiving antibiotic _____ for the last five days.
  c The drug can take up to four weeks to have a _____ effect.
4 infect – infection – infectious
  a Normally an _____ of animals, the virus can _____ humans by direct contact or food contamination.
  b _____ diseases accounted for one in three deaths in the mid-19th century.
5 transmit – transmission
  a Dengue is a viral infection which is _____ by mosquitoes.
  b Patients must be identified as early as possible to prevent unwanted _____ of the infection.

Treatment

C Pre-operative assessment allows an opportunity to **stabilize** any coexisting conditions, such as diabetes or high blood pressure, before the patient **undergoes** surgery. This minimizes the risk of complications during surgery and also alerts nursing staff to any conditions that may need **monitoring** post-surgery.

In the case of patients with **chronic** or **terminal** illnesses, the role of medical staff may be simply to ensure that the patient is comfortable and to **administer** pain relief as appropriate.

Glossary
pre-operative (*adj*): before an operation
coexisting (*adj*): existing together; here, two conditions in the same patient

Usage note *chronic, acute, terminal* and *fatal*
These words describe the state, progress or outcome of a disease, condition or injury in a patient.
An **acute** illness or injury has quickly become severe or dangerous and needs immediate treatment:
  • *an acute infection; acute heart failure*
A **chronic** condition is one that lasts for a long time. Patients with chronic conditions often have to manage their condition rather than being cured:
  • *chronic pain; chronic liver disease*
A **terminal** illness cannot be cured and will lead to death:
  • *terminal illness/cancer*
The adjective **fatal** is used to talk about injuries and accidents that cause death:
  • *a fatal injury*

3 Complete the text using the best form of the verbs in the box.

    administer   monitor   stabilize   undergo

After a patient has ¹_____ major surgery, they are admitted to an intensive care unit. Here they are closely ²_____ by specialist nursing staff who can ³_____ pain relief and other medication. Once their condition has ⁴_____ , they may be transferred to a general medical ward.

4 Choose the best word, *acute, chronic, terminal* or *fatal*, to complete the sentences.

1 In the emergency department, patients receive medical treatment for _____ illnesses or injury.
2 Research has identified that older workers are at most risk of a _____ injury as a result of a workplace accident.
3 After a _____ illness has been diagnosed, many people become anxious, depressed or angry.
4 Type 2 diabetes is one of the most common _____ conditions affecting older people.

5 Match the sentence halves. Use the highlighted words to help you.

1 Lowered immunity increases the risk of **contracting**
2 Any patients **exhibiting**
3 Most patients **undergoing**
4 It is important to **monitor**

a major **surgery** will require a period of IV fluid replacement.
b an infectious **disease**.
c **symptoms** suggestive of meningitis should be referred to a medical practitioner.
d **patients** closely throughout the course of treatment.

6 Write a short paragraph (three or four sentences) describing how a patient with a particular illness or injury might progress through the health care system. Try to use some of the vocabulary from this unit.

▶ EXAMPLE: When someone is diagnosed with diabetes, they may be admitted to hospital for a short period to stabilize their condition. Diabetes is a chronic condition and patients need to monitor their blood sugar levels daily. In serious cases, they may have to administer insulin via an injection.

40 Social sciences

Words to learn

enforce AWL
external AWL
humanitarian aid
index (plural: indices)
AWL

indicator AWL
international
development
literacy
norm AWL

per capita
poverty
prevalent
relief
sanction

standard of living
supplement AWL
value

International development

A **International development** is involved with international efforts to reduce **poverty** and inequality and to improve health, education and employment opportunities in the world's less-developed countries. While **humanitarian aid** and disaster **relief** provide short-term assistance, international development deals with policies to encourage long-term, sustainable development through effective political structures as well as via non-governmental organizations (NGOs) and other **external** bodies.

A number of **indices** can be used to measure development, including economic measures such as gross domestic product (GDP) or **per capita** income. Increasingly though, development has come to focus more on human and social **values** as reflected in the creation of measures such as the Human Development Index (HDI), which incorporates **indicators** of health (such as life expectancy at birth) and education (such as **literacy** rates), as well as **standard of living**.

Usage note *Third World, developing* and *emerging*

The Third World (or **Third World countries**) refers to poor countries in Africa, Asia and Latin America. This usage is now considered offensive by some people. More widely used terms are **developing** or **less-developed**:
• *developing countries/nations/economies*.
Emerging markets are countries where the economy is growing fast and shares some characteristics of developed economies:
• *an emerging economy/market*

1 Read text A and match the sentence halves.

1 Per capita income	a can be used as an indicator of health.
2 Literacy rates	b can be used as an indicator of standard of living.
3 Life expectancy at birth	c can be used as an indicator of education.

2 Choose the correct option to complete the sentences.

1 *Disaster relief / International development* requires a quick response and lasts only a few weeks.
2 The refugees are stuck in camps and dependent on *external / per capita* support for basic needs.
3 The *index / indicator* of multiple deprivation combines measures such as low income, poor housing and unemployment.
4 Priorities include the delivery of *humanitarian aid / disaster relief* to civilians in war zones.
5 There is recognition that economic growth reduces *literacy / poverty* only if accompanied by targeted economic and social policies.
6 We found substantial variation in monthly *per capita / standard* household expenditure.
7 The most common approach in economics is to measure a person's *cost of living / standard of living* by his or her income.
8 Due to the low *indicator / literacy* rates in some developing countries, health care messages have to be spread orally.

Social norms

B Culture can be seen as a system of shared beliefs, **values**, customs, and behaviours **prevalent** in a society and that are transmitted from generation to generation (Bates and Plog, 1990). Hofstede (1994), the management scientist, described these elements of culture as software of the mind, "the collective programming of the mind which distinguishes members of one category of people from another". The values in the culture are **enforced** by a set of **norms** which lay down rules of behaviour. These rules are usually **supplemented** by a set of **sanctions** to ensure that the norms are respected. Culture comprises a whole variety of different aspects, including religion, language, non-verbal communication, diet, dress, and institutions to ensure that the values and beliefs are transmitted from one generation to another.

Source: Hamilton, L. & Webster, P. (2009). *The International Business Environment.* Oxford: Oxford University Press. p.151.

Usage note countable and uncountable nouns

Some nouns in English that refer to general concepts are always uncountable, such as **poverty** and **literacy**. These nouns have no plural form and they are used with a singular verb:
  • *Poverty **is** widespread.*
Other nouns can be either countable (C) or uncountable (U) depending on their context and meaning:
development (U): the process of developing: • *international development is involved with …*
development (C): a new method, system, product or theory: • *recent developments in imaging techniques*
aid (U): money, food, etc. that is sent to help countries in difficult situations: • *humanitarian aid*
aid (C): sth used to help someone do a particular task: • *visual aids such as diagrams or graphs*
behaviour (U): the way that someone behaves: • *his behaviour towards his colleagues*
behaviour (C) (technical): the way that sb/sth functions or reacts in a particular situation: • *the customs and behaviours prevalent in a society*

---

3 **Complete the text using the correct form of the words in the box. Not all the words are needed.**

> enforce   norm   prevalent   sanction   supplement   value

School rules typically reflect the ¹_____ of the society at large, such as respect for others. They may also reinforce the social and cultural ²_____ of the local community through dress codes and codes of behaviour. The rules are set out by the school authorities and ³_____ by the teaching staff who have a range of possible ⁴_____ at their disposal, from keeping pupils behind after class through to exclusion from the school. New rules are introduced to reflect changes in the wider society, such as rules regarding the use of mobile phones and social media, especially ⁵_____ among children and teenagers.

4 **Match the sentence halves. Think about the highlighted noun and the verb form in the sentence as well as the meaning.**

1 The project has no regular funds, and thus all **aid**

2 An analysis of global trends showed how **poverty**

3 Over the past century, technological **developments**

4 NGOs warn of an outbreak of disease unless more **relief**

5 In some areas, economic **development**

6 A well-designed visual **aid**

a affects women disproportionately.

b has led to the overuse of natural resources.

c arrives soon.

d comes from voluntary contributions.

e adds greatly to the power of a verbal message.

f have radically changed the way we communicate.

41 Law

Words to learn

abolish
contract AWL
control
enhance AWL

harmonize
incorporate into AWL
instrument
legislation AWL

party
precondition
prohibit AWL
provision

require AWL
rigid AWL
seek to AWL
treaty

International law

A Schengen Agreement

Signed in Schengen (Luxemburg), the **treaty sought to abolish** border **controls** of private and commercial traffic between the signatory states. A second Agreement (Schengen II), signed in 1990, **enhanced** the **provisions** for common policing through the creation of the Schengen Information System. Immigration controls to third countries were **harmonized**, and external border controls to third countries enhanced. Originally signed by a core of European Community member states, it was **incorporated into** the EU by the Treaty of Amsterdam. Its members consisted of the EU countries, minus Great Britain and Northern Ireland. Although not members of the EU, Norway and Iceland were also members of the Schengen area. Upon enlargement in 2004 and 2007, the new eastern European member states were not automatically accepted as members, as these countries first had to adapt to the information systems and the **rigid** border controls which became a **precondition** for membership.

Source: Palmowski, J. (2008). *A Dictionary of Contemporary World History.* Oxford: Oxford University Press.

1 Choose the sentence that best summarizes the main idea in text A.

a The Schengen Agreement was designed to create stronger border controls within Europe. __

b The Schengen Agreement is part of the EU treaty which all member countries must be part of. __

c The Schengen Agreement aims to make movement between member countries easier. __

2 Match the words in the box to the more informal synonyms.

| abolish   enhance   harmonize   incorporate into   rigid   seek to |

1 strict: _____
2 make part of: _____
3 cancel: _____
4 improve: _____
5 make the same: _____
6 try to: _____

3 Choose the best word to complete the sentences. Use the glossary on pp.129–144 to help you if necessary.

1 There were no pollution *control / controls* and, in many cases, the emissions were released in residential areas.

2 The Council achieved agreement between federal and state governments to *harmonize / incorporate* firearms laws across Australian states.

3 The criminal justice reforms included *abolishing / enhancing* the death penalty.

4 Mental health laws contain *preconditions / provisions* for the police to detain such persons until they can be assessed by a doctor.

5 He argues that *enhanced / rigid* rules of behaviour do not encourage a positive working atmosphere.

6 The 1925 Geneva Protocol is an international *provision / treaty* that outlawed the use of chemical and biological weapons in war.

7 The review aims to identify ways of *enhancing / harmonizing* the quality of health care services.

8 The World Bank stresses that effective state governance is a necessary *precondition / provision* for economic development.

The work of a lawyer

B The vast majority of lawyers never appear in court at all. Rather they advise governments, businesses, and individuals about the law — what it allows them to do, **requires** them to do, and **prohibits** them from doing. Such lawyers undertake legal research (identifying the law — both **legislation** and court decisions — relevant to the client's circumstances), draft documents (such as letters of advice, **contracts**, and a wide variety of commercial **instruments**), and attend meetings and conferences with other **parties** and their lawyers.

Source: Menkel Meadow, C. (2008). Styles and skills of legal practice. In Cane, P. & Conaghan, J. (eds.). *The New Oxford Companion to Law.* Oxford: Oxford University Press.

Usage note general and specialist uses

In legal texts, common words are sometimes used with a specialist, legal meaning.
- *third* countries
(= countries which are not part of a particular legal agreement)
- *legal* **remedies**
(= ways of dealing with a legal problem)

4 Look at the dictionary entries for *instrument* and *party*.

1 Which sense of **instrument** is used in text B? __ 2 Which sense of **party** is used in text B? __

instrument (*noun*)
1 a process or system that is used to discover or describe attitudes, experiences, skills, etc.: *There was no instrument designed to measure academic motivation across subject areas.*
2 a tool or device used for a particular task, especially for scientific work: *optical/surgical/scientific instruments*
3 (law) a formal legal document: *The Act was amended by the passing of a statutory instrument.*

party (*noun*)
1 a political organization that you can vote for in elections and whose members have the same aims and ideas: *This book analyses the development of political parties in four Central and Eastern European countries.*
2 a social occasion, often in a person's home, at which people eat, drink, talk, dance, etc.: *birthday party*
3 one of the people or groups of people involved in a legal agreement or argument: *Both parties were seeking sole custody of their two children.*

5 Match the uses of the highlighted words in the sentences to the definitions.

1 The Commission relies on complaints from **third parties** for detecting infringements of environmental law.
2 The use of herbal **remedies** has been around for centuries.
3 A hygrometer is an **instrument** for measuring the level of humidity in the air.
4 The company included a 'sole supplier' **provision** in all contracts with its customers.
5 Statutory **instruments** are generally laid before Parliament for approval.

   a a person or group who is not directly involved
   b a formal legal document
   c a tool or device for a particular task
   d a condition in a legal document
   e a medical treatment

6 Choose the correct option to complete the sentences. Pay attention to the prepositions that follow the highlighted words. Use the list of dependent prepositions on pp.111–113 to help you if necessary.

1 International human rights law **seeks** *in establishing / to establish* minimum conditions for the treatment of prisoners.
2 **Provisions** *for / of* minimum rest periods were introduced with the Working Time Directive.
3 To be effective, the clause must be **incorporated** *on the / into the* contract at the time of the agreement.
4 She argues for human rights as an essential **precondition** *for / with* full democracy.
5 Employers are **required** *to provide / with providing* employees with health and safety information.
6 National rules may **prohibit** retailers *from opening / to open* their premises on a Sunday.

42 Politics

Words to learn

citizen
constitution AWL
cooperative AWL
coup

democratic
domestic AWL
faction
federal AWL

liberal AWL
overthrow
regime AWL
revolution AWL

scrutinize
state
unrest

Political beliefs

A In the aftermath of the Second World War, the US took the lead in seeking to encourage fundamental **liberal** principles within the institutions of the newly emerging international society. It attempted to establish a **cooperative** basis for power in a number of ways. Firstly, it aimed to provide a model for other **states** as a political system that was open and allowed different voices to be heard. Both foreign and **domestic** policy were closely **scrutinized** by the media, public opinion and opposition groups. The US also advocated a global free-trade **regime** on the basis that free trade brings benefits to all participants.

Usage note *country*, *nation* and *state*

Country, **nation** and **state** are all used to refer to a country as a political unit or to its government:
• *a newly independent country/nation/state*
Country and **nation** can also refer to an area where people live, its economy, culture, etc.:
• *a wealthy country/nation*
Some countries are divided into administrative areas with their own level of government. These can be called **states**, as in the US and India, or **provinces**, such as in Canada and China.

1 Do the pairs of words have a similar (S) or different meaning (D)?

1 domestic – foreign __
2 state – nation __

3 liberal – open __
4 scrutinize – examine __

5 cooperative – reluctant __
6 regime – system __

2 Match the use of the highlighted words in sentences 1–6 to the definitions, a–f.

1 The rules may vary across different regulatory **regimes**.
2 Mass opposition swept away authoritarian **regimes** in scores of countries.
3 In a short period, most colonies in Asia and Africa became independent **states** and members of the UN.
4 Mahabalipuram is an ancient city in the southern Indian **state** of Tamil Nadu.
5 In spite of more family-friendly policies, female managers still struggle to manage career and **domestic** life.
6 US **domestic** policy is increasingly susceptible to global events and issues.

a a country considered as a political unit
b an administrative area that forms part of a country
c of or inside a particular country; not foreign or international
d connected with the home
e a government
f a system of organizing something

Political systems

B A **federal** system is composed of a number of regional or state governments and is based on **democratic** principles that allow for the participation of **citizens** in the political process at both national and regional levels. Most experts agree that an effective federal system needs to operate under a written **constitution** that sets out the roles and responsibilities of the central and state governments.

3 In text B, does *state government* refer to the whole country or an area within a country?

4 **a** **Complete the table with an appropriate form of the highlighted words. Use the glossary on pp.129–144 to help you if necessary.**

Noun	Adjective
a written constitution	1 _____ reform
a 2 _____ of states	a federal system of states
a modern 3 _____	based on democratic principles
the participation of citizens in the political process She obtained British 4 _____	

b **Complete the sentences with the correct form of a word from the table.**

1 After three years of residence as a married partner, they may apply to become a British _____ .

2 The _____ rights to freedom of speech and of the press guarantee that journalists can write whatever they please.

3 The government's role in environmental affairs, both at the state and _____ level, grew steadily.

4 In _____ societies, policy tends to be dictated by the voters in the middle ground.

Political change

C The French Revolution, which began in 1789, was a political upheaval prompted by social and economic unrest. It led to the overthrow of the monarchy in France and the establishment of a republic in 1792. The Revolution initially failed to produce a stable government as different factions fought for power. The Revolution is generally considered to have ended in 1799 when Napoleon took power in a military coup.

Glossary
the monarchy (*n*): a country that is governed by a king or a queen
republic (*n*): a country that is governed by a president and elected politicians, with no king or queen

5 **Read text C. Mark the statements true (T) or false (F) according to the text.**

1 The French Revolution happened because of anger about the social and economic situation. __

2 After the Revolution, different groups worked together to govern the country. __

3 Napoleon came to power after an election in 1799. __

6 **Rewrite the sentences replacing the highlighted words with the correct form of a word from the box. Make any other changes needed.**

cooperative domestic faction liberal regime scrutinize unrest

1 The international community has thrown its support behind the new government _____.

2 Politicians need to balance politics at home _____ against the realities of globalization.

3 The role of the minister in the deal has been looked at closely and criticized _____ by the media.

4 During this period, the government adopted a more relaxed _____ approach to labour migration.

5 The party became divided as different groups _____ refused to compromise on key issues.

6 He managed to remain as leader through periods of social disorder _____ and even civil war.

7 This points to the importance of a transparent and international approach to the issue that involves working together _____.

7 **Write a short paragraph describing one of the following. Try to use words from this unit.**

- A particular political belief or perspective (see also Unit 23)
- The system of government in a country (see also Units 8–9)
- An example of political change in a country (see also Unit 13)

Words to learn

assemble AWL	component AWL	labour AWL	personnel
asset	developmental	life cycle	stakeholder
cash flow	human resources	manufacture	supplier
commodity AWL	in line with	outsource	workforce

Human resources

A **Human resources** are employees, **personnel**, or the **workforce** of an organization. The term has become increasingly fashionable in recent years and expresses the view that employees are a resource that must be harnessed and managed effectively alongside the other resources used by business organizations, such as capital, property, raw materials, and energy. Partly for this reason, some commentators are unhappy with this description of the workforce because it expresses the view of **labour** as a mere **commodity** or factor of production. Reflecting this unhappiness, some firms that aspire to practise 'soft HRM' (human resource management) refer to the employees as associates, members, partners, or **stakeholders**.

B 'Soft HRM' is a term used to describe the **developmental** aspects of managing people. It is an approach that emphasizes the need to treat employees as **assets** which must be looked after, trained, and developed in order to get the best out of them. In contrast, 'hard HRM' views people as factors of production which, like other assets, can be treated dispassionately **in line with** business requirements.

Source: Heery, E. & Noon, M. (2008). *A Dictionary of Human Resource Management.* (2 rev ed.). Oxford: Oxford University Press.

Glossary
dispassionately (*adv*): in a way that is not influenced by emotion

Usage note talking about employees

An **employee**, a **worker**, a **staff member** or a **member of staff** can refer to an individual who works.

• *a full-time employee; each member of staff*

Worker is especially used in compounds to talk about someone who does a particular kind of work:

• *a social/health worker; a manual/skilled/unskilled worker*

You can use **staff**, **personnel** or **workforce** to talk about all the people in a particular business:

• *medical/school staff; military/sales personnel*

Personnel and **staff** are plural nouns and they are followed by a plural verb form:

• *When staff are working under pressure …*

Workforce is a singular noun which is used with either a singular or a plural verb form:

• *Nearly half the workforce was/were employed in manufacturing.*

Labour (an uncountable noun) refers to workers considered as a general group:

• *skilled/local labour; labour costs; the labour market*

---

1 Read texts A and B and mark the statements true (T) or false (F).

1 'Hard HRM' views employees as resources, like property or materials. __
2 'Soft HRM' sees employees as valuable; they need to be supported and developed. __

2 Complete the statements using words or phrases from the box.

assets	commodity	in line with	stakeholder

1 A _____ can be anyone who has an interest in the activities of an organization, from employees and investors to suppliers and customers.
2 A company's _____ include all the things that it owns which have value, including cash, property and other resources.
3 Reducing a business's marketing budget _____ falling sales could actually worsen the situation.
4 We prefer not to think of people as a _____ that can be bought and sold like raw materials.

3 Choose the best word to complete the sentences. Think about both meaning and grammar.

1 There are severe shortages of qualified health *personnel / workforce* in many countries.
2 One former *employee / personnel* described how he often worked 12 hours without a break.
3 The survey found that a growing proportion of the *labour / workforce* are not getting work-related training.
4 Some clothing businesses have been criticized for using cheap *labour / workforce* abroad to produce their clothes.

Manufacturing

> **C** The first step in choosing a supplier is deciding whether to manufacture the product solely ourselves, or simply to buy the necessary components to make the product from outside suppliers. 'This choice is characterized as a "make or buy" decision, with the associated alternatives of insourcing or outsourcing' (Monczka, 2010).
>
> Manufacturing the product entirely ourselves would require large amounts of capital in order to cover the facilities needed to produce all the materials for the final product. This would be a huge cost and require the majority of our available capital, in turn leaving us with poor cash flow and no capital to invest in advertising and marketing of the product and brand – both of which are an essential part of the product's success in the early stages of its life cycle. Therefore, we have decided to outsource the components from outside suppliers who specialize in the given technology, and assemble the final product within our own factory.
>
> Source: student proposal

4 Read text C and answer the questions.

1 Does the student decide to insource or outsource the components for their product?_____
2 What is the main factor in their decision?_____

5 Match the processes, 1–4, to the descriptions, a–d.

1 marketing
2 cash flow
3 life cycle
4 outsourcing

a A product goes through four stages: its introduction to the market, followed by a period of sales growth before it reaches maturity and has its greatest sales, and then a period of decline as sales drop before the product is finally withdrawn.

b The movement of money into and out of a business is governed by the balance of receipts from sales (money coming in) and payments which the business needs to make (money going out).

c Sometimes a firm decides to use another company to supply some components or services it needs to produce its final product because it lacks the expertise or resources to do so in-house.

d The process involves planning and then effectively managing the pricing, promotion and distribution of a product to its customers.

6 Choose the correct word to complete the sentences. Use the glossary on pp.129–144 to help you check the word families if necessary.

1 To reduce emissions, they are opening more facilities to *assemble / assembly* products closer to the customer.
2 A number of car *manufactures / manufacturers* set up facilities in Malaysia to avoid tariffs imposed on imports.
3 The key *components / composed* of a communication system are as follows.
4 Most local parts *supplies / suppliers* lacked the production capabilities to meet the company's quality standards.
5 Any new product goes through various *developing / developmental* stages before its launch.

44 Economics and finance

Words to learn

borrower	debt	income AWL	market
crash	economy AWL	interest rate	mortgage
creditor AWL	evident AWL	lender	probability
crisis	financial AWL	loan	

The economy

A The global **financial crisis** that began in 2007–8 was the biggest shock to the capitalist **economy** since the Great Depression that originated in 1929. The **crash** in asset values, particularly share **market** values, sent shock waves through the global economy. An economic recession developed in many nations, with falling **incomes** and rising unemployment.

Source: Stilwell, F. (2012). *Political Economy: The Contest of Economic Ideas.* (3 ed.). Oxford: Oxford University Press.

Glossary
share (*n*): one of the units of equal value into which a company is divided and sold to raise money
shock waves (*n*): feelings of shock that people experience when something bad happens

1 Read text A and answer the questions.

1 Which events started in 1929 and in 2007–8 respectively? _____
2 Which do you think is more serious: a **depression** or a **recession**? (See note on p.101 for help) _____
3 As a result of the global financial crisis, which of these things increased and which decreased?
  a the value of assets, such as shares on financial markets: _____
  b average incomes: _____
  c unemployment: _____

2 Choose the best word to complete the sentences. Use the glossary on pp.129–144 to help you if necessary.

1 The City of London is home to one of the largest concentrations of banks and *financial / economic* institutions in the world.
2 One way that firms raise *finance / economics* is by offering shares for sale on the stock market.
3 European 'knowledge' workers are now competing with well-educated employees willing to work for lower incomes in developing *economies / economics*.
4 There is disagreement among *economies / economists* about how best to measure the cost of living in a country.
5 The environmental consequences of *financial / economic* growth within a country are rarely assessed.

3 Complete the sentences with the correct form of one of the verbs in the box. Use the list of collocations on pp.107–110 to help you if necessary.

> face   fall   grow   have   hit

1 Currently, the country _____ a serious financial **crisis**.
2 As people's **incomes** _____ , the state's tax revenues will also drop.
3 The economic **crisis** has _____ the company hard in many of its key markets.
4 China's **economy** _____ by 7.4% in 2014 – its slowest annual rate for a quarter of a century.
5 Six per cent of those questioned _____ an annual **income** of less than $15,000.

Financial Institutions

B The warning signs of the coming crash became **evident** during the emergence of the 'subprime crisis' in the United States in 2007. The egregious business practices of a range of financial institutions were the immediate cause of the problem. The financial institutions had been making **loans** to low-income people wishing to buy houses: these were known as 'subprime' loans because there was a relatively high **probability** that the **borrowers** would default. Indeed, both borrowers and **lenders** would become losers when the US housing price bubble burst and prices started to fall.

Source: Stilwell, F. (2012). *Political Economy: The Contest of Economic Ideas.* (3 ed.). Oxford: Oxford University Press.

C What might have caused the borrowers to default on their **mortgages**?
If their incomes dropped or they lost their job, then they wouldn't be able to make the repayments and they'd get further into **debt** with their **creditors**.
If **interest rates** rose, then the cost of repayments would go up, making them unaffordable for people on a low incomes.

Glossary
default (*v*): to fail to do something that you legally have to do, especially by not paying a debt
egregious (*adj*): extremely bad

4 Read texts B and C and answer the questions about the 'subprime crisis'.

1 Who did financial institutions lend money to? _____
2 Give two reasons why borrowers were unlikely to repay their debt. _____
3 Why did the lenders lose out when house prices fell? _____
4 What does the writer mean when he says that 'the US housing price bubble burst'? _____

5 Complete the sentences using the correct form of words from the box.

borrow   crisis   debt   evident   interest   lender   loan   market   probability

1 A mortgage is a _____ from a bank to buy a property.
2 Most _____ require buyers to have at least a 10% deposit before they will issue a mortgage.
3 Financial problems typically arise when people get into _____ and can't repay what they owe.
4 Banks are reluctant to lend money to people if there is a high _____ that they will default.
5 Lower _____ rates make it easier for businesses to _____ money in order to expand, thus stimulating the economy.
6 It has become increasingly _____ that in a globalized world, the economies of all countries are affected by changes in international financial _____ .
7 During the economic _____ in the 1970s, many companies were forced out of business.

6 Put the sentence parts into the best order to create a summary of texts A and B.

1 financial institutions had been issuing loans to low-income families. _
2 and the resulting lack of confidence in financial institutions led eventually to a global recession. _
3 but when property prices subsequently fell dramatically, _
4 lenders were left unable to recover the full value of the properties either. _
5 The global financial crisis began in the US in 2007 when it emerged that ⊥
6 because they were unable to repay their debt, _
7 Not only were these borrowers at high risk of defaulting _
8 As the full scale of this problem became evident, share market values crashed _

7 Write a short paragraph (three or four sentences) about one of the following topics. Try to use some of the vocabulary from this unit.

• The economy of a country you know
• The property market
• Credit cards

recession (*n*):
An overall decline in economic activity mainly observed as a slowdown in output and employment. It is not as severe or prolonged as a depression. A recession is often defined as real GDP falling for two successive quarters.

Source: (2010). *Oxford Dictionary of Economics.* (4 ed.). Oxford: Oxford University Press.

Words to learn

access AWL	discourse	implicit AWL	native speaker
channel AWL	disseminate	linguist	overtly
commentator AWL	finite AWL	mass media	publish AWL
content	formality	mediate AWL	

Linguistics

A The popular view of grammar is as a **finite** number of imposed rules that are unchangeable. However, according to **linguists**, the grammar of a language is a far more wide-ranging, complex and abstract system that is not **overtly** prescribed (Milroy and Milroy, 1999). Within this view, it is said that **native speakers** gain an **implicit** knowledge of language – a 'mental grammar' – as they learn the language (Milroy, 1998). There is also disagreement between what a standard grammar is: some would suggest that there is one grammar that should be applied to both written and spoken **discourse**. In this view, sentences that would not appear in a piece of careful literary prose would be classified as ungrammatical, but this brings about the issue of **formality**, as it is not appropriate to 'talk like a book'.

Source: student essay

Glossary
prescribe (*v*): to say what should be done or how it should be done

1 Match the sentence halves to create a summary of text A.

1 Most people see grammar as
2 Many linguists, however, would argue that grammar is
3 There is one view that a single set of grammatical rules
4 Others would point out that

   a applies to both spoken and written communication.
   b a fixed set of rules about a language.
   c there are clear differences between the way we write and speak.
   d a more complex system that speakers acquire naturally.

2 Match the highlighted words to keywords with an opposite meaning from text A.

1 Kennedy insisted on **informality** and ignored traditional structures. _____
2 A language has an **infinite** number of possible grammatical sentences. _____
3 The reasons behind the decision are made **explicit** in a formal report. _____

3 Complete the sentences using words from the box. Not all the words are needed.

discourse finite implicit implicitly linguist linguistic native speakers overt

1 This article shows some of the _____ features of Chinese that present challenges for Chinese-speaking learners of English.
2 Two professional translators, who were _____ of Chinese, translated the English document into Chinese independently.
3 Media reports and political _____ typically ignore this key underlying issue.
4 The _____ message conveyed here is that giving financial aid to these countries is not a good idea.
5 The software can recognize only a _____ set of spoken commands.

Media and communication studies

B In an 'information age' where so much information is widely available via the internet and other mass media, you might think that if knowledge is power, then this situation should lead to greater equality. However, many commentators have instead highlighted an 'information gap' between the 'information rich' and the 'information poor'. The information rich tend to be of a higher socio-economic status, be better educated and have better access to information technology than the information poor. This last factor is sometimes known as the 'digital divide'. This refers to the disparity between those who have reliable internet access and the skills to make full use of it and those who do not.

While information gaps exist between groups within societies, the greatest inequalities seem to be between more and less developed societies. Most of the channels of global communication are owned and controlled by media organizations based in more developed countries. This means that they not only have the resources to gather and disseminate more information, but they also maintain control of the flow and content of that information. Thus, a handful of multinational corporations mediate the flow of information globally, selecting which information is published or broadcast to audiences around the world.

Glossary
disparity (*n*): a difference, especially one that is considered unfair

4 Read text B and answer the questions.

1 Which three features characterize the information rich? _____
2 Which two factors are key to the 'digital divide'? _____
3 Note four ways in which media organizations control information. _____

5 Do the paraphrases (b) have roughly the same meaning as the original text (a)? Mark them (S) if they have a similar meaning and (D) if they have a different meaning.

1 a "… so much information is widely available via the internet and other mass media…"
  b A large amount of information can be found online and in the press. __
2 a "… many commentators have highlighted an 'information gap …"
  b Experts note the existence of an 'information gap'. __
3 a "… channels of global communication …" …
  b … international TV channels such as the BBC and CNN. __
4 a "… they […] have the resources to gather and disseminate more information …"
  b They are able to collect and interpret large amounts of information. __
5 a "… they maintain control of the flow and content of that information."
  b They can decide what information to make public, when and how. __
6 a "… a handful of multinational corporations mediate the flow of information globally."
  b A few international media organizations influence what information people around the world receive. __

6 Match the sentence halves. Use the highlighted words, the list of collocations on pp.107–110 and the list of dependent prepositions on pp.111–113 to help you.

1 She notes the implicit
2 Everyone should have equal access
3 The research team published
4 It is important to establish effective channels
5 Digital technologies allow us to disseminate

a an article in the Journal of Media and Communication Studies.
b information more widely than in previous centuries.
c message in the text regarding what constitutes 'good' or 'moral' behaviour.
d of communication within an organization.
e to educational resources.

Student writing: case studies

Case studies are used in a number of disciplines, including business studies, engineering and health sciences. The main aim of a case study is to demonstrate your ability to apply theoretical knowledge or analytical techniques learned during your course to a specific real-world situation: the case. A case study typically includes setting out the context and describing the case, followed by analysis, evaluation and recommendations.

A Microfinance is a method of improving the **standard of living** of people living in extreme **poverty** by providing very small-scale, low-**interest loans** to enable them to start a small, local enterprise (Last, 2007). Microfinance initiatives are aimed at individuals and communities who would not normally have **access** to **financial** services. Small-scale loans are used to fund small enterprises which provide an **income** for those involved. Once the initial loan has been repaid, larger loans can be taken out to expand the business. This case study looks at one such enterprise in a village in rural India and assesses the effectiveness of microfinancing in this case.

B Ten women in the village formed a group to take out a loan to breed goats and sell them. As the women were **illiterate**, the village health worker helped them to complete an application for a loan from a microfinance initiative. The **lender** first **required** the women to raise enough money to **demonstrate** their ability to eventually repay the loan. The women all had jobs as farm labourers and managed to set aside 100 rupees (Rs) each month for a year until they had collectively saved Rs 12,000. The lender then granted a loan of Rs 10,000 at an **interest rate** of 6% per annum for a term of one year. The group used the money to purchase five goats and each took turns caring for them. Each woman contributed monthly both to the cost of keeping the goats and to repaying the loan.

C However, after just two months, the women mutually decided not to continue repayments, leaving Rs 6,000 plus interest unpaid. After several missed repayments, the lender sent a letter to the women which they ignored. The lender took no further action since the costs of recovering the loan would have been greater than the size of the loan itself. After six months, the number of goats had expanded, so the women decided to sell the entire herd. In total, the women sold the herd for approximately Rs 50,000, distributing the profit equally and ending the business.

D The lender's inability to **enforce** the repayments in this case suggest that a more effective, local enforcement method is needed. As the **borrowers** were illiterate, it may be that they were not fully aware of the consequences of not repaying the loan. It is worth noting that the women could easily have repaid their loan but chose not to do so, seemingly unaware that although there were no **sanctions** in the short term, they had damaged their credit history and would not be able to apply for further loans in the future. In this sense, the enterprise was of limited success, providing some short-term gains, but not securing the women and their families a continued income in the longer term. In order to avoid such a situation, the lender could have used a trusted local person, such as the village health worker, to **mediate** between the lender and the women, ensuring they better understood the commitment they were making and also **monitoring** the progress of the enterprise.

1 Read the case study by an international development student. Which paragraph(s):

1 Describe the theoretical background? _____
2 Describe the details of the case? _____ / _____
3 Analyse the case? _____
4 Make recommendations? _____

2 Mark the statements true (T) or false (F) according to the text.

1 Microfinance is aimed at people who wouldn't usually be able to borrow money. __
2 The women stopped paying back the loan because they couldn't afford it. __
3 The lender didn't try harder to get back the money because it wasn't worthwhile for such a small amount. __
4 By selling the goats, the women could not use the business to support their families long-term. __
5 The writer recommends that the lender should not lend to people who are illiterate. __

Focus on collocation and patterns

3 Collocation can be about more than pairs of words. Longer 'chunks' of language, or patterns, are also commonly used together. Complete each 'chunk' that appears in the case study using two words or phrases from the box. Some of the phrases are used more than once.

> access   action   an ability   an income   for sb   no further   of sth   the consequences
> the effectiveness   the progress   to do sth   to sth

▶ EXAMPLE: have _access to sth_

1 provide _____   3 assess _____   5 be aware of _____
2 take _____   4 demonstrate _____   6 monitor _____

4 Match the sentence halves. Think about meaning, collocation and longer patterns.

1 A benchmark is a measure
2 The IMF provides short-term
3 Transportation issues frequently prevented
4 These changes mean greater participation
5 They found that local standards of care were not in line
6 The institution was facing

a monetary assistance to countries struggling with financial instability.
b individuals from receiving the care to which they were entitled.
c with current guidelines.
d of performance that serves as a standard for evaluating other results.
e a financial crisis due in part to falling membership.
f of stakeholders in the regulation process.

Focus on word formation

5 Rewrite the sentences using the correct form of the highlighted word shown. Make any other changes needed.

▶ EXAMPLE: They found no link between internet use and how students **perform** academically.
They found no link between internet use and _students' academic performance_. (*noun*)

1 This campaign provides a **demonstration** of the way in which direct action can have a major impact on policy.
This campaign _____. (*verb*)
2 There is clearer **evidence** of differences in ability in larger classes.
Differences in ability become _____. (*adjective*)
3 This approach makes the **implicit** assumption that the entrepreneur starts their new business in the same sector they previously worked in.
This approach _____. (*adverb*)
4 The study looked at how health care information was **provided** online in two different areas.
The study looked at _____. (*noun*)
5 **Finance** for the project was provided largely by local businesses.
Local businesses _____. (*adjective*)

Writing task

6 Write a short case study in your discipline. Use one of the ideas below or choose your own. Describe the background context and the details of the case, analyse it in relation to a theory or technique in your discipline and conclude by making a recommendation.

- A business case
- An engineering project
- A medical case
- A teaching situation
- A legal case or situation

Academic and language terms

adjective: a word that describes a person or a thing. For example, *serious, interesting* or *scientific* in *a serious illness, interesting research* and *scientific knowledge*

adverb: a word that adds more information about place, time, manner, cause or degree to a **verb** (*directly benefit*), an **adjective** (*severely ill*), a phrase or another **adverb**

affix: a **prefix** or a **suffix** ▶ Unit 30

citation: a summary, **paraphrase** or quotation from another piece of writing; when you cite something from a **source**, you usually give a **reference** to identify the original writer ▶ Unit 35

collocate: if one word **collocates with** another, they are typically used together. For example, *make* collocates with *decision*; we commonly say *make a decision*

collocation: a combination of words that are typically used together. For example, *make a decision* or *widespread use* ▶ Unit 31

countable noun: a **noun** that can be used in the **plural** (*numbers, ideas, people*) or with *a* or *an* (*a number, an idea, a person*)

dependent preposition: a **dependent preposition** is one that is typically used together with another word, such as a **noun** (*assessment of, insight into*), a **verb** (*overlap with, discriminate against*) or an **adjective** (*capable of, responsible for*). The choice of **preposition** depends on the word it is used with ▶ Unit 29

discipline: a subject of study, especially at university, such as history, chemistry or economics

emphasis: the use of language to show that something has special importance (*a crucial difference*) or that you are very confident about something (*this clearly demonstrates*) ▶ Unit 34

evaluation: in academic writing, **evaluation** is the writer's response to an idea based on evidence; whether it is valid, accurate, effective, etc. ▶ Units 24 and 25

hedging: in academic writing, **hedging** is the language a writer uses to show how they feel about an idea. It is used to make sure that you express ideas accurately and to avoid generalizations (*approximately half, possibly harmful, this could to some extent* …) and to express **stance** (*supposedly neutral, an apparent contradiction*) ▶ Unit 33

noun: a word that refers to a person (*scientist*), a place (*city*) or a thing (*book*), a quality (*accuracy*) or an activity (*development*)

noun phrase: a group of words in a sentence that behaves in the same way as a **noun**. For example, *the difference in temperature, individual members of the team* ▶ Unit 27

paraphrase: to express what someone has said or written using different words

part of speech: one of the classes which words are divided into according to their grammar, such as **noun, verb, adjective**, etc.

phrasal verb: a **verb** combined with an **adverb** or a **preposition** to give a new meaning. For example, *put forward, end up* and *lead to*

plural: a form of a **noun** or a **verb** that refers to more than one person or thing

prefix: a letter or group of letters added to the beginning of a word to change its meaning, such as *un* in *unnecessary* and *re* in *reassess*

preposition: a word, such as *in, from, to* and *of*, used before a **noun** or pronoun to show place, position, time or method

reference: in academic writing, a **reference** is a mention of a source of information. A **reference** is always used with a quotation or a **citation** to give details about the **source**

singular: a form of a **noun** or **verb** that refers to one person or thing

source: a text or person that provides information, especially for a piece of written work

stance: the view that someone has about something, based on evidence

suffix: a letter or group of letters added to the end of a word to make another word, such as *–ly* in *greatly* or *–ness* in *awareness*

synonym: a word or expression that has the same or nearly the same meaning as another word

uncountable noun: an **uncountable noun** cannot be made **plural** or used with *a* or *an*, for example *water, information* and *diversity*

verb: a word or group of words that expresses an action (such as *perform*), an event (such as *occur*) or a state (such as *exist*)

word family: all the forms or **parts of speech** of a word. For example, *conclude, conclusion, conclusive, conclusively, inconclusive*

word formation: the way in which words are made up of different parts, such as **prefixes** and **suffixes**

Collocations

Collocation is the way that words are typically used together. This can include various combinations: verb + noun (*attend a lecture*), adjective + noun (*ancient history*), adverb + adjective (*statistically significant*), etc. Learning and using these common combinations can make your writing more natural and easier to read. For more about collocations in academic writing, ▶ Unit 31.

The collocations in this list are common combinations which appear in this book. It is not a complete list and other collocations may also be possible with the words shown.

Learner's dictionaries often include useful information about common collocations. These might be shown in the example sentences or, sometimes, in a note at the end of the entry:

> ▸ ADJECTIVE + DISTINCTION **important • key, crucial • clear, sharp • fundamental, basic • fine • traditional • useful • conceptual**
> *Table 10.2 indicates the **key distinctions** between the supervisory board and the management board.* ◇ *Professionals draw fairly **clear distinctions** between traditional and modern irrigation systems.*
>
> ▸ VERB + DISTINCTION **make, draw • note • blur • maintain • introduce • recognize • emphasize**
> *Gronroos (1981) **draws a distinction** between what he sees as the strategic and tactical levels of internal marketing.* ◇ *Developments in computer technology in the late 1990s further **blurred the distinction** between hardware and software.*

adjective	+ noun	▶ Unit:
applied / computer / environmental earth / life / natural / physical	science(s)	2
computer / information	technology	2
environmental	impact / science	2
interdisciplinary	research / team	2
physical	sciences / force	2
marine / human	biology	2
ancient	history / times / civilization	3
literary	work / genre / criticism	3
anthropological	study / fieldwork / perspective	3
archaeological	site / evidence / remains	3
cultural	tradition / norms / diversity	3
informed	consent	7
manufacturing / retail	sector	8
physical	property	9
thin / surface	layer	9
sales	projection	10
preceding / following	section	10
demographic	trend / information	12
economic	depression / downturn	12
underlying	trend / cause / factor / motivation	12
dramatic	change / increase / fluctuation	12
social / political	upheaval	13
nationwide	survey	14
local	community	14
transport	route	14
widespread	use	14
ethnic	minority / group	15
social	status / class / group	15
first / future	generation	15
minority	group	15
marital	status / partner	15
physical	dimensions	16
the predominant	form / type	16
direct / contributing	cause	17
adverse	effect	19
factual / unsupported	claim	20
primary / secondary	data / source	20
comprehensive	review	20
key / theoretical / abstract	concept	21
alternative / working	hypothesis	21
real-world	implication / situation / example	21
critical	thinking / question / analysis / review	22

adjective	+ noun	▶ Unit:
credible	argument / source / account	22
valid / coherent / compelling	argument	24
realistic	goal	24
feasible / flexible	solution	24
robust	design	24
coherent	framework / system	24
comprehensive	review / list	24
feasible	option	24
compelling	reason	24
strong	incentive	31
quantitative / qualitative	(research) methods / data	31
gas / solid / liquid	phase (science)	31
initial / early	phase	31
challenging	work / task	32
inevitable	consequence / result	34
overwhelming	majority	34
laborious	process	R4
mean / average	value	37
electricity / power	generation	38
renewable	energy / source / resource	38
nuclear	power / plant / energy	38
infectious	disease	39
chronic / acute / terminal / serious	illness / condition	39
disaster / emergency / humanitarian	relief	40
literacy	rate / level	40
domestic	policy / politics	42
social / civil / political	unrest	42
economic	activity / development / growth	44
financial	institution / market / support	44
financial / economic / global / banking	crisis	44
finite	number / set	45
implicit	knowledge / message	45

verb	+ adjective	▶ Unit:
become	evident	44

adverb	+ adjective	▶ Unit:
weekly	intervals	10
directly	relevant	20
statistically	significant	24
severely	disabled / ill	34
fundamentally	different	34
severely / profoundly	deaf	R4

adverb	+ verb	▶ Unit:
seriously	undermine / affect / damage sth	34
greatly	reduce / increase	34

verb	+ adverb	▶ Unit:
benefit	directly / greatly	31
vary	enormously	34

noun	+ verb	▶ Unit:
a theme	emerges	4
a graph	illustrates / shows sth	5
a curve	indicates / represents sth	5
problems / issues / differences	arise / emerge	11
a problem / an issue	arises / recurs	19
an error / a problem	persists	25
a crisis	affects sth / occurs / hits sth	44
income	increases / rises / falls	44
an economy	grows	44

verb	+ noun	▶ Unit:
study for / complete	a degree / a master's / a PhD	1
receive	a degree / a BA / a BSc / a master's	1
complete / submit	an assignment / coursework	
complete	a dissertation / a project / a task	1
write	a dissertation	1
attend	a lecture / a seminar	1
develop	a (research) proposal	1
create	an outline	4
add / write	notes	4
outline	the structure	4
acknowledge / have	limitations	4
plot	a graph	5
produce	a curve	5
conduct / carry out	research / an experiment / a study / an analysis / a test / an interview	6
conform to	a format / a standard	6
perform	an analysis / a test	6
set up / use	equipment	6
set up	an experiment	6
yield / analyse / interpret	data / results	6
collect	data	7
confirm	the findings	7
obtain / select	a sample	7
divide into	groups / parts / sections / stages / types	8
found / establish	a company / an institution / an organization	11
commence / undertake	work / study / training	11
introduce / initiate	a change / a policy / reform	11
make	a modification / a transition	13
re-evaluate	a situation	13
amend	a law	13
transform	the way	13
experience	discrimination	15
exceed	a level / a limit	16
play	a part (in sth)	17
detect / resolve	a problem / an issue	19
impose	a limitation / a constraint / a requirement	19
meet	the requirements	19
provide	support / evidence / information	20
support	an argument / a claim	20
establish	the source	20
compile	data / a list / statistics	20
develop / test	a theory	21
make / question	an assumption	21
define	a term / a group	21
make	a generalization	21
evaluate	an argument / an effect / an impact	22
question	a point / an assumption / a view / an idea	22
make / offer / provide / give	an assessment	22
further	a cause / understanding / a goal	23
set	a goal	24
pose	a danger / a threat / a problem / a risk	25
undermine	effectiveness / confidence / credibility	25
discourage	investment / participation / smoking	25
restrict	the use / access / movement	25
conduct	a study / research / an interview / a survey	28
perform	a task / a function / a test	28
implement	a policy / a strategy / a change	28
utilize	a resource / technology / an approach	28
employ	a method / a strategy / a technique	28
exploit	an opportunity / a resource / technology	28
obtain	results / information / data / consent	28
acquire	knowledge / skills / a language	28
gain	access / an insight / an advantage	28
maintain	a level / a standard	28
provide / have / create	an incentive	31
commission	a report / a study / research	31

verb	+ noun	▶ Unit:
make	a distinction / an observation / a decision / a contribution	31
do	work / business / research / harm / damage	31
award	damages (law)	31
execute	an instruction (computing)	31
follow / give	instructions	31
execute	a plan	31
violate	an article / a convention (law)	31
violate	a rule	31
consult	a physician / a practitioner (medicine)	31
consult	a reference	31
generate	revenue / income	32
note	the importance / the difference / the increase	35
argue	the case / a point / the merits	35
suggest	an approach / a need / a link	35
summarize	the results / the findings / the data	35
have	the opportunity (to do sth)	R4
have	implications	R4
reduce	the risk	R4
reach	one's potential	R4
record	data / information / values	37
generate	electricity / power	38
contract / transmit / diagnose / treat	disease	39
exhibit / experience / report	a symptom	39
undergo	surgery / treatment / a procedure	39
administer	drugs / medication	39
monitor	a patient / sb's condition / sb's health	39
overthrow	the government / the regime / the monarchy	42
manufacture	a product / goods	43
face / experience	a crisis	44
have / earn	an income	44
make / repay / provide / grant	a loan	44
default on / grant / take out / pay	a mortgage	44
disseminate	information	45
publish	an article	45

Dependent prepositions

Many nouns, verbs and adjectives are typically followed by a particular preposition. Some words also appear in phrases with a preposition before them, for example *on average*. Learning these combinations can help to make your writing more accurate, more natural and easier to read. Some words are followed by different prepositions depending on the context or meaning. For example:

*Bad weather **resulted** in the closure of the airport.*

*Sleep problems sometimes **result** from the use of certain medicines.*

For more about preposition use, ▶ **Unit 29**.

The list here shows the most typical prepositions used with keywords that appear in this book. Other combinations may also be possible. You can find information about which prepositions to use with a word in a learner's dictionary.

Preposition before	Keyword	Following preposition	▶ Unit:
	access (n)	to sth	45
	accessible (adj)	to sb	9
	account (v)	for sth	19
	accumulation (n)	of sth	29
	adapt (v)	to sth	13
	adequate (adj)	for sth	16
	adjust (v)	for / to sth	12
	the **aim** (n)	of sth	7
	allocation (n)	of sth	29
	alteration (n)	to sth	29
	alternative (n)	to sth	18
	analysis (n)	of sth	22
	apply (v)	to sth / sb	21
	argue (v)	for / against sth	35
	assessment (n)	of sth	22
	associated (adj)	with sth / sb	32
	association (n)	with / between sth	29
	assumption (n)	about sth	21
	attitude (n)	of sb to / towards sth	27
	attribute (v)	sth to sth / sb	27
on	**average** (n)		33
	awareness (n)	of sth	24
	barrier (n)	to sth	19
	be based (v)	on / upon sth	21
	bias (n)	against / towards sth	22
	borrow (v)	(sth) from sb	44
	capable (adj)	of sth	29
(in the)	**case** (n)	of sth / sb	36
in (this / every)	**case** (n)		36
	citizen (n)	of a country	42
	collapse (n)	of sth	12
	comment (v)	on sth	35
	comparison (n)	of results / rates / groups, etc.	27
	comparison (n)	with sth / between sth and sth	27
	compatible (adj)	with sth	29
	be composed (v)	of sth	9
	concentration (n)	of sth (= amount of a substance)	27
	concentration (n)	on sth (= attention)	27
	concept (n)	of sth	21
	condition (n)	of sth	17
	be confined (v)	to sth / somewhere	14
	conform (v)	to / with sth	6
	the **consequences** (n)	of sth for sb / sth	17
	consist (v)	of sth	9
	constraint (n)	on sb / sth	19
	contact (n)	with sb / between sb and sb	29
	content (n)	of sth	45
in	**context** (n)		21
on the	**contrary** (n)		18
in	**contrast** (n)	(to sth)	32
	contribute (v)	to sth	17
	convert (v)	from sth to sth	29

Preposition before	Keyword	Following preposition	▶ Unit:
	convince (v)	sb of sth	22
	correlation (n)	with sth / between sth and sth	17
	correspondence (n)	with sth / between sth and sth	27
	critique (n)	of sth	35
in	debt (n)		44
	decline (n)	in sth	12
	defect (n)	in sth	25
	define (v)	sth as sth	21
	degree (n)	in sth (= university qualification)	1
	degree (n)	of sth (= amount / level)	27
	derive (v)	(sth) from sth	29
	deviation (n)	from sth	37
	diagnose (v)	sb with sth	39
	difference (n)	in sth / between sth and sth	27
	differentiate (v)	between sth and sth	18
	discourage (v)	sb from doing sth	25
	discrimination (n)	against sb / sth	15
	divide (v)	sth into parts, groups, etc.	8
without	doubt (n)		34
	downturn (n)	in sth	12
	effect (n)	of sth on sb / sth	29
	eliminate (v)	sth from sth / somewhere	11
	equal (adj)	to sth	37
	equivalent (adj)	to sth	30
	error (n)	in sth	25
	evaluation (n)	of sth	22
	evidence (n)	of / for / against / from sth	20
	example (n)	of sth	29
for	example (n)		1
	explanation (n)	of / for sth	29
to (an / some)	extent (n)		33
	failure (n)	of sth	25
	feature (n)	of sth	8
	flaw (n)	in sth	22
	fluctuation (n)	in sth	12
	formula (n)	for sth	37
	graduate (v)	from a university / with a degree	1
	impact (n)	of sth on sb / sth	29
	implications (n)	of sth for sb / sth	4
	impose (v)	sth on sb	19
	incidence (n)	of sth	27
	incorporate (v)	sth into sth	41
	independent (adj)	of sth	9
	indicator (n)	of sth	40
	infer (v)	sth from sth	21
	insight (n)	into sth	27
	instance (n)	of sth	36
for	instance (n)		36
in (this / one)	instance (n)		36
	integrate (v)	sth into sth	15
	interaction (n)	with sb / sth / between sth and sth	27
at	intervals (n)		10
	lack (n)	of sth	16
in / under / by	law (n)		3
	layer (n)	of sth	9
	lead (v)	to sth	17
	lend (v)	sth to sb	44
	limitation (n)	of sth	4
in	line (n)	with sth	43
	measure (n)	of sth	37
	member (n)	of sth	8
	migrate (v)	from somewhere to somewhere	13
	modification (n)	to sth	13
	multiply (v)	a number by a number	37
	nature (n)	of sth	29
	occurrence (n)	of sth	27
as	opposed (adj)	to sth	18
	outcome (n)	of sth	17
	parallels (n)	with sth / between sth and sth	29
	participate (v)	in sth	7

Preposition before	Keyword	Following preposition	▶ Unit:
	perceive (v)	sth as sth	23
	perception (n)	of sth	23
	precondition (n)	for sth	41
on	the **premise** that (n)		32
under	**pressure** (n)		23
	prevalent (adj)	in / among sb / sth	40
in	**principle** (n)		33
	prior (adj)	to sth	10
	probability (n)	of sth	44
	product (n)	of sth	17
	prohibit (v)	sb from doing sth	41
	property (n)	of sth	9
	proportion (n)	of sth	16
	provision (n)	of / for sth	41
in / within	a **range** (n)		12
at	a **rate** (n)		12
	rate (n)	of sth	12
	react (v)	to sth	22
	recognition (n)	of sb / sth	22
	refer (v)	to sth	35
with	**reference** (n)	to sth	35
with	**regard** (n)	to sth	32
	related (adj)	to sb / sth	15
	relationship (n)	with sb / sth / between sth and sth	15
	relevant (adj)	to sth	20
	rely (v)	on sth / sb	20
	repercussions (n)	of sth for sth / sb	17
	replace (v)	sth with sth	13
	representative (adj)	of sth	7
in (many / some)	**respects** (n)		33
	respond (v)	to sth	22
(in)	**response** (n)	to sth	13
	responsible (adj)	for sth	29
	restrict (v)	sth to sth	25
	result (v)	from / in sth	17
	results (n)	of sth	6
	round (v)	a number up / down / sth to sth	37
in	a **scenario** (n)		21
	shift (n)	in sth / from sth to sth	13
	shortcoming (n)	of sth	25
	source (n)	of sth	20
	square root (n)	of a number	37
	status (n)	of sth	15
	substitute (v)	sth for / with sth	13
	substitution (n)	of sth with sth	13
	the **sum** (n)	of several numbers	37
	supplement (v)	sth by / with sth	40
	supply (v)	sb with sth / sth to sb	38
	support (n)	for / from sth	20
in	**support** (n)	of sth	20
	symbol (n)	of / for sth	37
in	**terms** (n)	of sth	29
	theory (n)	of sth	21
	trace (n)	of sth	16
	transfer (v)	sth from sth to sth / sth between sth and sth	29
	transition (n)	from sth to sth	13
	variability (n)	in / of / between sth	37
	variation (n)	in / of / between sth	18
	vary (v)	in / with sth / from sth to sth / between sth and sth	18

Affixes

Understanding prefixes (at the beginning of words) and suffixes (at the end of words) can help you to work out the meaning of the word or the part of speech. For example, several common prefixes are used to express negative or opposite meanings: *un-*, *in-*, *de-*, *dis-*, *non-*. Some suffixes indicate a word's part of speech: *require**ment*** (noun) or *effect**ive*** (adjective). For more about affixes, ▶ Unit 30.

Prefixes

agro- / agri- connected with farming: *agriculture, agrochemical*

anti- **1** opposed to: *antisocial* **2** preventing: *antidepressant*

auto- **1** about or by yourself: *autonomy* **2** by itself; without a person to operate it: *automation*

bio- connected with living things or human life: *biological, biotechnology, biohazard*

cardio- connected with the heart: *cardiovascular*

co- together with: *coordinate, cooperate, co-worker*

dis- not; the opposite of: *disadvantage, disagree*

eco- connected with the environment: *ecosystem*

electro- connected with electricity: *electrochemical*

equi- equal; equally: *equivalent, equitable*

extra- outside; beyond: *extracellular*

geo- of the earth: *geothermal, geopolitical*

homo- the same: *homogeneous*

hyper- more than normal; too much: *hypersensitive*

in- / il- / im- / ir- / not; the opposite of: *inconsistent, impossible, illegal*

inter- between: *international, interaction*

micro- small; on a small scale: *microelectronics, microorganism*

mid- in the middle of: *mid-century, midwinter*

mis- bad or wrong; badly or wrongly: *misinterpret, misunderstand, misuse*

neuro- connected with the nerves: *neuroscience*

non- not: *non-standard, non-existent*

omni- of all things; in all ways or places: *omnipresent*

over- more than normal; too much: *overestimate, overwhelming*

post- after: *post-war*

pre- before: *presuppose, preoperative*

psycho- / psych- connected with the mind: *psychology*

quasi- partly; almost: *quasi-spherical*

re- again: *re-evaluate, reinforce, re-establish*

socio- connected with society or the study of society: *socio-economic, sociocultural*

techno- connected with technology: *technophobia*

tele- over a long distance; far: *telecommunications*

trans- **1** across; beyond: *transportation, transaction* **2** into another place or state: *transplant*

un- not; the opposite of: *unnecessary, unproductive*

uni- one; having one: *uniform, unilateral*

Suffixes

-able / -ible (in adjectives) **1** possible to: *flexible, disposable* **2** having the quality of: *visible*

-age (in nouns) **1** the action or result of: *breakage* **2** a process or state: *shortage* **3** a set of group of: *assemblage* **4** an amount of: *dosage, percentage* **5** a place where: *storage*

-al **1** (in adjectives) connected with: *developmental* **2** (in nouns) process or state of: *survival*

-ance / -ence (in nouns) an action, process or state: *inheritance, incidence, occurrence*

-ant / -ent **1** (in adjectives) that is or does sth: *persistent, ignorant* **2** (in nouns) a person or thing that: *opponent, immigrant*

-ate **1** (in adjectives) full of or having the quality of: *literate, accurate* **2** (in verbs) to give the thing or quality mentioned to: *automate, validate* **3** (in nouns) the status of function of: *graduate* **4** (in nouns) a group with the status or function of: *electorate*

-ee (in nouns) a person affected by an action: *employee*

-er / -or (in nouns) **1** a person or thing that: *manufacturer* **2** a person or thing that has the quality mentioned: *foreigner* **3** a person concerned with: *astronomer*

-ery / -ry (in nouns) **1** the group or class of: *machinery* **2** the state or character of: *recovery* **3** a place where sth is made, grows, lives, etc.: *fishery*

-fold (in adjectives and adverbs) multiplied by; having the number of parts mentioned: *fourfold*

-ful (in adjectives) **1** having a particular quality: *harmful* **2** an amount that fills sth: *handful*

-hood (in nouns) a state, often during a particular period of time: *childhood, adulthood*

-ify (in verbs) to make or become: *modify, classify*

-ism (in nouns) **1** the action or result of: *criticism* **2** the state or quality of: *professionalism* **3** the teaching, system or movement of: *capitalism* **4** unfair treatment or hatred: *racism, sexism* **5** a medical condition or disease: *alcoholism*

-ist (in nouns) **1** a person who has studied sth or does sth as a job: *psychologist, scientist* **2** a person who believes in sth or belongs to a particular group: *capitalist*

-ity (in nouns) the quality or state of: *legality, neutrality*

-ive (in adjectives) having a particular quality: *active, effective*

-ization (in nouns) the process of changing in a particular way: *industrialization, globalization*

-ize / -ise (in verbs) **1** to become, make or make like: *generalize, minimize* **2** to place in: *hospitalize*

-less (in adjectives) not having or doing sth: *useless, ceaseless*

-ly **1** (in adverbs) in a particular way: *greatly, seriously* **2** (in adjectives) having the qualities of: *scholarly* **3** (in adjectives and adverbs) at intervals of: *hourly*

-ment (in nouns) a state, action or quality: *development, requirement*

-ness (in nouns) a state or quality: *awareness, effectiveness*

-ous (in adjectives) having a particular quality: *ambiguous, continuous, infectious*

-ship (in nouns) **1** the state or quality of: *ownership* **2** showing status: *citizenship* **3** the group of: *membership*

-tion / -sion / -ion (in nouns) the action or state of: *reaction, submission*

-wide (in adjectives and adverbs) across an area: *nationwide, statewide, worldwide*

Answer key

Unit 1

1 1 3 2 3 3 1 4 2 5 3

2 1 graduated: v
2 graduates: n
3 undergraduates: n
4 graduation: n
5 graduate: v

3 1 dissertation
2 coursework
3 project
4 task
5 assignment

4 1 S (although *postgraduate student* includes master's and PhD students)
2 D (these could refer to the same person but in different roles – *supervisor*: helps a PhD student, *lecturer*: anyone working at a university who gives lectures)
3 D (*an academic* is someone who teaches or does research at a university)
4 D (a *research proposal* is the formal plan that must be written and accepted before a *research project* begins)
5 S

5 a 1 complete 2 submit 3 attend 4 write
5 undertake 6 develop

5 b 1 submit / complete (*complete* is a less natural alternative)
2 complete / submit
3 attend
4 writing / completing
5 develop
6 undertake / complete (*complete* is a less natural alternative)

Unit 2

1 1 physical 2 physicist 3 chemistry
4 chemist 5 geological 6 ecology
7 ecologist 8 biology 9 biological

2 1 geologists
2 biological
3 physics
4 scientific
5 ecologists
6 chemical

3 1 engineers
2 applied
3 technological
4 Civil
5 electronics

4 1 civil
2 natural
3 geology
4 chemistry

5 technology
6 geological

5 1 e 2 a 3 d 4 b 5 c

Unit 3

1 a 1 Societies, cultural
2 archaeologists
3 literature, civilizations
4 literary

1 b 1 anthropology
2 archaeology
3 ancient history
4 literature

2 a 1 c 2 d 3 e 4 a 5 b

2 b 1 times
2 studies
3 works
4 diversity
5 sites

3 1 economics 2 economically 3 law 4 lawyer
5 managerially 6 manager 7 political
8 politically 9 psychology 10 psychologist

4 1 commercially / economically (*economically* is a less natural alternative)
2 economics 3 legal
4 political 5 psychology
6 management / managerial

5 1 society 2 commercial 3 politically
4 cultures 5 legal 6 law

Unit 4

1 1 outline
2 outline, introductory, conclusion
3 headings, theme
4 draft

2 a 1 adjective
2 noun, adverb
3 noun, verb
4 noun, verb

2 b 1 outlining
2 introduction
3 thematically, theme
4 headed
5 conclude

3 1 emerge
2 create
3 Add
4 draws
5 outlines

4 1 Results
  2 References / Bibliography
  3 Conclusion (*the implications*)
  4 Abstract
  5 Methodology
  6 Introduction / Discussion / Conclusion
  7 Conclusion (*the limitations*)
  8 Discussion

5 1 appendix
  2 limitations
  3 thesis
  4 a literature review
  5 abstracts
  6 journal

Unit 5

1 1 plot, graph
  2 axis
  3 curve, distribution
  4 figure

2 a 1 show
  2 indicate

2 b 1 c 2 a 3 b 4 d

3 1 pie chart
  2 segment
  3 key
  4 bar chart
  5 axis
  6 label

4 1 pie chart
  2 key
  3 segment
  4 bar chart
  5 labelled
  6 visual

5 1 diagram
  2 plotted
  3 arrow
  4 segment
  5 Figure
  6 illustrate, visually

6 **suggested answers**
  1 shows the distribution of male heights
  2 shows what the different coloured segments represent
  3 represents the amount of rainfall in that month
  4 illustrate the flow of hot and cold air

Unit 6

1 1 c 2 d 3 e 4 a 5 b

2 1 methods 2 units 3 materials
  4 statistical calculations 5 equipment

3 1 statistics 2 calculate 3 analysis
  4 analytical 5 interpretation

4 1 calculate
  2 statistical
  3 analytical
  4 interpretation
  5 were analysed / are analysed

5 a 1 yields
  2 interprets
  3 conducts
  4 sets up
  5 analyses

5 b **suggested answers**
  1 4 2 3 3 1 4 5 5 2

Unit 7

1 1 6
  2 1
  3 2 / 3 (these happen in either order/together)
  4 2 / 3 (these happen in either order/together)
  5 7
  6 4 / 5 (these happen in either order/together)
  7 4 / 5 (these happen in either order/together)

2 1 investigate
  2 procedure
  3 data
  4 interpret
  5 findings
  6 flaws
  7 confirms
  8 biased

3 1 participate 2 participant 3 sample
  4 representative 5 distortion

4 1 participate 2 sample 3 representative
  4 distort 5 distortion 6 participants
  7 represent

5 1 b 2 e 3 a 4 c 5 d

6 **suggested answers**
  1 Participants
  2 target population
  3 distortions
  4 biased findings
  5 flawed
  6 confirm the

Review 1

1 **suggested answer**
  The writer is reflecting on the reasons for their choice of dissertation topic.

2 1 D 2 C 3 – 4 E 5 – 6 B

3 1 graduated, study
  2 complete / conduct, submit
  3 complete, conducted
  4 collected, conducted
  5 illustrate
  6 emerged / emerge
  7 acknowledge

4   1 of   2 with   3 in   4 in
    5 of   6 for   7 of   8 of

5   1 submission
    2 representative
    3 graduation / graduating
    4 assessment
    5 are proposing / propose
    6 distributed
    7 conclude
    8 academically

Unit 8

1   1 divided into
    2 classified
    3 class
    4 categories
    5 items
    6 criteria
    7 system
    8 classification

2   1 hierarchial   2 level   3 sector   4 overlap

3   1 a   2 e   3 b   4 c   5 d

4   1 S   2 S   3 D (*divide into* is to separate into parts or groups; *select* is to choose from a group of people or things)   4 S   5 S   6 D (an *item* is a single thing; a *level* is a position in a scale of size or importance)   7 S   8 D (an *overlap* is a shared area of activity, interest, knowledge, etc.; *division* is the process or result of dividing something)

5   suggested answers
    1 items
    2 select
    3 is clearly some overlap
    4 classify people / to categorize people
    5 feature of (*characteristic of* is a less natural choice)

Unit 9

1   1 interior
    2 layers
    3 core
    4 exposed

2   1 composition
    2 properties
    3 core
    4 layers
    5 accessible

3   1 agencies / bodies
    2 vehicle
    3 is comprised of / consists of
    4 organizations
    5 internal (*interior* and *internal* can both refer to the inside of a physical object, but only *internal* is used about processes that happen inside an organization)
    6 framework / structure

4   1 a property / properties
       b properties
    2 a vehicle / vehicles
       b vehicles
    3 a body
       b body
    4 a assembly
       b assembly

Unit 10

1   1 interval
    2 continuous
    3 frequent
    4 potential
    5 initial
    6 forecast
    7 period

2   1 potential
    2 initially
    3 frequency
    4 continuous
    5 projections

3   1 B   2 B   3 A   4 A   5 A   6 B   7 A

4   1 forthcoming
    2 preliminary
    3 prior to / preceding
    4 preceding
    5 subsequently
    6 sequence
    7 ultimately
    8 following

5   suggested answers
    1 2   2 5   3 8   4 3   5 4   6 7   7 6

Unit 11

1   1 c   2 d   3 b   4 a

2   1 found / establish   2 arise / emerge
       3 undertake / commence   4 initiate / introduce

3   1 arise / emerge
    2 undertake / have undertaken / are undertaking
    3 emerged / emerge
    4 commencing / undertaking
    5 initiate
    6 founded / established
    7 established, introduced

4   suggested answers
    1 The Inuit ceased / stopped travelling south to trade goods and the previous trading network was eliminated / ended.
    2 The Inuit began to abandon their traditional spiritual beliefs.
    3 Because there is no work for them.
    4 If their job is terminated / ended permanently.

5   1 was eliminated
    2 abandon
    3 suspended
    4 terminated

6 1 introduction
2 establishment
3 suspension
4 emergence
5 elimination
6 foundation
7 cessation

Unit 12

1 1 fluctuated
2 range
3 dramatic
4 stabilized
5 underlying
6 maintain
7 successive

2 suggested answers
1 stabilized   2 rose steadily / increased steadily
3 fluctuated (slightly)   4 within the range of
5 the underlying trend

3 1 I   2 D   3 D   4 D

4 1 h/k   2 b/i   3 f/j   4 a/e   5 d/l   6 c/g

5 1 in
2 within
3 in
4 for
5 of
6 in

Unit 13

1 1 expansion
2 shape
3 shift
4 migrate
5 in response to

2 1 expand   2 evolution   3 respond
4 migration (the noun *migrant* also describes a
person who migrates)   5 shift

3 1 shifted / evolved (*evolved* is a less natural
alternative)
2 expansion
3 respond
4 shaping
5 evolved / expanded (*expanded* is a less natural
alternative)

4 1 amend   2 modify   3 transform   4 upheaval
5 substitute   6 replace

5 1 c; modifications were made
2 d; making the transition
3 b; re-evaluate the situation
4 f; amend the laws
5 g; implementing the changes
6 e; social / political upheavals
7 a; transform the way

Unit 14

1 **Formal:** 1 property   2 housing   3 dwelling
Neutral: 4 house   5 home   6 tower block

2 1 nationwide
2 properties
3 regenerate
4 facilities
5 local communities
6 most deprived

3 1 regeneration   2 facilities   3 deprived
4 properties   5 constructing

4 1 F (if a problem is *widespread*, it exists over a large
area)   2 F (an *isolated* community is far from
other places and does not have good transport
links)   3 T   4 T   5 T

5 a 1 c   2 e   3 g   4 h   5 d   6 b   7 f   8 a

5 b 1 property (*property* is a more general word (it can
be a house, an apartment, etc.) and it is more
formal)
2 widespread (*widespread* and *common* can be
synonyms, but *widespread* emphasizes how
many people/places are affected by something
and *common* emphasizes how frequent/usual
something is)
3 isolated (*isolated* can mean that someone feels
separate from other people for many reasons;
remote is only about physical distance)
4 renewal (*renewal* and *regeneration* can both be
about improving and repairing something, but
renewal can also refer to making something valid
for a further period of time)

Unit 15

1 1 siblings
2 marital partners
3 generation
4 inheritance

2 1 marital partners
2 relationships between
3 modes of inheritance

3 1 siblings
2 generation
3 relationships between
4 inherits
5 partner
6 related to
7 spouses

4 1 c   2 d   3 b   4 f   5 a   6 e

5 1 into
2 to
3 against
4 of
5 between

6 a partner
c immigrant
d family member
e sibling
f spouse

7 suggested answers
ethnic group
ethnic minority
first generation
future generations
marital partner
minority group
social class
social group
social status

Unit 16

1 1 C: the number of people or things in a particular area or space
2 D: the mass per unit volume of a solid, liquid or gas

2 1 dimensions, volume
2 density, proportion

3 1 range
2 dimensions
3 proportion
4 volumes
5 density
6 scope

4 1 S 2 S 3 L 4 L

5 1 adequate
2 exceeded
3 traces
4 predominant
5 accumulate
6 sole
7 maximum
8 of a lack of
9 minimal

6 1 substances
2 paper
3 people
4 traffic
5 understanding
6 options
7 bodies
8 acid

Review 2

1 1 rapport 2 relationship 3 perspectives
4 counseller / client 5 counsellor / client
6 evaluate

2 1 T ("Counselling aims to enable clients to help themselves to reach a more satisfying level of living …")
2 F (Rogers put forward the six core conditions)

3 T ("Egan incorporated Rogers' core conditions into his set of counselling skills which are divided into three stages.")
4 T ("Stage one aims to build up a rapport between counsellor and client …")
5 F (The counsellor uses five skills to help patients view their life from different perspectives)
6 T ("This stage encourages the client and the counsellor to collaborate and consider possible plans of action …")
7 F ("the stages are not used in isolation, but can be completed simultaneously (=at the same time)")
8 T ("… and repeated in response to the client's needs.")

3 a 1 c 2 e 3 f 4 b 5 a 6 d

3 b 1 dramatic 2 re-evaluate 3 introduced
4 response 5 make 6 composed 7 thin
8 preceding 9 widespread

3 c 1 demographic trend
2 physical properties

4 suggested answers
1 its establishment in 1586
2 suspended all operations at the plant
3 the frequency of such extreme weather events
4 put into categories according to their level of need
5 initial period, employees tend to be resistant to new working practices / initial stage, employees tend to be resistant to new working practices
6 adequately explain this gap
7 significant modifications were made to the design
8 are more adaptable to changing environmental conditions than others

Unit 17

1 1 b 2 c 3 d 4 a

2 1 E, C 2 C, E 3 E, C 4 C, E

3 1 e 2 c 3 d 4 a 5 b

4 1 in
2 of
3 for
4 between
5 for

5 suggested answers
1 a correlation
2 motivations for / factors affecting
3 resulted from / was a consequence of
4 the consequences of / the repercussions of
5 play a part in
6 priority
7 to ensure that

Unit 18

1 1 Mefford
   2 Colvin *et al.*

2 1 ✓
   2 However (the ideas are not completely opposite; the second idea just expresses one possible disadvantage)
   3 An alternative (the ideas are not contradictory, they are just alternatives)
   4 ✓

3 1 Conflicting
   2 alternative
   3 contradictory
   4 as opposed to
   5 variation
   6 distinct

4 1 MZ
   2 Differences between MZ twins are only due to environmental factors; genetic and environmental factors affect DZ twins.

5 1 alike / similar
   2 common / similar
   3 identical
   4 dissimilar
   5 analogy
   6 similarities

6 suggested answers
   1 Levels of pay across the country vary (greatly / considerably).
   2 Identical methods and procedures were used for both experiments. / The methods and procedures used for both experiments were identical.
   3 There are (a number of) similarities between the two organizations. / The two organizations have a number of similarities.
   4 There is conflicting evidence from the two studies.
   5 Neither this study nor others examining this approach have demonstrated any serious harm to patients. On the contrary, results seem to suggest that in general it improves the quality of care.

Unit 19

1 a 1 C   2 A   3 B

1 b 1 A   2 C   3 B

2 a 1 S   2 S   3 D   4 S   5 D   6 S   7 D   8 D

2 b 3 recurring (*arise* means to happen; *recur* means to happen again)
   5 a barrier (a *barrier* is something that prevents somebody from doing something; an *aid* is something that helps them to do it)
   7 impairment is (*impairment* refers to a problem with the body or brain; *barrier* refers to an external problem)

8 resolve (to *pose* a problem means to present a problem; to *resolve* a problem means to find a solution)

3 1 constraint, limitation
   2 criteria, requirements
   3 contingency
   4 account for
   5 impose on

4 1 account for
   2 contingencies
   3 constraints / limitations
   4 criteria / requirements
   5 impose

5 1 effects
   2 limitations
   3 requirements
   4 resolved, recurred

Unit 20

1 1 F (a *fact* can be confirmed or measured; a *claim* is just something a writer states)
   2 T
   3 T
   4 F (an argument that relies on *unsupported claims* is weak)
   5 F (a critical reader will question arguments, but then they may decide to agree or disagree with them)
   6 T

2 1 evidence
   2 source
   3 rely
   4 reject, claims
   5 Factual

3 1 b   2 d   3 c   4 a

4 1 compile   2 establish   3 secondary
   4 comprehensive   5 relevant   6 reliable

5 1 compile / collect
   2 collecting / compiling
   3 establish
   4 isn't always reliable
   5 relevant to
   6 sufficient
   7 comprehensive
   8 secondary source, primary source

Unit 21

1 1 d   2 a   3 c   4 b

2 1 b   2 h   3 g   4 a   5 d   6 e   7 c   8 f

3 1 develop
   2 practical
   3 factual
   4 theory

4
1 b
2 e
3 f (b and d are also real-world examples)
4 d
5 a
6 c

5
1 theoretical
2 definitions
3 hypothesize
4 metaphor
5 generalize

Unit 22

1 1 S   2 D (a *logical* analysis is based on facts or evidence; a *critical* analysis is based on careful judgements)   3 S   4 S   5 D (a *critical* appraisal will consider both positive and negative points)

2 a 1 a point
2 make
3 thinking, questions
4 argument

2 b 1 assessment
2 critical
3 evaluate / question
4 credible
5 question

2 c 1 assessments
2 critical
3 question
4 evaluate
5 credible

3 1 stance
2 convince
3 objective
4 reaction
5 responses
6 put forward
7 ignore
8 recognize

4 1 assessing
2 react to
3 analysed
4 recognition of
5 respond to

Unit 23

1 1 demands for government action
2 interests
3 perception of
4 ideology

2 1 a
2 b
3 b
4 b

3 1 symbolic
2 further
3 interests / lobby groups
4 pressure
5 lobby groups / interests
6 perception
7 ideology
8 supporters

4 b Whether or not it is better to leave the skin covering burn blisters unbroken.
c Whether the US Declaration of Independence is a basic part of the law and constitution.

5 1 Opponents of
2 advocates
3 Reformers
4 ambiguous
5 reluctant
6 a controversial issue

6 1 support   2 lobby   3 advocate   4 reform
5 oppose

7 1 oppose
2 supporter / opponent
3 advocates / supports / opposes
4 lobbying / to lobby
5 reformer

Unit 24

1 suggested answers
1 To encourage people to eat more fruit and vegetables (specifically, at least 5 portions of fruit or vegetables per day).
2 The groups formed successful partnerships with local organizations and it raised awareness of the benefits of eating fruit and vegetables.
3 The participants didn't significantly increase the amount of fruit and vegetables they ate.

2 a 1 significant
2 important
3 statistically significant

2 b 1 important
2 significant
3 statistically significant

3 1 aware
2 promote
3 positively
4 awareness
5 the positives

4 1 invalid
2 undermine
3 dismiss, reject
4 confused, incoherent
5 unconvincing, weak

5 1 coherent
2 accept
3 valid
4 compelling

6 1 flexible
2 realistic
3 robust
4 feasible
5 straightforward

7 1 c, d   2 a, f   3 e, h   4 b, g

Unit 25

1 1 misleading
2 unnecessary
3 inconsistent
4 unsustainable
5 unproductive

2 1 equal (notice that we say *inequality*, but *unequal*)
2 realistic   3 reliable   4 adequate   5 significant
6 valid   7 advantage   8 agree   9 organized
10 interpret   11 understand   12 use (*misuse*
is a verb (and a noun) meaning 'to use in an
inappropriate way'; there is also a noun, *disuse*,
meaning 'a situation in which something is no
longer used': *The building had fallen into disuse*)

3 1 unnecessary
2 unequal
3 misuse
4 disorganized
5 discourage

4 1 g   2 b   3 f   4 e   5 d   6 a   7 c

5 a 1 c
2 d
3 b
4 a (it is possible to say 'discourage the use' and
'restrict investment', but these don't appear in
the texts)

5 b 1 problem, threat
2 confidence, credibility
3 participation, smoking
4 access, movement

5 c 1 restrict
2 undermines
3 discourages
4 posed

Review 3

1 suggested answer
Overall, the writer is for the idea of AFNs.

2 1 P   2 P   3 N   4 N

3 1 O (the prefix *un-* usually makes an
opposite)   2 S   3 O (*ambiguous* is not clearly
stated or defined; *evident* is clear and easily
seen)   4 S   5 S   6 O (*conventional* follows the
way that something is usually or traditionally
done; *alternative* is different from the usual way)

4 a 1 N   2 P

4 b 1 persistent, restrict, Adverse, pose, consequence,
barrier
2 promoting, response, Similarly, reliable,
scenario

5 1 makes
2 played
3 arise
4 set
5 provide

6 1 to
2 from
3 between
4 on
5 under

Unit 26

1 1 emitted
2 specific
3 reduction
4 pursue
5 voluntarily, commit, regulatory

2 1 volunteers
2 emits
3 pursue
4 regulate
5 specifically
6 pollute
7 requirements
8 commit

3 1 -tion   2 -sion   3 -able   4 -ify   5 -ize   6 -ly
7 commitment / agreement / government /
environment / requirement / management
8 regulation / pollution / action / organization /
situation / protection / legislation / intervention /
restoration / completion   9 emission / provision /
mission / profession   10 neutral / physical /
international / global / industrial / formal / thermal /
legal / social / impartial / essential   11 attainable
12 separate   13 specify   14 recognize   15 legally /
physically / specifically   16 partly / unfairly /
exactly / effectively / easily / voluntarily

4 suggested answers
1 assist the children with completion of the
questionnaire
2 gained independence
3 physical disability
4 restore business confidence
5 are mentally ill
6 specify (limits on) how long samples can be
retained
7 political neutrality

Unit 27

1 1 C   2 U   3 U   4 U   5 U   6 U   7 C   8 C

2
1. preference; was
2. cooperation; has
3. formations; are
4. diversity; increases
5. concentrations; were
6. occurrence; has

3
1. F (if female hormones have a 'protective effect' against cardiovascular disease, we can infer that women are less likely to suffer from the disease)
2. T
3. F (larger companies are better able to carry out meaningful comparisons because they work with a wider range of different clients)

4
1. a correspondence between company size and the use of systematic benchmarking
2. differences between the attitudes of parents and teachers toward classroom discipline
3. the traditional practice of cooking and eating together as a family
4. a suitable method for evaluating the effects of computer games on children

5
1. of; occurrence; was
2. of, to; attitude; influences
3. between; interactions; develop
4. of, of, on; perception; is
5. of, between; degree; is
6. between / in; Differences; are

Unit 28

1
1. utilize 2. employ 3. obtain 4. acquire
5. gain 6. conduct 7. perform

2
1. gaining
2. implemented
3. acquire
4. exploited / utilized
5. obtaining
6. perform

3 put forward, conform to, result in, dispose of, end up

4
1. forward
2. in
3. of
4. out
5. to
6. of
7. on / upon

5
1. recover
2. establish
3. exclude
4. deduce

6
1. deduce
2. resolve
3. fluctuated
4. exclude
5. undergoing
6. monitor
7. compiled

Unit 29

1
1. T
2. F (data have shown that air polluted with smoke can be harmful, but scientists do not yet know exactly which elements in the smoke cause the harm)
3. F (the two theories offer *compatible* explanations)

2
1. of
2. on
3. of
4. to
5. of
6. for
7. with
8. from
9. for
10. with

3
1. The paper defines the key risk factors *responsible for* the development of the condition.
2. The exact *nature of* this process is unclear.
3. Several explanations have been *put forward for* the existence of these gaps.
4. Any *alterations* made *to* the terms of the contract must be agreed by both parties.
5. Any such agreement between airlines must be *compatible with* competition rules.
6. From one perspective, education can be viewed simply as the *accumulation of* knowledge.

4
1. with
2. on
3. assessing
4. with
5. to
6. of supporting

5
1. between
2. from, for
3. with
4. of, in, of
5. of, in, to
6. of, on, of, for

Unit 30

1 a 1 c 2 h 3 f 4 b 5 g 6 e 7 d

1 b
1. uniform
2. equivalent
3. interactive
4. transportation
5. automation

2
1. equi
2. inter
3. micro
4. tele
5. trans

3
1. d; noun 2 a; adjective 3 e; noun
4. b; adjective 5 c; noun

4
1 employer
2 invisible
3 account
4 action
5 adulthood (you would say *young adults*, NOT 'early adults')

5
1 disposable
2 manufacturers
3 reconstruct
4 interpreter
5 limitless / unlimited
6 interviewees
7 unreliable
8 cooperative

Unit 31

1
1 commission 2 noun 3 provide 4 make
5 strong 6 noun 7 method / data 8 directly

2
1 commissioned
2 directly
3 strong
4 do
5 qualitative
6 made

3 a
1 chemistry
2 any, computer science
3 any, law
4 medicine, any

3 b
1 initial, gas
2 follow, execute
3 rule, article
4 physician / primary care physician, reference

4
1 any
2 SD; law
3 SD; medicine / health sciences
4 any
5 any
6 SD; media studies / communication studies
7 SD; physics / astronomy / science
(*astronomical observations* involve viewing the stars and the planets through telescopes, etc.)

Unit 32

1
1 c 2 a 3 b

2
1 costs, drawbacks
2 exercise
3 considerable
4 recognize, acknowledge

3
1 a Starting from the assumption that
   b Based on the idea that (*premise, assumption* and *idea* all describe a possible idea that may or may not be true; the phrase *given that* implies something that is already accepted as true)
2 a regarding

c in terms of (*with regard to, regarding* and *in terms of* can all simply mean 'about'; *connected with* describes a link between two things)
3 a when it comes to
   c connected with (*when it comes to* is slightly informal but fits in the context; *in association with* typically describes a relationship between people or groups, not things or ideas)
4 b In contrast (*as opposed to* is used in the middle of a sentence to contrast two opposite ideas; *on the contrary* implies that the previous idea was wrong or incorrect (rather than just different)

4
1 b 2 a 3 c

5
1 Revenue / Income, income / revenue, income
2 challenging
3 corporation, Organization

6
1 revenues
2 panel
3 challenging
4 organizations
5 considerable
6 cost
7 positives

Unit 33

1 see usage note

2
1 to some extent (*somewhat* also fits in terms of meaning, but would not be within commas)
2 approximately
3 typically / primarily
4 primarily / typically
5 on average (*approximately* also fits in terms of meaning, but is not typically used at the end of a sentence)
6 somewhat
7 principal

3
1 d
2 a
3 c
4 e
5 b (*supposedly* and *allegedly* are very close in meaning; *supposedly* typically refers to a commonly held belief that has not been proven, whereas *allegedly* is used when someone has made a claim (they have alleged something) that has not yet been proven)

4
1 D (*so-called* is used to show that you do not think that the word or phrase that is being used to describe somebody or something is appropriate; *arguably* is used when you are stating an opinion that you belive you could give reasons to support) 2 S 3 S 4 D (*apparent* is used when something seems to be true, but may not be so; *so-called* is used to show that you do not think that the word or phrase that is being used to describe somebody or something is appropriate)

5
1 typical
2 seeming
3 primarily
4 alleged

6 suggested answers
1 *Apparently / Seemingly / Arguably*, dietary habits are *typically / to some extent* established in childhood.
2 In India, *approximately* 30% of the population is under the age of 14.
3 *Apparently / Allegedly*, a great deal of criminal activity is conducted via the *so-called* 'dark web': a part of the World Wide Web which is not available via conventional browsers.
4 Although men and women *theoretically / seemingly* have equal political rights in many countries, *typically* men still dominate in parliaments around the world.

Unit 34

1
1 fundamentally
2 severely, seriously
3 entirely
4 enormously, greatly

2
1 Bias from inaccurate instruments can result in *seriously* misleading results.
2 The migration of workers to large cities has *greatly* increased the urban population.
3 These brands benefitted *enormously* from the growing popularity of physical fitness.
4 In this group of patients, short-term memory is *severely* impaired.
5 Several of the studies rely *entirely* on evidence from interviews with managers.

3 1 G 2 H 3 F 4 E

4 1 c 2 e 3 b 4 a 5 d

5
1 fundamental
2 overwhelmingly
3 entirely
4 severe
5 inevitable
6 unavoidable

Unit 35

1 a 1 i 2 ii and iii

b 1 in-text citation   2 quotation marks
3 ellipsis   4 footnote

2
1 refer
2 quote
3 paraphrase
4 cited

3 suggested answers
1 D: argue that "despite the popular prejudice that unions are bad for performance, serious academic inquiry has failed to provide hard facts that would support this position".

2 There are examples of paraphrase in all the extracts:
B: note the importance of …, suggest that a housing policy …, comment that each stakeholder …
C: summarize the food and nutrition …
D: maintained that unions …
E: the whole extract paraphrases ideas from the source
3 B: Macdowall *et al.* (2006), Bonneyfoy *et al.* (2004), Taylor *et al.* (2003)
C: (Department of Health, 2005)
D: Metcalf (1986), Nolan and Marginson (1990)
E: (United Nations 2008).
4 B: note, suggest, comment
C: summarize
D: maintained, argue

4
1 c
2 e
3 a (several of the verbs can be followed by *that*, but this one fits best in terms of meaning)
4 d
5 b

5 1 c 2 b 3 a 4 d

Unit 36

1 suggested answers
1 Via social media.
2 Not completely because it's indirect contact.
3 No, it's an important factor, but in some cases other factors may be more important.
4 Translation is a part of the process which influences how these people view Shakespeare.
5 Because a translator has to decide how to deal with cultural and political issues within a text, this influences how people around the world view Shakespeare.
6 The tree cover grows again quickly (and so helps improve the soil).
7 No, some signs of the impact continue for decades.

2
1 via
2 hence / thereby
3 nonetheless / nevertheless
4 albeit
5 whereby
6 thereby / hence

3
1 namely, in other words
2 for instance, a case in point
3 the former = campaigns targeted at the whole population; the latter = campaigns targeted at high-risk groups

4
1 namely
2 a case in point
3 the former, the latter
4 For instance

5 suggested answers
1 a case in point
2 in all cases
3 For instance
4 in this case
5 in some instances

Review 4

1 1 acknowledging limitations   2 implications
3 citations

2 The final two sentences show the writer's stance. They believe that an approach which combines learning sign language with spoken skills will be the most useful.

3 1 language
2 process
3 severely, profoundly
4 have
5 have
6 means
7 risk
8 reach

4 1 exploit
2 challenging
3 gain
4 fundamentally
5 seriously

5 1 The findings revealed insights *into* the relationships between different environmental indicators.
2 The long working hours of MPs are not always compatible *with* family responsibilities.
3 This method of sampling is not systematic *in* terms of spatial distribution.
4 'Pharmacokinetics' refers *to* the processes involved in the delivery of a drug to its target site.
5 They should be assessed separately since the relevant variables are different *in* each case.
6 However, transferring knowledge *from* individuals to the wider organization presents practical challenges.

6 a 1 obtain   2 attain   3 incidence   4 existence
5 adapt   6 modify   7 variation   8 difference
9 somewhat   10 to some extent   11 in terms of
12 with reference to

6 b 1 existence (if something *exists*, it is there; if something *occurs*, it happens)
2 a somewhat (*in many respects* doesn't fit because the percentage is only larger in one way)
3 with reference to (the article *refers to* (= cites) the studies)
4 adapt (*adapt* can be an intransitive verb – sth adapts; *modify* is a transitive verb – sb modifies sth)
5 attain (*attain + a goal* is a strong collocation, you don't 'acquire goals')

6 differences (*diversity* is an uncountable noun and doesn't fit grammatically with the plural verb 'were')

Unit 37

1 1 formula   2 squared   3 symbol   4 equal to
5 mean   6 sum of

2 1 of
2 for
3 of
4 of
5 to
6 in
7 from

3 1 rounded up / rounded, whole number   2 down
3 digits   4 multiplied by   5 recording

4 1 all the numbers can be described as *values*
2 4, 9, 75
3 4, 9

5 1 formula
2 number
3 multiplied
4 equal
5 deviations
6 record
7 measure
8 variability

Unit 38

1 1 C   2 C   3 A   4 A   5 A   6 A

2 a 1 install   2 generate   3 energy   4 renewable

2 b 1 performance   2 capacity   3 Hybrid
4 conventional

3 1 unconventional
2 uninstall
3 non-renewable

4 1 prototype   2 model   3 demonstrate
4 techniques   5 specifications   6 functions

5 a 1 installation   2 perform   3 specify   4 function
5 demonstration (*demonstrator* is also a possible noun form, but not linked to this meaning)

5 b 1 installation
2 specify
3 generate
4 performance
5 function / perform

Unit 39

1 1 F (*diagnosis* involves identifying the cause of an illness, but not treating it)   2 T   3 F (*symptoms* are changes in your body or mind that show you are not healthy)   4 T   5 T   6 F (a person usually starts to show symptoms when they contract a disease)

2
1 a diagnosed
  b diagnosis
  c diagnostic
2 a examine
  b examination
3 a therapist
  b therapy
  c therapeutic
4 a infection, infect
  b Infectious
5 a transmitted
  b transmission

3 1 undergone 2 monitored 3 administer
4 stabilized

4 1 acute
2 fatal
3 terminal
4 chronic

5 1 b 2 c 3 a 4 d

Unit 40

1 1 b 2 c 3 a

2 1 Disaster relief
2 external
3 index
4 humanitarian aid
5 poverty
6 per capita
7 standard of living
8 literacy

3 1 values 2 norms 3 enforced 4 sanctions
5 prevalent

4 1 d 2 a 3 f 4 c 5 b 6 e

Unit 41

1 a The Schengen Agreement was designed to create stronger border controls within Europe.

2 1 rigid
2 incorporate into
3 abolish
4 enhance
5 harmonize
6 seek to

3 1 controls
2 harmonize
3 abolishing
4 provisions
5 rigid
6 treaty
7 enhancing
8 precondition

4 1 3 2 3

5 1 a 2 e 3 c 4 d 5 b

6 1 to establish
2 for
3 into the
4 for
5 to provide
6 from opening

Unit 42

1 1 D (*domestic* is used to talk about things that happen inside your own country; *foreign* refers to other countries) 2 S 3 S 4 S 5 D (a cooperative person is happy to work with others towards a shared aim; a reluctant person hesitates before doing something because they do not want to do it) 6 S

2 1 f 2 e 3 a 4 b 5 d 6 c

3 an area within a country

4 a 1 constitutional 2 federation 3 democracy
4 citizenship

4 b 1 citizen
2 constitutional
3 federal
4 democratic

5 1 T
2 F
3 F

6 1 regime
2 domestic politics
3 (closely) scrutinized
4 liberal
5 factions
6 unrest
7 international cooperative approach to the issue / cooperative international approach to the issue

Unit 43

1 1 T 2 T

2 1 stakeholder
2 assets
3 in line with
4 commodity

3 1 personnel
2 employee
3 workforce
4 labour

4 1 They decide to outsource the components (i.e. to have them made by an outside supplier).
2 Cost is the main factor.

5 1 d 2 b 3 a 4 c

6 1 assemble
2 manufacturers
3 components
4 suppliers
5 developmental

Unit 44

1 1 the Great Depression, the global financial crisis
   2 a depression is more serious and longer lasting
   3 a decreased
     b decreased
     c increased

2 1 financial
   2 finance
   3 economies
   4 economists
   5 economic

3 1 faces / is facing
   2 fall
   3 hit
   4 grew
   5 had / have

4 **suggested answers**
   1 low-income people
   2 1) Because their incomes fell / they became unemployed. 2) Because interest rates rose and they couldn't afford the higher repayments.
   3 They couldn't recover the value of the properties by selling them.
   4 A period of high house prices came to an end very suddenly.

5 1 loan
   2 lenders
   3 debt
   4 probability
   5 interest, borrow
   6 evident, markets
   7 crisis

6 1 2 2 8 3 5 4 6 5 1 6 4 7 3 8 7

Unit 45

1 1 b 2 d 3 a 4 c

2 1 formality
   2 finite
   3 implicit

3 1 linguistic
   2 native speakers
   3 discourse
   4 implicit
   5 finite

4 **suggested answers**
   1 high socioeconomic status, good education, good access to IT
   2 reliable internet access and the skills needed to use the internet
   3 1) they have resources to collect more information, 2) resources to spread information, 3) they have control of the flow of information and 4) control of content

5 1 D (*mass media* is not just 'the press'/newspapers, but also TV and radio)
   2 S
   3 D (*channels of communication* refers to any way of communicating, not just TV)
   4 D (*disseminate* means 'spread', not 'interpret')
   5 S
   6 S

6 1 c 2 e 3 a 4 d 5 b

Review 5

1 1 A 2 B, C 3 D 4 D

2 1 T ("Microfinance initiatives are aimed at individuals and communities who would not normally have access to financial services.")
   2 F ("It is worth noting that the women could easily have repaid their loan but chose not to do so ...")
   3 T ("The lender took no further action since the costs of recovering the loan would have been greater than the size of the loan itself.")
   4 T ("... the enterprise was of limited success, providing some short-term gains, but not securing the women and their families a continued income in the longer term.")
   5 F (the writer recommends that the lender should use a trusted local person to mediate with borrowers, i.e. to help explain the process to them and to make sure they repay the loan)

3 1 an income for sb
   2 no further action
   3 the effectiveness of sth
   4 an ability to do sth
   5 the consequences of sth
   6 the progress of sth

4 1 d 2 a 3 b 4 f 5 c 6 e

5 **suggested answers**
   1 *demonstrates* the way in which direct action can have a major impact on policy / *demonstrates* how direct action can have a major impact on policy
   2 more *evident* in larger classes
   3 *implicitly* assumes that the entrepreneur starts their new business in the same sector they previously worked in
   4 the *provision* of health care information online in two different areas / the *provision* of online health care information in two different areas
   5 provided (most of) the *financial* support / assistance for the project

Glossary

abandon AWL /əˈbændən/ *v* **1** to stop doing sth, especially before it is finished; to stop planning to do sth U11 **2** to stop believing in sth or supporting a party, cause, etc. U11 WF **abandonment** *n*

abolish /əˈbɒlɪʃ/ *v* to officially end a system, practice, institution or law U41 WF **abolition** *n*

abstract¹ AWL /ˈæbstrækt/ *adj* existing in thought or as an idea but not as a physical thing U21 WF **abstractly** *adv*

abstract² AWL /ˈæbstrækt/ *n* a short piece of writing containing the main ideas of a research article, book or speech U4

academic AWL /ˌækəˈdemɪk/ *n* a person who teaches and/or does research at a university or college U1 WF **academia** *n*, **academically** *adv*, **academy** *n*

accept /əkˈsept/ *v* to believe or recognize that an idea is true or valid U24 WF **acceptable** *adj*, **acceptance** *n*

access AWL /ˈækses/ *n* the opportunity or right to use or get sth, or to see sb/sth U45 WF **access** *v*, **accessibility** *n*, **accessible** *adj*, **inaccessible** *adj*

accessible AWL /əkˈsesəbl/ *adj* that can be reached, entered, used or obtained U9

accountable /əˈkaʊntəbl/ *adj* responsible for your decisions or actions and expected to explain them when you are asked U30

account for /əˈkaʊnt fɔː(r)/ *phr v* **1** to give an explanation for or description of sth U19 **2** to be the explanation or cause of sth U19 WF **account** *n*, **accountable** *adj*

accumulate AWL /əˈkjuːmjəleɪt/ *v* **1** to gradually get more and more of sth over a period of time U16 **2** to gradually increase in number or quantity over a period of time U16 WF **accumulation** *n*

acknowledge AWL /əkˈnɒlɪdʒ/ *v* **1** to accept that sth is true or exists U4 **2** to accept that sb/sth has a particular quality, importance or status U4 WF **acknowledgement** *n*

acquire AWL /əˈkwaɪə(r)/ *v* to learn or develop a skill, habit or quality U28 WF **acquisition** *n*

active /ˈæktɪv/ *adj* always busy doing things, especially physical activities U30 WF **actively** *adv*, **activity** *n*

adapt AWL /əˈdæpt/ *v* **1** to change sth in order to make it suitable for a new use or situation U13 **2** (of a person, animal, plant, etc.) to change your/its behaviour in order to deal more successfully with a new situation U13 WF **adaptable** *adj*, **adaptability** *n*, **adaptation** *n*

adequate AWL /ˈædɪkwət/ *adj* enough in quantity, or good enough in quality, for a particular purpose or need U16 WF **adequacy** *n*, **adequately** *adv*, **inadequate** *adj*

adjust AWL /əˈdʒʌst/ *v* to change sth slightly to make it more suitable for a new set of conditions or to make it work better U12 WF **adjustment** *n*

administer /ədˈmɪnɪstə(r)/ *v* to give drugs or medicine to sb U39 WF **administration** *n*

adulthood AWL /ˈædʌlthʊd/ *n* (of a person, animal, fish, etc.) the state of being fully grown or developed U30 WF **adult** *adj n*

adverse /ədˈvɜːs/ *adj* negative and unpleasant; not likely to produce a good result U19 WF **adversely** *adv*, **adversity** *n*

advocate AWL /ˈædvəkeɪt/ *v* to support or recommend sth publicly U23 WF **advocacy** *n*, **advocate** *n*

agency /ˈeɪdʒənsi/ *n* (pl. -ies) (especially NAmE) a government department that provides a particular service U9 WF **agent** *n*

aid AWL /eɪd/ *v* to help sb/sth to do sth, especially by making it easier U19 WF **aid** *n*

aim /eɪm/ *n* the purpose of doing sth; what sb is trying to achieve U7 WF **aim** *v*

albeit AWL /ˌɔːlˈbiːɪt/ *conj* although U36

alike /əˈlaɪk/ *adj* very similar U18 WF **alike** *adv*

allegedly /əˈledʒd/ *adv* used to show that sth is stated as a fact although there is no proof U33 WF **allegation** *n*, **allege** *v*, **alleged** *adj*

allocation AWL /ˌæləˈkeɪʃn/ *n* the act of giving sth to sb for a particular purpose U29 WF **allocate** *v*

alteration AWL /ˌɔːltəˈreɪʃn/ *n* **1** a change to sth U29 **2** the action of changing sth; the process of being changed U29 WF **alter** *v*

alternative AWL /ɔːlˈtɜːnətɪv/ *adj* **1** that can be used instead of sth else U18 **2** different from the usual or traditional way in which sth is done U18 WF **alternative** *n*, **alternatively** *adv*

ambiguous AWL /æmˈbɪɡjuəs/ *adj* **1** that can be understood in more than one different way U23 **2** not clearly stated or defined U23 WF **ambiguity** *n*, **ambiguously** *adv*, **unambiguous** *adj*

amend AWL /əˈmend/ *v* to change a law, an agreement or a document slightly to improve or correct it or to reflect changing circumstances U13 WF **amendment** *n*

analogy AWL /əˈnælədʒi/ *n* (pl. -ies) a comparison of one thing with another thing that has similar features, usually in order to explain it; a feature that is similar U18 WF **analogous** *adj*

analyse AWL /ˈænəlaɪz/ *v* to examine the nature or structure of sth, especially by separating it into its parts, in order to understand or explain it U6 WF **analysis** *n*, **analyst** *n*, **analytic** *adj*, **analytical** *adj*, **analytically** *adv*

analysis AWL /əˈnæləsɪs/ *n* (pl. analyses /əˈnæləsiːz/) the detailed study or examination of sth in order to understand more about it; the result of the study U22

ancient /ˈeɪnʃənt/ *adj* belonging to a period of history that is thousands of years in the past U3

anthropology /ˌænθrəˈpɒlədʒi/ *n* **1** the study of the human race by comparing human societies and cultures and how they have developed U3 **2** the study of the human race by examining how humans behave and how their bodies work and have changed during their development U3 WF **anthropological** *adj*, **anthropologically** *adv*, **anthropologist** *n*

apparent AWL /əˈpærənt/ *adj* that seems to be true, but may not be so U33 WF **apparently** *adv*

appendix AWL /əˈpendɪks/ (pl. appendices /əˈpendɪsiːz/ or appendixes /əˈpendɪksɪz/) *n* a section of extra information at the end of a book, article or other document U4 WF **append** *v*

applied sciences /əˌplaɪd ˈsaɪənsɪz/ *n* (pl.) the areas of science concerned with studying the use of scientific knowledge to solve practical problems, for example engineering and computer science U2

approximately AWL /əˈprɒksɪmətli/ *adv* (abbr. approx.) in a way that is almost accurate or exact, but not completely so U33 WF **approximate** *adj v*, **approximation** *n*

archaeology /ˌɑːkiˈɒlədʒi/ *n* the study of cultures of the past, and periods of history by examining the remains of buildings and objects found in the ground U3 WF **archaeological** *adj*, **archaeologist** *n*

arguably /ˈɑːɡjuəbli/ *adv* used when you are stating an opinion that you believe you could give reasons to support U33

argue /ˈɑːɡjuː/ *v* to give reasons why you think that sth is right/wrong, true/not true, etc., especially to persuade people that you are right U35 WF **arguable** *adj*, **arguably** *adv*, **argument** *n*

arise /əˈraɪz/ *v* (arose /əˈrəʊz/, arisen /əˈrɪzn/) **1** (of a problem, opportunity or situation) to happen and start to be noticed U11 **2** to happen as a result of a particular situation U11

arrow /ˈærəʊ/ *n* a mark or sign (→), used to show direction or position U5

as opposed to /ˌæz əˈpəʊzd tu/ *phr* used to make a contrast between two things or people U18

assemble AWL /əˈsembl/ *v* to fit together all the separate parts of sth U43 WF **assembly** *n*

assembly AWL /əˈsembli/ *n* (pl. -ies) **1** (also Assembly) a group of people who have been elected to meet together regularly and make decisions or laws for a particular region or country U9 **2** the process of putting together the parts of sth U9

assessment AWL /əˈsesmənt/ *n* **1** the act of judging or forming an opinion about sb/sth; an occasion when this is done U1 **2** an opinion or a judgement about sb/sth that has been thought about very carefully U22 WF **assess** *v*

asset /ˈæset/ *n* **1** a person or thing that is valuable or useful to sb/sth U43 **2** a thing of value, especially property, that a person or company owns, which can be used or sold to pay debts U43

assignment AWL /əˈsaɪnmənt/ *n* a task or piece of work that sb is given to do, usually as part of their job or studies; the act of giving a task to sb U1 WF **assign** *v*

assistance AWL /əˈsɪstəns/ *n* help or support in the form of money, resources, information or practical action U26 WF **assist** *v*, **assistant** *n*, **unassisted** *adj*

associated with /əˈsəʊʃieɪtɪd wɪð/ *phr* if one thing is associated with another, the two things are connected because they happen together or one thing causes the other U32 WF **associate** *adj n v*

assumption AWL /əˈsʌmpʃn/ *n* a belief or feeling that sth is true or that sth will happen, although there is no proof U21 WF **assume** *v*

attainable AWL /əˈteɪnəbl/ *adj* that you can achieve U26 WF **attain** *v*, **attainment** *n*, **unattainable** *adj*

attitude AWL /ˈætɪtjuːd/ *n* a way of thinking or feeling about sb/sth; the way of behaving towards sb/sth that shows how sb thinks or feels U27

attribute AWL /əˈtrɪbjuːt/ *v* to say or believe that sth is the result of a particular thing U27 WF **attributable** *adj*, **attribute** *n*, **attribution** *n*

automation AWL /ˌɔːtəˈmeɪʃn/ *n* the use or introduction of machines to do work that was previously done by people U30 WF **automatic** *adj*, **automatically** *adv*

awareness AWL /əˈweənəs/ *n* **1** the fact of knowing that sth is true or exists U24 **2** concern or interest in a particular situation or development U24 WF **aware** *adj*, **unaware** *adj*

axis /ˈæksɪs/ *n* (pl. axes /ˈæksiːz/) a fixed line against which the positions of points are measured, especially points on a graph U5

bar chart /ˈbɑː tʃɑːt/ *n* a diagram that uses lines or narrow bars of different heights (but equal widths) to show different amounts, so that they can be compared U5

barrier /ˈbæriə(r)/ *n* a problem, rule or situation that prevents sb from doing sth, or that makes sth impossible U19

base upon /ˈbeɪs əpɒn/ *phr v* to use an idea, a fact or situation as the point from which sth can be developed U21 WF **base** *n*, **basis** *n*

benchmarking /ˈbentʃmɑːk/ *n* the process of judging the standard of sth in relation to other similar things U27 WF **benchmark** *n v*

biased AWL /ˈbaɪəst/ *adj* giving results that are not fair or accurate, often because of a lack of balance in the way that information has been collected U7 WF **bias** *n v*, **unbiased** *adj*

bibliography /ˌbɪbliˈɒɡrəfi/ *n* (pl. -ies) the list of books, etc. that have been used by sb writing an article, essay, etc.; a list of books or articles about a particular subject or by a particular author U4

biology /baɪˈɒlədʒi/ *n* the scientific study of the life and structure of plants and animals U2 WF **biological** *adj*, **biologist** *n*

body /ˈbɒdi/ *n* (pl. -ies) a group of people who work or act together, often for an official purpose, or who are connected in some other way U9

borrower /ˈbɒrəʊə(r)/ *n* a person or an organization that borrows money, especially from a bank U44 WF **borrow** *v*

calculation /ˌkælkjuˈleɪʃn/ *n* the act or process of using numbers to find out an amount U6 WF **calculate** *v*, **calculator** *n*

capable AWL /ˈkeɪpəbl/ *adj* having the ability or qualities necessary for doing sth U29 WF **capability** *n*, **incapable** *adj*

capacity AWL /kəˈpæsəti/ *n* (pl. -ies) the size or power of a piece of equipment, especially the engine of a vehicle U38

carry out /ˌkæri ˈaʊt/ *phr v* (carries, carrying, carried) to do and complete a task U6

a case in point /ə ˌkeɪs ɪn ˈpɔɪnt/ *phr* a clear example of the situation or problem that is being discussed U36

cash flow /ˈkæʃ fləʊ/ *n* the movement of money into and out of a business as goods are bought and sold U43

category AWL /ˈkætəɡəri/ *n* (pl. -ies) a group of people or things with particular features in common U8 WF **categorize** *v*, **categorization** *n*

cause /kɔːz/ *n* an organization or idea that people support or fight for U23 WF **cause** *v*

cease AWL /siːs/ *v* **1** to stop happening or existing U11 **2** to stop doing sth U11 WF **ceaseless** *adj*

ceaseless /ˈsiːsləs/ *adj* not stopping; seeming to have no end U30

challenging AWL /ˈtʃælɪndʒɪŋ/ *adj* difficult in an interesting way that tests your ability U32 WF **challenge** *n v*

channel AWL /ˈtʃænl/ *n* **1** a way of sending and receiving information or goods U45 **2** a television station U45 WF **channel** *v*

characterize, -ise /ˈkærəktəraɪz/ *v* to describe sth/sb in a particular way U8 WF **character** *n*, **characteristic** *adj n*, **characteristically** *adv*

chemistry /ˈkemɪstri/ *n* (pl. -ies) the scientific study of substances, including the study of their chemical structures, properties and reactions U2 WF **chemical** *adj*, **chemically** *adv*, **chemist** *n*

chronic /ˈkrɒnɪk/ *adj* (especially of a disease) lasting for a long time; difficult to cure or get rid of U39 WF **chronically** *adv*

circumstance AWL /ˈsɜːkəmstɑːns/ *n* (usually pl.) the conditions and facts that are connected with and affect a situation, an event or action U21 WF **circumstantial** *adj*

cite AWL /saɪt/ *v* to speak or write words taken from another writer or speaker; to give a reference, usually consisting of a name and date, that identifies the original writer or speaker of these words U35 WF **citation** *n*

citizen /ˈsɪtɪzn/ *n* a person who has the legal right to belong to a particular country U42 WF **citizenship** *n*

civil engineering /ˌsɪvl ˌendʒɪˈnɪərɪŋ/ *n* the design, building and repair of roads, bridges, canals, etc.; the study of this as a subject U2

civilization, -isation /ˌsɪvəlaɪˈzeɪʃn/ *n* a society, its culture and its way of life during a particular period of time or in a particular part of the world U3 WF **civilized** *adj*

claim /kleɪm/ *n* a statement that sth is true although it has not been proved and other people may not agree with or believe it U20 WF **claim** *v*

class /klɑːs/ *n* **1** one of the groups of people in society that are thought of as being the same social or economic level U15 **2** the way that people are divided into different social and economic groups U15 **3** a group of things that have similar characteristics or qualities U8 **4** (biology) a group into which animals, plants or other life forms are divided U8 WF **class** *v*

classify /ˈklæsɪfaɪ/ *v* (classifies, classifying, classified) **1** to arrange sb/sth in groups according to features that they have in common U8 **2** to decide which type or group sb/sth belongs to U8 WF **classification** *n*

coherent AWL /kəʊˈhɪərənt/ *adj* (of an argument, theory, statement or policy) logical and well organized; easy to understand and clear U24 WF **coherence** *n*, **coherently** *adv*, **incoherent** *adj*, **incoherence** *n*

coincidence AWL /kəʊˈɪnsɪdəns/ *n* the fact of two things happening at the same time by chance, often in a surprising way U17 WF **coincide** *v*, **coincidental** *adj*, **coincidentally** *adv*

collapse AWL /kəˈlæps/ *n* **1** a sudden failure of sth, such as an institution, a system, business or course of action U12 **2** a sudden fall in value U12 WF **collapse** *v*

collect /kəˈlekt/ *v* to bring things together from different people or places U20 WF **collection** *n*, **collective** *adj*, **collectively** *adv*

come into contact with AWL /ˌkʌm ɪntə ˈkɒntækt wɪð/ *phr* to meet sb or experience sth U29 WF **contact** *v*

commence AWL /kəˈmens/ *v* to begin sth; to begin to happen U11 WF **commencement** *n*, **recommence** *v*

comment AWL /ˈkɒment/ *v* to express an opinion about sth U35 WF **comment** *n*, **commentary** *n*, **commentator** *n*

commentator AWL /ˈkɒmənteɪtə(r)/ *n* a person who is an expert on a particular subject and talks or writes about it, especially on television or radio or in a newspaper U45

commerce /ˈkɒmɜːs/ *n* trade, especially between countries; the buying and selling of goods and services U3 WF **commercial** *adj*, **commercialize** *v*, **commercialization** *n*, **commercially** *adv*

commission AWL /kəˈmɪʃn/ *v* to officially ask sb to write, make or create sth or to do a task for you U31 WF **commission** *n*, **commissioner** *n*

commitment AWL /kəˈmɪtmənt/ *n* a promise to do sth or to behave in a particular way U26 WF **commit** *v*

commodity AWL /kəˈmɒdəti/ *n* (pl. -ies) a product or raw material that can be bought and sold U43

common /ˈkɒmən/ *adj* (commoner, commonest) (more common and most common are more frequent) shared by or belonging to two or more people, groups or things, or by the people or things in a group U18 WF **commonly** *adv*

communication AWL /kəˌmjuːnɪˈkeɪʃn/ *n* **1** (also communications) (pl.) methods of sending information, especially telephones, radio, computers, etc. U14 **2** communications (pl.) methods of travelling or transporting goods, such as roads and railways U14 WF **communicate** *v*, **communicative** *adj*, **communicatively** *adv*

community AWL /kəˈmjuːnəti/ *n* all the people who live in a particular area, country, etc. when considered as a group U14

compatible AWL /kəmˈpætəbl/ *adj* (of ideas, policies or methods) able to exist together or be used together, despite differences U29 WF **compatibility** *n*, **incompatible** *adj*, **incompatibility** *n*

compelling /kəmˈpelɪŋ/ *adj* that makes you think it is true or valid U24

compile AWL /kəmˈpaɪl/ *v* to produce a book, list, report, etc. by bringing together information from different places U20 WF **compilation** *n*

component AWL /kəmˈpəʊnənt/ *n* one of several parts that combine together to make a system, machine or substance U43

composition /ˌkɒmpəˈzɪʃn/ *n* the different parts that sth is made of; the way in which the different parts are organized U9 WF **compose** *v*

comprehensive AWL /ˌkɒmprɪˈhensɪv/ *adj* including all, or almost all, the items or information that may be concerned U20 WF **comprehensively** *adv*

comprise AWL /kəmˈpraɪz/ *v* (not used in the progressive tenses) to have sb/sth as parts or members U16

concentration AWL /ˌkɒnsnˈtreɪʃn/ *n* the amount of a substance in a liquid or in another substance U27 WF **concentrate** *v*

concept AWL /ˈkɒnsept/ *n* an idea; a basic principle U21 WF **conceptual** *adj*, **conceptually** *adv*

conclusion AWL /kənˈkluːʒn/ *n* **1** an opinion that you reach after thinking about all the information connected with a situation U4 **2** the end of sth such as a piece of writing or a process U4 WF **inconclusive** *adj*, **conclude** *v*, **conclusive** *adj*, **conclusively** *adv*

condition of /kənˈdɪʃn ɒv/ *phr* a situation that must exist in order for sth else to happen U17 WF **conditional** *adj*, **conditionally** *adv*, **precondition** *n*

conduct [AWL] /kənˈdʌkt/ *v* to organize and/or do a particular activity U6 WF **conduct** *n*

confidential /ˌkɒnfɪˈdenʃl/ *adj* intended to be kept secret U7 WF **confidentiality** *n*, **confidentially** *adv*

confined to [AWL] /kənˈfaɪnd tu/ *v* kept inside the limits of a particular activity, subject or area U14

confirm [AWL] /kənˈfɜːm/ *v* to state or show that sth is definitely true or correct, especially by providing evidence U7 WF **confirmation** *n*

conflicting [AWL] /kənˈflɪktɪŋ/ *adj* (of two ideas, opinions, reports, etc.) that cannot exist together or both be true U18 WF **conflict** *n v*

conform to /kənˈfɔːm tu/ *phr v* to agree with or match sth U28

consent [AWL] /kənˈsent/ *n* permission that you give for sth, especially sth that affects you personally U7 WF **consensus** *n*, **consent** *v*

consequence [AWL] /ˈkɒnsɪkwəns/ *n* (often plural) a result of sth that has happened U17 WF **consequent** *adj*, **consequently** *adv*

considerable [AWL] /kənˈsɪdərəbl/ *adj* great in amount, size or importance U32 WF **considerably** *adv*

consist of [AWL] /kənˈsɪst ɒv/ *phr v* (not used in the progressive tenses) to be formed from the people or things mentioned U9

constitution [AWL] /ˌkɒnstɪˈtjuːʃn/ *n* the system of laws and basic principles that a state, country or an organization is governed by U42 WF **constitute** *v*, **constitutional** *adj*, **constitutionally** *adv*, **unconstitutional** *adj*

constraint [AWL] /kənˈstreɪnt/ *n* a thing that limits or restricts sth or your freedom to do sth U19 WF **constrain** *v*, **constrained** *adj*, **unconstrained** *adj*

construct [AWL] /kənˈstrʌkt/ *v* to build or make sth such as a road, building or machine U14 WF **construction** *n*, **constructive** *adj*, **reconstruct** *v*, **reconstruction** *n*

consult [AWL] /kənˈsʌlt/ *v* **1** to go to sb for information or advice, especially an expert such as a doctor or lawyer U31 **2** to look in or at sth to get information U31 WF **consultancy** *n*, **consultant** *n*, **consultation** *n*, **consultative** *adj*

content /ˈkɒntent/ *n* the subject matter of a book, speech, programme, etc. U45

context [AWL] /ˈkɒntekst/ *n* the situation or set of circumstances in which sth happens and that helps you to understand it U21 WF **contextual** *adj*, **contextualize** *v*

contingency /kənˈtɪndʒənsi/ *n* (pl. -ies) an event that may happen but that is not certain to happen U19

continuous /kənˈtɪnjuəs/ *adj* happening or existing for a period of time without interruption U10 WF **continuously** *adv*

contract¹ [AWL] /ˈkɒntrækt/ *n* an official written agreement, especially one concerned with employment or selling sth U41 WF **contractor** *n*, **contractual** *adj*, **contractually** *adv*

contract² [AWL] /kənˈtrækt/ *v* to get an illness U39

contradict [AWL] /ˌkɒntrəˈdɪkt/ *v* (of statements or pieces of evidence) to be so different from each other that one of them must be wrong U18 WF **contradiction** *n*, **contradictory** *adj*

contribute [AWL] /ˈkɒntrɪbjuːt/ *v* to be one of the causes of sth U17 WF **contribution** *n*, **contributor** *n*

control /kənˈtrəʊl/ *n* **1** the power to direct how a company, country, etc. is run or to influence a process or a course of events U41 **2** (often in compounds) the act of restricting, limiting or managing sth; a method of doing this U41 **3** (often in compounds) a person, group or thing used as a standard of comparison for checking the results of a survey or an experiment; an experiment whose result is known, used for checking working methods U41 **4** a place where checks are made; the people who make these checks U41 WF **control** *v*

controversial [AWL] /ˌkɒntrəˈvɜːʃl/ *adj* causing a lot of angry public discussion and disagreement U23 WF **controversially** *adv*, **controversy** *n*, **uncontroversial** *adj*

conventional [AWL] /kənˈvenʃənl/ *adj* **1** based on what is generally believed; following the way sth is usually done U38 **2** (especially of weapons) not nuclear U38 WF **convention** *n*, **conventionally** *adv*, **unconventional** *adj*

conversely [AWL] /ˈkɒnvɜːsli/ *adv* in a way that is the opposite of sth U18 WF **converse** *n*

convert [AWL] /kənˈvɜːt/ *v* **1** to change the form, use or character of sth; to change from one form, purpose or system to another U29 **2** to be able to change or be changed from one form or purpose to another U29 WF **conversion** *n*, **convert** *n*, **convertible** *adj*

convince [AWL] /kənˈvɪns/ *v* to make sb/yourself believe that sth is true U22 WF **convincing** *adj*, **convincingly** *adv*, **unconvincing** *adj*

cooperation [AWL] /kəʊˌɒpəˈreɪʃn/ *n* the action or process of working together towards a shared aim U27 WF **cooperate** *v*, **cooperative** *adj*, **cooperatively** *adv*, **uncooperative** *adj*

cooperative [AWL] /kəʊˈɒpərətɪv/ *adj* involving working together with others towards a shared aim U42

coordination [AWL] /kəʊˌɔːdɪˈneɪʃn/ *n* the process of making the parts of sth or groups of people work together in an efficient and organized way U27 WF **coordinate** *v*, **coordinator** *n*

core [AWL] /kɔː(r)/ *n* **1** the central part of an object U9 **2** the central inner part of a planet or star U9 WF **core** *adj*

corporation [AWL] /ˌkɔːpəˈreɪʃn/ *n* (abbr. **Corp.**) a large business company, or a group of companies that is recognized by law as a single unit U32 WF **corporate** *adj*

correlation /ˌkɒrəˈleɪʃn/ *n* a connection between two things in which one thing changes as the other does U17 WF **correlate** *v*

correspondence [AWL] /ˌkɒrəˈspɒndəns/ *n* (formal) a connection between two things; the fact of two things being similar U27 WF **corresponding** *adj*, **correspondingly** *adv*

coup /kuː/ *n* (pl. **coups** /kuːz/) a sudden change of government that is illegal and often violent U42

coursework /ˈkɔːswɜːk/ *n* work that students do during a course of study, not in exams, that is included in their final grade U1 WF **course** *n*

crash /kræʃ/ *n* a sudden serious fall in the price or value of sth; the occasion when a business suddenly fails U44 WF **crash** *v*

creative AWL /kriˈeɪtɪv/ *adj* involving the use of skill and imagination to produce sth new U3 WF **creation** *n*, **creatively** *adv*, **creator** *n*, **recreate** *v*

credible /ˈkredəbl/ *adj* that can be believed or trusted U22 WF **credibly** *adv*, **credibility** *n*

creditor AWL /ˈkredɪtə(r)/ *n* a person, country or an organization that sb/sth owes money to U44 WF **credit** *n* *v*

crisis /ˈkraɪsɪs/ *n* (pl. crises /ˈkraɪsiːz/) a time of great danger, difficulty or confusion when problems must be solved or important decisions made U44

criterion AWL /kraɪˈtɪəriən/ *n* (pl. criteria /kraɪˈtɪəriə/) a standard or principle by which sth is judged, or with the help of which a decision is made U8 U19

critical /ˈkrɪtɪkl/ *adj* **1** involving making fair, careful judgements about the good and bad qualities of sb/sth U22 **2** expressing disapproval of sb/sth and saying what you think is bad about them/it U22 WF **critically** *adv*, **criticism** *n*, **criticize** *v*

critique /krɪˈtiːk/ *n* a detailed and usually critical examination and analysis of a system, situation, set of ideas or work of art U35 WF **critique** *v*

crucial AWL /ˈkruːʃl/ *adj* extremely important, because it will affect other things U34 WF **crucially** *adv*

cultural AWL /ˈkʌltʃərəl/ *adj* connected with the customs, beliefs, art, way of life or social organization of a particular country or group U3 WF **culturally** *adv*, **culture** *n*, **cultured** *adj*, **uncultured** *adj*

curve /kɜːv/ *n* (statistics) a line on a graph (either straight or curved) showing how one quantity varies with respect to another U5 WF **curve** *v*

data AWL /ˈdeɪtə/ *n* (pl.) facts or figures, especially when examined and used to find out things or to make decisions U7

debt /det/ *n* **1** a sum of money that sb owes U44 **2** the situation of owing money, especially when you cannot pay U44 WF **debtor** *n*

decline AWL /dɪˈklaɪn/ *n* a continuous decrease in the number, strength, value, etc. of sth U12 WF **decline** *v*

deduce AWL /dɪˈdjuːs/ *v* to form an opinion about sth based on the information or evidence that is available U28 WF **deduction** *n*, **deductive** *adj*

defect /ˈdiːfekt/ *n* something that is wrong with or missing from sb/sth U25 WF **defect** *v*, **defective** *adj*

define AWL /dɪˈfaɪn/ *v* to say or explain what the meaning of a word or phrase is U21 WF **definition** *n*, **definable** *adj*, **redefine** *v*, **undefined** *adj*

degree /dɪˈɡriː/ *n* **1** a qualification obtained by a student who successfully completes a university or college course U1 **2** (BrE) a university or college course, normally lasting three years or more U1

democratic /ˌdeməˈkrætɪk/ *adj* **1** (of a country or system) controlled by representatives who are elected by the people of a country; connected with this system U42 **2** (of an organization or society) based on the principle that everyone has an equal right to be involved in making decisions U42 WF **democracy** *n*, **democratically** *adv*

demographic /ˌdeməˈɡræfɪk/ *adj* connected with the population and different groups within it U12 WF **demographic** *n*, **demographically** *adv*, **demography** *n*

demonstrate AWL /ˈdemənstreɪt/ *v* **1** to show sth clearly by giving proof or evidence U38 **2** to show and explain how sth works or how to do sth U38 WF **demonstrable** *adj*, **demonstrably** *adv*, **demonstration** *n*, **demonstrator** *n*

density /ˈdensəti/ *n* (pl. -ies) **1** the number of people or things in a particular area or space U16 **2** (physics) the mass per unit volume of a solid, liquid or gas U16 WF **dense** *adj*, **densely** *adv*

deprived /dɪˈpraɪvd/ *adj* without all the things that are necessary for people to live a happy and comfortable life U14 WF **deprive** *v*, **deprivation** *n*

derive AWL /dɪˈraɪv/ *v* (be) derived from sth to come or develop from sth U29 WF **derivation** *n*, **derivative** *adj* *n*

detect AWL /dɪˈtekt/ *v* to discover or notice sth that is difficult to discover or notice U19 WF **detectable** *adj*, **detection** *n*, **detective** *n*, **detector** *n*

developmental /dɪˌveləpˈmentl/ *adj* **1** developing or being developed U43 **2** connected with the development of sb/sth U43 WF **develop** *v*, **developed** *adj*, **developing** *adj*, **development** *n*

deviation AWL /ˌdiːviˈeɪʃn/ *n* (statistics) the amount by which a single measurement is different from a fixed value such as the mean U37 WF **deviate** *v*

diagnosis /ˌdaɪəɡˈnəʊsɪs/ *n* (pl. diagnoses /ˌdaɪəɡˈnəʊsiːz/) the act of discovering or identifying the exact cause of an illness or a problem U39 WF **diagnose** *v*, **diagnostic** *adj*

diagram /ˈdaɪəɡræm/ *n* a simple drawing using lines to explain where sth is, how sth works, etc. U5

differentiate between AWL /ˌdɪfəˈrenʃieɪt bɪtwiːn/ *phr v* to recognize or show what makes sb/sth different U18 WF **differentiation** *n*

digit /ˈdɪdʒɪt/ *n* any of the numbers from zero to nine U37 WF **digital** *adj*, **digitally** *adv*

dimension AWL /daɪˈmenʃn/ *n* a measurement such as length or height; the size or extent of sth U16 WF **dimensional** *adj*, **multidimensional** *adj*

direct /dɪˈrekt/ *adj* happening or done without involving other people or factors; having no one or nothing in between U17 WF **direct** *adv* *v*, **direction** *n*, **directly** *adv*

discipline /ˈdɪsəplɪn/ *n* a subject of study, especially in a university U1

discourage /dɪsˈkʌrɪdʒ/ *v* **1** to try to prevent sth from happening or to prevent sb from doing sth, especially by making it difficult to do or by showing that you do not approve of it U25 **2** to make sb feel less confident or enthusiastic about doing sth U25 WF **discouragement** *n*, **discouraging** *adj*

discourse /ˈdɪskɔːs/ *n* **1** written or spoken communication, especially a discussion within society about a serious subject U45 **2** (linguistics) the use of language in speech and writing in order to produce meaning U45

discrimination AWL /dɪˌskrɪmɪˈneɪʃn/ *n* the practice of treating sb or a particular group in society less fairly than others U15 WF **discriminate** *v*, **discriminatory** *adj*

disorder /dɪsˈɔːdə(r)/ *n* an illness that causes the body or the mind to stop working correctly U39

dispose of AWL /dɪˈspəʊz ɒv/ *phr v* to get rid of sb/sth that you do not want or cannot keep U28 WF **disposable** *adj*, **disposal** *n*

disseminate /dɪˈsemɪneɪt/ *v* to spread information or knowledge so that it reaches many people U45 WF **dissemination** *n*

dissertation /ˌdɪsə'teɪʃn/ n a long piece of writing on a particular subject, especially one written for a university degree U1

dissimilar AWL /dɪ'sɪmɪlə(r)/ adj not the same as sb/sth else U18 WF **dissimilarity** n, **similar** adj, **similarity** n

distinction AWL /dɪ'stɪŋkʃn/ n a clear difference, especially between people or things that are similar or related U31 WF **distinct** adj, **distinctive** adj, **distinctively** adv, **distinctly** adv

distinctly AWL /dɪ'stɪŋktli/ adv in a way that is clear and easily noticed; showing a clear difference U18

distortion AWL /dɪ'stɔːʃn/ n a change in facts or ideas that makes them no longer correct or true U7 WF **distort** v, **distorted** adj

distribution AWL /ˌdɪstrɪ'bjuːʃn/ n the way that sth exists or is shared over a particular area or among a particular group of people U5 WF **distribute** v, **distributive** adj, **distributor** n, **redistribute** v, **redistribution** n

diversity AWL /daɪ'vɜːsəti/ n a range of things or people that are very different from each other; the fact of including such a range U27 WF **diverse** adj, **diversely** adv, **diversification** n, **diversify** v

divide into /dɪ'vaɪd ɪntu/ phr v to separate into parts or groups; to make sth separate into parts or groups U8 WF **division** n

domestic AWL /də'mestɪk/ adj 1 of or inside a particular country; not foreign or international U42 2 connected with or happening in the home; used in the home U42 WF **domestically** adv

dominate AWL /'dɒmɪneɪt/ v to control or have a lot of influence over sth/sb, especially in a negative way U34 WF **dominance** n, **dominant** adj, **domination** n

downturn /'daʊntɜːn/ n a fall in the amount of business that is done; a time when the economy becomes weaker U12

draft AWL /drɑːft/ n a rough written version of sth that is not yet in its final form U4 WF **draft** adj v, **redraft** v

dramatic AWL /drə'mætɪk/ adj (of a change or an event) sudden, very great and often surprising U12 WF **dramatically** adv

drawback /'drɔːbæk/ n a disadvantage or problem that makes sth a less attractive idea U32

earth science /'ɜːθ saɪəns/ n science concerned with studying the earth or part of it. Geography and ecology are both earth sciences. U2

ecology /i'kɒlədʒi/ n the study of the relation of plants and living creatures to each other and to their environment U2 WF **ecological** adj, **ecologically** adv, **ecologist** n

economic AWL /ˌiːkə'nɒmɪk/ adj connected with the trade, industry and development of wealth of a country, an area or a society U3 WF **economical** adj, **economically** adv, **economics** n, **economy** n, **uneconomical** adj

economy AWL /ɪ'kɒnəmi/ n (pl. -ies) 1 (often the economy) the relationship between production, trade and the supply of money in a particular country or region U44 2 a country, when you are thinking about its economic system U44

electronics /ɪˌlek'trɒnɪks/ n the branch of science and technology that studies electric currents in electronic equipment U2 WF **electronic** adj

eliminate AWL /ɪ'lɪmɪneɪt/ v to remove or get rid of sth/sb U11 WF **elimination** n

ellipsis /ɪ'lɪpsɪs/ n (pl. ellipses /ɪ'lɪpsiːz/) 1 (grammar) the act of leaving out a word or words from a sentence deliberately, when the meaning can be understood without them U35 2 three dots (…) used to show that a word or words have been left out U35

emerge AWL /i'mɜːdʒ/ v (of facts or ideas) to become known U11 WF **emergence** n, **emergent** adj

emission /i'mɪʃn/ n 1 an amount of sth, especially gas or light, that is sent out into the air U26 2 the production or sending out of sth, especially gas or light U26 WF **emit** v

employ /ɪm'plɔɪ/ v to use sth such as a skill, method, device or word for a particular purpose U28 WF **employee** n, **employer** n, **employment** n

employee /ɪm'plɔɪiː/ n a person who is paid to work for sb U30

end up /ˌend 'ʌp/ phr v to find yourself in a place or situation that you did not intend or expect to be in U28 WF **end** n

energy AWL /'enədʒi/ n a source of power that can be used by sb/sth, for example to provide light and heat or to work machines U38 WF **energetic** adj, **energetically** adv

enforce AWL /ɪn'fɔːs/ v to make sure that people obey a particular law or rule U40 WF **enforcement** n

engineering /ˌendʒɪ'nɪərɪŋ/ n the activity of using scientific knowledge to design and build things U2 WF **engineer** n, **engineer** v

enhance AWL /ɪn'hɑːns/ v to increase or further improve the good quality, value or status of sb/sth U41 WF **enhancement** n

enormously AWL /ɪ'nɔːməsli/ adv very; very much U34 WF **enormity** n, **enormous** adj

ensure AWL /ɪn'ʃʊə(r)/ v to make sure that sth happens or is definite U17

entirely /ɪn'taɪəli/ adv in every way possible U34 WF **entire** adj

environmental AWL /ɪnˌvaɪrən'mentl/ adj 1 connected with the natural world; connected with the ways in which the natural world is damaged or protected, especially by humans U2 2 connected with the conditions that affect the behaviour and development of sb/sth; connected with the conditions in which sb/sth exists U2 WF **environment** adv, **environmentally** adv, **environmentalist** n

equal to /'iːkwəl tu/ phr the same in size, quantity, value, etc. as sth else U37 WF **equal** n v, **equality** n, **equalize** v, **equally** adv, **inequality** n, **unequal** adj

equipment AWL /ɪ'kwɪpmənt/ n the necessary items for a particular purpose or activity U6 WF **equip** v

equivalent AWL /ɪ'kwɪvələnt/ adj equal in value, amount, meaning or importance U30 WF **equivalence** n, **equivalent** n

error AWL /'erə(r)/ n a mistake, especially one that causes problems or affects the result of sth U25 WF **erroneous** adj, **erroneously** adv

establish AWL /ɪ'stæblɪʃ/ v 1 to start or create an organization, system or practice that will last for a long time U11 2 to discover or find proof of the facts of a situation U20 WF **establishment** n

ethical AWL /ˈeθɪkl/ *adj* **1** connected with beliefs and principles about what is right and wrong U7 **2** morally correct or acceptable U7 WF **ethic** *n*, **ethically** *adv*, **unethical** *adj*

ethnic AWL /ˈeθnɪk/ *adj* connected with or belonging to a race or people that shares a cultural tradition U15 WF **ethnically** *adv*, **ethnicity** *n*

evaluate AWL /ɪˈvæljueɪt/ *v* to form an opinion of the amount, value or quality of sth after thinking about it carefully U22 WF **evaluation** *n*, **evaluative** *adj*, **re-evaluation** *n*, **re-evaluate** *v*

evidence AWL /ˈevɪdəns/ *n* the facts, signs or objects that make you believe that sth is true U20 WF **evident** *adj*, **evidential** *adj*, **evidently** *adv*

evident AWL /ˈevɪdənt/ *adj* clear; easily seen U44

evolve AWL /iˈvɒlv/ *v* to develop gradually, especially from a simple to a more complicated form; to develop sth in this way U13 WF **evolution** *n*, **evolutionary** *adj*

examination /ɪgˌzæmɪˈneɪʃn/ *n* a close look at sb/sth, especially to see if there is anything wrong or to find the cause of a problem U39 WF **examine** *v*

exceed AWL /ɪkˈsiːd/ *v* to go beyond what the law, an order or a rule says you are allowed to do U16 WF **excess** *n*, **excessive** *adj*, **excessively** *adv*

exclude AWL /ɪkˈskluːd/ *v* **1** to deliberately not include sth in what you are doing or considering U28 **2** to decide that sth is not possible or is not the cause of sth U28 WF **exclusion** *n*

execute /ˈeksɪkjuːt/ *v* **1** (computing) to carry out an instruction or program U31 **2** to do a piece of work, perform a duty, put a plan into action, etc. U31 WF **execution** *n*

exhibit AWL /ɪgˈzɪbɪt/ *v* to show a particular sign, quality or type of behaviour U39 WF **exhibit** *n*, **exhibition** *n*

expand AWL /ɪkˈspænd/ *v* to become greater in size, number or importance; to make sth greater in size, number or importance U13 WF **expansion** *n*, **expansive** *adj*

exploit AWL /ɪkˈsplɔɪt/ *v* to use sth well in order to gain as much from it as possible U28 WF **exploitation** *n*

expose AWL /ɪkˈspəʊz/ *v* to show sth that is usually hidden U9 WF **exposure** *n*

external AWL /ɪkˈstɜːnl/ *adj* coming from outside the place, organization or situation that is affected U40 WF **externally** *adv*

facility AWL /fəˈsɪləti/ *n* (pl. -ies) buildings, services and equipment that are provided for a particular purpose U14

faction /ˈfækʃn/ *n* a small group of people within a larger one whose members have some different aims and beliefs from those of the larger group U42 WF **factional** *adj*

factor AWL /ˈfæktə(r)/ *n* one of several things that cause or affect sth U17 WF **factor** *v*

factual /ˈfæktʃuəl/ *adj* based on or containing facts U20 WF **fact** *n*, **factually** *adv*

failure /ˈfeɪljə(r)/ *n* an act of not doing sth, especially sth that you are expected to do U25 WF **fail** *v*

feasible /ˈfiːzəbl/ *adj* that is possible and likely to be achieved U24 WF **feasibility** *n*, **feasibly** *n*

feature AWL /ˈfiːtʃə(r)/ *n* something important, interesting or typical of sth such as a system, structure or place U8 WF **feature** *v*

federal AWL /ˈfedərəl/ *adj* having a system of government in which the individual states of a country have control over their own affairs, but are controlled by a central government for national decisions U42 WF **federation** *n*

figure /ˈfɪgə(r)/ *n* (abbr. **fig.**) a picture or diagram in a book, that is often referred to by a number U5 WF **figure** *v*

financial AWL /faɪˈnænʃl/ *adj* connected with money and finance U44 WF **finance** *n*, **financially** *adv*, **financier** *n*

finding /ˈfaɪndɪŋ/ *n* information that is discovered as the result of research into sth U7

finite AWL /ˈfaɪnaɪt/ *adj* having a definite limit or fixed size U45 WF **infinite** *adj*, **infinitely** *adv*

flaw /flɔː/ *n* a mistake or weakness in sth that means that it is not correct or does not work correctly U7 WF **flawed** *adj*

flexible AWL /ˈfleksəbl/ *adj* able to change to suit new conditions or situations U24 WF **flexibility** *n*, **flexibly** *adv*, **inflexible** *adv*

fluctuate AWL /ˈflʌktʃueɪt/ *v* to change frequently in amount, size or quality U12 WF **fluctuation** *n*

following /ˈfɒləʊɪŋ/ *adj* **1** next in time or order U10 **2** that will be mentioned next in a piece of writing or a speech U10 WF **following** *n prep*

footnote /ˈfʊtnəʊt/ *n* an extra piece of information that is printed at the bottom of a page in a book U35

forecast /ˈfɔːkɑːst/ *v* to say what you expect to happen in the future, based on information that is available now U10 WF **forecast** *n*, **forecaster** *n*

for instance AWL /fər ˈɪnstəns/ *phr* for example U36

formality /fɔːˈmæləti/ *n* (pl. -ies) correct and formal behaviour U45 WF **formal** *adj*, **formally** *adv*, **informal** *adj*, **informality** *n*, **informally** *adv*

format AWL /ˈfɔːmæt/ *n* the general arrangement, plan or design of sth U6 WF **format** *v*

formation /fɔːˈmeɪʃn/ *n* **1** the action of forming sth; the process of being formed U27 **2** a thing that has been formed, especially in a particular place or in a particular way U27 WF **form** *n v*

former /ˈfɔːmə(r)/ *pron* (pl. **the former**) the first of two things or people mentioned U36 WF **former** *adj*

formula AWL /ˈfɔːmjələ/ *n* (pl. **formulae** /ˈfɔːmjəliː/ or **formulas**) (mathematics) a series of letters, numbers or symbols that represent a rule or law U37

forthcoming AWL /ˌfɔːθˈkʌmɪŋ/ *adj* going to happen, be published, etc. very soon U10

found AWL /faʊnd/ *v* to start sth, such as an organization or institution, especially by providing money U11 WF **founder** *n*

framework AWL /ˈfreɪmwɜːk/ *n* **1** a set of beliefs, ideas or principles that is used as the basis for examining or understanding sth U9 **2** a system of rules, laws or agreements that controls the way that sth works in business, politics or society U9

frequent /ˈfriːkwənt/ *adj* happening or doing sth often U10 WF **frequency** *n*, **frequently** *adv*, **infrequent** *adj*

function AWL /ˈfʌŋkʃn/ *n* the action or purpose that sb/sth has in a particular situation; the ability that sb/sth has to perform a particular job or role U38 WF **function** *v*, **functional** *adj*, **functionality** *n*, **functionally** *adv*

fundamentally AWL /ˌfʌndə'mentəli/ *adv* in an important and basic way U34 WF **fundamental** *adj*

further /'fɜːðə(r)/ *v* to help the progress or development of sth U23 WF **further** *adv*

gain /geɪn/ *v* to obtain sth, especially sth that is needed or wanted U28 WF **gain** *n*

generalization, -isation /ˌdʒenrəlaɪ'zeɪʃn/ *n* a general statement that is true in most situations U21 WF **general** *adj*, **generalize** *v*, **generally** *adv*

generate AWL /'dʒenəreɪt/ *v* to produce energy, especially electricity U38 WF **generation** *n*

generation AWL /ˌdʒenə'reɪʃn/ *n* **1** all the people who were born at about the same time U15 **2** a single stage in the history of a family U15 **3** the production of sth U38

geology /dʒi'ɒlədʒi/ *n* the scientific study of the earth, including the origin and history of the rocks and soil of which the earth is made U2 WF **geological** *adj*, **geologically** *adv*, **geologist** *n*

goal AWL /gəʊl/ *n* something that you hope to achieve U24

graduate¹ /'grædʒuət/ *n* **1** a person who has successfully completed a course of study, especially a person who has a first university degree U1 **2** (NAmE) a person who has completed their high school studies U1 WF **graduation** *n*

graduate² /'grædʒueɪt/ *v* **1** to get a degree, especially your first degree, from a university or college U1 **2** (NAmE) to complete a course in education, especially at high school U1

graph /grɑːf/ *n* a diagram, consisting of a line or lines, showing the relation between two or more sets of numbers U5

greatly /'greɪtli/ *adv* very much U34 WF **great** *adj*

harmonize, -ise /'hɑːmənaɪz/ *v* to make systems or rules similar in different countries or organizations U41 WF **harmonization** *n*, **harmony** *n*

heading /'hedɪŋ/ *n* a title printed at the top of a page or at the beginning of a section of a book U4

hence AWL /hens/ *adv* for this reason U36

hierarchy AWL /'haɪərɑːki/ *n* (pl. -ies) a system, especially in a society or an organization, in which people are organized into different levels of importance from highest to lowest U8 WF **hierarchical** *adj*

humanitarian aid /hjuːˌmænɪˌteəriən 'eɪd/ *n* money, food, etc. that is sent to help countries in difficult situations U40

human resources /ˌhjuːmən rɪ'sɔːsɪz/ *n* **1** people's skills and abilities, seen as sth a company or organization can make use of U43 **2** (abbr. HR) the department in a company that deals with employing and training people U43

hybrid /'haɪbrɪd/ *adj* (of a vehicle, machine or system) using two different types of power, for example petrol and electricity U38 WF **hybrid** *n*

hypothesis AWL /haɪ'pɒθəsɪs/ *n* (pl. hypotheses /haɪ'pɒθəsiːz/) an idea or explanation of sth that is based on a few known facts but that has not yet been proved to be true or correct U21 WF **hypothesize** *v*, **hypothetical** *adj*, **hypothetically** *adv*

identical AWL /aɪ'dentɪkl/ *adj* similar in every detail U18 WF **identically** *adv*

ideology AWL /ˌaɪdi'ɒlədʒi/ *n* a set of ideas and beliefs that an economic or political system is based on, or that influences the way a person or group behaves U23 WF **ideological** *adj*, **ideologically** *adv*

ignore AWL /ɪg'nɔː(r)/ *v* to fail to consider an important aspect of sth U22 WF **ignorance** *n*, **ignorant** *adj*

illustrate AWL /'ɪləstreɪt/ *v* to make the meaning of sth clearer by using examples, pictures, etc. U5 WF **illustration** *n*, **illustrative** *adj*

immigrant AWL /'ɪmɪgrənt/ *n* a person who has come to live permanently in a country that is not their own U15 WF **immigrate** *v*, **immigration** *n*

impairment /ɪm'peəmənt/ *n* (technical) the state of having a physical or mental condition which means that part of your body or brain does not work correctly; a particular condition of this sort U19 WF **impair** *v*, **impaired** *adj*

imperative /ɪm'perətɪv/ *adj* very important and needing immediate attention or action U34

implement AWL /'ɪmplɪment/ *v* to start to use a new plan, system or law U13 WF **implementation** *n*

implicit AWL /ɪm'plɪsɪt/ *adj* **1** forming a necessary part of sth U45 **2** said or written in a way that suggests sth without expressing it directly U45 WF **implicitly** *adv*

impose on AWL /ɪm'pəʊz ɒn/ *phr v* to give sb rules or limits that they must work within U19 WF **imposition** *n*

incentive AWL /ɪn'sentɪv/ *n* something that encourages you to do sth U31

incidence AWL /'ɪnsɪdəns/ *n* the number of times sth unpleasant, such as a disease or crime, happens in a particular group or particular situation U27 WF **incident** *n*

income AWL /'ɪnkʌm/ *n* the money that a person, region, country, etc. earns from work, from investing money or from business U44

inconsistent AWL /ˌɪnkən'sɪstənt/ *adj* **1** if two statements, etc. are inconsistent, or one is inconsistent with the other, they cannot both be true because they give the facts in a different way U25 **2** tending to change too often; not staying the same U25 WF **consist** *v*, **consistency** *n*, **consistent** *adj*, **consistently** *adv*, **inconsistency** *n*, **inconsistently** *adv*

incorporate into AWL /ɪn'kɔːpəreɪt ɪntu/ *phr v* to include sth so that it forms a part of sth U41 WF **incorporation** *n*

independent /ˌɪndɪ'pendənt/ *adj* **1** not under the control or authority of sb/sth else U9 **2** done or given by sb who is not involved in a situation and so is able to judge it fairly U9

index AWL /'ɪndeks/ *n* (pl. indices /'ɪndɪsiːz/) a sign or measure that sth else can be judged by U40 WF **index** *v*

indicator AWL /'ɪndɪkeɪtə(r)/ *n* a sign that shows you the state, existence or level of sth U40 WF **indicate** *v*, **indication** *n*, **indicative** *adj*

inequality /ˌɪnɪ'kwɒləti/ *n* (pl. -ies) the unfair difference between groups of people in society, when some have more money, power or opportunities than others U25 WF **equal** *adj*, **equality** *n*, **unequal** *adj*

inevitable AWL /ɪn'evɪtəbl/ *adj* that you cannot avoid or prevent U34 WF **inevitability** *n*, **inevitably** *adv*

infectious /ɪn'fekʃəs/ *adj* (of a disease) that can be passed easily from one person or animal to another, especially through the air they breathe U39 WF **infect** *v*, **infection** *n*

infer AWL /ɪnˈfɜː(r)/ v (-rr-) to reach an opinion or decide that sth is true on the basis of information that is available U21

infrastructure AWL /ˈɪnfrəstrʌktʃə(r)/ n the basic systems and services that are necessary for a country or an organization to run smoothly, for example buildings, transport, and water and power supplies U14

inheritance /ɪnˈherɪtəns/ n the money or property that you receive from sb when they die; the fact of receiving sth when sb dies U15 WF inherit v

initial AWL /ɪˈnɪʃl/ adj happening at the beginning; first U10 WF initially adv

initiate AWL /ɪˈnɪʃieɪt/ v to make sth such as a process or an action begin U11 WF initiation n, initiative n

in line with /ˌɪn ˈlaɪn wɪð/ phr similar to sth; so that one thing is closely connected with another U43

in other words /ˌɪn ˈʌðə wɜːdz/ phr used to introduce an explanation of sth U36

in principle AWL /ˌɪn ˈprɪnsəpl/ phr if sth can be done in principle, there is no good reason why it should not be done although it has not yet been done and there may be some difficulties U33

in response to /ˌɪn rɪˈspɒns tu/ phr as a reaction to sth that has happened or been said U13

insight AWL /ˈɪnsaɪt/ n an understanding of a particular situation or thing U27 WF insightful adj

install /ɪnˈstɔːl/ v to fix equipment into position so that it can be used U38 WF installation n, uninstall v

instruction AWL /ɪnˈstrʌkʃn/ n **1** instructions detailed information on how to do or use sth U31 **2** something that sb tells you to do U31 **3** (computing) a code in a program that tells a computer to perform a particular operation U31 WF instructive adj, instructor n

instrument /ˈɪnstrəmənt/ n **1** a process or system that is used to discover or describe attitudes, experiences, skills, etc. U41 **2** a tool or device used for a particular task, especially for scientific work U41 **3** (law) a formal legal document U41

integrate AWL /ˈɪntɪɡreɪt/ v to become or make sb become accepted as a member of a social group, especially when they come from a different culture U15 WF integral adj, integration n

interaction AWL /ˌɪntərˈækʃn/ n **1** the effect that two things have on each other U29 **2** the way that people communicate with each other, especially while they work or spend time with them U29 WF interact v, interactive adj, interactively adv

interest /ˈɪntrest/ n **1** the price of borrowing or lending money for a particular period of time (usually given as a proportion of the original amount at an annual rate) U44 **2** a connection with sth that affects your attitude to it, especially because you may benefit from it in some way U23 **3** a group of people or companies that are in the same business that they want to protect U23

interest rate /ˈɪntrest reɪt/ n the price of borrowing or lending money for a particular period of time (usually given as a percentage of the original amount at an annual rate) U44

interior /ɪnˈtɪəriə(r)/ n the inside part of sth U9 WF interior adj

in terms of /ˌɪn ˈtɜːmz ɒv/ phr used to show what aspect of a subject you are talking about or how you are thinking about it U29

internal AWL /ɪnˈtɜːnl/ adj involving or concerning only the people who are part of a particular organization rather than people from outside it U9 WF internally adv

international development /ˌɪntəˌnæʃnəl dɪˈveləpmənt/ n the process of making a country or area richer and more successful, and of reducing poverty and inequality in these places U40

international relations /ˌɪntəˌnæʃnəl rɪˈleɪʃnz/ n (pl.) the way in which countries behave towards each other or deal with each other U3

interpret AWL /ɪnˈtɜːprɪt/ v to explain the meaning of sth U6 WF interpretation n, interpretative adj, misinterpret v

interval AWL /ˈɪntəvl/ n **1** a period of time between two events U10 **2** at (...) intervals phr with time between U10

intervene AWL /ˌɪntəˈviːn/ v to become involved in a situation in order to improve it or stop it from getting worse U26 WF intervention n

introduce /ˌɪntrəˈdjuːs/ v to bring sth, especially a product, system, law or idea, into use or operation for the first time U11 WF introduction n, introductory adj

introduction /ˌɪntrəˈdʌkʃn/ n the first part of a book, report or speech that gives a general idea of what is to follow U4

investigate AWL /ɪnˈvestɪɡeɪt/ v to find out information about a subject or problem by study or research U7 WF investigation n, investigative adj, investigator n

isolated AWL /ˈaɪsəleɪtɪd/ adj **1** far away from other places, buildings or people U14 **2** without much contact with other people or other countries U14 WF isolate v, isolation n

item AWL /ˈaɪtəm/ n a single object or thing, especially one that is part of a list, collection or set U8

journal AWL /ˈdʒɜːnl/ n a newspaper or magazine that deals with a particular subject or profession U4

key /kiː/ n a list explaining the symbols used in a map, plan, table, etc. U5 WF key adj

label AWL /ˈleɪbl/ v (-ll-, US -l-) to attach a label to sth; to write information on sth in order to identify it U5 WF label n

labour AWL /ˈleɪbə(r)/ n workers, considered as a group, especially people who use their hands or physical strength to do their work U43 WF labour v

lack /læk/ n the state of not having sth or not having enough of sth U16 WF lack v

latter /ˈlætə(r)/ pron (pl. the latter) the second of two things, people or groups that have just been mentioned, or the last in a list U36 WF latter adj

layer AWL /ˈleɪə(r)/ n a quantity of sth that lies over a surface or between surfaces U9 WF layer v

lead to /ˈliːd tu/ phr v (led /led/) to have sth as a result U17

lecture AWL /ˈlektʃə(r)/ n a talk that is given to a group of people to teach them about a particular subject, often as part of a university or college course U1 WF lecture v

legal AWL /ˈliːɡl/ adj connected with the law U3 WF law n, legally adv, legality n, illegal adj

legislation AWL /ˌledʒɪsˈleɪʃn/ n a law or set of laws passed by a parliament U41 WF legislate v, legislative adj, legislator n, legislature n

lender /ˈlendə(r)/ n an organization or a person that lends money U44 WF lend v, loan n

level /ˈlevl/ n a position or rank in a scale of size or importance U8

liberal AWL /ˈlɪbərəl/ adj **1** willing to understand and respect other people's behaviour and opinions, especially when they are different from your own; believing people should be able to choose how they behave U42 **2** wanting or allowing a lot of political and economic freedom and supporting gradual social, political or religious change U42 WF liberalism n, liberalization n, liberalize v, liberally adv

life cycle /ˈlaɪf saɪkl/ n the period of time during which sth, for example a product, is developed and used U43

life sciences /ˈlaɪf saɪənsɪz/ n (often **the life sciences**) the sciences concerned with studying humans, animals or plants U2

limitation /ˌlɪmɪˈteɪʃn/ n a limit on what sb/sth can do or how good they/it can be U4 U19 WF limit n v, limited adj

linguist /ˈlɪŋgwɪst/ n a person who studies languages or linguistics U45 WF linguistic adj, linguistics n

literacy /ˈlɪtərəsi/ n the ability to read and write U40 WF literate adj, illiterate adj

literature /ˈlɪtrətʃə(r)/ n pieces of writing that are considered to be works of art, especially novels, plays and poems (in contrast to technical books and newspapers, magazines, etc.) U3 WF literary adj

literature review /ˈlɪtrətʃə rɪvjuː/ n part of a piece of academic writing which describes previous research that is relevant to the main point of the paper U4

loan /ləʊn/ n money that an organization such as a bank lends and sb borrows U44 WF loan v

lobby group /ˈlɒbi gruːp/ n a group of people who try to influence politicians on a particular issue U23 WF lobby n v

located AWL /ləʊˈkeɪtɪd/ adj if sth is located in a particular place, it exists there or has been put there U14 WF locate v, location n, relocate v

logical AWL /ˈlɒdʒɪkl/ adj following or able to follow the rules of logic in which ideas or facts are based on other true ideas or facts U22 WF illogical adj, logic n, logically adv

maintain AWL /meɪnˈteɪn/ v **1** to cause or enable a condition or situation to continue U12 **2** to keep sth at the same level or rate U12 **3** to state strongly that sth is true, even when some other people may not believe it U35 WF maintenance n

management /ˈmænɪdʒmənt/ n the act of running and controlling a business or similar organization U3 WF manage v, manager n

manufacture /ˌmænjuˈfæktʃə(r)/ v to make goods in large quantities using machinery U43 WF manufacturer n, manufacturing n

marital /ˈmærɪtl/ adj connected with marriage or with the relationship between a husband and wife U15

market /ˈmɑːkɪt/ n **1** business or trade; the amount of trade in a particular type of goods U44 **2** a stock market or financial market; a place where commodities or currencies can be bought and sold U44 WF marketable adj, marketing n

mass media /ˌmæs ˈmiːdiə/ n sources of information and news such as newspapers, magazines, television and the internet, that reach and influence large numbers of people U45

material /məˈtɪəriəl/ n things that are needed in order to do a particular activity U6

maximum AWL /ˈmæksɪməm/ adj (abbr. max) as large, fast, etc. as is possible; the most that is possible or allowed U16 WF maximization n, maximize v, maximum n

mean /miːn/ n (technical) the value found by adding together all the numbers in a group, and dividing the total by the number of numbers U37 WF mean adj

measure /ˈmeʒə(r)/ n a standard unit used for stating the size, quantity or degree of sth; a system or scale of these units U37 WF measure v, measurement n

mechanical /məˈkænɪkl/ adj **1** connected with the physical laws of movement U2 **2** connected with machines and engines U2 WF mechanic n, mechanics n, mechanism n

mediate AWL /ˈmiːdieɪt/ v (technical) to influence sth and/or make it possible for it to happen U45 WF mediation n

mental AWL /ˈmentl/ adj connected with the state of health of the mind or with the treatment of illnesses of the mind U26 WF mentality n, mentally adv

metaphorical /ˌmetəˈfɒrɪkl/ adj connected with or containing metaphors (= sth that represents another situation or idea) U21 WF metaphor n, metaphorically adv

method AWL /ˈmeθəd/ n a particular way of doing sth U6 WF methodical adj, methodological adj, methodology n

migrate AWL /maɪˈgreɪt/ v (of a lot of people) to move from one town, country or place to go and live and/or work in another U13 WF migrant n, migration n, migratory adj

minimal AWL /ˈmɪnɪməl/ adj very small in size, amount or extent U16 WF minimally adv, minimization n, minimize v

minority AWL /maɪˈnɒrəti/ n (pl. -ies) a group within a community or country that is different because of race, religion, culture or language U15 WF minor adj

misleading /ˌmɪsˈliːdɪŋ/ adj giving the wrong idea and making people believe sth that is not true U25 WF mislead v

model /ˈmɒdl/ n **1** a simple description, especially a mathematical one, of a group of complex systems or processes, used for understanding or explaining how sth works U21 **2** an object that is a copy of sth, usually smaller than the original object U38 WF model v

modification AWL /ˌmɒdɪfɪˈkeɪʃn/ n the act or process of changing sth in order to improve it or make it more suitable; a change that is made U13 WF modify v, unmodified adj

monitor AWL /ˈmɒnɪtə(r)/ v to watch or check sb over a period of time, so that you can see if any problems develop and take action to stop or correct this U39 WF monitor n, monitoring n

mortgage /ˈmɔːgɪdʒ/ n a legal agreement by which a bank or similar organization lends sb money to buy a house, etc., and they pay the money back over a particular number of years; the sum of money that they borrow U44

motivation AWL /ˌməʊtɪ'veɪʃn/ n **1** a reason or reasons for doing a particular activity or behaving in a particular way U17 **2** desire or willingness to do sth U17 WF motivate v, motivated adj, motive n, unmotivated adj

multiply /'mʌltɪplaɪ/ v to add a number to itself a particular number of times U37 WF multiple n, multiplication n

namely /'neɪmli/ adv used to introduce more detailed information about sth that has just been mentioned U36

nationwide /ˌneɪʃn'waɪd/ adj happening or existing in all parts of a particular country U14 WF nationwide adv

native speaker /ˌneɪtɪv 'spiːkə(r)/ n a person who speaks a language as their first language and has not learned it as a foreign language U45

natural sciences /ˌnætʃrəl 'saɪənsɪz/ n sciences concerned with studying the physical world. Chemistry, biology and physics are all natural sciences. U2 WF nature n

nature /'neɪtʃə(r)/ n the basic character or qualities of sth U29 WF natural adj, naturally adv

network AWL /'netwɜːk/ n **1** a complicated system of roads, lines, tubes, etc. that cross each other and are connected to each other U14 **2** a group or system of people or things that are connected to each other U14 WF network v

neutral AWL /'njuːtrəl/ adj **1** not supporting or helping either side in a disagreement, competition, etc. U26 **2** not belonging to or supporting any of the countries that are involved in a war U26 WF neutrally adv, neutrality n, neutralization n, neutralize v

nevertheless AWL /ˌnevəðə'les/ adv despite this fact U36

nonetheless AWL /ˌnʌnðə'les/ adv despite this fact U36

norm AWL /nɔːm/ n a standard or pattern of behaviour that is typical of or accepted within a particular group or society U40

note /nəʊt/ v to mention sth because it is important or interesting U35 WF note n

nuclear AWL /'njuːkliə(r)/ adj using, producing or resulting from energy that is produced by splitting the nucleus of atoms U38

objective AWL /əb'dʒektɪv/ adj not influenced by personal feelings or opinions; considering only facts U22 WF objective n, objectively adv, objectivity n

observation /ˌɒbzə'veɪʃn/ n the act of watching sb/sth carefully for a period of time, especially to learn sth U31 WF observe v, observer n

obtain AWL /əb'teɪn/ v to get sth, especially by making an effort U28 WF obtainable adj, unobtainable adj

occupation AWL /ˌɒkju'peɪʃn/ n a job or profession U15 WF occupancy n, occupant n, occupational adj, occupier n, occupy v

occurrence AWL /ə'kʌrəns/ n **1** the fact of sth happening U27 **2** the fact of sth existing or being found somewhere U27 WF occur v

omission /ə'mɪʃn/ n **1** the act of not including sb/sth or not doing sth; the fact of not being included/done U25 **2** a thing that has not been included or done U25 WF omit v

on average /ˌɒn 'ævərɪdʒ/ phr at the level that is usual U33 WF average adj v

on the contrary /ˌɒn ðə 'kɒntrəri/ phr used to introduce a statement that says the opposite of the last one U18

opponent /ə'pəʊnənt/ n **1** a person who disagrees with sth and tries to change or stop it U23 **2** the person, organization or animal that sb/sth is fighting or competing against U23 WF oppose v, opposed adj, opposition n

outline /'aʊtlaɪn/ n a description of the main facts or points involved in sth U4 WF outline v

outsource /'aʊtsɔːs/ v to arrange for sb outside a company to do work or provide goods for that company U43 WF outsourcing n

overlap AWL /ˌəʊvə'læp/ v (-pp-) to cover part of the same area of interest, knowledge, responsibility, etc. U8 WF overlap /'əʊvəlæp/ n

overthrow /'əʊvəθrəʊ/ n the act of taking power by force from a leader or government U42 WF overthrow v

overtly /əʊ'vɜːtli/ adv in a way that is open and not secret U45 WF overt adj

overwhelming /ˌəʊvə'welmɪŋ/ adj very great or very strong; so powerful that you cannot resist it or decide how to react U34 WF overwhelmingly adv

panel AWL /'pænl/ n a group of experts who give their advice or opinion about sth U32

parallel AWL /'pærəlel/ n **1** a person, situation or an event that is very similar to another, especially one in a different place or time U29 **2** a comparison between two things U29 WF parallel adj v, unparalleled adj

paraphrase /'pærəfreɪz/ v to express what sb has said or written using different words, especially in order to make it easier to understand U35 WF paraphrase n

participant AWL /pɑː'tɪsɪpənt/ n a person who is taking part in an activity or event U7 WF participate v, participation n, participatory adj

partner AWL /'pɑːtnə(r)/ n the person that sb is married to or having a sexual relationship with U15 WF partnership n

party /'pɑːti/ n (pl. -ies) one of the people or groups of people involved in a legal agreement or argument U41

per capita /pə 'kæpɪtə/ adj for each person U40 WF per capita adv

perception AWL /pə'sepʃn/ n an idea, image or a belief you have as a result of how you see or understand sth U23 WF perceive v, perceived adj, perceptive adj, perceptively adv

perform /pə'fɔːm/ v to do sth, such as a piece of work, task or duty U6 WF performance n, performer n

performance /pə'fɔːməns/ n how well or badly you do sth; how well or badly sth works U38

period AWL /'pɪəriəd/ n a particular length of time U10 WF periodic adj, periodical n, periodically adv

permanent /'pɜːmənənt/ adj lasting for a long time or for all time in the future; existing all the time U11 WF permanence n, permanently adv

persist AWL /pə'sɪst/ v to continue to exist U25 WF persistence n, persistent adj, persistently adv

personnel /ˌpɜːsə'nel/ n the people who work for a business, an organization or one of the armed forces U43

phase AWL /feɪz/ n a stage in a process of change or development U31 WF phase v

PhD /ˌpiː eɪtʃ ˈdiː/ *n* the abbreviation for 'Doctor of Philosophy', a university degree of a very high level that is given to sb who has done research in a particular subject U1

phenomenon AWL /fəˈnɒmɪnən/ *n* (pl. phenomena) a fact or an event in nature or society, especially one that is not fully understood U21 WF **phenomenal** *adj*, **phenomenally** *adv*

physical AWL /ˈfɪzɪkl/ *adj* connected with a person's body rather than their mind U26

physical science /ˌfɪzɪkl ˈsaɪəns/ *n* (also **the physical sciences**) the areas of science concerned with studying natural forces and things that are not alive, for example physics and chemistry U2

physics /ˈfɪzɪks/ *n* the scientific study of matter and energy and the relationships between them, including the study of forces, heat, light, sound, electricity and the structure of atoms U2 WF **physical** *adj*, **physically** *adv*

pie chart /ˈpaɪ tʃɑːt/ *n* a diagram consisting of a circle that is divided into sections to show the size of particular amounts in relation to the whole U5

play a part in /ˌpleɪ ə ˈpɑːt ɪn/ *phr* to be involved in sth U17

plot /plɒt/ *v* (-tt-) to mark points on a graph and draw a line or curve connecting them; to show information on a graph U5

political /pəˈlɪtɪkl/ *adj* connected with the state, government or public affairs U3 WF **politically** *adv*, **politician** *n*, **politics** *n*

pose AWL /pəʊz/ *v* to create a problem that has to be dealt with U25

positive AWL /ˈpɒzətɪv/ *n* a good or useful quality or aspect; the aspects of a situation that are good or useful U24 WF **positive** *adj*, **positively** *adv*

potential AWL /pəˈtenʃl/ *adj* that can develop into sth or be developed in the future U10 WF **potential** *n*, **potentially** *adv*

poverty /ˈpɒvəti/ *n* the state of being poor U40

practice /ˈpræktɪs/ *n* a way of doing sth that is the usual or expected way; a custom or habit U27 WF **practicable** *adj*, **practical** *adj*, **practically** *adv*, **practise** *v*, **practitioner** *n*

preceding /prɪˈsiːdɪŋ/ *adj* happening before sth or coming before sth/sb in order U10 WF **precede** *v*, **precedence** *n*, **precedent** *n*, **unprecedented** *adj*

precondition /ˌpriːkənˈdɪʃn/ *n* something that must happen or exist before sth else can exist or be done U41 WF **condition** *n*

predominant AWL /prɪˈdɒmɪnənt/ *adj* largest or most frequent; most obvious or important U16 WF **predominance** *n*, **predominantly** *adv*, **predominate** *v*

preliminary AWL /prɪˈlɪmɪnəri/ *adj* happening or done before a more important event or action U10 WF **preliminary** *n*

premise /ˈpremɪs/ *n* a statement or an idea that forms the basis for a reasonable line of argument U32

pressure /ˈpreʃə(r)/ *n* the feeling that it is necessary to do sth; the action of making sb feel this; the problems caused by this U23

prevalent /ˈprevələnt/ *adj* that exists or is very common at a particular time or in a particular place U40 WF **prevalence** *n*

primarily AWL /praɪˈmerəli/ *adv* mainly U33

primary AWL /ˈpraɪməri/ *adj* containing information obtained by research or observation, not taken from from other books, etc U20 WF **primarily** *adv*

principal AWL /ˈprɪnsəpl/ *adj* main; most important U33 WF **principally** *adv*

priority AWL /praɪˈɒrəti/ *n* (pl. -ies) **1** something that you think is more important than other things and should be dealt with first U17 **2** the condition of being considered or treated as more important than other things or people U17 WF **prioritize** *v*, **prioritization** *n*

prior to /ˈpraɪə tu/ *prep* before sth U10 WF **prior** *adj*

probability /ˌprɒbəˈbɪləti/ *n* (pl. -ies) how likely sth is to happen U44 WF **probable** *adj*, **probably** *adv*, **improbable** *adj*

procedure AWL /prəˈsiːdʒə(r)/ *n* a series of actions done in a particular order and way, especially the usual or correct way U7 WF **procedural** *adj*, **proceed** *v*

product of /ˈprɒdʌkt ɒv/ *phr* a person or thing that is the result of sth U17 WF **produce** *v*, **production** *n*, **productive** *adj*, **productively** *adv*, **productivity** *n*, **unproductive** *adj*

prohibit AWL /prəˈhɪbɪt/ *v* to stop sth from being done or used, especially by law U41 WF **prohibition** *n*, **prohibitive** *adj*, **prohibitively** *adv*

project AWL /ˈprɒdʒekt/ *n* a piece of research work done by a school or college student U1 WF **project** *v*, **projection** *n*

projection AWL /prəˈdʒekʃn/ *n* an estimate or forecast of a future situation based on what is happening now U10

promote AWL /prəˈməʊt/ *v* **1** to help sth to happen or develop U24 **2** to help sell a product or service or make it more popular by advertising it or offering it at a special price U24 WF **promoter** *n*, **promotion** *n*, **promotional** *adj*

property /ˈprɒpəti/ *n* (pl. -ies) **1** a quality or characteristic that sth has U9 **2** land and buildings; a particular piece of land or a particular building and its surrounding land U14

proportion AWL /prəˈpɔːʃn/ *n* a part or share of a whole U16 WF **proportional** *adj*, **proportionally** *adv*, **proportionate** *adj*, **proportionately** *adv*

protective /prəˈtektɪv/ *adj* providing or intended to provide protection U27 WF **protect** *v*, **protection** *n*

prototype /ˈprəʊtətaɪp/ *n* the first design of sth from which other forms are copied or developed U38

provision /prəˈvɪʒn/ *n* a condition or an arrangement in a legal document U41 WF **provide** *v*

psychology AWL /saɪˈkɒlədʒi/ *n* **1** the scientific study of the mind and how it influences behaviour U3 **2** the way that people think and therefore behave in a particular situation U3 WF **psychological** *adj*, **psychologically** *adv*, **psychologist** *n*

publish AWL /ˈpʌblɪʃ/ *v* **1** (of an author) to have your work printed in a newspaper, magazine, etc., or printed and sold to the public U45 **2** to make information available to the public U45 WF **publication** *n*, **publisher** *n*, **unpublished** *adj*

pursuit AWL /pəˈsjuːt/ *n* the act of trying to find, obtain or achieve sth U26 WF **pursue** *v*

put forward /ˌpʊt ˈfɔːwəd/ *phr v* (putting, put) to suggest sth for discussion U22

qualitative AWL /ˈkwɒlɪtətɪv/ *adj* connected with or measuring the quality of sth, rather than with how much of it there is U31 WF **qualitatively** *adv*

quantitative /ˈkwɒntɪtətɪv/ *adj* connected with or measuring the amount or number of sth rather than its quality U31 WF **quantitatively** *adv*

question /ˈkwestʃən/ *v* to have or express doubts about sth U22 WF **question** *n*, **questionable** *adj*

quotation marks /kwəʊˈteɪʃn mɑːks/ *n* a pair of marks ('') or ("") placed around a word, sentence, etc. to show that it is what sb said or wrote, that it is a title or that you are using it in an unusual way U35

quote AWL /kwəʊt/ *v* to use words from another speaker or writer in your writing or speech, showing clearly that the words are from this source U35 WF **quotation** *n*

random AWL /ˈrændəm/ *adj* done, chosen, etc. so that all possible choices have an equal chance of being considered U19 WF **randomly** *adv*, **randomness** *n*

range AWL /reɪndʒ/ *n* **1** a variety of things of a particular type U16 **2** the limits between which sth varies U12 WF **range** *v*

rank /ræŋk/ *v* (not used in the progressive tenses) to give sb/sth a particular position on a scale according to quality, importance, success, etc.; to have a position of this kind U8 WF **rank** *n*

rate /reɪt/ *n* a measurement of the speed at which sth happens U12

reaction AWL /riˈækʃn/ *n* what you do, say or think as a result of sth that has happened U22 WF **react** *v*, **reactionary** *adj*, **reactive** *adj*, **reactor** *n*

realistic /ˌriːəˈlɪstɪk/ *adj* sensible and appropriate; possible to achieve U24 WF **realistically** *adv*, **unrealistic** *adj*

real-world /ˈrɪəl wɜːld/ *adj* existing in the real world and not specially invented for a particular purpose U21

recognize, -ise /ˈrekəgnaɪz/ *v* (not used in the progressive tenses) to admit or to be aware that sth exists or is true U22 WF **recognition** *n*, **recognizable** *adj*

record /rɪˈkɔːd/ *v* **1** to keep a permanent account of facts or events by writing them down, filming them, storing them in a computer, etc. U37 **2** to show a particular measurement or amount U37 WF **record** *n*, **recording** *n*

recover AWL /rɪˈkʌvə(r)/ *v* to get back the same amount of money that you have spent or that is owed to you U28 WF **recoverable** *adj*, **recovery** *n*

recur /rɪˈkɜː(r)/ *v* (-rr-) to happen again or a number of times U19 WF **recurrence** *n*, **recurring** *adj*

re-evaluate /ˌriːɪˈvæljueɪt/ *v* to think about sth again, especially in order to form a new opinion about it U13

reference /ˈrefrəns/ *n* a mention of a source of information in a book, an article, etc; a source of information that is mentioned in this way U4

refer to /rɪˈfɜː tu/ *phr v* (-rr-) to mention sb/sth, usually in a way that gives particular information about them U35 WF **reference** *n v*

reformer /rɪˈfɔːmə(r)/ *n* a person who works to achieve political or social change U23 WF **reform** *n*, **reform** *v*

regenerate /rɪˈdʒenəreɪt/ *v* to make an area, institution, etc. develop and grow strong again U14 WF **regeneration** *n*

regime AWL /reɪˈʒiːm/ *n* **1** a government, especially one that has not been elected in a fair way U42 **2** a method or system of organizing or managing sth U42

regulation AWL /ˌregjuˈleɪʃn/ *n* **1** an official rule made by a government or some other authority U26 **2** the act of controlling sth by means of rules U26 WF **deregulate** *v*, **regulate** *v*, **regulator** *n*, **regulatory** *adj*, **unregulated** *adj*

reinforce AWL /ˌriːɪnˈfɔːs/ *v* to make a feeling, idea, habit or tendency stronger U30 WF **reinforcement** *n*

reject AWL /rɪˈdʒekt/ *v* to refuse to accept or consider sth U20 WF **rejection** *n*

related to /rɪˈleɪtɪd tu/ *phr* connected by a family relationship or by marriage U15

relationship /rɪˈleɪʃnʃɪp/ *n* the way in which a person is related to sb else in a family U15 WF **related** *adj*, **relation** *n*, **unrelated** *adj*

relevant AWL /ˈreləvənt/ *adj* closely connected with the subject you are discussing or the situation you are thinking about U20 WF **irrelevant** *adj*, **relevance** *n*

relief /rɪˈliːf/ *n* food, money, medicine, etc. that is given to help people in places where there has been a war or natural disaster U40 WF **relieve** *v*

reluctant AWL /rɪˈlʌktənt/ *adj* hesitating before doing sth because you are you do not want to do it or because you are not sure that it is the right thing to do U23 WF **reluctance** *n*, **reluctantly** *adv*

rely on AWL /rɪˈlaɪ ɒn/ *phr v* (relies, relying, relied) to need or depend on sb/sth U20 WF **reliable** *adj*, **reliably** *adv*, **reliance** *n*, **reliant** *adj*, **unreliable** *adj*

remote /rɪˈməʊt/ *adj* (remoter, remotest) far away from places where other people live U14 WF **remotely** *adv*

renewable /rɪˈnjuːəbl/ *adj* (of energy and natural resources) replaced naturally or controlled carefully and therefore able to be used without the risk of none being left U38 WF **non-renewable** *adj*, **renew** *v*, **renewal** *n*

repercussion /ˌriːpəˈkʌʃn/ *n* (usually pl.) an indirect and usually bad result of an action or event that may happen some time afterwards U17

replace /rɪˈpleɪs/ *v* **1** to remove sb/sth and put another person or thing in their place U13 **2** to change sth that is old, damaged, etc. for a similar thing that is newer or better U13 WF **replacement** *n*

representative /ˌreprɪˈzentətɪv/ *adj* (technical) (of a sample or piece of work) containing or including examples of all the different types of people or things in a large group U7 WF **misrepresent** *v*, **represent** *v*, **representation** *n*, **representatively** *adv*

require AWL /rɪˈkwaɪə(r)/ *v* (not usually used in the progressive tenses) to make sb do or have sth, especially because it is necessary according to a particular law or set of rules U41 WF **requirement** *n*

requirement AWL /rɪˈkwaɪəmənt/ *n* **1** (often requirements) something that sb needs or wants U19 **2** something that is necessary according to a particular law or set of rules U19

research proposal /ˈriːsɜːtʃ prəpəʊzl/ *n* a formal suggestion or plan that gives a detailed description of what sb aims to discover from their research and how they plan to do this U1 WF **propose** *v*, **proposition** *n*

resolve AWL /rɪˈzɒlv/ *v* to find an acceptable solution to a disagreement or problem U19 WF **resolution** *n*, **unresolved** *adj*

respectively /rɪˈspektɪvli/ *adv* in the same order as the people or things mentioned U36 WF **respect** *n v*, **respective** *adj*

response AWL /rɪˈspɒns/ n a spoken or written answer U22 WF **respond** v, **respondent** n, **responsive** adj, **responsiveness** n, **unresponsive** adj

responsible /rɪˈspɒnsəbl/ adj being the cause of sth U29 WF **irresponsible** adj, **responsibility** n, **responsibly** adv

restore AWL /rɪˈstɔː(r)/ v to bring back a situation or feeling that existed before U26 WF **restoration** n

restrict AWL /rɪˈstrɪkt/ v to limit or control the size, amount or range of sth U25 WF **restriction** n, **restrictive** adj, **restrictively** adv, **unrestricted** adj

result from /rɪˈzʌlt frɒm/ phr v to happen because of sth else that happened first U17 WF **result** n

retain AWL /rɪˈteɪn/ v to keep sb/sth; to continue to have sth and not lose it or get rid of it U28 WF **retainer** n, **retention** n, **retentive** adj

revenue AWL /ˈrevənjuː/ n (also **revenues**) money that a government receives from taxes or that an organization receives from its business U32

revolution AWL /ˌrevəˈluːʃn/ n an attempt, by a large number of people, to change the government of a country, especially by violent action U42 WF **revolt** n, **revolutionary** adj, **revolutionize** v

rigid AWL /ˈrɪdʒɪd/ adj (of rules, methods, etc.) very strict and difficult to change or adapt WF **rigidity** n, **rigidly** adv U41

robust /rəʊˈbʌst/ adj **1** (of a system, an organization, a method or evidence) likely to remain successful, strong or valid, even in changing or difficult circumstances U24 **2** physically strong and unlikely to break or be damaged or destroyed U24 WF **robustly** adv

round to /ˈraʊnd tu/ phr v to increase or decrease a number to the next highest or lowest whole number U37

route AWL /ruːt/ n a fixed way along which a bus, train, etc. regularly travels or goods are regularly sent U14 WF **route** v

salary /ˈsæləri/ n (pl. -ies) money that employees receive for doing their job, especially professional employees or people working in an office, usually paid every month U32

sample /ˈsɑːmpl/ n a number of people or things taken from a larger group and used in tests to provide information about the group U7 WF **sample** v, **sampling** n

sanction /ˈsæŋkʃn/ n a course of action that can be used, if necessary, to make people obey a law or behave in a particular way U40 WF **sanction** v

scenario AWL /səˈnɑːriəʊ/ n (pl. -os) a description of a possible series of events or situations U21

scope AWL /skəʊp/ n the range of things that a subject, an organization, an activity, etc. deals with U16

scrutinize, **-ise** /ˈskruːtənaɪz/ v to look at or examine sth carefully U42 WF **scrutiny** n

secondary /ˈsekəndri/ adj (of writing) based on other books, etc, not on direct research or observation U20

sector AWL /ˈsektə(r)/ n a part of an area of activity, especially of a country's economy U8

seek to AWL /ˈsiːk tu/ v (sought /sɔːt/) to try to do sth U41

seemingly /ˈsiːmɪŋli/ adv in a way that appears to be true but may in fact not be U33 WF **seeming** adj

segment /ˈsegmənt/ n (geometry) part of a shape separated from the rest by at least one line or plane; the line between two points U5 WF **segment** v, **segmental** adj, **segmentation** n

selection AWL /sɪˈlekʃn/ n the process of choosing sb/sth from a group of people or things, usually according to a system U8 WF **select** adj v, **selective** adj, **selectively** adv, **selector** n

seminar /ˈsemɪnɑː(r)/ n a class at a university or college when a small group of students and a teacher discuss or study a particular topic U1

sequence AWL /ˈsiːkwəns/ n a set of connected events, actions, numbers, etc. that have a particular order U10 WF **sequence** v, **sequential** adj, **sequentially** adv

seriously /ˈsɪəriəsli/ adv to a degree that is important and worrying U34 WF **serious** adj

set up /ˌset ˈʌp/ phr v (setting, set) **1** to start a process or a series of events U6 **2** to build sth or put sth somewhere U6 **3** to make a machine ready for use U6

severely /sɪˈvɪəli/ adv very badly or seriously U34 WF **severe** adj, **severity** n

shape /ʃeɪp/ v to have an important influence on the way that sth is done or the way that sb/sth develops U13

shift AWL /ʃɪft/ n a change in position or direction U13 WF **shift** v

shortcoming /ˈʃɔːtkʌmɪŋ/ n a fault in a piece of research, a plan, a system, etc. U25

sibling /ˈsɪblɪŋ/ n a brother or sister U15

similarity AWL /ˌsɪməˈlærəti/ n (pl. -ies) a feature that things or people have that makes them like each other U18 WF **dissimilar** adj, **similar** adj, **similarly** adv

so-called AWL /ˌsəʊ ˈkɔːld/ adj used to show that you do not think that the word or phrase that is being used to describe sb/sth is appropriate U33

social /ˈsəʊʃl/ adj connected with society and the way it is organized U3 WF **socialize** v, **socialization** n, **socially** adv, **society** n

sole AWL /səʊl/ adj **1** only; single U16 **2** involving only one person or group U16 WF **solely** adv

somewhat AWL /ˈsʌmwɒt/ adv to some degree U33

source AWL /sɔːs/ n a text or person that provides information, especially for study, a piece of written work or news U20 WF **source** v

specification AWL /ˌspesɪfɪˈkeɪʃn/ n a detailed description of how sth is, or should be, designed or made U38 WF **specific** adj, **specifically** adv, **specifics** n, **specify** v, **unspecified** adj

specify AWL /ˈspesɪfaɪ/ v to identify sb/sth clearly and definitely; to state a fact or sth that is required clearly and exactly U26

spouse /spaʊs/ n (formal or law) a husband or wife U15

square /skweə(r)/ v (pp **squared**) to multiply a number by itself U37

square root /ˌskweə ˈruːt/ n (mathematics) a number which, when multiplied by itself, produces a particular number U37

stabilize, **-ise** AWL /ˈsteɪbəlaɪz/ v **1** to become firmly established and not likely to change; to make sth do this U12 **2** (of a patient or their medical condition) to stop getting any worse after an injury or operation; to make a patient or their condition do this U39 WF **instability** n, **stability** n, **stabilization** n, **unstable** adj

stakeholder /ˈsteɪkhəʊldə(r)/ *n* a person or company that is involved in a particular organization, project or system, especially because they have invested money in it U43

stance /stæns/ *n* the opinions that sb has about sth and expresses publicly U22

standard of living /ˌstændəd əv ˈlɪvɪŋ/ *n* (pl. standards of living) the amount of money and level of comfort that a particular person or group has U40

state /steɪt/ *n* **1** (also **State**) a country considered as an organized political community controlled by one government U42 **2** (also **State**) an organized political community forming part of a country U42 **3** (also **the State**) the government of a country U42 WF **state** *adj*

statistical AWL /stəˈtɪstɪkl/ *adj* connected with statistics (= a collection of information shown in numbers) U6 WF **statistic** *n*, **statistics** *n*, **statistically** *adv*, **statistician** *n*

statistically significant /stəˌtɪstɪkli ˌsɪɡˈnɪfɪkənt/ *adj* having a result that is different from what would be expected from random variation or errors U24 WF **statistical significance** *n*

status AWL /ˈsteɪtəs/ *n* the social or professional position of sb/sth in relation to others U15

steadily /ˈstedɪli/ *adv* gradually and in an even and regular way U12 WF **steady** *adj*

straightforward AWL /ˌstreɪtˈfɔːwəd/ *adj* easy to do or to understand; not complicated U24

strengthen /ˈstreŋθn/ *v* to make an organization, a position or an argument stronger or more powerful U24 WF **strength** *n*, **strong** *adj*, **strongly** *adv*

structure AWL /ˈstrʌktʃə(r)/ *n* the way in which the parts of sth are connected together, arranged or organized; a particular arrangement of parts U9 WF **restructure** *v*, **structural** *adj*, **structurally** *adv*, **unstructured** *adj*

submit AWL /səbˈmɪt/ *v* (-tt-) to give a proposal, application or other document to sb in authority so that they can consider or judge it U1 WF **submission** *n*

subsequently AWL /ˈsʌbsɪkwəntli/ *adv* afterwards; after sth else has happened U10 WF **subsequent** *adj*

substitute AWL /ˈsʌbstɪtjuːt/ *v* to take the place of sb/sth else; to use sb/sth instead of sb/sth else U13 WF **substitute** *n*, **substitution** *n*

successive AWL /səkˈsesɪv/ *adj* following immediately one after the other U12 WF **successively** *adv*, **succession** *n*

sufficient AWL /səˈfɪʃnt/ *adj* enough for a particular purpose; as much as you need U20 WF **insufficient** *adj*, **sufficiently** *adv*, **sufficiency** *n*

suggest /səˈdʒest/ *v* to put forward an idea or a plan for other people to consider U35 WF **suggestion** *n*, **suggestive** *adj*

summarize, -ise AWL /ˈsʌməraɪz/ *v* to give a summary of sth U35 WF **summary** *n*

sum of AWL /ˈsʌm ɒv/ *phr* the total amount resulting from the addition of two or more numbers, amounts or items U37 WF **sum** *v*

supervisor /ˈsuːpəvaɪzə(r)/ *n* a person who supervises sb/sth (= makes sure everything is done in a correct or safe way) sb/sth U1 WF **supervision** *n*, **supervise** *v*

supplement AWL /ˈsʌplɪment/ *v* to add sth to sth in order to improve it or make it more complete U40 WF **supplement** *n*, **supplementary** *adj*

supplier /səˈplaɪə(r)/ *n* a person or company that supplies goods U43 WF **supply** *v*

support /səˈpɔːt/ *v* to help to show that sth is true or correct U20 WF **support** *n*, **supporter** *adj*, **supportive** *adj*

supporter /səˈpɔːtə(r)/ *n* a person who supports a political party, an idea, etc. U23

supposedly /səˈpəʊzɪdli/ *adv* according to what is generally thought or believed but not known for certain U33 WF **suppose** *v*, **supposed** *adj*

suspend AWL /səˈspend/ *v* to officially stop sth for a time; to prevent sth from being active, used, etc. for a time U11 WF **suspension** *n*

symbol AWL /ˈsɪmbl/ *n* a sign, number, letter, etc. that has a fixed meaning, especially in science, mathematics and music U37 WF **symbolic** *adj*, **symbolically** *adv*, **symbolism** *n*, **symbolize** *v*

symbolic AWL /sɪmˈbɒlɪk/ *adj* containing symbols; being used as a symbol U23

symptom /ˈsɪmptəm/ *n* a change in your body or mind that shows that you are not healthy U39 WF **symptomatic** *adj*

system /ˈsɪstəm/ *n* an organized way of doing sth; an organized set of ideas or theories U8 WF **systematic** *adj*, **systematically** *adv*

systematic /ˌsɪstəˈmætɪk/ *adj* done according to a system or plan, in a thorough, efficient or determined way U27

target population /ˈtɑːɡɪt pɒpjuleɪʃn/ *n* a group whose behaviour a researcher wishes to investigate U7

technique AWL /tekˈniːk/ *n* a particular way of doing sth that involves using a special skill or process U38

technological AWL /ˌteknəˈlɒdʒɪkl/ *adj* connected with or using technology U2 WF **technologically** *adv*, **technology** *n*

terminal AWL /ˈtɜːmɪnl/ *adj* (of an illness or a disease) that cannot be cured and will lead to death, often slowly U39 WF **terminal** *n*, **terminate** *v*, **termination** *n*

terminate AWL /ˈtɜːmɪneɪt/ *v* to end; to make sth end U11

theme AWL /θiːm/ *n* the subject of a talk, piece of writing, etc.; an idea that keeps returning in a piece of research or a work of art or literature U4 WF **thematic** *adj*, **thematically** *adv*

theoretically AWL /ˌθɪəˈretɪkli/ *adv* in a way that is possible in theory but unlikely in practice U33

theory AWL /ˈθɪəri/ *n* (pl. -ies) a formal set of ideas that is intended to explain why sth happens or exists U21 WF **theoretical** *adj*, **theoretically** *adv*, **theorist** *n*

therapeutic /ˌθerəˈpjuːtɪk/ *adj* designed to help treat an illness U39 WF **therapist** *n*, **therapy** *n*

thereby AWL /ˌðeəˈbaɪ/ *adv* (formal) used to introduce the result of the action or situation mentioned U36

thesis AWL /ˈθiːsɪs/ *n* (pl. theses /ˈθiːsiːz/) a statement or an opinion that is discussed in a logical way and presented with evidence in order to prove that it is true U4

to some extent /tə ˌsʌm ɪkˈstent/ *phr* used to show that sth is partly true or has some effect, but is not completely true or effective U33

trace AWL /treɪs/ *n* a very small amount of sth U16 WF **trace** *v*

transfer AWL /træns'fɜː(r)/ v (-rr-) to move from one place to another; to move sth/sb from one place to another U29 WF transfer /'trænsfɜː(r)/ n, transferable adj, transference n

transform AWL /træns'fɔːm/ v to completely change the appearance or character of sth/sb, especially so that it is better U13 WF transformation n

transition AWL /træn'zɪʃn/ n the process or a period of changing from one state or condition to another U13 WF transit n, transitional adj

transmit AWL /træns'mɪt/ v (-tt-) to pass sth from one person to another U39 WF transmission n

transportation AWL /ˌtrænspɔː'teɪʃn/ n a system for carrying people or goods from one place to another using vehicles, roads, etc U30 WF transport n v, transporter n

treaty /'triːti/ n (pl. -ies) a formal agreement between two or more countries U41

trend AWL /trend/ n a general direction in which a situation is changing or developing U12

typically /'tɪpɪkli/ adv used to say that sth usually happens in the way that you are stating U33 WF atypical adj, typical adj

ultimately AWL /'ʌltɪmətli/ adv in the end; finally U10 WF ultimate adj

unavoidable /ˌʌnə'vɔɪdəbl/ adj impossible to avoid or prevent U34 WF avoid v, unavoidably adv

undeniably /ˌʌndɪ'naɪəbli/ adv used to show that you think sth is true or certain, or that it cannot be denied U34 WF deniable adj, denial n, undeniable adj

undergo AWL /ˌʌndə'ɡəʊ/ v (undergoes /ˌʌndə'ɡəʊz/, underwent /ˌʌndə'went/, undergone /ˌʌndə'ɡɒn/) to experience sth, especially a change or sth unpleasant U39

underlying AWL /ˌʌndə'laɪɪŋ/ adj important in a situation but not always easily noticed or stated clearly U12 WF underlie v

undermine /ˌʌndə'maɪn/ v to make sth, especially sb's confidence or authority, gradually weaker or less effective U25

undertake AWL /ˌʌndə'teɪk/ v (undertook /ˌʌndə'tʊk/, undertaken /ˌʌndə'teɪkən/) to make yourself responsible for sth and start doing it U11 WF undertaking n

undoubtedly /ʌn'daʊtɪdli/ adv used to emphasize that sth exists or is definitely true U34 WF undoubted adj

uniform AWL /'juːnɪfɔːm/ adj not varying; the same in all parts and at all times U30 WF uniform n, uniformity n, uniformly adv

unit /'juːnɪt/ n a fixed quantity that is used as a standard measurement U6

unnecessary /ʌn'nesəsəri/ adj more than is needed U25 WF necessarily adv, necessary adj, necessity n

unproductive /ˌʌnprə'dʌktɪv/ adj not producing very much; not producing good results U25 WF produce v, product n, production n, productive adj, productively adv, productivity n

unrest /ʌn'rest/ n a situation in which people are angry and likely to protest against the government or their employers U42

unsupported /ˌʌnsə'pɔːtɪd/ adj (of a statement, etc.) not proved to be true by evidence U20

unsustainable AWL /ˌʌnsə'steɪnəbl/ adj that cannot be continued at the same level or rate U25 WF sustain v, sustainability n, sustainable adj, sustenance n

upheaval /ʌp'hiːvl/ n a big change that causes a lot of confusion, worry and problems U13

utilize, -ise AWL /'juːtəlaɪz/ v to use sth, especially for a practical purpose U28 WF utility n, utilization n

valid AWL /'vælɪd/ adj based on what is logical or true U24 WF invalid adj, invalidate v, validate v, validation n, validity n, validly adv

value /'væljuː/ n **1** the amount represented by a letter or symbol; a size, number or quantity U37 **2 values** beliefs about what is right and wrong and what is important in life U40 WF valuable adj, value v

variability AWL /ˌveəriə'bɪləti/ n the fact of sth being likely to vary U37 WF invariable adj, variable adj n, variably adv, variance n, variant n, variation n, variety n

variation AWL /ˌveəri'eɪʃn/ n a change or difference, especially in the amount or level of sth, usually within particular limits U18 WF vary v

vehicle AWL /'viːəkl/ n something that can be used to express your ideas or feelings or as a way of achieving sth U9

via AWL /'vaɪə/ prep by means of a particular person, system, etc. U36

violate AWL /'vaɪəleɪt/ v to go against or refuse to obey a law, an agreement, etc. U31 WF violation n

visible AWL /'vɪzəbl/ adj **1** that can be seen U30 **2** that is obvious enough to attract attention easily U30 WF invisible adj, visibly adv, visibility n

visual AWL /'vɪʒuəl/ adj of or connected with seeing or sight U5 WF visually adv, visualize v, visualization n

volume AWL /'vɒljuːm/ n **1** the amount of space that an object or a substance fills; the amount of space that a container has U16 **2** the amount of sth U16

voluntary AWL /'vɒləntri/ adj done willingly, not because you are forced U26 WF voluntarily adv, volunteer n v

whereby AWL /weə'baɪ/ adv by which; because of which U36

whole number /ˌhəʊl 'nʌmbə(r)/ n (mathematics) a number that consists of one or more units with no fractions (= parts of a number less than one) U37

widespread AWL /'waɪdspred/ adj existing or happening over a large area or among many people U14

with reference to /ˌwɪð 'refrəns tu/ phr used to say what sth refers to or is about U35

with regard to /ˌwɪð rɪ'ɡɑːd tu/ phr concerning sb/sth U32 WF regard v

workforce /'wɜːkfɔːs/ n **1** all the people who work for a particular company or organization U43 **2** all the people in a country or an area who are available for work U43

yield /jiːld/ v to produce or provide sth, for example a result, information or a profit U6 WF yield n

KEY

abbr.	abbreviation	phr v	phrasal verb
adj	adjective	pl.	plural
adv	adverb	prep	preposition
AWL	*Academic Word List*	pron	pronoun
conj	conjunction	sb	somebody
n	noun	sth	something
NAmE	North American English	v	verb
phr	phrase	WF	word family